BLOOD AND COIN

THE RANGER ARCHIVES: VOLUME TWO

PHILIP C. QUAINTRELL

Cover Illustration by Chris McGrath
Book design by Bod:Dog Design
Edited by David Bradley

ISBN: 978-1-916610-19-4 (paperback)
ASIN: B0B3BD8WTC (ebook)

Published by Quaintrell Publishings

For Margot, my lion cub...

ALSO BY
PHILIP C. QUAINTRELL

THE ECHOES SAGA: (9 Book Series)

1. Rise of the Ranger

2. Empire of Dirt

3. Relic of the Gods

4. The Fall of Neverdark

5. Kingdom of Bones

6. Age of the King

7. The Knights of Erador

8. Last of the Dragorn

9. A Clash of Fates

THE RANGER ARCHIVES: (3 Book Series)

1. Court of Assassins

2. Blood and Coin

3. A Dance of Fang and Claw

THE TERRAN CYCLE: (4 Book Series)

1. Intrinsic

2. Tempest

3. Heretic

4. Legacy

THE WHISPERING MOUNTAINS
GRIMWHAL
BHAN DORAL
KHALDARIM
DHENAHEIM
THE VENGORAN MOUNTAINS
THE KING'S LAKE
SILVYR HALL
NAMDHOR
HYNDAERN
SKYSTEAD
THE WHITE VALE
ILLIA
NIMDUHN
WOOD VALE
KELP TOWN
THE KING'S INN
IKIRITH
GREY STONE
THE EVERMOOR
SNOWFELL
LIRIAN
BLEAK
THE NORD
VANGARTH
CARSTANE
THE WILD MOORES
ELETHIAH
WEST FELLION
QAMNARAN
THE NARROWS
THE MOONLIT PLAIN
ILYTHYRA
LAKE NUBIA
HALLA
TREGARAN
AMEERASKA
THE ARID LANE
THE HOX
THE OLD GARDEN
KARATH
SYLA'S GATE
SYLA'S PASS
THE UNDYING MOUNTAINS
ITHILIA
LAKE RAND
THE BLACK LAKE

VERDA
THE LONELY WASTES
THE SPEAR
LONGDALE
HOGSTEAD
THE BLACK WOOD
THE OLD WELL
DUNWICH
ARKWELL
THE UNMAR
OS
STOWHOLD
KORKANATH
SELK ROAD
VELIA
SSH
DRAGORN
TOWER OF DRAGORN
THE LIFELESS ISLES
THE WILLOWS
RDRA
THE ADEAN
SHALARIA
THE CRYSTAL SEA
THE AMARA
THE DARVUN MOUNTAINS
ELANDRIL
THE ELMEER FOREST
MOUNT GARGANAFAN
THE ESSIANT LAKE
LAKE KAHEARE
THE Q'OL
AYDA
THE RED MOUNTAINS
ATILAN'S LANDING
DROWNERS' RUN
THE HOOK OF THE WORLD
THE TRIDENT
THE FLAT WASTES
DRAGONS' REACH
MALAYSAI
THE GREAT MAW
DAVOSAI
GRAVOSAI
THE LIVING SEA

DRAMATIS PERSONAE

Asher
Ranger

Baal
Gladiator

Borvyn Murell
Lord of Dunwich

Danagarr Stormshield
Dwarven smith

Darya Siad-Agnasi
Right hand of Viktor Varga

Deadora Stormshield
Child and daughter of Danagarr and Kilda

Doran Heavybelly
Ranger

DRAMATIS PERSONAE

Kad Gorson
Magistri

Kilda Stormshield
Dwarven Healer

Lucas Farney (The Fang)
Trigorn emissary

Malak
Chief henchman to Viktor Varga

Nasta Nal-Aket
Father of Nightfall

Rhaldor Kavarion
Mage

Salim Al-Anan
Gladiator

Tyvarnus
Previous arena champion

Undvig
Mage

Viktor Varga
Leader of Crime Guild

CHAPTER 1
BETWEEN WORLDS

Howling Matron *- What devil gave birth to such a creature I could not guess nor would I care to meet it, for this offspring of evil is wretch enough. It boasts a dozen pincer legs, giving this beast its scurrying speed. Its carapace, sizeably comparable to a horse, is plated like armour and capable of chipping our blades and keeping back our arrows.*

And what hellish sight its monstrous jaws are. Upon attack, the largest of the Matron's armoured plates retreats just enough to reveal the six blood-red tentacles that surround a razored beak. It will howl almost continuously, altering its pitch until it finds one that disorientates its prey. Once thoroughly dazed, those tentacles will have you; then there's no getting away from that beak.

All that in mind, you'll be wanting to tackle this monster with a spear— to give those tentacles something to do. Then push the beast back and lever it up to expose its soft underbelly. That said, I would advise bringing another ranger into the contract. If that's not possible, you're going to need more preparation time. First, hunt down a Narkul - you're going to need the natural acid their mushrooms produce as it's one of the few things capable of burning through the Matron's carapace.

Just try not to die extracting the acid from the Narkul first.

***A Chronicle of Monsters: A Ranger's Bestiary, 12th Edition,
Page 13.***

Keldrik The Grey, Ranger.

The Iron Valley—a corridor of snow and ice that dissuaded even the bravest of men from crossing The Vengoran Mountains. To its south lay Illian, the sprawling realm of man and his many kingdoms. To the north, the dwarf lords ruled over the land of Dhenaheim in their halls of cold stone.

Halfway between the two, along the western edge of that wild valley, a ranger stood in the blasting winds, his green cloak swept aside. Piercing blue eyes roamed over a wall of ice through which an arched entrance had been carved. Beyond the surrounding barrier, set into the base of the mountains, dwelled a breed of man not idly met.

They called themselves The Jarat. North and south of the valley, however, they were known to both man and dwarf as *barbarians*.

Standing in the snow, Asher adjusted the white furs anchoring his cloak and gripped Hector's reins a little tighter. He could feel the unease that ran through the horse, tempting it to bolt. "Steady," he uttered, his gaze caught by the skulls mounted on pikes inside the entrance.

It wasn't the most welcoming of sights but, then again, it wasn't supposed to be. Skulls on display were always a warning and only the most foolish would proceed without a second thought. Giving this particular job that second thought, the ranger had to wonder if the coin was worth it—barbarians weren't exactly known for making deals with outsiders, let alone honouring them.

To his left, beyond the curtain of hair that blew in the wind, Asher heard the snow crunching under boots and hooves alike. It was the first time he had heard the approaching stranger, though he had caught glimpses of him during his journey through the valley. Instead of a dark figure on the horizon now, the stranger was standing a little more than ten feet away, his destination apparently the same.

Asher took a breath, wondering if violence was to occur much earlier in the day than he had anticipated. Keeping one hand on Hector's reins, the ranger turned to regard the potential foe, wondering if *he* was the stranger's target. It wouldn't be the first time he was someone else's quarry.

A flicker of surprise flashed across Asher's face, cutting through his usual expression of stoicism. As his eyes roamed over the figure and his strange mount, the ranger's fingers slowly clasped the hilt of the broadsword on his hip. Had the figure been any man of Illian, Asher would likely have maintained a casual demeanour or, perhaps, gripped the concealed dagger at the base of his back. But the stranger who had followed him into the valley from the south was no man.

"What's the matter?" came the stranger's growling voice. "Ye look like ye've never seen a dwarf before."

Asher required an extra moment to grasp the events that had led to this unusual meeting. "You don't hail from Dhenaheim," he remarked by way of a reply, his head nodding to Illian, behind the dwarf.

"I suppose I don'," he said cryptically, before taking a long swig from a flask. The belch that escaped his lips was loud enough to inform the inhabitants of the entire valley that there were intruders in their land. It was also strong enough to carry the aroma of ale all the way to Asher's nose.

After wiping his thick beard, the dwarf swept back his hood to reveal a mane of blond hair pulled tight into a ponytail. His skin was weathered and marred by deep lines that exaggerated his features. Small dark eyes peered out from his prominent brow and puffy cheeks, though they possessed a lack of focus that suggested the dwarf was suffering the influences of whatever was inside his flask.

Nightfall's training, a way of thinking Asher could never

escape, pressed upon the ranger to assess the potential threats that accompanied the dwarf. There were many.

His armour, bulky and mismatched as it was, covered a good portion of his body, including one particular pauldron adorned with three bony spikes, likely taken from a beast of some description. The hilt of a sword poked over his right shoulder, its length and blade type hidden from view. In one gloved hand there rested a single-bladed axe, its size perfect for both throwing and close combat. Then there was the mount standing beside the dwarf. To call it a hog was an insult, for the animal was twice that size if not more, its hardened tusks ringed with armoured bands. The saddle and supplies strapped around its barrel of a body appeared cumbersome and heavy, yet the beast bore it all on strong legs with no sign of fatigue. Then there were the scars that decorated its hide, a tapestry that spoke of a lifetime of violence.

The dwarf's ragged cloak blew in the wind, revealing a pair of small daggers on his belt and a modest axe, a toy compared to the one in his hand. Much like his mount, everything about this dwarf told a tale of violence.

Asher gripped his broadsword a little tighter.

"'ave ye taken the measure o' me then?" the dwarf asked after the flask left his lips for a second time. "Perhaps ye'd like to take a look inside me saddlebags as well."

Asher caught himself and focused on the dwarf's face again. "You're a hunter," he concluded.

"Aye," the dwarf agreed. "What gave me away?" he laughed.

"Might I ask of your intended prey?" By Asher's last syllable, his knuckles had now whitened around the hilt of his broadsword.

The dwarf made a face. "My *intended* prey?" he echoed mockingly. "Careful, laddy, ye're giving too much away. Now I know two things abou' ye." A stubby finger ran up and down the ranger's attire. "Ye're a hunter too. I'd also say ye're well-educated. I would then *deduce*," he emphasised with that same mocking expression, "that ye've received enough trainin' to know what ye're doin' with all that hardware ye're carryin'."

It was an impressive speech and even more impressive deduction for someone so inebriated. "I'm inclined to say the same about yourself," Asher told him.

The dwarf drained the last of his flask and gave Asher another look up and down, his lips tight. "Ye got a name, hunter?"

"I do," the ranger answered.

The dwarf chuckled lightly. "I'm not 'ere to hunt any man. At least not today," he added, stuffing his empty flask into one of his saddlebags. "Though it's a curious thing that ye'd suspect I'm 'ere for yerself, eh?"

Asher knew well enough that if he kept his mouth shut, more information would come spilling out of the dwarf, some of his inhibitions dampened by the alcohol.

After spoiling the air with a cloud of hot vapour, the dwarf announced, "Doran Heavybelly's the name!"

Asher raised an eyebrow. "*Heavybelly?*" he repeated incredulously.

The dwarf looked to be taking the ranger's insulting tone in his stride. "Aye. Doran, son o' Dorain, o' *clan* Heavybelly. Ye 'ave a problem with me name, laddy?"

Asher relaxed his muscles a notch. "I meant no offence, Doran, son of Dorain. I am unaccustomed to the ways of your people."

"Good for ye," Doran said with another, quieter burp. "Would ye prefer I simply call yerself *hunter*?"

Asher paused, wondering how many weeks, or even months, it had been since he introduced himself to someone by name. "I'm not a hunter," he corrected. "I'm a ranger. And my name is Asher."

"Asher," the dwarf echoed aloud, his head nodding along. "Well met, I suppose. An' what in the name o' Grarfath is a *ranger*?"

Asher opened his mouth to describe his profession when he realised he had never been required to do so before. He stumbled over what would be the best explanation before succinctly replying, "I hunt monsters."

The dwarf's bushy eyebrows creased his forehead. "So... Ye're a hunter then."

Asher wanted to argue the differences but that would only lead to more talking, and he had already said more in the last few minutes than he had in the last few weeks. "Something like that," he said instead.

Doran shoved a thumb into his armoured breastplate. "Me too. Monsters, people, whatever needs trackin' down really."

That sounded more like a bounty hunter to Asher, but he wasn't about to get into it with the dwarf. "So you heard about the job?" he reasoned, tilting his head towards the icy archway.

"Aye. Came straight from Dunwich. Me axe has felt naught but the soft touch o' snow for too long."

Asher didn't hide his confusion. "You mean *Namdhor*?"

Reaching for a pocket-sized flask hanging from his belt, a single guttural noise blurted from the dwarf. "Eh?"

"The job," Asher continued, somewhat exasperated now. "It came from Namdhor, not Dunwich."

"Namdhor?" Doran licked his lips after a mouthful from his flask. "I've come from Dunwich, laddy."

Asher's exasperation was quickly turning into frustration. "The people of this tribe only reached out to Namdhor. You *must* have come from the city."

Doran chewed it all over. "Big hill on a lake. Grim to the eye."

Asher nodded along. "That's Namdhor."

"It's Dunwich, ain' it?"

"It's the capital in the north. Hard to mistake," the ranger added with some condescension.

Doran shrugged. "All yer towns an' cities look the same to me."

Asher shook his head. "It doesn't matter. You're here for the job they're offering—The Jarat?"

"That I am," the dwarven hunter stated. "From memory—which I'll admit, isn' what it normally is—the coin they're offerin' ain' nearly enough to be shared."

"On that," Asher replied determinedly, "we agree, son of Dorain."

Doran chewed his lips and looked upon the ranger with narrow eyes, his axe tapping the ground beneath the snow. "What are we to do then, laddy?"

Asher's heart rate increased a few beats and the tension in his muscles returned. His answer, he knew, would manifest itself in the form of action, as it so often did, but a flicker of movement caught his eye and turned him to the archway. There, standing between the skulls was a small boy, his wiry frame hidden beneath grey furs.

"Ye can see 'im too?" Doran asked, blinking his eyes. "Praise Yamnomora," he muttered.

Asher attempted to soften his features, though his hand refused to let go of the resting broadsword. "Well met," he said to the boy. The child's only response was to turn on his heel and flee, disappearing into the narrow entrance that cut through the ice. "Wait!" Asher called after him.

To his left, the dwarf was clambering onto his saddle and making ready to follow the boy. Asher, his limbs unaffected by alcohol, was able to climb onto his own saddle in half the time and spur Hector into the opening.

The route beyond the archway proved to be a winding maze through the piled snow and sheer walls of ice. It eventually offered more than one path though, thanks to the fresh snow that blanketed the ground, the ranger had no trouble tracking the child's footprints.

By the time he had found his way past the surrounding fortification of ice and into the barbarians' camp, Doran and his strident mount had caught up.

Remaining in their saddles, the two hunters scrutinised the living conditions of The Jarat. Two dozen huts, most with smoke rising from their makeshift chimneys, were dotted from left to right and all connected by ropes decorated with natural chimes and feathers.

Dogs ran between the homes, some of which diverted to the intruders and barked their distinct alarm. The response from the human inhabitants was slower than Asher had expected but, when they did finally confront the strangers in their midst, they were all wielding weapons of some fashion. It didn't take the ranger long, however, to see the truth of those who formed a jagged line between them and the rest of the tribe. They were mostly teenagers, if not children. The slowest, and therefore last, to arrive were the elders amongst the tribe, though they too held themselves well and with weapons in hand.

"I'm not seein' many warriors," Doran commented from his lower perch.

Asher agreed, even if he didn't say as much. What he did see, however, was fear—an unusual sight where the barbarians were concerned. Then again, he considered the information he had received in Namdhor from the old woman and young child who had accompanied her from this very place. At each end of life's spectrum, they had travelled beyond the familiar and into the dangers of civilised man to offer coin—likely taken from wayward travellers—in exchange for help.

Though they had offered less than half his normal rate, Asher had been keen to get away from the cities and towns, for a while at least. He had spent the last four years wandering from city to city, but they steadily overwhelmed him, often leading him to take refuge in the wilds of the world. A paid job in The Iron Valley had sounded ideal.

"There's a reason they need our help," the ranger said to the dwarf.

"Do ye speak their tongue, laddy?"

Asher boasted a wealth of knowledge where the numerous languages of Illian were concerned, but he knew only a handful of words used by The Jarat. "Not as well as I'd like," he replied, eyeing the tip of a spear angled up at him.

"Words are only half o' it," Doran explained. "Almost every other word is spoken with their hands. Let *me* do the talkin'."

Asher looked down at the dwarf, his scepticism laid bare.

The dwarf licked his lips. "Ye don' strike me as the kind to jus' walk away. So we either split the coin or fight until only one o' us is standin' to collect."

Asher considered those options, though he only needed a couple of seconds to see sense. "Talk," he instructed reluctantly.

Doran slowly climbed down from his saddle and raised his hands, the universal sign for *I pose no threat—please don't kill me.* A handful of scrawny teenagers advanced a step and thrust their spears towards the dwarf's face. To his credit, the son of Dorain didn't so much as flinch.

After surviving the next few seconds, the dwarf started to speak in their language, integrating his fingers and hands into the speech. More than once he indicated Asher astride his horse. This was more than uncomfortable since he had no idea what was being said about him and there were still weapons being pointed in his direction.

One of the elders amongst the defensive line eventually spoke up, his response as foreign in Asher's ears as Doran's opening statement. Again, gestures were thrown the ranger's way.

"What's he saying?" Asher demanded.

Doran motioned for him to climb down and join him before replying to the elder with hand signals alone. "They accept that we're 'ere to hunt their monster down. I've tried to haggle on the price a bit, but they want us to speak directly with their chieftain abou' it."

Two of the younger barbarians stepped forward to take control of Hector, at which Asher drew his broadsword an inch. Unease rippled through The Jarat and their weapons began poking the air around the ranger, their guttural language barking commands at him.

"Leave it, laddy," Doran advised. "They won' hurt the animals."

Asher dropped the blade back into place but was sure to let the threat linger in his eyes.

The pair were escorted through the camp, to its most western edge, where an overhang of jagged rock sheltered a throne of bones and animal skin rugs. A man, passing through his eighth decade perhaps, was seated on the throne, his frail body drowning in blankets and furs. Servants were at his beck and call, waiting attentively either side of the throne. A closer inspection informed Asher they were not servants. They were slaves. Their wrists were bound by rope, though they had been given enough slack to allow them to perform their tasks. An iron collar, however, offered no slack at all as it circled their necks, though the collars remained free of any tether for the moment.

Doran cleared his throat and straightened his armour-laden shoulders. He began his presentation anew with the chieftain's eyes and ears for an audience. The dwarf was quickly silenced by the subtle flex of the old man's gnarled fingers. The Jarat leader said something in his native tongue and the hunters were prodded forward, bringing them closer to the throne. Asher had to wonder how good the chieftain's eyes were, a necessity where their language was concerned.

After another command was given, it seemed Doran had been granted permission to speak again. The son of Dorain brought his hands up and blended them into his speech, in which the entire tribe had become enthralled. The young and the old, for there was no in-between, watched the dwarf and listened to his words while flashing Asher regular looks of growing curiosity. Eventually, the chieftain replied, though his own hand signals were considerably ill-defined.

"What's he saying?" Asher asked quietly.

"Apparently, this is all that's left," Doran told him, gesturing to the tribe. "They lost their strongest to the beast."

"All of them?" the ranger queried in disbelief.

"When their raidin' party never returned, more were sent to look for 'em. Only one returned, an' with a tale o' a monster on his tongue."

"They sent hunters," Asher reasoned.

The dwarf nodded. "They sent hunters. Who never returned. So they sent more. None were seen again. Now it's jus' those who don' know how to wield a weapon, an' those who can' even lift a weapon. They must 'ave been desperate to seek help so far south as Dunwich."

"Namdhor," Asher quickly corrected. "And, from what I've heard, the iron tribes are at constant war. There's no one out here to help them."

"He won' budge on the price," Doran added with a shrug. "An'

I'm pretty sure whatever they pay us with won' be recognised by the kingdoms o' Illian."

Asher didn't much care. "Can they take us to the last place they know the monster was sighted?"

"Aye."

"What of its description?"

Doran turned back to the chieftain and relayed the question. "It's the usual," the dwarf said with a sigh. "Fangs, claws, an' an *insatiable* hunger. Nothin' useful."

"It'll do," Asher said. "Tell them to take us there now."

The dwarf again spoke in The Jarat's language and the chieftain mumbled a reply, his hand waving them away. "They won' take us now," Doran reported.

"Why not?"

"Night approaches an' they won' risk any o' their young beyond the camp's borders after dark. Lost too many I suppose. They've offered us lodgin' for the time bein', an' I'm inclined to take it given the thirst I can feel in me throat."

Asher wanted to argue against any rest, eager to be on with the hunt, but he had no words to offer that The Jarat would either understand or care for. With a reluctant sigh, he accompanied the dwarf to a rounded dwelling that looked like the flat earth had simply bubbled over in a mound of mud. Asher paused on his way inside to make sure the mounts were being seen to, not far from their hut.

It wasn't long after the flaps of material fell back into place behind the ranger that the dwarf was thrusting a flask into his chest. Seeing little choice but to accept it, Asher took the drink while Doran moved on to stoking the fire, its smoke allowed to escape through the holes poked into the domed ceiling.

"They'll take us at dawn," the son of Dorain reassured. "Until then, *ranger man*, might I suggest we come to trust each other a bit more."

"That isn't going to happen," Asher replied honestly.

The dwarf appeared more intrigued than taken aback. "Whether ye like it or not, laddy, we're huntin' this beastie together. A tenuous alliance won' cut it. I'm only askin' to know how ye hunt. Yer methods an' the like."

Asher eyed the son of Dorain. "You seem less drunk than you were before," he observed.

Doran chuckled to himself as he removed yet another flask from the depths of his satchel. "Easily fixed, ranger man!" The dwarf popped the top and drank heartily, filling the small dwelling with the sweet smell of honey mead. "Go on now," he encouraged, gesturing to the flask in Asher's hand. "It'll keep ye warm."

"It'll keep me *slow*," Asher retorted.

"Well there's naught but sleep to be had until dawn, so what's it matter?" Doran swigged his mead some more before asking, "So, where do ye hail from, lad? I've seen all the kingdoms ye kin 'ave to offer an' I can' place ye."

Asher didn't want to answer the question and decided to drink from the flask in a bid to delay his response. It was bitter, though he detected enough of the Duke's Ale to appreciate the flavour.

"I'm from all over," he finally answered.

Doran kept his gaze on the ranger from across the fire. "All over?" he mused. "Funny, most with markin's like that," he said, looking directly at the black fang tattooed beneath Asher's left eye, "tend to hail from The Wild Moores."

Asher paused with the rim of the flask on his lips. It was an unusually insightful observation from one who claimed to confuse Namdhor for Dunwich. He drank some more of the ale and returned the dwarf's gaze. "You're very familiar with Illian and its people."

"Well, it's always good to know an Outlander when ye see one," Doran remarked casually. "From experience, it never works out when they see ye first."

Asher was inclined to agree, though he wasn't in the mood to say as much. "I'm not an Outlander," was all he offered in return.

"Obviously," Doran said with a burp on his lips. "There's no Outlander alive that knows the word *intended*," he added with a laugh from deep in his chest. "It does compound me intrigue though."

"I am no more intriguing than the dwarf roaming the kingdoms of Illian and hunting monsters for barbarians."

"Indeed," Doran agreed. "Me own tale, however, is most certainly longer than yer own. By abou' two hundred years I'd wager."

Asher's hand was working without conscious thought, bringing his flask repeatedly to his lips. "Two hundred years," he echoed, his eyes taken by the flames of the fire. Two centuries of life sounded like torment to the ranger, whose dreams still tempted him with the release of death.

A particularly loud crackle was unleashed by the fire and Asher focused on the dwarf again. At least he tried to. Doran's outline was so blurry there appeared two or three of him at times. A question began to form in the ranger's mind but he struggled to voice it.

"This is a nice sword," Doran commented, his hands having pulled Asher's broadsword halfway out of its scabbard. "It's no dwarven blade mind ye, but it'd get the job done."

Asher held a warning hand out, though it was slower to rise than normal and his entire arm left an echo in its wake. "That's... That's mine," he managed, his words slurred.

Doran gave a toothy grin. "I know, laddy. It's all yers!"

Asher followed the dwarf's eyes and discovered all of his weapons and gear had been piled up, on Doran's side of the fire. Alarming questions began to vie for supremacy in the ranger's mind, no one finding its way to the surface.

"I'll be takin' that back now." The son of Dorain shuffled round the fire and reclaimed his flask of Duke's Mead. "Don' worry," he continued. "Ye're goin' to 'ave the best sleep o' yer life."

Asher felt the dwarf's hand press into the side of his face and slowly push his head down to the ground. The change in orientation was enough to rob the ranger of all sense.

~

A blistering cold washed over Asher and he awoke with a start. Drenched in icy water, the ranger gasped before his breathing increased.

Standing before him was Doran Heavybelly, an empty bucket in hand. "Mornin', sleepy head!" he declared cheerfully. "It looks like ye had a little too much to drink last night."

Asher scowled at the mischievous grin spreading the dwarf's beard. "What did you poison me with?"

"Me kin call it *Morndin Thord*," he explained, with a touch of his native language. "That's Mountain Stone to ye. The Duke's Ale is the only thing bitter enough to mask its taste. Most o' me people use it to help 'em sleep, but yer soft brains can' handle it. Knocks ye out cold an' quickly too. Though, I've got to say, ranger man, ye surprised me. I've never seen a human stay awake for so long after his first sip."

Asher tried to rise and found his movement restricted by a pressure around his neck. One of the iron collars, forced only upon slaves, was ringing his neck and chained to the wall. To that end, he realised they were no longer inside the bubbled hut, but somewhere along the outer edge of the camp, where the natural rock wall could be used as an anchor for the chain. His hands were bound by rope and connected to another length of rope that had been tied around his waist.

"What have you done, dwarf?" he growled.

"A good hunter always bargains," the son of Dorain began. "I got the chieftain to increase the pot but, even then, it's hardly worth sharin'. As it turns out, the tribe's lost their cook—killed by the monster. So," the dwarf drawled, "I might 'ave convinced 'em that ye're an *excellent* cook, the best in the north in fact!"

Asher pushed against his restraints and attempted to assault his scheming foe, but Doran remained a few inches beyond his reach.

"Come on," the dwarf insisted. "It's not *that* bad. Better than sufferin' me axe buried in yer head, eh? Jus' make 'em some meals, do a bad job o' it, an' they'll probably let ye go before long."

"I'm a slave!" Asher hissed.

Doran waved the notion away. "Somethin' tells me ye're a man o' means." He wagged his finger at the bindings. "I've no doubt ye'll find a way out o' this, jus' not before I line me pockets with some well-earned coin."

Asher leaned forward as much as he could and fixed the dwarf with a glare. "Pray to your gods, Doran, son of Dorain. Pray that the monster out there gets you before I do."

The dwarf was still smiling. "I'm sorry, laddy. Ye jus' picked the wrong job. Look on the bright side: ye'll get to see the tribe thrive again after I take care o' the beastie." Doran began to walk away before he remembered something and turned back to the ranger. "I nearly forgot. Ye'll be needin' this." Asher looked down at the wooden ladle thrown between his resting knees. "I hear they're big fans o' broth!"

CHAPTER 2

BE CAREFUL WHAT YOU BARGAIN FOR

Centaur - The scourge of The Moonlit Plains, to be sure. Most would describe these creatures as part man, part horse. They'd be wrong. There's no shred of man to be found in these beasts. Now, I know the legends as well as anyone—ancient friends of the even more ancient elves. But whether they were once friends to the elves or not, one thing that isn't a legend is their brutality towards humans. Stray too far from The Selk Road while traversing The Moonlit Plains and it's said you'll meet your end by way of a Centaur. And they would be right. Why the beasts hate us so much has been debated by scholars of The All-Tower for centuries but we rangers know the truth, don't we? Centaurs are like any animal we hunt—they're territorial. The Plains are theirs, it's that simple. But, sometimes, it's they who stray from their territory. In these cases, most contracts for a Centaur will come out of Vangarth or Tregaran. But be warned, they hunt and live in teams of forty or more. They are not likely to be brought down.

A Chronicle of Monsters: A Ranger's Bestiary, 12th Edition, Page 238.

Hadrik Delaney, Ranger.

. . .

The tundra of The Iron Valley offered little but unrelenting winds and bouts of blinding snowfall. It was nothing a hearty dwarf couldn't handle, his bones made from Grarfath's mountains and his weathered skin woven by Yamnomora.

After a few decades of living south of The Vengoran Mountains, however, where the word of man held sway, Doran Heavybelly had grown accustomed to winters most dwarves would refer to as summer. And so the son of Dorain was thankful for the track that cut through the edge of the valley, where the land rose up either side and protected him from those unforgiving winds.

He didn't need to ask the young Jarat if this was the spot where their kin had been attacked—it was obvious. Old blood stained the stone walls and various limbs were poking out from the most recent snows.

Doran climbed down from his Warhog and elbowed the animal's head. "Keep yer nose out o' it, Pig," he instructed, stopping the aptly named hog from rummaging beneath the snow.

Crouching down, the dwarf moved some of the snow aside and yanked on two frozen fingers. The rest of the hand came with them until the torn and jagged wrist was revealed. Inspecting the bone, Doran concluded that it had been snapped by teeth—a powerful bite. Noticing the young Jarat observing his investigation with some trepidation, the son of Dorain quickly buried the limb again. For all he knew, the hand could have belonged to one of their parents.

Moving to the flat wall of rock on his left, where a large volume of blood had been splattered, Doran pressed his fingers into the grooves where three strong claw marks had raked from up to down. Judging by the size of the marks and the length of the overall scar left in the stone, he decided the monster in question was two or three times his size.

"Well," he said, turning back to the Warhog, "at least we're in for a decent fight."

Looking up at the mountain that bathed in the morning sun,

Doran searched for any sign of the monster's dwelling. This was, after all, the territory it had carved out for itself; there must be shelter somewhere that offered even beasts refuge from the extremes.

"*Are there any caves nearby?*" he asked in the barbarian tongue.

One of the older Jarat pointed to the curve in the path, where it presumably led to the base of the mountain.

"*Alright,*" he replied in thanks. "*Get yourselves home and be quick about it.*"

Doran was tempted to escort them back to the tribe and retrace his steps after making certain they were safe but, by all reports, the monster had only ever attacked at night. Beckoning Pig to follow him round the bend, the dwarf took both his sword and axe in hand, the vanguard to his hunt.

The narrow route curved one way then the next before opening up into a clearing that fronted a wide cave. The pair only had to walk a few feet inside to come across numerous bones and gnawed skeletons.

"I'd say this is it," Doran remarked, eyeing the darkness beyond. "Alright, keep that fat head o' yers on a swivel." Returning the sword to its place over his shoulder, the dwarf proceeded to remove the unlit torch protruding from one of his saddlebags and the flint to ignite it. "Shall we?" he continued, once the flames were brought to life.

The shadows of the mountain hollow retreated with every step. "What are ye thinkin' then?" he asked of the Warhog. "A Dweller? Nest o' Clackers? A *Stonemaw*?" The latter amused the dwarf, for the legendary Stonemaw was said to have been so immense it could have consumed the entire tribe in one mouthful. "Jus' remember, *Viktor* wants whatever it is alive. We're not to be upsettin' the likes o' him."

Pig came to a sudden halt. Doran knew better than to ignore the hog's animal senses. Holding the fiery torch away from himself, the son of Dorain directed the light into every nook and cranny his eyes failed to pierce. He froze when the eyes of another caught that light, revealing their hard gaze.

Doran smiled.

"An' what might *ye* be?" the dwarven hunter questioned, his anticipation rising to gleeful heights. "Care to make a new friend?" he asked the creature, indicating the axe in his hand.

Those reflective eyes slowly rose up in the darkness and, with every foot they rose, Doran's glee wavered a little more. It was damned big. Though he had jested, if this was indeed a Dweller he was as good as dead already. While Doran wondered if this was to be the day he would meet the Mother and Father in the flesh, the monster lurched forward, bringing its head into the furthest reaches of the light. It wasn't a Dweller.

Doran raised one bushy eyebrow. "What in all the hells are ye supposed to be?"

The monster's long arms, noticeably longer than its legs, braced against the cave floor and bent just enough to broadcast its intentions. Doran leapt to the side with hardly a moment to spare before the fiend was lashing out. Its body revealed by the torchlight now, the dwarf could see its scaled physique and sloping head, its features reminding him of a lizard. Experience told him it was a Gobber, but the son of Dorain had never seen one to boast such an impressive size.

One of its long arms swept out wide and three thick claws came for Doran's head. He dropped and rolled aside while Pig charged in and brought its tusks to bear. The enormous Gobber roared before the Warhog barrelled it over, spoiling the air with reptilian blood. The monster was quick to recover, however, and backhanded the hog with its knuckled fist.

"Oi!" Doran bellowed. "No one but me hits the pig!"

The Gobber hissed, its razor-sharp fangs revealed in all their deadly glory. Enraged, Doran didn't care what advantages the beast possessed. He was going to hard steel and that's all there was. With axe and torch, he ran at his enemy. The Gobber used its extended arms to propel itself, giving the dwarf just enough space to skid under it and hack once with his axe. The creature shrieked and continued on to the other side of the cave.

Doran took in the sight of blood on his blade and smirked. "Now ye're goin' to get it," he uttered determinedly.

Turning again, this particular Gobber proved more intelligent than those of its kind Doran had faced before. The monster launched itself up into the ceiling and clawed its way over the dwarf. The son of Dorain swore in the language of his kin and dived to one side, narrowly avoiding the crushing bulk that came for his life. As he rose to his feet, the Gobber was upon him, its claws raking his armour from shoulder to gut. The force of it pushed him back and a second blow took him from his feet.

The Gobber's lizard-like head darted down towards the dwarf, its salivating maw stretching wide. Taking to his axe with two hands, the torch left by his side, Doran raised his weapon and lodged it between the monster's snapping jaws. Infuriated, a hardened flap of scaled skin expanded along either side of its neck, a hood of sorts. Doran had seen certain snakes display the same feature, often used to make the animal appear larger than it was.

His blood boiling with the fight, the dwarf cared little for size now. Nor did Pig.

The Warhog rammed the Gobber in its midriff, its tusks again piercing its hide. The son of Dorain was gifted a reprieve and he used it to find his feet and pick up the torch. He flicked his axe and splattered thick saliva up the nearest wall. With a war cry on his lips, the dwarven hunter raced back into battle.

Only seconds later, both Doran and Pig were thrown aside and forced to the cave floor again, bloodied and bruised for their effort. The Warhog grunted and shook its snout while the son of Dorain spat a mouthful of blood onto the cold stone and muttered of his need for a hard drink. Not far away, the hulking Gobber was stalking the edges of the cave, its eyes trained on them.

"Viktor can keep 'is bloody coin," Doran grumbled, as he rose to his full height again. "I'm thinkin' yer hide will make for a great saddle," he said, his smile revealing the blood coating his teeth.

The creature reared its head and let loose a threatening hiss that filled the cave and the surrounding tunnels. Only moments later the cave began to fill with the shape of Gobbers more familiar to the dwarf, their size akin to the Warhog. Doran wasn't one to back down from a fight, whatever the odds, but the same could not be said of Pig, whose judgement was often sounder.

The Warhog bolted. Doran's instinct was to chastise the animal and his mouth opened to do just that, but it was a yelp of surprise that came forth instead. His ankle having become tangled up in the rope that had spilled out of the saddlebags, the dwarf was quickly on the flat of his back for a third time, only now he was unceremoniously dragged from the cave and with a pack of Gobbers in pursuit.

They were fast, swiftly propelled on their long arms, but none were so fast as the big one. The beast flattened two of its smaller kin in its desire to catch up with its next meal.

Pig, however, had no intention of being the next meal and sprang from the cave entrance without delay. The mount darted through the clearing with a shower of snow kicked up in its wake. His point of view upside down, Doran could only watch the giant creature as it skimmed the arch of the cave and emerged into the light. One leap and its front claws dug into the ground mere inches from the dwarf's head.

Leaving the clearing behind, Pig charged along the weaving path, sending Doran skidding left and right. A pained grunt escaped his lips every time his armour scraped against the rock and bit into his muscles. Before long, the Warhog's hooves were pounding through the attack site, where one of the severed hands was kicked up and sent into the dwarf's face.

"Watch where ye're goin'!" he barked.

The racing monster was soon upon them again. Doran rolled his shoulders and twisted his torso out of the way, evading an incoming claw by inches. He returned the attack with one of his own and lashed out with the axe, though the blade had no more luck than the creature's claws.

As The Iron Valley opened up, the adjacent mountains no more than a thin black line on the horizon, Pig doubled its efforts and cut a straight line across the land. Beyond the western edge of the valley, it seemed the monster was loath to enter the tundra and leave its territory. Its claws dug in and brought its considerable bulk to an abrupt halt on their trail.

The dwarf waited until it retreated into the mountains before heaving himself up and tugging hard on the rope. After numerous, and exhausting attempts, it finally snagged on a rock, breaking free of the saddle, and the son of Dorain's momentum saw him tumble through the snow for several feet.

His breath laboured, the dwarf still managed to curse the hog. When he eventually sat up—and it was some time—Pig had come to its senses and returned to him.

He looked back to the western mountains. "We might need to rethink this," he admitted reluctantly.

Nearing noon, hours after his encounter with the monster, Doran Heavybelly entered the Jarat camp with his head hanging low. Pig trotted in beside him with no such shame and quickly went off in search of scraps.

Many of the younger barbarians ran up to the dwarf and required a brief recounting. Explaining why he hadn't returned with the beast's head compounded his shame.

"*We were just getting the measure of each other,*" he told them, including one of the elders who would likely report directly to the chieftain. "*I'll head back out at dawn and see the job finished,*" he promised.

Following his nose, the son of Dorain made his way into the heart of the camp, where something of a queue had formed. One by one, The Jarat were receiving a bowl of something steaming. On the other side of a makeshift counter stood the ranger and a couple of other slaves—a man and a woman, likely claimed in a skirmish with an opposing tribe. While two of them were preparing food, Asher was stirring a large pot with his new ladle before filling the bowls.

His eyes, a shade of blue even the sky would envy, found the dwarf on his approach and promised death if he wandered too close. Still, the son of Dorain had questions and there were none among the barbarians who could answer them.

Daring to go around the counter and join Asher, Doran looked from the young Jarat to the enslaved ranger, unsure exactly how to begin. "It's goin' well then?"

Asher glanced at the dwarf between servings. "You found the monster," he concluded.

Doran's fingers unconsciously ran over one of the claw marks on his breastplate. "Aye, that I did. Big bugger it is too."

The ranger looked past the dwarf. "You didn't slay it," he stated, seeing no evidence of the kill.

"I've got it right where I want it," Doran defended half-heartedly.

"What is *it* exactly?"

Doran noticed Asher give a hand signal to one of the young boys as he took the bowl from the ranger. *To survive*, were his silent words. Dwarves and humans alike would have said something along the lines of, *you're welcome*, but in The Iron Valley such words had no place. Anything, if not everything, that was given was merely to survive and to be appreciated as such. In this instance, Asher had given the boy food *to survive*.

"Ye're a quick learner," he complimented.

"I thought it best since I'm to *die* here," the ranger quipped dryly. Asher looked the dwarf in the face for a moment before an amused smile curled his lips. "You don't know what it is, do you?"

The son of Dorain attempted to look offended before his embarrassment showed through. "I think it's a Gobber," he said gruffly.

"You don't know a Gobber when you see one?" Asher asked, if a little mockingly.

"I've seen plenty o' Gobbers, laddy." A shadow overcame his furrowed brow. "But not like this. It was bigger than a horse an' damned strong I can tell ye. It looked like a Giant standin' next to the other Gobbers."

Asher paused in his stirring before scooping another bowlful for a waiting Jarat. "It's a Hobgobber," he declared evenly.

Doran was stumped. "Ye mean like Hobgobber's Ale?"

The ranger blinked once and slowly. "Yes, like the ale," he replied with obvious exasperation. "Except the real thing will tear your head off, as you've seen. Hobgobber, Royal Gobber; they've gone by a few names. They're the male of the species."

Doran raised an eyebrow. "So the rest o' 'em are…"

"The females," Asher finished. "For a hunter, you don't know much about your prey."

"Well I don' jus' hunt beasties, ranger man," Doran retorted angrily. "There's plenty o' dumb humans out there with prices on their heads."

"Bounty hunting is a messy profession," the ranger opined. "I prefer to keep it simple."

"Good for ye," the dwarf remarked, growing tired of the man already. "It's not goin' to get much simpler than this," he added spitefully, nodding at the pot of stew.

Asher continued to stir the food a while longer, ignoring the comment. "Are you going to ask me then?"

Doran tensed his jaw and looked anywhere but at the ranger, battling with his next words. "How exactly do ye kill a Royal Gobber or whatever?"

Asher waited until he had served two more people before answering. "The same way you kill anything—stab something it can't live without. Take that sword for example," he continued, flicking his jaw at the weapon strapped to the dwarf's back. "Run it through the Hobgobber's brain, heart, vital organs and it'll go down."

"Oh," Doran replied sarcastically, "is that how ye kill somethin'? It's a wonder I've lived as long as I 'ave without knowin' where to put me sword."

"You asked," Asher pointed out.

"Perhaps ye'd like me to tell ye where to put that ladle?"

Asher knocked the wooden spoon against the rim of the pot. "I could kill a Hobgobber with this if I had to," he said with no hint of a boast.

Doran chuckled at the preposterous image. "Sure ye could, laddy. Would that be with or without yer wrists bound?"

"You'll just have to wait and see," the ranger said quietly.

"What's that supposed to mean?" Doran spat, confident an insult had been weaved between Asher's words.

"*You* might be forgettable to a Hobgobber," the ranger explained, "but that hog of yours..."

The dwarf turned to his left and caught sight of Pig between the huts, its head poking through someone's doorway. "Speak plainly."

"Your mount could feed a Hobgobber for days," Asher said simply. "It's not going to let that kind of prey just slip away."

An edge of panic entered Doran's voice. "What are ye sayin'?"

"Gobbers can be exquisite trackers if the prey is worth it. They can cross miles, even if it takes them far from their hunting grounds."

The son of Dorain chewed over that. "Ye don' know what ye're talkin' about. The beastie gave up the hunt an' turned back."

The ranger just nodded along. "Like you said: I don't know what I'm talking about."

Doran huffed and marched away before he gave in to his violent inclinations. His path was soon blocked by four children playing a game beyond his dwarven comprehension. He watched them run off, his imagination carried away by dark thoughts of the horrors a Royal Gobber could inflict upon the camp.

"Bah!" he grumped, dismissing Asher's predictions. The man had less than forty winters behind him—what did he know?

CHAPTER 3
PROVING A POINT

Humming Swarm *- Twenty-six years. That's how long I've been in this business. That's a long time for a ranger. I tell you this because in all my years on the job, only once have I come across a contract for a Humming Swarm.*

The swarm I was contracted to destroy was on the west coast, not far from Ameeraska. The little buggers prefer a hot and dry climate. They also devour their prey within three to five seconds and they leave naught but nibbled bones in their wake. The closest creature I could compare them to is a piranha fish—if it had wings.

Most mistake them for leaves, and a whole swarm will fill the branches of a fully-grown tree. Unfortunately, each individual Hummer (my preferred name for them) is no bigger than the end of your finger, so your sword, axe, bow— whatever your preference—is of no use with these monsters. You could swing at them for hours and hit naught but air. Not that they'd give you the chance.

The only way to kill the critters is with smoke. Since they sleep at night, I would suggest creeping under the canopy and starting a few fires. Either that or don't take the contract. The latter is probably more sensible.

A Chronicle of Monsters: A Ranger's Bestiary, 12th Edition,
Page 366.

Arslef, Ranger.

After a short reprieve in the middle of the afternoon, Asher and his ladle had been forced back to the pot where the evening meal was to be cooked. While his wrists were kept in their bindings, the rope connecting them to his waist had been removed, allowing him more movement to prepare the food.

To his left, Ghali and Henuun—slaves from a tribe he couldn't name—were dicing meat and vegetables before tossing them into the pot. Try as he might, Asher had only succeeded in learning a handful of words alongside their names, and the words he had learned served only to aid in the cooking.

Though there was nothing to like about his enslavement, the ranger found an island of solace in the simplicity of his new job. He prepared food, he cooked it, and then he served it, feeding the entire tribe in the process. Every now and then he was granted a glimpse of Hector. The ranger was growing concerned that bits of the horse would soon cross his table, there to be added to the broth.

It wouldn't come to that, he told himself. The half-witted dwarf had seen to events that would soon provide the required opportunity.

Sheltered by the natural walls that surrounded the camp, the flames blazing on the torches were able to withstand the growing winds that accompanied the night. In the gloom, Asher served young and old, slopping their hot broth into one bowl after another. A small portion was allowed to be shared between the slaves.

Once they had finished their meagre meals and the bowls had all been collected, it was time to wash everything, ready for break-fast at first light. Asher went about his duties without a word, his focus constantly shifting from the camp's main entrance to the top of the surrounding walls. If the Hobgobber had indeed tracked the hog's scent, it would most certainly have detected the cooking meat on the air by now.

Finished with the pot, Asher discreetly took the single knife they were permitted to use and seated himself on a small bench behind Ghali and Henuun. He didn't have long before the knife would be reclaimed by one of the older Jarat—the blade only given to them while food needed preparing. Henuun turned around and shot the ranger a questioning look but said nothing in protest. Using his fellow slaves as shields, he began to whittle the handle of the ladle, turning it into a sharpened point.

Soon after, as a full moon continued its journey across the heavens, the knife was taken and the slaves commanded to their feet. Single-file, they were escorted to their dwelling, a form of shelter more suited to animals. With the ladle slotted neatly between his arm and vambrace, the ranger prepared himself for a sleepless night of waiting and watching.

Thankfully, neither was required.

A scream of dread tore through the barbarian camp. The two adolescents escorting them braced their spears and turned in the direction of the alarm. The slaves were quickly forgotten in the face of a possible attack and soon abandoned in search of the fight. Ghali and Henuun made a dash for their pathetic shelter, a place that couldn't protect them from monster or man.

Asher did what he always did. He followed the sound of violence.

Weaving between the huts, his heading north, the ranger caught sight of Doran sitting over a log with his trousers around his ankles and a bucket waiting to be filled. He was clearly flustered by the interruption and alarmed by the ruckus around him. Asher would have paused to offer the dwarf a smug grin, but the next scream he heard suggested someone had been injured.

Clearing the huts, he got his first sight of the monster that had terrorised The Jarat. There was no mistaking it: the huge beast could only be a Hobgobber. Asher had seen an illustration of the creature in A Chronicle of Monsters: A Ranger's Bestiary but the artist had failed to get the Royal Gobber's truly superior size across.

As the male of the species perched on the lip of the surrounding ice wall, two female Gobbers leapt into the camp, their jaws snapping incessantly. Proving that no matter their age the barbarians of The Iron Valley were hard folk, three of the children, no older than thirteen years, rushed the incoming monsters and speared them with brutal efficiency. The adolescents who had been escorting Asher and the slaves emerged from behind a line of hanging furs and added their crude blades to the tribe's defence, killing two more of the female Gobbers.

A rumbling snarl accompanied the steaming breath of the Hobgobber. Its muscles tensed beneath green scales, a prelude to its inevitable jump. Asher was shouting at The Jarat to move as he himself was running towards the lurching beast. One of the elders with more sense barrelled into the young men and knocked them aside, sparing them from the Royal Gobber's descent.

The ground shook under its weight, its reptilian eyes homed in on the approaching ranger. By now, Asher was the only one in the camp running towards the fiend, his advance an obvious contrast to The Jarat's retreat.

The coming violence played out in Asher's mind, a place where the chaos of battle was all so serene and calculated. He pictured the killing stroke and his hand tightened around the ladle, the pointed shaft angled down.

As the gap closed between them, the ranger used the Hobgobber's speed to his advantage. Unable to change its direction fast enough, the beast could do nothing but watch the ranger leap to one side, into the hut on his right. Its claws dug in to take some momentum away, but it was too late. By the time it was skidding past the hut, Asher had used one foot to reverse his jump and gain some height in the process. Before the monster knew what had happened, the ranger was on its back, the top of his bindings wrapped around its thick neck.

Asher clenched every muscle, his limbs gripping to the scaly hide with all his strength. The Royal Gobber thrashed and shrieked, bruising the ranger's arms and legs. Following through the scenario his mind had conjured, Asher thrust the sharpened ladle into the softer skin of the monster's neck folds. Warm blood spilled over his hands and the frustrated shrieks evolved into pained grunts.

Stabbing the creature again and again, Asher slammed the palm of his hand onto the scoop of the ladle, hammering the shaft further into its throat. After another inch was covered, the Hobgobber's voice grew distorted until the distinct sound of drowning found Asher's ears. Then the blood began to ooze out of the monster's mouth and its legs wobbled.

Death had come for it, and Death would take it.

As it fell forwards under its top-heavy weight, the ranger was thrown to the ground, his wrists still bound. Only then did Doran Heavybelly burst forth from between two huts, his axe buried in the head of a common Gobber. Unable to slow down following that blow, the dwarf tripped over the corpse of his own kill and landed beside Asher in a heap of limbs with a face full of snow.

"I see you found your trousers," the ranger quipped between breaths.

The dwarf pushed himself up and dragged his hand through his long beard, relieving it of snow. "I was abou' to do that," he informed, looking at the dead Hobgobber.

"I thought as much," Asher replied, picking himself up.

Doran groaned under the weight of his armour but it didn't stop him from finding his feet and rising beside the ranger. His head tilted to take in the corpse and another, more aggrieved, groan escaped his lips.

"Ye've got to be kiddin' me." The son of Dorain stepped forward and tapped the end of the ladle with his boot. "Ye jus' had to, didn' ye?"

Asher's lip began to curl into a smirk when the spears of his masters preceded their arrival. Young and old looked from the Royal Gobber to Asher, his feat of skill and bravery seen by most. They parted for the chieftain, who was much taller and his shoulders broader than his throne had suggested. That said, the older man was using his staff for support more than a symbol of status. His guttural language filled the night air, every syllable as foreign to Asher as the next.

The ranger turned to regard Doran. "He had better be talking about my freedom or the next utensil is going up your—"

"I'll take care o' it," the dwarf assured, his hand coming up to wave the threat away. The exchange that took place between barbarian and dwarf felt an eternity.

"Yer freedom is acceptable," he eventually reported. "But the coin..." The son of Dorain caught himself and cleared his throat. "He says the coin is mine, since ye were me slave an' I brought ye 'ere."

Asher tensed his jaw and worked hard at keeping his immediate thoughts and feelings to himself. "Tell him you want Ghali and Henuun instead of the coin."

"What?" Doran snapped in surprise. "They've got nothin' to do with us, laddy. This is their way."

Asher met the dwarf's eyes and delivered his ultimatum with an even tone. "If I walk out of this camp with only you by my side, Doran, son of Dorain, I give you my word there will be blood."

The dwarven hunter glanced at the protruding ladle, firmly lodged in the Hobgobber's throat, before delivering his terms to the chieftain. There was some back and forth between them, enough to make Asher wonder whether they had asked for too much.

"They can go free," Doran finally informed him. "But they want to keep the corpse," he added, nudging the Hobgobber. "By tradition, the kill is yours to—"

"They can have it," Asher cut in, raising his hands to present the taut rope that bound his wrists.

A pink dawn gave way to an ocean of blue sky, a contrast to the carpet of pure white that lay across the floor of The Iron Valley.

Asher met the open land astride Hector, his gear and supplies returned to him. His last night with The Jarat had been one of celebration that saw the entire tribe feed off the Royal Gobber.

It hadn't tasted too bad.

Now, with the barbarians behind him, the ranger listened and watched Ghali and Henuun offer him a handful of words. "They're thankin' ye again," Doran translated.

Asher responded with a nod and polite smile—their freedom was to be his only reward for this particular journey. He could live with that.

After watching them take off to the west, the ranger shifted his shoulders to look down on Doran. "Take a care, master dwarf," he began. "Should we meet again I might recall all too easily the deal you struck."

The son of Dorain straightened his back astride his Warhog. "Is that a threat, ranger man?"

Asher offered him a look in place of any words, and a look with steel behind his eyes. His answer given, the ranger guided Hector took to the south, to Illian.

CHAPTER 4
DARKWELL

Dopplegorger *- Once you've learnt of these demons you'll have enjoyed your last night in a tavern or upon the cosy bed of some sleepy inn. I thank the gods Dopplegorgers are rare (almost wiped out in the fourth century of the Third Age).*

These monsters will infiltrate villages or towns, lurking on the outskirts until they find a suitable candidate (often a loner with little to no family). Once they do, they not only kill their victim but assume their identity. I am yet to understand how they accomplish their devilry, but it seems they skin the victim and then proceed to wear it. Beyond this, the fiends are able to transform their bodies until their resemblance is flawless.

It is then that the fox is able to walk among the chickens. Should you find yourself hunting one of these monsters, be sure to thoroughly question everyone—leave no stone unturned. Their level of intelligence is only passable in brief encounters; extensive questioning will reveal them. Just make sure your sword is in hand when you do.

A Chronicle of Monsters: A Ranger's Bestiary, 12th Edition, Page 241.

Borvun the Butcher, Ranger.

S ix Months Later...

Falling back on the skills of his previous career, Asher always felt in control of his environment, and moving through the world of man without being noticed was second nature to him: a state of existence he had become accustomed to, preferred even. And so, to enter a city with the eyes of many tracking him was akin to walking the streets with naught but his bare skin for company.

The inhabitants of Darkwell watched Asher as he rode down the central avenue with the utmost interest. It wasn't the broadsword resting on his hip that caught their eye, nor the folded bow and short-sword strapped to his back.

It was the two severed heads that hung from one side of his saddle.

They had all heard, no doubt, of the monsters plaguing The Selk Road just south of their home, but seeing them in the flesh was something entirely different. Then there was the man himself, the ranger who had defeated the savage beasts and now presented them so openly. Asher could make himself appear diminutive if he wished, a talent that allowed him to pass through most places without a trace, but moving unseen and unheard was foolish when parading his work. After all, he required payment.

The decapitated heads were dropped unceremoniously on the desk, a desk that belonged to the captain of Darkwell's city watch. The only person to hold more authority was Lord Gudson, the lord in those parts.

Captain Faerson pushed himself back from the edge of the desk, his brow furrowing with disgust and irritation. "What in the hells are they?" he growled, looking up at the ranger before him.

"Stravakin," Asher answered in his gruff voice.

"What?" the captain demanded, glancing at two of his men for support.

"Bone eaters," Asher told him simply, gesturing to the monsters' pale and pointed beaks. "They were the fiends plaguing your southern road," he continued, aware that the Stravakin had restricted the ebb and flow of merchants of late.

"That doesn't explain why they're on my desk," Faerson fumed.

"Better there than on the road," the ranger remarked, with little thought given to his tone.

The captain sucked on his teeth, contorting his expression into something close to a sneer. "I said we'd pay you to kill the monster. I'm not paying you more for two of them."

Asher refrained from sighing, the conversation going like so many others. "Stravakin always come in pairs. I told you that when I took the job."

"I find it suspicious," Faerson replied with no care given to his own tone, "that you already knew what kind of beasts were stalking the road. A con man perhaps?"

Asher stepped forward, a physical and obvious response to the offence. The two watchmen reached for their swords but kept them sheathed when the ranger did no more than stand a little closer to the desk.

"I knew they were Stravakin from the description of the bodies you found," he explained. "I told you there would be two and you told me to *just deal with it.*" The ranger stepped back and nodded his chin at the heads. "It's been dealt with. The coin is double."

"Double?" The captain almost choked on the word. "The coin I was paying you was already generous, Ranger. If you want more I suggest you find your way to Palios and demand the rest from them—the southern road is more theirs than ours anyway."

Palios was south of The Unmar River, too far to be concerned by the Stravakin just beyond Darkwell's border. It was an absurd suggestion and the captain knew as much.

Asher took a composing breath. "The coin is double," he repeated.

Captain Faerson reached into the drawer, on the left of his desk, and retrieved a leather purse of coins. It wasn't double, that much was obvious as he placed it in front of Asher. "Take it or leave it, Ranger," the captain instructed. "Either way, you *will* be leaving now."

Again, the watchmen rested their hands on the hilts of their swords: a clear threat. Asher's instincts fought for superiority, demanding that he give in to his training and let his muscle memory take over. How easily he could kill all three of them.

But that was not his way. Not anymore.

The ranger stepped onto the streets of Darkwell with the coin purse tied to his belt. He admired the blue sky of summer, taking what little pleasure there was to be had in the moment. Such were the risks of taking a contract in the city, he knew. Still, the payment was higher than anything he could have expected from a town or village.

Guiding Hector by the reins, he led the horse through the heart of Darkwell, where its oval theatre dominated a large crossroads. Mid-afternoon, the theatre was closed, though the streets around it were still chaotic with foot traffic. The surrounding buildings, three storeys all, offered a variety of shops and places to enjoy a good meal.

Asher knew he had a choice: buy one large and exquisite meal or buy a good bed for the night and something bland that would simply fill his stomach. Though often frugal, as any smart ranger would be, Asher had no problem these days with making a bed out on the land, and killing Stravakin was hungry work.

"Come along, Hector," he bade. "I see dumplings in our future."

After securing the horse to one of the exterior posts, the ranger entered The Lion's Crown, a tavern so named for the sigil of the north's ruling family, the Tions. By the time Asher's hot meal—a large plate of beef stew and dumplings—was being put in front of him, The Lion's Crown was filling up with patrons from all walks of life. No one had entered the tavern without being scrutinised by the ranger, even if it had only been a passing glance.

As was habit, Asher would be ever vigilant in crowded places.

Crowds were the perfect environment for Arakesh, offering a palette of culture that they could adopt and acclimate to. Thankfully, their numbers being so few, it was a rare thing to cross paths with an assassin of Nightfall, and in a realm so large as the six kingdoms rarer still. Regardless, Asher assessed every individual around him, searching for any hint of a facade.

After another hour of enjoying his Velian mint tea while his hearty meal digested, the general hubbub of the tavern changed, a single voice growing louder amongst the patrons. Looking around, it seemed one customer had entered The Lion's Crown without the ranger's notice, though his voice more than made up for his physical stature.

"Can no one help me?" the dwarf beseeched as he came into view. "Not one o' ye?"

Asher eyed the dwarf, somewhat astounded. It wasn't Doran Heavybelly—a dwarf not easily forgotten. But what were the chances of meeting another of his kin in as little as six months?

Where the son of Dorain had possessed a tight ponytail and bushy blond beard, this child of the mountain was almost hidden from the world by the wild greying hair that met his beard to form a mane around his hard face. Without the hunter's armour, this dwarf could be seen for all he was and none would describe him as anything but strong. The muscles in his forearms were coiled like ropes and defined by worming veins. His hairy chest looked to be escaping his shirt, revealing slabs of muscle. Perhaps this one didn't need armour.

"How can ye deny me help?" the dwarf continued, turning from person to person. "Would ye deny each other the aid I ask for? No ye wouldn'!" he accused. "I'm one o' ye! I live in Darkwell! This is me home! This is me family's home!"

"You don't live here, dwarf!" one of the patrons barked.

"Get back to the forest!" another chipped in maliciously. "Where you belong."

"We live out there because the lord won' grant us permission to live among ye!" the dwarf retorted. "But I must be one o' ye, because he still taxes me! Not to mention the work I do for ye! There's no better smith in the whole damn city!"

The barman groaned. "Be gone with you, dwarf! You're upsetting my customers and you're not welcome here!"

The burly dwarf planted his feet like the roots of a mountain. "I ask for yer aid now," he began anew, if somewhat exasperated, "because, together, we might be able to deal with the Troll. It won' jus' stop with me an' mine. Oh no! It'll find its way 'ere an' ye'll all suffer its wrath!"

Asher's attention was immediately sharpened by mention of the monster. He bore no inclination to get involved with the dwarf or in his dispute with the people of Darkwell, but Trolls and the like were his business. Also, his coin purse was lighter than it should have been.

"Out with you!" came the responding chorus.

In the silence that followed, the ranger pushed himself up, causing his chair to drag across the floor. As all eyes turned to Asher, his own gaze fell upon the dwarf. The smith looked him up and down, perhaps wondering if the man with more weapons than limbs was friend or foe.

"You may join me, smith," Asher said, his eyes flitting to the adjacent chair.

"The hells he will," the barman interjected.

With one look, Asher conveyed the inconvenience, if not the injury, that would occur should anyone prevent the pair from sitting together. A tentative moment existed between every patron and the ranger before the dwarf accepted the invitation and took up the offered seat. Since there were no further protests, Asher sat back down and gave the surrounding men and women one lasting look that suggested they get on with their business. Only when the murmur of conversation began again did the ranger acknowledge his companion.

"My name is Asher," he said, not often the first to speak his name.

"Well met, Asher," the dwarf replied with something of an

embarrassed smile. "I am Danagarr, son of... Well, it doesn' really matter to be honest. I'm a smith by trade."

"So I heard," Asher replied. "I'm a ranger."

Danagarr looked away, his memory at work. "I've heard o' ye folk—monster hunters right? Not seen one round these parts for years."

"There aren't many of us left," Asher told him, confident that he was, in fact, the only man in Illian who called himself a ranger. "But I'm here now, and it sounds like you have a monster problem."

"Too right I do," Danagarr intoned, leaning over the table. "A damned Troll if ye can believe it. An' close to the city. Not that *they* care."

"You've been to the watch?"

"Aye, o' course. They wouldn' hear it. I even tried to get an audience with Lord Gudson but I was laughed away by those who serve 'im."

"How have you survived it so far?" Asher enquired.

"Distractions, traps, sacrificin' the odd bit o' livestock we keep. I had one close encounter a week past—I ended up hidin' in a hollowed-out log like some bug." Danagarr shook his head, a hint of shame in his expression. "A dwarf hidin' from the likes o' a stinkin' Troll..."

"Trolls are not easily beaten," Asher offered reassuringly.

"I couldn' risk leadin' it back to me family. Me wife an' daughter... I couldn' let anythin' happen to 'em."

Hearing about a wife and daughter surprised the ranger, though such a thing was perfectly normal, expected even. Asher could have accepted a single dwarven smith, but a whole family living in the world of man was most unusual. He wasn't one to pry, however.

"I would offer you my services," he said instead, "if we could agree on payment."

Danagarr nodded along, taking the measure of the ranger again. "Ye've experience with Trolls?"

The easy lie surfaced before the truth, but Asher managed to hold on to it. "No," he answered honestly. "Though I have slain a Giant. A larger monster there is not."

"A Giant, eh?" Danagarr considered. "That's impressive. Ye've proof?"

"No," Asher said again. "Giants are hard trophies to carry around," he added with some sarcasm. "But I don't expect coin up front. If I can't kill the Troll you needn't be concerned with my skill or payment."

"Fair enough," the dwarf agreed. "When can ye start?"

Asher considered his empty plate and dwindling supply of mint tea. "Right now," he replied. "We can discuss payment on the way."

Danagarr slapped his hand on the table. "At last! A man o' action! Unlike the rest o' ye!" he bellowed as he stood up from the table. "Let's be off then; I'd not be away from me Deadora an' Kilda any longer than I need to."

Asher noted that neither the barman nor patrons could meet his eyes as he trailed the dwarf out of The Lion's Crown.

~

Somewhere between life and death, Doran Heavybelly gripped his reins, holding fast to Pig as the animal traversed the short journey across Darkwell's stone bridge. The dwarf was able to heave himself up just enough to spit blood, most of which splattered against his boot. The effort sent an agonising twinge through his back and a stabbing pain behind his shoulder.

"Keep goin', laddy," he rasped to his Warhog.

Groaning as he did, the son of Dorain managed to reach over his pained shoulder and tug the bony spike protruding from between his armoured plates. He examined the dark spine, coated in his blood, and let it fall to the ground.

In the late summer sun, there was still a healthy flow of travellers and merchants moving in and out of the city. Every one of them paused in their activity to stare at the dwarf, curious about his kind more than his obvious injuries. Doran was used to it. Though, right now, he didn't much care one way or the other.

Where any human would have been offered immediate aid, the son of Dorain was ignored by the watchmen at Darkwell's gate. If anything, they eyed him with suspicion and chose to overlook the blood that oozed from his multiple wounds. Again, Doran was used to it.

Pushing himself up as much as his injuries would allow, the dwarf was able to guide Pig through the markets and into the heart of the city.

"What foul beast walks our fair streets?" came a threatening call from ahead.

Doran found a patrolling watchman and his friends, their firm stances enough to grant them a wider berth from everyone else. "Grarfath's beard," he muttered to himself. "It's *my* foul beast," he replied, bringing the Warhog to a stop in front of them.

The loudest amongst the watchmen rested his hands on his hips. "You are granted more rights than you deserve, Danagarr Stormshield. I will not permit this wild creature to walk my streets."

Doran sighed and wondered if he had the strength to beat the men back. Then again, if he did put them in their place, more of their ilk would replace them and he would inevitably find his way behind the bars of a cell.

"'Tis me mount, good sir," the dwarf replied, changing tack. "He won' hurt ye or yer folk. Ye 'ave me word."

"The word of Danagarr Stormshield means little to me... *little man*," he added with a wicked edge to his voice.

Doran's hand squeezed the leather of Pig's reins, freeing a trickle of blood from a small cut on his knuckle. "I'm not Dana-garr," he said with little patience, his fatigue biting into his muscles. "Nor am I a Stormshield," he told them, his own clan a notch lower in Dhenaheim's hierarchy. Seeing their confusion, the son of Dorain continued, "Doran Heavybelly's the name, fellas."

"*Another* dwarf?" one of the watchmen complained.

"Is this an invasion?" another voiced with his own brand of humour.

There was a time when Doran would have confidently invaded Darkwell with a mere handful of his kin. Of course, there were none among his clan who would stand beside him now.

"I'm jus' passin' through," the dwarf explained, struggling to keep his head up.

The lead watchman looked over his shoulder, clearly bemused. "Passing through? To where? The sea? Can dwarves even swim?" he queried, much to the amusement of his comrades.

"Danagarr," Doran announced with blood on his lips. "I'm 'ere to see Danagarr."

The watchman said something in response but the words were lost on Doran, his attention getting away from him. The light of the sky was becoming too much and the constant buzz of the human world swirled around the son of Dorain like a closing storm. His hand lazily wandered down, over his armour, until it found the edges of another spine protruding from under his ribs.

"I need..." he drawled. "I need... Danagarr."

With that, Doran Heavybelly slipped from his saddle and met the hard ground, his world reduced to a soundless abyss.

CHAPTER 5

THE STORMSHIELDS

Naerwitch - These be demons of the dark I say. The pitch-black is their home and they know it well. How these cave-dwellers are able to detect their prey remains a mystery but, make no mistake, they will find you. And while you will need fire to hunt them down, the light will not deter them. It's for this reason we believe Naerwitches lack eyes altogether. These creatures move on six legs, though it should be noted that some have been discovered to possess eight or even ten. I hesitate to describe their feet but it is a feature that remains unique to these monsters. It doesn't matter how many legs they have, they all walk on feet that look exactly like human hands.

Why this is the case remains as much a mystery as their perception. As for killing a Naerwitch, aim for their protruding torso and swing hard—you don't want to get into a prolonged fight while your fire is dying. Once you lose the light, you lose your life.

A Chronicle of Monsters: A Ranger's Bestiary, 12th Edition, Page 359.

Anther Grane, Ranger.

. . .

East of Darkwell, where the land continued without sight or sound of civilisation, a small wood blocked any view of The Adean, though its lapping waves filled the air with their constant rhythm. Asher could smell the salt too and wondered just how close the sea was beyond his sight. They never made it far enough to tell, Danagarr's homestead emerging from between the trees.

The ranger guided Hector in on foot, the reins pulled taut in one hand. It was by no means a large house, though it possessed a welcoming quality to it, a look that suggested it was cosy inside. Asher also guessed it had been built by Danagarr himself, the proportions suited to his kin alone.

Off to one side, though connected to the house by a pergola that had long been overrun by ivy, stood a squat building that lacked the comfortable features of the main home. Even from a distance, Asher could see the forge and a variety of tools favoured by a smith. Further still were a handful of pens with animals roaming about inside. The pen housing a family of pigs was currently being tended to by a dwarven female who had failed to note their arrival.

"Kilda!" Danagarr called cheerfully enough.

Kilda turned to see their approach, her beaming smile quick to fade upon sighting Asher. Suspicion, and a small degree of trepidation, infringed on her expression. The people of Darkwell, if not all of Illian, had treated this family poorly.

A moment later, a small dwarven girl came bounding out of the house, excited to see her father. Danagarr scooped her up and held her tight. "Deadora!" he said with so much love in his voice.

By now, Kilda had left her duties and crossed the small yard to claim her daughter's hand while she nestled into her father's arms. Vibrant green eyes fixed on Asher and never strayed as she asked a question in the tongue of Dhenaheim.

Danagarr held up a reassuring hand. "He's a friend," the dwarf declared in the common speech of man. "I *think*," he added, offering the ranger a sly look. "Asher, this is me family: Kilda an' Deadora Stormshield."

Kilda held on to her reservations. "An' why, exactly, 'ave ye made friends with me husband, Asher?"

"Kilda," Danagarr intoned.

"I have offered my services... Lady Stormshield," he added, entirely unsure how to address her.

"Yer ears corked?" she retorted. "The name's Kilda. I ain' no *lady o' Illian.*"

Asher managed to contain his chortle, though the hint of a smile pushed at his stubbled cheeks. "My trade is that of a ranger," he began again.

"Yer 'ere to slay the Troll?" she questioned, an air of disbelief about her.

"So he intends," Danagarr put in, a hand ushering them all inside while he walked Hector to the stable. "It'll be dark soon," he pointed out, his gaze roaming the woods beyond.

Bowing to walk under the doorframe, Asher entered the dwarven dwelling, pleased to see that the ceiling rose with the pointed roof. He stretched to his full height and briefly examined the natural clutter of family life. Part of him craved it while another part feared it. Families were so rooted, like a tree that had carved out its place in the world. Asher's life was more akin to a river, always on the move and impossible to capture.

"Come," the smith bade, walking in behind the ranger. "Sit with us. There's enough food for one more stomach."

"Especially when it's a stomach as small as a human's," Kilda quipped on her way past.

Asher relieved himself of weapons and gear and took the offered chair, though his knees came up uncomfortably past his waist.

As twilight gripped the realm, lamb pie was served in four tin bowls. Deadora had placed her chair next to Asher's, where she might better take in the exotic ranger. After every mouthful of pie, the girl would pause to look up at him, her curious eyes drawn to his scars or the black fang tattoo under his left eye. More than once, her mother gave instruction not to stare, but the young one was not to be deterred.

"So ye believe ye can kill this Troll that wanders our lands," Kilda stated halfway through the meal.

"This has already been discussed," Danagarr interjected. "Asher 'ere has slain himself a Giant."

Kilda appeared less impressed than her husband had. "An' what are ye expectin' in return?" she asked plainly.

Asher simply looked at Danagarr, who had made his offer on their journey out of Darkwell.

Kilda rolled her eyes and turned to the smith. "What did ye promise?"

Danagarr took one more mouthful of pie, perhaps the last he would enjoy. "Twelve hundred," he answered quietly.

"Twelve fifty," Asher corrected, much to Danagarr's annoyance.

"Twelve fifty?" Kilda shrieked. "We'll 'ave to sell all the damned pigs to..." The dwarf stopped herself before their argument was aired in front of company. With a more controlled tone, she said something in her native language. Whatever the exchange, it resulted in husband and wife taking themselves off into another room.

"He's in for it now," Deadora chimed in with amusement.

Asher, however, was not amused. A tinge of guilt was seeping in, making him doubt the price he had haggled. Was it too much? He knew it wasn't: the monster in question was a Troll after all. In fact, he was well within reason to at least double his fee. But it seemed the loss of coin would severely impact them as a family. It felt different to his normal contracts, where the coin had come from multiple sources saved up over time or from the coffers of royalty.

"How many monsters 'ave ye killed?" Deadora enquired while chomping through a piece of lamb.

Surprised by the question, and unaccustomed to conversing with children, Asher didn't have a response of any kind prepared. "I've..." He cleared his throat. "A lot," he finally answered.

"Me too," she replied, bringing out a rare smile of real amusement in the ranger.

A sudden bang against the front door wiped the smile from the ranger's face. His heart quickened and his muscles tensed. While one hand gripped the scabbard of his broadsword, the other reached for the hilt, ready to free the steel.

Deadora harboured no such caution. The dwarven girl hopped down from her chair, thick braids swinging over her shoulders, and made for the door. Asher called for her to wait, glancing nervously at the door through which her parents had disappeared.

As another heavy thud impacted the door, Deadora opened it and jumped back with a gasp. Asher drew his sword an inch, taking an instant dislike to the man in the doorway. He was a watchman of Darkwell by the look of him, a fact that spoke nothing of the man's virtues.

"Delivery," he said with half a scowl.

Danagarr and Kilda came storming out of their room and quickly put themselves between the watchman and Deadora. "What are ye abou'?" the smith demanded.

The watchman rose to his full height and walked back into the yard, where four more of his fellow officers stood. "This one's with you apparently," he said, gesturing to another dwarf thrown over the saddle of a...

Asher blinked hard, sure the twilight was playing tricks on his sight. It was a Warhog, and a familiar one at that. But the chances of running into that Warhog and its cantankerous owner again were surely too slim.

"I don't like strays bleeding all over my city," the watchman berated. "Keep to yourselves, dwarves, or next time he'll find his way into a cell." With that, the five men took to their horses and departed.

Danagarr and Kilda rushed out to meet the Warhog and guide it towards the house. "Doran," the smith hissed.

"Get 'im inside," Kilda urged, taking the Warhog to the same shed Hector had been shown to.

Danagarr half-carried the Heavybelly, who looked to be struggling to stay on his feet. Asher had already left his chair behind and removed all the obstacles from the table. There was no mistaking Doran Heavybelly, though his blond hair and beard were matted with mud and partially stained with blood. His mismatched armour was in need of repair, with every plate and scrap of leather showing signs of recent battle.

"By the Mother an' Father," Danagarr agonised, "ye look worse than usual, Doran."

The son of Dorain lay flat on the table, his bloodshot eyes set adrift. "Ye should see... the other guy."

Kilda arrived moments later and barked instructions to relieve the dwarf of his armour. "Deadora, ye will observe," she told the girl. "If me skills are to be yers one day, ye need to know what ye doin'."

"Give me a hand," the smith said, gesturing for Asher to mirror his actions and unstrap the spiked pauldron.

Removing the plate, the ranger quickly discovered one of the causes for Doran's current state. He plucked the smooth spine from deep in the dwarf's shoulder and held it up to the light.

"What's that?" Danagarr asked, unbuckling one side of Doran's chest piece.

Asher looked down at the son of Dorain and saw the truth of his wounds. "He got on the wrong end of a Rakenbak," he explained, his meaning quite literal since the many thousands of spines the monster possessed were located on its back.

Doran's hand clamped around Asher's wrist, a spark of life finally in his dark eyes. "Ranger man?" he voiced, before his disorientation was complete and the dwarf's head fell firmly onto the table.

Quite stunned, both Danagarr and Kilda looked from Doran to Asher. "Ye know each other?" the smith questioned.

Asher placed the Rakenbak spine on the table. "We've met before," was all he offered.

"There'll be time for this later," Kilda cut in, her hands waving their words away. "I need to see what I'm dealin' with so be on with it."

Stripped to his trousers alone, not only were Doran's recent injuries detailed in the light but a lifetime of accumulated scars. It was a familiar canvas to Asher, who saw an almost identical body every time he bathed. Most, if not all of Doran's scars, had been made by steel, not fang and claw. The dwarf might call himself a hunter, the ranger thought, but he had not always been.

Deadora followed her mother's instructions and heaved a particular box onto the chair. Kilda lifted the lid to reveal items and tools more often attributed to healers.

"I'm goin' to need more Dain Paste," she announced after rifling through the contents. "Deadora, go into the kitchen an' bring me some Grindel Powder an' a bowl o' water."

Asher watched as Kilda used a combination of hands and tweezers to carefully remove the other spines that had found their way past Doran's armour and through his leathers. She then cleaned every wound with water and filled the bloody gaps with green paste.

"Ye know o' the beast that did this to 'im?" Kilda eventually asked without looking up from her work.

"A Rakenbak ye called it," Danagarr spoke up.

"In size and shape it's akin to a bear," Asher described. "But its back is protected by thousands of those," he said, indicating the collection of spines.

Kilda spared the ranger a glance. "Are they poisonous?"

"No," he replied, having read A Chronicle of Monsters from cover to cover several times. "But they're brutes," he went on. "Very strong, very territorial. If you can see one, you're in its domain and you're as good as dead." The ranger immediately looked to Deadora, regretting the extra detail he needn't have added.

"Don' worry abou' her," Kilda informed, catching Asher's introspection. "Deadora needs to know how the world works south o' Vengora."

Kilda went about her work in silence for a time. They assisted in turning Doran left and right to give her a better look at his back.

They found only bruising and a few streaks of blood, which Kilda had Deadora clean up.

When it was finally time to apply the bandages, Danagarr looked to Asher and made an observation. "Ye don' carry any ill will towards our kind. An' ye seem to know Doran 'ere. Am I to take it that ye're friends?"

Asher tried to categorise the nature of their short-standing acquaintance. "We're not enemies," he concluded, the best he could offer.

"That's better than most would say after meetin' the first-born son o' Dorain," Kilda sniped.

"He has his moments," Danagarr defended.

Asher looked from husband to wife and back. "You know him well?"

"Well enough," the smith replied.

"Too well," Kilda opined.

"Easy," Danagarr bade. "There's not many who can forge armour to the measurements o' a dwarf," he continued. "At least there's not many who will try. There's none but meself in the realm o' man that knows how best to go abou' it."

"An' it needs fixin' *a lot*," Kilda remarked, applying another bandage.

"You didn't travel from Dhenaheim together?" the ranger enquired innocently enough.

Both adult dwarves shared a look before Deadora spoke up. "No," she said, oblivious to the silent conversation her parents were having.

"Dee!" Danagarr chastised, before saying something to her in dwarven speech. "Apologies," he said to Asher, a smile forced onto his face. "Doran's past is his own an' not ours to tell."

Asher understood and refrained from asking any more questions, be it about Doran or them. Instead he helped to move the lump of a dwarf onto Deadora's bed, the child assigned to her parents' bed for the night.

After the evening's dramatic events, once Deadora was settled in bed, the Stormshields cleared up the mess left in Doran's wake and again joined Asher at the table. "I thank ye for yer assistance," Danagarr voiced, a weary look about him. "I haven' met many who would help our kind so easily."

"Will ye be chargin' us for ye services?" Kilda asked bluntly.

"The Troll is my business," Asher assured. "Can you tell me any more about it?"

Danagarr raised an eyebrow. "Such as?"

"The look of it," the ranger cajoled. "There exist varieties of Troll. Knowing which one would aid in the hunt."

The smith shrugged. "The only reason I've survived what encounters I've had is because I *don'* stop to look at it."

"It always comes from the north," Kilda said more helpfully.

"Aye, that it does," her husband confirmed. "Reckon it's got some territory up on the cliffs."

Asher heard Danagarr's assessment but his attention was drawn to the water in his cup. "I would say it's expanding its territory," Asher commented lazily. "Has it ever come here?"

"No," Danagarr replied, as if the answer should be obvious. "Do ye think the timber would still be standin' if it had? No, I've always managed to lead it away before doublin' back."

Asher continued to watch the surface of his drink, noting the rhythmic waves that rippled out from the centre. Looking up, Kilda had placed her fingertips onto the table top having detected the subtle vibrations for herself.

"What's the matter?" Danagarr demanded, seeing their growing concern.

Kilda threw her husband an exasperated expression. "That damned forge o' yers has dulled yer senses," she spat, hurrying about the room.

"What's goin' on?" the smith asked.

Now Asher was on his feet and matching Kilda's speed as he dashed from candle to candle, dousing them all. "Something big approaches," he whispered.

Danagarr's concern quickly turned to panic and he made for Deadora. "Leave her," Kilda hissed. "Better she remains asleep."

"We're to jus' hope it passes then?" the smith complained.

"Without any light we might just blend in," Asher pointed out.

"An' without noise," Kilda added, a finger to her lips.

Asher wanted to correct her, aware that both Trolls and Giants lacked a good sense of hearing. Given the tense atmosphere and growing quakes beneath their feet, the ranger decided keeping quiet on all accounts was for the best.

Positioning himself by the window beside the front door, Asher crouched down and flattened his shoulder to the wall. With one finger, he moved the curtain an inch and peered out into the night. The earth shuddered four more times, each one getting stronger, until it stopped completely. Asher didn't take that as a good sign. He narrowed his eyes and looked left and right, sure that the Troll must be scrutinising the building it had come across.

The ranger replied to Danagarr's questioning expression with a shake of the head. Then came the unmistakable squeal of a distressed pig, shortly followed by the sound of splintering wood and a sudden end to the animal's terror. Danagarr gritted his teeth and moved to retrieve what appeared to be an ornamental hammer from the wall.

"Don' be daft!" Kilda warned.

"I can' let it eat all the livestock—we *need* 'em."

Asher was about to offer cautioning words of his own when Deadora's scream filled the house.

"Dee!" her father bellowed, already rising to his feet.

The swiftest among them, Asher cleared the table and bounded through the bedroom door before the Stormshields. The dwarven girl was standing by the window, a witness to the Troll's savagery. Her scream, however, was a beacon for the Troll and it reacted as its instincts demanded.

"No!" Asher snapped, dashing across the room.

He was too late. The monster had only to reach down and its tree-like arm penetrated the roof and most of the wall. The ranger was struck by a swinging beam and sent across the bed and into the wall. As Danagarr and Kilda rushed into the room, they were forced to watch the Troll scoop up their howling daughter.

The smith growled in his father's tongue and hurled his

hammer at the beast. The Troll cried out and staggered back, its knee taking the full brunt of the dwarf's wrath.

On the other side of the room, Asher used the wall to pull himself up and get a look at the nightmare unfolding around him. The Troll still held Deadora in its grip—one squeeze and the girl would be crushed. Save cutting the beast's hand off, the ranger knew there was no way of convincing it to let her go.

Angered by the pain in its knee, the Troll lowered its head towards the hole it had punched through the roof and unleashed a deafening roar that displayed its hammer-like teeth. Its moment of defiance was ruined by Doran's Warhog. The dwarven mount had broken free of its dwelling and charged tusks-first into the Troll's ankle. The monster staggered again and hopped on one foot, all the while maintaining a hold on Deadora.

"Let her go, ye animal!" Danagarr shouted, as he pushed his way through the debris that hung from the shattered wall.

The Troll paid the dwarf no attention, too busy trying to stamp on the Warhog. Eventually, the lumbering beast swiped at the mount with its free hand and sent it flying across the yard. Danagarr was too slow to evade and was subsequently barrelled over by the mount.

With only a butcher's knife in hand, Kilda was next to enter the yard and face the Troll. Asher didn't hesitate to back her up, his two-handed broadsword firmly gripped. The monster was still nursing its ankle when it noticed fresh opponents. It gave them another roar and stepped forward to flatten them, but its ankle crunched beneath its bark-like skin and the beast faltered, falling onto one hand for support.

The ranger lunged forwards, his weapon coming up into a two-handed swing. The Troll looked up just in time see the steel before it tore a red line down one side of its hideous face. The wound added to the pain in its ankle and, it seemed, the monster had endured all the fight it could. Without any further aggression, it turned on its good heel and limped away from the homestead. Asher and Kilda gave a short chase but, even with a limp, the monster's superior stride allowed a hasty escape.

"Deadora!" Kilda yelled, her breaking heart all too easy to hear.

Asher knew better than to give chase on foot, his energy surely needed for the inevitable confrontation. Instead, he turned away from the fleeing Troll and ran for Hector. He paused on his way, casting an eye over Danagarr, who was clearly struggling to rise. Beside him, the Warhog had already risen onto its hooves and shaken the blow off: a hardy animal if ever there was one.

"Wait," the smith groaned. "I'm comin' with ye."

Asher looked back at the Troll, its hulking frame already vanishing into the night. The ranger cursed under his breath and helped Danagarr up, only to discover that the dwarf had a similar injury to the monster.

"You can't walk properly," he stated.

"Never mind 'im!" Kilda shrieked, storming towards them. "I can see to 'im! Get after Deadora!" she commanded, her chest heaving.

Asher looked back at Danagarr, who offered a resigned groan of defeat. "Bring her back to us," he uttered.

"Aye," Kilda agreed, shoving Asher towards his horse. "Brin' me daughter back, Ranger, an' ye can 'ave *all* our coin! Jus' go!"

Asher nodded his understanding, sharing a portion of their urgency. The promise to see Deadora returned was on the edge of his lips, but the ranger knew better than to make promises he couldn't keep.

Pausing only long enough to strap all his gear on, Asher was soon astride Hector and galloping off into the night, his heading north.

CHAPTER 6
JOINING THE HUNT

Greyking - *Like the Arkilisk, the Greyking is another sub-species of the Basilisk, which is itself a sub-species of the incredibly rare King Basilisk. Firstly, I would like to talk about their size as I'm sure that would be on any ranger's mind when something as big as a Basilisk is mentioned. The Greyking sub-species fits nicely between the dog-sized Arkilisk and the Basilisk which, of course, is comparable to a horse. I believe the largest Greyking on record was just shy of seven-feet in length, so no easy beast to bring down.*

Unlike those of the broader species, the Greyking does not possess a venomous bite. That's not to say its bite can't kill you—it most certainly can. However, depending on the season, the Greyking will either remove your limb with a single bite or implant a number of eggs into your body.

I, personally, have come across two victims who believed they had survived their encounter with a Greyking by some miracle. Of course, once those eggs mature they poison the blood, resulting in a deadly fever. Once the victim has died, the newly-hatched Greykings begin to eat their way out.

It is not a sight for the faint-hearted.

A Chronicle of Monsters: A Ranger's Bestiary, 12th Edition,
Page 444.

Eletta Gelding, Ranger.

Doran's heavy eyelids failed against his rising mind, a mind that demanded answers. Where was he? What had happened to him? Why was there pain? He knew immediately, though, that the mattress and sheets upon which he lay were not those ever found in a dungeon cell. That was always a good sign.

Then he saw it, his memory flashing an image of the Rakenbak across his eyes. His hand instinctively reached for the wound he had received from that first swiping blow. A shooting pain spread out from his shoulder where his fingers had probed the injury.

Very much awake now, the dwarf pushed himself up into a sitting position, his face moving into a ray of golden light. Doing his best to ignore the pain he had caused, Doran ran tentative fingers over the bandages he had no recollection of applying.

The dwarf decided to chalk the fight up to a draw. He definitely hadn't lost.

"Ye damned fool," he muttered to himself.

Pleased to have survived the battle without any broken bones, the son of Dorain began to examine his surroundings. It was a child's room, that much was clear from the scattered toys and small items of clothing.

Deadora.

The name came to him and, with it, he remembered his last moments of clarity, before succumbing to his wounds. How exactly he had gone from collapsing in the street to sleeping in Deadora's room escaped him though.

His spine cracked in several places on his way to his feet and a nauseating wave tried to sit him back down. "Come on, Heavybel-ly," he encouraged, "ye've had worse."

Making his way to the door, he heard frantic discussion taking place on the other side. He knew Danagarr's voice and that of his wife, Kilda—he hoped he hadn't caused them too much distress. His parched tongue failed to bring any moisture to his dry lips as he opened the door to greet them.

The apology he had already begun to prepare never made it past those cracked lips. Something was *wrong*. Kilda's face was puffy and red, her eyes glassy from the tears that still streaked her cheeks. She stopped her desperate pacing when Doran came into view, leading Danagarr to swivel in his seat. The older smith looked much like his wife, his distress all too easy to see. Then there was his leg, propped up on a stool and wrapped in a tight bandage.

"What's happened?"

~

The son of Dorain stared at the devastation wrought by the Troll. He could imagine the lumbering arm smashing through the roof and dragging most of the wall out with it. How could he have slept through all this, he demanded of himself.

The dwarf looked hard at the spot where Deadora had been standing. The thought of that monstrous hand taking her in its grip enraged him. Turning to see the Stormshields, their suffering increased his thirst for vengeance.

"*I'm so sorry,*" he said again in their shared language. "*I should have been here to help you, not sleeping.*"

"*You couldn't even open your eyes, Heavybelly,*" Kilda reminded him.

"*Aye, the best we could have done is throw you at it,*" Danagarr voiced. "*And I'm sure I can't throw you that far,*" he added as an afterthought.

"*You're sure he said his name was Asher?*" Doran checked. "*Green cloak. Short-sword on his back. Not a big talker.*"

"*That's him,*" Danagarr confirmed. "*I told you; I met him in The Lion's Crown. He took off after the beast.*"

"He's dead," Kilda announced, her hope long since abandoned.

"Dead?" Doran questioned.

"His horse returned to us hours ago," Danagarr explained.

"His horse alone," Kilda specified. *"The ranger's dead."*

Doran took on their burden. *"I'll join the hunt myself,"* he vowed. *"Where's Pig? My gear?"*

"You're in no state to be facing down a Troll," Danagarr began, before Kilda stepped forward.

"Your armour is already in the workshop," she said flatly, *"awaiting Danagarr's hands. Your weapons are in the other room. I'll get Pig ready for you."*

The dwarven hunter gave her a tight nod, seeing a mother who would sacrifice anything or anyone to get her daughter back. *"If there's a place for my axe in this fight,"* he promised, *"you can bet I'll be staining it with Troll blood."*

Kilda mirrored his tight nod, aware that his oath could see him dead. *"Go, son of Dorain. Prove the strength of Thorgen still lives in your bones."*

Mention of his distant ancestor caught Doran. Thorgen Heavybelly had been a dwarf of history's note, a hero known to all the clans of Dhenaheim. Never could he be compared to Thorgen, nor ever would he be. The idea that he could do anything that tied his deeds to him felt like an insult to his lineage. Doran Heavybelly was to die no more than an exile now.

The son of Dorain swallowed his pride and buried his past beneath Deadora's need of him.

While stuffing his face with one cold chicken leg after another, and downing as much water as he could handle, Doran donned his shirt, collected his axe and sword, and marched across the courtyard to Danagarr's workshop. His armour was in a heap by the forge and still marred by the Rakenbak's claws and fangs. Smears of his own blood tarnished the blue trimming that edged the grey plates.

"I see you're keeping your armour in good nick," Danagarr called sarcastically, limping from the house. *"Whatever you fought, it packed a punch and then some."*

Time against him, Doran waved away the notion of armouring up. Instead, he strapped the sword over his back and hefted his axe, ready to attach it to Pig's saddle. The Warhog was already being escorted towards him, the reins soon handed over by Kilda.

"*I* will *return with her,*" he promised from his saddle.

"*See that you do, Heavybelly,*" Kilda replied, her words clipped.

His oath given, Doran turned his Warhog to the north. He would return with Deadora… or die trying.

CHAPTER 7

TROLL WITH A VIEW

Banefisher *- Devils of sea and land I say. They plague the coasts from north to south paying the weather no heed, for neither heat nor blistering cold can bother them. Their outer layer is that of a crab, a natural armour that can also lend them the appearance of a rock should they curl up on the beach. Upon their two feet—webbed claws—they stand at six-feet tall. Now these beasts are fast on land and even faster in the water, so mind your surroundings.*

I've seen the buggers eat, or consume I should say. They have four rows of translucent fangs and an extendable jaw that can fit a man's face neatly inside. Don't let them get that close. You're going to need something with a bit of weight behind it if you're to crack their shell exterior. I would recommend a war-hammer or spiked mace even.

A Chronicle of Monsters: A Ranger's Bestiary, 12th Edition, Page 139.

Hamish Harclaw, Ranger.

Not for the first time, Asher looked back over his shoulder in the hope of seeing Hector wandering in the distance. Again, there was naught but himself on the dirt path and, again, the ranger cursed his cowardly mount. As soon as they had caught up with the fleeing Troll, the horse reared up, turned tail, and bolted back the way they had come.

In his fall from the saddle, which hadn't occurred without some pain, Asher had reached out for purchase and found only the coiled rope attached to the side of the saddle. And so now he was left to hunt the Troll on foot, an exercise that consumed much of the night and reduced the odds of Deadora's survival.

With the rope slung over his shoulder, the ranger followed the Troll's footprints, each track a deep impression on the land. It was also clear to see that the beast was still limping. Asher hoped the injury would play to his advantage in the fight to come.

As the dawn crested the world, its favourable light piercing the trees ahead, Asher heard the sound of The Adean, its untamed waves crashing into the white cliffs of The Shining Coast, reminding the land that it would never cease its assault. Asher related to the eternal clash, as a man who would never stop hunting his prey.

And now, having tracked his target through the night and into the morning, the ranger's tenacity had paid off.

In the Troll's wake, Asher descended a crumbly path that curved down to the beach and strode over the soft sand towards the vertiginous cliff—a white wall that towered over the coast.

It was there that the Troll's deep footprints stopped. The ranger craned his neck and followed the immediate line up to the top. There was no missing the smooth patches where the Troll's hands and feet had worn the stone down over several years. It was something of a climb though, at least from a human's perspective.

That was all the thought Asher gave it.

The ranger looped the rope over his head to secure it and removed his fingerless gloves—the hard calluses would aid his ascent. Of course, he only had to think back to his days under Nightfall's tutelage to recall climbs far deadlier than this.

At least there was only a Troll on the other end this time.

His jaw braced in determination, Asher concentrated on the rough stone and continued his arduous journey. The higher he climbed the more stunning the view became, the ocean stretching to the east as far as the eye could see. Where most might allow their minds to wander at such a vista, pondering, perhaps, the fabled elves that lived beyond that horizon, Asher only grew more focused. He cared naught for such things.

There was only the fight.

In this case, however, a young girl's life hung in the balance—providing she hadn't been killed on the Troll's journey—and so the ranger paused when he finally gripped the top of the cliff. He raised his head so that only his eyes cleared the short grass. Scanning the terrain, he discovered a wide grassy shelf that ended at another, even higher, cliff. At its base sat a large hovel in the white stone—so large, in fact, that a Troll was able to sit inside and stoke the flames of its fire.

Asher cursed his luck. It was a Mountain Troll.

Not only were they the biggest of their race, they were also the most intelligent, being the only Trolls capable of starting a fire. That said, this particular Mountain Troll was not so big as to be compared with a Giant. Its attack on Danagarr's house had shown it to be no taller than the highest reach of the roof.

Scanning the area around the Troll, Asher tried to spot any sign of Deadora. The ranger narrowed his eyes, believing the girl might be on the other side of the fire. If she was, he deduced the dwarf to be sitting up and, therefore, alive. He wouldn't know for certain until he got a closer look—no easy thing with a mere handful of boulders scattered across the flat surface.

The Mountain Troll took a deep and staggered breath, a prelude to an almighty sneeze by the look of it. Asher took what might be his only moment to climb over the edge unseen. As the monster's nose and mouth exploded, harassing the flames of its fire, the ranger heaved himself onto the grass and crawled as fast as he could to the nearest boulder, where he rolled to one side and concealed himself fully, the large rock now between him and the monster.

The ranger waited. If the Troll had spotted him the ground would surely be shaking. Confident he had arrived without notice, Asher carefully drew the short-sword from over his shoulder. The hourglass blade caught the morning light and gleamed as if it hadn't been stained with the blood of countless innocents over the years. How many times had he wanted to get rid of it? Yet it felt like an extension of himself—a weapon he had wielded since his earliest years.

Now was not the time to dwell on such thoughts. He would put the short-sword to good use.

Sitting back against the boulder, the ranger fiddled with his belt until the required pouch came loose. It felt awfully empty. Popping the cork from the hard leather neck, he proceeded to pour the black contents over the blade. Indeed there wasn't much and he chastised himself for making so little nearly a month past. He had made several potions, poisons, and elixirs over those few days —the standard preparations of any ranger—but the Oylish poison had been far from his priority at the time. Still, it was enough to coat the tip of the short-sword and some of its biting edge.

Moving to his right, Asher tilted his head to look out from the side of the rock. Hunched over, the Troll's shape was closer to that of a ball, its bark-like hide curving up from its hip and round to its brow. There, a pair of eyes, too large for a skull that size, gazed into the fire with a child-like wonder. The light of the flames exaggerated the pink hue of the creature's chest and rounded belly, a contrast to the chalk white of its rough posterior hide. According to A Chronicle of Monsters, its eyes and midriff were its weak points, vulnerable to steel.

Desiring a glimpse of a living breathing Deadora, Asher threw a pebble at the back wall of the alcove, hoping to give the Troll enough cause to turn around. It didn't. The ranger sighed and picked up another rock, this time taking aim at the monster itself. The missile bounced off the tough hide of its shoulder and turned the creature's head, a questioning grunt rumbling from its throat. Asher dashed and skidded to the next boulder, allowing him to approach the shelter from the left now.

With the fire positioned to one side, relief flooded the ranger as he finally caught sight of the dwarven girl. Deadora was sitting with her feet crossed and arms wrapped around her body. There were no bindings to speak of, though tying up a small girl was far too delicate a job for the large and blunt fingers of a Mountain Troll. Seated only ten feet away from the hulking beast, Deadora must have been too terrified to move.

Shifting back behind the cover of the boulder, Asher ran through the imminent confrontation in his mind. He had received no training for this kind of encounter during his time in Nightfall, and so those memories only served as a foundation for his overall plan. Over the four years since becoming a ranger, he had tackled all manner of creatures, but none so big as a Troll—even an adolescent Troll as he suspected this one was. Of course, there was the Giant he had slain outside of Hogstead, but that job had gone from bad to worse and offered him little in the way of ideas.

Surprise seemed his best and only chance of saving Deadora. The bestiary also recommended a surprise attack: one that incorporated the Troll's hearing impairment and preferably a long-range weapon such as a spear. He had no spear in his arsenal but he did have his folded bow and a quiver full of arrows. Considering the Oylish poison at his disposal and the bow on his back, the ranger began to see an assault that would tip the fight in his favour. Potentially.

Readying himself in a crouched position, the ranger took steadying breaths and adjusted the hilt of the short-sword between his fingers. His other hand curled up behind his back and freed the folded bow attached to the quiver.

There was no denying it. He loved this part.

Springing from concealment, Asher launched his short-sword

at the Mountain Troll. The blade spun end over end, creating a circle of steel as it cut through the air. Its journey came to an end in the monster's chest, though it wasn't nearly long enough to have caused serious harm. It did, on the other hand, enrage the Troll, who swiped the short-sword from its body and let loose an ear-splitting roar.

It was nothing Asher hadn't heard before. And so, unfazed as he was, the ranger flicked the notch on his bow and set off a series of cogs built into the limbs. In the blink of an eye, the weapon was fully extended and being nocked with an arrow.

The first shot struck the beast just under its square jaw, in the softer skin of its throat. It was enough to make the Troll stumble on its way up to its feet. It tried to roar again but the arrow proved troublesome, causing it to cough and choke on its own breath.

Asher glimpsed Deadora scrambling to the far side of the alcove, her little body pressed against the stone in terror. Intending to keep the monster as far away from the girl as possible, the ranger began backing up towards the eastern edge, releasing arrow after arrow to draw his foe in the same direction. The Troll's large eyes had no trouble finding the pesky human that continued to lodge twigs in its soft midriff.

Expending his last arrow, Asher discarded the bow and pulled free his broadsword. The arrows themselves had caused an apron of blood to stain the Troll's large gut, but they weren't enough to put it down for good. Still, the projectiles had done their job and led the creature away from the fire and into the fight.

Now he would finish this with steel.

Halfway across the meadow, the Mountain Troll groaned and slowed down, its thick arms extending to prop itself up. The beast shook its head with what little mobility its stubby neck provided. Shaking its head, however, only increased its dizziness and the monster staggered all the more.

Asher grinned menacingly. The Oylish poison was already hard at work inside his enemy's veins, slowing it down. Taking advantage of the Troll's acute discomfort, the ranger charged ahead. One swift strike across its throat or a successful thrust into one of its eyes would bring an end to the fight before it could even begin.

The Troll, though, had no intention of dying so easily. At the last moment, it managed to raise a hand and meet Asher's blade with the rough hide of its forearm. The blow was jarring, leaving the ranger with little sensation between his wrists and elbows. But the worst was yet to come. The beast had only to push its arm out and Asher was taken with it, thrown from his feet.

Keen to avoid a hard collision with the ground, the ranger tucked his knees up and turned his fall into a backwards roll. He came up with the broadsword quickly locking into two hands again, the blade angled at his foe. Thankfully, the Oylish poison was proving its worth and preventing the Troll from moving with any significant speed. So too was it slowed by the injury inflicted by the Warhog, the monster's ankle requiring extra care while pivoting. This gave the ranger just enough time to dive aside and evade the incoming hammer-stroke of a very heavy fist.

Again, his momentum was turned into a roll and Asher was able to come up swinging. The steel of his blade swept out wide and caught the beast around the back of its knee, where the flexible skin was vulnerable. The arrow that remained lodged in its throat dampened the cry of pain, but it did nothing to stop the hulking monster from lashing out with a backhand.

Asher ducked, plotting to come under the arm and land a devastating wound across the Troll's gut. Slow as the beast was though, its proximity to the ranger made completely avoiding the blow impossible. Two rock-like knuckles impacted against the back of his shoulder and sent him spinning away. Disorientated by his own rapid rotation, the ground was a shock when it rose up to greet him with its unrelenting embrace.

Still, his muscle memory had adhered to the years of training he had endured and maintained some semblance of a hold around the hilt of his sword. Aware of the open hand coming down on him, he let his instincts take momentary control and waved the blade from left to right, cutting a red line across the Troll's palm. The monster recoiled with a yelp that sounded like a rock slide.

Now, instead of trying to pick him up, the beast clenched its uninjured hand and raised it high.

Asher swore.

Then he moved.

If the shudder that ran through the earth was anything to go by, rolling away had saved his life. The lumbering creature wasn't done though, its sluggish hand rising again. Asher rolled back the other way, over the new divot in the ground, and avoided the second attack. The third attack revealed some of the Troll's intelligence for, this time, it dragged the back of its hand towards the ranger rather than lifting it again. Asher was inevitably caught in the path of those three fingers and tossed back into the air.

A cloud of fine dust, the same chalk white as the cliff, filled the air around Asher's impact. His blade clattered against the ground beside him, his fingertips still touching the basilisk hide wrapped around the hilt. The ranger could feel an intense heat against his left cheek and he opened his eyes to a blazing fire. Both his ears and his body detected the slow and thunderous feet of the Troll. Were it not for the poison slowing it down, Asher was sure he would have been barrelled into the fire.

Using the precious time his preparations had granted him, the ranger picked himself up while simultaneously grabbing one of the smaller logs protruding from the edge of the fire. He was careful to keep his new weapon hidden from the incoming Troll.

The time was upon him, he knew. If he didn't end this soon, the larger foe would simply wear him down until he could barely lift his sword anymore. Beyond that there was little hope that Deadora would see home again.

Having gauged his enemy before engaging it, Asher visualised the imminent encounter. He saw his movements unfold and the Troll's expected reaction. Providing the Troll positioned itself as he imagined it to, there was one manoeuvre left to him that would ensure victory in as little as three steps—as long as he didn't miss.

The monster spat a mouthful of blood across the ground and limped after him. Asher waited. Timing was everything. The Troll attempted to snarl at its prey but, harassed as it was by the poison, the reverberation that ran through its head proved too much, forcing it to blink hard to keep sight of the ranger. Of course, sight mattered little at such close range and its bleeding hand came up to attest as much.

His patience having paid off, Asher finally burst into action. He slipped into the pre-planned movements and tossed the burning log underarm. The flying log took the Troll square in the face, stopping its attack and bringing its hands up to its eyes.

Step one complete, the ranger lunged forward and scored a gash across his enemy's stomach. He continued to drag the blade through its pink flesh as he dashed around to its rear. As soon as the steel was free again, he wasted no time landing a second strike to its harder posterior, thereby alerting the monster to his new location.

Step two complete, Asher prepared to execute step three and moved to give the Troll space to turn around. While continuing forward, away from the awkward pivot of his foe, the ranger brought his broadsword up in one hand to extend the arc of his intended swing. A moment later and the beast was pursuing him again. Its own forward momentum, however, worked against it.

Darting away from the monster, Asher's sword hand dropped down and round until his arm was behind him and level with his shoulder. Before reaching the apex of his swing, the ranger released the broadsword and let it fly. Partially blinded by the hot ash and slowed by the Oylish poison, the Troll could do nothing but step into the spinning weapon.

Only when it was buried to the hilt, deep inside the monster's exposed throat, did the blade halt its journey. The beast ceased any assault upon the ranger and wrapped its hands around its neck, though neither could prevent the inevitable. Once the gurgling came to an end, the Troll wobbled on the spot and let loose one final groan.

Asher casually stepped to one side and observed his enemy's ground-breaking fall. Its head turned to the side, the ranger was able to take hold of his broadsword and yank it free, his boot planted firmly against the Troll's jaw. He shook the blade twice to relieve it of as much blood and gore as possible before returning it to his scabbard.

All three steps completed and his enemy dead, Asher turned his attention to the trembling dwarf. Deadora remained plastered to the wall, her fear surviving the death of her would-be killer.

"It's alright," he began, keeping his voice low and soft on his approach. "It can't hurt you now. It's dead."

With tears in her eyes, the girl looked from the Troll to the ranger before crashing into his legs. Asher cupped the back of Deadora's head, somewhat unsure how to comfort her any more than he already had. "It's alright," he repeated. "You're safe now. I'm going to take you home to your parents."

Deadora required another minute of gentle sobbing before she was happy to let go of Asher's legs. She thanked him repeatedly despite being told it wasn't necessary. Since she refused to leave his side or go anywhere near the Troll's corpse, the young dwarf accompanied him in retrieving his short-sword and bow.

His gear reclaimed, the ranger set himself to his next task: getting back down the cliff. There was only one thing that he could securely tie the rope to, and so the Troll served one last purpose in death. Happy with the knot around the creature's wrist, he proceeded to throw the rest of the rope over the cliff side and position Deadora over his back.

"Hold on tight," he said, giving the small wrist around his neck a squeeze. The ranger carefully lowered himself over the lip and began a slow but steady descent, his feet braced against the rock. "Don't look down," he advised after feeling her squirm.

They were still too high to feel the ocean's spray, but a quick glance revealed a familiar dwarf waiting for them at the bottom.

"Well ain' it a damned good mornin'!" Doran Heavybelly yelled up. "Ye got her, lad!" he cheered.

"Doran!" Deadora called down with glee.

"Stop moving," Asher said gruffly, the dwarf's weight shifting just enough to pause their descent.

Then the rope, taut with their weight, wobbled.

The ranger frowned and cast his eyes back up the line. It

wobbled again. Impossible was the word that came to Asher's mind. The Troll was dead. It couldn't be a problem with the rope—if it was growing loose, it wouldn't wobble so much as slip. Yet a strong vibration was running down the entire length and through his hands.

"What's the hold up?" Doran queried, seeing that they were within ten feet of the bottom.

Without warning, the rope went up. Asher's feet were taken from the cliff face and he shouldered the rock. A questioning sound of alarm came from the son of Dorain, who was helpless to do anything. Meanwhile, the ranger attempted to counter the ascent by letting his hands slip down the rope. It was no use, not with the speed of their new climb.

There was nothing for it. "Catch her!" Asher bellowed.

"What?" Doran shouted back.

The ranger gripped Deadora by the wrist and untangled her from his body. "What are ye doin'?" she demanded, her terror quick to return.

Asher ignored the girl and looked down again. It was too far for himself, the fall more than capable of killing him. But weren't dwarves said to be as hard as the stone that birthed them?

"Catch her!" he yelled again.

A stream of obscenities flowed free from Doran's lips as he pushed the Warhog away. With Deadora's chances of survival slipping away one foot at a time, Asher let go of her. The sudden descent elicited a brief scream until the air was taken from her lungs impacting against Doran. The son of Dorain gave the girl the safest landing he could by dropping himself to the ground as he caught her.

Asher continued to look down, making certain the young Stormshield had survived. His fear abated when she rolled off the dwarven hunter and met his gaze. Whatever happened next, he had saved her life.

It wasn't long before *whatever happened next* was happening right then. The rope pulled him over the edge of the cliff top. With more scrapes and cuts added to his list of injuries, Asher stood up and looked from the Troll's corpse to his new enemy.

If there was such a thing as luck, the ranger knew then that his was long spent.

"Let's get it over with," he growled, drawing his broadsword once more.

~

Doran's first breath after catching Deadora was a wheeze. Then he coughed so hard he was sure his lungs must have come out. Rolling to one side, he shook his head as if such a thing would free him of the pain in the back of his skull. It didn't.

"Doran!" The young girl's hands came to rest on his shoulder and ribs.

"I'm alrigh', lass," he reassured, though the truth of that statement was yet to be seen. Digging into his dwarven grit, the son of Dorain found his way back to his feet with a reminder of why his armour was so useful. "Let's be seein' ye then," he said, thrusting his chin into the air.

Deadora was able to stand—a good sign where her bones were concerned. Doran put a finger to her chin and moved her face one way then the other, checking for further injury. All in all, the girl had come through the ordeal with hardly a mark. That was a shame, Doran thought. Scars made for excellent stories.

"Ye'll live," he concluded. "Which is more than I can say for the ranger man," he added, craning his neck. There was no sign of Asher now, though the rope appeared to have been kicked back over the edge, its end a few feet from the ground.

"Ye 'ave to help 'im, Doran," Deadora beseeched.

"No," the dwarf disagreed, while clicking his fingers to beckon Pig. "What I need to do is get ye back to yer parents."

"Ye can' leave him up there!" she protested.

"I can an' I will," Doran replied. Without asking for her permission, the dwarf scooped up Deadora and unceremoniously plonked the girl on his saddle. "Hold on to this," he told her, indicating the rise in the saddle.

"I won' leave without Asher!" the little Stormshield continued. "He saved me life!"

"He'll be fine," Doran promised. "Besides, he's a *ranger*. Dyin' on the job is what they do."

His last word was almost drowned out by a pained cry and an ear-splitting roar. The dwarf glanced up at the cliff. *He'll be fine*, he told himself this time. Gripping the saddle, preparing to mount the Warhog, more of the battle drifted down and got lodged in his ears. A reluctant thought was now worming its way into the son of Dorain's mind.

Doran sighed. "He's goin' to be the death o' me," he muttered. "Hold this," he said, handing Deadora the reins. "Pig's goin' to take ye home. If he gets distracted jus' give 'im a swift kick. He'll soon smell yer mother's cookin'."

"Ye're goin' to help 'im?" the girl asked hopefully.

"Aye," the dwarven hunter replied dourly. He gave the Warhog a smack on the rump and sent it running back the way they had come.

With that out of the way, Doran turned back to the cliff. It was quite the climb for a dwarf, but he was confident it was nothing his strong arms couldn't handle. Strapping his axe over his back, there to clash with his sword, he set himself to the task of being a damned fool.

After ascending twenty feet, the son of Dorain was actually thankful his armour had been left behind. And so he continued the climb, his feet stepping in time with his hands. The closer he got the more he heard Asher's sword swinging and some monster retaliating. Every now and then the cliff face would be shaken by some impact or other. Then there were times when the rope was flicked from side to side and the dwarf feared he would be cast into the sea.

As any child of the mountain could boast, however, Doran's grip was unrelenting. Coated in sweat, his muscles stinging, the son of Dorain heaved himself up until he finally reached the grassy top. Groaning as he did, the dwarf pulled himself up enough to see what was happening. Following the rope he was still holding led to a dead Troll, its wrist proving a suitable anchor. Off to the side was a far more gruesome sight to behold.

A second Troll, bigger than the dead one, was crawling across the ground with a three-fingered hand clutching at a severe gash in its throat. Blood was pumping between those rocky fingers, the precious red liquid spoiling the earth. From the brief glimpse he got of the creature's midriff, its throat wasn't the only wound it bore.

Movement further to Doran's left led him to the one who had brought both Trolls down. Asher was staggering around a boulder, his bloody broadsword used as an aid more than a weapon. Patches of his face appeared bruised and swollen with a sheen of sweat and blood gathering in the creases of his pained expression. The ranger was slowly making his way towards the fleeing Troll, but he soon faltered and fell to his knees. It was only then that Doran noticed how low the man's right arm was hanging.

"I'm comin', laddy." The words were squeezed out of Doran as he attempted to roll onto the grassy top.

The sound of shattering rock was always a familiar sound to dwarven ears—and often a welcome one given that so many were masons—but this time the sound was accompanied by a loss of footing for the son of Dorain. Refusing to aid him any further, part of the cliff edge broke away and Doran fell below the lip. His sharp yelp was short-lived when his hands succeeded in grasping the rope a little tighter. Saved from death, the dwarf looked down at the nauseating distance that stretched between his dangling feet and the ground.

"Come on, Heavybelly," he said to himself.

One hand after the other reached up for more rope and brought him closer to the top of the cliff again. He imagined the ranger to be dead by now. If he hadn't succumbed to his wounds, the surviving Troll had only to swat him with one hand to finish the job. Rather than pause to get a lay of the land this time, Doran continued his ascent until he was completely over the edge and officially on the grass.

The dwarf's lungs and burning hands demanded that he rest for a moment, but he needed to help the ranger who had saved Deadora's life. Rising to his feet, the son of Dorain took a single step before sheer surprise halted him in his tracks. His mouth fell open and his brow furrowed in confusion. Though his mind worked furiously to understand what his eyes were reporting, he had no choice but to stare.

Asher was standing on the back of the Troll's arching neck like some fabled hero of old, his sword plunged deep into the beast's head. Sighting the dwarf, the ranger used both hands to remove the blade and jump down.

He didn't have a scratch on him.

Dumbfounded, Doran took another step. He looked from the dead Trolls to the ranger. As Asher approached, the dwarf scrutinised the human's features. He still had the sweat and blood streaking his face, and there were tears and gashes in his leathers with blood stains around the jagged fringes, only there were no wounds to explain any of it.

"You look like you've never seen a couple of dead Trolls before," Asher commented, his sword disappearing inside the scabbard on his hip.

"I'm not sure what I've seen," Doran uttered, more to himself than the ranger. "Ye were injured," he began, his voice still uncharacteristically quiet. "No," he continued, louder now, "ye were damn near dead yerself."

Asher gave himself a once over. "What are you talking about?"

"I saw ye!" Doran insisted, moving round the man to get a better look at the whole scene. "Ye were right there, broken like some rag doll!"

"I think that climb has robbed you of sense, master dwarf," Asher replied, his voice too even for a man who had just battled not one but two Trolls.

"Don' *master dwarf* me, ranger man!" Doran fumed, a stubby finger pointed up at Asher. "I know what I saw."

Asher was beginning to look bored with the conversation. "Where's Deadora?" he asked with more concern.

Doran was still chewing over recent memory. "I sent her home with Pig," he answered offhandedly.

"Pig?" the ranger echoed incredulously, his mouth curling into a tight smile of amusement. "You named your mount *Pig*?"

"Well it's a pig ain' it?" the dwarf spat in frustration.

Asher rubbed his hands together, ridding them of excess dirt. "I suppose so," he agreed.

"Ye were bleedin'," the son of Dorain told him forcefully. "Yer arm was hangin' by a thread. Ye were on yer knees. Then..." His arm came up to gesture at the latest Troll sent to the next life. "Then ye were jus' standin' there like nothin'... I don' understand."

Asher rolled his right shoulder. "The arm's fine." One of his fingers ran down his face and collected some dry blood. "That's not mine." He half turned to look at the Troll. "And I tripped over a rock. *That's* all you saw." The ranger folded his arms. "The more interesting thing, son of Dorain, is your presence up here."

Doran was about to continue his argument when his defences came up and demanded to be voiced. "What o' it?" he questioned.

Asher leaned down ever so slightly. "Did you come all the way up here to... *help* me?"

The dwarf made to speak not once but twice, failing each time to articulate anything intelligible. "Bah!" he spat, waving a hand between them. "I came to make sure the job got done right. I didn' want that blasted Troll botherin' me kin again."

Asher didn't look convinced. "Hmm," was all he said.

"An' I can see they won' be troublin' folk again," Doran continued in the absence of any real reply. "So... I suppose I'll be climbin' down again," he added with little enthusiasm.

"I suppose so," Asher repeated, patting the dwarf on the shoulder as he made for the edge.

The ranger began his descent first, leaving Doran with the view all to himself. He gave the bloody scene one last look, his memory replaying the haggard and broken appearance of Asher. The dwarf knew what he had seen, as unbelievable as it now was. It had been as real as what lay before him that very moment.

As he reached down to grip the rope, an odd thought crept to the forefront. When Asher had rolled his shoulder to prove it wasn't injured, he had rolled his *right* shoulder. According to the ranger, he had never been wounded in the first place, so he couldn't have known which arm had been dislocated. Yet he displayed the same one Doran had seen hanging abnormally low.

The dwarf didn't like any of it. Not one bit.

CHAPTER 8
A GIFT FROM THE GODS

Red Daliad - At two-feet tall, these monsters might not appear all that threatening, especially since they seem all legs with an almost indiscernible body. But hunt these beasts with caution in your step. Should you wander into their nest (see A Charter of Monsters, Page 212, for known locations) they will quietly, almost innocently, approach you with feigned curiosity. Do not be fooled. They regard you as naught but prey.

When close enough, the Daliads will leap for you, their hooked legs fanned out. It is then that you will see their mouths, located on the underside of their small body. They'll take chunks out of you while their hooks barb your skin to keep them anchored.

One of my earliest contracts was to exterminate a nest, just west of Vangarth. There were two of us, in fact, and I was the novice. I watched my mentor disappear, his body overtaken by these red monsters. Now, depending on the size of the nest, you can either take your sword to the task or—as I did—use a portion of the contract money to hire a mage. If you take the latter route, for the larger nests, insist that the mage uses a freezing spell. The Daliads have a curious resistance to fire. I will continue to research the reason for this.

A Chronicle of Monsters: A Ranger's Bestiary, 12th Edition,
Page 409.

Rogaer the Blueblood, Ranger.

The silent trek back to the Stormshield homestead was insufferably long, and not because Hector had fled from the trail. Walking beside Doran Heavybelly for an entire day was a form of slow torture in Asher's opinion, a topic that had been covered extensively in Nightfall.

Every time he glanced down at his travel companion, the dwarf was already eyeing him, and with great suspicion at that. He had every right to be suspicious, the ranger admitted, if only to himself. The dwarven hunter hadn't missed the truth of his dire situation on the cliff top.

He could still recall the pain of his injuries, in particular his dislocated shoulder.

Asher glanced down at the hard lump beneath the dark leather of his fingerless glove. Were it not for the mysterious black gem he would have died a hundred times over by now, and long before he encountered that second Troll.

The ranger knotted his fist, feeling the iron band of the ring that held the gem. Keeping its existence secret was second nature to him, whatever *it* was. He considered the last person to see him use it. It hadn't ended well for Everic, a young assassin with too much ambition and naught but vengeance in his heart. Asher couldn't imagine Doran sharing that same fate, though the dwarf had only to touch it and he would be undone.

The ranger blinked hard and sighed in his bid to rid himself of the incoming questions that surrounded not only the gem but his entire past, before Nightfall buried its hooks in him. As always, he was in a place where those answers could never be found. He had only the path ahead of him.

Thankfully, that path eventually gifted him the sight of all three Stormshields.

They stood together in their yard and welcomed the hunters with beaming smiles and enthusiastic waves. The ranger couldn't say he was accustomed to either, though he did quietly enjoy it.

The intuitive fight to control his smile failed when Doran tripped trying to avoid the scurrying chickens that passed underfoot.

"Beware the deadly chickens, master dwarf," the ranger quipped, with an easy laugh.

Doran picked himself up and dusted his arms down. "Bloody chickens," he grumbled.

"Ye are most welcome!" Danagarr called, one hand propping him up with a stick.

Even Kilda looked pleased to see the weary ranger, breaking away from her family to greet him. "Won' ye come inside? Ye must be hungry."

Deadora ran until she collided with Asher's legs. Her embrace of genuine affection was foreign to the ranger but, much like the welcome he had received, he enjoyed this too.

"Come along," Kilda bade.

Doran watched the family guide Asher towards the house. "Am I invisible?"

The ranger looked back at him over one shoulder. "Definitely not," he said with disappointment.

The dwarf's grumbling response went unheard as they were ushered into the house. Kilda was quick to tend to the meal, increasing the volume of food to feed the extra mouths. Deadora appeared to have overcome her recent captivity or, at least, her young mind had failed to engage with it yet. The memories would either surface in time or be buried beneath layers of mental fortitude forever. Now she babbled almost continuously about Asher's heroics in slaying the Troll. Doran was given a brief mention for his part in saving her at the last minute.

Danagarr listened to it all, fascinated, if a little disturbed. "*Two Trolls* ye say?"

"A male and a female," Asher confirmed, as he sat back to give Kilda space to put down his bowl of soup.

"My apologies, Ranger," the smith continued. "Had I known it were two I would 'ave... Well, I don' know what I would 'ave done. I'm jus' sorry I can' compensate ye for two."

"We can never truly compensate ye for what ye've brought back to us," Kilda added, pausing on her way round the table to grip Deadora's shoulders.

Asher took a breath, considering one last time what he had been thinking about on his journey back from the cliffs. "Deadora's life is payment enough for me," he said sheepishly, aware of the reaction his words would elicit. "You can keep your coin," he specified.

The Stormshields froze and simply stared at the ranger.

"Ye don' want... Ye don' want payment?" Danagarr stuttered.

Asher took a mouthful of soup. "No."

Kilda hurried back around the table and threw her arms around him. "There be no man or dwarf like ye! Thank ye!"

Uncomfortable again, Asher patted the dwarf's arm.

"Is there nothin' we can give ye?" Danagarr pleaded. "Ye've more than earned it."

There was one thing the smith could do for him. "I would ask for *something*, besides your generous hospitality."

"Name it," Kilda told him.

Turning in his chair, Asher reached for his gear propped up against the wall. He removed the short-sword from its scabbard and displayed it in both hands. It was clear for all to see that the tip of the blade had snapped off.

"The Troll shattered the steel," Asher explained, recalling the monster's swipe that removed the weapon from its chest. "If you could fix it..."

Danagarr held out his hands and accepted the broken sword, his experienced eyes running over the weapon from end to end. Then, quite curiously, he looked at his wife. Kilda returned the look with an approving nod.

"I can fix it for ye," Danagarr humbly informed him. "Or… I could make ye somethin' better. How attached to the blade are ye?"

The offer took Asher by surprise, though the dwarves would have had to employ a high level of scrutiny to identify the subtle change in his expression. "In truth," he replied, "I would happily destroy the weapon if it didn't feel such a part of me. I've been using it since… Well, for as long as I can remember."

Doran raised a bushy eyebrow, clearly interested by the unexpected answer.

"I can forge ye an identical weapon," Danagarr assured. "But it'll be much *stronger*. Lighter too."

Doran's curiosity shifted to his fellow dwarf and became all the more obvious. "Ye can' mean what I think ye mean," he said cryptically.

The smith quieted the son of Dorain with a gesture, his attention fixed on the man who had saved his daughter's life. "Please. Let *me* do somethin' for *ye*," he proffered.

Asher wasn't sure what to make of the unsaid conversation between all the dwarves. "It will be identical?" he checked.

Danagarr tilted the blade one way then the other, his eyes running from hilt to broken tip. "Single grip. Hourglass shape. I can even make it to the same dimensions—ye won' even need to purchase a new scabbard."

Asher examined his blade from across the table. It was a wretched thing that tied him to countless deaths. It was time for something new. "Then I would accept this gift," he finally replied.

The smith looked pleased. "Very good. Ye'll 'ave to stay with us a few days mind. Me hands aren' as quick as they used to be."

Asher glanced from Danagarr to Kilda and back. "If you'll have me."

"There will always be a place for ye 'ere," Kilda announced warmly. "Heavybelly," she went on, her tone significantly lower. "Ye can have the chair."

Doran looked at the armchair in question before casting a scornful expression towards the ranger. "I've slept on worse," he remarked.

"An' ye still can if ye don' show some gratitude," Kilda snapped. "This ain' Grimwhal."

The son of Dorain waved his hands in the air, his surrender and apology all given at once. "'Tis an honour as always," he mumbled.

"Right," Danagarr declared excitedly. "I'll get to it!"

Kilda planted a firm hand on the smith's shoulder and kept him seated. "Eat first," she instructed. "Ye know what ye're like around that forge."

Danagarr acquiesced and propped the broken blade against the table leg. "Let us eat!" he urged eagerly.

Asher enjoyed his tomato and herb soup, though he wolfed it down so fast his tongue hardly had time to taste it. Kilda served pork chops soon after, which were closely followed by a joint of lamb. Apparently, it was dwarven culture to serve what every human would call two meals in one. Not one to complain, the ranger cleaned every plate he was served and welcomed the slice of carrot cake that signalled dinner's end.

In the waning summer sun, Deadora opted to fall asleep in her mother's arms rather than be put to bed alone. Kilda appeared happy with the development and kept the girl close as they continued to chat around the table. To save himself from the inevitable questions about his life, Asher offered to help board up the damage created by the Troll, but the Stormshields had already made sufficient immediate repairs to the boarding. Then he offered to wash up but Kilda refused to let him.

At a natural break in the conversation, the ranger could feel the dwarves' curiosity leaning towards him. "You said you didn't come down from Dhenaheim together," he said, steering the conversation before it could get to him.

A brief moment was shared between the three dwarves. "No we didn'," Danagarr said lightly. "Kilda an' meself 'ave been callin' Illian our home for... What? Seventy years?"

"Sixty-eight," Kilda corrected.

The smith nodded in agreement. "Doran, ye came down..."

"After that," the son of Dorain stated flatly.

"Aye, that's abou' right," Danagarr replied quietly.

"It's unusual no?" Asher probed. "Your people don't often come south of the mountains."

"True enough," Danagarr disclosed. "All dwarves are children o' the mountain; we don' often choose to live under a sky."

"Where did you hail from in Dhenaheim?" Asher asked innocently enough, his drink rising to his lips.

Doran gave a loud sniff that cut through the air. "Ye've a lot o' questions, eh?"

Kilda shot him a look as sharp as any blade in the ranger's arsenal. "Ye'll mind yer manners where me guests are concerned, son o' Dorain."

Addressing the tension, Danagarr said, "As ye might 'ave guessed, Asher, we're abound with secrets 'ere. Now yer deeds thus far 'ave shown ye to be a friend more than a mere ally. Can we trust ye with our words, for they are powerful things?"

Asher didn't have any friends and he was friend to none—who would he tell?

"Words *are* powerful," the ranger agreed. "And you have mine."

Danagarr studied his face for a moment longer. "That'll do."

Doran huffed and sat back in his chair with folded arms. Whatever he muttered to himself remained with him alone.

"I didn't mean to pry," Asher said apologetically.

The smith held up a hand of reassurance. "There's no offence taken. It's jus' our experience o' humans is... Well, it ain' good."

"We're from a place called Hyndaern," Kilda told him, while swaying a little to soothe Deadora.

"I've never heard of it," Asher admitted.

Danagarr chuckled. "I don' suppose ye would 'ave. But there's not a dwarf in all o' Dhenaheim who doesn' know o' clan Stormshield an' the kingdom o' Hyndaern. Second only to the Battleborns," he added with pride.

Again, Asher was lost as to the significance. "There's a hierarchy among the clans?"

"Oh aye," the smith replied. "A rigid one at that. It hasn' changed in centuries."

"The Battleborns rule," Kilda informed evenly.

"Always 'ave," Danagarr commented. "Always will."

"Then there's us, the Stormshields," his wife continued. "Though... I suppose it's *them* an' *us* now."

Danagarr reached over and squeezed her knee. "*Us* is enough," he said, the words sounding like a mantra.

"So Deadora was born on Illian soil," the ranger concluded.

"Aye!" The smith's response was all pride. "Perhaps the first dwarf to *ever* be born south o' Vengora."

Asher was relaxed enough that some of Danagarr's joy for his daughter reflected in the ranger's expression. He couldn't recall a time he had ever experienced such a thing. Then again, he had never known family or been around one. He was enjoying it.

What followed was a pause, an absence of any more information. Entirely unsure where the line was, however, he refrained from asking any further questions.

After a pause, Kilda said coyly, "We've gone this far. Ask if ye would know, Ranger."

Asher let Doran have his sigh before speaking again. "You couldn't stay in Hyndaern?"

Danagarr interlocked his fingers on the table top and looked Asher in the eyes. "What do ye know o' magic, lad?"

Unconsciously, the ranger glanced down at the black gem, now exposed on his finger for all to see. "I know of it, though I do not practice it."

"But it wouldn' be illegal if ye did," the smith pointed out. "Illian has schools for such a thing. Mages an' the like. The same cannot be said o' Dhenaheim, at least not like down 'ere. Our kin frown on the works o' magic."

"I didn't know dwarves used magic," Asher admitted, keeping the conversation going.

"The schemes o' elves," Kilda chimed in.

Danagarr gestured at his wife. "That an' worse is all they 'ave to say. *But,*" he emphasised, "that's not to say it isn' practiced among the clans, it's jus' difficult. Ye see, we dwarves have what ye might call a *natural resilience* when it comes to magic. It don' conjure so easily for us but, then again, it don' harm us as much either."

"Then what use do you have of it?" Asher enquired.

"Oh, magic has its uses when it comes to matters o' the crown," Danagarr explained. "Them that know the ways are able to communicate across the mountains without movin' a muscle." The smith shrugged. "Good for puttin' kings face to face without bein' in the same room. That sort o' meetin' can lead to wars."

Asher's attention shifted with his suspicions and his gaze landed on Kilda. "I was a healer by trade," she confessed under the scrutiny. "The skills me husband speaks o' are his own."

The pride that shone through Danagarr appeared to be spoiled by a hint of shame. "Me an' mine are known as *clerics*," he said. "We're treated as outcasts most o' the time, but when I started combinin' me knowledge o' magic with me skill in the forge…" The smith cut himself off with a breath, his memory proving too hard to recall perhaps.

"Ye were considered *dangerous*," Kilda stated.

Danagarr nodded along solemnly. "Word was gettin' abou'. Apparently it reached as high as King Gandalir 'imself. Soon enough, there was a warrant for me arrest."

"We fled," Kilda reported, her words unusually soft considering the weight they held.

"It's next to impossible to find shelter outside o' yer clan," Danagarr explained. "Illian was our only option. Execution or a life in the mines are all that await us should we ever return."

"I'm sorry to hear that," Asher responded. "I'm to take it then," he began, glancing at Doran, "that your friendship is an unusual one."

"Indeed it is," Kilda was quick to reply, though the dwarf exhibited a flash of amusement as she caught Doran's eye.

"Doran 'ere is a Heavybelly," Danagarr went on. "They're below the Stormshields but above the Hammerkegs, Goldhorns an', o' course, the Brightbeards. Right in the middle o' it, aren' ye?"

"Isn' he always?" Kilda added, to accompany Doran's grumble.

Asher's curiosity had now shifted entirely to the son of Dorain.

"And what did they kick you out for?" the ranger asked, aware that his barbed words would elicit a strong reaction from the dwarf. It was uncharacteristic of him, he knew, but something about Doran riled him.

It was probably because he had bartered him into slavery, he realised.

"None o' yer business," Doran grunted.

"Being a terrible hunter then," Asher concluded.

Doran's face crumpled into a severe scowl. "I'm a damned good hunter," he proclaimed with a thumb pressing into his chest.

"Tell that to the Rakenbak that nearly turned you inside out," the ranger quipped.

The dwarf's sharp retort was held back in favour of a demand. "How do ye know abou' that?"

Asher gestured to the bowl sitting on the side in the kitchen. "You were covered in spines. You know you're not supposed to attack them from behind, don't you?"

"Bah!" Doran snapped, swivelling in his chair to properly engage. "I know how to take down a Rakenbak, ranger man. An' I also know I don' need to tell ye a thing abou' meself *or* where I've come from."

"He's a prince," came a small voice, turning all eyes on Deadora.

"Ye're supposed to be sleepin'," Kilda said softly, wrapping the girl up more in her arms. "An' *ye're* too loud," she told Doran more sternly.

The dwarven hunter held up his hands by way of apology. Then he offered Deadora an affectionate smile. "I'm glad someone thinks so highly o' me." His expression soon hardened after returning his attention to the ranger.

"If you're a prince I'm the king of Velia," Asher said quietly, his cup coming up to his lips.

"For all we know ye are," Danagarr said, his tone suggesting he was defending Doran to a degree. "Ye must 'ave some history o' yer own, eh? How does one get into the business o' huntin' monsters anyway?"

Asher could feel the walls of his mind coming together, separating his conscious mind from the truth of his past, lest he spill secrets that should never be uttered. At the same time, his training was weaving an elaborate lie that would fill in the gaps for the dwarves and remove any suspicion.

"I was an assassin," he began seriously, "trained from childhood to kill any and all. Then, I saw the truth of my deeds and exiled myself. Hunting monsters feels like a good way to atone and it makes perfect use of the skills I already have."

There was a brief pause between them. Then all three adult dwarves laughed together, Kilda's hand covering Deadora's ear to keep her somewhere close to sleep.

"An assassin," Danagarr repeated, his face red with amusement.

Even Doran was still chuckling to himself. "That was a good one, ranger man."

Asher forced his own smile, as if he was in on the joke he had told. "In truth, I was recruited by a man named Geron Thorbear. He brought me into the rangers. Unfortunately, they all turned out to be con artists and murderers." The latter robbed the dwarves of their amusement.

"Murderers?" Danagarr probed.

Asher nodded along, his gaze lost to the hot liquid inside his cup. "They were killing people and planting monsters they could place the blame on. Then all they had to do was slay it and get the coin."

"Ugly business," Doran remarked.

"What did ye do?" Kilda enquired.

Asher had only to close his eyes and he was returned to The Ranch, where the walls had been decorated with blood and bodies lay strewn across the floor. Then there were the Mendal brothers, their arteries opened while they slept.

"The Graycoats saw to their end," he lied. "All but one," he added soberly.

"That Geron fella?" Danagarr reasoned.

"His real name was Kradamir Damakas. He had been a slaver in a previous life. Made himself a lot of enemies in The Arid Lands." Asher paused to wet his lips before placing his empty cup down. "I had him returned to those enemies."

The dwarves appeared very interested now. "What happened to 'im?" Doran asked.

"His fate is known only to those who now own his life. Though I imagine he has been thrown into a very dark hole and left there to rot."

"A fitting end for a slaver," Kilda declared with disgust in her voice.

"Indeed," Asher agreed, his eyes pointedly shifting to Doran.

"Come on now," the dwarf protested. "Ye can' lump me in with their kind. I'm no slaver!"

Danagarr looked from warrior to warrior. "What's he talkin' abou', Doran?"

Not for the first time in such company, Asher's smile found its way to the surface. "You haven't told them how we met?"

Doran squirmed about in his seat. "Not exactly," he replied sheepishly.

"Doran Heavybelly," Kilda pronounced. "What did ye do?"

When the answer failed to come forth, Asher spoke for him. "He sold me to the barbarians of The Iron Valley so we wouldn't have to share the coin."

Kilda's mouth fell open. "Doran—"

"I wasn' really goin' to leave 'im there," the son of Dorain insisted. "Besides, I could see he was a capable lad. Them barbarians were naught but young an' old. They couldn' keep ye imprisoned."

"I still had iron around my neck," Asher pointed out.

Kilda held her daughter a little tighter and leaned forward. "If *ye* think ye're leavin' 'ere with any supplies ye're sorely mistaken, Heavybelly. An' ye've seen the last o' a warm bed an' all."

Doran's mood took a dive into new depths. "Ye couldn' 'ave kept that between us?" he fumed at the ranger.

"I told you there would be repercussions should we ever meet again," Asher reminded him. "Consider yourself lucky those repercussions don't include *steel*."

The son of Dorain gritted his teeth and his fists knotted together. "Easy," Danagarr bade, dropping a heavy hand on Doran's shoulder. "Ye'll be takin' no action against the man who saved me daughter's life."

"I caught her!" Doran carped.

"I know," the smith said, patting the Heavybelly. "An' that's why we're goin' to look past this ugly business with the barbarians. Ain' that right, Asher?" he added meaningfully.

Asher waited a breath. "That's right."

Danagarr turned back to Doran, who had unclenched his jaw now and relaxed a notch.

"Perhaps an apology?" Kilda suggested.

"I'm not apologisin' to the likes o' 'im," the dwarven hunter fumed.

The smith put his hands up to calm things down. "Why don' we get some fresh air, eh?"

Kilda looked at the night sky beyond one of the windows. "I'm takin' Deadora to bed," she announced before turning to her husband. "Don' stay up *all* night," the healer added knowingly.

Danagarr watched his wife and daughter disappear before turning giddy eyes on the hunters. "What's say we put all this nonsense to bed an' see to yer payment in proper?"

"Ye're serious abou' that?" Doran questioned.

The smith slapped an excitable hand on the table. "Follow me, boys."

With his stick to aid him, Danagarr led the way out of the front door, across the yard, and just beyond the tree line of the dirt path. Along the way, he had instructed Doran to pick up the shovel resting against the stable wall.

"Right 'ere," the smith announced, tapping a patch of ground with the end of his stick. "Get to diggin'," he ordered.

Doran shook his head. "I'm havin' no part in this. It's wrong I tell ye."

Danagarr nodded at Asher. "Then hand it over an' quit yer whinin'."

Asher caught the shovel mid-air and hesitated before ploughing it into the dirt. "What exactly am I going to find under here?"

The smith offered a mischievous grin. "The treasure o' kings, good ranger. The treasure o' kings."

No more enlightened, Asher drove the shovel down and began to dig. He only had to work the ground for a few minutes before he struck something solid, something man made. No, he corrected, whatever this was, it had been crafted by dwarven hands—a fact that only added to the growing mystery.

"Lend 'im a hand then," Danagarr requested of Doran.

The son of Dorain groaned but gave no protest. Together, the two hunters heaved a mud-covered chest from the hole in the ground. Without opening it, the smith commanded that they follow him to his forge. The chest was an awkward thing to carry between a man and dwarf; a fact that continued to fuel their tension.

"Put it on 'ere," Danagarr called over his shoulder as he rounded the only table in his workshop.

Aided by torchlight, Asher got his first real look at the chest. Its design alone confirmed to him it hadn't been made by a human. There was no keyhole but rather an intricate affair of silver cogs and small bronze levers, and on every surface at that. Were he instructed to open it he would have no idea where to begin.

The smith approached the chest. "It's been a while," he noted, his thumbs wiping clumps of dirt from between the various mechanisms. "Give me a moment."

Doran tutted. "Don' tell me ye've forgotten the combination, Danagarr. Ye've got the most valuable thing in all o' Illian sittin' in front o' ye."

"Shut it, Heavybelly," the smith replied, his hands hovering over the chest. "I've got it."

One by one, the dwarven smith twisted a cog here, switched a lever there, and rotated the corresponding dials. After fiddling with something on every side of the chest, the lid finally sprang open half an inch. Danagarr clapped his hands together and rubbed them in anticipation. Using a finger on each side, he carefully lifted the lid, which came away as a completely separate piece.

Asher peered inside, wholly unimpressed at the *king's treasure*. At a glance, he counted six ingots of what appeared to be pure silver. Never one to be tempted by wealth, it did nothing to excite the ranger, though he was beginning to wonder why the Stormshields would struggle to afford his fee.

"He doesn' know what it is," Danagarr commented with half a smile.

"O' course he doesn'," Doran said. "It belongs to the children o' the mountain."

The smith waved the notion away. "It's known that our ancestors used it for barterin' with human kings an' the like."

"The Stormshields maybe," the son of Dorain commented. "Clan Heavybelly knew better."

"What is it?" Asher queried, tired of their bickering already.

Danagarr picked up one of the ingots and displayed it in two hands. "Pure silvyr," he whispered.

The ranger blinked. "Silvyr's a myth."

The smith offered the metal bar and Asher accepted it. He was immediately surprised by how light it was, especially considering how hard it felt between his fingers. Moving it around, the ranger inspected every side and angle, wondering if it contained a detail that would explain the dwarves' great interest in it. There was nothing worthy of note. It was as plain as steel in appearance.

"It's a clear night," Danagarr said, regarding the star-speckled sky beyond the forge's canopy. "Take it out," he advised. "Reacquaint it with the moon."

Asher couldn't see the value in such a bizarre thing but, then again, he apparently couldn't see the value in the ingot itself. And so he walked away from the forge and planted himself beneath the night sky. The moon was almost full upon its throne in the heavens. Sure that he was about to be the butt of some dwarven joke, the ranger looked back down at the ingot in his hands.

Finally, he was impressed.

The ranger had never seen anything like it, though he had certainly heard of the legendary mineral. Every which way he turned the ingot, its metallic surface sparkled like the stars above, as if it had been inlaid with the finest of diamonds. After marvelling at it for a few more seconds, Asher partially covered it with one hand, testing the obvious hypothesis. Shadowed from the moon, the silvyr returned to its former look of dull steel.

Joining the smith again, he said, "Is this what I think it is?"

"A gift from the Father 'imself," Danagarr replied sincerely.

"He ain' goin' to understand that," Doran commented.

The smith rounded the table. "Jus' because he don' believe in the right gods don' mean the right gods don' believe in 'im. After all, it can only be Grarfath's will that it's come to be his."

"Gibberish," Doran declared flatly.

Danagarr was apparently ignoring the son of Dorain. "A long time ago," he began, his tale directed at Asher, "when we children o' the mountain were naught but a mere thought to the Mother an' Father, a great gift was hurled from the stars so that we might find it one day. It landed in Dhenaheim an' *shook* the earth. Some even believe it was this event that allowed the first o' our kin to break away from the mountain stone an' find life."

"That's grand talk for a *mine*," Doran opined dryly. "That's to say, it's a bloody big hole in the ground."

Danagarr rolled his eyes at the dwarf. "*A bloody big hole in the ground* ain' exactly a gift, but what was *inside* the hole... Now there was a gift only a god could give. *Silvyr*," he said with wonder, the word striking a chord deep in Asher's memory. "Stronger than steel, yet as light as glass. The only thing more indestructible is Grarfath 'imself. An' Yamnomora o' course."

Asher absorbed it all, taking it for the myth it was, and handed the ingot back to the dwarven smith. "You're going to reforge my blade out of this?"

Danagarr smiled wildly. "That I am."

CHAPTER 9
THE POWER OF SILVYR

Ghola *- If I'm being honest—and I know I've been discouraged by my peers to voice as much—it would be easier to relocate the village or town plagued by a Ghola than to kill the monster.*

I have checked the records and found only one instance of a ranger killing a Ghola. The records are limited, however, as that same ranger died from injuries only moments after defeating the beast.

Luckily for all of us, Ghola dwell solely in the mountains. They rarely venture beyond them, only doing so if they feel their territory is threatened. Such was the case of Harvest Snows, a small village outside of Longdale. As you know, this area of the world is nestled well within the stony walls of The Vengoran Mountains (known colloquially as Vengora).

As you might not know, Harvest Snows no longer exists. Or, rather, it is no longer inhabited. Should you happen across the village site you will find naught but the shell of a village. From what I can tell of the records from the time, the village was in the process of expanding, soon to become a town in fact. That must have been when the Ghola felt threatened.

Now, the reason I suggest relocation over tackling the monster is their speed. Ghola can only be described as supernaturally fast, despite appearances being likened to a human. Before dying, the ranger who fought the beast described it as no more than a blur with claws.

A Chronicle of Monsters: A Ranger's Bestiary, 12th Edition, Page 409.

Folaf Ingerson, Ranger.

After another day and night on the Stormshield homestead, Asher walked outside to a glorious summer's day. While Danagarr worked every hour his gods had given him in the workshop, the ranger assisted Kilda with a variety of odd jobs, the largest of which concerned a more permanent solution to the damage caused by the Troll.

Trusted with some of their coin, Asher returned to Darkwell and purchased the supplies required to fix the wall and roof, though he personally had no experience in the labour of such a job. Thankfully, Doran did.

Though reluctant to work alongside the ranger, the dwarf accepted his help with the arduous task and, together, they spent most of that second day in silence, getting it done.

Now, as the afternoon rolled into a bright and pleasant evening, Asher retrieved his shirt and tossed it over one glistening shoulder. He was pleased with the honest work, perhaps the first piece of honest work he had ever done. There was a new kind of satisfaction to be enjoyed, a satisfaction that accompanied construction as opposed to the death and destruction he was more accustomed to.

But it was still there, bubbling under the surface. That itch to unleash and put a lifetime of violent skills to better use. The fight would always live in him, he knew. No matter how fast he ran or how far he travelled it would accompany his every step, ignited by every beat of his heart.

Though only a number of days, it felt too long since he had felt the weight of his weapons. The weight of wood was certainly no substitute. Coated with sweat, he looked across the yard, to the forge. It was oddly quiet considering the noise that had come out of it for two days. It increased the ranger's anticipation which, for a man who had very little to look forward to in life, was quite something.

"Ye should take a look," Doran said from behind. The dwarf nodded at the workshop. "'Tis an honour to see so skilled a smith as Danagarr work the likes o' silvyr. Ye can bet no human has ever witnessed such a sight."

Asher appreciated the suggestion and made his way over to the forge. Danagarr was a dwarf possessed, his eyes lost to the wonders of his creation. He was sitting on a small stool, simply staring at the short-sword resting on his black anvil. Equally black were his hands and his face, neither escaping the grime of such laborious work. But the smith didn't care about his looks. Right then, in that moment, there was only him and his creation.

And what a fine creation it was.

The ranger stepped into Danagarr's eye line and the dwarf sprang to life. "Ye're 'ere!" he cried with glee. "I've jus' finished it," the smith informed, though he cast a confused glance at the sky. "I think."

"You've been still for some time," Asher told him.

The smith chuckled. "It's always the way. The work takes over. It's like channellin' the Father 'imself." Asher approached the anvil and shot the dwarf a questioning look. "Wait," Danagarr beseeched, jumping onto his good foot. "It's customary to hand the weapon from maker to wielder, so's it knows who it truly belongs to."

Asher quite liked that detail and refrained from taking the short-sword from its place on the anvil. Instead, he held out his hands and waited for the smith to transfer the weight. It turned out there wasn't much weight at all. A sandy brown leather met his palm and fingers as he gripped the hilt and hefted the weapon in one hand. The ranger rolled his wrist to get a better feel for the balance. Pure was the word that came to mind, the weapon beyond compare.

The pommel was simple, tapered to its elegant end. Of course, Asher's eyes were quickly drawn to the blade itself. There was no guard between hilt and the hourglass curve of the sword, making it one smooth piece of weaponry. The fuller that ran down the middle of the silvyr was etched with curious dwarven hieroglyphs.

"The work of a cleric," he quietly commented.

"Aye," Danagarr replied, his shame and pride once again fighting for dominance. "The magic I've worked into it is subtle compared to the power ye humans are capable of. But it'll give the edge an extra bite when dealin' with the monsters o' the world."

And what an edge it was, Asher concluded, his finger bleeding from the lightest touch. "The calibre of this weapon is more than you owe me."

"There is no price for the life o' me daughter," Danagarr stated without a hint of hyperbole. "An' besides, I've naught else to do with it. I can' sell any o' it for its true worth—only kings an' queens can afford it. An' who's to say they won' 'ave me killed an' jus' take it? Me an' mine are barely considered *people* down 'ere."

Asher couldn't argue with that logic. The dwarves of Dhenaheim had the monopoly on silvyr, the most valuable mineral in the world, and here was this vulnerable family with six ingots.

"How did you come to have so much of it?" Asher asked, his blue eyes still fixed on the exquisite blade.

Danagarr shifted on his good leg and his gaze dropped. "I suppose I sort o'... *stole* it."

Asher finally tore his attention away from the sword and raised an eyebrow at the dwarf. "I didn't peg you for a thief, Master Stormshield," he said without any real judgement.

"Desperate times," the smith explained. "Gettin' out o' Hyndaern after me warrant was issued was damned hard. Then there was trekkin' across Dhenaheim an' reachin' Illian. We needed more than jus' coin to get us out. The forge I was workin' in had a small store o' silvyr; I think it belonged to one o' the lords. He probably wanted somethin' ridiculous to be made out o' it like a bloody chair. Anyway, I took all I could carry. I fled the forge with eleven bars that day. Now I 'ave five."

"I would have done the same," Asher affirmed, though the ex-assassin had no doubt he would also have left a trail of bodies in his wake.

Danagarr responded with a look of appreciation where his conscience was concerned. "So ye like the blade?" he enquired, as if the ranger could have any other feelings towards it.

Words of heart-felt appreciation didn't come naturally to Asher, and so the ranger could only offer the blade another look of admiration. Danagarr beamed and patted him on the arm.

'I get the sense it's in experienced hands," the dwarf commented, though Asher's attention had already been diverted by a familiar noise in the distance.

The ranger narrowed his sight to look between the trees and lay eyes on the horses, their hooves beating hard on the dirt path that led to the Stormshield homestead. He caught glimpses of them on their approach and was immediately beset with an uneasy feeling. Danagarr followed his gaze and, judging by the hammer he picked up, had arrived at a similar feeling.

"Doran Heavybelly!" the lead rider bellowed from astride his horse. "Stand and be seen!"

Across the yard, Doran was ushering Kilda and Deadora back into the house. "I'm standin'!" the dwarf yelled back with defiance in his voice. "Ye'll 'ave to do the seein' for yerself, laddy!"

Indeed the riders did spot the son of Dorain as they rounded the blocking trees. Doran presented himself as a sentinel before the house, his broad chest and knotted fists a clear warning to any who might try and cross him.

Partially concealed behind the central post of Danagarr's work-shop, Asher watched the scene unfold, sure in his bones that the fight he had been itching for was upon him. With a gesture, he kept the smith from interfering. It was always better to understand all the pieces on the board before making the first move. In this particular match, they were faced by five men, all of whom dismounted their rides. Four of them took positions behind the apparent leader. They had an ill-look about them, a demeanour that spoke of no regard for the laws of the realm.

The ranger kept himself to the shadows beneath the workshop's canopy and took note of their weapons. Each possessed a sword, though they remained on their hips. For now. Two of them also carried a small hand axe and a bow each, while the remaining three could only boast of knives. The leader appeared the most experienced of the group and the scar that ran up from his eye and into his reddish hairline spoke of a violent past. He swept his long coat out so the leather material gathered behind his sword. His threatening stance, however, had no effect on Doran, who continued to stand with his feet firmly rooted.

"Corrigan," the dwarf greeted evenly.

The man named Corrigan adopted a cocky stance, with one thumb hooked into his belt and his head on a tilt. "Doran Heavy-belly," he replied, his tone reminding Asher of a hunter upon catching their prey. "It's not easy for a dwarf to hide in Illian, is it?"

"I wasn' hidin'," Doran told him, his knuckles pale.

Corrigan gestured to the homestead. "This looks a lot like hiding. Though you were foolish to seek out your kin. Apparently there isn't a soul in Darkwell who doesn't know about this place."

Doran took a breath. "Viktor sent ye?"

"Why else would I be out in the middle of nowhere talking to the likes of you?" Corrigan retorted. "You failed to bring back the Hobgobber. For that failure alone you should be dead by now. But Mr Varga saw promise in you, dwarf. So here you are, with your second chance." The thug looked left and right. "Where's the Rakenbak?"

Doran nodded at the trees behind the group. "It's right there."

The head of every man, including Corrigan's, swivelled to make certain they weren't about to be flanked by a man-eating monster. The humiliation did nothing for Corrigan's mood, nor did Doran's hearty laugh.

"Ye should o' seen yer faces," the dwarf chortled.

Corrigan unclenched his jaw. "From the look of *your* face I'd say you already faced the Rakenbak. Proved too much did it?"

Doran's amusement evaporated. "I can tell ye, lad, they look a might different in the wild. Maybe *ye* should hunt one down."

Corrigan looked to have seen some humour in that. "I hunt a different prey," he said rather menacingly. "Speaking of which, if you have no Rakenbak to hand over, you're going to have to come with us. Viktor doesn't take kindly to failure."

"I'm not goin' anywhere with ye lot," Doran made known. "I don' work for Viktor, I'm jus' a freelancer. Ye can take the coin back he gave me an' our business will be concluded."

"We're past that," Corrigan reported. "Because of your promise, Viktor made promises to others, others who were expecting a Rakenbak. Their disappointment reflects poorly on the boss, makes him look like he can't deliver on his word. All that lands on your short arse, I'm afraid."

"Yer boss should know better than to make promises abou' things he can' see to with his own two hands," Doran advised.

Corrigan gave a short sharp laugh. "I'll let you tell him that yourself, though something tells me you won't be walking away with your *own* hands."

"I'm not budgin'," the dwarf reiterated.

"Anywhere else and that might be an issue," Corrigan reasoned. "But this is no place to make a stand, Heavybelly." The man's narrow eyes looked beyond the hunter, to Kilda and Deadora in the doorway. "Too much collateral here," he added threateningly.

Doran rolled his shoulders and squared his jaw. "Hear me, fellas, an' hear me well," he announced, his voice dropping. "*I'm* the line. Cross me an' ye'll never see home. It's that simple."

A ripple of hesitation passed through the five men. Their courage was renewed when Corrigan stepped forward and drew his sword, a sharp sneer escaping his lips. Asher had seen this in men before. So often did they try to drown their fear with anger. Foolish. Fear makes a man think before he acts and, had Corrigan done just that, he would know that Doran was no ordinary foe. He might also have discovered the ranger approaching him before he made it as far as the yard.

"Best be leaving now, boys," Asher said gruffly, his new silvyr blade held low in one hand.

Confusion, it appeared, looked right at home on Corrigan's simple face. "Who in the hells are you?" he demanded.

"I'm the man you're going to think about every time you feel the pain," Asher told him plainly.

Despite the limited intelligence Corrigan likely possessed, he still knew a threat when he heard one. A flick of the head sent one of the other four towards Asher, his blade already out and flashing in the low sun.

The ranger twisted his short-sword around and batted the incoming steel away—child's play. In the same fluid movement, he had also stepped forward and snatched his opponent's wrist with his free hand. Asher both heard and felt the small bones break when he snapped the wrist down, beyond its natural rotation. As if he had no choice, the man dropped his sword and fell at the ranger's mercy, still in his iron grip. A solid boot to the face put him on his back and out of the fight.

Such a swift end to the confrontation surprised the other men, who all stared at Asher with wild concern. Doran took his opportunity and charged ahead, barrelling into Corrigan with enough force to lift him off his feet. A second later and he was being crushed between the ground and the dwarf, who fell upon him with pummelling fists.

Asher stepped over the man he had left writhing in the dirt and presented himself as an easy target for the next one. Sure enough, he was soon looking down the length of a thrusting sword. He sidestepped the obvious attack and then shifted his shoulders to evade the swing of another enemy. The ranger darted in with a hammering fist and caught the second foe across the jaw, a blow that broke the bone and sent the man tumbling to the ground.

Calling on all his rage to blind him to any fear, the first attacker rounded on Asher with a new thrust. He missed again, unable to keep up with the ranger's footwork, and came again and again with vicious swings of his sword. Asher deflected and blocked the steel, until colliding with the silvyr for a third time spelled its end and shattered the sword into two halves.

The ranger cast an impressed eye over his weapon while the thug looked at his own in despair. Then he tried to kill Asher with the jagged half that remained in his hand. Asher knocked the half blade aside and shoved an elbow into his opponent's face, a precursor to locking the man's wrist in a vice-hold that added more broken bones to his already broken nose. As he fell in agony, the fool with the mangled jaw found his feet again and decided he would kill Asher with the small axe that had been tucked into his belt.

It was a poor decision.

Moving like a viper, the ranger dashed one way, backhanding his silvyr blade to slice through the haft of the axe, before darting back in and locking his foe's arm into an unbreakable hold. His elbow, however, was most definitely breakable. Asher applied the necessary force and his ears were filled with the man's desperate scream before he let him crumple to the ground.

Only feet away, Doran had got himself into a scrap of his own having moved on from Corrigan to challenge the last of their wretched group. While their mouthy leader writhed around, cupping his swollen and battered face, the son of Dorain had intercepted the remaining would-be killer and wrestled him to the ground.

On his approach, Asher happily watched Doran stand up, take the man's arm in both hands, and plant a heavy boot in his chest. One strong tug dislocated the arm and sent a spasm of pain through the rest of his body.

Between Asher and Doran, however, Corrigan had renewed his courage and found the strength to rise. As he did, a slender dagger was drawn from his belt and with it the promise to use it. His face was inflamed and discoloured from dwarven fists, but it did nothing to hide his vexation. Oblivious to the ranger behind him, Corrigan made for the dwarf with murder in his eyes. He would have succeeded too were it not for Asher's intervention.

Corrigan grunted when his wrist was twisted and pulled,

bringing his entire arm up behind his back. It was there that Asher broke his thumb and Corrigan's grunt was transformed into a pained cry. A foot to the back of his knee and a shove between his shoulders sent him into the dirt with the rest of his thugs.

"I was goin' to handle it," Doran assured, kicking the slender dagger into the bushes.

"Sure you were," Asher replied, turning to take in the whole group of intruders.

They were a sorry sight, beaten and broken, as they did their best to try and stand without the use of all their limbs. "You don't know what you've done," Corrigan spluttered through bleeding lips. "Viktor's going to—"

"What?" Doran interjected. "What's the big man goin' to do? Everyone knows he never leaves 'em four walls o' his. So all he can do is send more o' yer sorry selves." The dwarf barked a laugh. "Send 'em I say. I'll kick 'em all into next week; an' that's the lucky ones!"

With nothing but a scornful look to cast, Corrigan led his horse away using his good hand. The rest were quick to follow him or, at least, as quick as their new injuries would allow. Asher and Doran walked behind them and watched the group disappear down the muddy path.

"Doran Heavybelly!" Kilda fumed. "What nonsense 'ave ye brought to me door now?" The son of Dorain was halfway through a shrug and the beginning of an answer when Kilda held up a finger to silence him. She looked down at Deadora. "Right. It's supper for ye an' early to bed." Again, her finger came up but, this time, it was to silence the girl. "As for *ye*," she continued, looking back at Doran, "there'll be no supper until an explanation comes tumblin' out o' yer stupid mouth." The dwarven hunter clearly wanted to protest but, instead, bowed his head and offered not a word.

While Kilda ushered Deadora inside, Danagarr crossed the yard at a limp. "I'm gettin' mighty tired o' the drama that follows ye, Heavybelly." Doran could but nod his head and catch his breath.

Tearing his sharp gaze from the other dwarf, the smith bent

down, an awkward manoeuvre given his wounded leg, and picked up the pointed half of the thug's broken sword. He examined the steel with awe before searching for the silvyr blade in Asher's hand.

"Bet ye've never done that before?"

Asher glanced at the shattered weapon. "I can't say I have." He raised the silvyr blade. "Not a single mote of damage," he commented, uncharacteristically bewildered.

"Nor will there ever be," Danagarr informed him with a smile. It quickly faded as a thought crossed his mind. "Be warned though, Asher. Even without the light o' the moon to betray it, the power o' silvyr cannot be mistaken. If any learn ye possess such a weapon, they'll undoubtedly kill ye for it."

Doran walked past them on his way to the house. "I'm not so sure he's worried abou' that, Danagarr," he remarked with a suspicious eye on the ranger.

Upon reflection, Asher had to wonder if he had tipped his hand in the fight, displaying one too many moves not known to the common warrior, whatever their profession. It was that urge to fight, to unleash. As much as he hated it, the need to inflict pain, to exert his control over a weaker opponent was a pressing need that Nightfall had instilled in him. In time, he hoped it would at least fade.

"I appreciate the warning," he said to the smith. "I will keep it in mind."

CHAPTER 10

OLD BLOOD

Dathrak - *In the cities, I have oft heard the pigeons be referred to as 'rats with wings'. If such a phrase was to be coined for Dathraks, it would be something akin to 'a Basilisk with wings'. In truth, one of the strongest theories I've come across actually suggests the Dathraks are distant cousins of dragons.*

If the true size of dragons is to be believed, then Dathraks are considerably smaller. That's not to say they aren't large monsters in their own right. The largest recorded possessed a body close in size to a shire horse. Believe me when I tell you, a Dathrak will have no trouble snatching you in its claws and returning you to its high nest (see A Charter of Monsters, Page 112, for known locations).

On two legs, their stance is not dissimilar to that of a vulture's. Their snout is even beak-like, with a razored hook on the end. 'Tis their hide that sparks the debates regarding their relation to dragons. Dathraks are scaled from head to tail and hard it is too, harder than any scales a Basilisk might boast. See below for list of viable poisons and proven traps.

A Chronicle of Monsters: A Ranger's Bestiary, 12th Edition, Page 266.

Arn Grawly, Ranger.

Once again, in the late twilight, the ranger found himself sitting amidst an uncomfortable tension around the Stormshields' table. Kilda had purposely held back any food—from all of them—and now sat across from Doran with daggers in her eyes.

"Ye think it isn' hard enough livin' 'ere, under the shadow o' humans, without ye bringin' more trouble down on our heads?"

Doran held up his hands and shook his head. "I didn' mean for this to happen," he began, sparing a glance at Asher. "I didn' think they'd find me 'ere."

"Dwarves don't move around Illian unnoticed," Asher felt like pointing out.

"What are ye still doin' 'ere anyway?" the dwarven hunter spat. "Ye killed the Trolls an' ye got ye reward. Shouldn' ye be on yer way?"

The ranger leaned forward. "I'm still here because your *friends* might come back in the night."

"Bah!" Doran grunted. "That lot won' be back. They've wounds to lick."

"Silvyr or no silvyr," Danagarr said, looking at Asher, "ye know how to handle yerself. Ye snapped those fellas like kindlin'."

"I could o' takin' 'em all," Doran seethed. "I was jus' too busy reshapin' Corrigan's face," he mumbled.

Asher ignored the son of Dorain's meaningless defence and replied to Danagarr. "I've had my fair share of brawls with men like that. I've grown accustomed to treating them like... *kindling*," he echoed.

Doran was scrutinising him with those suspicious eyes again, but he held his tongue, for a change. Instead, he looked at the food sitting on the counter behind their hosts. "Couldn' we 'ave a *little* somethin'? I beg ye. Knockin' men on their arses is hungry work."

"They threatened Deadora." Kilda's response sounded like a

threat in itself. "Ye get food when ye tell me exactly who they are, Doran."

The son of Dorain sat back and sighed, his gaze drawn to his tapping finger. "They work for Blood an' Coin."

"Don't we all," Asher was quick to reply.

Doran shook his head. "No. Blood an' Coin is a... Ye've heard o' the fightin' pits right? Two men in an arena. They don' stop until one o' 'em can' stand or... they're *dead*."

Asher nodded along, well aware of the illegal fights and, more importantly, the lucrative betting that accompanied them. He had been tempted to participate more than once to earn some extra coin for supplies and the like. In the end, he had refrained, not wishing to risk exposure.

"Well," Doran continued, "Blood an' Coin is like that, only it's *more*. More everythin'. It's run by the rich for the rich. Only the wealthiest can afford entry. Hells, the lowest buy-in to any bet would cripple the average person."

The ranger digested the information at speed, but there was one key piece missing that intrigued him most of all. "Where does the Rakenbak come into this?"

"An' *ye* for that matter?" Danagarr chimed in.

Doran kept his mouth shut, answering Asher's question with a knowing look.

"You must be joking," the ranger replied, putting it together.

"What?" Kilda asked.

"I did say it was *more*," the dwarven hunter reminded them.

"They're betting on monsters fighting monsters," Asher concluded aloud, for the sake of the Stormshields.

"They pit humans against humans too," Doran detailed. "But when it comes to the monsters, the meaner the better. Or exotic. Fangs an' claws are always good, but the crowds are generally swayed by somethin' with a little extra."

"So that's where you come in," Asher reasoned. "You hunt down and capture the monsters they want."

Doran shrugged. "They 'ave hunters o' their own, but every

now an' then—when Viktor wants somethin' with a little more bite—there's room for freelancers like meself."

Danagarr wagged a finger. "Ye mentioned 'im earlier, this Viktor."

"Aye," Doran replied hesitantly, as if he'd rather not speak about the man. "Viktor Varga. He's Corrigan's boss. An' the rest."

The name struck Asher somewhere deep in his memory and drew his brow into a knot. How did he know that name? Had he heard it before? The ranger was sure he hadn't met the man. "Who is he?" he finally asked.

The son of Dorain let his eyes rest over the ranger for a moment. "Are ye sure ye want that answerin', laddy? Viktor's not a man to be knowin'."

"I've met my fair share of sullied men," he told the dwarf.

"Not like Viktor Varga ye haven'. His operation is run out o' Dragorn." Just the name of the island nation put a sour expression on the Stormshields' faces. "O' all the rot in the realm o' man, can ye tell o' a place worse than that?" Doran went on. "No kings or queens there. Jus' a council o' thieves an' murderers with sixty-thousand people under their thumb."

"You're talking about the crime guilds," the ranger said.

"Aye. Four o' them there are. The Fenrigs, Yarls, Danathors, an', o' course, the worst o' the lot, the Trigorns. Ye spent any time over there?"

Asher recalled a handful of memories from his time on the city-island, a time when he had killed in the name of Nightfall. "Some," he admitted. "But it's been a while."

"Well I imagine nothin's changed. The seats on the rulin' council are still held by the four guilds an' they each manage their own quarter o' the city. They control who an' what comes an' goes an' they own a good deal o' the docks in Velia. Barossh too."

"Which of the four guilds does Varga belong to?" Asher asked.

"None," the dwarf replied, his answer surprising the ranger.

"Then how is Blood and Coin allowed to operate?"

"Viktor's old blood," Doran explained. "When yer ancestors

conquered Dragorn—what, a thousand years ago—there were *five* crime guilds that set up shop, but one o' 'em was significantly smaller than the rest. While the big four warred it out for their piece o' the island, the Vargas settled in an' started workin' *all* the angles. Weapons, supplies, information—it all went to the highest bidder. They became this kind o' neutral guild that worked for *an'* against 'em all. This monster business is jus' Viktor's latest venture to increase his vast coin collection. He's also a nasty bugger who'd do anythin' for a *single* coin. An' I mean *anythin'*. Some o' the stories abou' 'im... Well, they'd keep ye up at night, put it that way."

"You seem to know quite a bit about him," Asher remarked.

"I like to know who I'm in business with," Doran told him.

"Corrigan mentioned the Hobgobber," the ranger probed, following his curiosity. "The one we were hunting in The Iron Valley?"

"Aye, the same. Viktor didn' know exactly what it was, only that it were nasty enough to terrorise the likes o' The Jarat. I told Corrigan what it was, he told Viktor an' Viktor, apparently, wasn' best pleased to hear o' its demise."

"But you were negotiating with the tribe," Asher pointed out.

Doran licked his lips, hesitant to elaborate. "I had..." He cleared his throat. "I had hoped to get rid o' the monster for The Jarat *an'* deliver it in one piece to Viktor."

Asher narrowed his eyes at the dwarf. "You mean you were trying to get paid *twice* for the same monster?"

Kilda leaned over the table. "Because he's a greedy sack o' hammers!" she blurted. "An' I'd say ye knew this Viktor would want ye head if ye didn' deliver on yer word."

The son of Dorain retreated somewhat. "I knew he'd be displeased. I jus' didn' think his reach went beyond Dragorn."

"Ye damned fool," Danagarr chastised, with a shake of his head.

"He'll get the message now," Doran insisted, gesturing at the yard. "Corrigan will take his sorry self back to that gods-forsaken island an' Viktor will know I'm not to be pursued."

Asher didn't see it that way, his own conclusion far darker.

"Or," he countered, "Viktor will send more, and more skilled at that—"

Doran was already waving his hand. "Bah! Let 'em come for me. Me axe will do the speakin' next time."

"He might not send them for *you*, son of Dorain," Asher pointed out, his gaze shifting to the Stormshields.

"Us?" the smith snapped, his concern evident.

"They have no way of tracking Doran," the ranger told them. "The only reason they found him here is because they knew where he was hunting the Rakenbak, and everyone in Darkwell knows a family of dwarves live on the outskirts. If Viktor decides to retaliate —and he sounds like a man who will—there is only one place he will come."

There was a pregnant pause before Kilda leapt across the table, her hands reaching for Doran's throat. "What have ye brought down on us, ye son o' a—"

Danagarr's powerful arms caught his wife before she cleared the table and kept her from throttling the dwarven hunter. "Easy," he repeated again and again. "Ye can be sure o' this?" he asked the ranger when Kilda was finally calm enough to take her seat again.

"I know how men like him think," Asher replied. "If he really wants Doran, he'll go through anyone he has to."

"Ye've doomed us!" Kilda spat. "Ye've put Deadora in danger!" she added, twisting the knife.

"I'm sorry—" Doran attempted before Kilda cut him off.

"I'll kill *ye* before they come for *us*," she promised.

"They might not come," he argued, though with little conviction.

"They *won'* come if ye're dead," Kilda stated.

"No one's killin' anyone!" Danagarr interjected, his hands coming up between them.

"What exactly did you promise him?" Asher asked, leading the conversation.

Doran took a breath and settled back into his chair again. "A Rakenbak. A live one."

The ranger considered the logistics, difficult as they were. "And how were you going to transport a living Rakenbak to Dragorn?"

"I sent word to his people in Velia, the ones that control the docks. Told 'em where to meet me with a wagon, a *big* wagon. They were supposed to pay me the remainder o' me fee an' ship the beast to Dragorn."

Asher looked away, his finger lightly tapping the table top. He was already considering how to fix the situation and protect the Stormshield family before considering *why* he would do such a thing. There was no coin to be earned in keeping these people safe. He was a ranger, a drifter who wandered the wilds and breezed through the world of man.

Getting involved with the crime guilds was... *loud*. Such an overt act, a display of his abilities, went against his instincts. Staying in one place, even a place as vast and busy as Dragorn was a mistake. After all, he had defeated the court of assassins, but that didn't mean he could walk freely. If he made too much noise in the world he was likely to disturb Nightfall, a nest of Arakesh who would willingly descend upon him with wrath and ruin.

Though he could see a way through Doran's mess, he declared to himself that he was no one's saviour and nor did he wish to be. But then a burning question presented itself and prevented his mind from moving on.

Was he content to atone by slaying monsters alone? And for coin no less.

As images of Thomas Murell began to stir in the ranger's mind, images that would take him to a dark place that questioned his own existence, Danagarr's voice cut through his thoughts.

"What are ye thinkin', Asher?" he asked.

Now was his moment to walk away, he knew. He had only to offer no solution and simply wish them the best of luck. Having already saved their daughter and slain the Trolls he was under no obligation to aid them any further.

But then he thought about the young girl sleeping in the room behind Danagarr. As far as Asher was concerned, her fate had been sealed by Doran's blunder. He then thought of another young girl whose fate had once been in his hands. Esabelle Murell was still alive today because he hadn't walked away.

"Asher?" the smith voiced again.

"If Viktor Varga wants a Rakenbak," he said, his path chosen, "then we'll give him one." He turned to Doran. "Can you still get word to his people at the docks?"

The dwarf turned a curious eye on the ranger. "Aye," he drawled. "When ye say *we*..."

"I mean you and I will track down that Rakenbak and personally deliver it to Viktor's feet. In person, with the monster and an apology, he might just overlook your mistakes. Obviously, you'll have to give him back whatever he's already paid you," he added as a matter of fact.

From the expression contorting Doran's face, he wasn't entirely happy with the plan. "See 'im in *person*? Ye mean actually go to Blood an' Coin? Ye did hear the part where I said it's in Dragorn?"

"It's the only way to know for sure whether he's forgiven you," Asher replied.

"An' if he doesn' ye can bet me head will roll," the dwarf contested.

"If that's the case," Asher laid out, "then there would be no reason to harm the Stormshields."

Doran opened his mouth to further his complaint but Asher's logic kept the dwarf's words from spilling out.

Hearing the likely conclusion said out loud tempered some of Kilda's ire. "Ye bloody fool, Doran."

"Ye would help?" Danagarr asked sceptically, looking towards Asher.

"If ye come with me," Doran said, "ye're likely to share the same fate, whatever that may be."

"This doesn' have to be yer fight," the smith added.

Asher glanced at the bedroom door beyond Danagarr. "It is now," he made known. He looked at Doran, half expecting the dwarf to protest his assistance but, instead, the son of Dorain responded with an appreciative nod. "We don't have long," he continued. "Corrigan and his men are ahead of us. If we leave for

Darkwell now you can get a raven to Velia before they report back to Viktor. If he knows you're coming to him it might buy us some time before he sends anyone else back here."

Doran took a second to think it all through. "Aye, ye're right. There's no time to wait for the dawn."

Kilda stood up first. "What do ye need?" she offered.

"You have already given enough," Asher reassured.

The healer shook her head. "If ye're to travel through the night ye won' be findin' anythin' in the city. Ye'll need supplies, food an' the like. I can sort that for ye."

The ranger nodded his thanks. "Give my farewell to Deadora," he said, rising from his chair.

"An' mine," Doran chimed in.

Kilda looked the dwarven hunter in the eyes. "See this through, Doran, an' all is forgiven."

The son of Dorain swallowed and nodded his understanding. "I'll see it done, one way or the other."

With that, the hunters saw themselves reunited with their gear, weapons, and mounts. Asher gave Danagarr his thanks once again for the addition of his silvyr blade, a payment greater than he had earned, in his own eyes.

After Kilda stuffed their saddlebags with supplies, the ranger swept his green cloak over the back of Hector and set the horse to the dirt path. Doran paused in his wake and offered the Stormshields a handful of words in their native tongue, to which they responded in kind.

Putting the homestead behind them, man and dwarf took up the hunt.

CHAPTER II
UNLIKELY COMPANIONS

***Urgal** - It is highly unlikely you will ever encounter this creature, but there are two accounts in our oldest archives that detail Urgals, and so I have chosen to make an addition to our growing bestiary.*

Having thoroughly read the reports from our long dead colleagues (it should be stated that neither man ever met, with forty years between the death of one and the birth of the other) I can see that their descriptions of an Urgal are identical. And disturbing.

The Urgals were seen north of Snowfell, at the base of The Vengoran Mountains. This alone would suggest that their species inhabits the area. There are local myths and legends about Urgals, though most in The Ice Vales refer to them as Goblins.

At a reported three-feet tall, they are green of colour with large pointed ears. They've sharp teeth and lethal nails on their six-fingered hands. Now for the disturbing part.

According to both late rangers, the Urgals they encountered could speak and even wore clothes, if a little shabby in their appearance. Furthermore, it was reported by both that the creatures possessed a level of intelligence on a par with a human. It was the creatures who named themselves as Urgals, in fact.

The second ranger to meet an Urgal made note of tools hanging from

several belts around its waist, though their purpose was never recorded.
Nor was their reason for being around Snowfell.
With that, they remain a mystery.

A Chronicle of Monsters: A Ranger's Bestiary, 12th Edition,
Page 478.

Elswyn Palona, Ranger.

As it will, the moon traversed the heavens and swept with it the blanket of stars, before the sun returned in its stead. Through that night and day, Asher and Doran put mile after mile behind them until, once again, the moon held sway over the world and rest finally called to them.

Throughout their journey, Doran had glanced at the sky, imagining the raven he had dispatched flying ever southward, to Velia. It would reach the city long before Corrigan did and his message would travel further still to Viktor himself. Doran prayed to the Mother and Father that it would be enough to hold back any immediate retaliation where the Stormshields were concerned.

He would never forgive himself if anything happened to that family.

What would his own family say if they knew he harboured such concern for Stormshields? Ridicule would be the least of his worries, the dwarf knew. But, then again, his family couldn't possibly think any lower of him than they already did, so what did it matter?

Doran shook his head, hoping the thoughts would simply fall out of his ears. He rarely dwelled on his family and realised he must be tired. Judging by the lack of feeling below the waist, he knew he had certainly been in his saddle too long. Thankfully, the ranger had already steered them off The Selk Road, and beyond an outcropping of rocks that would conceal them for the remainder of the night.

Without a word, they went about setting up their makeshift camp; a couple of bed rolls either side of what was to be their fire. Pig and Hector rested on the ground, satisfied to be off their hooves for a while. Doran sorted through their supplies of food and drink while Asher gathered the necessary firewood.

"There ain' much to choose from," the dwarf complained, scrutinising their rations. "An' we've got to be sly with it since we're cuttin' across the land an' missin' out Palios altogether. The next tavern's not till Velia," he added, salivating at the thought of a cosy warm ale.

"We can hunt if needs be," Asher said gruffly, his first words for many hours.

"True enough," Doran grumbled, too tired to think about hunting right then. His mood was lifted, however, when he came across some linus grass and arakan spices. The son of Dorain was quick to retrieve his pipe before turning to hold it all up for the ranger to see. "Do ye smoke, laddy?"

"Can't say I do," Asher said with hardly a glance at the pipe.

Doran shook the pouches in his hand. "Sweet an' spicy! It'll make up for the lack o' any puddin'. Ye'll see."

While Asher took a mouthful from his waterskin, the dwarf joined him and crouched over the firewood. Leaving the pipe and spices on the ground, he retrieved the flint from his pocket and went about sparking a flame, eager to get on with the evening.

"Damned thing," he cursed under his breath. "Come on," he urged the insufficient spark.

Asher continued to watch him, unimpressed. "Get the food," he instructed. "I'll see to the fire."

"I can do it," Doran insisted.

The ranger looked past him, at the saddlebags attached to Pig. "Get the food," he repeated evenly.

The dwarf slowed his words down. "I can do it."

"If you can do it why is there no fire?" Asher jibed.

"There's no fire," Doran snapped, "because ye're not givin' it enough space to breathe!"

"You think *I'm* the one taking up too much space?" Asher retorted.

The son of Dorain let loose a low grumble as he returned to the task of creating a spark. His hands worked furiously to no avail. "Bah!" he finally growled. "Ye do it then, ranger man." He tossed the flint to the ground and walked back to his Warhog with rage pumping through his veins.

Quite aggressively, he rummaged through the saddlebags until he was handling the right food. He heard Asher mutter something behind him and, sure that it was an insult, he turned around, ready to demand that the ranger say it again, only louder and to his face. He failed to find the words, however, in light of the large flames that now sat at the centre of their little camp. The dwarf was stumped.

"How did ye do that?" he asked.

Asher tossed the flint in his direction and Doran caught it between the food he was holding. That was, apparently, the only answer the ranger was giving.

The dwarf scowled on his way back to the fire, his curiosity growing all the more where his travel companion was concerned. Too much about the human didn't make sense to him, and they were usually such a simple breed to understand.

There was only more silence to follow as the hunters consumed their food and drink. When Asher finished his waterskin, Doran offered him some of his own, though it most definitely wasn't water.

"Duke's Mead again?" the ranger said to the dwarf's outstretched arm. "You'll forgive me if I don't drink anything you offer me."

Doran frowned. "Come on now, we're past all that aren' we? Besides, what's the use in druggin' ye now?" he pointed out.

"Bait for the Rakenbak?" Asher suggested.

"Now there's an idea," the son of Dorain mused, before he broke into a throaty laugh. "I mean ye no ill will, ranger man. We're on the same side."

"Until that doesn't suit you," Asher stated.

Doran could feel the air of confidence that surrounded the man, suggesting he was more than ready for what he considered an inevitable betrayal. "*I'm* the one who's wary o' *ye*, lad. Odds are high that we're *both* goin' to die on this path. Yet 'ere ye are, with nothin' to gain for yerself. Combine that with what I've seen o' ye so far an' ye're addin' up to one strange fella."

"What you've seen of me?" Asher echoed, looking up from the flames.

"Ye made a mockery o' Viktor's men," Doran recalled. "Now they weren' exactly Graycoats, I'll admit, but they were fighters all, each one havin' earned their way into the guild with violence an' blood. I don't believe some mere *ranger* possesses the skills you unleashed on them."

"Is that right?" Asher now appeared lost to the flames again.

"Aye," the dwarf argued. "Anyone can take part in a fight, but it takes *real* trainin' to break yer opponent instead o' killin' 'em. That kind o' restraint ain' easy."

"Well you're right about that," the ranger agreed without elaborating.

Doran eyed his companion for a moment longer. "Then there's what I saw on that cliff," he announced. When Asher ignored the comment, the dwarf doubled down. "I know what I saw. Ye shouldn' o' walked away from that fight yet 'ere ye are. How many can say they brought down *two* Trolls without so much as a scratch?"

"I'm good at what I do," Asher responded calmly. "I don't have to defend that."

"An' what abou' the fire?" Doran went on.

Asher returned the dwarf's frown. "I used the flint *you* gave me."

"That don' explain how ye made it so big so fast! An' I didn' even hear ye strike the damned flint!"

The ranger tensed his jaw and nodded along. "So you don't trust me because I'm a skilled fighter and I'm good at starting fires." Continuing in this sarcastic vein, he said, "And *I* don't trust *you* because... Oh, that's right. Because you drugged me and sold me into slavery."

Doran threw his arms up. "That again? Are ye never goin' to let that go?"

Asher had nothing to say and so the pair sat in silence again.

It was some time later when Asher finally broke the tension. "You're sure this is the way to the Rakenbak?"

"O' course I'm sure," the dwarf said with a shrug. "South o' 'ere. We'll 'ave to cross The Unmar, but it ain' much further than that. There's some ruins nestled in the wood beyond the river. That's where we'll trap it."

The ranger half turned to retrieve a leather-bound book from his saddlebag. Without explanation, he flicked through the pages before opening the covers wide and placing it on the ground in the firelight.

"What's that then?" Doran enquired.

Asher flashed a brief glance up at the dwarf, his eyes pulled back to the pages as if by some unseen force. "It's a book," the ranger said.

Doran couldn't help his look of mock surprise. "A book? Well, I've never seen one o' those before."

The comment was clearly noted for what it was and Asher diverted his gaze across the fire again. "It's a bestiary," he finally told him.

"Bestiary? Ye mean a book abou' monsters an' the like?"

"That's *exactly* what it is," the ranger replied dryly.

The dwarf nodded, wilfully ignorant of his companion's tone. "Has it got anythin' abou' Rakenbaks?"

Asher paused before responding. "Yes. *That's* why I'm reading it."

Seeing the ranger's exasperation grow and grow, the son of Dorain continued to push and push. "Well what does it say, lad?"

Asher stopped himself from reading any further. "I don't know because I haven't read it yet."

"I thought ye would 'ave read it a few times, what with ye bein' a ranger an' all."

The ranger unknotted his jaw. "I have. But it's been a while and I've slain a lot of other monsters since then."

Doran made an expression of understanding and raised his hands apologetically. He waited three more seconds, letting Asher sink back into the pages, before probing further. "Does it say anythin' abou' traps?" The dwarf worked furiously to contain his amusement as the ranger sighed and let his head drop. "Because ye know," he continued, "we should probably avoid the spines—"

Asher stood up, cutting the dwarf off, and rounded the fire to hand over the book. "See for yourself," he instructed, before returning to his bed roll.

"Oh," Doran said with a hint of forced surprise. "I suppose I could take a look." He inspected the front cover first. "A Chronicle o' Monsters: A Ranger's Bestiary. Hmm. A bit wordy ain' it?" he remarked. "Heavy too. Ye take this everywhere with ye? Ye ever thought abou', ye know, jus' rememberin' it?"

One of the ranger's fingers drummed his knee at speed. "There's a lot to remember," he pointed out. "There's a whole wide world of monsters out there."

Doran flicked the side of the book. "That's right. I keep forgettin'. Ye humans 'ave limited space in there," he said, pointing to his own head. "Ye weren' built to last like me kin. Ye know, the oldest recorded dwarf made it jus' past two thousand years. When ye're puttin' century after century behind ye, ye need to be good with the ol' memory."

Asher was clearly pained by the conversation, not to mention the offence laced throughout. "And there I was," he replied, "thinking you had nothing but stone between your ears."

"If I was to hit ye with me head it'd feel like stone, I can tell ye that."

The ranger looked across the flames with predatory eyes. "If I wanted to, dwarf, I could drop you like a stone."

Doran slammed the book shut. "Why don' ye come over an' give it a try?"

Asher had the appearance of a wild cat, ready to pounce.

"You're infuriating," he seethed, his left eye twitching ever so slightly.

"I don' even know how to spell infuriating. But what I do know is: every time I look at yer face, me fist knots up." Doran felt the tension finally snap with his last word.

Man and dwarf collided, their feet kicking up sparks and disturbing the fire before their combined weight took them into the gloom. They hit the ground and rolled over each other, their fists hammering wildly at anything. All manner of obscenities and curses escaped their lips as they fell upon one another with fury. The next time Asher came up on top, the ranger locked Doran's arm in a hold while simultaneously thrusting his other elbow into the dwarf's clavicle, a move that inflicted pain on two fronts.

The dwarf was having none of it. "A head o' stone, ye say."

The son of Dorain gripped Asher by the hair and brought their heads together with a pounding slam. It was more than enough to convince Asher to release his hold on the dwarf and roll aside. Doran tried to sit up but soon discovered his arm had gone to sleep and his shoulder ached deep in the bone. He ended up falling in the dirt under his own weight and lying side by side with the groaning ranger again.

"What in the hells did ye do to me arm?" the dwarf panted.

Asher finally removed his hands from his forehead. "I can't see straight," he complained.

The pair slowly turned their heads to regard the other, each weighing up the odds of their fight beginning anew.

"The arakan spice," the ranger announced.

"Eh?"

"I'll try the arakan spice."

Doran's blank expression erupted into laughter.

Awake far later than they should have been, and with a pipe each gripped between their teeth, the odd companions sat in contemplative silence. They both sported bruises and fresh cuts, but they had expelled the anger that had continued to build in them over the last few days.

Asher removed the pipe from his mouth and peered inside the bowl, where the arakan spices burned. "It's not bad," he opined.

"It's got a pleasant after taste," Doran replied wearily. "'ere, try the linus grass."

The hunters swapped pipes. "Too sweet," Asher said, offering the pipe back.

"Ye get used to it," the dwarf told him. "I'm... I'm sorry abou'... *all that*, back there. I was lookin' to rile ye up."

"I'm sorry about the..." Asher nodded at Doran's arm. "Is it feeling any better?"

The dwarf rolled his shoulder. "Still numb, but the pain's gone." Doran regarded him. "Where did ye learn to do somethin' like that?"

Staring into the fire, the ranger hesitated with his answer. "My father."

"He a ranger too?"

"No."

Doran remained silent, waiting for the rest of Asher's response. When it became awkwardly clear that he was done, the son of Dorain took his pipe in hand. "Ye not a talker, I'll give ye that. But I know a lie when I hear one. Told enough o' 'em meself," he added with a short chortle.

Asher turned to look at him. "I wasn't lying."

"I know. But ye also weren' tellin' the whole truth. I've done enough o' that too."

The ranger fiddled with the fingerless glove on his right hand. "Not telling you everything is a mercy," he said quietly.

The dwarf gave a short laugh again. "Ain' that the truth." He held out his pipe. "I'll smoke to that."

Asher agreed and knocked his pipe against Doran's. "We should probably make a plan if we're to capture this Rakenbak alive," he suggested.

"The ruins are another hard day's ride," Doran said. "There'll be time on the journey. Now, I'm all for restin'."

The ranger gave no protest, allowing the pair to seek out their bed rolls and get as comfortable as the natural earth would allow.

In the quiet that followed, the son of Dorain turned his head to the sky so that Asher could hear him. "An' erm... I am sorry abou' the whole... *slave* business."

The ranger didn't move, already asleep apparently.

The dwarf sighed. He wasn't sure he had it in him to say that again.

CHAPTER 12

A DAY IN THE LIFE OF A RANGER

Harkon - Vicious aquatic hunters, the Harkons could best be described as eel dogs. They hunt in fresh water such as lakes and rivers (see A Charter of Monsters, Page 203, for known locations). They can reach up to twenty feet and weigh up to four hundred pounds.

It's a myth that these creatures possess a venomous bite—as far as humans are concerned that is. To the fish it shares a habitat with, the bite of a Harkon means death within seconds. That's not to say their bite doesn't mean death for a human, for their jaws are extendable and capable of taking a limb, given the opportunity. A fully grown female could snap a man in half.

As with any monster who calls the water their home, Harkons can be difficult to hunt (see below for suitable list of bait).

When it comes to killing them, I would recommend using poisoned bait. Failing that, you're going to need a spear and a lot of patience.

Good hunting.

A Chronicle of Monsters: A Ranger's Bestiary, 12th Edition, Page 169.

Cal Phesto, Ranger.

. . .

As Doran had said, the distance between their camp and the banks of The Unmar was a hard day's ride. Asher, however, always enjoyed such a day. Time in the saddle didn't bother him—he had certainly endured far worse—and even the company was beginning to grow on him, though he would never admit such a thing. The ranger had decided it was easy to travel with the dwarf given that he too preferred to ride in silence. The value of this could not be overstated.

Of course, he had suffered a painful headache for the entire journey. Doran's head was comparable to a hammer, and Asher had been hit by enough hammers to know. He wasn't the only one suffering. The ranger had caught glimpses of the dwarf slipping his hand beneath the spiked pauldron to rub his sore shoulder. Doran's pain didn't lessen Asher's, though it did make him feel better.

With the sun beginning to set below the western horizon, the hunters found a shallow section of The Unmar River and crossed to its southern bank. Only a hundred feet away stood a wall of trees that concealed the land belonging to the kingdom of Alborn.

"What've ye stopped for?" the son of Dorain questioned astride his Warhog. "The ruins are further still."

Asher climbed down and took Hector by the reins, his gaze set to the wood. "If the Rakenbak is as big as you say, this tree line is likely the edge of its domain."

"Aye," Doran agreed. "So we won' be catchin' it out 'ere."

"It'll catch the scent of our mounts before it does us," the ranger explained. "We're best leaving them here and finishing the hunt on foot."

Doran frowned. "Yers might be good for nothin' but carryin' yer hide, but Pig 'ere is a warrior bred."

Asher scrutinised the Warhog, its snout entirely lost to the interior of a hollow log. "I'm sure it is," he said evenly. "But it also *stinks*. Surprise will be our best chance at capturing the Rakenbak alive. We'll lose that opportunity if it comes looking for..."

An idea occurred to the ranger.

"Oh no," the dwarf began, catching on. "Ye're not usin' me pig as bait. Forget it."

"We need something to lure the beast into our trap," Asher pointed out. "What better than a fat juicy pig?"

"He's not *fat*," Doran protested. "That's how they're bred! Solid as the mountain stone I tell ye!" He waved the idea away. "Besides, ye said we could use somethin' simple, like a rabbit carcass. Ye even said we could sprinkle it with some arakan spice!"

Asher nodded along for he had suggested just that. "Because it would prove a scent powerful enough to intrigue our prey," he said, repeating his words from earlier. "But there's a *big* difference between a curious Rakenbak and a Rakenbak blinded by the delicious aroma of a *fat* juicy pig. We don't want it questioning its environment. The pig will make us all but invisible."

The dwarf chewed over the logic, desperate, by the looks of him, to come up with a better solution. "Damn," he relented with a sigh.

~

After securing Hector to one of the trees, the hunters threw their saddlebags over their shoulders and proceeded to enter the wood. Doran led his Warhog by the reins with his sword slung over his back and axe ready in hand. Given the need to capture the monster alive, Asher was tempted to instruct the dwarf to leave his axe behind. Such a weapon often guaranteed death—something easily imagined in the hands of Doran.

In truth, the ranger was eager to free his new weapon and see what it was capable of. Much like Doran's axe though, he imagined the silvyr blade was a weapon better for delivering death than taking anything alive. Still, he yearned to wield it.

Just before true dark enveloped the world, the companions came across the aforementioned ruins. It was no more than a collection of ancient arches and a few broken walls, its original shape impossible to deduce. While Doran began to pile up some of the Warhog's food—the only method the dwarf knew of to keep Pig in one place—Asher was drawn to something only a hunter could be: animal dung.

It was a considerable pile and smeared up a portion of a shattered wall. The ranger crouched down and picked up a small handful. It was dry and cold, a day old perhaps. It was also Rakenbak dung.

"This is the right place," he voiced, and quietly so.

"I did say as much," Doran replied. "Ye didn' 'ave to go siftin' through the likes o' that," he added with a disgusted expression.

Asher stood up and surveyed the surrounding area, searching for a good place to wait for the Rakenbak out of sight, and preferably up wind of the pig lest the creature discover them first. "We haven't got long," he voiced. "Rakenbaks like to hunt at night."

Doran tied a piece of rope to a nearby tree and secured it around Pig's harness, giving the animal enough slack to move but not to run away. "Do ye need time to prepare that stuff ye bought in Darkwell?"

The ranger placed his saddlebag on the ground and retrieved the slick weed and kern oil. "It'll only take a minute. Get the net ready."

While Doran unfolded the net he had purchased for the previous hunt, Asher filled his small mixing bowl with the slick weed and poured the kern oil over the top. Using the pommel of his dagger, the ranger crouched down and ground it all together, just as the bestiary advised. Satisfied with the paste he had created, Asher began covering his arrowheads in it.

"You're sure it was a female?" the ranger asked, always doubting the dwarf.

Doran stopped his work with the net. "How many times are ye goin' to ask me that, lad? Aye, I'm sure it were a female."

Asher turned from his preparations to look at some of the tracks he had noted on their way in to the ruins. There were a lot of them, which suggested this location was either frequently visited by the Rakenbak or there was more than one of them. The ranger didn't feel like being surprised again.

"And you're sure there was only one of them?"

The son of Dorain sighed into his chestplate. "Aye," he answered wearily. "Ye might not be able to count Trolls, but I can count Rakenbaks. Are ye sure abou' that paste o' yers?" the dwarf snapped back.

"This is just another day for me," Asher replied casually.

Moving about the ruins, the ranger acquainted himself with its layout. Fighting Rakenbaks was always a case of remaining fluid since standing your ground was a death sentence. Strike and move, the bestiary instructed. He also noted the likely entrances from where the beast might appear, though it was getting so dark now that its tracks were impossible to see.

"Damned thing," Doran grumbled from the other side of the broken wall.

Asher rounded the obstacle to see the dwarf struggling with the net. "It's knotted," he observed.

"Ye don' say," Doran replied.

"You any good with that thing?" the ranger asked, his doubt audible.

"I know how to throw a bloody net," came the frustrated response.

Asher picked up the other side of the net and inspected the hooks that added weight to it. Some were rusted while others appeared blunted and barely attached to the rope. "Who conned you into buying this?"

The son of Dorain spared the ranger a scowl. "I wasn' conned," he insisted. "There's no better haggler than a dwarf."

Asher wasn't convinced. "Have you ever caught anything with this?"

"Aye," Doran growled. "A Rakenbak."

The ranger raised a sceptical eyebrow. "You mean the Rakenbak that nearly killed you? The same Rakenbak we're here to capture?"

The dwarf finally had the net laid out in his hands. "Don' worry abou' it. Ye jus' hit it with them arrows o' yers an' I'll net it while it's nice an' drowsy."

Asher was shaking his head, his own frustration showing through where Doran's memory was concerned. "It's not going to be drowsy," he reminded. "The slick weed will make it hack up whatever's in its gut. That's when we strike."

"Right, right," the dwarf agreed, hardly listening. "None o' that's goin' to matter after I've introduced it to me axe."

"We need it alive, remember," the ranger stated. "We only need to exhaust it."

"What?" Doran barked. "What am I supposed to do then, jus' give it the run abou'? Do I look like a runner?"

Asher was starting to wonder if the son of Dorain had listened to anything he had told him about their prey. "Rakenbaks need a constant supply of food. On empty stomachs their weight proves too much and they slow. We can use the ruins to our advantage."

"I'll take ye word for it, ranger man. Where I'm from, we tend to jus' knock things on the head until they don' move anymore."

The ranger was inclined to believe him. "Knocking an angry Rakenbak on the head," he mused. "I don't know why that didn't work for you the first time." Doran continued to stare up at him, his jaw firmly set. "Come," Asher finally bade, his amusement well concealed. "We can wait over there."

The world turned and the heavens with it while the hunters sat in wait. The ruins were cast in the pale light of the moon, unlike Asher and Doran who sat in the arched hollow of a great root. The natural walls helped to keep their scents contained, whereas the unmistakable smell of Pig continued to permeate the wood.

More than once the Warhog had tried to break free of its restraint, going so far as to gnaw on the rope that bound it to the tree. Doran had insisted his knot was sufficient, however, and that the rope would hold long enough to lure the monster.

"It should be 'ere by now," the dwarf complained in what he considered to be a hushed tone.

"Quiet," Asher replied, far more accustomed to waiting for his prey.

"Maybe it's moved on," Doran theorised.

"Quiet," Asher repeated.

"I thought ye said it didn' 'ave good hearin'."

The ranger slowly turned his head to look at the dwarf in disbelief. "That's Trolls," he said with no lack of exasperation. "How much of what I say do you actually hear?"

"Abou' half," Doran answered, without skipping a beat.

Asher was about to respond, and not too kindly, when the bark of the arched root audibly strained. Both hunters froze and looked up, unable to see what had applied the pressure. The root groaned again and something exhaled a sharp breath. Dead ahead, the Warhog stood perfectly still, its dark eyes looking at whatever was resting directly above them. Without warning, the pig broke into a mad sprint, taking it in the other direction, towards the ruins. The rope went taut, however, and the animal was momentarily brought down.

The Rakenbak was revealed.

The hulking monster pounced from the root and landed not far in front of the hunters. Doran started forward before Asher placed a firm hand on his arm and shook his head. When the dwarf questioned him with a look, the ranger held up a single finger and spun it around, informing his companion that they couldn't attack from the back, where a wall of spines covered it from head to ankle.

By now, Pig had found its hooves and was testing the real strength of Doran's rope. All the while, the Rakenbak slowly approached, oblivious to the hunters at its flank. Asher indicated for Doran to creep out to the left while he moved to the right. The ranger winced at the sound of dwarven armour scraping together but, thankfully, the salivating monster was too occupied with its delicious prey to notice anything else.

As he moved, Asher nocked an arrow and searched for that all important angle if he was to pierce its hide instead of seeing his attack ricochet off its spiky back. Matching his pace, Doran came up on the Rakenbak's left with the net held ready in both hands. It was a simple plan, he knew, but anything else would likely over-complicate things for the dwarf. Simple or not, there were variables the ranger wasn't used to working with. One such variable was Doran himself, a hunter with an opposing style to Asher's.

The other was Pig.

While the animal was trapped within a circle of the tree, the Rakenbak was content to approach slowly, saving its precious energy. But the Warhog's attempts to break free finally bore fruit. The rope snapped and it bolted, forcing the monster to give chase. The Rakenbak's initial acceleration was impressive for its size, a testament to its sheer strength.

It also unravelled Asher's simple plan.

The arrow he had been aiming was let loose on the world only to find naught but air in the place of a target. That was, of course, until it sailed beyond and into the tree a few inches from Doran's head. The dwarf naturally jumped back and threw his hands up in the air at the ranger.

A low growl rumbled out of Asher's throat. "This is why I work alone," he grumbled to himself, nocking another arrow.

Only a second later and Pig was dashing around the ruins and coming back towards them. The Rakenbak was close behind, its hardened shoulder pushing through a corner of stonework to pursue the Warhog. It unleashed a roar, filling the woods with the sound of its most dominant predator.

It was also the roar of a *male* Rakenbak.

"That's not a female!" the ranger hissed at the dwarf.

"What does it matter?" Doran called, as Pig raced past.

Asher ignored the question—*he* would remind the wood who the real predator was. Raising his bow, taking aim, and firing the arrow was all instinct to the ex-assassin. The poisoned missile flew over Pig's head and carried on into the monster's torso, a slab of muscle covered in mottled yellow fur.

Undeterred by the arrow in its chest, the Rakenbak leapt at him, its bear-shaped head following closely behind two front paws of razored claws. The ranger dived to his left and tucked into an evasive roll. Mid-rise, one hand was already reach over his shoulder for the next arrow. Asher fired again, and with only a moment's aim since he had expected the beast to have turned on him. The monster did no such thing, avoiding the arrow altogether.

It wanted the pig.

The Warhog zig-zagged to evade those powerful jaws and the Rakenbak kicked up a wave of dirt as it turned sharply to pursue. A moment later and both were lost from sight again, returned to the ruins.

"The males are harder to kill," Asher panted, his chest heaving. "It takes a lot more slick weed to stop them."

"Well ye've got more arrows haven' ye," Doran pointed out, with no more than a gesture. "So stop yer complainin' an' start hittin' it!"

Asher was reacquainted with the twitch in his left eye. "Get ready to throw the net on its next pass," he ordered through gritted teeth.

Sure enough, the Warhog soon returned, retracing its steps at speed. Asher backed off and nocked another arrow while Doran closed the gap to intercept the beast. There was no missing the Rakenbak's approach, its every step pounding the earth.

Finally displaying the skills of an experienced hunter, Doran threw his net like a professional. It spun on an angle and blocked the monster's path with perfect timing. The Rakenbak was immediately entangled, the beast's own speed working against it. More dirt was kicked up and roots broken as the creature fell forwards and skidded several feet, tumbling over its limbs again and again.

Asher pulled his bow string and brought the end of the arrow to the familiar anchor point at the base of his ear. He waited two heartbeats, giving the Rakenbak time to fight the net and present him with its mottled front. The first arrow was swiftly followed by a second, both boring into their intended target. The monster cried out, though the missiles were to be irritants rather than deadly blows.

"Hit it again!" Doran bellowed.

The ranger didn't require such instruction. Since he was dealing with a male, he knew *every* arrow would likely be required.

The next arrow cut through the air and stabbed into the Rakenbak's gut, adding a third dose of poison. The fourth missed the mark when the beast staggered into a tree and presented Asher with its hard back. Still, the ranger nocked another arrow and prepared to fire.

"Hit it!" the dwarf encouraged.

"I need it to turn!"

"I'll get it to turn," Doran assured.

"Don't—" Asher tried to warn, but it was too late.

The son of Dorain was already drumming his axe and sword together and shouting at the monster. The Rakenbak did indeed take note of the dwarf, its pointed head swivelling to locate the obnoxious sound. An almighty roar split the air and the angered beast tore the net in half as it burst into action.

"Run!" Asher cried, letting loose his arrow.

The Rakenbak barely noticed the arrow that pierced its side, its predatory mind focused on Doran. Now at full speed, Asher's chances of hitting it with any more arrows was severely reduced, and he needed to make them count. Instead, he ran for the ruins and watched Doran disappear beyond the first broken wall and the Rakenbak behind him.

"Doran!" the ranger called.

The sound of pounding paws, incessant growls, and dwarven war cries echoed through the ruins. Asher weaved between the weathered stone with cautious footing. Rush the wrong corner and he could come face to face with a charging Rakenbak. Hearing Doran's axe and sword swing and clatter, the ranger moved to the east, pausing here and there to check the way ahead. He caught sight of the beast hurtling past an archway before it met the son of Dorain in battle again.

Approaching from the opposite direction, Asher hopped over a low wall and nocked an arrow, his aim rising to meet the monster's imminent reappearance. Doran was seen first, manoeuvring from left to right to evade the raking claws. As he retreated step by step, the Rakenbak was eventually revealed, the beast standing on its hind legs to tower over the dwarf.

The ranger's bow gave a resounding *twang* and his next arrow was quickly embedded in the monster's midriff. This time it recoiled, its roar distorted by some grievance. Doran threw himself into the fight and scored a lashing strike with both sword and axe across his enemy's legs.

"Get out of there!" Asher yelled. The dwarf's fighting style was too rooted.

The Rakenbak brought its front weight down and with it came a hammering spread of sharp claws. The son of Dorain stepped back and took the hit to the chestplate in place of his head, though the blow was still powerful enough to knock him back off his feet. From his back, and without much thought, the dwarf hurled his axe at the advancing beast. On all fours now, the beast had only to bow its head and the axe found naught but a carpet of hard spines that ran back from the creature's forehead.

Asher had watched it all out of the corner of his eye while navigating the last of the ruins between them. He noted its steps were becoming sluggish and an unpleasant wet cough reverberated up through its throat. The slick weed was finally beginning to work. Even so, Asher nocked another arrow and took aim. The margin between a sluggish Rakenbak and a Rakenbak that couldn't move for vomiting so much was as considerable as the margin between life and death.

The arrow sank into the softer skin around the top of the shoulder joint and startled the monster, though not enough to stop it from advancing on Doran. The dwarf was quick to shake off the attack that had floored him and find his feet again, and now with Asher at his back. The ranger could see the son of Dorain's instincts rising dangerously close to the surface, instincts that told the dwarf to attack his foe while it was slowing.

"We need it alive," Asher reminded him.

Doran wasn't listening. He darted in and swung his dwarven sword, his aim high to cut down through his enemy's face. Regardless, the Rakenbak wasn't out of the fight for its life or its prey yet.

One backhand took Doran from his feet and through the top half of a broken wall. Asher would have winced on behalf of the dwarf if he hadn't seen it coming and made plans of his own.

The window was brief—the time it took the Rakenbak to flex its mighty arm—but he had been trained to use any and all opportunities when it came to bringing down his target. And so, while Doran had neared the end of his short charge, the ranger had dropped into a crouch, nocked another arrow, and taken aim at where he predicted the creature's arm would be.

The arrow found its home in the bicep and increased the dose of poison yet again.

The Rakenbak staggered into the stone archway on its left and knocked two of the remaining slabs free, each shattering on its impregnable back. A single jet of vomit shot from its maw and soaked the ground and splashed up the walls.

Spying the ranger, the creature ceased its dramatic episode and offered him a defiant roar.

Given the Rakenbak's proximity, Asher simply dropped his bow rather than collapse it and return it to his back. His hands free, the ranger drew his silvyr short-sword before assuming an aggressive fighting stance. Its priorities shifting, however, the monster pushed its weight through the rest of the arch and ploughed through another wall before Asher lost sight of it.

"Where'd it go?" Doran demanded, his feet finding uneasy steps through the debris of his previous impact.

"Do you have another net?" Asher asked him quickly, his eyes scanning the gloom of the ruins.

The dwarf rolled his injured shoulder. "I've got a couple o' hooks an' some rope, but that's it."

The ranger retrieved his bow and took the time now to collapse it and see it returned to its rightful place. "We need to spread out," he instructed. "It'll be getting weaker, but that feeling will only drive it to find food."

Doran was nodding his understanding. "An' we're still the prey, eh?"

Asher jutted his chin to the north, indicating the direction the dwarven hunter should take, while he took the ruins to the south. They didn't have a particularly large area to search, but it was the Rakenbak's area, not theirs. The pair cautiously ringed the exterior of the ruins, listening for any sign of their quarry.

The ranger halted and pressed his back to the nearest wall when he heard the beast emptying its guts. Confusingly, the sound appeared to come from both the interior of the ruins and the wood beyond. Then its heavy footsteps turned him around and he glimpsed its hind legs disappearing behind the curve of the ruins.

Retracing his path, Asher peered around the corner and waited, watching for any movement. Nothing. Then it vomited again, the noise pulling the ranger back into the ancient stonework. Cocking his head to the right, he heard Doran's armour and wondered how the dwarf hunted anything successfully.

Similarly drawn back in, the son of Dorain appeared not far away and waved his hand to catch the ranger's eye. He raised his hands questioningly and made a face, though his features were concealed by the shadows. Asher replied with a shrug before gesturing with his blade, ushering the dwarf on. For just a moment, both were captivated by the silvyr as it was kissed by the moon, the blade sparkling from end to end.

The Rakenbak moved on Asher's left, turning him down a different path. After a few steps he crossed a fresh patch of vomit. It wouldn't be long before the creature's stomach was empty and its muscles would begin paying the price.

"Asher!" Doran cried.

The ranger spun on his heel and darted through the ruins. He heard the distinct sound of a sword slicing through flesh before the Rakenbak let loose a weary roar. Asher skidded under the next arch, hoping—for the sake of the Stormshields—that Doran hadn't just killed the beast.

Very much alive, the Rakenbak had the dwarf's chest plate and pauldron between its jaws. It attempted to thrash Doran about but, in its weakening state, the monster struggled to raise the considerable weight. Likely concerned that his armour would soon give way to fangs and pressure, the son of Dorain stabbed the Rakenbak again and again, spilling its blood across his boots.

"Doran!" Asher growled.

The Rakenbak relented and staggered back, leaving Doran to lean against the broken wall and catch his breath. Asher joined his companion and ran a critical eye over the dwarf. There seemed nothing that would prove fatal, though stitches would definitely be needed for the gash that tore through his right eyebrow.

"Why does it keep comin' for me?" Doran complained.

"Easy prey," the ranger quipped. "Now *run!*"

The dwarf muttered some retort before pushing off the wall and hefting his sword. "Run?" he echoed.

The ranger paused after hopping over the nearest wall. "We need to tire it, not fight it. Run!"

The Rakenbak stopped hurling its guts and growled at the son of Dorain. "Runnin' ain' exactly me strong suit," he complained, but the dwarf followed Asher over the broken stone all the same.

The monster gave chase, though its weakened state now prevented it from simply pushing its way through the ruins. Navigating it just as the hunters did, the Rakenbak only grew more exhausted. Asher glanced over his shoulder and saw the creature ten feet behind Doran. There was desperation in its dark eyes. It needed food and it needed it *now.*

Soon, Asher was beyond the ruins and into the trees, and with Doran close on his heels yelling something in his native tongue. His foreign profanities were quickly followed by the Rakenbak. It was notably slower with the slick weed polluting its veins, but the animal was close to matching the dwarf's speed.

A sharp squeal and a roaring snort preceded Pig's arrival. The Warhog shot out of the woods and charged into the Rakenbak from the side, its tusks ploughing through the monster's hind legs. The beast tripped and was flung at an awkward angle into a tree, where its momentum and weight threatened the integrity of the roots.

Asher came to an abrupt halt and Doran with him. Seeing the damage inflicted on the Rakenbak from where he stood, the ranger could but sigh. The beast was still alive, that much was obvious from its feeble attempts to rise, but it wouldn't be charging with its back left leg in such a condition.

"Ha!" Doran celebrated. "We got it!"

The ranger wasn't sharing in the glee. "Give it a few minutes," he warned. Even an exhausted Rakenbak was still capable of killing them if it clamped its jaws around a limb.

"What's wrong with ye?" the dwarf barked. "We did it!"

"How appeased will this Viktor be when we deliver a Rakenbak that can't fight in his arena?"

The son of Dorain frowned at the question. "It'll be alrigh'," he insisted, without much real thought as to the extent of the problem. "He wanted a Rakenbak—that's what he's got."

Asher grunted. "We'll see."

CHAPTER 13
DEADLY NEGOTIATION

Fade - A nightmare of the Shadow Realm, of that there is no doubt (see Monsters of the Deep World). 'Tis a plane of existence that should never have been tampered with, but I could write a book on the arrogance of mages.

The Fades are either brought through from their world and let loose or they find a way through to our world due to a mistake on the mage's part. Either way, they will seek to create chaos in our world. Fortunately, in most cases, these creatures of the abyss are taken care of by the mages of Korkanath (they don't want magic's reputation to be tarnished after all).

Rangers are called upon when these monsters find people—and they will find people. They seem to be drawn to civilisation, as if we are no more than play things for their entertainment.

Fades are categorised by their appearance: unnaturally tall and thin, cloaked in black, they attack with claws the size of your hand. Unlike Wraiths, kin from the Shadow Realm, salt will not aid you in your fight. It is known, however, that Fades cannot cross iron. Even a fallen sword is as impassable as a stone wall. This makes for subtle traps—use them well.

A Chronicle of Monsters: A Ranger's Bestiary, 12th Edition,
Page 453.

Kasira Cornwell, Ranger.

Having secured the creature with numerous ropes and straps pooled from both hunters, Hector and Pig had succeeded in dragging it from the woods and further south, to the predetermined meeting point. It wasn't far from The Selk Road, but the natural rise and fall of the terrain kept them hidden from any inquisitive travellers.

Doran climbed down from his saddle and cracked his spine, his eyes ever vigilant where the barely-conscious Rakenbak was concerned. "How long will it stay like that for?" he asked, his hand never far from the axe strapped to his Warhog.

"Until it gets food," Asher replied in his usual gruff tone.

The dwarf chewed over the information. "Can it die?"

"Everything can die," the ranger said, unhelpfully.

Doran eyed his irritable companion. "Do ye need yer beauty sleep or what?"

Asher appeared to have no reaction to the question, though he did eventually respond. "I don't think either of us will be getting much sleep, not while we're in the company of Varga's men."

As usual, Doran's natural reaction to any general concern was to shrug it off. "We'll be done with this business soon enough. We deliver the beastie, I offer me *heart-felt* apologies, an' we get out o' there. Easy."

The ranger sighed. "There's every chance the Rakenbak will die before we make it to Dragorn," he said stiffly. "And even if it does survive the journey, Viktor could reject the condition of the beast. Your pig has *crippled* it."

The son of Dorain was shaking his head, his irritation rising to match the ranger's. "I suppose that's the problem with havin' such short lives, eh? Ye humans 'ave to do all o' yer worryin' at once."

Again, Asher showed no outward sign that the dwarf's words had impacted him. "Someone is coming," he announced, his upturned gaze leading Doran's eyes to the southern rise.

Indeed, the ranger was proved correct only a few seconds later when two horses, towing a large carriage, topped the hill. The driver was a new face to Doran but he recognised the older man seated beside him. That particular thug had taken custody of a Sandstalker from the dwarf almost a year ago. The horses were directed down the slope where a curve in the hill would bring them to the meeting place.

Asher looked down at the dwarf, unimpressed. "Two?" he questioned. "It will take a lot more than four of us to move the Rakenbak."

"Ye see the fancy-lookin' fella, next to the driver? He's a *mage*."

Asher's posture shifted subtly, so he now appeared more rigid than before. "A mage?"

"Aye, that's what I said. Viktor likes to surround 'imself with 'em. From what I've heard," he added quietly, "they're not *proper* mages."

"How so?"

"Supposedly, they're all failed students from that magic school, the one out in the ocean."

"Korkanath," Asher said, naming the school.

"Aye, that's the one. They don' know everythin', but they know enough to turn ye inside out." Asher gave no response, turning the dwarf's attention up to him. The prejudice that ruled his features was obvious to see. "What's the matter with ye? Got somethin' against mages?"

"Hmm," came Asher's guttural response. "I'm yet to meet one I haven't had to kill."

The comment struck the dwarf, adding to the growing list of questions that surrounded the ranger, but he kept his reply light. "Well 'ere's hopin' this one makes the list."

"You know him?" Asher asked.

"We've met," Doran informed, letting his dour feelings towards the mage be heard in his voice.

"Anything I should be concerned about?"

The dwarf raised a hand to calm the ranger. "Ye jus' sit there an' look dangerous."

His jaw firmly set, Asher's focus turned back to the carriage. Though Doran would never compliment the ranger, the dwarf could see that he had no trouble pulling off the look. Indeed, there was something about Asher that unsettled the son of Dorain. Perhaps, he thought, it was the animal he glimpsed in the ranger every now and then, the one that appeared to dwell just beneath the skin, waiting to be unleashed. He had seen such beasts before, in both men and dwarves, though they were few and far between. Thankfully.

"Ye took yer bloody time!" he called out to Varga's men. "This thing ain' goin' to stay dopy forever ye know!"

The horses were brought to a stop and the two men made the small jump to the grassy earth. The driver immediately turned on his heel and went about opening the doors at the back of the carriage—a silent operative in the illegal affair. Doran gave him no further thought and, instead, raised his chin to look upon the approaching passenger.

Like the last time they had met, the man was immaculately dressed beneath his flowing blue cloak, a cloak that somehow defied the dirt that clung to everyone else's. As he had then, Doran tried to gauge his age but humans were hard to pin down given the oppression they suffered under the reign of time. He had decided Varga's man was either in his early fifties or sixties. Were he a dwarf, Doran knew, anyone looking as he did would be in his fifth or sixth century. But he wasn't a dwarf. He was just a man and would likely die of old age before the son of Dorain grew his first grey hair.

Of course, there was more to this man than met the eye, a fact that made him very useful to Viktor Varga. The dwarf let his hands rest on his belt, where he could quickly retrieve the small throwing axe should he require it. All the while, his eyes scrutinised the shadows within the man's cloak.

"Doran Heavybelly," the thug announced, his accent suggesting he had ties to royalty. His tone added to this possibility, suggesting he considered the dwarf to be no better than the mud beneath his expensive boots.

"Kar..." Doran stumbled over the name. "Kal..." The dwarven hunter shook his head and offered a helpless shrug.

"Kavarion," the man declared with notable pride. "Rhaldor Kavarion."

Doran wagged his finger. "That's it—"

"And who is this?" Kavarion interjected, tilting his head up towards the ranger.

"His name's not to bother ye," Doran told him. "He's with me an' that's that. Now," he said, stepping aside to give Kavarion a clear view of the Rakenbak, "as ye can see, Viktor's prize is very much alive but it ain' goin' to stay that way unless we get on with it."

"Do you imagine it's that simple?" Kavarion questioned before his eyes finally left Asher and found the dwarf.

"It *is* that simple," Doran insisted, glancing at Kavarion's concealed hands.

"I read your missive myself," Kavarion went on. "You really believe that late delivery and an apology will suffice?"

Doran clenched his teeth together and threw a purse of coins at the man's feet. "An' his money back."

Kavarion's eyebrows danced across his forehead as he considered the addition. "My master will appreciate the latter, and even the apology, but the late delivery has left a sour taste in his mouth." Rhaldor's hand moved inside his cloak, causing Doran to slide his own hand across to the head of his throwing axe.

"We will travel with you," Asher said, his addition to the conversation enough to cut through the mounting tension.

"He speaks," Kavarion replied with a hint of curiosity.

"Asher," Doran warned.

"We will travel with you," the ranger continued, "to Dragorn. There, Doran will give his apology in person."

"That won't be enough, *Asher*," Kavarion informed. "I am not just here for the beast," he added, his gaze falling on Doran.

"He can have the next one for free," Asher stated, pausing Kavarion's obvious intentions.

"The next one?"

"Asher," Doran growled.

"Whatever monster Mr Varga desires," the ranger explained, "he can have it for free. We will hunt it and deliver it *on time*."

The new offer gave Rhaldor Kavarion a real reason to stay his hand and consider the terms. "Asher," he began, drawing out the ranger's name. "You wouldn't be the same man Corrigan spoke of, would you? He returned as we were leaving to meet you. That was a lot of Mr Varga's employees you broke. Going before my master might not be so wise."

"Your master needs to employ better men," Asher said flatly.

A hint of amusement flashed across Kavarion's face. "Where Corrigan and his goons are concerned, we are in agreement. Still, once you step foot on Dragorn, I cannot speak of your fate, *either* of you. Should we conclude our business here and now, however, I can guarantee you both a swift and painless death."

"Well that is most kind," Doran replied dryly.

"Shall we?" Kavarion queried lightly, his right hand appearing from the confines of his cloak and with a wand no less.

Doran had been dreading its appearance, but he had also been expecting it. As the wand was so arrogantly brandished before them, the son of Dorain was raising his small axe and taking aim.

"You would test your steel against my magic?" Kavarion questioned incredulously.

"Me steel'll do the job," Doran assured. "It's ye *speed* I'm to test."

"We'll take our chances with your master," Asher interrupted, still seated calmly in his saddle. "With the Rakenbak and the coin at your feet, he gets *two* monsters for free *and* an apology from

Doran. Should he then desire it, Mr Varga never has to see either of us again. But I would say the deal is *his* to consider, not *yours*."

Kavarion's wand dipped and he raised his chin to look upon the ranger. "You are a curious specimen, Asher. Most curious. Perhaps the simple truth is; you don't know who you're dealing with. If you did," he added, his voice an octave lower, "you would have gladly chosen death this day. But," he said sharply, his wand held low now, "if it's an education you seek I shall not stand in your way. You may accompany us to Dragorn and *request* an audience with my master. Thereafter your life is in his hands."

"This is acceptable," Asher said, before making eye contact with Doran.

The son of Dorain scowled, frustrated that the ranger had spoken for him. He was also irked to have had his hand stayed. The axe would have flown beautifully.

"Aye," he grumbled, lowering his weapon. "Let's be gettin' on with it then. Dragorn ain' exactly round the corner. We'll be lucky if the beastie survives the trip."

Kavarion navigated the dwarf to stand beside the Rakenbak. "Given that you are still drawing breath, Master Heavybelly, I would say you've already used all your luck."

With that, the mage swept his cloak aside with some flare and flourished his wand. While his lips moved incessantly, the spell he uttered could not be heard as he raised his hand and pointed the wand down. Limb by limb, the Rakenbak began to levitate from the ground. Walking side by side with the floating monster, Kavarion slowly guided it to the back of the carriage until he was able to place it down inside. The driver then moved in to close the doors and lock them with three heavy padlocks and two thick bolts.

Satisfied with his cargo, the mage returned to his seat behind the horses. "Velia is two days' ride from here," he stated.

"We'll be right behind ye," Doran assured, though he had no intention of being within earshot of the mage. In fact, the dwarf gestured for Asher to hold back while the carriage cleared the rise and disappeared from sight. "Two monsters!" he exclaimed. "Did that Rakenbak hit ye in the head, laddy? I thought we were to be squared with the one an' an apology. Hells, I've even given the coin back! More business with Viktor only gives 'im more opportunities to put our heads on the choppin' block!"

Asher was watching the rise as if he could still see Kavarion. "We had to sweeten the deal."

"Oh did we now?"

"That mage was sent to kill you and that's exactly what he would have done."

"Bah! He'd 'ave tried. If ye'd 'ave kept ye mouth shut he'd be tastin' me steel right now."

The ranger tapped his horse into motion. "He would have put a hole in your head and then *I* would have been forced to put one in *his*."

Doran snorted with amusement. "Is that right, ranger man? Kavarion's quick enough to kill me but not ye?"

"That's about right," Asher remarked over his shoulder. "Then the driver would have been able to report what he'd seen so I would have had to kill him too. And when neither you or the mage turned up, Viktor Varga would send someone to look for you and they'd start with the Stormshields. So I'd have to kill whoever he sent." The ranger shrugged with exasperation. "The list goes on and on. This is the easiest way."

The dwarf grumbled to himself. Now that they were actually on course to meet Viktor Varga in person, he was starting to wonder if it would have been easier to relocate the Stormshields. Upon further consideration, Doran decided it would be safer to meet Varga rather than tell Kilda her family had to go into hiding.

CHAPTER 14
A STORM IS COMING

Kruid - A good old-fashioned monster if ever there was one. If you're yet to accept a contract on one of these beasties, perhaps you haven't spent enough time in The Arid Lands, typically Karath. Kruids hail from The Undying Mountains, a place no man can say much about. Adding to the mysteries of the mountains are the Kruids themselves. It is unknown why they only appear during the summer months, though I would guess it has something to do with their food supply.

When it comes to slaying these monsters, you would be better off sharing the contract with another ranger, maybe even two. They're easy enough to kill, but they're big. The best description I can give would be to compare a Kruid to a scorpion, except they can reach twenty feet in length.

Now, as long as you have a sharp enough sword, you'll do just fine. I would suggest assaulting as a team so you can distract the beast, specifically its pincers. Keep them busy, and you can attack from the sides.

A Chronicle of Monsters: A Ranger's Bestiary, 12th Edition, Page 459.

Robyn Kobb, Ranger.

After topping the rise and joining The Selk Road, just beyond their meeting place, the journey to Velia was simple enough. The road was almost a straight line down The Shining Coast and offered several places to make camp overnight. Asher and Doran had deliberately set up their camp away from Kavarion and the carriage and, even then, taken it in shifts to keep watch.

By late afternoon, on the second day, the towering gates of Alborn's capital finally stood before them. Velia was a bustling city, vibrant with life and activity be it night or day. The gates were always open and packed from edge to edge with merchants, travellers, and wagons. Spread out across the flat plain of grassland was the lower town and, further still, the swarming markets that couldn't fit inside the city walls.

Overseeing it all were the first four kings of old—Alborn's most prestigious rulers who had established the region's foundations and sprawling docks. Of the four statues that lined the curving outer wall, only one had been constructed to give the appearance that the king was looking down on the Velians.

Once upon a time, that was a detail Asher would never have given a moment's thought to. In the years since he had abandoned the life of an Arakesh, however, he had begun to research parts of the world that had nothing to do with the art of killing. He now knew that the king looking down on everyone was King Tradabor, the first to rule Illian's eastern lands after Gal Tion's empire shattered into its current six nations.

Looking up into those featureless stone eyes, Asher wondered what the king had witnessed in his time. Wars, plague, peace and prosperity—Velia had seen it all over the last thousand years. The ranger was certain, though, that King Tradabor had never seen a man and a dwarf pass through Velia's gates side by side. And with an imprisoned Rakenbak no less.

Asher was beginning to worry for the health of the creature. They still needed to find the ship, cross The Adean, and acquire an audience with Viktor Varga. The Rakenbak would be dead by then, he was sure of it.

As he had on the journey south, Rhaldor Kavarion turned in his seat to spot them behind the carriage. He motioned with one hand to inform the hunters they would be turning right after entering the city. It came as no surprise to Asher, who knew the outer-most road would lead them round to the docks. It had been many years since he had taken that route and crossed the sea to Dragorn. There weren't enough years, however, to rob him of the memory. Or her face.

Serena Trigorn.

That had been his target's name. As a young assassin, Asher had stalked her for no more than an afternoon, having decided her escort was less than adequate to protect her. Her family—one of the ruling four—were rich and possessed enough power to feel untouchable, comfortable within the folds of their crime guild. Serena, however, was a cousin or a niece—he couldn't quite recall —and, therefore, existed on the fringes of the inner circle. It was a dangerous place to be during the silent war that was eternally waged between the guilds.

As Hector took him through the city, keeping him above the constant foot traffic that cut between them and the leading carriage, Asher's memory clawed for dominance and brought back that fateful night.

Adopting the garb of a nobleman, he had been granted entry to the prestigious tavern that Serena favoured. Blending in was second nature to him and he was soon moving freely without a hint of suspicion from the rich patrons. He was simply a mirror to them—his demeanour, speech pattern, and even his choice of words taken straight from their world and used against them: a wolf parading as a sheep.

To Serena, however, there was something about him that was just different enough to make him stand out. Something roguish, rugged even. Asher had used that to his advantage and spent most of the evening seducing her. Feigning his level of intoxication, the Arakesh inevitably left with her, loosely followed by the two guards. They didn't know it then, but their imminent failure to protect Serena would result in their deaths too. Asher had suspected such a fate for them, but the young assassin hadn't a care.

In the privacy of her chambers, some time after midnight, Asher accomplished his dark mission. He could still feel her neck snap as if her head was in his hands that very moment. A pall of shame overcame the ranger, the guilt so heavy a burden it sagged his shoulders. Serena had been one of the innocents, one of his targets who didn't deserve an ounce of violence. But her name had been knotted into a length of red string and with it her death had been assured.

Then it struck him, the memory finally surfacing from deep in the ranger's memory. Deep in the *Assassin's* memory. That particular piece of red string, coded with the target's name and last-known location had been knotted with the name and location of another. The patron who had paid for Nightfall's services.

As they approached the open portcullis that led out to the docks, Asher's finger and thumb ran over the knots in his mind, as they had all those years ago. His hand squeezed Hector's reins, the name coming to him clearly.

Viktor Varga.

The crime lord's reasons for wanting Serena dead were his own and a younger Asher hadn't cared enough to investigate. Back then, the assassin had been single-minded when it came to his targets or, more specifically, the will of the Father, Nightfall's ruthless monarch. The voice of his old master came back to him so easily, a melody in his ear that could command of him anything.

Before his memories of Nasta Nal-Aket surfaced and took him down a path of misery, the ranger urged Hector to catch up to the head of the carriage. "Mage," he greeted in his gruff manner. "We need to feed the Rakenbak if it's to survive the rest of the journey."

By the expression on Kavarion's face, Asher might as well have informed the man that the sky was blue. "The beast is your concern, Ranger. But know the ship won't wait for you."

Asher gave the mage a look of grim determination as he turned Hector away from the carriage and returned to Doran.

"What were that abou'?"

"We need to find something to feed the Rakenbak," Asher told him.

The dwarf eyed the carriage. "The mage perhaps?"

"Tempting," Asher muttered. "We need raw meat," he specified. "Just enough to keep it alive."

Doran thumbed over his shoulder at the street they had just passed. "There's a butcher's shop round the corner if I recall. Damned good pork chops."

The ranger continued to stare at the dwarven hunter.

The son of Dorain met his stare with an air of confusion. "What are ye abou'?"

"The *meat*," Asher emphasised, looking over the dwarf's head.

Doran's confusion increased. "Aye. Go an' get whatever ye think'll do the trick."

"*You're* getting the meat," Asher asserted.

"Why 'ave *I* got to get the meat? It's yer idea!"

"This entire situation is of *your* making," Asher reminded him. "Getting the Rakenbak to Viktor alive is your responsibility. So, *buy the meat*."

The son of Dorain grumbled incessantly as he steered Pig to the left. "How much?" he barked at the departing ranger.

"A lot," he replied, keeping up with the carriage. "And be quick about it!" he called over his shoulder.

Within the hour, they had navigated the busy streets, passed through the eastern gate, and taken to the vast docks that joined the land and the sea. It was there Asher laid eyes on The Mer Seed, easily the largest ship in the dock, with three masts and fully rigged. There had to be four, perhaps even five decks contained within its hull. The ranger had to wonder if the grand size of the vessel said more about its owner than anything else.

Cutting it close, Doran eventually returned with a hefty

package of raw steaks and a lighter purse—the latter being the chief cause of his scowl.

Asher greeted the dwarf with a nod, though he only spared him a glance. The ranger's concern lay with the Rakenbak, which had been hidden beneath a tarp while Kavarion levitated it from the carriage towards the ship's hold. It appeared The Mer Seed had been designed with the transport of monsters in mind. Having already seen Hector safely aboard, nestled in the bowels of the ship, Asher now stood on the deck and watched the Rakenbak as it was lowered into a central hold. The walls of this hold were lined with steel bars. Its cover had been constructed with heavier timbers and reinforcements too, safely hiding and containing the illegal cargo.

Satisfied that the creature had been carefully placed in its temporary pen, Asher walked over to the port side railing, curious as to why Doran was yet to board. "What's the hold up?" he asked, spotting the dwarf below.

The son of Dorain didn't respond straight away, his attention turned to Pig as the Warhog was escorted into the hold by one of the deckhands. "I got the meat," he said, adjusting the package under his arm.

"I can see that," Asher said, his curiosity growing. "So why are you still down there?"

Doran licked his lips and looked around, eyeing the passing sailors with a degree of suspicion. "I don' like ships," he replied sheepishly.

The ranger twisted his mouth to hold any amusement back. "You don't like ships?" he echoed, his questioning tone more than enough to bore down to the unsaid truth.

The dwarf sighed and checked who was within earshot again. "I don' like the water," he muttered, his voice just loud enough to reach Asher on the deck.

"Well which is it?" the ranger pressed, enjoying himself a little too much. "Ships or water? Or perhaps it's—"

"I can' *swim*," Doran growled, grappling with his composure.

And there was the truth, begrudgingly given. "That's what the ship's for," Asher informed him. "So get up here—the Rakenbak needs that meat."

"I 'ave a process, a'right," Doran snapped. "This ain' me first time. Jus' give a dwarf a minute."

In his own time, the son of Dorain breathed a sigh into his chest and took the first step on the ramp. "Bloody island," he cursed on his way up. "The water's no place for a child o' the mountain," he said a little louder. "It's not our domain," he continued, his knuckles paling with every grip of the railing. "It's not *yers* either, I'll point out. It shouldn' be disturbed."

"The *meat*, Heavybelly," Asher coaxed.

After watching the fatigued creature slowly consume one steak after another—each one dropped right in front of its mouth—the ranger observed the crew cover the monster hold and slot several bolts into place.

Apparently, the Rakenbak wasn't the only cargo bound for Dragorn. The Mer Seed's crew, under Kavarion's direction, began loading crate after crate of fresh supplies into an adjacent hold.

The sun was kissing the horizon beyond Velia by the time the sails were being hoisted. The mage flicked his wand up and filled them with a blast of air, pushing The Mer Seed away from the docks at speed.

Asher braced himself against the starboard railing and watched civilisation fade into the twilight.

Though most would argue that civilisation awaited them at the end of their journey, the ranger considered otherwise. Asher knew the truth of their destination. Dragorn was far from civilised, whatever facade it might wear. They were sailing into a nest of bloodsucking Vorska.

A crack of thunder woke Asher with a start. His hammock, along with the lantern hanging from the ceiling, was swaying from side to side, and it was certainly moving more than it had been when he got in. Another hammer stroke erupted from the heavens and the ranger knew he had caught all the sleep he was going to.

With what little rest he had gained, Asher emerged on the top deck and inhaled the night air through the lashing rain. He had needed it, that spray of cold water and a gulp of fresh air. His dreams had quickly twisted themselves into nightmares, as they so often did. He had relived the murder of Serena Trigorn over and over again. How many times had he cracked her neck in the last few hours? How many times had he felt Viktor Varga's name on that length of red string?

The ranger felt like he needed to dive into the churning ocean to cleanse himself of the death that clung to him. Added to that, he was now plagued with a question that had remained dormant for a decade. Why had Serena had to die? Living with the kill and the blood on his hands was hard enough, but now he wanted answers.

It was foolish to hope he might learn something from his time in Dragorn for an investigation could reveal his past as an Arakesh. Asher knew he had to bury his feelings on the matter. Serena was dead and there would be no undoing that. She was one of countless victims who had died in vain, sentenced to an early grave by Viktor.

His emotions rose to battle that fact. Serena Trigorn was one of countless victims who had died in vain and been sentenced to an early grave by *him*. Serena was simply a common strand in a web of deaths where he and Varga collided.

"Bury it," he whispered to himself, before stepping away from the door.

The Mer Seed was awash in the cool moonlight that found the only gap in the racing clouds. Its sails were full now without the aid of Kavarion's magic. Up on the command deck, one of the crew defied the drenching rain and fought the wheel to keep them on the right heading.

Here and there, deckhands saw to the sails' constant adjustment, a necessity when dealing with the wrath of Mother Nature. Asher was no sailor, but even he knew the mounting storm was about to become a problem for them. Then there was Doran, a problem all on his own. The dwarf was right where Asher had left him, his back pressed to the main mast. He was also in the way, though any of the crew who dared tell him so received a biting threat.

"If you're not going to rest," Asher advised on his approach, his voice rising above The Adean's aggressive waves, "at least let them do their job. They're the only thing keeping you out of the water."

The dwarf's eyes shifted in his head and landed briefly on the ranger before returning to a dead stare. "I'm a'right, thanks."

Asher considered his companion's rigid stance and the pile of armour on the deck beside him. "You don't look alright."

Doran briefly tore his eyes from the horizon to track Asher's gaze upon his armour. "So I don' sink," he snapped. "An' where's the damned mage?" Doran demanded, likely wishing to change the subject.

The ranger shrugged, though it was hard to tell with the ever-increasing roll of The Mer Seed. "I haven't seen him since he went below deck."

"Shouldn' he be usin' that wand o' his an' gettin' us there faster?"

Asher walked across the deck, his honed sense of balance portraying ease of movement. "It's hardly a storm," he lied, before stamping his right foot twice into the decking. "Solid," he assured. "It can even take *your* weight."

"Ye're funny, ranger man," Doran said, his palms plastered to the mast.

The smile spreading across Asher's face fell away in an instant. The securely-bolted hatch over the monster's hold was out of place.

"What is it?" the dwarf demanded immediately. "What's wrong?"

The ranger moved to see around the central mast and caught sight of the driver who had brought the Rakenbak to the docks. The young man was swaying in time with the ship, one hand in his pocket while the other picked fish from an open barrel. Every fish he retrieved from the barrel was casually tossed down into the monster hold.

Alarmed by the scene, Asher burst into a stride and confronted the man from across the opening. "What in the hells are you doing?" he growled.

By the edge of the hold now, he peered into the shadows below. There wasn't a fish in sight, every one eaten by the Rakenbak, which was now on all four paws and slowly pacing up and down with an obvious limp.

Soaking wet and without a care, the driver shrugged with barely an apology about him. "I heard what you said about it needing food," he said, as if that was explanation enough.

Asher couldn't fathom the stupidity, and in a brewing storm of all times. "We needed it alive, not awake! Now it's going to—"

The Rakenbak roared, drowning out both him and the storm. The ranger looked down at its hide of spines and soon found its black eyes looking back at him. Its strength was almost fully returned, a fact that made him question the hold's durability.

"Why's that blasted thing makin' a racket?" Doran fumed from the mast, his feet edging around it.

"How long have you been feeding it?" Asher barked.

Again, the driver shrugged, oblivious to the potential calamity he had caused. "A while," he supposed.

The ranger had to fight the urge to navigate the hold and break the young man's nose. "Fool," he hissed, reaching for the hatch instead. "Give me a hand with this," he commanded. The driver rolled his eyes, failing to see the danger he had placed them in. "Doran, go and fetch Kavarion! Without any slick weed we're going to need magic!"

"Why don' *ye* get him?"

"Doran," Asher glowered, reaching down to begin pushing the wet roof back into place.

It was at that moment the driver miscalculated his footing in time with the sway. The slippery deck got the better of the young man and his left leg shot out from under him. He kicked the barrel of fish over the deck and landed on the edge of the monster hold.

Asher was moving only a second later but the young man's legs had already fallen over the side and into the Rakenbak's domain. Terror-stricken, he scrambled and screamed for help.

"Get out!" Asher bellowed as he dived to grab the driver's hands.

It was too late of course. The Rakenbak had recovered enough to dig those deadly meat hooks into the wall, its head rising up to meet its victim's dangling legs. Hefted by its front claws, powerful jaws dragged the young man down as Asher tried desperately to pull him up. The creature's strength, however, far surpassed the ranger's. Any grip that existed between him and the driver was torn apart.

Asher remained on his hands and knees, helpless to do anything but watch the butchering that splattered the hold with blood. The driver was dead within seconds of impacting the floor, his throat having been locked between the Rakenbak's jaws.

Very soon, the beast would convert that young man into unbridled power.

The ranger hurried to his feet and returned his efforts to the hold's cover. "Quickly!" he yelled at Doran.

Though reluctant, the dwarf managed to peel himself away from the mast and add his strength to the effort. Together, they slid the roof into place and shoved the bolts into their housing.

"What's all this?" Kavarion's familiar, if irritating, voice called from the other side of the mast. The mage appeared with his wand upturned and a shimmering spell dancing over his head to combat the pouring rain. "What are you doing?" he asked upon discovering the hunters and scattered fish.

"Yer damned driver fed 'imself to the beastie," Doran unhelpfully explained.

"He fell in," Asher specified, his concern mounting with every second the Rakenbak metabolised the young man. "Rakenbak's are excellent climbers," he elaborated, gesturing to the hold they had just secured.

Once again, the mage turned an uninterested expression on the matter, no concern given to the young man who had just died a gruesome death—the same young man the mage had travelled with for days to reach this point. "The roof is reinforced," he stated, "as are the walls." His last word was punctuated by a violent shudder that rippled out from the monster hold.

"They're strong," Asher told him. "Even more so when their stomachs are full."

Again, the ship bucked under another impact from within the hold.

"Maybe," Doran suggested, "a spell or two would convince it to sleep?"

Kavarion opened his mouth but the next quake was accompanied by the sound of a defiant roar that robbed him of words. Suitably disturbed, the entire crew had now joined them on the deck to investigate.

"I am not aware of any spell that will put a Rakenbak to sleep," the mage finally answered. "Any magic I might employ will rip the beast in half." The next impact almost took their balance. "Perhaps that is the best course of action," he reasoned.

Doran huffed. "In other words ye're a useless—"

"Shh," Asher interjected, his hand coming up to halt the dwarf's insult. "It's stopped."

Along with the crew, they waited anxiously in the absence of another impact. Nothing. They couldn't even hear the Rakenbak growling anymore.

"You see," Kavarion said arrogantly. "The walls are reinforced for just this occasion." The mage smoothed down his dry robes. "Though I would suggest you find some way to subdue the monster before we dock—my master doesn't like a scene to be made of his business."

Kavarion swivelled on his heel and began a meaningful stride that would see him returned to below decks. He only made it a few feet before the sound of snapping wood gave him pause. He turned back to the monster hold, where all eyes had quickly been drawn. That single sound then turned into a frenzy of clawing, hammering paws, and splintering wood.

"What's it doing?" the mage spat.

Though he didn't like to picture it, Asher had a pretty good idea about what was happening down there. "You said the walls are reinforced. What about the floor?"

The look on Kavarion's face was all the answer required.

"Slide it back!" Doran shouted, his hands reaching for the edge of the hatch.

Asher kicked the bolts out of place while two others offered their strength and helped the dwarf pull the roof back. It was just as the ranger had envisioned, only the Rakenbak had taken to its destructive task with a haste he couldn't have imagined. The monster had burrowed as if its life was at stake, its claws tearing down through the ship to reveal candlelight illuminating the lowest deck.

Kavarion aimed his wand, perhaps the only person among them who could stop the Rakenbak with immediate effect. His magic banished the night for a brief second, a blinding flash that concealed the magic that erupted from his wand. Whatever the spell, it seared through a handful of the creature's spines and marked its hide with a crater no bigger than a closed fist. That is to say, it did nothing at all to deter the Rakenbak.

Doran looked from monster to mage in disbelief. "Rip it in half, eh?"

Kavarion contorted his jaw and thrust his arm out, unleashing a salvo of magical blasts. Though any one of those blasts was more than enough to kill a man, and an armoured one at that, it did no more than spur the Rakenbak on. Soon, the front half of the beast was buried beneath its devastating work. Finally, the integrity of the monster hold utterly compromised, the Rakenbak's weight fell through the broken beams and created an even larger hole.

Then came the screams.

"It's loose in the ship!" one sailor cried.

Asher imagined the beast charging through The Mer Seed, its hulking size tearing every doorframe to splinters as it roamed from cabin to cabin. The hardier sailors, those who could sleep through all manner of storm, would be slaughtered in their hammocks or pulled apart in the cramped conditions. Those were not the conditions he would choose to meet an angry Rakenbak.

The crew who had witnessed the monster's escape fell into chaos, making a mad dash in every direction. Some drew weapons while others hid wherever they could. They would all die, Asher knew. None of them could fight a Rakenbak and those that tried to conceal themselves were hiding from a keen predator, the apex in its environment.

The ranger squinted into the rain, searching desperately for any sign of land. There was naught but rolling waves and staccatos of lightning.

"We need to kill it," Asher announced, flashing Doran a reluctant expression.

"Brace!" came the warning from the command deck.

Asher dropped down and clung to the edge of the monster hold, but everything was wet, too wet to find purchase. The unforgiving wave slammed into the port side and gave no quarter, tilting the ship down to starboard and flinging the ranger across the deck. The heel of his boot caught Doran in the face and together they slammed into the railing.

They were the lucky ones.

Three others struck the railing and were bowled over, gladly swallowed whole by The Adean and its churning waves. Asher spared a glance at the man controlling the wheel—he wasn't there. The crew who found their feet again seemed to have forgotten about the monster beneath their feet, their attention turned to controlling the ship. It all felt pointless to Asher, who had already come to the conclusion that The Mer Seed was now at the mercy of the ocean.

"This is *yer* fault!" Doran berated, holding on to a stray length of rope for dear life. "I should never 'ave stepped foot on this damned thing!"

Asher ignored the dwarf and narrowed his eyes on the horizon. Every flash of lightning revealed a hidden world beyond the night. A black silhouette stood out in the distance. Dragorn. The island was only a mile away now and, without the helmsman, they were being driven rapidly towards it.

"We're still on course!" the ranger shouted over the pelting rain, choosing to relay the silver lining of their dire situation. "But we need to kill the Rakenbak!"

The ship leaned wildly again and the son of Dorain swore at the black heavens. "Where's me damned axe?" he growled, resorting now to crawling on all fours in a bid to retrieve his piled armour and weapons.

Another wave was hurled by the sea and the ship leaned drastically to one side, sending the dwarf's armour and weapons over the edge and into the inky abyss. Doran let loose a bellowing curse, adding a heavy fist to the wet deck as he did.

Asher waited for that brief moment when The Mer Seed was level before darting to the door beneath the command deck. Fighting a Rakenbak in very close quarters was by no means the wisest choice, but there was every chance those close quarters could be used to his advantage given the beast's cumbersome size.

A new injury, stinging his right shoulder, attempted to demand his attention as he drew the silvyr short-sword from his back. The ranger considered calling on the power of the black gem on his finger, but something else demanded his attention. Something much bigger.

The destruction that accompanied the Rakenbak gave it away only a moment before it burst through the door and surrounding framework. This fleeting moment was all Asher had and he used it to dive aside and evade the rampaging beast.

Doran was waving his hand at Kavarion and barking something unintelligible when he caught sight of the monster limping across the top deck. The mage, however, was too busy barking his own orders at the crew to listen to the dwarf's warnings. It was the Rakenbak's own roar that finally turned Kavarion around—his face stricken with deathly fright. His wand came up but not before the beast's front paw. That meaty limb swiped at his face and hurled him across the ship.

Not one to back down—even from a fight he couldn't possibly

win—Doran set himself low into a crouch, his arms held out wide. "Come on then, beastie," he baited, his fear of the sea forgotten in the shadow of the Rakenbak.

Slipping and skidding over the wet decking, Asher pushed the wild crew aside to reach his companion. "Doran!" he yelled, the dwarf's name washed away in the crashing of another wave.

One of the sailors collided with the ranger in his bid to get away from the monster. On land, it would have been no more than a jarring interaction, an irritation. On a ship, at sea, in the middle of a storm, it was enough to send both men down to the deck. Asher cried out when his own short-sword nicked his left eyebrow, adding a trickle of blood to the rain that ran down his face.

Flat on the deck, he was eye to eye with Kavarion. The mage was dead. His head had been dealt such a blow that it was pointed over his right shoulder, his neck a mangled and contorted mess of torn flesh.

Asher felt nothing for the man's death and quickly absorbed the event like a cold void that took no prisoners.

Amid the rhythmic assault of waves coming over the side, the ranger pushed himself up and glimpsed a nightmare beyond the main mast, a nightmare covered in sharp spines. "Get back!" Asher shouted at the son of Dorain, who had so far succeeded in outmanoeuvring the Rakenbak.

One brave sailor, too young to know that he was entering a fight he couldn't hope to win, charged at the monster and thrust a spear into its spiny hide. It did no more than inform the Rakenbak that more potential prey was at its back. Turning to claw the man, the beast staggered on its wounded hind leg, though it was still powerful enough to tear the spear from the sailor's grip, leaving the weapon lodged in its hide. Simultaneously, the shaft of the spear whipped across Doran's face and the Rakenbak snapped its jaws shut around the young man's head.

Asher was splashed with the blood, but it didn't stop him from skidding across the deck on his knees, the silvyr blade held out. Its fine edge sliced through the monster, adding another wounded leg to its list of growing injuries. Its hind legs barely able to support its weight anymore, the Rakenbak fell upon the sailor locked in its jaws. To a chorus of lightning and lashing rain, the monster unleashed a roar from deep in its chest.

"Now ye've done it," Doran said, a streak of blood tattooed across his face as he came up on the ranger's side. Asher handed the dwarf his silvyr blade and drew his broadsword. "Why do ye get the big one?"

The ranger responded with no more than a sideways glance before angling his sword at the beast and edging away from his companion. The two hunters positioned themselves to attack from opposite sides, though they were constantly hampered by the relentless storm that threatened to take them from their feet. The Rakenbak had no such problem, its claws rooted into the wooden deck while its black eyes shifted from man to dwarf.

Asher lunged first, his attack was no more than a feint to draw the monster towards him. Fortunately, Doran didn't require an invitation to know his part in the strategy. The silvyr blade rolling around in his hand, the dwarf darted in and slashed at the creature's side, where the hide of spines ended and the fur began. Reeling from the wound, the Rakenbak dismissed Asher and turned on the son of Dorain. At least it tried to. The injuries to its hind legs not only slowed it down but forced the beast to rely on its front paws to take the weight.

In came the ranger's broadsword.

The steel chopped into the Rakenbak's right front leg and went no further than breaking the bone therein. The creature growled and fell flat to the deck as Asher slid his blade free. Doran was there again, ready to slay the beast that had once sent him bleeding in retreat. The tip of the silvyr blade plunged into the back of the monster's neck without protest, severing flesh, muscle, and bone in one smooth action.

Asher let his sword arm relax, the end of his blade knocking once against the deck.

Doran marvelled at the silvyr in his hand. "Ye're a lucky man," he commented between laboured breaths.

Asher accepted the words without response. He was

exhausted, his body having worked to fight both the sea and the monster. While the latter was no more of a concern, the Adean's cold embrace continued to reach up and claim The Mer Seed as its own, another relic to add to its collection on the ocean floor.

The bow of the ship ascended towards the black heavens before dipping back to the dancing waves, offering a glimpse of Dragorn. Asher saw the sprawling docks before the storm robbed him of footing and dragged him down to the hard deck. Despite the knock to the back of his head, the ranger managed to hold on to that image of the docks and the feeling of impending doom it burdened him with.

They had seconds.

He tried to warn the dwarf, urging him to find something, anything to hold on to, but no more than a murmur escaped his lips. It was then that calamity struck The Mer Seed, ending its journey across The Adean. Like an arrow from a bow, the intemperate sea expelled the ship at speed, driving it through the outermost docks. Along with the surviving crew, Doran was instantly flung across the deck, though the dwarf's flight was brought to a swift end when he ricocheted off the mast and was sent sprawling across the deck.

Similarly, Asher lost control of his place in the world when he was cast across the wet deck like a skipping stone. He impacted various objects that had escaped their lashings in the chaos, each adding new cuts and gashes to the ranger, until he left the deck altogether, hurled through the jagged doorway and tossed down the steps that led into The Mer Seed's bowels.

An eerie silence fell upon the ship and a pitch darkness, as thick and black as The Adean's lowest depths, took hold of the ranger.

CHAPTER 15

INTO THE SPIRAL

***Skitter** - Sometimes referred to as Ice Spider. These buggers start out life no bigger than your hand and can grow to the size of a small house. If you come across the latter, leave well alone. No contract reward is worth the risk.*
I should also say, if you come across the smaller ones, there will be hundreds of them and their mother, one of the big ones, won't be far away. Leave them all alone too.
Anything in-between is manageable. They appear to go through a phase in their adolescence that sees them isolate themselves, especially the males. When taking them on, use fire. Their icy hides are so sensitive to heat that even light has been known to burn them.

A Chronicle of Monsters: A Ranger's Bestiary, 12th Edition, Page 238.

Elgor Thrice-Bitten, Ranger.

The world came back to Asher in pieces. His senses breathed in the environment, creating a disjointed reality. An unwelcome light pressed down on his eyelids, though it could not be said to be as painful as whatever he was lying on. The floor beneath him was uneven, the boards broken at awkward angles, and wet to the touch. The smell of the sea was strong, but not strong enough to overcome the scent of damp wood and lingering mould. The ranger knew where he was yet couldn't put a name to it, the individual words eluding him as much as any cohesive thought.

Ship. He was on a ship. The Mer Seed. His reasoning mind then attempted to retreat—it cared little for his surroundings right now. He just wanted to go back to sleep, to the blissful folds of oblivion. The distant squawk of a seagull pierced the air, however, irritating his state of fatigue.

His initial movement intensified the pain in his back and he felt a panoply of other wounds bite at his body. It was enough to add some adrenaline to his blood and see his senses rise from the haze. Disturbed by the hot pain in both his back and head, Asher's left hand blindly explored the area in question, just beneath his ribs. Like the tentacles of an octopus, the ranger's fingers wrapped around the hard edges of wood, a fragment from the debris.

The Rakenbak!

The monster suddenly filled his mind, tearing through the haze that hid his thoughts. He recalled fighting the beast on the deck after it had burst forth. It was dead, he remembered with relief, the killing blow delivered by the dwarf.

"Doran," he rasped, his throat horribly dry.

Again, his memory was peeled back to reveal the last image he had concerning the son of Dorain. Had he survived The Mer Seed's impact? This question led the ranger to the quandary of time. How long had he been lying unconscious?

His survival instincts, unwavering as they were, brought a swift end to his meagre worries—*his* life was the priority. Looking at his hand, slick with blood, he decided the shaft of wood protruding from his side was to be the death of him. He also had no idea how long it was, but it was a good bet that at least one of his internal organs had been pierced. Then there was the injury to the back of his head, a wound that had matted his hair with blood.

It wasn't the first time Death had taken the opportunity to coil its cold and reaching hand around him. Perhaps now, after years of defiance, he would finally succumb to its machinations. The Arakesh that dwelled within, a creature woven into every fabric of his being, simply refused such an end. He would live, as he had been commanded to lesson after lesson.

Turning his attention to his right hand, Asher noted the lump beneath his fingerless glove. There, concealed against prying eyes, the black gem lay secured in its iron ring. The mystery of it would normally stab at him, igniting his curiosity like a rising fire, but not today. Today, he just needed it to work.

The ranger strained as he rolled slightly onto his right side, a pained groan on his lips. Again, his left hand gripped the shaft of wood that intended to kill him. He took three deep breaths and gritted his teeth. Pain was an old friend, he told himself. It reminded him he was alive and, if he was alive, he could always get back up.

He pulled it free.

His groan expanded in magnitudes until it became a short cry of agony. Then the blood came, soon to be absorbed by his already bloodied green cloak. Clenching his right fist, the ranger poured his will into the inexplicable gem. *Heal*, he said over and over in his mind. There was a moment of pain before relief eventually came, the muscle and skin knitting back together as if the wound were being cast back through time.

Patting the area down, Asher discovered naught but healthy skin. Death would have to wait.

Rising to his feet, feeling no more than the lack of food and water now, the ranger turned his head left and right, checking his head wound had also healed and left no lingering damage.

He paused at the bottom of the steps, most of which had been shattered beneath the Rakenbak's stomping weight. Looking up through the ragged hole that had been left in the monster's wake, a pale blue sky, streaked with the pinks and golds of a new dawn, greeted him. It made for a better view than the raging sky that had last hung over him.

One boot on the nearest step and the ranger paused again, though it was not what he saw that gave him cause for alarm. He could hear voices. Men. At least four. They were moving about the top deck. Friend or foe was never a consideration. Until extensively proven otherwise, all were foe.

Falling on the skills of his previous career, Asher crept up the broken steps and emerged cautiously onto the deck. The Mer Seed was an unsalvageable wreck. So too was the ship it had ploughed into. The masts of both had snapped like trees struck by lightning and lay strewn across the decks, their many sheets entangled among the debris. Adding to the grim landscape were the bodies of those who had not survived the impact. As with Kavarion, Asher felt nothing for them.

How could he with the *Assassin* rising to the surface in this moment of uncertainty?

Checking one of these bodies, crouched by its side, was a broad man, his ample stomach spilling over the belt looped around his breeches. Without conscious thought, the ranger profiled the stranger. On the mainland he would have been easily identified as a mercenary, a sword for hire. On Dragorn, however, everyone owed allegiance to someone. Unhindered in his investigating The Mer Seed, it was likely the man was on Viktor Varga's payroll. That made him no more than a thug, the closest thing to an animal in Asher's eyes.

Beyond him were two more, both facing the bow of the ship and oblivious to the ranger's presence. This gave him a moment longer to settle into his surroundings and discern the truth of his situation. Hearing more voices from further down the ship, it became clear that there were more thugs on the top deck, concealed behind the mess of broken masts and draping sails.

Edging out from under the overhang, where the ship's wheel sat, the ranger half crouched to spy the men amongst the debris, careful not to disturb the man rummaging through the corpse's pockets. He spotted a handful of others in a tight circle, their attire and weapons identifying them as more thugs.

Moving to get a better look, he saw past the wreckage and was quickly drawn to the obvious leader of the group. From past experience, Asher knew that these types of men always followed the biggest and strongest of their breed, and this particular thug was easily the largest. Then there was the way he carried himself, his confidence tipping into arrogance after years of coming out on top. The leader's dark skin stood out against his blood red leathers, cut off at the shoulders to reveal muscled arms and powerful hands. Long and decorated dreadlocks were draped over his shoulders and down his back.

The ranger's focus held on the leader's right hand, his fingers clenched around the silvyr short-sword. Reclaiming the rare blade would have taken its place at the top of Asher's priority list had he not seen Doran, doubled over on the deck and surrounded by the thugs.

A sardonic grin spread across the leader's dark features. "The son of Dorain," he drawled, holding his arms out, the silvyr catching the morning rays.

"Greetin's, Malak," the dwarf replied wearily, before spitting blood at the man's boots.

"This is quite the entrance," Malak stated, glancing at the portion of ruined docks beyond The Mer Seed. "This is not how my master likes to conduct business."

"I came to straighten things out," Doran explained, finally raising himself up on his knees. "To make a deal."

"A deal?" Malak questioned bemusedly. "The mage sent word of your *deal*." He gestured to the bodies caught in a web of sheets. "He made mention of the monster," he went on, half turning to take in the corpse, its array of spines angled at the sky. "Your deal's as dead as they are."

"That's up to Viktor," Doran pointed out.

Malak made a mocking attempt to find his master among their number. "It looks like you're just dealing with me today, dwarf."

The thug raised Asher's silvyr blade so that the tip rested under Doran's jaw. "Besides," he added with a jovial disposition now, "Mr Varga would only have you executed anyway. Might as well be getting on with it, eh?"

"That's mine," Asher growled, his voice like gravel. His sudden appearance gave the thugs a start, especially the man crouched only a few feet away.

"And who in the hells are you, mate?" Malak enquired, still feeling very in control of the evolving situation.

"That short-sword," the ranger said. "It's mine."

"Short-sword?" Malak questioned, eyeing the blade in his hand. "You must be mistaken, mate; this is no more than a knife. *My* knife to be exact." His declaration of ownership made, he gave the man next to Asher the nod.

Displaying more of the misplaced arrogance their type were known for, the balding sellsword advanced on the ranger without feeling the need for a weapon in hand. Without looking at his approaching foe, Asher cranked his arm just once and slammed a fist into the man's eye. It whipped his head back and sent him in quick retreat, but not before the ranger pressed the attack and delivered not one but three successive elbow-strikes to his temple.

The thug hit the deck with no more sensibility than one of the heavy planks of wood that littered it.

From the port side, the two men Asher had caught sight of earlier rushed him. Were it not for the ring, he would have been dead on his feet, little more than a punching bag for Viktor's criminal employees. As it was, the ranger cracked his neck to one side and faced the fools.

He weaved to the right, narrowly evading the first's wild swing, before chopping the side of his hand into the man's throat. Without halting his flow, Asher shifted his shoulders to one side and let the fist of the second sail past his nose with an inch to spare. In a two-handed grip, he locked the thug in a hold with one hand around his neck and the other tugging on the back of his shirt. Like a bag of grain, the man was thrown into the deck where he received a swift heel to the face.

As the world faded to black for him, his comrade staggered and stumbled into the port railing, his hands clasped around his throat. Quite casually, with his gaze set on Malak, Asher shoved the man overboard and onto what little remained of the dock below.

"Like I said," the ranger repeated, "that's *mine.*"

Malak's brow pinched in a brief moment of consideration as he reassessed the man before him. But still—big and strong as he clearly was—the leader could only see the more diminutive figure that challenged him.

"Well come and take it then," he replied happily, his smile drawing out into a look of hunger.

Asher made to move, content to teach the swine a lesson while taking back his weapon, but that warrior's sixth sense knocked against the inside of the ranger's skull, informing him of unseen danger, something his other senses had detected. He was being flanked, and by someone who could move almost as silently as himself.

Turning on his heel, Asher merely glimpsed the woman who curled a roundhouse kick into his jaw. The blow was more accurate than it was strong, sending the ranger back several steps rather than flooring him. The disorientation, however, was more than enough for the newcomer to stride forward and bring a pair of curved daggers to bear. Asher fell into defensive measures and gave in to his body's instincts. He flowed with those blades, always moving ahead of them and avoiding the steel by a hairsbreadth.

With enviable speed, the woman shot towards him and planted a boot in his chest. Her whole body curled back on itself, dragging her other leg in a perfect arc until she kicked the ranger in the face again. As he landed on his back, she landed on her feet with effortless grace.

Asher was slower to rise than he would have preferred, but his mind was trying to work its way past the pain and place that distinctive fighting style. He had seen it used before, that very move in fact. Using what remained of the mast to pick himself up, he laid eyes on his new attacker. Her blades spun between scarred fingers, drawing his attention to the hilts, bejewelled with rubies.

For most, they would be a display of both power and wealth, but they were so much more in their owner's hands.

Her head was razored smooth, allowing all to see the intricate pattern of thick lines and fine glyphs that had been tattooed into her sun-kissed skin. Her dark eyes, absent the crowning brows, bored into the ranger, as if she too were unravelling him. Her long coat of leather hide clung tightly to her body and fanned out at the waist, reminding Asher of the Graycoats—if they could afford such quality. Small gold rings followed the curve of her ears though they were not her only piercings. Each side of her nose was decorated with golden studs and yet two more golden rings curled around her bottom lip. It was all so uniform and symmetrical that it spoke of the woman's inner workings, a discipline that had been imposed upon her just as Asher's had been imposed upon him.

The answer then emerged from his musings and observations. Standing before him was a Shadow Witch, a Merikarni in the southern tongue of The Arid Lands, from where she had certainly originated. It had been some years since he had encountered one of her ilk, and the Arakesh in him immediately looked down on her, inferior as she was.

"You are the one Kavarion referred to as *Asher*," she stated, her accent confirming her heritage.

"And you are?"

"I am Darya Siad-Agnasi," she told him, a hint of pride in her voice.

Asher dissected her name, recognising the Calmardran dialect. Siad-Agnasi... Daughter-of-none. It was a title reserved for the slaves of The Arid Lands, the perfect recruits as far as the Shadow Witches were concerned.

"Let's just kill them and be done with it," Malak complained.

"If our master did not wish to hear them out," Darya replied, her tone clarifying her place above the brute, "they would never have set sail from Velia."

"We only came to make a deal," Asher said, his hands still raised to fight.

"You have bound yourself to the indebted," the Shadow Witch

admonished, one of her daggers pointing towards Doran. "Until my master's judgment is passed, you belong to him. As do your weapons, your clothes, and the very skin that holds you together."

"You wouldn't like me as a prisoner," Asher warned.

Darya narrowed her dark eyes at the ranger. Then they shifted to Doran. "Cut off the dwarf's ears," she instructed coolly.

The son of Dorain reacted to the order with explosive action, but the swift pummelling he received kept him at his captors' mercy. Malak was only too happy, it seemed, to put the silvyr blade to work.

"No!" Asher blurted, stepping in his companion's direction.

Darya held a hand up, delaying the gruesome act. Her lips pursed as she again scrutinised the ranger. "How very telling," she purred. "You will comply or the dwarf will lose parts that do not grow back."

Asher sighed and locked eyes with Doran, who could only respond with an apologetic shrug. He had no answer but to lower his hands and stand at ease.

Satisfied, the Shadow Witch returned her finely-crafted daggers to the sheaths on the front of her belt. "Search them both," she commanded, her voice lowered to one of authority.

Every ounce of Asher's discipline was required to prevent him from snapping the neck of the man who patted him down. His torn and blood-stained cloak was detached and taken away after the folded bow and quiver were claimed from his back, each handed to another thug and removed from the ship. After that, he was instructed to lift his arms so they could disassemble every piece of his leather armour, eventually leaving him with just a shirt, trousers, and red blindfold looped around his belt. The only things returned to him post inspection were his boots, which he was informed would be needed for their journey into the heart of the city.

"Gloves, jewellery," Darya listed, jutting her heart-shaped chin at the ranger's hands. "The dwarf too. I can see rings and a neck-lace. All belong to Mr Varga."

Asher's heart rate increased, rising into his throat where it attempted to rob him of breath. He had seen more than once what happened to those who handled the black gem. For reasons known only to the ring, it would not permit the touch of any but the ranger. The moment it was in the hand of another, his secret—and perhaps his most powerful weapon—would be revealed. He wouldn't be able to offer answers as to why its victim lay at his feet, foaming at the mouth while their body spasmed.

Slowly, he removed his fingerless gloves and let the natural light kiss the black stone. It drank in the rays and sat on his finger, a dull and uninteresting thing to the likes of someone who walked around with golden piercings and ruby-studded daggers.

"Come along," Darya cajoled, ushering the thug who had parted Doran from his rings and necklace.

Asher dropped his gloves to the deck and twisted the ring off his finger, eyeing the man on his approach. He was holding a small sack purse that now jingled with the dwarf's belongings. Utilising his window of opportunity, Asher stepped forward—a brash action that saw several swords pointed in his direction—and put the ring inside the open purse himself. He was sure to raise his hands and step back, his gaze entwined with Darya's.

"Bind their wrists," the Shadow Witch said evenly, encouraged to do so, perhaps, by the ranger's sudden movements.

Shoved into place behind Doran, Asher was marched off The Mer Seed and down the ramp. Crowds had gathered along the maze of docks and moorings, onlookers who only dared to spectate the activity aboard Viktor Varga's vessel. Peering back over his shoulder, the ranger surveyed the damage their arrival had caused, sinking small boats, scraping some of the larger ships, and, ultimately, ploughing into another ship of equal size. All in all, it was a costly docking.

The sound of horses brought Asher to a halt, a fact that irked Malak behind him. "Did I tell you to stop?"

The ranger ignored him, his attention having shifted further down the dock, where a team of men were directing three horses from The Mer Seed's hold. The horse in the middle was Hector, his reins taut between him and Viktor's thug.

"That's my horse," Asher started towards his mount before Malak pushed him back in line.

"An' that's me pig!" Doran croaked, sighting his Warhog being taken with the horses.

"I told you," the Shadow Witch, said, standing as straight as an arrow, "all that was yours, is now Mr Varga's. Come."

Asher and Doran shared a look that showed some of their silent concern for what lay ahead.

After following the curve of the city's outer wall, a stretch of stone that encircled all of Dragorn, the company arrived at the main gates; two slabs of iron that, together, could have matched The Mer Seed in length. Asher gave the vista behind him one last look, wondering if and when he would ever see outside of Dragorn's high walls again. There were towns in Illian that could have fitted inside the docks alone, but his eyes were naturally drawn to the open ocean and the freedom it represented. Sadly, much of The Adean was obscured by the profusion of scattered warehouses, all of which were busy with the activity of imports and exports—the lifeblood of the island nation.

"Keep moving," Malak ordered, pushing the ranger on and through the gates.

Asher envisioned himself turning on the henchman and breaking his neck. Of course, were he to do that one of Darya's daggers was sure to find its home in his back.

The city quickly swallowed them up, a warren of alleys and narrow streets that cut between buildings stacked upon buildings. For the most part, Dragorn appeared to have been cobbled together, with only the occasional tower or crossroads displaying any sign of considered architecture. Then there were the people. There were too many of them, like ants crawling over each other in their underground kingdoms. They sat on the rooftops, hung out of the windows, and shuffled through the streets. Even the Shadow Witch and her armed escorts could only create so much space for those in tow. And, of course, there were the animals. Stray cats and dogs were everywhere, getting under peoples' feet and stealing food from stalls.

The temptation was to use the population to his advantage. Disappearing in Dragorn was child's play for the likes of a novice thief, and an Arakesh was no novice. Opportunity after opportunity presented itself to the ranger and his instincts urged him to act. But Doran had no hope of following him. The loudmouth would end up before Viktor Varga and, without Asher to help navigate negotiations, he was sure to meet his end.

Another chance to escape presented itself. Of course, he would be doing so without any of his gear or even Hector. But the survivor in him didn't care. None of those things were worth his freedom or his life. Not even the ring.

Finding its way through the cracks of his training, a sound and logical thought occurred to Asher.

Even if they stood their ground and defeated their captors, they would never make it off Dragorn alive. Viktor controlled swathes of the docks and was likely owed by half the city. That would be a lot of eyes and ears to avoid and neither of them had the coin to bribe their way onto a ship. Asher's chances of survival were higher having been trained to blend in and lie his way through suspicious questions, but there was no mistaking Doran, likely the only dwarf on the island. His ultimate death was assured.

The ranger turned to his right and considered his stout companion.

Did he really care whether Doran died or not? It wasn't that long ago the dwarf had betrayed him to the barbarians and, now, the son of Dorain had caused enough of a problem that Asher was likely to die standing beside him. If Doran died, the Stormshields would be safe, the family leverage to no one. Wasn't that his only motivation for accompanying the annoying dwarf? If he slipped away now, he could be on the mainland by dawn and returned to the life he had carved out for himself.

Asher watched the opportunity come and go, his feet keeping him in line with the others. He cursed himself; as if he wasn't already. The ranger could only assume that the cold calculating killer inside him was truly broken, for he could not let Doran Heavybelly die.

On the ship, Asher had entertained the idea that the son of Dorain had perished in the collision and it had cut him in a way he hadn't expected. There was something about this dwarf that bonded them: something kindred that the ranger couldn't yet define. For all their differences, a quiet, but persistent, voice in his mind told him they were the same.

Doran caught him looking his way. "I'm... I'm sorry abou' all this, laddy. I know this wasn' how it were supposed to go."

Asher nodded his appreciation, aware by now that apologies didn't find their way easily to the dwarf's lips. "You know this lot?" he asked, thrusting his chin at the Shadow Witch.

"Aye," Doran answered quietly. "I've had the pleasure once before. Darya. She's Viktor's right hand. I've never seen her in a fight until today an', from what I'd heard, she lived up to her reputation."

Asher regarded the young woman. "She is a Merikarni, a Shadow Witch," he quickly translated.

"Eh? What's one o' 'em?"

"You see those glyphs on her head. They are the tenets of her order, The League of Silk and Ink."

"I'm still not followin'," Doran said, with a shake of his head.

"She's an assassin," Asher explained, his words lost to the hubbub around them. "The League operate out of Ameeraska."

"Did ye say assassin?" The dwarf chortled. "That explains how she were able to put ye on yer arse."

The ranger moved past the remark. "It doesn't explain why she's in the employ of a crime guild. The League usually keep their dogs on a tighter leash."

Doran gave something of a shrug, his features screwed into a knot. "Might have somethin' to do with all the time Viktor spent down there. Years apparently. All the while he were mixin' with the worst o' the worst, before he took over from his father. Maybe he struck a deal with 'em. I don' know."

The ranger absorbed the information, his mind building a profile of Viktor Varga with every step. "And him?" he queried, his eyes shifting to his shoulder.

Doran glanced at Malak with derision. "He's a general, o' *sorts*. He runs the men, the thugs an' scoundrels that Viktor likes to employ. Watch 'im, Asher, because he'll be watchin' *ye*," the dwarf guaranteed.

Asher understood, and he would be watching *everything* until they were back on Illian soil. "They're taking us to the arena," he observed.

"Viktor does most o' his work out o' there. He's got his own little paradise though, *outside* o' the city."

"Outside?"

"On one o' the northern islands in The Lifeless Isles," Doran detailed. "I've heard it's a fortress."

Asher added the information to his profile and continued to walk within the tight confines of their escort. They were heading deeper into Dragorn, where the streets seemed to spiral into a central heart.

It was there that the ranger laid eyes on Blood and Coin.

CHAPTER 16

HERE BE MONSTERS

Cruul - A Cruul, pronounced 'Cruel', is well suited to its name. These monsters—a distant cousin of the Hell Hag—dwell in deep lakes, the darkest depths their home.

The majority of their bodies are made up of tentacles, and long ones at that. They reach up, towards the surface, and wrap a single tentacle around their victim's leg. Once their human prey is ensnared, they will drag them down and then let go, allowing the person to swim back to the surface. This is by design. The Cruul wants its victim to shout for help, thereby bringing more into the water.

With up to a dozen tentacles, the beast can easily drag down numerous people. There is no escaping it then. There are no records in the older archives that detail any ranger ever killing a Cruul. Most are slain when the problem is escalated to the local lords or even kings and queens, who have access to court mages.

A Chronicle of Monsters: A Ranger's Bestiary, 12th Edition, Page 333.

Suesh Nas-Arteese, Ranger.

. . .

There was a brief pause at the end of the journey while the horses and Warhog were handed to others awaiting their arrival. Using what time he had, Asher craned his neck to take in the arena.

Oval in shape, its dimensions made it the largest building in the area. There were no windows or arches to allow light inside—or prying eyes for that matter. Even if it had possessed windows, the voluminous canopies that spread out from its roof and connected to the surrounding buildings would have kept out the light.

This was a dark place for dark things. Perhaps, Asher mused, he would fit right in.

"Gentlemen," Darya addressed. "If you would follow me."

Led by the Shadow Witch and guarded from the rear by Malak and his men, Asher and Doran were taken into the belly of the beast. Without any windows, torches were required to light the way beyond the arena's gate and interior double doors. It lent the arena a forbidding and gloomy atmosphere that reminded the ranger of a dungeon, of which he had seen his fair share.

It wasn't long before the raucous sound of Dragorn died away. In its place there came a new sound, quiet at first. But, with every step, the chorus grew louder and more terrible.

Asher recognised some of those noises, though he had never heard them all together before. One of Darya's escorts quick-stepped ahead and opened the next door for her and, with it, the disturbing sounds became almost deafening.

Monsters.

Lots of monsters.

Asher looked down the corridor from where their roars, shrieks, and howls originated. He couldn't help but feel glad that they were heading in the opposite direction. Meeting Doran's eyes, it appeared he shared the sentiment.

The last door to be opened brought back the blinding light of a blue sky. The ranger raised a hand to shield his eyes, noting that they were now in the heart of the arena, its oval shape laid bare by an open-top roof. They were led down the steps and instructed to wait by the edge, though neither man nor dwarf required such instruction.

There was a Lumber Dug in the centre of the sandy arena.

Asher had never seen one in the flesh—or stone rather. He had read about them in A Chronicle of Monsters and, truthfully, found them hard to imagine. There was no denying his eyes, however.

At ten feet tall, the Lumber Dug lurched on two legs of jagged stone, the natural armour that almost covered its entire body. It was hard to say how many digits the monster's hands possessed for, when they were knotted into fists, they looked no different to boulders.

Despite numerous chains and the thick collar being used to restrain the creature, the Lumber Dug still noted their arrival and turned its head to spy them with its single eye. It was a small movement for the cumbersome beast, but the sound of grating rocks filled the arena. The beast tilted its head one way then the next to see the hunters past its horn, a curved protrusion of stone that extended from the middle of its hideous face.

The Lumber Dug took offence at the newcomers and set every plate of its armour into a state of vibration, its equivalent of a roar. The edges of the individual plates of stone collided with each other, creating the sound of a rockslide. Having only read about it, the ranger hadn't fully grasped the way it would make him feel. Standing in its presence now, though, some primal part of his mind told him to get as far away from that sound as possible.

A low-level buzz cut through the arena as a luminous whip unfurled, seemingly from nowhere, and coiled around the Lumber Dug's neck, just above its collar. Asher followed the glowing whip back to its source—a wand tip. Another of Viktor's mages twisted her wrist and the whip tightened around the creature's throat, dragging it down to all fours and bringing an end to its defiant vibrations.

The subsequent silence was soon replaced by the laughter of one individual, who added applause to his amusement. For all of

Asher's fatigue, the ranger dug into his reserves and focused. The next few minutes would dictate how many people had to die for his survival.

The laughing man walked into view from the other side of the Lumber Dug. He wasn't alone, Asher's eyes quickly drawn to the hooded figure that followed in his wake. By the figure's frame he guessed it to be a woman, though he cared little for the stranger's sex. The ranger was more interested in the wand she held. *Another* mage. It seemed Viktor really did collect them.

"Excellent," the laughing man praised, and with a beaming smile that flashed all of his teeth. "Is this not an outstanding speci-men?" he mused, his accent a mix of more than one culture.

The ranger didn't respond, his mind too busy analysing the man who could only be Viktor Varga. By appearance alone he esti-mated his age to be somewhere in his early fifties, though his frame suggested he kept his body in the shape of a younger man. A strong square jaw, freshly shaved, laid the foundation of his harsh features and sunken grey eyes. His hair, cleaned and cut in keeping with his wealth, was a sandy blond with signs of grey creeping in at the edges.

His style of dress aligned with what Doran had told him about Viktor's time in the south, in the baking realm of The Arid Lands. His robe, tightly fastened around his waist stopped an inch above the floor, but the quality of the deep blue fabric—much like his silky hair—accentuated his success in life. There was no obvious weapon to be seen on his person, though that didn't mean he was unarmed. He certainly wasn't without protection, given the mage at his side.

"Do you not like my latest addition?" Viktor continued, looking hurt. "Or is it that you do not know the creature you look upon, son of Dorain?" Varga gave the dwarf a patronising tilt of the head. "You might be the *worst* monster hunter I have ever employed."

"It's a Lumber Dug," Asher stated flatly, unamused by the whole situation.

Viktor's eyes snapped to the ranger and he corrected his stance to that of a nobleman. "Oh, forgive my rudeness," he began apologetically. "We have not met. I... am Viktor Varga," he said with a broadening smile. "And you, I believe, go by the name *Asher*. A ranger no less!" he added with a hint of giddiness. "And a good one at that. Besides helping our mutual acquaintance here with a certain Rakenbak, you know a Lumber Dug when you see one. Impressive."

With one finger, Viktor beckoned them onto the arena floor. Malak stepped down behind them, his proximity an encouragement to move forward or suffer a painful price. Asher and Doran shared a look before putting a foot on the hard sand, each aware that they were potentially walking to their own execution.

The stony beast didn't take well to their approach, but its attempt at vibrating again was interrupted when the mage tightened the magical leash.

"Tell me, Asher," Viktor enquired. "Do you know why they are called Lumber Dugs?"

Asher took a breath, finding Varga's conduct rather tedious. "Because of its walk," he explained. "It *lumbers* from side to side to see past its horn."

Viktor's smile returned with ease as he pointed a finger at the ranger. "Tremendous!" he commended. "Doesn't it feel good to have knowledge? There is no better currency. I, myself, am a man who likes to know things. I pride myself on it. When someone asks me a question I like to know the answer. Better yet, I like to hold that answer at a price." The crime lord looked Asher up and down. "To that end I find you quite frustrating. Since hearing of your involvement in my affairs I have reached out to several contacts, none of whom can tell me anything about you. You walk alone in the world and with no name or title to trace any history." He gave a short laugh. "I know nothing about you.

"Well," he added with a subtle shrug, "I do know a few things, I suppose." Viktor pointed at the faded tattoo under Asher's left eye. "Seeing you in the flesh, I now know you have spent time in The Wild Moores. How exciting! What is that? A black fang?" Varga rubbed his angular jaw in thought. "A hunter tribe!" he exclaimed, startling the Lumber Dug. "Yes, that's it. The black fang, a mark of the hunter amongst the Outlanders I believe." The crime lord scrutinised him again. "You are no Outlander though. How could you be?" he questioned, gesturing at Asher's clothing, as if that was enough to differentiate him from the wild Outlanders.

"But that only adds to the intrigue," he went on, enjoying the sound of his own voice. "Who could you be that the savage Outlanders not only let you live, but marked you as one of them?"

Viktor walked between him and the Lumber Dug with no care for the danger that placed him in, so confident was he. No, not confidence. *Knowledge.* Varga knew he was safe but not because of the glowing leash. It had only been a flicker but Asher had seen it, rippling in the light and dancing over his form in a multitude of colours. The crime lord was being shielded.

The ranger let his eyes drift to the mage whose face remained in shadow beneath her hood. Asher didn't know much about magic, but he knew casting a constant shielding spell—an invisible one at that—was extremely taxing. The hooded mage was either well-skilled in her craft or, as was more likely, Viktor had his pet mages rotate to ensure he was shielded at all times.

"Then there's what you did to my men," Viktor said, bringing Asher's mind back to the arena. He watched as Varga gave Malak a nod, who, in turn, called out a familiar name.

From one end of the arena, Corrigan and his four compatriots shuffled through the open gate and sheepishly made their way across the sand. They lined up, displaying their variety of wounds, all of which were bandaged or held in slings. Not one of them had escaped the fight without a limiting injury and a degree of humiliation.

Doran looked up at Asher with amusement. "Get a look at this lot," he whispered. The ranger mirrored the dwarf's wry smile.

"Hold your tongue, Heavybelly," Viktor commanded, his tone momentarily altering his demeanour. "I'll get to you."

Asher heard every knuckle crack in Doran's left hand. "It was self-defence," the ranger declared, looking over the damage he had wrought upon the men.

"I'm sure it was," Varga agreed, having returned to his light approach. "It's not *why* you broke my men so much as *how* you broke them. I have seen all manner of fighter from Namdhor to Karath and, I can tell you, it is rare to find a warrior capable of not only facing multiple opponents but walking away without personal injury. The wounds you inflicted were sufficient to end any further threat without causing death—quite the skill."

"You would rather I'd killed them?" Asher posed.

By now, Viktor had walked around the hunters, putting *them* between him and the Lumber Dug. "You might as well have," he answered casually. "Not only did you end their threat to you but their ability to threaten *anyone*. It will be months before any of them are fully recovered, perhaps longer. That's a lot of coin spent on useless assets."

Viktor's next nod of the head was directed at the mage, a woman of Darya's age who, thus far, had focused all of her attention on the glowing leash she had conjured around the Lumber Dug's neck. The signal understood, the mage ceased her spell and the whip retracted into nothingness an inch from the tip of her wand. She then flourished her slender weapon and sent a wave of condensed air and sand into the back of Corrigan and his men. All five of them lost their footing and cried out as they were flung several feet across the arena.

There were more yells of pain when their already broken limbs impacted the floor and failed to support them. Broken bones, however, were now the least of their worries. All five men had been hurled into the Lumber Dug's personal space, where even its anchored chains would offer no protection.

Asher braced himself a second before the carnage began.

A single vibration rippled through the Lumber Dug's body and it exhaled sharply from its nostrils. That was all the warning Corrigan and his men got. Then the monster reared up on its back legs and raised its heavy fists. In what short time they had left, the injured men tried to scramble back, but it was all for naught.

When those fists came back down they dented the hard floor having gone right through the thugs. Again and again, the Lumber Dug hammered the arena beneath it, giving in to the rage of a caged beast. Of the spectators, only Asher and the Shadow Witch didn't flinch when the blood splattered over their clothes and faces. Further telling of his enchanted shielding, not a drop touched Viktor's immaculate robes.

Their bodies pummelled into pieces in a matter of seconds, Corrigan and his allies found the violent end their careers had destined them for.

Viktor held his hands up, marvelling at the creature's destructive capabilities. "Isn't it wonderful?" He stepped forward again, leaving the monster to its fresh meal. "I had hoped to pit it against the Rakenbak. That will be most difficult now that it slumbers at the bottom of The Adean."

Asher could only imagine the effort and man power required to shift the Rakenbak's body over the side of The Mer Seed and into the ocean. Before he could entertain ideas about harnesses and loading cranes, his attention sharpened on Varga, his hands now clasped behind his back as he planted himself in front of Doran.

"I suppose that brings us to you, son of Dorain."

"Viktor—" Doran began.

"I gave you a second chance," Viktor cut in. "The Hobgobber was disappointing but I saw potential in you. I wonder now, of course, if I was more curious about the power of dwarves. My curiosity is often my greatest weakness, after all. At any rate, you have been found wanting, a poor reflection on your kin. The Rakenbak proved too hard a prey for you alone and, even with aid, you have failed to bring it to me. I even lost a mage, a ship, and most of my cargo in the process."

"It's a little more complicated than that," Doran attempted, by way of an explanation. "An' ye can' blame me for the loss o' yer ship."

"Take heart, Master Heavybelly," Viktor interjected, with a cold smile and a raised hand. "Your life is about to simplify."

Asher tensed, sensing a killing blow coming his companion's way. He glanced at Darya and then Malak, though neither moved a muscle to suggest they were about to act on a silent order to kill the dwarf. Beyond them, the mage regarded only the Lumber Dug, prepared to take action should it break away from its meal.

"You came to make a deal, yes? What was it Kavarion wrote? The Rakenbak, return of the deposit I gave you and, oh yes, another monster of my choosing. Somewhere in there I believe there was mention of an apology." Viktor looked around. "No Rakenbak, no coin, no reason to believe you could deliver a monster of my choosing, and..." The crime lord looked down at Doran's legs. "Shouldn't you be on your knees if you're apologising?"

The dwarf's exterior hardened like that of the Lumber Dug's natural armour. "There's only *one* I bow to," he told Varga, "an' ye're not 'im."

Stood beside him, Asher slowly closed his eyes and held on to his sigh.

There was a look in Viktor's eyes that the ranger knew all too well. He wasn't a man to be told no or defied in any way. To do so was a personal slight that challenged his authority, the very thing that defined him. Typically, in these circumstances, he had seen men such as Varga erupt and exact their wrath upon the defiant. But the psychotic expression that held Viktor's face was wiped away by the smile of a man in perfect control.

"As stubborn as the mountains that birthed you," he observed. "Perhaps you need breaking first." Viktor stepped aside and gestured at the ragged body parts. "Incompetent as he was, Corrigan brought back some interesting news of his time on the mainland. The *Stormshields* I believe they are called..."

Asher felt his reality lurch as he instantly connected the violent fate of Corrigan and his men to the family of dwarves. What horrors Viktor could unleash upon them, upon that little girl. Their guaranteed safety was the only reason they had made the treacherous journey and here they were being threatened over something as ridiculous as an apology.

"Doran," Asher insisted as calmly as he could, reminding him of the plan.

"Listen to your friend, Doran," Varga advised. "Your apology

might be the difference between life and death for that poor family," he added.

The dwarf glanced at the ranger, his hands fidgeting by his
side. Asher assumed he was deciding whether to bend the knee
and apologise or take his chances and assault the crime lord. The
latter, however, wouldn't end well for the dwarf when he was
repelled by the mage's shield. Since Doran had most likely missed
Viktor's defensive measure, the ranger began to formulate the
order in which he would kill those around them.

The mage should have been harmless as far as Asher was
concerned, her magic nullified by the black gem on his finger, but
absent the ring he was susceptible to her spells. That made the
mages priority one. The distance, however, between him and the
spell-casters was cause for alarm for either had only to turn their
wand on him and end his threat. He would go for Malak first then.
A swift blow to his throat would render him next to useless, a
malleable shield that would take the first spell on the ranger's
behalf. From his corpse he would take back his silvyr short-sword
and throw it at Darya, all the while positioning himself to keep
Viktor between him and the mage...

Asher's stratagem came to nothing when Doran dropped to his
knees and bowed his head.

"I apologise for failin' ye," the son of Dorain offered, fear in his
voice. "If ye would allow it, Asher an' I would hunt down any
monster o' ye likin'. Then, if it would please ye, our business would
be done."

Viktor looked down on Doran with satisfaction. "That feels
good," he replied, bringing his shoulders up and sighing with
relief. "Like a weight lifted from my shoulders. Apology accepted,
Master Heavybelly." The crime lord took a breath. "Apology or not,
there is still the matter of your *debt*. Much like the monster you
promised me, the deposit I gave you is beyond the reach of us both.
And, if I'm being honest, I don't have faith in you to procure any
monster."

"If ye give me a chance I can—"

Viktor tutted and wagged his finger in Doran's face. "Some

would argue that I was already being soft when I gave you a *second* chance. How would I look giving you a third? No," he said shaking his head. "Any position of power, be it a king or the head of a humble guild, is a precarious one. You must always balance *reward* and *fear*," he explained, raising a hand to represent each. "For those who earn it, I line their pockets with more coin than they know what to do with. For those who raise arms to defend my house, I offer protection from the other guilds. But then there are those who fail me, the ones who make me *bleed*. One drop of blood, just *one*... and the sharks will come."

On his knees, Doran looked up at the crime lord with obvious regret. "Viktor, ye don' 'ave to—"

"SILENCE!" Varga's voice erupted from nowhere, his face frozen in a manic rictus. A moment passed before the crime lord composed himself and straightened his robes, a tight smile cutting his expression in half. "Examples, Master Heavybelly. Examples must be made lest my house be exposed to those who would *take* it." Viktor looked over Doran to lay eyes on his Shadow Witch. "Have the Stormshields butchered and spread the word."

"NO!" Doran bellowed. As one of his feet came up, there to launch him into the crime lord, Darya brought one of her daggers down over the dwarf's shoulder and a portion of his throat.

Viktor clasped a wrist behind his back and looked down on the son of Dorain. "And have their heads brought back, would you. I would have Doran see them one last time before he joins them."

"No," the ranger stated calmly, if immediately.

His moment of glee interrupted, Viktor turned a scornful expression upon the ranger. "Excuse me?"

"The Stormshields are off the table," Asher exacted, haunted now by images of their gruesome murder.

Viktor giggled, his shoulders bobbing. "I didn't realise we were negotiating."

"We came here to make a deal," the ranger said, his eyes tracing the jagged lines of the Lumber Dug's rough exterior.

"So you did," Varga replied, somewhat bemused. "Though I fail to see what a lowly ranger might offer to save the lives of four *doomed* dwarves. And yourself, of course," he added, as if Asher's life was of no consequence. "Your naivety in befriending him was *your* mistake. Killing any and all connected to the son of Dorain will add to the example."

"Forget about the Stormshields and release Doran from his debt," the ranger began, his gaze fixed on Viktor now.

The crime lord frowned, his eyes narrowing on the ranger. "Perhaps you didn't hear my little speech about examples—it was quite poignant, I thought," Viktor added, clearly enjoying himself.

"Leave the Stormshields be," Asher repeated slowly, "and put Doran on a ship back to Illian. Give me your word... and I will fight for you."

Viktor folded his arms and rubbed his smooth chin, perplexed it seemed. "Well now you're making me curious," he said, his smile creeping back. "Tell me, why would I forego this show of strength for one more fighter on my roster? And do consider your answer, Asher," he went on in a theatrical manner, his arm outstretched, "because I'm picturing all five of your heads adorning the main gate. It's going to look spectacular!"

The laugh that followed sank into Asher's skin like barbs, bringing with it the petrified expression on Deadora's face, there until she rotted.

"You don't have any fighters like me," Asher told him, pressing his nails into the palms of his hands.

"Is that so?" Viktor replied incredulously.

Asher didn't answer him immediately, his years of training and subsequent instincts digging their claws in. He was not to utter it. Never. To no one. Only death would follow, for him *and* those around him. But it was his last card to play and the Stormshields deserved everything he had to give.

It was almost painful to say the words, but say them he did. "I am an Arakesh."

His revelation filled the arena and left complete silence in its wake. That was until Malak sniggered and loosely pointed the ranger's own short-sword at him. "He's lying," the thug condemned. "You're talking about bedtime stories, mate."

Still, Malak did not move against Asher; waiting on the word of his master, who now regarded the ranger with a new level of scrutiny, his suspicions easy to see. "Prove it," he said quietly, a glance spared for Darya.

Asher knew of several ways to display the abilities unique to the students of Nightfall, but he knew of a quicker way to cut through Viktor Varga's personal disbelief. "Serena Trigorn," he announced.

The name struck the crime lord a second before the others. He was notably more rigid, his air of superiority clearly deflated.

In the absence of a response from Viktor, Asher continued down the rabbit hole. "It was just over a decade—"

Varga's hand shot up, silencing the ranger. "Not... another... word." His grey and calculating eyes washed over everyone, his inspection forcing another moment of silence upon them, save for the sound of the Lumber Dug chomping through Corrigan's left leg. "You must be tired from your journey," he eventually said, his mood changing like the wind. "Take them both to the cells," he ordered without looking at anyone in particular. "Feed them both."

Malak bit his lip, his brow furrowing to knot his eyebrows together. "We're not killing them?"

"NOW!" Viktor screamed, wiping Malak's face of all expression. "No one is to speak to them," he added, already walking away.

It should have been a moment of relief for Asher: after all—and if nothing else—Doran was still breathing. But, instead, the ranger was left feeling hollow, emptied of a secret so precious it could have been entwined with his soul.

CHAPTER 17

HELL IS AN ISLAND

Narkul - Known as the Mushroom Folk to some, these monsters do not actively hunt out human prey, though they are more than capable of killing humans.

When left to themselves, Narkuls will simply get on with their lives but, should their territory be disturbed, they will not only protect it but consume those who have wandered into their path.

Their true form is unknown due to the sheer number of mushrooms that protrude from every inch of their bodies. We do know they are capable of standing on two feet and possess two stubby arms.

Their main form of attack is to rear up and burst a number of mushrooms on their chest. The spores and flesh that explode from these mushrooms will melt you to the bone. If harvested correctly, this substance can be used as a weapon against other monsters.

Killing Narkuls is relatively easy, though it does feel cruel to kill an animal for no more than defending its territory. Still, a contract's a contract.

A Chronicle of Monsters: A Ranger's Bestiary, 12th Edition, Page 118.

Wovun Bhear, Ranger.

Doran's blood boiled at the sight of Malak's toothy grin, a predator's smile upon cornering its prey. Viktor's chief thug slammed the wall of bars into place, securing the dwarf in one of the cells beneath the arena.

His grin broadening all the more, Malak offered his own version of a farewell. "Gut you later, Heavybelly."

Oh, how Doran wanted him to try. Even with his body crying out for rest, the son of Dorain would have welcomed the fight and the opportunity to wield his fists like hammers, Malak strewn on his anvil.

Hard as it was, the dwarf watched him leave without riposte, his ire saved for someone else. That someone had been shoved into the opposite cell and the sliding gate sealed behind him. Asher watched every move his jailers made, as if the ranger was making notes about them individually.

The moment they were left alone in the gloom, Doran started forward and gripped the bars, his face pushed between them. "What in all the hells were that abou'?" he fumed, his guilt pouring into a melting pot of emotions he hadn't been raised to truly process.

"That was about saving your life," Asher replied calmly, his attention having already shifted to the iron cage that imprisoned him. "You're welcome," he added dryly.

Doran stumbled over his response, his thoughts and emotions tumbling on top of each other. "Don' *welcome* me, laddy!" he barked. "I didn' ask no one to save me! Never 'ave! Never will! An' who are ye to do such a thing?" he questioned, his tirade growing with every breath. "I've met more o' yer kind than I can rightly stomach an' ye're all the same. Then *ye* come along... Ye do an' say things that make no bloody sense. A man with yer skills should be as bad as the rest o' 'em, worse perhaps. Ye shouldn' be helpin' the Stormshields for nothin'. Ye definitely shouldn' o' accompanied me!" The dwarf was pacing now, his paranoia, curiosity, and guilt colliding into each other as they fell out of his mouth. "Do ye want me in yer debt? Is that it? Ye've seen what little I 'ave to offer."

Asher briefly paused the inspection of the lock on his gate. "Are you done?" he asked, bored by his tone.

Something close to a laugh escaped with Doran's disbelief. "I've not even started, I can tell ye!"

The son of Dorain sighed. He considered offering up a prayer to Grarfath and Yamnomora, but if there was any chance the Mother and Father were looking beyond The Whispering Mountains, he didn't want to draw them to his shame.

Movement in Asher's cell drew him back to the ranger. "Now what are ye doin'?" he demanded.

Lying flat on his cot, Asher rolled away from the dwarf. "Getting some sleep," he replied. "You should think about doing the same."

"Are ye havin' a laugh?" Doran questioned, helpless to do anything but watch the man fall asleep. "Bah!" He pushed himself away from the bars and put all of his fury into the singular task of pacing his cell.

At some point, the dwarf had allowed himself to sit down. Inevitably, his eyes had closed and his thoughts drifted until sleep finally ensnared him. His sleep was like that of a stone, his mind closed off to the world as much as it was to his dreams.

When next he woke, after untold time, it was to the sound of gargling gibberish.

"Eh?" he grumbled, rising from the depths of his rest. He started awake at the sight that greeted him. "What in the hells…"

One of Viktor's thugs, employed as a jailer, was pinned to Asher's cell, his face squeezed between the bars. Though the ranger was hidden beyond the squirming thug, his hands could be seen clasping the front and back of his victim's neck. The jailer thrashed and lashed out however he could, desperate to prise Asher's fingers from his windpipe.

"These are Novian cells," Asher said in a strained voice, his head tilting to see Doran.

"What?" the dwarf questioned, stunned by the quiet violence taking place in front of him.

"They're fitted with Hyperia locks," the ranger continued, "and the hinge bolts are Karathan-forged by the look of them."

To Doran's ears, Asher had told him they were imprisoned behind nonsense cells that were fitted with nonsense locks and the hinge bolts were made in the capital of The Arid Lands.

"They're good then," the dwarf reasoned, somewhat bemused now as he returned to his feet.

"*Very* good," Asher confirmed through clenched teeth. "They're used in the south to... house slaves."

Doran came to rest his elbows against the bars of his cell, noting the thug to be on his tiptoes. "Ye know a fair bit abou' dungeons," he concluded, hardly interested in the topic.

"Enough to know I can't open them from the inside." With his final word, the jailer went limp in the ranger's grip, his vigorous protests at an end.

Keeping the jailer elevated by the throat, Asher tugged sharply on the keys attached to the man's belt. His prize in hand, he let the body fall to the floor and turned his attention to the lock. After cycling through four of the keys on the ring, he successfully opened the sliding door and stepped into freedom.

"What are ye doin'?" Doran demanded.

"He's going to kill you," Asher stated.

Doran was momentarily dazed by the prediction. "What's that?"

Asher stepped over the body with the required key pinched between finger and thumb. "He'll keep the Stormshields under threat to keep me fighting, but I can't guarantee Viktor won't slit your throat if he thinks he already has enough leverage."

A deep line cut through Doran's brow as he watched Asher insert the key into the lock of his cell. "Why would he even spare 'em jus' for ye? Gods be damned, Asher! What in the hells is goin' on 'ere?"

Asher slid the bars out of place. "Soon, Viktor is going to want proof I am what I say I am. When he gets it, he *will* give me his word to leave the Stormshields alone. I need you back in Darkwell to make sure he doesn't renege on the deal."

"I'm not goin' anywhere, laddy," Doran assured. "I've not come this far to run away. I'm seein' this through." The dwarf grabbed the bars and slid them shut.

"Don't be a fool," Asher warned, sliding the bars open again.

"No one," Doran replied as a matter of fact, "is *dyin'* for me." The dwarf emphasised his final word by closing the gate.

"You need to protect them," the ranger insisted.

"I need to make things right with Varga," Doran countered. "There'll be somethin' I can offer him—there's always a deal to be made."

The ranger looked to be considering the gate but he refrained from sliding it open. Instead, he let his head sink towards his chest and sigh in defeat. "You're a stubborn son of a... *Dorain.*"

The dwarf chortled. "That I am, laddy. Besides," he continued, throwing his hands up, "we both know there's no gettin' off this wretched island without Viktor's notice. If he doesn' own it, someone who owes 'im owns it; that's how this city works."

Without locking Doran's cell, Asher turned away, stepped over the jailer, and shut himself behind his own bars once more. Appearing weary, despite his recent sleep, the ranger dropped onto his cot and rested his elbows on his knees.

"I should also say," Doran went on, "this whole thing was *yer* idea. So..." The son of Dorain put his back to the wall and slid down to the floor.

"I should say," Asher mimicked, "this whole thing is *your* fault. You could have gone anywhere," the ranger pointed out, "but you had to go to the Stormshields."

"A'right, a'right," Doran groaned. "I'd like to see where *ye'd* go in a land where ye're one o' four humans."

Asher was shaking his head. "It doesn't matter," he uttered.

"When I make the deal with Viktor, just keep your mouth shut and use your freedom to ensure their safety."

The dwarf tucked his chin up towards his mouth and eyed the ranger from his cell. "Ye seem mighty sure o' this deal." When Asher said nothing, his gaze cast to the floor, Doran's frustration bubbled over. "How can ye be so damned sure?" he growled. "Who are ye? Really? What was all that abou'?" he demanded, gesturing up to the concealed arena. "What's an *Arakus*? Who was that woman ye mentioned?" He reached out and gripped one of the bars. "For the love o' Grarfath, ye stopped Viktor in his tracks. We should both be dead an' the Stormshields with us!"

"It's *Arakesh*," the ranger corrected, drawing the sound out.

The pronunciation felt trivial to Doran, who could only echo the name with a tense shrug. "Why would that stump Viktor Varga?"

"Because he's a man who enjoys collecting the rarer things in life," Asher explained, though, in truth, it did nothing to help the dwarf understand anything.

"Speak plainly, lad, or gods help me, I'll come over there—"

Asher cut the dwarf off and raised his voice to be heard over the unravelling threat. "I'm an *assassin*, Doran."

Dumbstruck, the dwarf stared at the ranger. He must have misheard him.

"An assassin?" he echoed incredulously. "Like the witch lady?"

Asher shook his head. "The League of Silk and Ink are a smaller operation. They recruit women only. They're proficient killers all, but their training cannot be compared to that of an Arakesh."

"Still," Doran reasoned, "ye're a killer for hire?"

"It's more complicated than that," Asher mumbled.

The son of Dorain made a face. "Ain' that complicated, lad. Men like Varga want someone dead an' they pay ye to do it for 'em. Simple."

The ranger was pinching the bridge of his nose. "I didn't... Arakesh aren't paid per kill. It doesn't work like that."

There was that absurd word again—just the sound of it made Doran's nose crinkle. "Why do ye keep callin' yerself that?"

Asher held on to his answer for a few seconds. "Arakesh is elvish for assassin. Most people don't know that though. To the common man, the name is merely tied to an ancient order of killers."

The dwarf ran a hand through his tangled beard. "Ye're not jokin'?" he questioned, his disbelief demanding it.

"I'm not known for joking," the ranger replied.

The dwarf didn't argue with that. "Who was the lass?" he asked. "The one ye mentioned to Viktor."

Asher slid off his cot and joined Doran on the floor, his position mirroring the dwarf's. "Serena Trigorn," he announced, his voice laden with guilt.

"Trigorn?" Doran checked. "She belonged to one o' the big four then?"

"She was just born into the wrong family," Asher replied miserably. "Why Viktor wanted her dead I don't know. I didn't ask questions back then."

Doran turned to lay eyes on his companion. "*Viktor* wanted her dead?"

The ranger's nodding response was subtle. "I murdered her for him. That's why her name meant something. It's also why the name Arakesh meant something to him."

Doran took a breath, doing his best to absorb it all. "I'm to take it ye walked away from this path?"

"I did. Four years ago."

By a dwarf's counting that might as well have been four weeks ago. "So," he began, attempting to wrap his head around the revelation, "only *four* years ago ye were killin' folk for coin?"

Asher had never looked so uncomfortable in front of Doran. "Not exactly," he said hesitantly. "Nightfall doesn't pay... I told you it's complicated."

Doran scrutinised the ranger, usually so confident and sure of the words he had carefully chosen to utter unto the world. "This has got ye all tied up in knots ain' it? An' what's Nightfall? Ye know, the more ye go on the more made-up it all sounds."

"Nightfall is part of the legend to most," Asher answered darkly. "It's where Arakesh are trained. To me it was... home."

Doran chewed over it all, the gears in his mind clunking round and round. "But ye don' get paid?" he reiterated incredulously.

The ranger remained silent for a couple of heartbeats, his thoughts his own. "Not directly. Coin is just a means to an end. Payment is taken by Nightfall as a whole for... upkeep and the like."

That made no sense to the dwarf, a being brought up in a culture that thrived so much on transaction and trade that it was almost entwined with their religion. "Then why in Grarfath's name were ye killin' folk?"

Asher opened his mouth to answer before his lack of words caused it to close again. Doran didn't miss, however, the glassy appearance in the ranger's eyes, caught in the torchlight.

"For Nightfall," he eventually offered in despair of himself. "For the Father. For honour. Hells, for the god of shadows." Shaking his head, Asher rose from the cold and dusty floor to drop onto the cot chained to the wall. "I actually don't know why. Conditioning I suppose. Your training begins in childhood. It's all I've ever known."

Doran could see the toll such talk was taking on the man. "The Father?" he still probed with all the acuity of a hammer.

Asher's glassy eyes found him across the way. "The leader of Nightfall," came his clipped response.

"So this Arakesh is all some big secret, eh? I mean, I've been 'ere for decades an' never heard o' one."

"They're only a legend to those who can't afford an Arakesh's blade," Asher told him.

"Hmm. All the Viktors o' the world then," Doran concluded, aware that this breed of man was all too common in Illian.

"Unfortunately."

"A'right," the dwarf declared. "Let's say I believe ye, ranger man. Why would Viktor be so keen to 'ave an Arak... an Ara... Bah! Damned elves an' their damned words! Why would Viktor make any kind o' deal jus' to 'ave ye in his arena? There's got to be plenty o' trained killers out there."

Asher contemplated the dwarf's question for a moment longer than was conversational etiquette. "I have a feeling you'll see why soon enough. Giving him Serena Trigorn's name was enough to stay our execution, but it won't be enough to make a deal. Viktor's going to need proof I'm a real Arakesh. Then you'll understand why."

Doran rolled his eyes, his companion being as cryptic as ever. "Well, ye'll be makin' a deal with the only *real* monster in this bloody place!" he exclaimed. "Instead, ye should jus' put those assassin skills o' yers to good use an' send Viktor to the next world. If ye'd been straight with me from the beginnin' I would o' suggested *that* before *this*!"

The ranger was mindlessly rubbing the skin on his right index finger. "He's shielded," he informed the dwarf.

"So? Jus' kill his guards before ye kill 'im."

"He's shielded by magic," Asher specified.

Doran turned to see the man. "Magic?" he questioned.

"I caught a glimpse of it in the arena," the ranger explained. "It was being moulded to his shape by the hooded mage."

"Well... I'll admit that complicates things but..." The son of Dorain could only shrug. "I'm sure a man o' yer means will figure it out."

Under a pall of depression, Asher replied, "I don't do that anymore."

"Ye're not goin' to get very far in 'ere, lad, if ye're not up to killin' some folk."

"I'll end a man if he seeks my death," Asher stated evenly.

"I'm pretty sure Varga falls into that category," Doran replied.

The ranger scraped the back of his head against the wall as he shook it in response. "Killing Viktor won't keep the Stormshields safe now. Whoever takes over will conclude his affairs and likely with a great show of violence to solidify their new crown. No, I either play his game or dismantle his entire operation, one body at a time."

"The latter sounds good to me," the dwarf opined.

"And me," Asher agreed. "But I can't guarantee the family's safety while I'm slaughtering half of Dragorn."

One dead end after another frayed Doran's already deteriorating mood. "There's got to be somethin' we can do. Anythin'! Anythin' that means ye don' 'ave to fight for that shit o' a man!" Again, the ranger's lack of response only increased the dwarf's ire. "I didn' ask ye to do this," he grizzled, the weight of another person's life pressing upon him. "I tried to tell ye what kind o' man we were dealin' with."

"I expect nothing from you, Doran," Asher said plainly.

"Well why not?" the dwarf fumed. "By rights ye should 'ave killed me in The Iron Valley. Instead, ye're abou' to offer up yer life to save me an' me kin."

"Who says I'm going to die here?"

"Everyone dies here!" Doran yelled. "Those indebted to Viktor end up no better than slaves for the arena. They don' get out, Asher. No matter how many fights they win it's never enough to pay 'im back. An' if ye don' die fightin' he'll feed yer to one o' his pets for no more than entertainment. Every drop o' blood in this place makes him coin. He's goin' to spill yers until ye've nothin' left to give."

There was a pause. "Does that trouble you, Heavybelly?" Asher enquired, his head tilted in a curious fashion.

Doran grumbled incoherently. "Makes no difference to me, ranger man. Die in 'ere or die out there—yer fate's yer own. I owe ye nothin'. *Nothin'*, ye hear?" The dwarf was sure his tone and words were enough to convince Asher as much, even if they didn't convince *him*.

"Just keep them safe," the ranger said without argument.

Asher's response dug into Doran's conscience all the more. A heavy silence sat between them for a short while, interrupted only by the sudden and obnoxiously loud snort of the jailer. That answered the question of whether Asher had killed the man, though the dwarf had hardly cared either way.

"Why'd ye walk away from the life?" the dwarf eventually asked, finally putting some work into softening his harsh tone.

"I became very good at ending lives," the ranger answered after a moment's contemplation, his head resting back against the wall. "One night, I ended the wrong life. Something... *broke* in me. Or perhaps I saw the part of me that was already broken," he uttered as an afterthought, almost oblivious to his dwarven companion. Asher cleared his throat and took a breath. "Now I hunt monsters and save hapless dwarves in distress."

Asher's comment elicited a short sharp laugh from Doran. "An' ye said ye don' joke," he remarked. Continuing his silent trend, Asher kept his mouth shut and his eyes on the ceiling. "So that's what this is then," the son of Dorain said, filling the silence. "The reason ye helped the Stormshields for naught but Kilda's cookin'. Why ye'd forsake the next job an' good coin to accompany me. I mean, ye must 'ave known this couldn' end any other way," he added, gesturing to the bars that surrounded them. "Hells, this even explains why ye demanded the barbarian slaves be set free. Ye're a man tryin' to right all yer wrongs, eh?"

"Something like that," Asher replied glumly.

"I know abou' that," the dwarf replied solemnly, pursing his lips. "An' I know the Stormshields are mighty glad ye changed careers. Deadora would be Troll food if it weren' for ye. Gods know I wasn' there to help..." He turned over his hand to scan the myriad cuts and bruises, all acquired during his unorthodox journey ashore. "At least this assassin business explains the way ye carved yer way through Corrigan's boys." His choice of wording brought up gruesome images of the Lumber Dug.

"If they're the best Viktor can conjure," Asher stated, "then I'll *win* my freedom long before you see the Stormshields again."

Doran grinned, appreciating the dwarven mettle the ranger exhibited. "Ye're confident, laddy, I'll give ye that." And his confidence made sense now, knowing what he did about the man. There was still one aspect of his companion that gnawed at the dwarf. "So, are ye goin' to tell me how ye did it then?"

Asher lifted his head from the wall. "Did what?"

Doran met his eyes. "I know what I saw on that cliff top. Then there's the way ye started that fire. There's more to ye than jus' an assassin."

Asher's finger held his attention for a moment longer. "I'll tell you. After you tell me who he is."

The dwarf frowned at the preposterous statement. "Who *who* is?"

"In the arena, you told Viktor you bow only to *one*."

Doran turned away from the ranger. He didn't want to answer that question. He didn't want to talk about any of it. He looked down at his hands again. They were red up to his elbows, slick with the blood of those he had laid low. There were so many. Though his memory traversed decades, the dwarf could still feel the weight of his axe being taken by the body he buried it in. Or the satisfying pressure applied to his sword when it passed through his foe. No, he thought. Not foe. It had taken him too long to see the distinction. Now, however, he knew the appropriate word.

Kin.

The blood that would stain his skin for evermore was that of his people. He couldn't undo that and, even with a dwarven life-span, knew he could never atone for all the death and carnage he had wrought.

Still, his companion, the man he was most certainly to share death with, had spoken his truth, damning as it was. Perhaps, Doran considered, it would be cathartic to voice his sins before that final breath. Not that such a thing could purify his soul or purge him of the deeds that lay behind him. He was simply one dead man talking to another.

"Me father," Doran said. "He's the only one that can put a bend in me knee."

"Ye have a lot of respect for him," the ranger observed.

The truth of that almost made the dwarf laugh. "Not really. He's somethin' o' a relic. A product o' his own father's shapin' hands, I suppose. He doesn' mean to be the way he is, there's jus' no other way for 'im to be is all." Doran sighed as the flood of memories swept over him, moments from a time and place he had tried to bury deep. "I should 'ave been a son in his eyes but... he treated me no better than ye would a weapon."

"Yet you would still bow to him?" Asher commented, the confusion audible in his voice.

"Aye," Doran replied, aware of the conundrum. "But what else can ye do when ye father's King Dorain, son o' Dorryn, wielder o' Andaljor, an' ruler o' Grimwhal? He's a few more titles I think, but..." The dwarf shrugged and shook his head.

Asher sat forward from the wall. "Deadora was telling the—"

"Truth," Doran finished with a slow blink of his eyes. "Aye she was. But she's too young to know any better."

"You're a *prince*?" Asher's shock was mixed with a hint of amusement.

The dwarf hated the title. "Aye, but not like yer flowery ones who sail through the halls o' their big castles. To be a prince in Dhenaheim—to be the future king—ye 'ave to *lead* yer armies. Ye 'ave to be the tip o' the spear. It's the strongest who rule, not the richest."

The ranger continued to watch him for a moment. "You're royalty?" he asked in disbelief.

"It's hard to believe, I know."

Asher adjusted his sitting position, his eyes wandering before refocusing on Doran. "Why are you here? In Illian?"

"That's a story older than yerself," the dwarf remarked.

"The best ones usually are," Asher replied. He fell silent after that, leading Doran to the ranger's expectant gaze. "*I'm* not going anywhere."

The son of Dorain groaned and knocked the back of his head into the wall. "I'm no bard, laddy."

"Perhaps you should learn," Asher suggested. "It's not a bad way to earn some extra coin. Imagine the tale you'll have to tell if you survive this."

The image of Asher recounting any tale to an audience made Doran laugh. "Is that what ye do then? Tell stories in taverns between loppin' off heads."

"It's not a skill I need," the ranger boasted. "I always get my monster," he added with a cocky grin.

"In this place it's the other way around, lad."

Again, Asher had fallen silent, evidently waiting for Doran to stop skirting around the subject of his past. It had been decades since he had spoken about it. He wasn't even sure where to start anymore.

"Fine," he relented. "But ye 'ave to tell me what happened on that cliff."

The ranger nodded his agreement.

Doran pushed his knees up and rested his arms over the top, a dead stare given to the adjacent wall. "Ye recall what the Stormshields said abou' the hierarchy in Dhenaheim? There's six clans in all. The Battleborns sit at the top an' the Brightbeards reside at the bottom. I was born in Grimwhal, to the Heavybellys—it sits right in the middle o' that hierarchy."

"Grimwhal is a... city?"

"O' sorts. Dwarven kingdoms are built like the roots o' a tree, sprawling beneath the mountain. Grimwhal's probably similar in size to Dragorn," he added as an extra detail, happy to put off his personal tale a while longer.

Asher's silent regard encouraged the dwarf to continue. "The clans all follow a strict rule when it comes to war," he said. "Ye can attack the clan above ye but not below. Ye can defend o' course, but retaliation can become overly political. Ye need permission from Silvyr Hall—the Battleborns—to strike at a lesser clan an' ye need a damn good reason. More often than not, such things are done in secret. As long as the lesser clan can never prove who's attacked 'em, it's like it never happened."

"Did you lead such attacks?" Asher enquired.

"An' the rest," Doran muttered. "Me father considered strikes against the Hammerkegs an' Goldhorns—hells, even the Brightbeard—as no more than trainin' where I was concerned. He wanted to make sure I could kill me own kin without remorse. Only when the blood on me hands didn' bother me was I properly integrated into the army. I had to work me way up to War Mason

—a general. The only way to do that, o' course, was by cuttin' swathes out o' the Stormshields' army. On top o' that, it were me duty to execute any deserters. I can' even count the number o' heads I've separated from shoulders, be 'em Stormshields or Heavybellys."

A barrage of memories forced themselves upon the dwarf. He was suddenly transported back to the bitterly cold plains of Dhenaheim, moments away from smashing into the front line of hardened Stormshields. With every swing of his axe and sword, lives blinked out of existence and the halls of Grarfath swelled in the heavens.

"After every victory, we'd pile up the Stormshield bodies an' burn 'em for all o' Dhenaheim to see. A show o' strength," he said, pitying his old beliefs. "The children o' the mountain 'aven' known *real* strength since the days o' Vengora."

"Vengora?" Asher echoed. "Your people used to live in The Vengoran Mountains?"

"Oh aye. If ye can find ye way in, there's a whole world o' dwarven history in 'em mountains. Back then we were one people, united under one banner."

"But you fractured into six kingdoms," the ranger concluded. "Just like the kingdoms of Illian."

"Aye, a cruel bond between our two peoples if ever there was one."

"What happened?"

Doran licked his lips, happy to be given a brief diversion from his own tale. "We lost the war. We had no choice but to retreat to The Whisperin' Mountains in Dhenaheim."

"War?"

Doran's mood turned sour, spoiled by the stories he had been brought up on and the hate he had been conditioned to harbour. "It's no war yer people will know of."

"Who were you fighting?"

The dwarf finally turned to look Asher in the eyes. "The orc," he said gravely, his memory cast back to the sculptures and mosaics he had studied in his youth.

"I've never heard of them," the ranger confessed.

"No fouler creature has walked the earth since their defeat. An' they *were* defeated. Wiped *out*," he emphasised with a cutting motion of his hand. "An', even then, they were only beaten because me ancestors formed an alliance with the elves. Can ye imagine that? Dwarves an' elves fightin' side by side!"

"Sounds fascinating," Asher commented, though his tone suggested he was ready to return to Doran's history.

"They were dark days," the son of Dorain replied, repeating his grandfather's words. "We never recovered afterwards. The six clans took shape an' war was all we knew. An' I was damned good at it," he told the ranger, hating himself all the more. "Fathers, brothers, sons... I cut 'em all down. There were years—decades— where I enjoyed it, lived for it. If I wasn' on the battlefield I was no better than a caged animal. There was only Grimwhal's glory. Me father's approval," he added, delving further into the truth.

"What happened?"

Doran had been dreading this part, for his mind recalled all too easily the sight that had left his soul bereft of honour. "For two days we fought 'em," he began, his voice a shadow. "The Stormshields had raided one o' our outposts," he explained before going on, thereby delaying the inevitable. "We couldn' prove it, o' course, but we knew it were 'em. There were a number o' ways we could 'ave retaliated, but me father wanted to make 'em feel it an' I wanted the fight. So we marched on the barracks at Addakarr, only five miles north o' Hyndaern itself. It would 'ave been a major blow to their infrastructure, potentially weakenin' 'em enough to allow me clan to usurp their place in the hierarchy."

Looking at his hands again, they appeared to be dripping with blood.

"After two days o' slaughterin' each other, I found a moment to breathe. I looked around an'... There was nothin' but bodies as far as the eye could see. Every inch o' snow was red with blood. I wasn' even holdin' me own weapons anymore. At some point I had picked up a Stormshield warhammer an' started killin' 'em with their own iron. I could taste the blood o' me kin on me lips. At me feet there were naught but *bits* o' folk, young an' old.

"An' then I saw it—me own future. Surrounded by the dead an' the dyin', it all became so clear. There was only ever going to be another battlefield. We were goin' to kill each other until there were more dwarven bones than snow litterin' the ground. The wheel would keep turnin' an' we would keep grindin' each other to pulp. It broke me," Doran said, mirroring Asher's analogy. He ran a hand down his face and over his beard. "So I jus' walked away. I didn' say anythin' to anyone. I jus' turned around an' walked away. I left me kin to keep fightin' an' vowed to never take another dwarven life. To this day I don' know the outcome o' the campaign."

For a time there existed nothing but silence between the two companions.

"I know little of the battlefield," Asher eventually voiced, "but I know what it means to have blood on your hands, to be haunted by the dead."

"I was a damned coward," Doran blurted, his anger bubbling up to the surface. "I knew the way o' me people was wrong, but walkin' away was the easy way out. I should 'ave jus' died on the field or put me head on the block."

Asher was nodding along. "I too used to believe I had taken the coward's path. I couldn't live with myself but I couldn't end it either. I see now that it takes more strength to *choose* another path and live with what you've done. The coward's way out, Doran, would have been to let yourself be killed on that battlefield."

In all the years since his self-imposed exile, the dwarf had never considered such a view. "That's one way o' lookin' at it," he managed, his feelings somewhat raw now. In truth, he was thankful for the opposing outlook. Adopting it, he knew, would take time.

"For what it's worth," the ranger continued, "I'm glad you found your way to Illian. If I hadn't met you, I wouldn't know how good a ranger I am." There was a mocking note in his voice as he reclined against the wall once more. "As it turns out, I'm *very* good."

The banter brought a much-needed smile to Doran's face and he welcomed the levity. "I'm twice the monster hunter ye are, laddy," he retorted with a thumb in his chest. "An' ye owe me an explanation o' ye own now. Deal's a deal."

"Does it really matter?" the ranger questioned. "According to you we're both destined to die in here anyway."

"So humour the walkin' dead," Doran countered. "We dwarves hate a mystery ye know."

As the ranger sat forward again, his mouth opening to set that final piece of the puzzle into place, the sound of approaching feet drew their attention to the passage between them. Darya and six of Viktor's hired thugs entered the space.

The Shadow Witch brought them all to a stop as she looked upon the sleeping jailer, his keys resting on his back. She reached out to Asher's cell, her fingers exploring the bars, before sliding it open with no protest from the lock. One of the guards opened Doran's cell with identical ease.

Asher looked from the guard to Darya and simply shrugged under her scrutiny. "He was tired."

She wasn't entertained by his answer. "Bind their wrists," came the command, her hands resting on the hilts of those fine daggers.

Doran let out a long groan. "We were in the middle o' somethin' actually."

Darya turned to lay her gaze over the dwarf. "That you certainly are," she said, knowingly.

For some reason, being beneath her cutting smile, the son of Dorain couldn't help but think about Corrigan and his men as they scrambled helplessly beneath the Lumber Dug.

CHAPTER 18
KILL OR BE KILLED

__Wither__ - Forest dwellers—the darker the better. In fact, a prevailing myth surrounding these creatures suggests they possess some ability to darken the areas they inhabit.

At six feet tall, they are entirely covered in coarse black hair. Beneath all this hair stands a beast not unlike a wolf. This likeness ends, however, when taking into account the ram-like horns on their heads.

Exclusively meat eaters, these monsters have no problem eating humans should they cross paths. Of course, it is not very often the two encounter each other, as most people avoid these strangely dark areas of the forest. When a contract arises though, and they do from time to time, you need to know how to tackle the creatures.

Firstly, they live in groups of male or female. The two only mix when it comes to mating season during the autumn. From studies, there seems no difference between the male and females when it comes to facing them, but it should be noted that the females are more territorial.

__*A Chronicle of Monsters: A Ranger's Bestiary, 12th Edition, Page 398.*__

__*Galus Kroma, Ranger.*__

. . .

His steps retraced, Asher found himself standing under a starry night in the middle of the arena again. The Lumber Dug was gone, though its recent presence was still evident by the large patch of red sand just off from the centre. Even the ragged remnants of Corrigan and his men had been removed. There was no removing the foul odour, however, a distinct smell created when a person's insides had become their outsides.

It reminded the ranger of Nightfall, where torture and death were a way of life. He imagined many fighters entering the arena only to be set upon by the gruesome scent, and all to the background cheers of a crowd that desired their bloody demise—enough to cripple the bravest of men.

Though he certainly didn't find any pleasure in the odour, Asher was disturbed by his level of comfort in the midst of it. The thought was fleeting, given his rising instincts, but he did wonder, as he had done many times over the last few years, if he was more monster than man.

"Welcome back!" Viktor called from the stands above, the real monster in the room. The crime lord rubbed his hands together before placing them on top of the wall. He looked down on his captives with a smile as slashing as any blade. "I've been considering your *deal*."

"I fight and the Stormshields are forgotten," the ranger clarified, his wrists bound neatly in front of him. "Doran goes—"

Viktor held up a hand. "The details can wait. First, I would have proof you are what you say you are," Varga said, raising a finger with his spreading grin. "I would add, should your claim be proven false, I will have you both peeled to the bone and the lovely Stormshields with you." A quick nod of the head sent his men into retreat, Doran dragged away with them.

Asher turned to watch over his shoulder, observing the dwarf as he was forced up the steps and thrust onto the bench as if he were no more than a paying spectator. Darya, however, remained close to the ranger and perfectly motionless: a display of impeccable control.

Returning his attention to the crime lord and Malak beside him, Asher held up his bound wrists.

"Would a true Arakesh require such freedom?" Viktor enquired.

The ranger dropped his arms and exhaled through his nose. "My sword then?" he asked, looking to Malak.

The thug flexed his arms and adjusted the blade on his belt, a weapon he considered no better than a mere dagger. "You've no sword up here, mate."

Viktor moved and Malak froze. The crime lord removed the short-sword from the brute's belt. "You are permitted this…" He trailed off, quite taken by the blade. "'Tis remarkably light," he marvelled, turning the weapon over and over. "Wonderfully so…"

"It's no better than a toothpick," Malak remarked.

"Yet you have so quickly taken ownership," Varga countered.

Malak averted his gaze, smart enough to know when he should keep his mouth shut.

Viktor enjoyed the feel of the short-sword a moment longer before tossing it to one end of the arena, far from the ranger's grip. The silvyr tip drove into the sand and stood proud, awaiting its master. Beyond the exquisite weapon, however, six men—gladiators all—were already entering the arena and soon standing sentinel between Asher and his prize.

The ranger's eyes roamed over them, his critical assessment honed after years of carefully picking his fights. For the most part, their protection was hard leather, though each of them possessed a piece of iron armour, be it a pauldron, cuirass or a pair of vambraces. One of them wore a helmet fitted with a visor to conceal and protect his face.

Their weapons were another matter, far more varied than the average group of fighters. A spear, twin axes, a sabre, two-handed hammer, a mace on a chain, and a pair of spiked knuckle-dusters.

The ranger had fought with and against all weapon groups, and that was before he had been allowed beyond Nightfall's dark halls. Using the time available, he ran through various scenarios, routines, and strategies that could be utilised against these particular foes. It was also important to note, though, that these men were fighters all. Though their training could be called into question, they were accustomed to violence, pain, and pushing themselves to the limits.

Asher reminded himself that he wasn't to enjoy it too much.

"My champions!" Viktor declared. "Murderers, rapists, thieves, and killers for hire," he rattled off. "You might have noticed Dragorn has no prison nor dungeon. The great houses dole out justice and, more often than not, those who escape immediate execution find themselves being donated to my arena. But the men you see before you... They *chose* to fight in this mighty arena and with no chance of freedom. They *will* die in here, on this very sand. They just love the fight," he added with a shrug. "So trust me when I tell you, Asher, none of these men will stop until you are dead. Either they walk away or you do."

Kill or be killed. The ranger's conscience—an element of his new existence that he couldn't seem to escape—attempted to wrestle with the concept, reminding him that, with a bit more care, he could immobilise them instead. Asher tried to reason with it, comparing the situation to being set upon by a gang of thieves on the road. Sending *them* into Death's waiting arms would have been inevitable and beyond his control, for he was only doing what anyone would do in those circumstances.

The scenes playing out in his mind began to change from bloodshed to broken bones, his tactics shifting. The tally of dead that lay behind him didn't need to get any bigger, even if those he would kill were the worst of humanity.

His internal argument came to a swift end when his right hand came across the red blindfold looped around his belt. Just the feel of the fabric weighted the argument against his conscience. Now he *wanted* to fight. He wanted to let the Nightseye elixir flowing through his veins take over and let him assume the role of predator. He could already feel the satisfying pressure against his blade as the silvyr edge sliced through his enemies. The ecstasy of it.

The *Assassin* wanted out.

Removing the red fabric from his belt, he held it up and locked eyes with Viktor. The crime lord was illuminated with joy and he clasped his hands together. "Of course," he said with great pleasure. "Darya, if you would cover his eyes..."

Aware of Nightfall's existence, as all League members were, the Shadow Witch understood perfectly why she had been instructed to blindfold him. While she moved behind him, Asher exhaled a long and slow breath, as if he were expelling the ranger within. That man had no place in this fight.

As the fabric was wrapped around his eyes, he became the *Assassin* once more. The gladiators before him vanished from traditional sight but, with the consuming darkness that followed, all their secrets were laid bare. That, and so much more.

It had been some time since Asher had embraced true darkness and touched the world as an Arakesh. For just a moment, the input threatened to overwhelm him. Clenching his fists and setting his jaw firmly, instinct and muscle memory worked to slip his mind back into that of an Arakesh. Only seconds later and he was in command of his senses and able to process the details of his environment.

First was the chorus of heartbeats, an orchestra of drums that played out of tune with each other. The fastest was Viktor's, though his rapid heart rate was only one aspect of his excitement. His muscles were just as tense as the gladiators and he was even sweating more than any of them. It didn't take the assassin long to find the hidden blade concealed inside the right sleeve of his robes, though the condition of the hilt suggested it was rarely handled.

Then there was Doran's heartbeat, easily the strongest and slowest in the arena. It was a testament to his body's natural power and long life. He was fidgeting in his seat, his bindings chaffing against his wrists. He was blinking sweat from his eyelashes, his gaze fixed on Asher. As the dwarf breathed, the assassin could both hear and feel the hairline fractures two of his ribs had suffered, though they appeared to cause him no pain.

Darya had walked away by now, stepping out of the arena to

join her master up in the stands. Unlike Viktor—who carried the scent of lilac and honey—she wore no perfume. Another distinction she boasted was her lack of sweat, her body clearly accustomed to a hotter environment.

Asher licked his lips and tasted the steel of her daggers—Karathan steel. They were tools of death and expensive tools at that. A gift from her rich employer no doubt. She bore no current injuries and her skeleton moved with ease. By the smell of her breath, he knew she had eaten in the last two hours—a steak. Though that meant nothing, it compounded the image of a predator he had already assigned to her.

On the other side of Viktor, Malak leaned over the edge of the wall on his elbows, the scent of two women clinging to his skin. He had enjoyed their intimate company at some point in the last day and night and not bathed in-between.

The thug's body possessed one significant injury, and it was an old one judging by the feel of the scar on his left hip. Deeper, the assassin could feel where someone's sword had swiped through Malak's hip and chipped the bone. Asher knew immediately that he wouldn't be able to pivot to his left with any great speed. Not that such a detail mattered right now, for his opponents were those on the sand.

The gladiators appeared calm to the limited senses of those around the arena but, to Asher, they were preparing to fight or die. Their heart rates had steadily increased as Darya walked away and a time of violence approached. Their bodies were a canvas that spoke of a lifetime of brutality and savagery. It made estimating their ages difficult, since the movement of both their skeletons and overlapping muscles had taken so much damage in a relatively short period of time.

Their skin tone and elasticity aided him, informing the assassin that all six men were between twenty-five and forty years old. On the cusp of turning forty himself, the majority of his opponents were younger it seemed. It was no bother. Youth never stood up to experience, and the one they faced this day was a dragon among men, a creature of innate experience in the art of death.

With the exception of his hearing, his senses detected the old blood that marred their various weapons. It was likely that none of them were cleaned on purpose, to complement their menacing appearance. To Asher it was no more than an acrid taste in his mouth, one that was soon to be replaced by fresh blood.

As the gladiators began to advance and spread out, the assassin absorbed the feedback from his silvyr short-sword, too far to grasp. The metal was new to his heightened senses, a mineral he had never tasted, touched or smelled before. Try as he might, there was nothing to compare it to. It was simply alien to all that he knew of the world—a weapon from the heavens indeed. Adding to its mystery, he couldn't detect a single imperfection in the blade, though he easily felt the bite of its edge, like a physical tear in the fabric of reality.

Taking advantage of their cautious approach, Asher crouched down and placed the flat of his hand to the ground. There was something else beneath his feet, nagging at the edges of his senses. Through touch, he connected to the chambers below and built an image in his mind, an image of monsters.

They slithered, crawled, and stalked around their cages, growling, roaring, and hissing with hunger and rage, as if they themselves had been swallowed by some enormous beast that was slowly digesting them. He felt claws rake down stone walls and tentacles coil around iron bars. Blood and Coin had its very own hell.

"What's he doing?" came Malak's hushed voice from above.

Viktor gave half a laugh. "I have no idea," he replied with mounting anticipation.

"He can't see anything," the thug pointed out.

Varga smiled enough to flash his teeth. "It is said that Death itself grants an Arakesh with its vision, revealing those who are doomed to die."

Still crouched and now surrounded by the gladiators, Asher was slowly fading into the background as the *Assassin* rose up in him. The entire scenario took him back to his youth, when those of his cohort would be pitted against him, and all under the ethereal gaze of Nasta Nal-Aket who, in this case, had been replaced by Viktor Varga. He was a poor substitute, even if he did hold all the cards.

Asher felt the change in air pressure behind him as the spearman stepped forwards, his boot displacing the grains of sand. It was silent to all others, but Asher heard the tip of the spear as it cut through the air on its way up. That informed the assassin that his opponent planned on thrusting down, through his back.

Resist as he might, a wry smile pulled at the corner of Asher's mouth. It felt good to unleash—a relief even.

The shaft of the spear darted down through the air, but its pointed end found naught but sand. Having pivoted on his left knee, Asher was now facing his enemy and with a handful of sand snapping up to greet him. The gladiator staggered back, his vision irritatingly obstructed. The assassin pounced, springing up to drive the edge of one hand into the man's exposed throat. His breathing now obstructed as well, the gladiator instinctively panicked and, as predicted, raised his hands to his throat in favour of maintaining a hold on his spear.

Asher could feel the weapon falling through the air, his senses appraising him of its position relative to himself with better precision than his eyes alone could ever have achieved. In the grip of his bound hands, the assassin twisted the spear around and plunged it into his enemy's bare chest.

It might have taken less than a second for the steel tip to push through from chest to back but, to Asher, it was a prolonged moment in which he felt the varying vibrations through the shaft as the weapon tore through skin, muscle, and arteries before exposing fresh blood on the other side. The killer that had been carefully nurtured in him from childhood relished it. The cold and calculating *Assassin* that had resulted from that nurturing also knew that five seconds had passed since the fight began. One down. Five to go.

Letting his opponent fall to the ground, and with the spear still lodged in his chest, Asher remained where he stood, head bowed. He didn't have to wait long.

The next to attack came at him with an axe in each hand. His face trapped behind the steel plate of a visor, Asher could hear the man's heavy breathing inside. It was the creak of leather around his right shoulder, combined with the taste of bloody steel as one of the axes went from low to high, that built the perfect image of events. The assassin's body responded as if they were in the midst of a choreographed dance. His shoulders weaved left then right, keeping time with his retreating steps, and evaded every swing of the curved blades.

Quite deliberately, however, Asher was moving backwards towards the largest of the gladiators, who gripped his two-handed hammer with pale knuckles. The assassin felt almost every muscle working in that particular gladiator's body as he hefted the hammer and swung it around. Using the axe-man's limited vision against him, Asher had manoeuvred him into range of that incoming hammer. All the assassin had to do was duck at the last second.

That solid casting of iron came around with all the gladiator's strength behind it and caught the axe-man's right hand instead of Asher. Following the now flying axe, the assassin turned his crouch into a roll and came back up with the weapon in hand. Behind him, the axe-man was crying out and nursing his mangled hand while the hammer-wielding brawler pursued Asher.

His responses limited by the binding around his wrists, Asher adapted his tactics. Rather than launching the axe at his enemy's chest—a killing blow that came at the expense of the time lost to raise the weapon over his head—the assassin tossed the axe underarm at his opponent's feet. It was enough to make the gladiator stumble mid-charge and fall forwards, his hammer extended clumsily. Not one to waste an opportunity, Asher held out his hands and snatched the weapon as its wielder was on his way down to meet the ground.

Continuing his momentum, the assassin exploded with energy and charged the axe-man. At the last second, Asher leapt high and brought the hammer up with him, its unforgiving end swinging to meet the gladiator's exposed jaw. He heard the jawbone crack and felt the pressure of his enemy's teeth shattering against each other. His visor thrown clear from his head, the axe-man flew from his feet and impacted the sand. On his back, choking on his own blood, the man was helpless to do anything but observe his end as Asher fell from his leap and reversed the hammer's swing. The last thing he saw was that hammer before it staved his skull in and painted the sand red.

The original wielder of the hammer looked back from his place on the ground to see that his weapon had been used against a comrade. He let loose a primal growl and picked himself up, along with the axe Asher had thrown at his feet.

Again, Asher left the hammer where it was, standing at an awkward angle in the middle of a man's skull. Facing the largest of them, he listened to his senses and waited for his instincts to respond to the information they were relaying. Time to free his hands, he decided.

The brute came at him with all the finesse of a backstreet brawler, believing his raw strength would be enough to end the contest. He likely had a history proving that to be true—how else had he arrived at this moment? Against an Arakesh, however, he might as well have turned that axe against himself.

One step back and his arms raised, Asher was positioned precisely where he needed to be in order to break his binding. The axe, as foreseen in his mind, chopped down between his wrists and sliced neatly through the rope. Again, his tactics shifted, his mind slipping further into attack over counterattack.

Moving forward, he slapped both of his newly freed hands over the gladiator's ears, instantly discombobulating the man. He would have followed up the attack with another, were it not for the gladiator approaching from his right. He heard the small bones clicking inside the man's hands as he balled them into fists around his spiked knuckle-dusters.

The assassin thrust an elbow into the big man's solar plexus, knocking him back to allow space for hand-to-hand combat with his fellow gladiator. Again, the style of fighting brought to bear was that of an amateur who had relied on his strength and indifferent attitude towards violence to get this far. Asher batted the incoming punches away and countered every time with a blow to one of the man's nerve clusters. Soon, the pain was enough to slow him down and the assassin took advantage.

With a two-handed grip, he first snapped his foe's wrist before popping his shoulder out of place. His agonised yell was cut short when Asher kicked his knee out with a bone-breaking crunch before swiftly snapping his neck with one powerful tug.

The body hit the sand and joined the other two.

That left the big man, who was still unsteady on his feet, along with the swordsman and the mace-wielder. That spiked ball was spinning round and round, its chain a constant rattle. Even without his acute senses, it would have been easy to predict where the cumbersome weapon was coming from. Of course, what none of the gladiators had realised was the general direction in which Asher had been manipulating the fight from the very beginning.

Now, as the mace came swinging in to claim his head, the assassin had but to roll under it—to his left—and the silvyr blade was once again his to wield. Blindfolded in red and with short-sword in hand, Asher had reclaimed the appearance of an Arakesh.

While the armed gladiators regarded each other with some unease, the big man returned to his senses and dashed back for his hammer—for all the good it had done him so far. In Nightfall, the slow learners were soon weeded out, and always at the expense of their life. Asher saw no reason why that shouldn't apply to a gladi-ator's life.

Rather than rush the two closest to him, the assassin calmly walked towards them, his weapon held low so as to conceal his intended move. The mace-wielder, the more aggressive of the two, attacked first. He was, of course, a slave to the requirements of such a weapon. In order to utilise its deadly ability, the gladiator had to give it some momentum, an action that involved the overextension of the upper body. Such an opening was inexcusable and not to be missed.

He could almost hear Nasta whispering as much in his ear.

Asher moved like a viper, cutting low and to the side while the mace was still on its way up. It was his first time bringing the silvyr to bear against flesh. Though he had killed just as easily with steel, the silvyr was far more satisfying in the way it sliced through his enemy. Had his senses not detected the blood and felt the internal organs split apart around the blade, he might have questioned whether he had even struck the man.

A large gash in his waist—so considerable that a portion of his severed intestines spilled out—the mace-wielder fell to his knees before collapsing face-first into the sand. Over his dead body came the leaping swordsman, but Asher had heard every part of his body hurtling towards him. The steel sabre rolled continuously, weaving one way then the next while the assassin effortlessly deflected the swiping edges.

In came the hammer-wielding brute and, once again, with no care for his fellow gladiator. Asher didn't even try to block the swinging weapon. Instead, he batted the sabre away and evaded the iron hammerhead with an unorthodox twist of his body, a manoeuvre that took him momentarily off his feet. As he landed, one hand reached out and scooped up the fallen mace.

It had been many years since the assassin had handled such a weapon. It was an inelegant tool of death, even in the hands of a surgical killer, but it had its uses. Swinging it around was enough to keep the big man at bay while his silvyr blade arced wide and scored a red line across the swordsman's chest and arm, the edge slicing easily through his leathers, flesh and even his armoured pauldron.

Utilising the mace's momentum, Asher swung it around one more time, sending the ball high and the chain taut. Unfortunately for the swordsman, who was reeling from his new wound, what went up had to come down, and down the mace came. The spikes were buried in the gladiator's foot and the weight behind it drove most of it into the sand beneath. Pinned to the spot and racked with agony, the swordsman was helpless to prevent his death, a fate brought about by Asher's silvyr blade as it plunged directly through the centre of his face and out of the other side.

Content to wield his short-sword alone, the assassin abandoned the mace and turned his head over one shoulder, as if he were regarding the big man. At last, surrounded by the dead, the brute hesitated in his advance.

Asher twisted his weapon so the silvyr blade rested up against the back of his arm. The final act of the dance played out in his mind and his body quietly prepared to respond. All he had to do was wait.

The big man glanced at Viktor in the stands. Despite the assassin's lack of vision, he felt the fine muscles in Varga's face tense and his jaw shift up and forwards into a stern expression.

"You heard him," Asher said gruffly, his chest heaving. "You're going to die here, on this very sand."

The gladiator churned his fear into anger and grim determination. He used it to fuel his charge, though he only achieved two steps before Asher flicked his short-sword at him. The exquisite blade spun through the air, cut the hammer in half, and found its resting place in the brute's skull. The assassin was already there to meet his fall, one hand snapping out to reclaim his weapon from the descending corpse. Joining his brothers, the big man added his blood to the sand, just as his master had prophesied.

Viktor Varga was already laughing. The sound of his singular applause filled the stunned arena. "Outstanding!" he praised. "Truly... Outstanding."

Asher remained very still. The Arakesh had tasted blood but it wasn't satiated. Under no threat, however, the *Ranger* began to return, assuming control and revealing the death that had been dealt by his hands. His chest heaving, head hanging low and dripping with sweat, Asher added the body count to his tally.

There was no escaping who he really was. *What* he really was.

CHAPTER 19

THE DEAL

Husk *- These skeletal monstrosities haven't been seen for some time, though they are worthy of note in our fine bestiary. Their origins are unknown to our order of hunters and, perhaps, even the mages of Korkanath. What we can all agree on, however, is that magic had its part to play.*

The beasts do not have brains or working minds as we do—they do not even possess organs. Their bodies are capable of reshaping to match whatever prey has endured the misfortune of crossing it. They simply engulf their victim from head-to-toe, wrapping around them like strips of filthy cloth, and leech every ounce of energy. You see, these creatures are not named for their appearance, but for the manner in which they discard their prey.

Steel, neither sharp nor blunt, will aid you here. Fire is key when it comes to destroying Husks. Until fire and flame are required, pray to the gods that the monsters stay in seclusion.

A Chronicle of Monsters: A Ranger's Bestiary, 12th Edition, Page 68.

Beregor Nine-Fingers, Ranger.

. . .

All could see inside Doran Heavybelly's mouth, for his jaw had fallen out of place and refused to go back together. It had been stuck like that from the moment he had observed Asher impale the first gladiator, using his own spear no less. From there on, the fight had only escalated until it reached unbelievable heights.

Until that moment, the dwarf had believed he possessed too many years to ever be surprised, but now he was beyond surprised, shocked even. He knew Asher to be a good fighter—that much he had witnessed against Corrigan and his men—and since learning of his past as an Arakesh, the son of Dorain was led to suspect that the ranger had been holding back during that particular fight. Taking in the bloody massacre that now surrounded his companion, he could see what *not* holding back looked like.

Doran shook his head. Grarfath only knew how he had accomplished such a feat while blindfolded, never mind having bound wrists for a good deal of the fight.

Glancing at his armed guards, he could see that Asher's display was having a similar effect on them as well. In fact, their attention had wandered so far from the dwarf in their custody that the son of Dorain had to wonder if this was his chance to escape. With him out of the equation, Asher would have no need to make a deal and, judging by his skill with any weapon, there was unlikely to be anyone in Viktor's employ capable of stopping him from leaving.

Of course, the pair would have nowhere to go beyond the arena walls. The island was a closed fist, each digit a controlling guild, Viktor's included. They would find no allies and no one stupid enough to take a bribe from fugitives of Blood and Coin. The only way back to the mainland was with Varga's permission... or over his dead body. Doran knew which he would choose.

Resigned to his fate, whatever it might be, he could only hope now that Asher had the words to match his fighting prowess. After all, there was still a deal to be made.

"Outstanding!" the crime lord called. "Truly... Outstanding!"

Unfazed by the killer that currently dominated the arena, Viktor made his way down the steps and onto the sand. Even Doran, an ally of Asher, was unsure if he would purposefully put himself within six feet of the ranger at that moment, magical shield or not. His breathing was still laboured, his shoulders hunched like an animal ready to spring. Then there was his blood-lust from the fight, clearly still bubbling under the skin.

With his hooded mage at his back, Viktor—confident he was untouchable—approached Asher with open arms, a gesture to encompass all the bodies. "An Arakesh!" he declared. "In *my* arena. Extraordinary!"

Close behind him, Darya and Malak manoeuvred themselves into striking positions should Asher prove unruly. Both appeared to be seeing the ranger as Doran did, their weapons already freed and in hand.

"In all the realm," Viktor continued, "I have never seen such a thing. Even the Graycoats pale in comparison." He gave a short sharp laugh. "And to think, I thought you were all just daggers in the shadows. When, in fact, you are so much *more*."

Asher tossed his short-sword into the sand between them, an unthreatening action, but action enough to see Darya raise her blades and Malak his one-handed axe.

"I fight," Asher rasped. "You leave the Stormshields alone. Doran goes free."

Viktor took a long breath before signalling for the dwarf to be brought down. Doran didn't appreciate the rough hands hooking under his arms and manhandling him into the arena but he didn't offer protest, eager to see this deal to a swift end.

"Obviously," Varga said, his attention returned to Asher, "I must have you fight. How could I not? Word of an Arakesh on the sands of Blood and Coin will draw an audience from all four corners of the realm." His expression soured upon sighting Doran, brought before him. "But I see no reason why I should let the dwarf keep his head. Master Heavybelly is already in my house, his fate—like yours—in my hands. Why not have you fight *and* him executed?"

Asher took another breath, his eyes still hidden behind his red blindfold. "I fight," he repeated. "Doran goes free. It's the only way I know the Stormshields will be safe. It's also the only deal I'm making. Kill him," he said, removing his blindfold, "and I will fight like any other."

Doran didn't need to scrutinise Viktor's face to know that Asher had just found his leverage. An Arakesh in his clutches, it seemed, was worth making a deal for.

Varga responded with a smile that didn't quite reach his eyes. "These terms are acceptable."

The son of Dorain felt some relief at hearing the words from Viktor's own mouth, though he was thinking entirely about the Stormshields. How foolish he had been, selfish even, to have put them in so much danger. He vowed there and then to leave them be after ensuring Varga kept his word. There was, of course, Asher to consider. Doran looked up at him, a man sacrificing his freedom and life for them. Whatever his past deeds, the ranger had honour, a rare and valuable quality whatever the race.

"Wait," the dwarf blurted. "What are the conditions o' his term? How long is he to fight for ye? How many victories will buy his freedom?"

Viktor put his hands together before opening them into a shrug. "I'm afraid this particular contract has no such stipulations. There will be no freedom, just as there was no freedom for these gentlemen," he pointed out, gesturing to the dead.

"That isn' right!" Doran exclaimed.

"No, it *isn't*," Viktor agreed, looming over the son of Dorain. "Whose fault do you think that is? Hmm? 'Tis *your* debt that must be paid, master dwarf. Yet you have nothing to offer. And so it is Asher here, our hero in red, who must take on the burden! Yes, hero in *red*... I like that," he said, becoming distracted by possible theatrics. "I want you to stand out. A red cloak perhaps. To match your blindfold."

Ignoring the crime lord, Doran turned to the ranger. "Asher it's too much!" he fumed, his guilt rising higher and higher. "Ye can' take this deal."

"Master Heavybelly is quite right," Varga agreed, circling them now. "You don't have to take this deal, not at all. I already have a missive scribed and with a raven. Without further command it will be set free and deliver word to my people in Velia. From there, they will seek out the Stormshields and bring them here and... well, you both know what happens next."

"I want to see him leave," Asher said, as if Doran had never spoken. "On a ship. At first light."

Viktor looked to Malak questioningly and the brute replied, "The White Horse is due to set sail at dawn."

The crime lord clapped his hands once and held them together. "Excellent. You can watch Master Heavybelly leave our fair island aboard The White Horse at sunrise. Malak will see to the details." Viktor clasped his hands behind his back and swivelled on the spot.

"I want me pig," Doran declared, and with more confidence than one in his position should have. It was the royalty in him, he decided, standing firm behind his demand.

"Excuse me," Viktor said calmly, if somewhat irritated.

"Me Warhog. Ye've got 'im. I want 'im back."

Again, Viktor looked to Malak, the matter so insignificant he hadn't a clue what the dwarf was talking about. The thug gave his master a nod, confirming the claim to be true.

"I am not so petty a man as to keep the beast. The mount will be returned to you." With that, Viktor attempted his exit one more time only to give himself reason to pause. "Oh, one last thing, good dwarf. Should you step foot in my city again, I cannot speak for your safe departure. Best keep to the mainland I think."

Doran so desperately wanted to have the last word, and a threatening one at that. Instead, he offered the back of Varga's head a determined grimace. The feeling of helplessness that overcame him then was akin to a blade in the gut, a debilitating pain that rooted him to the spot. He was soon uprooted, however, when Malak severed his bindings and shoved him towards the edge of the arena. The rest of the thugs, including the Shadow Witch, saw to Asher's personal escort.

Beyond the sands of the arena, the pair were unceremoniously marched through the halls of Blood and Coin until they were outside its walls. They were kept too far apart to barter words while Pig was retrieved from the stables and returned to the dwarf. How he wanted to say something to Asher, anything to relay the shame and guilt that shadowed every corner of his mind. Or perhaps a simple thank you, two small but meaningful words he had yet to muster.

Happy to see him, Pig pressed the flat of his large snout into Doran's hip. "Easy, big fella," he bade, wary of the animal's tusks. "We're gettin' out o' 'ere." Looking to Asher with such a statement, he was saddened to see the ranger's head held low, his gaze seeking naught but his own feet. He was a man resigned to his grim fate.

"Let's move," Darya ordered, calling above the din of the raucous streets.

Indeed, the pale light creeping across the sky suggested that the new day was leaning into the night. By the time they reached the docks again the dawn would be unquestionable.

And so they made their way through Dragorn's streets, working their way out of the spiral now. Those who still danced with merriment and hurled drunken insults cared little for the time of day, or night as some would argue. In fact, it seemed the whole city failed to keep time. There were markets that never closed, taverns that never stopped serving, and even children playing across the rooftops.

One thing Doran noticed that he had missed on his way into the city were the sigils painted on various walls. The first few blocks were all marked by a rose of thorns, the mark of house Danathor he knew. Then, closer to Dragorn's outer wall, he began to see a painted fist with a single coin perched on the index finger, as if it was about to toss it into the air. After a moment's thought, the dwarf recognised it as the sigil of house Trigorn, one of the more powerful crime guilds. Everything belonged to someone on the wretched island.

Ushered through those imposing gates and into the breaking

dawn, Asher and Doran were once again on the vast docks of Dragorn. Much like the city inside, the docks were still full of life, the business of business never resting.

Malak took point and led them through the maze of jetties and quays, taking them further out to sea with every step. The ship they were brought to, The White Horse, was nowhere near the wreckage of The Mer Seed. It was a smaller vessel, its crew having been drawn to the port side to see the passenger being imposed upon them. Seeing a dwarf was clearly a surprise for most, though their pointed stares were nothing new to Doran.

While they waited for Malak to square things with the captain, Doran edged forward to see Asher past the line of thugs that separated them. The ranger remained a mute, a silent sentinel that stood where he was instructed. The dwarf licked his lips. If he was to speak to him it had to be now. The moment he stepped onto The White Horse he would lose the opportunity, possibly forever.

One of the thugs stepped forward, barring the way. Doran craned his short neck and met the man's eyes. "Unless ye fancy goin' for a swim, laddy, I suggest you put yerself somewhere else."

A little unsure how to proceed, the man looked back at Darya for support. The Shadow Witch considered the dwarf's obvious intentions before finally nodding her approval. His path clear, Doran left Pig where he was and approached Asher.

"Ye're a damned fool for makin' this deal," he began, perhaps a little too brashly.

"The Stormshields would disagree," Asher said softly, his gaze as distant as the horizon.

Doran wondered if a part of him was still in that arena. "I suppose I would too," he replied. "Ye've done more for me than any human before ye. Hells, ye've done more for me than any dwarf." Doran swallowed, aware of the ears listening to the exchange. "I'm sure Danagarr an' Kilda would say the same. I'll be sure to tell 'em what ye did 'ere."

Asher simply nodded in return.

The dwarf hesitated with the foreign words on the edge of his lips. "Thank ye."

The ranger looked down at him, his face still splattered with blood. "Live well, Doran Heavybelly. And make sure the Stormshields do the same."

Doran wasn't sure if he would have preferred Asher to yell at him, to curse his bones and all his endeavours. "I see it in ye, lad," he said, garnering a look of curiosity from the ranger. "It's the same demon that lives in me. It *enjoys* the bloodshed. Craves it. Take it from one who's walked that path for too long—don' let it rule ye. Don' let this place win."

Asher bowed his head a notch, taking the advice without comment.

Malak called down from the deck of The White Horse, ending their time together. Doran knew he owed Asher more than a thank you—even a thousand wouldn't reset the scales. But what else could be done? The ranger needed to stay and he needed to leave or an innocent family would suffer a terrible fate. The son of Dorain was never one for physical affection, but he managed to pat Asher's forearm and offer a slight squeeze. It was the best he could do.

With Pig secured in the hold, Doran reluctantly came to stand by the port side. So weighed down was the dwarf that his fear of the ocean failed to rise through his own stormy thoughts. He looked down on his one-time companion. It felt wrong, to sail away and leave the ranger to be swallowed up by the monstrous island. How many years, decades even, would this haunt him? How many times would he return to this moment in his memory and wonder if he could have done something differently?

His fingers clenched around the wooden rail, his knuckles paling under the intense pressure. No, he said to himself. No. He would not, could not, leave Asher to die in this place. If there was even a scrap of honour left in his Heavybelly bones then he would find a way to free him. The how of that escaped him for now, but it did nothing to temper the determination he felt in that moment.

As the ship began to slip away from the dockside, the son of Dorain thought desperately of a way to communicate his intentions without alerting Viktor's dogs. He just needed the ranger to survive, to do whatever he must to see the day of Doran's return. Survive... The word stuck in his mind. Perhaps there was a way after all.

Prising his hands from the rail, the dwarf presented them to the ranger and chopped the edge of one into the palm of the other and then swept it across his outstretched fingers. He watched Asher intently, daring to hope that he remembered something of the sign language used by the northern Jarat. It had been months since that moment, in the freezing wastes of The Iron Valley, but it was the one phrase he recalled his companion had learned. He had only used the latter half of that phrase, a single word that Asher could wield like a flaming sword in the darkness of his inevitable torment.

It felt like an eternity passed between them, a time in which Doran's hope dwindled.

Eventually, the ranger gave him a single nod of the head and mimicked the hand signal.

Survive.

CHAPTER 20
HERE TO DIE

Scelda - Known as Gremlins to those who call The Shining Coast their home. Scelda, excellent climbers, burrow in and out of the white cliffs in the east. The people of Velia and Barossh, in particular, have started many a legend about these small creatures. Most of them are absolute twaddle, the spindled tales of storytellers with nothing better to do. Ask any along the coast and they will warn you of Scelda, the baby-snatchers! 'Tis ludicrous, of course, since these so-called Gremlins prefer to eat stone over meat. The only real threat these monsters have ever posed was nigh on three centuries ago, when they displayed a liking towards the hewn stone of Velia's walls. Small as they are, however—and none have ever been recorded as being taller than one's knee—it would take hundreds, if not thousands, to weaken Velia's walls. Still, if you piss the little bastards off you can imagine the bite these stone-eaters are capable of. Best kill them quick, eh?

A Chronicle of Monsters: A Ranger's Bestiary, 12th Edition, Page 227.

Old Bill, Ranger.

· · ·

Dragorn soon closed in on the ranger again, the gates and impressive port replaced by high walls and a bustling city. He held on to the crisp image for as long as possible, his feet mindlessly following his armed keepers through the chaos of the streets. Within that image he recalled Doran's hand gesture over and over again, as he departed over the waves of The Adean.

Survive, he had said. Easier said than done in a place like this, and that was without being pitted against all manner of men and beasts. And what did the dwarf even mean? That question burned in Asher but, worse still, it sparked something he knew better than to hold on to.

Hope.

How many had died across the eons clinging to such a nebulous tether? How many had been tormented horribly only to perish believing to the bitter end that something would come along and take them away from the dark? The sentiment had been scrubbed from the emotional index of every Arakesh, and from a young age too. No one was coming for them. No one would save them.

"*Grit your teeth,*" Nasta Nal-Aket would instruct. "*Embrace the pain. Fight to survive.*"

It had been some time since his old mentor's voice had rung so clear in his mind, but his words always came back with clarity. Now, more than ever, they held truth, for the dwarf would not prove to be his saviour. Only a fool would believe the son of Dorain was coming back, having hatched some ludicrous plan to free him. Doran's feet would touch Illian soil and he would taste his freedom once again. With that, he would vanish into the world, unlikely to give Asher a second thought until the centuries had piled up.

Though he believed that to be the truth of the matter, he also knew the dwarf cared about the Stormshields enough to make sure they were safe before returning to his old life. That was what really mattered, that was what the ranger held on to. Besides, Asher told himself on those dusty streets, he hadn't put himself into this situation thinking it was temporary. He would not go gently, but he would inevitably meet his end in that arena, just like the men whose lives he had ended.

But a spark there had been. A kindling of hope in the dark. It offered a glimpse of the future, any future, in which he was again in control of his destiny; the path his to choose.

How the dwarf would rescue him he did not know and that, in itself, was a thought that led him right back to Nasta's teachings. He could not imagine Doran saving him because there was no way to save him. As that sank in, Asher gritted his teeth until it hurt, the pain embraced as an old friend. He would fight because that's all he knew. And then, one day, he would fall on those sands as he was meant to. Maybe then, after suffering for so long, he would find peace.

As the arena swelled into view, even that sentiment grew weak, much like his hope.

Bidding farewell to the sun and its surrounding blue sky, the ranger let his head drop and entered the gloomy halls of his new prison. Where Darya had led before it was now Malak who instructed his direction. Darya, curiously, could now be found at the ranger's back. Asher decided it was a strategic development in light of recent revelations where his training was concerned.

He was returned to the same Novian cell, where Hyperia locks and Karathan-forged hinges and bolts would contain him. Darya herself kept the keys to the cell—they were taking no chances this time. The keys were not the only thing she possessed. Poking out of her left pocket was the end of his blindfold, the red easily noted against the black of her long coat. The Shadow Witch caught him looking at it and removed the length of fabric, there to dangle it beyond his reach.

"What are you without this?" she questioned, an edge to her melodic tone. "You Arakesh... Always so arrogant. You believe all pale in your shadow—"

"We don't make shadows," Asher interrupted. Even as he said it he regretted it; an immature response that had been just as ingrained in him as hand-to-hand combat. Then there was his use of *we*. How could he have referred to himself as an Arakesh? The ranger couldn't help feeling there was more filth on him in that moment than there was clinging to his cell.

Like a viper, Darya hissed and stepped closer to the bars as if baiting him. "You poison your veins with elven magic and think you can call yourselves the best assassins in the world."

Asher's stoical expression faltered, betraying his surprise.

"Yes," the daughter-of-none purred. "The League knows about the origins of your elixir. Playing with elven alchemy doesn't make you the best. It makes you *weak*."

She didn't know the *whole* truth, Asher decided. The League of Silk and Ink believed Nightfall was merely dallying with elven secrets. If only they knew of Alidyr Yalathanil, an elf of unknown centuries who had been present for Nightfall's inception. For most, meeting an immortal of the old world would be the greatest honour of their life, a story they would pass down the generations. Asher had wished more than once that he had never met the cruel elf or tasted the addictive elixir of his making.

"Perhaps you are right," he replied, his words surprising enough to take some of the venom out of the Shadow Witch's expression. "But neither of us can escape the truth of what we are." Asher locked her dark eyes with his. "Killers," he said, with dripping derision.

Darya's smooth head tilted to one side. "Why would you want to be anything else?" she asked.

Her response was unexpected and kept the ranger from forming any argument.

"What a broken little bird you are," the Shadow Witch continued patronisingly. "It is one thing to walk your own path, but quite another to forget what you are. What you will *always* be." Darya's eyes roamed over the cell. "In here, you will forget again. Whatever you have become, whatever you have made of yourself, it will fade. From now till the day you drop dead in the arena, there will only be the next fight."

Asher dwelled on how little she knew him. The latter was all he had ever known. Still, he did not correct her. Instead, he held her gaze until she walked away, taking the guards with her.

Left with some food and water, the rest of the day trickled by without further event. The ranger paced what little floor he had, sat in every corner, and pulled on every bar. There was nowhere left to explore and no weaknesses to exploit. And so he slept, if only in brief intervals and, even then, very lightly.

After untold hours of boredom, the ceiling was set upon by thunderous waves that rained dust upon the ranger. The cacophonous sound of voices accompanied the barrage until it became the background noise of Asher's existence. Only when the cheering began did he know for sure that the evening's games had begun in earnest. There were peaks and troughs in the crowds' excitement and, every now and then, he heard the distinct sound of some beast unleashing its roar.

When, at last, he saw another face, it was that of Malak. He entered with a broad grin and several thugs at his back, all of whom were laughing at some unheard joke. Malak's amusement increased at the sight of the ranger.

"Well if it isn't the myth, the legend, the bogeyman himself!" he announced mockingly. "You're looking a little cooped up in there, mate. Maybe I'll throw you in with the Sandstalkers for a bit. They'll give you a run around." His fellow goons found the empty threat hilarious.

Asher simply stared at him, a lion waiting for the opportune moment to strike. "I'm wondering," he eventually said, his voice and tone carefully measured, "what punishment Viktor would exact on his new champion if I were to put my thumb through your eye." Such musings wiped Malak's grin off his face.

"Easy, little man," Malak bade, daring to come within a few inches of the bars. "If you're a naughty boy the master's going to send for that lovely little family of dwarves. I'll be sure to personally cut them up in front of you."

The ranger let his imagination do what it did best and run through vivid scenarios in which he brutally murdered Malak. Then, upon returning to reality, he unclenched his fist and reluctantly let go of his mounting anger. For all the thug's posturing and empty threats, he wasn't wrong about the leverage Viktor held over him.

Offering no retort, he stood up and held his arms out, wrists pressed together. "I'm assuming it's my turn," he said, flicking his head towards the arena. A part of him was hoping that to be true, for he desperately needed somewhere to put his rage and fury.

"Your time's coming, mate," Malak told him, his hungry grin reaching for his eyes. "But not tonight. Bind him," he commanded of the others.

Asher made no protest, though he enjoyed watching the men try to mask their squirming as they bound his wrists and escorted him from the cell. They marched him through the labyrinth, avoiding the public areas, and up two levels. Here, there was a notable increase in security, with stairwells and hallways under the watchful eyes of Viktor's guards. With Malak in the lead, however, they were given no scrutiny and allowed open access.

As they walked down a particularly wide corridor, the only one to have been dressed with grand statues of muscled fighters and sculptures of various monsters, the door at the far end opened and torchlight poured out. Amicable chatter could be heard before Asher glimpsed Viktor Varga clasping a man's forearm. They were momentarily obscured by obvious guardsmen, though not men under Viktor's employ by their appearance. Uniformed in well-fitted armour that cut off at the shoulders, these guards wore iron helmets that cut a triangle down to their chins. Their job, it seemed, was to ensure the hallway was clear of threats before their lord exited the chamber.

"...and please," Viktor was saying, "give my humblest regards to Lady Trigorn. I shall have something special for her visit," he added with a mischievous smirk.

Asher was brought to a halt and directed to one side by numerous hands. He observed Malak's rigid stance, as if the big man was trying to blend in with the statues that lined the walls. Here was a man who knew when he was the little fish, Asher thought. That made him pay close attention to the man entering the hallway. He was a few inches taller than Varga and, like the crime lord, his clothes spoke of wealth but his posture and demeanour spoke of an elevated position. Were they in Illian, the ranger would assume the man to be royalty or a Lord at the very least. On Dragorn, however, it simply meant he was a ruthless criminal with significant wealth.

His hair was a shade of blond so vibrant he couldn't possibly have been born to natives of Dragorn. The man flashed a smile at Viktor and revealed a long front tooth that resembled a fang. It was the man's only imperfection, though he made no effort to conceal it.

"Thank you for the entertainment, Viktor," the wealthy stranger replied on his way out. The ease with which he wielded Varga's name compounded his high station. "My Lady will grace your house of blood soon, I'm sure." The stranger's cloak of cerulean blue swept out behind him as he strode away, his armoured guards stepping to keep him perfectly centred between them. He paid Asher and the others no attention, as if they weren't even there, but Asher paid everyone around him the utmost attention. The details mattered. In the case of this man, the most important detail was the brass pin he wore on the exterior of his cloak, where it crossed his chest. A closed fist with a coin resting flat on top. He was a Trigorn. The ranger didn't know what he was to do with this knowledge, but he certainly wasn't going to forget it.

A beckoning gesture from Viktor saw the ranger manhandled down the remainder of the hall and into the chamber beyond. Varga had already turned away before they entered, his attention turned to the open balcony that looked out over the arena. Darya stood to one side, her form naturally finding the available shadow in the room. Lounging on one of the plush sofas was the same mage who had earlier that day restrained the Lumber Dug. Her level of comfort suggested she was, perhaps, more than just another tool at Viktor's disposal.

"Leave," the crime lord commanded casually. "All of you," he added, turning his head towards Darya without actually laying eyes on her. The Shadow Witch hesitated, throwing Asher a wary glance. "I will be fine," Viktor assured, a subtle gesture cast towards the second mage in the room, hooded in shadow and standing sentinel in the corner. "Besides, Asher here poses no threat to me. Isn't that right?" he asked, finally pivoting to see the ranger.

Images of Deadora Stormshield filled Asher's mind. He gave an affirmative bow of the head.

Satisfied, Viktor returned his gaze to the arena below while the chamber was emptied of surplus occupants. Darya slowed as she passed the ranger, her eyes threatening a painful death should he try anything foolish. Of course, a single day in Nightfall's dark halls would redefine the meaning of a painful death for the Shadow Witch—not that he intended to tell her as much.

As the door closed behind her, leaving the two men and the silent mage alone, Asher felt a surge within him, as if the Arakesh was stepping out of his body and reaching to break Viktor's neck. The mage would surely kill him, and swiftly too. The ranger pressed his nails into the palms of his hands and used the pain to regain some mental fortitude. There was something about being in this place that gave the *Assassin* more power over him. He realised then the utter truth in Darya's earlier warning—Blood and Coin would be the death of the *Ranger*.

"Come, come," Varga urged, a hand out to guide the ranger to his side. "You won't have come across this on your travels," he promised.

Asher studied the crime lord as he moved to the railing. Though their surroundings were adequately illuminated by the torches and hearth in the middle of the room, true sunlight was better for discerning the presence of a mage's shield. The mage's presence, however, was confirmation enough that the crime lord was well protected.

"Do you know what they are?" Viktor asked, his question leading the ranger to the battle below.

Still distracted by murderous thoughts, Asher required another moment to focus on the fight taking place on the arena sands. Looking down over the heads of hundreds, he spotted first a three-legged creature, its flesh a putrid green and mottled red. Three bony limbs extended from its narrow rib cage, one of which protruded from the centre of its chest and ended with three serrated claws. A slender neck rose up to a head of nightmarish features. Asher had never come across one in the wild, but he had seen the drawings, always depicting its head like an open flower.

A flower it was not.

Every petal, as it were, had row upon row of curved fangs and suckers that would drag everything in towards a smaller circular mouth of teeth.

"It's a Yarxal," he determined, much to Viktor's glee.

"You're quite right! And the other?"

Not far from the Yarxal, another predator of the wilds lurked on the sands. The ranger identified it immediately as one of the Sandstalkers Malak had recently threatened him with. The creature stomped its six pointed legs, producing small plumes of sand about it. Its spider-like body rose up at one end and formed a torso not unlike that of a man, with two well-muscled arms that extended from the shoulders. That was where any similarity ended. Those arms ended in five long protrusions of sharp bone that had been known to pierce steel. Like the Yarxal it was pitted against, its head was not for the faint-hearted. Continuing its spider-like qualities, the Sandstalker's head was a terrifying amalgamation of man and arachnid, with gleaming fangs dominating its jaw.

Asher named the beast and Viktor praised his knowledge. "What's your coin going on?" he enquired, as if they were no more than spectators standing next to each other.

Had he any coins, Asher knew, he would shove them down Varga's throat until he choked on them. His murderous fantasies aside, the ranger considered the question. Indeed, Viktor had been right about the spectacle of it for neither monster would ever encounter the other in their natural habitats. Sandstalkers preferred hot and dry climates while Yarxals were rarely found outside of swamps. Considering the torrid weather of Dragorn's summer, the latter would be extremely uncomfortable and disorientated.

"The Sandstalker is going to win," Asher stated confidently.

Viktor pursed his lips and folded his arms. "Why do you say this?"

"The Sandstalker is in its element," the ranger explained.

"But the Yarxal is equal in size," Viktor posed, "perhaps even strength."

Asher gave a subtle shake of his head. "It doesn't matter. The Yarxal won't be able to penetrate the Sandstalker's hard exterior. And it doesn't have the Sandstalker's speed. They're active predators—everything about them is designed to hunt down their prey and overcome it with sheer ferocity. Yarxals are natural trappers. They wait for their prey to stumble across them and..."

The ranger trailed off as the Yarxal's outer arms braced the Sandstalker's out wide, preventing it from bringing those pointed fingers to bear. While the Sandstalker looked to be steadily overcoming the Yarxal's strength, it was helpless to stop the Yarxal from engulfing its spider-like head with its enveloping petals. Suckers and teeth dug in and sealed off the Sandstalker's air supply. The two staggered from side to side, though it became obvious the Sandstalker was faltering, its back legs trembling. A minute went by in silence, the crowd subdued by the unexpected turn of events.

Unable to breathe, the Sandstalker dropped, its limbs and pincer legs hanging limp as it remained secured in the Yarxal's gruesome mouth. Having become the prey, the Sandstalker was subsequently drained of all its internal liquids, sucked out by the Yarxal.

"You see," Viktor gloated, "armour, speed, predatory skill... It guarantees nothing. The Yarxal knew what the Sandstalker needed more than anything." The crime lord held up a hand and clenched it into a fist. "And then it took it away."

Varga's message wasn't lost on Asher. Still, he didn't feel like bartering words with the madman, and so he continued to watch the Yarxal. The fight over, and many out of coin, two people, a man and woman, entered the arena from the side gate. The confidence with which they approached the monster informed the ranger that they were two more of Viktor's mages.

Its meal disturbed, the Yarxal released its prey, now a shrivelled husk within its chitinous shell, and turned on the obvious mages, its petal lips spread wide. The woman lashed her wand out, her spell a familiar glowing whip that coiled around the creature's neck. Her partner stepped closer to the beast and thrust his staff at it, the end exploding with a forceful mist and specks of ice. The Yarxal cried out in its strangely melodic and enticing voice, but the cold soon took it. Only seconds later and it had become sluggish and docile, making it all the easier for the woman to levitate the monster and guide it from the arena. The man performed the same spell and removed the Sandstalker's carcass.

"Do you know who that was?" Viktor asked, having walked away to pour himself a cup of wine so red it was almost black.

Slightly vexed by the sudden change in topic, Asher tore himself away from the view and faced the room as the crime lord was taking a seat in a plush armchair. The ranger glanced at the door, realising who Viktor was referring to.

"He's a Trigorn," Asher answered.

Viktor contorted his jaw. "Yes and no," he replied, with a vague clarification. "That was Lucas Farney, though he's known as *The Fang* in most circles." Varga tapped one of his front teeth. "By blood or name he cannot claim to be Trigorn, yet he is awarded all their privileges. He is awarded such because of his proven loyalty. When the Trigorns require someone to be intimidated or simply removed from the equation, they take Mr Farney's leash off. I hear he's quite the artist when it comes to his work." Viktor pointed a lazy finger at Asher. "Perhaps you have that in common," he added, as an afterthought.

It was tempting to consider the numerous *artistic* ways in which he could kill the man before him, but the ranger let them go... for now. "So," Asher surmised, "he would be the one sent after you should the Trigorns learn of your involvement in Serena's death."

As if a lever had been flipped, Viktor's jovial demeanour fell away, leaving something as still and hard as marble in its place. "What a peculiar web we have found ourselves in. That the gods could weave such a tapestry of events as to bring us together." Varga's grey eyes bored into him as the tension mounted. "Do you recall her death?" he finally asked, bringing the wine to his lips.

Again, Asher glanced at the door, where Lucas Farney had stood. This was why he had been brought here—the ranger had dangled Serena's death and now it was hanging over the crime lord.

"I do," he said, his voice catching.

Viktor's head twitched to one side, relaying his expectation for more.

"I snapped her neck," Asher reported, against the rising tide of guilt and shame.

Varga nodded as if satisfied, leading Asher to wonder if he had just been tested. "Did you enjoy it?" he enquired.

Asher's blazing gaze turned on the man. "No," he lied, well aware of the exhilaration he had felt after the deed had been done.

Viktor appeared to be analysing him. "I don't believe you."

The ranger held his captor's gaze. "And I don't care," he retorted.

Viktor put his wine down and opened his arms. "This is a safe place, Asher," he assured, his easy-going facade leading the way again. "In these walls, you can just be you. You don't have to pretend." The crime lord shrugged and gestured to the arena. "Like all the others who step onto those sands, you are here to die. Why not live out your final years being who you were meant to be?"

"Why am I here?" Asher demanded, irritated by the tedium of the conversation and rope binding his wrists.

"I just told you," Viktor said, wandering back towards the railing. "You're here to die. Not before I make some coin first, of course..."

"Why have you had me brought *here*?" the ranger specified.

"Concerned I won't take your secret to the grave?" It was subtle, but Varga's right eye twitched. He wasn't accustomed to being spoken to by someone who didn't either fear or respect him.

"Do you know who she was?" Viktor asked, again avoiding the mention of Serena's name as well as answering Asher's question. "Do you know who she was to Lady Trigorn? That is, Lady Isabella Sorgova Trigorn, the sitting head of the *entire* Trigorn commerce guild."

"*Commerce guild?*" Asher echoed with a scoff. "I thought you said we didn't have to pretend here?"

Viktor added an easy shrug to his equally easy smile. "Theirs is a dynasty of criminals that predates even my own—though I like to think we didn't all start out that way. Besides, referring to one's business as a *crime guild* is a little candid."

The ranger didn't care much either way. "Serena was a cousin or some such."

"She was Lady Trigorn's *favourite* niece," Varga informed him. "Daughter to her dead sister, the late Sybil Trigorn. Now *there* was a woman who could drink you under the table," he added with a chortle.

"You're afraid of the Trigorns," Asher concluded. With only a few words he had, again, brought an end to Viktor's genial manner.

The red wine flew from his cup and clashed with the fire of the hearth like a hissing beast. Swiftly, Varga moved to the table beside Asher and placed his cup upside down on the surface, trapping a spider as he did so. Its spindly legs could still be seen through the frosted glass that lined the rim of the cup.

"A Radonian Red-back," Viktor commented, his hand pressed down on the bottom of the cup. "Quite poisonous. It doesn't matter what deal you Arakesh have struck with Death, one bite would send you into its waiting arms within the hour." His cold grey eyes looked up at Asher. "But while I have it trapped here, the poison is harmless. Now isn't that better for everyone?"

"Not the spider," Asher pointed out.

"The spider is naught but a mindless animal. It has impulses and instincts and nothing else."

"Then why not kill it?"

Viktor's sniggering amusement grew into a quiet laugh. "You believe you are the spider?" He laughed again, louder this time. "No, my dear ranger, *I* am the spider. The cup is the four ruling guilds of Dragorn. *This* is how they view me. A poisonous creature that, at any moment, could crawl out of the shadows and kill them. You see, over the years, I have acquired information, *secrets*, of what keeps their guilds so high on their pedestals. Now, as you can probably imagine, this places my house in a precarious position. I am, to many, a loose end. And so we have the *cup*. A prison of their making and with their hands always pressing down. It is, however, an *illusion*."

Varga lifted the cup and the spider scurried away, over the edge of the table.

"It is *my* illusion," Viktor elaborated. "I have spent a long time ensuring that all four guilds believe they hold power over me. I bow to their restrictions, I pay their taxes, and I bend the knee to each with a grand show of loyalty. But what I know could position them into open war by day's end."

"Then why haven't you?" Asher questioned. "You could rule the whole damn place then."

"Because it's bad for business," Viktor answered honestly. "Secrets, whispers in the dark, bargains struck behind closed doors... They are all tactics best used in a shadow war, such as the one this island has known since we settled here. I like it that way. Open, bloody war on the streets would be... well, *expensive*."

Seeing the city through Viktor's description, it seemed his was the controlling guild. Though how much of it was self-delusion remained to be seen from inside the crime lord's personal domin-ion. To Asher, however, a man who had navigated numerous underworlds across the realm, it wasn't too much of a stretch to believe Viktor's claims. It was often the secret-keepers of the world who put kings on thrones, orchestrated wars, and—in Dragorn's case—ran entire cities. But like so many of the world's power brokers, Viktor shared their weakness.

"And how expensive would it be," the ranger posed, taking aim at that weakness, "if Lady Trigorn discovered your role in her niece's death?"

Varga gave a devilish smile and wagged a finger at Asher. "You silver-tongued dog, you." He put his hands up as if placed at the point of a sword. "You've got me. You are free to go at once. Neither yourself or the lovely Stormshields will ever hear my name again, I swear it." The crime lord broke into hysterics, his face brightening to scarlet. "I admire your guile, I really do. It's exactly what I would do in your position." Viktor gave an overdramatic shrug. "It's what I do every day in fact. You find their secrets and you leverage them for everything they've got!"

Still laughing to himself, Varga took a seat on the cushioned sofa that overlooked the arena. "Sadly, the secret you find yourself in possession of is no secret at all. Who do you think charged me with Serena's demise?"

Asher put it together in moments, though the answer made little sense to him. "Lady Trigorn."

Viktor responded with his broad grin. "The very same."

"You said Serena was her favourite niece."

"And she was. But you mustn't think of Lady Trigorn as you would any other. Nor any of the guild heads for that matter," he continued, as if he wasn't one of them. "There is only one thing that matters, one thing that guarantees their survival, if not their luxury."

"Coin," the ranger stated.

"Coin," Viktor echoed, nodding his head, his eyes taken in by the new fight below—two gladiators locked in battle. "Sybil, her sister, was becoming something of a problem: a power struggle in the wake of their father's death. It wouldn't look good to have one so high up as Sybil killed, especially after their father's recent passing. So Lady Trigorn came to me and requested that I have her sister's attentions directed anywhere but the throne."

"So you had Nightfall murder her daughter."

"Technically," Viktor said, his finger coming up to point at the ranger, "I had *you* murder her, though it's all semantics, I suppose. Serena's death drove Sybil mad with more wrath than even the gods could conjure." The crime lord giggled at the memory of it. "She too came to me. Paid me handsomely to find her daughter's killer. I eventually pointed her to the Bolivar crime family. Ever heard of them?"

"Can't say I have," Asher replied, his stomach sinking with every fresh detail Varga provided.

"That's because Sybil had them wiped out—*all* of them. Families too. They were based out of Velia; controlled a valuable portion of the docks there. Of course, they're *my* docks now," he added smugly. "And you! You were perfect for the task," Viktor complimented offhandedly, as if Asher had been stood there waiting for such praise. "I needed an outsider, someone Sybil could never find and trace back to me. Not that it really mattered in the end," he said casually, crossing one leg over the other. "Only a year later and Lady Sybil caught the grey lung and died anyway."

Asher's stomach finally hit rock bottom. Viktor had laid it out, stripping the potential secret of any power it might have offered the ranger. Worse still, Serena's death had been for absolutely nothing. He had murdered that young woman in her prime for no more than the machinations of those too greedy to realise they already had the whole world in their hands. And, ultimately, it had left him with naught but blood on *his* hands.

"Have I answered the question to your satisfaction?" Viktor enquired. "I invited you here tonight so you wouldn't lose sleep wondering how you might use Serena's death to your advantage. I want you focused on the *fight*."

The crowd below roared as one, the final blow delivered to one of the duelling gladiators. Viktor smiled and applauded before rising from the sofa and making his way to the door. Upon opening it, Malak and his fellow goons stood to attention in the hall beyond, ready to take custody of the ranger.

"I have enjoyed our little chat," Varga beamed, one arm outstretched to indicate Asher should leave. "Think about how soundly the lovely Stormshields will be sleeping tonight. Perhaps that will give you some comfort, for tomorrow your new life begins in earnest."

Asher looked from Viktor to Malak before a subtle movement drew him to the floor. There, creeping between them was the Radonian Red-back, oblivious to the giant gods that stood observing it. The ranger made a point to step on it in front of Varga, their eyes catching in the wake of its extermination.

CHAPTER 21

HARD GROUND

Hell Hags - You best be having some years behind you before taking on a contract for a Hell Hag. One wrong move—or if you're too stupid to plan ahead—and you're Hag food. These wicked specimens of life call swamps their home, and the worse the better. If you can't see through the water or you feel the trees around you have gathered to defy the light, you're probably right in the middle of their lair.

Now, I've heard some talk of this evolution rubbish, as if monsters can change according to their environment, but no one can argue that Hell Hags were designed by the very scaled hands of demons themselves.

Atilan protect us.

To see a Hag from the shore, you would think you were watching some poor girl drowning in the swamp, even crying out for help, arms flailing. You'd be wrong. And if you dived into the water to save that girl, you'd be dead too. That girl—at least what you can see of her—is the humanoid bait that protrudes from the top of a Hag's back. The spider-like creature that dwells below the surface is a monster you wouldn't soon forget. They vary in size, but I've never seen one dredged out of the water that was smaller than my horse.

You can see below the numerous methods used against Hell Hags over the years but, more than anything, you're going to need a big set of lungs.

A Chronicle of Monsters: A Ranger's Bestiary, 12th Edition, Page 50.

Veador Hemsmith, Ranger.

T he moon, its crescent tips so sharp they could have been forged by dwarves, sat high upon its dark throne in the sky. Its appearances were brief, masked by the rushing clouds that swept over Velia and unleashed a torrent of rain upon its stone.

Doran thanked Grarfath and Yamnomora for the sight of the city, dismal as it was. For nearly eighteen hours he had suffered the to and fro of The Adean as The White Horse speared its way to the mainland.

The son of Dorain dashed for the ramp as soon as it touched the decking of the harbour, his strong hands shoving any and all aside. There was no stopping the turmoil inside his gut, however. The contents of his stomach forced their way up and out, splattering over the boards and into the black water that lapped against the struts of the jetty.

There came groans of disgust from various sailors and onlookers, but none louder than Doran's. "Sorry," he grunted, staggering across the decking. He was soon crawling on all fours until he could sit with his back to a crate and appreciate the lack of a sway.

Some time passed while moorings were seen to and copious supplies ferried from the vessel. The dwarf waited happily enough, content to be as still as possible for as long as possible. Eventually, the familiar squeals of his faithful Warhog found him, turning the dwarf to the open hold further down The White Horse.

"What a sorry sight we are, eh?" he put to the pig, which snorted and snuffled in response.

With deep breaths, Doran rose and found his feet, unsteady as they were. He had no intention of mounting the Warhog in his present condition, for the sway of the ride would upset his still sensitive stomach. Instead, he took Pig by the reins and guided the animal through Velia's port, where his boots finally touched rocky ground and he praised the Mother and Father all the more.

Entering the city via the eastern gate, the son of Dorain passed through the torchlight of a guard post. Velian soldiers, marked by the region's sigil—the howling wolf—cast suspicious glares over the dwarf. It never mounted to enough, however, that they gave up their game of Gallant, the slick cards played over a small dilapidated table.

Accepted into the city, its dark folds and harsh corners were empty for the most part, the late hour given over to vagabonds and street urchins bereft of a home. Taverns here and there continued to cater to the merry, with men and women stumbling out into the night, oblivious to the rain which fell in relentless sheets. Doran was merely thankful for the cool air and the lashing drops of cold rainwater, a far cry from the recent stifling weather on Dragorn.

It then struck the son of Dorain what little he had to his name. The Adean had swallowed up his weapons and armour, leaving him with naught but the clothes on his back, all of which had seen better days. Adding to his troubles, Pig's saddlebags had been picked clean by whoever had claimed him after The Mer Seed's violent arrival. The dwarf looked longingly at one of the taverns, its warm light beckoning him. It would not be a warm welcome, however, in the absence of coin. And being a dwarf, he decided, would probably only make things worse for him.

Doran came to a halt and sighed, the noise lost in the rain. Amidst the high walls of Velia, there was no escaping the fact that he was in the middle of civilisation, a place where coin and trade kept one alive. How was he to reach Darkwell without supplies or even a weapon with which to hunt and defend himself?

A young couple almost fell out of the nearest tavern, laughing arm in arm. Doran was tempted to ask them for help—just a coin or two—but asking for charity felt beneath him. Sometimes there was no getting away from the prince that dwelled within him, within his very blood. What descendant of Thorgen could ever beg for help, be it mercy or coin? Instead, he watched them pass him by, their laughter only increasing as they looked upon him and his obviously different stature.

It was there in the dark of night, his head sunk towards his chest and his clothes plastered to his skin, that Doran Heavybelly considered his pride. Unlike the pride that might plague most, be they human or dwarf, his was royal pride, a wholly different animal. It was a wall, as physical as any that guarded Velia's inhabitants, that stood between him and what he needed. Was it so beneath him to accept his dire situation and ask others for help? Even a coin or two would make a difference.

"Bah!" he growled, quashing his insecurities with anger.

The son of Dorain approached the next person to exit the tavern, an older man by the deep lines that shadowed his face and the knotted grey hair that fell over his cheeks.

"Might I bother ye for—" Doran's plea was cut short by some unintelligible interruption and a severe wave of the hand. The dwarf's jaw faltered in response to the rejection and notable derision. Still, he swallowed the response that came to mind and turned to the next patron departing the tavern. It was a younger man this time, alone and, perhaps, recently spurned by the expression etched into his youthful face. "I'm sorry to bother ye, lad, but might I—"

"What in the name of Atilan are you supposed to be?" the young man cut in, looking down on Doran as if he were a king faced by an ungrateful serf.

The beginnings of a harsh retaliation were on the tip of Doran's tongue, but something about the way he looked over him, to the streets beyond, gave the dwarf pause. When the young man slipped away, almost hugging the tavern wall as he did, the son of Dorain turned back to investigate.

Trouble was waiting for him. Just as he had suspected.

In a word, that was exactly what the five men loitering on the corner were. Two blocks down, they were easily seen through the curtain of rain, their features mostly concealed by hoods and their bodies hidden beneath cloaks and ponchos.

Doran tugged on Pig's reins. "Let's see where this goes, eh?"

Continuing up the street, away from the gang of menacing strangers, dwarf and Warhog followed Velia's outer wall until they came across an alleyway, its dimensions relatively suitable in Doran's eyes. A quick glance over his shoulder gave him a glimpse of the gang: they were certainly following him. The son of Dorain squared his jaw and entered the alley, guiding Pig to the other end, where a stone wall blocked the way.

Moments later, those same five men appeared at the mouth of the alley, there to be caught in one of the intermittent shafts of moonlight. Doran didn't miss the glint of steel amongst them.

To his left was the back door of some establishment. Doran gave the handle a hard pull to check that it was locked. "That should do," he muttered, knotting Pig's reins around it. "Ye sit this one out."

His attention soon returned to the hardy men. He could see that they had encroached into the alley and now blocked it from wall to wall. Doran could see the knuckle dusters, knives, and small clubs they had brought out.

"Evenin', lads," the dwarf greeted, friendly enough. "Now, the way I see it, ye're either too stupid to know what ye're gettin' into 'ere, or ye're under the heel o' Varga an' ye've got no choice. If it's the latter, I feel for ye, because I've seen what he does to his broken toys, an' well..." Doran shrugged. "I'm abou' to break all o' ye."

None gave away their true intentions, at least not beyond their proclivity for violence, and they certainly didn't take Doran's promise of injury seriously. The son of Dorain offered them a wry smile—hindsight could be painful.

Seeing the imminent fight coming his way, Doran reached for the axe that should have been on his belt. It was a good thing then, he decided, that Grarfath had seen fit to grant him two steel maces for fists.

The first to come at him wielded a knife, the serrated edge slashing through the rain drops to cut his face. Doran moved—

faster than his attacker had apparently anticipated—and let the blade thrust harmlessly past his left ear. A strong dwarven hand then seized the thug's wrist and squeezed like a smith's vice. A sudden jerk yanked the man towards him or, more specifically, towards his incoming fist. That mace of knuckles slammed into the thug's cheekbone with such force he was rendered unconscious before he dropped to the puddles.

The quick and seamless victory gave the remaining four good reason to hesitate. While they reassessed their target, Doran took the time to bend down and retrieve the fallen dagger.

"Who's next?"

The shortest of the four answered the question, lunging at him with his equally small club. The son of Dorain, a veteran of countless wars and skirmishes, deflected the meagre weapon with a simple backhand of his adopted knife. Going on the offensive, Doran then barrelled into his foe, though not before sinking the blade into the short man's right leg. His immediate cry of pain was terminated when he fell to the ground, there to be buried beneath the dwarf. A swift impact from Doran's forehead sent the thug into blissful oblivion.

A hard kick was planted into the dwarf's ribs, shoving him off the man and into the adjacent wall. In the process, he lost his hold of the knife, still lodged in the leg of the other. Looking up through the rain, he belatedly glimpsed a blurry figure descend upon him with another powerful kick, this time to the head. Were he a man, such a blow would have robbed him of all sense.

But Doran Heavybelly was no man.

He stopped the next kick with his arm and managed to reach up as that same attacker brought a knife down on him. The dwarf intercepted his enemy's wrist with only a few inches between his neck and the tip of the blade. Still, even with two hands pressing down on the hilt, there was little the man's strength could do against the iron will of a Heavybelly dwarf.

"I've had enough o' ye, laddy." With his free hand, Doran slapped his palm into the side of the thug's face and shoved his head into the wall.

The man's weight fell over him as the last two advanced with knuckle dusters and a club. With the length of his body pressed to the alley wall, the son of Dorain had but one direction to go. Taking a firm hold of the man on top of him, the dwarf rolled towards his foes. The wretch wielding the club tripped over them and landed where Doran had been lying, while the other managed to jump aside at the last second.

The soldier in Doran told him the knuckle duster was his immediate priority; the man still on his feet. Of course, the dwarf couldn't see him through the blond hair rain-plastered to his face.

As his weight fell upon his feet again, that first blow of steel caught him in the jaw and nearly sent him back to the ground. Staggering to the alley wall, his jaw already throbbing, he finally swept the hair aside only to see another steel-ridged fist coming his way. The second punch landed with success and closed his right eye while also sending him reeling into Pig.

The Warhog had been fighting its restraints the entire time, testing the strength of the locked door. Seeing its only companion of many years bloodied and bruised gave the animal a new and raw well of rage. The handle and some of its surrounding wood burst out, rending the whole door, as Pig charged.

The thug saw what was coming for him all too late. He slipped and skidded in the puddles in his bid to turn and run, though even on a dry night he would never have outpaced a dwarven Warhog. Unforgiving tusks brought the man down and ensured the local watch would find at least one body come the morning.

Seeing his dead comrade beneath a seemingly wild hog, the last thug and his club decided the fight wasn't worth his life. Keeping as far away as he could from Pig, the man bolted for freedom.

"Come 'ere!" Doran growled.

The dwarf leapt the gap between them and tackled his fleeing enemy to the ground with powerful arms wrapped around his waist. Squirm and writhe as he might, there was no getting away from the son of Dorain when his weight was bearing down. Doran roughly turned the man over and snatched the club from his hand before holding it threateningly high.

"What are ye abou'?" he demanded of the thug. "Who sent ye? Hmm?" The club's position above them both was adjusted, increasing the threat of it. "Speak boy!"

"Get off me!" came the protest, his efforts to break free doubled.

Doran bought the club down but not to strike his foe. Instead, he placed it horizontally over the man's neck and pressed down with both hands. "Was it Viktor?" he fumed. "Were ye sent by Viktor Varga to kill me?" The response was garbled as both the club and the pouring rain obstructed the man's ability to breathe. Doran let up, but only a notch. "Answer me," he growled, "an' yer head won' end up inside the mouth o' me pig."

"Undvig," was the rasp that came back.

"Undvig?" the son of Dorain spat, the name unknown to him.

"Undvig," the thug tried again, his airway almost entirely blocked.

"An' who is this *Undvig* exactly?"

The man desperately pawed at Doran's forearms and the dwarf relented another notch. "Mage! He's a mage!"

Doran sighed. "So Viktor then," he concluded, lending the name all the disdain he could muster. "If this Undvig don' skin ye alive, laddy, ye tell 'im Doran Heavybelly's a free dwarf." Lifting the club, he backhanded the man across the temple, striking him unconscious.

Rising from his crouch, Doran slumped against the nearest wall and caught his breath, feeling the pains of his new injuries setting in. Come the morn, his face would be black and blue with swellings like hillocks distorting his features. A small price, he decided, for walking away with his life. The man beneath Pig could not boast such a thing.

Taking in the sight of the others, there was no missing the scattered coins that rattled under the barrage of rain. They had spilled out from his purse when the first man had struck the ground.

Doran's hungry eyes examined the other men, noting that each possessed a similar purse knotted to their belts.

"Would ye look at that, Pig," the son of Dorain remarked, pushing off from the wall with some renewed vigour. "It seems our luck's on the turn."

Gathering a few of the weapons and all the coins, Doran stored them in the Warhog's saddlebags and departed the alleyway. Before he lost sight of them, however, he turned back to look at the men Viktor had sent to put him in the ground. Word had clearly been sent ahead of his arrival, be that communication by magic or bird.

It was then, more than ever, that he felt the need for urgency. If Viktor could break his end of the deal to see *him* dead, he would certainly break it further and fulfil his threat to murder the Stormshields, and all so that he might make an example.

And how would Asher know from within the confines of his cell?

A righteous growl rumbled deep in the son of Dorain's throat. He would not stand for the treachery.

"Come along, Pig," he bade, leading the Warhog from the alley. "I think we've a few more skulls to crack before we see the end o' this."

CHAPTER 22

HOME SWEET HOME

Royal Gobber - *I'm sure you will agree that slaying Gobbers is nothing short of fun for the experienced and exhilarating for the recruits, but—and there is a but my fellow rangers—a Royal Gobber is a completely different beast.*

Coming in at somewhere between seven and eight feet, these behemoths are sheer walls of muscle, rage, and speed.

Not much is known about them, though we believe they are asexual creatures and responsible for hatching the lesser Gobbers that trail them. Like I say, we believe. This is only a theory and there are many credible theories where these beasts are concerned. I've heard it said that the Royal Gobbers serve to impregnate some kind of Queen Gobber, though there has never been any proof that such a monster exists.

When it comes to killing these things, well, you just need to know your way through the beats of a good fight. They don't go down easily, being known for taking a damn good beating before giving up. Personally, I found a nice heavy axe to the skull did the trick. On the third swing.

A Chronicle of Monsters: A Ranger's Bestiary, 12th Edition, Page 172.

Mosef Gibbs, Ranger.

"Wakey, wakey, mate!" Those three words, all from the mouth of Malak, cut through Asher's meditative rest.

Leaning against the bars, Viktor's chief thug flashed a broad smile of yellowing teeth. Behind him were five more of his ilk, each wielding a weapon. He was to be escorted somewhere then. The rattle of keys and the sound of bolts retracting into their locks almost set the ranger's instincts off.

In any other circumstance, this would be his moment of escape. In the few seconds that had passed he had already devised the swiftest methods to neutralise all six combatants. Two of them would die—unavoidable. Three would be maimed for life, their injuries preventing them from finding decent work ever again. The last would wake up with a severe concussion and question his own identity for a few hours.

Deadora's bloody face sat squarely in front of Asher's vision, her last and dying expression one of great pain. It was enough to quieten the *Assassin's* voice in his mind and stay his hands.

"Today marks the beginning of the end," Malak declared, sliding the gate aside. The thug looked purposefully at the ranger's hands and raised his eyebrows. "Wrists," he ordered.

Soon after, Asher was being marched through the arena's labyrinth of hallways and up to the third floor. A pair of guards noted their approach and unlocked the double doors at their back, letting the light in.

Asher narrowed his eyes against the blinding touch of the sun, though he could still see the bridge before him. The rails were higher than the norm and adorned with small spikes where anyone might place their weight to jump over the side. Its entire length was sheltered by a flat roof that was in need of repair. With a man either side, a hand gripping his arms, the ranger walked across the bridge and got a glimpse of the city below. Dragorn was a mass of activity, a chaos that could only be understood by those born and raised on the island. Before he could take in even a portion of what was going on, they had passed through another set of double doors that granted entrance to the building behind the arena.

While the noise of Dragorn was soon left behind, it was quickly replaced by a different kind of ruckus. It opened old memories for Asher, taking him back to his youth in Nightfall.

Malak continued to lead the way, bringing the ranger to a narrow walkway that followed the interior of the new building and its rectangular shape. Trained to think and observe in a particular way, he first noticed the guards stationed regularly all the way around. Like the arena, it had no roof to keep out the oppressive summer sun and its central floor was covered in baking sand.

Tracking that familiar sound to its source, Asher looked upon dozens of men fighting in pairs across the sand. The sounds they made—the grunts and laboured breaths—were those that had accompanied his training, but the clash of their weapons was that of wood against wood. In Nightfall, the ranger recalled with pained memory, the Arakesh sparred only with steel so they might know its bite and learn never to flinch.

"Home sweet home!" Malak exclaimed with open arms. "Come. Let's introduce you!"

After passing through two more locked gates and being escorted down the steps, Asher was standing on the sands of the training arena. The fighting had come to a stop and those that had been sitting lazily around the arena's edges stood up to stare at the newcomer.

"Morning, gents!" Malak shouted, drawing them in all the more. "This is Asher!" he continued, stepping aside to present the ranger like a new piece of meat for them to enjoy. "He's the reason Tyvarnus and the rest haven't come back!" The thug laughed to himself before elaborating, "He made a bloody mess of them, he did! Anyway..." Malak slapped him on the back. "Be sure to make him feel at home!"

"DID I SAY STOP?" The berating question turned Asher to his

right, while the rest of Viktor's indebted and Dragorn's most damned renewed their one-on-one battles.

The man approaching from the right was a veteran of many fights, evident by the tapestry of scars he so proudly wore. The most evident, of course, was the patch concealing his left eye, though what ruin lay beneath remained to be seen. His bald head was far from smooth, with dents and ravines stretching across the scalp. The tone of his skin was that of Darya's—another of Viktor's collection pieces from The Arid Lands perhaps.

Upon reaching Asher, the man could now be seen to be a foot smaller than the ranger and was possibly two decades his senior. In a simple tunic, however, his broad shoulders pulled the fabric taut to reveal the landscape of his muscled torso. Asher's first guess placed the man as once being a soldier in the emperor's army, his rank high enough that he had tasted command.

Malak sighed and made no effort to hide it. "This is Kad Gorson, the magistri here. He'll tell you when to eat, sleep, and bleed."

Gorson placed himself directly in front of Malak. "We've been here before, you and I," he began, unwavering in his hard stare. "Out there, you can do whatever it is mad dogs do. But in here," he said, a thumb pressed back into his own chest, "Mr Varga has given me complete control. So don't come in here and give these boys cause to question my authority." He gave Asher no more than a cursory glance. "Why are you parading this one?" he demanded.

Malak looked to be swallowing his pride as he was, once again, put in his place by another of Viktor's organisation. "He's the assassin—"

"I know *who* he is," Kad interrupted, finally looking the ranger in the eyes. "Mr Varga has already spoken to me about him. I was also told that he is not to be... *broken in*." The magistri eyed Malak again. "You dangling him like bait makes that all the harder."

Maintaining his stoical demeanour, Malak spat on the ground beside Gorson. "Just have him ready to fight," he sneered, before facing Asher. "His first match is tomorrow tonight," he added with a sharp smirk.

"I require no instruction," Kad replied evenly, his arm outstretched to show Malak the way out.

Asher watched the brute leave the same way they had entered, but his attention was stolen by Kad Gorson when the man drew a small knife from his belt. The blade cut through the ranger's bindings, as all the while its owner explored every facet of Asher's blue eyes.

"Come with me, *assassin*."

The title wasn't appreciated but Asher followed the magistri all the same. Though training had resumed, the ferocity had calmed down enough for the individual fighters to get a better look at the new inmate. Some tried to pick him apart with scrutiny, looking at him as they puckered their lips in a kiss, an attempt to display their superiority. These were the fighters, the men who, for whatever reason, had found themselves in Viktor's arena and didn't shy away from the brutality of it all.

It was these men that made the *others* stand out. Amidst the natural gladiators were those who had lived relatively ordinary lives until their debt had landed them in this hell. They were scrawny and timid or old and meek; resigned to a submissive lifestyle until they were thrown to the wolves in the real arena.

If only it *were* wolves.

Brought to an empty cell, one of many that lined the floor of the training ground, Kad nodded at the pathetic excuse for a bed. "This is you. When you're not training this will be your whole world. You get three meals a day and all the water you need. Step out of line and that will all change dramatically. You should know, there are no weapons over here." Asher thought of the steel blade on the magistri's hip and knew that wasn't an accurate statement. "Everything is kept in the armoury across the way, where you'll be equipped before your fights."

Asher heard it all but he was meeting the many glares of his fellow gladiators, his own assessment ongoing.

"It's at this point I would usually recommend keeping to yourself," Kad advised. "Making friends in here is a bad idea. Makes it all the harder when it comes down to you or them. But Mr Varga told me about you, about what you *are*. I get the feeling you don't need such a recommendation."

"You'd be right," Asher said, noting one man in particular, his eyes blazing with animosity where the ranger was concerned.

"Mr Varga fancies you his new champion," Gorson went on in his Karathan accent. "The title comes with privileges. You don't have to share this cell with anyone. It's also the only one with four walls and a door. Once a week you're allowed a *visitor* at night, though you don't get a choice; it's just whoever the local brothel send. After every fight, you have the option to bathe, alone I might add. You'll soon come to learn that solitude is hard to come by in here. Appreciate it while you can."

Seeing so many indentured men sparring on the training ground hammered that home to him. There would be little to no privacy—the idea of being seen at all times was disturbingly uncomfortable. Asher entered his new abode, a lion shuffling into its cage.

"What are you doing?" Kad questioned, turning the ranger back. "Sun's up. Hit the sand, assassin." The magistri stepped aside, clearing the short path from Asher's cell to the training ground.

"You said you know what I am," the ranger reminded.

"There are no exceptions," Gorson told him. "You're either catching your breath or training."

"I don't need to train."

"No exceptions," Kad repeated.

Asher's protest was worn in his expression, though he still exited his cell and moved to the edge of the training ground, where the sand was contained by a lip of stone. "That one wishes me dead," the ranger remarked, indicating the gladiator who continued to relay his violent intentions through a cold hard stare.

"That's Baal," Kad informed him. "Tyvarnus was his brother."

There was that name again. "He was the champion before me," Asher concluded.

"You met him in the arena I believe. Big man." Gorson nodded his chin at Baal. "He had no love for his brother, but blood's blood.

First chance he gets he's going to kill you. So will others, those who would rather not face you in the arena. Killing a man is easier in here."

"They are welcome to try," Asher commented.

Kad cocked his head to look up at the ranger with his only eye. "Mr Varga has impressed upon me the importance of your health. It seems he has big plans for you. I'll do what I can but it's a jungle in here and I can't be everywhere. I'll tell the guards as much but that's no guarantee."

Asher regarded the magistri. "I too can offer no guarantees."

Kad groaned to himself. "Just keep your head down and try not to stray from the training ground alone. I don't want bodies showing up all over the place." The magistri began to walk away, pausing only to issue one last command. "Pick up a practice sword, assassin."

The ranger turned to the rack against the far wall, where several dozen wooden swords rested. Many were stained with old blood, proving that most objects were a weapon in the right hands. Asher examined six of them before choosing the sword with the fewest chips in its edges.

The shape and size were similar to his broadsword, though they were all single-handed. The feel of it was all wrong, the weight and balance simply off. He missed the monster-killing weapon he had wielded for the last four years, now lost to The Adean or salvaged by another.

"SWITCH!" Kad Gorson bellowed.

Half of the fighters rotated to their left, the choreography having been predetermined by the magistri no doubt, and faced a new combatant. Asher watched them move through their routines before attempting to score the killing blow as it were. Though accustomed to violence, none displayed the discipline born of regimented training outside of the techniques the magistri had shown them. It was in their fighting, however, that the ranger knew his hunch had been right about Gorson's origin—their attacks and defences were taken straight from Karath's army. It was a style of fighting Asher had only seen in the southern empire. Not that it explained how Kad Gorson had wound up in Viktor's pocket to begin with.

"Water?"

The question took Asher from the fighting and to the man on his right, a figure that had been lurking on his periphery for several minutes. Laying eyes on the man, the ranger had to wonder if calling him such was an overestimation. He couldn't have seen twenty summers yet and his frame suggested he hadn't seen twenty hot meals either. Asher took the offered waterskin and put the rim to his nose first, searching for any notes of poison. Detecting none, he drained the skin, quenching the thirst he had tried to ignore.

"I'm Mouse," the young man said, his voice befitting of the name.

"I didn't ask," Asher replied, handing the waterskin back.

The humanity that had taken root in him over the last four years yearned to make a connection with the young man, to enquire of his name and history, to protect him even, for he surely needed it in a place like this. But what room was there for humanity in this gods forsaken hell? If Mouse wasn't to be monster food he would meet his end by any other, Asher included.

Nevertheless, the ranger's focus sharpened to a point when Mouse was shoved aside, replaced by a shirtless fool who believed his chiselled physique made him intimidating. His long hair scrunched into a knot at the back of his head, the gladiator was two inches taller than Asher and he enjoyed every inch of it as he looked down his nose. So close was he that a stale breath, tainted by old fish, washed warm over the ranger's face. At the man's back were two others, equally muscled and equally beguiled by their own appearance.

"Assassin," the gladiator considered, drawing out the title. "My name is Grift. You should remember it well, for when you arrive at the feet of the gods and they ask you how you got there, it will be my name you utter."

Asher heard every word, despite the fact that his attention had wandered to another man not far away. He was sitting on the ground, in the corner of the courtyard, his hands hanging limp over his bent knees. While everyone else had turned to watch the encounter Grift had instigated, this other man continued to stare dead ahead, his sight lost to space and time. His long dark hair was matted with sweat and his black goatee was neatly trimmed—an unusual sight among the dishevelled lot that occupied the training ground. Like Kad Gorson, this man obviously hailed from The Arid Lands.

It was more than just his appearance, however, that pulled Asher in. There was something more to the stranger, a quiet resolve about him that spoke of a very different background to those he shared this hell with.

"You like hiding in the shadows?" Grift had continued. "Stabbing folk in the back when they're not looking." The fool chuckled to himself. "We've had assassins in here before. They don't last. There's no place for blades in the dark. In here, on the sand, you face your opponent and—"

Asher powered his head forward, driving it into the gladiator's chest. It took the air from him and launched the ignorant halfwit into the pair behind. One of the two, the only one to have stayed on his feet, moved on the ranger with a closed fist. That same fist was knocked away but not by Asher. Kad Gorson had emerged from the sand and caught the gladiator's knuckles with a wooden baton. His second strike was swift and merciless, impacting him in the centre of the chest. Now, like the one who had tried to intimidate Asher, he too was on the ground struggling for breath.

Swifter still did the magistri turn on Asher, bringing the wooden baton to rest against his jaw. He left it there a while, his frustration ebbing out in waves of hot fury.

"You said to keep my head down," Asher quipped, breaking the tension.

Gorson sneered and shoved the ranger back before swivelling on the three gladiators. "Get up!" he barked. "You're going to lap the court until you drop. If you stop, *I* will drop you. Understand?"

All three nodded on their way back to their feet. The largest of the three was pressing a hand to his chest where Asher's head had made itself known. He gave the ranger a lasting look, a promise of retribution, but Asher had returned his attention to the quiet stranger in the far corner. Even the violence had failed to turn his head.

"And you!" Kad hissed, facing Asher again. "Hit the sand! Gemmel, you're out—get some water!"

The ranger looked for Gemmel and moved to take his place. He now stood opposite a man of similar height and weight to himself, though his morning had clearly been more taxing judging by the sheen of sweat that clung to him. He faced Asher in a crouching stance, his shoulders hunched, knees bent, and sword pointed at his foe. It was a good stance, but his eyes told the ranger exactly where he was going to put his sword. When the magistri commanded they begin again, Asher had only to deflect the side of the wooden blade and hammer the pommel into the man's face.

For the second time that day, he put someone on the ground.

It garnered more than a few onlookers, Kad Gorson included. Asher shrugged.

"SWITCH!"

Unsure what to do, the ranger stepped with those either side of him until he was facing a new opponent. The gladiator looked from Asher to the man cupping his nose on the ground beside him. With a hint of trepidation, he assumed the stance Gorson had drilled into him and presented Asher with a high sword, tightly gripped in both hands. When the order to begin came, shortly after Kad had instructed the injured gladiator to take himself off, that high sword came down on the ranger as only it could.

The ranger lunged forward and reached up to grab his opponent's wrist. It halted the downward stroke and left the gladiator's entire body exposed. Asher pummelled his sword hand into the man's gut, lifting him to his toes, before bringing his wooden blade around to strike at the back of his knees. Flipped the other way now, the gladiator landed hard on the top of his back. Again, the quick execution brought more attention down on the ranger. This time, however, he didn't shrug under the magistri's scrutiny but, instead, offered the man an expression that repeated his disinterest in training.

"SWITCH!" The word came out as a growl this time.

The next opponent watched the last crawl off the sand until his eyes inevitably found Asher waiting for him. The ranger stood with his practice sword held low, casually even. Judging by the tattoos that had been layered upon each other, stretching from his wrists to this jaw, this man had spent time in the employ of all four major crime guilds. From all his time working within their spheres of violence, it seemed he had developed an edge of arrogance when it came to fighting. He slapped his sword twice against the side of his head and roared.

Then Asher put a boot in his chest.

The impact displaced the sand before his body curled up like a closing flower. Coughing and spluttering inevitably followed, all between desperate breaths for air as the gladiator rolled from side to side. The ranger looked pointedly at Kad Gorson, questioning with his eyes alone how long the magistri would let this go on for. When Kad looked past Asher it turned the ranger around, his grip tightening around the wooden hilt. Baal was standing there, his own opponent having simply backed off. An empire of tension existed between them and pulled everyone's attention to it. Curiously, the vengeful gladiator remained where he stood, no more than a threatening sculpture of muscle.

"Baal!" Kad yelled on his way across the shady ground. "Get some water! Asher!" The magistri gestured to the ranger's cell. "Take a break! The rest of you, switch!"

Asher dropped his so-called weapon where he stood and made for his cell, careful to navigate the new bout of sparring. Gorson met him by the edge of the training ground and clasped one hand around the ranger's arm.

Conscious thought was required to prevent the reflexes that demanded he break the man's fingers.

"You've been out here five minutes, assassin," he hissed. "You might have training but most of these boys don't. It's my job to give them every fighting chance I can in that arena. Knocking them on their arse isn't going to help. They need real *instruction*."

With more care than he would normally give, Asher removed the hand around his arm and looked down at the magistri. "Your job is to make sure they don't die too *fast*," he corrected. "And what instruction does a man need when he's faced by one of those monsters your master keeps beneath the arena? I've fought all manner of creature in all manner of hell. Trust me; they don't have the time to learn anything that will keep them from the jaws of some *thing*. They're all going to die on that sand." The ranger entered his cell and took a seat on the cot.

Gorson held his gaze a moment longer. "And *you*, assassin," he pointed out. "There is no *them* and *you*. The arena devours *all* eventually."

Left with that searing truth, Asher stared at the blank wall of his cell and asked himself but one question. How many centuries would Deadora Stormshield enjoy for a few short years of his torment?

Whatever the answer, it was enough to give the weary ranger some peace of mind.

CHAPTER 23

GETTING OUT OF DODGE

Cruxta *- Wherever the dead have fallen, these monsters will be sure to appear. They move in small packs of three or four, all with a nose for the stench of rotting flesh. Make no mistake, though Cruxta prefer the taste of the dead, they will settle for the living. If there is a big enough battlefield, where chaos reigns, they have even been so bold as to begin feasting amidst the fighting. It should also be known, if the battle goes on and on, that more packs will arrive. This can be advantageous as the packs will consider each other rivals and fight amongst themselves.*

I have to say, in most cases, we rangers are not called upon in these circumstances. The last contract I accepted for a pack of Cruxta was in an old crypt just outside of Kelp Town. This is more typical for our line of work.

If it's possible, I would recommend hunting them during the day, while they sleep in their nest (see A Charter of Monsters, Page 301, for typical locations).

Don't however, think that light and dark will have a part to play beyond their natural sleep periods. Cruxta have no eyes but rather a whole face of nostrils. And a mouth. A very big mouth in fact. I should probably have mentioned the mouth earlier. Anyway, back to the nostrils. Always approach from up wind.

A Chronicle of Monsters: A Ranger's Bestiary, 12th Edition,
Page 35.

Kalem Bifson (oldest ranger on record).

There was no mirror in the closet-like room, but Doran didn't need to see his reflection to know there were lumps and bumps on both his face and ribs. His stubby fingers probed a particular bruise beneath his right eye, the touch enough to make him flinch. The dwarf cursed Viktor Varga, the treacherous wretch.

With only enough room to stand on the spot, Doran donned his clothes—a simple shirt and breeches. Both were partially damp from the rain the previous night. The shirt, off-white in its colour, also possessed spots of blood here and there. With nothing else to wear, however, the dwarf got on with it and scooped up the purse of scavenged coins on his way out.

With meaningful strides, he made his way downstairs and bid the owner of the inn his farewell. It had taken some time to find anywhere that would take his coin at such a late hour and, even then, the room he had been offered was not a fair exchange for the price he had paid. But his journey required several days of relentless trekking and hard riding. He needed to start it well if he was to arrive with any strength.

Continuing his purposeful momentum, Doran moved briskly from shop to shop and market stall to market stall. One by one, he purchased the supplies he would need, favouring waterskins over the typical ales and ciders for a change. He didn't have nearly enough to buy replacements for his weapons and armour, but he was able to procure a new cloak, though, without a tailor, it dragged horrendously through the streets.

Deciding he would take a knife to it once he was on the road, the son of Dorain made his way to the local livery, where Pig had slept the night—another drain on his limited purse. The Warhog returned to him, the dwarf took stock of his saddlebags. A small club, two knives, and a pair of knuckle dusters. A pitiful cache of weapons if ever he saw one, but it was all he had and he could use any one to reasonably defend himself. His father's war masters had seen to that.

"I hope they fed ye well, boy," Doran said, guiding the Warhog on foot. "We're hittin' the road hard today."

Navigating the streets of Velia and its ever-increasing foot traffic, the dwarf was full of *excuse mes* and *do ye minds* as so many failed to properly see him. He had half a mind to let Pig lead the way out; there would be no missing the animal that moved tusks-first.

Rounding the corner, having backtracked almost half of his path from the previous night, a crowd had gathered in the street. The dwarf required an extra moment to recognise his surroundings since it all looked so different in the daylight. He licked his lips nervously. On the other side of the crowd was the alley where he had fought for his life. It was also where Pig had killed a man.

"Hells," he grumbled, suddenly urged to wipe the tusks of his Warhog clean.

Moving cautiously, he found an opening through the crowd and glimpsed the alley beyond. There was no more than a human-shaped lump, covered by a Velian cloak, where the dead man would be. Stepping here and there were men of the watch, cloaked and armed, likely investigating the area. Velia was a rich city and didn't suffer the likes of murder to tarnish its reputation.

There was no sign of those he had injured or the one he had spoken to, the thug who would deliver his message to Undvig the mage. Doran decided they were either in custody or they had been lucky enough to come to their senses before the watch came across them. One way or another, Viktor Varga would learn of his survival. Hopefully, the crime lord would come to understand that Doran Heavybelly was not to be trifled with and would leave him be.

That didn't help with the leverage Viktor held over Asher, he thought resolutely. Nor did it ensure the Stormshields were kept out of harm's way.

"Time we were gone," he muttered to Pig, guiding the animal away from the crowd.

The son of Dorain froze and the Warhog with him.

Leaning against the corner of the adjacent building, arms folded, and wand lightly tapping his own shoulder, was Undvig the mage. Doran had never seen the man before and only known of him for less than a day, yet he knew without a doubt that the man watching him from across the street was, indeed, Undvig. Tall and slender, his bushy chestnut beard made up for the lack of any hair on his narrow head. Scrutinising his dress, Doran couldn't decide whether the man was a monk or a vagabond. It didn't really matter so long as he wielded that wand.

Without making a scene, Doran began to slowly walk away, his sight shifting sideways to keep Undvig in his peripheral vision. The mage pushed away from the wall in lazy pursuit. The dwarf couldn't help but peer over his shoulder, where he then noted four others in Undvig's wake. He cursed his luck and wondered if Grarfath would ever look favourably on him again.

Determined to reach the Stormshields, the son of Dorain scrambled onto his saddle with all haste. Looking back again, his pursuers were mounting horses, determined to catch him. Doran hollered at those in his way and rammed his heels into Pig. Now he had made a scene. The sudden disturbance, created by a bolting Warhog, was cause for more than one person to cry out or scream. Then came Undvig and his thugs, their mounts adding to the mayhem. They knocked aside any who got in their way and drew the attention of the watch, making all the more mess of it.

Velia's densely populated streets didn't welcome the chase, aiding neither Doran nor Undvig. Pig squealed almost continuously, like a ringing bell that alerted all to an imminent calamity. Still, the Velians couldn't always move quickly enough, forcing the dwarf to redirect the Warhog down side streets and through alleyways. It wasn't long before he felt lost, though he could not lose his pursuers. The mage led the way by the tip of his wand.

The first spell was deafening and, thankfully, not aimed at the son of Dorain. Daring to steal a glance over his shoulder, Doran observed the watch stumble and stagger down the road, which was now filled with brick dust and smoke. The wall to their left— part of the archway they had all passed under—had been struck by the mage's magic and exploded in a shower of debris. By the time Pig had put another street behind them, Undvig and his men alone were in the chase. Such a bold move, however, was sure to bring a lot more of the watch down on them, perhaps even the king's soldiers.

"How in the hells do ye get out o' 'ere?" Doran raged, his head turning swiftly and repeatedly to find the right route.

Another ear-piercing crack split the air and the market stall beside the dwarf was blown to splinters. A multitude of fruits was sent in every direction, splattering Doran with sweet juices to add to his already stained shirt. Worse still, the explosion scattered the dense herd of shoppers and startled Pig, sending the mount charging.

"Get out o' the way!" Doran bellowed, his hands constricting around the reins.

Undvig unleashed a staccato of lightning, the spell's edges tinted violet. Riding as he was, however, the mage's aim was far from accurate and even less so with such a dispersed spell. The dusty road, hard-baked by Velia's summer, was kicked up in a violent bloom by branches of the lightning. One such branch caught the side of another market stall and set it alight, including the sheets of cotton displayed thereon.

Through the screams and mad scurries of the terrified Velians, Doran attempted to take back control of Pig's reins and guide him through the chaos. He desperately wanted to look back and check on his pursuers, but he didn't dare take his eyes from what was in front of him, lest they trample a child in their escape.

"This way, ye big lump!" the dwarf barked with great exertion, his whole body heaving to the left. Pig followed the command and barged its way through a corner of stacked crates as it made the sudden turn.

With some open space in front of him, the son of Dorain turned over his shoulder and spotted Undvig and only three of his thugs now. Their horses were shoving people aside and leaping over the debris Pig left in their wake, but the gap between them was definitely increasing.

"Come on, big fella!" he encouraged, patting the Warhog's thick hide. "Keep it up!"

Slowing at the next junction, it became clear to the dwarf that things were escalating inside the walls of Velia. Dead ahead, two blocks away, the main gates were slowly being shut as word reached them about the dangerous chase. Adding to his troubles, a group of soldiers, clad in shining armour emblazoned with the howling wolf, were fast approaching from the south while a group from the city watch sprinted in from the north. With Viktor's men rushing up from behind, Doran had no destination but those closing gates.

"Ye've led the armies o' Grimwhal, lad," Doran uttered to his mount. "Get us out o' this damned city."

Pig grunted. Doran hunkered down.

It was not often that the animal displayed even an ounce of its rigorous dwarven breeding but, when the mount did, it was clear why it was granted the title of *Warhog*.

Like a bolt from a ballista, Pig shot away from the junction and the closing fist of enemies. More than a few people were forced to dive aside in order to avoid the animal's considerable bulk and unforgiving tusks. When it became clear to Doran, however, that there were simply too many people crowding the road, he nudged the Warhog to the left and let the mount figure out the new route its master had already determined.

Up went Pig, defying gravity with Doran's girth atop it, leaping from one lone crate to a stack of barrels and through a stall selling trinkets. The dwarf braced himself for the inevitable landing, but the saddle still struck a blow that quatered his eyes.

There came no reprieve from the Warhog, who dashed sharply around the next stall and cut through a gap between the crowds. Having crossed the road on a diagonal, Pig again used the market supplies to its advantage and gained height as it continued its mad dash for the gates. Doran was sure to brace himself a little higher in the stirrups for the next impact.

It still hurt.

Growling through the pain, the son of Dorain dared a backwards glance for those that wished him dead rather than imprisoned. Undvig and his creeps had apparently stopped short of the junction, likely having heard the commotion created by the armoured soldiers approaching from their left. But the chain of events started by the spell caster was still unfolding and Doran really didn't want to get stuck in the city with a bunch of killers on Viktor's payroll.

Two blocks down and a courtyard opened up before Doran and Pig. Their last obstacle was the circular fountain that dominated the space, the structure having long ago replaced the city's first well that had served the elves when the realm was considerably younger. The Warhog leapt the small wall and splashed through the shallow water without a care, passing the statue of some ancient queen.

So narrow were the gates now that three men abreast would have had to squeeze to fit through. Calls came out from everywhere for the gates to be closed all the quicker, but manpower was no match for Warhog power. Pig left the fountain behind, sped past the merchants complaining about the closing gates, and hurtled through the gap. The dwarf's knees grazed the thick wood of each mighty gate on the way out, but the great beyond was freedom, nay life itself.

Like coming up for air, Doran inhaled the green pastures of Alborn's flat plains having rushed through the ramshackle town that survived outside Velia's main entrance. Now, under the hopefulness of summer's blue sky, the son of Dorain headed north. He prayed to Grarfath and Yamnomora both that the Stormshields remained unharmed.

CHAPTER 24
THE FALL

Dhisha - *I have no intention of dying by the fang or claw of any monster but, if I had to choose one of their foul kind to end my days, it would be a Dhisha.*

I am fairly confident in stating that there is no other creature in the realm that kills its prey quite like one of these beasts. You can see from the crude drawing below what they look like, but it does nothing to explain how their unique venom works.

Dhisha will always attack their prey while they sleep (they have not mastered lock and key but they have no trouble opening doors). When they attack, a pair of retractable fangs, so fine as to be mistaken for strands of hair, will sink into the victim's skin and do a number of interesting things.

As the venom is not powerful enough to paralyse a person, it instead seeks out the mind, working its way into their very thoughts. Those who have survived these attacks state the same thing. They are all-consumed by their dream-like condition to a point that the mind chooses not to wake up. The victims also stated that this was accomplished through some shadowed figure in their mind, a figure who grants them three wishes. They are then able to play out their greatest fantasies while the Dhisha drains them of life.

I don't know about you, but I know what my three wishes would be.

**A Chronicle of Monsters: A Ranger's Bestiary, 12th Edition,
Page 344.**

Ryfe Fenlock, Ranger.

After a long day of listening to men spar and curse each other, be that on the training grounds or across the tables over their meals, Asher noted the last of the iron bars slamming shut beyond the walls of his cell. With that, all of Viktor's toy soldiers were locked in their cages inside a much bigger cage constructed on an island-sized cage. There were no more depths to this hell.

Asher considered sleep but he was yet to hear the lock in his own door fall into place. Rest would not come until he was certain none could sneak up on him, a practice he had established as a child in Nightfall. When the footsteps came, accompanied by the rattle of keys, the ranger assumed the moment was upon him.

He was wrong.

The door opened with a creak and to the gloom of a twilight sky. Filling its frame was the squat magistri, Kad Gorson, his wooden baton in hand. Asher made no move to stand and greet the man but, instead, tightened his grip around the patchy blanket that had been left on the cot for him. It wasn't much, it was certainly no baton—or even a knife such as the one on Gorson's belt—but the ranger knew of at least three ways he could kill the man with it.

"Assassin," Kad greeted before entering uninvited. He was immediately followed by another, the gladiator who Baal had shoved aside earlier that day. "This is Jorvyn," the magistri introduced in a hushed voice.

Asher's eyes narrowed for a moment. "Why do I care?"

Kad closed the door behind them and indicated for Jorvyn to stand against the wall, past Asher. "Jorvyn's fighting tonight."

The ranger looked from the gladiator to the magistri. "Fighting who?" he asked, with hardly a care for the answer.

"Not *who*," Gorson said. "*What*."

Asher recalled the sounds he had heard from beneath the arena, a cacophony of starving monsters. "What does this have to do with me?" he asked, leaning back against the wall beside his cot.

Kad crossed his arms, though the movement was likely in response to the discomfort he was trying to hide. "You said you had faced all manner of monster. Mr Varga told me you were some kind of hunter."

"A ranger," Asher breathed, feeling that life drift ever further from him.

"I can't train men to fight monsters," Gorson continued.

"I don't think your master cares," the ranger remarked, his interest yet to be sparked.

Kad made no comment on Viktor. "I thought you could give Jorvyn some advice, anything that might aid him."

Asher's gaze shifted to the gladiator. He was doing his best to conceal the fear bubbling under the surface, but it seemed so obvious to the old Arakesh. It was there to see in his eyes, as if he was seeing his own death playing out right in front of him.

Fear.

So often it was believed to be a weakness in the strong, a broken link in a warrior's armour. How wrong they all were. Fear didn't cripple the mind. Fear kept men alive. Let the brave and courageous run into the fires of an honourable death. Asher would *survive.*

"What are you fighting?" he asked of the dead man.

"I don't know," he admitted, his dry voice breaking.

"I've heard it's a *Drayga*," the magistri announced, declining to meet Jorvyn's eyes.

Asher's memory was immediately taken back four years, to the swamps just south of Snowfell. There he had taken on a contract to rid the town of creatures described by the locals as pale men. Men they were not. The pod of Drayga had been easy to locate or, more accurately, they had easily located the ranger on his hunt.

"What in the hells is a Drayga?" Jorvyn demanded.

"White demons, pale men, swamp fiends…" Asher shrugged. "Whatever you want to call them, they're the worst kind of monster."

"How's that?" Kad enquired, seeing Jorvyn retreat into himself.

"Most monsters just hunt for food or kill defending and claiming territory," the ranger explained as a matter of fact, "but Drayga hunt for the love of it. They *enjoy* taking down their prey, hungry or not."

The magistri glanced at the gladiator before directing his next question at the ranger. "You have faced their kind, yes? What about killing it?"

"I've fought Drayga," Asher confirmed, "though I would need my book to tell you everything about them."

"Book?"

"It will be with my horse," Asher instructed. "A Chronicle of Monsters; it's a bestiary—"

Kad was shaking his head. "I won't be able to get that before the fight, if at all."

"I'm already dead," Jorvyn muttered to himself.

"They're easy enough to kill," Asher stated, assuming the gladiator knew how to wield a real sword. "They've no natural armour, just a pale flesh that slices like ours."

"What else?" Kad pressed, tapping the vein.

The ranger recalled what he could from the book but his knowledge from those pages was secondary to the visceral memory of actually fighting them. "They have poor eyesight," he informed after a moment's thought. "They're adapted to life in swamps and bogs. Don't ask me how, but they sense the ripples in the water to find their prey."

"There won't be any water in the arena," Kad pointed out, though his tone offered little hope that it would make a difference where Jorvyn's fate was concerned.

That statement sat with Asher, drawing out words from the bestiary. "They must be keeping the Drayga in a bath of some kind," he theorised, wondering how elaborate the cells were beneath the arena.

Kad shrugged. "I have been into the pits below, but I make a point for my own sanity not to linger nor peer into the cages."

"Why do you say that?" Jorvyn asked of the ranger.

"Drayga don't just live in the swamps," Asher began, "they *need* them. When its skin begins to dry, it'll crack and cause pain. If you can't outright kill it, keep your distance and wait it out."

"It can die from this?" Gorson asked, his hands coming down to rest on his hips.

The ranger chewed over his reply. "I don't know," he said honestly. "The ones I fought were in a swamp and I don't recall everything in the bestiary." Seeing the despair creep into Jorvyn's features, Asher added, "It would certainly give you an edge. The Drayga's pain might give you an opportunity to strike it down."

Jorvyn swallowed. "How big are they?"

"No bigger than the average man," Asher told him. "Skinnier too. If you can land a decent blow, it *will* go down."

The magistri glanced back at the door. "We need to go," he said. "You need to get ready." Without ceremony, Kad opened the door and ushered Jorvyn outside.

"You know he's a dead man," Asher uttered, giving Gorson pause over the threshold. "Whether that's tonight or next week. Why are you bothering?"

Kad struggled to meet the ranger's gaze but, when he did, there was unquestionable resolve in his dark eye. "I told you. It's my job to give these boys every fighting chance. I take that seriously."

"Don't fool yourself," Asher added as the magistri began to close the door behind him. "You might not be the fall that kills them, but you're still the one that pushes them off the cliff."

The door remained open a crack, the magistri's hand faltering on the handle. With no response, he closed the door and locked it.

～

Whether it was mere minutes or, indeed, hours, the ranger could not say how long he had slept before his door was being opened again. He recognised the guard, his face etched into Asher's memory, having seen him patrolling the walkway around the training ground.

"Move!" he barked, hammering his baton against the door.

The guard quickly moved on and opened the next cell. Stepping out, Asher could see that all of Viktor's fighters were being let out. The ranger rubbed his eyes and pinched his nose before scrutinising the moon—an hour then, maybe two, he deduced.

There came no more instructions from the guards, and there were a dozen more now, not including a handful on the walkway surrounding them. Asher counted seven arrows being aimed at the mass of prisoners.

"We're going to the arena," said a small voice.

Asher turned to see Mouse close on his heels. "Why?"

"We're allowed to watch the matches," the malnourished boy replied.

Asher steeled himself—he wasn't a boy and he shouldn't think of him as one. Mouse was a man, even if he hadn't been able to call himself one for very long. "I'd rather sleep," he remarked, falling in with the flow of gladiators.

One behind the other, and under constant guard, the men were escorted up and across the bridge where the arena awaited. Once inside the wretched place, they were taken down and spread out along a narrow corridor that reached all the way around the arena's oval shape. From there, the arena floor was level with their necks, allowing them to observe the match through the barred grates that lined the bottom of the sandy ground. It also kept them relatively out of sight from the hundreds of highborns that filled the seats above.

To the ranger's left, Mouse stretched himself on his tiptoes to peer between the bars. Asher looked easily over his head to the man standing beside Mouse. It was the olive-skinned stranger from the corner of the courtyard. Absent his sweat, the man's dark hair flowed down his back in a thick mane. Up close, the ranger could see his strong jaw and combed goatee and moustache. It was his stance that gave him away. The man was a rigid plank, his muscles long honed to keep his body from ever slouching. Asher's best guess placed the stranger as an ex-soldier, like Kad Gorson. It still didn't sit right with the ranger. There was something else about him, a discipline that even the magistri didn't display.

Accustomed to knowing who surrounded him at any moment, the question mark over his fellow gladiator irked Asher. For now, like all others, he would simply be labelled as a threat until proven otherwise.

"LADIES AND GENTLEMEN!"

The booming voice drew Asher's gaze to the man standing on the opposing arena wall. Another of Viktor's collected mages, a failure of Korkanath's teaching. The announcer was speaking with his wand held beside his face, the tip just in front of his lips, where it magnified his voice.

"FOR TONIGHT'S ENTERTAINMENT, YOUR GRACIOUS HOST, THE DARING VIKTOR VARGA, BRINGS YOU NIGHTMARES FROM BEYOND THE WALLS OF OUR FAIR CITY!"

The portcullis at the arena's south end began to open, turning spectators and gladiators alike to the newcomer. It was Jorvyn, now attired in hard leathers and wielding an axe and sword.

"A DESERTER FROM THE NORTHERN ARMIES OF YOUNG KING MERKARIS! HE FLEES THE RAGING BATTLES OF THE FROSTED LAND, A COWARD WITH NAUGHT BUT HIS WEAPONS!" The crowd erupted in a chorus of jeers and slurs. "BUT," the announcer added, creating a dramatic pause to enhance the experience, "WHAT STRANGE AND DARK REALM HAS HE STUMBLED UPON? HE KNOWS NOT WHERE HE IS! HOW IS HE TO FIND HOME AGAIN? LITTLE DOES THE COWARD KNOW, HE WILL HAVE TO FIGHT TO SEE EVEN THE DAWN AGAIN!"

The northern portcullis began to open, the chains rattling with every link that moved to draw it up. Though Asher felt very little for Jorvyn, he was still disheartened to see not one but three Drayga enter the arena. Their pale hides, clinging to their skeletons beneath, were dripping wet. Large circular mouths dominated the entire front half of their heads, which sloped up and back to a rounded point. Within those mouths were three to four rows of sharp teeth designed to shred their prey's skin and muscle. As they stepped onto the dry sand, two of Viktor's goons tossed buckets of water over the wall, drenching them further. Waiting them out was going to be an arduous task.

"What are they?" Mouse asked, with trepidation.

His question was answered by the announcer. "DRAYGA! THE SWAMP DEMONS OF ILLIAN!"

While everyone else took in the nightmarish features of the Drayga, Asher looked to Jorvyn. Credit to him, the man wasn't shaking with fear or soiling himself. His jaw was set and he never looked away from the monsters that stalked towards him. Still, courage wasn't always enough to keep one alive.

As the announcer's voice faded away, the surrounding crowd of vile spectators filled the space with their cheers. Most, it seemed, were shouting for the gladiator to be torn apart. To them, Jorvyn's gruesome death was no more than a sum of coins, their winnings for a well-placed bet.

Asher pressed himself closer to the wall and angled his head to better see Viktor's viewing box. The master of Blood and Coin was a shadowed figure watching from his perch of safety, nestled, most likely, within his protective shield.

Turning what fear he might have into rage, Jorvyn clapped his axe and sword together and roared at the three monsters. Whether the Drayga had all been captured from the same pod or not, they knew instinctively how to hunt together. As one, they slowly spread out on their upturned feet of claws. Within seconds, Jorvyn had an enemy to his left and right as well as in front.

Asher had already moved through the scenario in his mind and knew the best strategy would be an offensive approach. Jorvyn needed to move and move quickly before they acted collectively. If he could take one of them down in the first few seconds his chances of survival would increase dramatically.

But he didn't move.

All three Drayga advanced as if the constant chittering they produced had informed the others of their intentions. Jorvyn swung his sword out wide—enough to halt the charge of two. The third, however, brought its claws down and knocked the gladiator's axe from his hand. Its second and more savage swipe drew red lines down Jorvyn's arm, exposing the muscle beneath. Naturally, he cried out and staggered away from them, his sword continuing to slash in a desperate effort to keep them at bay.

Asher exhaled through his nose. It was a terrible start for the man, who now only had one good arm.

One of the other Drayga bolted towards him and evaded the gladiator's thrust. As it skidded through the sand beside him, one of its clawed hands raked another set of bloody lines, only it was his ribs that took the punishment this time. Through the subsequent pain, though, Jorvyn retained enough grit to swing his blade and score a successful strike. The Drayga wailed, the noise reverberating in ear-piercing waves, as blood oozed from the wound that cut across its bony chest.

The only female Drayga among the three—easily identified by the dark stripes on the thighs and upper arms—tilted its head of teeth towards its injured kin. There came no warning; the female simply lunged at it. Through sheer force the female pinned the other Drayga to the sand and immediately buried its mouth in the gaping wound. Blood exploded into the air as the dying beast writhed under the assault.

It soon stopped when there was no heart in its body to pump what little blood remained.

It was an unexpected twist that Asher hadn't predicted—likely born of starvation where the female Drayga was concerned. The ranger was yet to determine the way it would affect Jorvyn's chances of survival. The crowd certainly hadn't taken well to the death. Their cheers had turned sour for there was only one death they desired.

"Come on, Jorvyn!" some of the gladiators called from down the line.

The surviving male took the female's distraction as an opportunity. It dashed in from Jorvyn's right, claws slashing at the air.

With one hand, the gladiator bore the weight of his sword and swung from high to low. Though he suffered another swipe of claws, he severed the creature's right hand from its wrist. Pressing the advantage, Jorvyn pivoted to strike again, this time landing a backhanded swipe across the monster's slender neck. Had he been an inch closer, he would surely have decapitated the fiend. Instead, the Drayga's head hung by a few strands of flesh as it dropped to the sand.

The gladiators cheered, as if they saw their own victory in Jorvyn's. The paying audience, however, drowned them out with their thunderous jeers.

While so many focused on the dead Drayga, Asher kept his attention on the female. Its bulbous black eyes swivelled on Jorvyn. He was, by far, the better meal. Compared to a Drayga, his insides were practically fat with juicy organs.

It slowly rose onto its three-clawed feet, back hunched and hands splayed out wide. Thick blood dripped from every facet of its mouth, a stark contrast to the chalk white of its body. Jorvyn was sporting three wounds now and it showed in his sluggish movements. Similar to the female Drayga, he was slightly hunched, feet braced apart, though his sheen was that of sweat rather than water.

"One good swing," Asher muttered to himself, hopeful almost.

The Arakesh in him fought for supremacy urging him to dampen whatever emotions might get the better of his senses. Why should he care what happened to this man? This was a place of survival and death, a place where he could thrive if he let the *Assassin* out.

Man and beast collided in a bid to end the contest. It was quick, a blink of the eye and a flash of steel and claw. Jorvyn was too slow, his weapon requiring too much effort to raise and swing where the Drayga had but to lash out with pale and bony hands.

The creature simultaneously gripped his sword arm and clamped its circular jaw around the gladiator's neck, all before driving him to the ground. Jorvyn's fate was that of the female's first victim, and what a bloody mess it was.

A ripple of dismay passed through the gladiators as they witnessed their own end on that red sand. Tonight had been Jorvyn's time. The rest of them were simply in a queue.

The crowd jumped to their feet and erupted in cheers and hollers, their bloodlust filled as much as their purses now. The Drayga was permitted to consume considerably more of Jorvyn's body before one of Viktor's mages stepped into the arena and wrangled it with magic. All the while, the gladiators had nowhere to look but at the ravaged corpse.

"Show's over!" one of the guards yelled, his statement punctuated by the sound of a heavy door being opened beside him.

Slowly but surely, they filed out of the surrounding gutter and were escorted back to their cells. "A damn shame," Mouse voiced on their way back. "He nearly had them for a minute there."

Against his better judgment, Asher replied with a question. "What did he do?"

Mouse looked up and back at the ranger, both surprised and, perhaps, delighted by the response. "Jorvyn? He tried to rob one of the highborns as they left the arena. Mr Varga's guards caught him and well..." He shrugged with his bony shoulders, Jorvyn's fate sitting heavily on all of them now.

Asher recalled the importance Viktor placed on the use of examples. It wouldn't be good for business if the patrons felt unsafe visiting the arena.

"Can I ask," Mouse began in his small voice, "how *you* came to join us?"

Something of the predator that lived within Asher looked back at the young man and it swiftly ended their conversation.

Upon their return to the courtyard and the surrounding cells, the ranger took one last look at the stranger from The Arid Lands, beyond Mouse. Indeed, the way he walked declared his confidence and strength.

Asher had nowhere to put that curiosity and so it sat with him inside his cell. The door was inevitably locked, leaving the ranger with only the light of a single candle in the corner of his room. While considering the mystery around the stranger from the south, he also considered the hard facts he now knew about his environment.

The likes of Baal and Grift were the most obvious threats outside of the arena. Asher was confident he could defend himself against them, though he didn't know what punishment awaited those who killed Viktor Varga's *investments*.

Mouse was harmless, though his entire character poked at the humanity clinging to the ranger. From a mental or emotional standpoint, Asher considered the young man a long-term threat. He would need to quash that sooner rather than later.

Then there was Kad Gorson, a magistri who seemed to walk the line between being just another of Varga's thugs and a decent man who truly wished to help those bound to this life. Time would tell, the ranger knew, which side of that line the magistri leaned towards the most. Though he was a threat to the rest of the gladiators, Asher knew he was safe thanks to Viktor's mandate where his champion's health was concerned.

The grounds themselves would prove an issue were he to attempt any kind of escape. To do so would put the Stormshields in danger, but his mind couldn't help but strategise the scenario.

The inner walls of the courtyard were spiked, like the bridge that connected them to the arena. The only gate that led up to the walkway and beyond was locked at all times and manned by two guards. By the time he scaled it they would either be ready with weapons drawn or the archers would take him down. Even if he did get on the other side in one piece, the outer walls of the main building were too high and too smooth to climb up and over.

After giving some thought for several minutes, the ranger decided it was probably for the best if he didn't devise a plan of escape.

With that came the creeping hopelessness of his situation, nay his life. This was to be the end of him, trapped in a gloomy cell when he wasn't being forced to kill others. He was momentarily cast back to The Lion's Crown and his invitation for Danagarr to sit with him. Little had he known, nor could he have ever guessed, that such a small thing would put him on a path that, ultimately, led him right back to where he had started.

He had swapped one hell for another.

Before desperation and misery took its firm hold, Asher reminded himself that this fate was no more than he deserved. Lying back on his cot, the ranger closed his eyes and welcomed the nightmares of his past, lest he forget the murderer he was.

CHAPTER 25
PREPARATIONS

Broxon - A bullish monster that enjoys the taste of cattle over a human. That said, the loss of cattle is often the catalyst for a contract to be drawn up. Thus enters the ranger.

My first description was, perhaps, deliberate as Broxon resemble bulls. That is in shape and by the horns on their head. All else is quite different. For starters, they are twice the size of any bull. Their hide is difficult to look at, well, at least it is for those unaccustomed to the musculature of any animal. You see, Broxon hide is the deep red of muscle, as if the beasts have been stripped of their skin. That would certainly explain their bad temperament.

There are a number of ways to slay a Broxon, some easier than others. By far the easiest way is to poison the beast with suitable bait, but I would advise killing the monster the old-fashioned way. Granted this comes with greater risk, but doesn't such a thing always come with greater reward?

A fully-grown Broxon can feed a village for a week. They taste like pork of all things. Now, if you can put the beast down with steel instead of poison, you can then sell the carcass and add the coin to your reward.

*A Chronicle of Monsters: A Ranger's Bestiary, 12th Edition,
Page 49.*

Fenley Klum, Ranger.

Asher welcomed the light of the new day. The candle had failed to hold through the night and, with the ensuing darkness, the Nightseye elixir in his veins played hell with his sleep. Rest was almost impossible when he could hear the men in the adjacent cells and the conversations between the patrolling guards.

Then there were the various smells that clung to his room, the odours of more than just Tyvarnus. Asher had been able to detect the lingering scent of two previous champions before the big man, not to mention the visitors they had all enjoyed.

Even the taste of his own sweat on the air was repugnant. That, at least, was better than the odour of the numerous rats who shared the building with the gladiators.

When his door, at last, opened wide, the ranger almost burst out of his cell and onto the training ground. The relief of ordinary senses was its own ecstasy.

Instruction from the guards was hardly needed to direct the gladiators to their first meal. The large chamber was located through the only open corridor that led away from the training ground. Breakfast had already been laid out by staff unseen and the men took to their preferred seats with no more than murmured conversation between them.

With nowhere else to put himself but opposite Mouse, Asher picked up his bowl of whatever they were calling the gruel and turned back to his cell. Kad Gorson was blocking his way, the smaller man's frame somehow magnified in the corridor's entryway.

"All meals are eaten in here. No exceptions."

The ranger sighed and pivoted on his heel. Mouse was smiling at him, a hand out to gesture at the empty seat. Asher placed his weight down with little care and the man beside him shuffled away. On the other side of the table, Mouse gazed at him expectantly, but the ranger had nothing but a shadowed glower for the young man.

Beyond the diminutive gladiator, if he could boast of such a title, Asher noted Baal on the adjacent table. He too had his eyes on the ranger. A few seats down was Grift who, more overtly, stared at Asher while mouthing, *you're a dead man*. Neither of them unnerved him and so he put his head down and consumed the sorry excuse for breakfast.

The rest of the morning played out just as the previous day had. The magistri split them up into groups and put them through their fighting routines and physical exercises. For those who failed to live up to Gorson's standards, he reminded them of Jorvyn, though not before reacquainting them with his baton.

Since fighting routines offered little to Asher, he used the opportunity to build on his assessment of every man he was now imprisoned with. Those accustomed to a life of violence were easy to identify, and they used Gorson's military knowledge to make themselves all the worse.

The gladiators who had little experience of violence, those who had likely failed to pay their debt to Viktor, were clumsy and dropped their wooden sword more often than not. Asher tried not to look them in the eye or commit their faces to memory, they who were to be fodder for the cheering masses.

The physical exercises were a welcomed retreat from it all, a chance to pour all of his focus into a single and mindless task that made his muscles burn.

Completing his sixty-fifth press up, a shadow overcame him, drawing his focus like the string of a bow. Coming out of the press up, he was sure to grab a handful of sand until he noticed Mouse's bony feet, at which he relaxed and rose to no more than a sitting position.

"Water?" the young man offered.

With sweat dripping off the end of his nose and running down his bare torso, Asher happily accepted the skin and drained it before handing it back. Mouse's small voice began wittering on about something—the ranger's approaching debut perhaps—but Asher's gaze had found the stranger from the south, exercising by the adjacent wall. His long mane of black hair was gathered tightly in a knot behind his head, revealing a lean yet well-muscled back as he pulled himself up repeatedly on the two beams of wood that protruded from the wall.

When he lowered himself to the ground, and in such a controlled manner, the gladiator from the southern empire turned around. His torso rippled with muscles that had been tended to for years, decades even. There was a difference between his honed physique and the bulky physiques of the violent criminals Viktor had turned into gladiators.

He was a *warrior*.

It occurred to Asher that he had yet to see the stranger sparring on the sand. Seeing him fight would reveal so much more to the ranger, a master of every style known to the realm of man.

"Who's he?" he asked bluntly, cutting Mouse off.

"Who? Him?" Mouse ran one hand down his jaw and glanced at Kad Gorson in the distance. "That's Salim..." The young man trailed off, clearly trying to remember something. "Al-Anan!" he exclaimed, before reducing everything about himself. Indeed, Mouse possessed quite the skill when it came to retreating into himself, as if he were no more than the furniture.

"Salim Al-Anan," Asher put together, eyeing the warrior who slowly raised his legs up and over his head, his weight balanced on his hands alone. "Who is he? Who *was* he?" he corrected himself.

Mouse could only shrug before glancing at Gorson again. "I think he knows the magistri from... before."

That was easy enough to believe given their apparent origins. "Is that why he doesn't have to spar?" the ranger enquired, concerned that his every question only enamoured Mouse.

"He does spar," Mouse reported, nodding his head. "No exceptions," he added, his voice a poor imitation of the magistri's. "But he doesn't spar with any of us. Only with the magistri. You'll probably see for yourself later—they usually spar when the sun's lower."

The ranger again tuned out Mouse as he focused on Salim. He didn't know why the warrior from the south held his attention so, besides his inability to assign him the correct level of threat he posed. Sitting there, in the baking sun, Asher wondered if he saw something else in Salim, something the other men didn't possess. But why did that matter? Was he looking at Salim Al-Anan and hoping he saw an ally? Or, worse still, was he looking at the man and hoping he saw someone who could help him escape this place?

The latter was a path that led nowhere, but a shard of hope had lodged itself in Asher's heart. For all the logic he applied to his miserable situation, a part of him clung to the hope that he would taste freedom again.

And the idea of an ally in hell was just a good way to get stabbed in the back. He would let it all go and focus on the one thing that had been drilled into him since his earliest days in Nightfall.

He would survive.

～

After lunch, and another round of threatening stares from various gladiators, Asher was pulled aside by Kad Gorson as the rest filed onto the training ground.

"You're done for the day," the magistri told him. "Mr Varga wants you ready for tonight."

Asher looked over the men. "Who am I fighting?" he asked, the question having been on his mind all morning.

"I haven't told them yet," Kad replied, his voice somewhat hushed despite the hubbub.

"*Them?*" the ranger echoed.

"Mr Varga wants a show, not an execution. And I'm not telling you before I tell them. But what I am going to do is have you escorted across the bridge. You're going to spend the rest of the day over there."

Asher straightened his back all the more. "Afraid they'll try and kill me before the fight?"

"I heard what you did to Tyvarnus and the others," Kad said, pointedly. "I'm concerned your opponents will die before their intended time."

Something about Gorson's words stuck to the inside of the ranger's head. It struck him then that he was, undoubtedly, a part of Viktor's gruesome business. The men around him had no other purpose than to die, and to die as spectacularly as they could. His role in that was integral.

For the first time since striking his deal with Varga, Asher wondered if he had given up too much, for he was debased again to the level of an animal on a leash. Just as he had done with the Father of Nightfall, he now awaited the command to kill from his master.

Walking under guard, the training ground behind him, the ranger took a deep breath, as if such a thing would cleanse him of those plaguing and selfish thoughts. A young dwarf got to live, a girl more deserving of life than any of the condemned gladiators. Asher reminded himself that he was included in that sentence. For the murder of Thomas Murell—a child of Deadora's age—he would have been justly executed, and the boy was one of countless others who had felt the sting of his blade.

Reacquainted with the first cell he had occupied in the arena, the ranger was left to himself for most of the afternoon; his only visitor was an unnamed thug who brought him food and water.

Asher turned to yet more physical exercise. He needed something to do, anything to keep his hope from gaining any more of a foothold while, simultaneously, keeping his hopelessness at bay. In truth, he wished to feel nothing at all—to become a numb killing machine.

For all his efforts, for all the pain he pushed himself through, *humanity* clung to him like a parasite. It was a creature from which there was no escape.

"He's not coming back," the ranger uttered to himself, every word breathed out as he completed a sit-up.

And why would Doran come back? Whatever kindred tether might have existed between them, the dwarf was no friend. Asher had neither friends nor allies. To have either was to trust them and the world had shown the ranger that such a construct was for the foolish and the soon to be dead.

He thought of Geron Thorbear. He had trusted him, a man who was not even the real Geron Thorbear. Pausing his exercise, Asher spared the old slaver a moment's thought and wondered if he too was sitting in a cell somewhere in The Arid Lands and thinking of him, the one who had delivered him unto the likes of a vengeful Kali Ras-Sabeem. It seemed unlikely. Chances were high that Kradamir Damakas—his real name—was long dead, and what an awful death he would have suffered for his crimes against the Karathan lord.

His thoughts returning to Doran Heavybelly, Asher would never make a comparison between the dwarf and Kradamir. But that didn't mean the son of Dorain was to be trusted beyond safeguarding his kin in Darkwell.

No... He was truly alone.

The sound of rattling keys and a creaking door informed him otherwise. Viktor Varga strode between the cells with his usual shadows: Darya Siad-Agnasi and the hooded mage. In their wake were four brutes, four more than either the Shadow Witch or mage required to safeguard their master. As was typical for the crime lord, he presented with a beaming grin, a stark contrast to the dark line that kept the Shadow Witch's jaw shut.

"It's time to get ready!" Viktor declared, his hands rising. "Come, come!"

The ranger was escorted to another part of the arena's ringed interior, his wrists bound as he was moved from one place to the other. The new chamber was larger than any other he had seen besides the arena itself, with high windows that offered a view of the night sky. To his right was a legion of weapons, real ones, hanging on the wall. The arena, it seemed, had collected every type of sword, axe, and spear, and everything else in-between.

To his left stood a cage twice the height of an average man but it wasn't for the likes of an animal or a monster. Inside, Asher spied numerous items and belongings hanging from racks on the grated bars, with all manner of sundries piled on the three tables therein.

After being left to stand in the middle of the room, the ranger continued to peruse the items beyond his reach. He soon spotted his green cloak, folded up on the edge of a table, next to his brown leathers. Not far away, he discovered his folded bow resting against his quiver, which still retained a handful of arrows. None, however, were quite so significant as the small sack purse on the other side of his cloak. He recognised it as the same purse he had been forced to give up his ring to, as Doran had given up various pieces of jewellery.

He envisioned the black gem in his mind and recalled the familiar touch of it. Not only that, he recalled the security of it. If the ring was returned to him his survival would be all but guaranteed. So too would his torment be extended. Better, he thought, to die as any man should and be done with this wretched place.

Still, he couldn't help but desire it.

In recent years, he had learned that the gem had more to offer than good health. He thought of the fires he had learned to start with naught but a wave of the hand. Asher knew he had only scratched the surface of its capabilities, but his training had always shunned magic. It was a thought pattern he couldn't shake.

Not that any of it mattered anymore. He could desire the relic all he wanted; it wouldn't change the fact that it lay beyond his grasp. There was only one possession Viktor permitted and the strip of red fabric was looped around Darya's belt.

"Tonight," Varga began, "is your grand reveal! Now, obviously, there are those who doubt what you are, but that hasn't prevented the heads of the Fenrigs, Yarls, *and* the Danathors from attending."

"No Lady Trigorn," Asher observed, sure that her absence had likely irked Victor at some point that evening.

"Sadly no," Varga confirmed, his cheerful demeanour withstanding. "Though Lucas Farney sits in her box. Once he sees the truth of you, I have no doubt Lady Trigorn will grace our fine establishment. But don't you concern yourself with the spectators,

Asher." The crime lord came to stand behind the ranger, his hands creeping up and over his shoulders until his grip was firm and his voice was in Asher's ear. "All you have to think about are those heartbeats. One by one, you will bring them to a halt. And don't forget," he added, his voice rising above a whisper now, "it's important to enjoy yourself."

Varga clapped him on the shoulders and moved away, gesturing, instead, for two others to approach the ranger. "This is Fengil and Roin," he introduced, neither man appearing particularly happy about their job. "They will dress you appropriately and, when the time is right, you will be granted access to the arena." He glanced at the overbearing gate that arched behind him, and only a second before something large and heavy barrelled into it from the other side. This was followed by a growl from one of mankind's nightmares and a loud cheer from the rich mob. "That would be our friend, the Lumber Dug," Viktor informed with a finger in the air. "It seems it's met its match in the Broxon. They're just warming up the crowd."

Asher knew of the second creature, though only from reading the bestiary. There was no comparison between a Lumber Dug and a Broxon in the book but, from the description he had read, it was easy to believe they were similar in their considerable mass. The ranger in him was curious to see the monster in the flesh but, catching sight of that red cloth, tucked into Darya's belt, banished such curiosities and, with it, the *Ranger* that dwelled within.

"What do you think?" Viktor's question brought Asher back to the present, where Fengil and Roin were presenting him with a black cuirass of hardened leather. "Having seen you fight," Varga went on, his hand running up and down the cuirass, "I know how important flexibility is. I don't want you weighed down by plate or mail. Besides, this lends something to the *assassin look*, don't you think?" The crime lord flicked a finger and Roin left Fengil holding the cuirass while he retrieved a cloak hanging on the adjacent wall. "To flow over the back," Viktor said with a flourish of the hand.

"It's red," Asher pointed out, seeing the jarring contrast to the black.

"'Tis a provocative colour, yes?" Viktor teased. "I have had it dyed to match your blindfold, you see. I want you to look the part of the villain *and* the hero at the same time. The crowds must bay for your blood while cheering you on." Varga urged Fengil and Roin to get on with dressing him. "Tonight will be your reveal," he continued, ever the champion of his own voice, "but it is also no more than a teaser, a sample of things to come. There hasn't been time for our friends in Illian to make the journey to witness the feats of a real Arakesh but, after tonight, word will spread of just how *real* you are. Then, the world will come and, with them, their coin."

Asher let Fengil and Roin undress him and fit the cuirass, their slender hands seeing to the knots and clasps. It was snug but too fine to offer any real protection should he be grazed by the edge of steel. The arching vambraces were better, having been fitted with two lengths of iron. After stepping into a pair of dark trousers he went through the uncomfortable process of allowing the two men to strap leather pads around his thighs. It was all for show, a fact that was no more evident than when they attached the red cloak to his cuirass.

Viktor beheld him, his arms crossed and one hand cupping his mouth. "Perfect," he muttered from behind his fingers. "Perfect!" he exclaimed, his hands coming out to clasp Fengil and Roin on the shoulder. "Gentlemen, you have surpassed yourselves."

"Who am I fighting?" Asher demanded, cutting through the moment.

Working through the sour taste in his mouth, Viktor replied, "Does it matter? Surely you haven't made friends of that horrid lot? Trust me when I tell you, Asher, every one of them is a criminal of the worst kind. I mean, think about it," he added with a short sharp laugh. "There isn't a soul on this island who wouldn't be locked up were they on Illian soil. So how wicked do you think your cellmates are—those who have been so evil as to be impris- oned by criminals of the highest order?"

Asher thought on the men he had assessed just that day and

knew many of them were no more than ordinary citizens who couldn't repay their debt.

Not wishing to dwell on such a harsh truth, he held Viktor's gaze only a moment longer. "How many am I fighting?" he asked, rather than comment on criminals sentencing criminals.

Varga stood a little straighter. "Four," he answered in a clipped tone.

"Four?" Asher repeated, incredulous. "I faced more proving myself to *you*."

"I am considerably harder to impress," Viktor told him with a tight smile. "And besides, I do not wish to overstretch you on your first night. As I said, this is but a sample of more to come." A screeching roar pierced the chamber and the ground gave a small quake. "It sounds like the Broxon doesn't have much left in it," Varga reasoned. "We should all retire and leave our champion here to his last preparations."

"What about my sword?" Asher's question came with an advancing step towards Viktor and Darya's exquisite daggers flashed in the torchlight.

Varga flexed his fingers alone to stay any further action. "Your weapon," he said, turning back to Asher, "will be awaiting you on the sands. I don't want you killing them too fast now," he added with a mischievous grin, as if he wasn't talking about the deaths of four men.

The ranger held Darya's piercing gaze until she disappeared from sight, departing behind her master. Only moments later and he was alone in that place, save for the two guards left either side of the gate. Neither could look him in the eyes, though they maintained a hand on the hilts of their swords at all times.

Asher tried to ignore their presence. He found a spot in the centre of the great gate and poured himself into it. When that gate finally opened, he would be neither man nor ranger.

He would be Arakesh once more.

CHAPTER 26

FOR ALL THE WORLD TO SEE

Dredling - *A parasite to be sure. These squid-like creatures will secure themselves to travellers who wander through bogs and the like, finding purchase under the concealment of clothing. Most prefer a nice juicy calf. Once they are attached, they will immediately begin to poison the mind of the host, turning them violent and mad. This usually results in death before the Dredling is discovered.*

There have been numerous cases of Dredlings injecting their eggs into their host and forcing the victim to seek out civilisation before the offspring slither out of their mouth to find hosts of their own.

There are signs to look out for, of course, before the violence begins. The eyes of the host are always extremely bloodshot for the first few days. Then they begin to turn black. By this stage, madness will have its firm hold. Other signs include a slight tremor in the hands, loss of appetite, paling skin, and muttering to oneself.

If you can identify a Dredling host before their eyes turn black, there is a chance you can save their life, though you must sever the limb. This, however, might result in their death anyway.

A Chronicle of Monsters: A Ranger's Bestiary, 12th Edition, Page 459.

Selene (the Maiden of Snowfell), Ranger.

"LADIES AND GENTLEMEN! LORDS OF DRAGORN! BLOOD AND COIN IS NOT DONE WITH YOU YET! YOU WERE PROMISED SOMETHING SPECIAL! TONIGHT, YOU WILL WITNESS THAT WHICH HAS NEVER BEEN SEEN IN THE LIGHT AND 'TIS ONLY WHISPERED OF IN THE SHADOWS! BY THE GRACE OF VIKTOR VARGA... AN ARAKESH!"

To the sound of thunderous cheers, the gate was pulled up like the maw of a monster, hungry to consume Asher whole. The red cloak trailing at his ankles, the *Assassin* walked onto the sands of the arena.

His first steps seemed to have a physical effect on the exclusive audience, each spectator dampening their strident anticipation. By the time the gate had closed behind him, there came not a sound but for his footfalls crunching the hard sand. Hundreds of eyes gazed at him, their intrigue holding their tongues.

Looking at them all, there were too many to spy any individual face. Instead, Asher turned his head high to the open roof, where the night's sky glittered like diamonds—absent the moon. Then there was Viktor, the shadowed figure watching from the rails of his viewing box. Asher didn't need to see his features to know he was grinning.

Movement to his right brought his attention to Darya Siad-Agnasi, the lithe Shadow Witch. Her long coat fanned out below her waist, revealing a row of small daggers strapped to her left thigh. Nothing was more alluring to Asher, however, than the strip of red cloth she held in her hands.

The way she approached, the blindfold held out ceremoniously for all to see, transported Asher's memory back to the very first time he had been given the fabric. Then, as a child, it had been tied around his head by Nasta Nal-Aket and his life in the dark had truly begun.

No words were exchanged between the trained killers as she

came to stand behind him—they had done this before. Asher took one last look at the spectators, all whispering to each other with eyes fixed on him. The *Assassin* craved what was coming next, the intoxication of being connected to everything.

Darya's hands looped over his head and brought the red blindfold down over his eyes and across the bridge of his nose. By the time she was finished tying the knot, Asher's mind had been cast into the darkness, a place where the predator came to life. It awoke in him, already hungry, already craving the fight.

Drawing down on years of training, Asher was able to anchor his mind in a place where the influx of stimuli couldn't overwhelm him. Had he been naught but a novice in the ways of the Arakesh, the Nightseye elixir would have informed him of every detail in the arena, from the number of grains of sand under his boots to the food lingering on the breath of every spectator. It would have been blinding to his senses as a whole and crippled his ability to fight.

But a novice he was not.

A master of disciplined training, Asher stood in the midst of it all and assimilated every piece of information at his own pace. Besides the mix of sweat and the old blood staining the sand, the assassin could smell, taste, feel, and hear a preposterous volume of coins inside the arena—the perfume of the rich. Asher could feel the cool metal as if there were coins between his fingers. The mineral tasted bitter in his mouth and he could smell the various hands the coins had passed through before settling in their purses.

For just a moment, a second of clarity, Asher wondered at what point those small pieces of metal outweighed the value of life itself.

But the moment was shattered when all of his senses detected the silvyr blade being drawn from its scabbard on Darya's back. Now there was a mineral worth fighting for. Its hourglass shape sang out to the assassin as it caught the air. His mind comprehended its impossible edge and he yearned to wield it. It was jolting then that the Shadow Witch didn't offer it to him but walked away, returning to the side gate and the steps.

It was all dramatics, of course. That much was obvious when

Darya tossed the short-sword high into the air and, apparently, with little care. Her own training showed through, though, the blade thrown to come down directly on top of Asher. First there came a collective gasp from the audience, their conclusions foregone as they watched the spinning weapon hurtle towards the blind man.

To Asher, the sword's velocity and the ever-changing angle of the hilt was all so clear. He could feel the air pressure shifting between him and the weapon as the gap grew shorter. He had but to raise one arm and snatch the hilt mid-fall, as if it had been drawn to his hand by some spell. The second collective gasp expanded into an erupting roar, the audience now just as hungry for bloodshed as the *Assassin* within.

Through the cheers, Asher heard the chain links as the gate at the other end of the arena was opened. Out walked four gladiators, four men doomed to die under the still heavens. Viktor had kept things nice and simple it seemed, with each gladiator wielding a single weapon. Asher felt the length of a two-handed longsword, its edge slightly dulled from lack of care. Another wielded an axe, its haft bound tightly with a leather strap that stank of old sweat and fear. The third, and closest, strode onto the sand holding a spear, its hardwood pole that of a hickory tree judging by its taste. The fourth and last gladiator followed the curve of the arena wall, a spiked mace resting casually over one shoulder.

They had no idea who—or *what*—they were up against.

Asher reasoned as much by the lack of fear they each exhibited. Their heart rates were rising, but steadily as was to be expected given the environment they had walked into. It was that same environment, surrounded by onlookers and cheers, that had apparently prevented the men from recalling what happened to the six gladiators who had preceded them.

Asher considered their point of view, the sheep looking at the blind wolf. To them he was at a severe disadvantage. But what they would learn all too late was that a blind wolf was still a wolf, and they were the very creatures he had been bred to hunt.

"FOUR CRIMINALS!" the announcer's voice boomed, the

enchanted volume enough to make Asher turn his head down and away. "'TIS THESE FOUR WHO HAVE WRONGED THE PEOPLE OF DRAGORN, THEIR CRIMES PUNISHABLE BY DEATH! BUT THEY HAVE FLED IN THE NIGHT. THEIR FREEDOM," the mage explained, gesturing to the gate beyond Asher, "IS SO CLOSE THEY CAN ALMOST TOUCH IT! BUT THE BENEVOLENT LORDS OF DRAGORN REACH OUT WITH HANDS OF JUSTICE. THEY SEEK THE SKILLS OF AN ARAKESH, AN ASSASSIN OF THE FABLED NIGHTFALL, TO HUNT THESE CRIMINALS DOWN AND DELIVER DESERVED DEATH!"

While the announcer detailed the pointless story, Asher detected his fellow gladiators watching from the observational gutter that traced the arena's wall. He didn't need eyes to feel the scorn in Baal's gaze or the contempt in Grift's. Then there was Mouse, who peered between the bars. Curiously, his was the calmest heart rate of them all. Even Salim, on the other side of the arena tonight, displayed more agitation, though he certainly felt composed, rigid almost, as if his entire body was tensed all the time. If Asher was to guess, he would say the southerner hated everything about Blood and Coin.

A particularly ear-piercing cheer from the crowd brought the assassin back to his place on the sand. The announcer, apparently, had finished the last flourishes of his tale and now the rich of Dragorn thirsted for violence unlike any they had ever seen.

No further encouragement required, the spearman took the first shot. Asher heard the pole leave his opponent's sweaty grip and the steel tip slice through the air. His aim was true, the spear having traversed just over half the arena to where the assassin stood. For the time it sailed on its murderous course, the baying mob grew quiet, caught somewhere between hope and wonder. When Asher pivoted his shoulders with all the effort of a man navigating a crowded street, the audience watched the spear continue its journey into the sand and, once again, erupted in cheers.

For all the crowd's excitement, the gladiators comparatively grew hesitant. Their strides became cautious steps and heads turned to regard each other with brows furrowed in question. The sheep were beginning to wonder just how blind the wolf was.

With no weapon now, the gladiator hung back and started to edge his way around the wall to retrieve his spear. The other three wielded their sword, axe, and mace in front of them, ready to attack or defend.

The assassin remained terrifyingly still.

Silvyr blade held low at his side, Asher let the men approach. With every step he could feel their confidence ebbing and their fear rising. They had likely heard the same legends as everyone else and believed him to be no more than one of Viktor's tales to bring in the larger bets. But they had all seen the blind man evade the spear if not catch his weapon from the air.

Having made his way around the arena, the spear was back in its owner's hands. It also meant that the assassin was surrounded on all sides by those who intended him harm. The imminent violence and overall threat of the gladiators was akin to needles slowly pressing into his skin, forcing the killer out to defend him.

Nasta Nal-Aket's voice whispered in his mind. *Survive...*

It was also the last word Doran had said to him, another rein-forcement to the very foundation of his instincts. Whether he was to kill his target or not, he *must* survive. It was the imperative that had long become the driving force behind his every action in a fight.

There was nothing he could do about enjoying it.

Believing he had naught but his ears, the swordsman came at him without a sound, his blade sweeping in from on high. The gladiator didn't know that it was his shifting bones that sounded in Asher's sensitive ears, informing the assassin of his every move and proximity.

The silvyr blade snapped up while Asher himself slid to one side. The blades collided but the gladiator's was deflected away, leaving everything above his neck vulnerable to counterattack. It would have been so easy. Asher had only to reverse his grip on the short-sword and slash it across his enemy's throat. But the *Assassin* wanted the gladiator to know that he faced something more than himself, something more than a man even. Hammering that superiority home, Asher tapped the pommel of his hilt into his foe's temple and sent him staggering away with a bloody gash.

It had all taken no more than a second, a second in which he could have reduced their number from four to three.

Maiming the man had certainly ignited the crowd. It was as if they too could taste the gladiator's blood on the air or, indeed, take the scent of it into their lungs. They lived for it, desired it. They hadn't seen anything yet.

The mace came in soon after, a low swing to break Asher's left leg. The assassin simply raised the imperilled limb and avoided the spiked ball. At almost the same time, the axeman swung for his head, forcing Asher to immediately tilt away and move forward into the available space. It was there that the spearman returned to the fight and thrust the tip of his weapon towards the assassin's face.

To Asher it was all so like a dance that he had rehearsed countless times, for his opponents offered no form of attack he hadn't encountered before. And so he dodged from left to right and grasped the pole of the spear as it shot past his head. Holding it firm, and without looking, he knew to manipulate the spear up and to the side, thereby blocking the incoming axe. The blow was jarring, though not enough to snap the weapon in two, as Asher's plan required it to be. Down came the silvyr and cut through the hickory wood as if it were no more than a twig.

Now, Asher possessed both his short-sword and the tipped end of the broken spear. He twisted the latter between his fingers and side-stepped into the charging mace wielder. Before the heavy weapon could be brought to bear, the assassin buried most of the spear end into his opponent's chest. His acute senses felt the edge of the spear's blade slice neatly through the artery that fed the heart before piercing his back.

Never one to add a flourish to his kills, for a dead man was a dead man and required no extra effort to see him to the next life, Asher yanked the spear end out and launched it under arm at the gladiator who had once laid claim to the weapon. With no more than a broken piece of hickory wood to defend himself—and lacking the reflexes of an Arakesh—the gladiator received the end of his spear back. He died instantly, his body forever marked by the protrusion from his skull.

Again, the crowd leapt from their seats with disgusting glee. They drank it in, invigorated by the splatter of blood and ease with which two lives had winked from existence. So too did Asher savour the moment, his talents unleashed to their full potential.

The swift and brutal deaths hadn't escaped the remaining gladiators, those with the sword and axe. Both men refrained from pressing the attack and favoured a short retreat.

All three were now beyond the reach of each other. The gladiators looked around, their confusion and fear added to the melting pot of information they inadvertently shared with the assassin's enhanced senses.

The urge to attack was enticing, to continue the bloodshed. But there was more fun to be had in the art of defence and counterattack. It was also a good way to display a wider variety of skills, for attacking would lead to a quick death as neither man could keep him at bay. And so the assassin held his ground and gave the gladiators some time to think about their next move. If they were smart, they would form a strategy that utilised their abilities in harmony, forcing Asher to defend on two fronts.

But the axeman harboured more fear than his comrade. His weight was balanced differently, keeping him on the balls of his feet and with his knees slightly bent. The nervous energy he held in his muscles would add to the speed with which he might flee the ensuing violence. Though his instincts favoured flight over fight, unlike the swordsman whose stance had him rooted to the spot, the axeman had nowhere to go. Only the victor walked off the sands.

As expected, the swordsman alone lunged at him. Asher met the incoming blade with his own and proceeded to block and deflect the succession of blows that followed. Mindful of his footwork, and that of his second opponent, the assassin began to place himself between the two gladiators, angling his back towards the axeman. There was no better bait for a coward than an easy kill.

While meeting or evading the swordsman's every blow, Asher heard the axeman take a breath and hold it, a precursor to an exertion of great effort. In this case, he was lifting his weapon high, the haft gripped between cracking knuckles and sweaty palms. The bait taken, the gladiator was locked into his actions with nothing to do but bring that axe down onto Asher's unsuspecting head.

But there wasn't so much as a displaced grain of sand that Asher didn't know about.

Having not only anticipated the rear attack but also manipulated his ongoing duel, the assassin was able to kick the swordsman back before pivoting and dashing to one side as the axe swung down. In the span of a heartbeat, Asher was no longer where the axeman needed him to be, yet he was unable to halt the downward stroke of his heavy weapon. Using his momentum against him, Asher raised his short-sword, snapping it out to the side in a curling arc. The rare metal cut upwards, slicing through the gladiator's wrists and the end of the haft with clean precision.

As the head of the axe dug into the sand, so too did the swordsman land on his back—unaware that his comrade had just lost both of his hands.

While the axeman stood, frozen in a moment of silent shock and rising terror, the crowd screamed for his death. It wasn't just that, Asher realised. They were revelling in the gladiator's torment. They liked to see the final blow coming and it was all the more intoxicating if the victim knew it too.

Sickened, bile rose in Asher's throat.

The *Assassin* within him was hushed, dampened by rolling waves of humanity that refused to be quashed. The axeman dropped to his knees, staring at the bloody stumps where his hands had been all his life. It wouldn't be long before the balance of pain and shock was outweighed and searing agony set in.

Asher stepped forward and thrust his short-sword into the man's heart. It wasn't the dramatic execution the crowd had wanted, but it killed the gladiator in an instant and ended his suffering.

That left only one. The swordsman had witnessed the death as he scrambled backwards over the sand, too afraid to turn his back on the murderous assassin. But Asher's lust for the fight had fled, leaving him deflated, shoulders hunched, and head bowed. Slowly, his free hand crept up his face and hooked under the blindfold. He removed it and made no effort to combat the painful disorientation. It was fleeting, however, and he soon looked upon his work as well as the frightened survivor.

The mob jeered, the aestheticism ruined for them. Without the blindfold he was just another accomplished fighter. There were also calls for the swordsman's head, the crowd not to be satisfied until the victor emerged. There was also the matter of their bets, all of which would be hinging on the death of one of them.

But the *Ranger* couldn't. He couldn't close the gap and drive his blade through the other. Instead, he turned his head and looked up, towards Viktor Varga's viewing box. The crime lord now stood in the torchlight, his expression clearly absent his typical smile. Conveyed in that expression was Viktor's oppressive command to finish the fight or face the consequences.

When the ranger made no move to do so, Varga looked to the shadowed mage who stood not far from him, beyond the light. Asher narrowed his eyes but failed to discern what was happening until it was too late.

Receiving no such instruction from his mind, Asher's sword arm was thrown out to the side and the silvyr blade launched from his hand. It struck the remaining gladiator in the throat as he attempted to stand, sending him back to the sand where he would drown in his own blood.

The ranger was disgusted.

It appeased the mob, their final cries of elation reaching a new crescendo. Asher turned back to the viewing box and scrutinised the mage who had manipulated his arm and sword from afar, her robes lapping up the shadows about her. As his mind would, Asher noted that Viktor appeared to employ four mages, including the announcer. He had nothing to do with that fact, but he couldn't help the way his mind compiled information.

"YOUR VICTOR!" the announcer declared, extending the roar of the crowd.

Asher stood in it, soaking up the praise for being no more than a proficient killer. And how naked he felt, the truth of Nightfall laid bare for all the world to see. Breaking that tenet was akin to breaking his own bones and he felt it now, caught in the gaze of so many.

Before he could dwell any further on the secrets he had spilled with his actions, a mage stepped onto the sand where Darya had stood before the fight. The mage flicked her head at the gate, motioning for him to make his way over. Asher glanced at the wand in her hand before complying and leaving his silvyr blade where it rested in the gladiator's throat.

In truth, he couldn't get off the sand quick enough.

Silenced by the weight of his actions, Asher stood motionless, his arms raised while Fengil and Roin undressed him. The black cuirass creaked once the straps were untied and the leather removed from his body. Fengil, or possibly Roin, commented quietly that it would require a thorough clean. The ranger didn't need to look at it to know the armour was splattered with blood.

The vambraces were slid from his forearms, each slick from his opponents' injuries. As they were removed, the blood on his hands was smeared across his fingers.

He could feel the cloak bunched around his ankles before it was taken away. Like everything else it would need to be washed, though it seemed unlikely that they would be able to get those darker patches of red out of the fabric.

By the time he was back in his own clothes, the weapons chamber had welcomed Viktor, Darya, and Malak. Viktor was clapping his hands on approach, carefully stalked by the Shadow Witch, whose fingers remained close to one of the daggers on her belt. Malak was doing his best to appear unimpressed, though he was the only one who kept his distance from the blood-soaked Arakesh.

"That was wonderful!" Varga praised, his advance sending Fengil and Roin into retreat. "The whole city will be talking about you! Soon, the entire realm will—"

Asher snapped, his discipline forsaken in the face of such evil.

Viktor's next word died in his mouth as the ranger lunged at him and wrapped one hand around his jaw and the other around the back of his head. It was a move of execution—one of many in Asher's repertoire. He had only to twist his arms and the crime lord would cease to be, his neck broken.

Darya reacted, though she would have been too late to save her employer had Asher followed through with the execution. As it was, one of her daggers came to press against the side of his neck while the other had found the gap between his ribs, the tip needling his skin there. Beyond them all, Malak fell into a braced position, his one-handed axe freed from his belt. He was useless so far away.

Nobody moved. A fragile tension filled the chamber. Even so, Viktor remained unnaturally calm and flexed the fingers of one hand, urging the Shadow Witch to back off.

Asher had yet to take his murderous gaze from Varga's grey orbs, though he could see the edges of the shield flaring around his grip. It was so fine a thing that he could barely make out the gap between his hand and Viktor's jaw, but it was likely stronger than a steel plate.

"I might not be able to run you through," Asher growled, "but your magic can't stop me from turning your head so fast it snaps your neck."

The truth of that statement slowly, but surely, removed Viktor's smug grin. Perhaps, Asher pondered, this was the first time he had ever been assaulted and thus had never considered being killed in such a manner. Either way, it pleased the ranger greatly to see the crime lord squirm, even if it was subtly.

"Darya, my dear," Viktor called, with just enough slack around his jaw to do so.

Asher watched the Shadow Witch sheath one dagger and retrieve a slender strip of blue fabric from a pouch on her belt. She handed it to her master who then raised it for the ranger to better examine.

"Had you those keen senses of yours you would know exactly what this is," Viktor began. "'Tis a ribbon," he went on to explain. "Specifically, a little girl's ribbon. Can you guess which little girl once owned this?"

Asher's eyes shifted instantly between Viktor and the silky ribbon. There was only one girl it could have belonged to.

"Little Deadora Stormshield," Varga said melodically.

The ranger pressed himself even closer to the crime lord. "If you've—"

"She is perfectly safe," Viktor interjected reassuringly. "I had this taken from her home and sent here in the clutches of a raven. Of course, the lovely Stormshields have no idea a ruthless killer has crept into their home and robbed them."

Asher's grip faltered.

"That's it," Varga purred. "Kill me and the next raven that leaves this island will deliver their fate in its claws. When next you see the Stormshields, it will be in the arena facing some monster of nightmares."

The ranger's eyes glazed over, his rage snuffed out like a blown candle. He had seen red. He had seen evil in human form. The over-whelming desire to murder Viktor had claimed him in that moment. He had *needed* to, lest Viktor command him to take more lives on the arena's sands. But there was no defying the hard logic of his situation. Viktor could have the dwarven family killed before he even made it back to The Selk Road.

And what promise was Doran? How long could he defend them for? What was to stop Viktor's man from sneaking up on the dwarf and slitting his throat? No... This was the only way.

Asher's hands fell by his side again and his gaze grew distant, skimming over the top of Viktor's head into nothingness.

"Very good," Varga praised softly. "I understand," he said, running his hands down Asher's chest to smooth out the wrinkles. "Your blood must be boiling after all that," he added with a glance at the gate behind the ranger. "However…"

Varga exploded in a controlled burst of action; an impressive display having been stood so casually still. It also surprised Asher, who took the pointed elbow to his solar plexus. The blow was both accurate and powerful enough to knock him back and drop him to one knee, the air snatched from his lungs.

"If you *ever* touch me again," Viktor fumed, looking over the gasping ranger, "I will drag those dwarves here and skin them in front of you! Don't think I won't take the loss and happily feed you to my Vorska!"

His threat delivered, the crime lord backed off to straighten his robes out and clear his throat, his composure always quick to return. "Now that we've got that ugliness out of the way, I would compliment your display in the arena. You certainly captured the crowd. Hells, even The Fang looked eager for more!"

His breath coming under control once again, Asher managed to pick himself up and face the man. He had no doubt his face was flushed and his eyes watery—Nasta Nal-Aket had delivered just such a blow many times during his training. Like then, he wasn't permitted to strike back. Instead, he was to bear it, another brick in the walls of his fortitude.

"Very good," Viktor remarked lightly, satisfied to be looking up at the ranger again. "I think we will give you a few days. Yes," he agreed with himself. "Your legend will grow from tonight. When next you fight the coins will flow all the more easily. And you *will* fight," Varga determined, his tone dropping ominously. "I don't know what that was at the end there, but you are not to remove your blindfold and you will kill *every* last man I pit you against. If Alissandra is forced to intervene again," he warned, gesturing to the shadows of the chamber's doorway, "*I* will be forced to seek out more *severe* ways of motivating you. Am I understood?"

Asher was able to pierce the shadows around the doorway just enough to discover the outline of the mage who upheld Viktor's shield. He simply nodded, having said everything he felt like saying to the crime lord.

"Excellent!" Varga beamed, his hands clapping together. "Have Asher here escorted back to the training grounds. I think he's earned a hot soak in the baths."

~

The journey back was a blur, his reluctant steps those of a man resigned to his bloody destiny. Returned to the training grounds, Dragorn's unofficial prison, Asher was paraded along the sands, where all could watch him from between the bars of their cells. They had all witnessed his abilities in the arena, and had witnessed him whittle their number down by four.

Asher kept his head down and followed Kad Gorson, who had taken custody of him at the gate, through the narrow corridors, beyond the training area. They passed the tables and chairs where they ate during the day and entered the baths, of which there were twelve to choose from.

The magistri directed him to the only one that had steaming water in it. The Karathan gave some instruction about cleaning the blood off and the allotted time he had in the water, but the ranger had retreated into himself, where the words of others were no more than noise.

Upon Kad's departure, Asher relieved himself of his clothes and boots and stepped down into the bath dug out of the floor. He immediately submerged his head and let loose a roar worthy of the monsters caged beneath the arena.

CHAPTER 27

A ROYAL WELCOME

Jaxyl - A monster of cruel design and, in my opinion, further proof that something truly wicked has put monsters on our fair Verda. You will know a Jaxyl when you come across one or hear of their description. In fact, I have never met a witness who didn't tell me they had seen a creature of wolf and ram. 'Tis an apt description. To put it simply, they possess the head of a very angry ram (with four eyes mind you) and the body and claws of a wolf.

Something drives these beasts to rage. They roam the wilds with a very particular look in their four golden eyes. You've probably seen that look, in a tavern or pub, before a fight breaks out. It's as if the Jaxyls go looking for trouble, and not always for sustenance. They just like to kill, as if they've something in them that must be unleashed.

Killing them is just as easy as swinging your sword into the right body part. Just be sure to avoid those horns though—even at a short charge a Jaxyl will break your legs.

A Chronicle of Monsters: A Ranger's Bestiary, 12th Edition, Page 427.

Sabine The Red, Ranger.

. . .

What bitterly cold days had followed the son of Dorain's dramatic departure from Velia. How often he had looked up at the grey sky and wondered where the summer had gone, though never more so than when he made camp beside Pig, be that under the low branches of an old oak or by the banks of a stream.

Still, he had rationed his supplies well and utilised the streams as he happened across them, including the rushing waters of The Unmar. To save time—and such a precious thing that was—the dwarf had cut across the land, turning away from The Selk Road where it veered inland, towards Palios. Just as he had with Asher, on their journey south, Doran traversed the shallows of the river and continued north until he, once again, found the road that took him directly to Darkwell.

Under the usual scrutiny, he made his way through the city astride his Warhog. Eager though he was to push on with all haste and exit the city's rear gate, situated in the east, Doran kept Pig to a steady trot. The scrutiny he could handle, but there was no time to deal with the city watch face to face—he needed to *see* the Stormshields.

By the time he had put the streets behind him and the eastern gate was passing over his head, the world finally remembered what season it was in. Rays of warmth shone down on the later afternoon, breaking through the splitting clouds and returning the surrounding forest to its green vibrancy.

Taking the less-beaten track that wound up the rising land and through the trees, Doran demanded one last burst of energy from Pig, spurring the mount into the fastest run it could manage. When the smell of the ocean found its way to his nose, the dwarf pulled on the reins and began to dismount before the Warhog had come to a complete halt.

Moving a few steps away from the weary animal, the son of Dorain cocked his head to one side, listening. They weren't far from the Stormshield homestead, meaning he was either to hear Deadora playing as she would or Viktor's men making a ruin of the place. He heard neither thanks to Pig's heavy breathing. Turning to regard his noisy companion, the Warhog planted itself firmly on the ground and laid its snout out flat.

The dwarf sighed. "Ye stay 'ere then."

Taking naught but a small club and one of the daggers, Doran finished the rest of the trail on foot, and cautiously so. He knew the family owned a donkey, often required when towing Danagarr's cart into the city and back, but the hoof prints he discovered on the way were those of large horses and freshly imprinted at that.

It gave him a terrible feeling in his gut.

Pressing on, careful with his choice of steps, he finally heard signs of life. He stopped on the outskirts of the homestead, where one of Danagarr's sheds offered some cover. He waited, sure that the voice he had heard was not that of a fellow dwarf.

"We've been here since the dawn, Revus!" the same voice called out, a complaining tone to it.

"He's got a point, Rev," another spoke up, a little closer to the shed. "If them dwarves were 'ere we'd 'ave found 'em ages ago."

"Shut it! Both of you!"

Doran tracked the rebuttal across the courtyard, to the chicken coop. There stood a man, frustrated and tired by the hunch in his shoulders, who had known a life of violence. There didn't seem one feature about Revus's face that hadn't been injured at some point in his life. His hair was shaved and badly so, with clumps and tufts jutting out here and there. His appearance aside, Revus was broad of arm and shoulders alike with an ugly two-headed axe hanging low in one hand. Doran knew exactly what that weapon had been brought for.

"You were all there," Revus reminded. "You all heard what Undvig's message said. The boss wants the dwarves dead and we aren't to return until it's done."

One of the others stepped into view, his protest already visible in his expression. "Yeah but—"

"Is it done?" Revus interrupted. "Is it done?" he repeated, a pitch higher.

The other sighed in response. "No," he muttered.

"The boss also said," the third and closer thug pointed out incredulously, "that he wants their *heads*."

Revus shrugged. "What of it?"

The thug mimicked the leader's shrug. "So we've got to cross the country with *three heads in a bag*?"

The second thug appeared confused, though that might have been his resting expression. "Oh aye," he said, as if the minor detail had only just occurred to him. "Do we even have a bag?"

Revus held his hands up, head shaking in despair. "We'll figure it out when we actually *have* the heads."

The third of the witless fools looked about the homestead. "And when will that be? 'Cos just thinking about that sweet Velian ale is making me thirsty."

"That's if we make it back to Velia," the second added, "what with the trail of blood we'll be leaving behind us and all. We'll be lucky if we make it as far as Palios."

"Fine!" Revus blurted, exasperated. "You two can go back to Velia. But," he said sharply, one finger pointing, "when you get there without a bag full of heads, what do you think Undvig's going to do to you? Because I reckon he'll stick that wand of his between your legs and—"

"Alright, I get it!" the second insisted, his face screwed up even more than usual.

Revus grinned. "Well it's either that or he sends you both to Mr Varga himself. You heard what happened to Corrigan and his boys right?"

Thugs two and three regarded each other. "Let's just be finding them, then," the second said for them both.

"You checked the floorboards?" Revus questioned, pointing at the house with his axe. "These are dwarves remember—they're like badgers or something. I've heard it said they all live underground north of the mountains."

"I checked," the third replied, his tone suggesting this wasn't the first or even second time Revus had asked about the floor-boards. "I'm tellin' you, they ain' in the house. They ain't in any of the buildings!"

Revus grumbled something under his breath before turning to the trees. "Ratcher!" he yelled. "Ratcher! You out there?"

The rustle of bushes sounded not far from Doran. "Over here, Rev," came the reply from a fourth.

"Well?" Revus demanded.

"I found tracks," the fourth reported, missing the figure of Doran, who had crouched beside a holly bush. "I can't make heads or tails of them though. They're everywhere and they lead nowhere."

Revus turned away and growled, his mounting frustration punctuated by the swing of his axe and its impact to the roof of the chicken coop. The chickens were sent into a frenzy and darted in every direction, their wings flapping rapidly. Doran used the distraction to move, taking up a new position where he could see all four men without obstruction.

"Where in the hells are you dwarves?" Revus practically shrieked, yanking his axe out of the coop.

Ratcher turned to the second and quietly asked, "Did you bring up the thing about the heads?"

The second gave a resigned shrug. "We need to find a sack or something," was all he said in a hushed tone.

"Where are you?" Revus shouted again.

Doran pressed his back flat to the stable and slunk down into a crouch. He had the same question as Revus and, just like the thug, he couldn't answer it. Wherever they were, it wasn't in the hands of Viktor Varga, a fact he thanked the Mother and Father profusely for. He added an extra thanks that, despite arriving after Viktor's hired goons, he had still arrived in time to confront them before they bloodied their weapons. Perhaps there was still a little of the gods' favour shining down on him.

Adjusting his position to observe the thugs again, the dwarf's eyes passed over the wall of the stable and spotted something between the gaps in the boards. His mind required an extra moment to process what he had seen and so he gave a double take before focusing on the stable's interior.

There, peering out from a messy pile of hay, were a pair of eyes. They were watching Viktor's men through the open door of the stable. Moving closer to the gap between the boards, he was able to make out the edges of a trap door within the bundle of hay—the Stormshields were hiding *under* the stables.

"Psss," Doran hissed quietly.

Danagarr's eyes turned to him, wide and alarmed. Doran put his mouth over the gap and pressed a finger to his lips. The dwarven smith appeared to nod before slowly retreating beneath the stables, the trap door closing softly above him. The son of Dorain expressed his relief through a deep sigh—he could still vividly picture Varga's threat towards the family in his mind.

Now he just had to convince Revus and the others to be on their merry way.

"Why don't we just burn the house down?" Ratcher suggested, thrusting his slab of a chin at the Stormshields' home.

"Aye," the second thug agreed. "Let's smoke them out!"

Revus was already shaking his head. "The smoke will bring scouts from Darkwell," he told them. "We don't want the watch to deal with."

The third of the witless goons shrugged his lanky shoulders. "They ain't goin' to care! It's no crime to burn a few dwarves."

The man's words turned Doran's blood to fire. *He* would die first.

With his knife and club in hand, Doran waited for the others to turn back to Revus for instruction before stepping out from behind the stable. He crept up on the man, his boots treading softly on the hard dirt. The club struck the thug on the back of his left knee, dropping him down to Doran's height. There came no hesitation from the war-forged dwarf, his dagger plunging cleanly through the side of his foe's neck. And there he held him, gargling blood on one knee, pinned in place by the knife in his throat. It felt good.

The brief, but definitive, assault garnered the attention of the others. Their shock and disgust was just as satisfying as a fresh pint of Hobgobber's Ale on a hot day. Doran drank it in.

"It seems to me," the son of Dorain began, taking advantage of their stunned surprise, "that ye boys 'ave a short memory. It wasn' that long ago yer predecessors were standin' where ye are now. We sent those fellas back to Varga with their tails between their legs." Doran adjusted his grip on the hilt, eliciting a slow gasp from the dying thug. "I'm in no mood to break bones today," he continued, sure he had their attention. "And ye can bet I've no problem putting monsters like ye in the ground. So," he drew out, while simultaneously sliding his knife free, "ye've a decision to make."

As blood spurted from the gash in his throat, the thug fell onto his face, his journey to death assured. This focused the others all the more.

"Ye can either piss off back to Velia an' take whatever's comin' to ye," Doran continued, "or—an' this is me personal preference—ye can stay an' take yer chances with me. But I warn ye, lads," he added, reversing his grip on the knife, "if ye choose the latter, I won' be showin' ye the mercy o' broken bones."

Indeed, the dwarf was of a mind to beat them all bloody before delivering the killing blow. The fact that they could entertain the idea of murdering a child made them worse than any of the monsters under Viktor's arena. Better, he decided, to simply rid the world of them and quickly, before they consumed any more of its precious air.

The only thug who remained nameless made to advance, his short-sword gripped in one hand. Doran recognised the arrogant smirk ruling the fool's expression. Here was another human believing his height made him in every way superior to Doran when, in truth, he simply didn't know what killing machines dwarves were.

The son of Dorain hoped someone would inform him as such in the next life, for he would be too dead to ever learn it in this one. While the former would forever remain a mystery, Doran's knife—launched from his hand—ensured the latter came to pass with immediate effect. The thug had just enough time to look down at the hilt protruding from his chest before Death swooped in and claimed him, leaving naught but a corpse to hit the ground.

"Next," Doran spat with glee, his head turning sharply to Ratcher.

The largest of the gang retrieved a simple mason's hammer from his belt. A proficient weapon, in Doran's opinion, as it required little skill to wield yet it delivered significant damage. It was also, of course, utterly useless if the wielder's hand was too broken to actually grip it.

Doran met his opponent's backhand with a strong block that brought his club across Ratcher's knuckles. The hammer dropped, Ratcher gripped the wrist of his broken hand and cried out in pain. Doran, however, couldn't be doing with the racket and sought to silence the man as quickly as possible. To that end, he slammed the club up between the thug's legs, a debilitating blow that took the air from Ratcher's lungs and dropped him to his knees. The dwarf didn't even take a breath before snapping his enemy's neck.

That left one.

Doran turned around to lay eyes on Revus. He hadn't moved an inch. Gone was his bravado, snuffed out like the lives of his friends, if monsters could claim to have such things. Now, there was an almost imperceptible tremble in the hand holding the full weight of his two-handed axe. Revus swallowed hard and licked his lips, clearly trying to decide in which direction he should flee.

The son of Dorain cracked his neck to one side. "I'm to be killin' *ye* now," he said gruffly.

Revus tore his eyes from the dwarf, where they then flittered over the three dead bodies behind him. Proving he had better survival skills than the others, the thug let go of his weapon and ran. Survival skills hardly mattered, however, if he couldn't outrun a flying axe.

"Ye dropped this!" Doran yelled, as he threw the weapon from over his head, two hands firmly gripped around the haft.

In the span of a heartbeat—Revus's last as it was—a blur of steel and wood closed the gap. Its journey came to a sudden stop when one of the curved blades sank deep into his back, throwing him forward to the ground.

The woods surrounding the homestead were eerily quiet in the wake of Death's arrival. There was no bird song nor even a rustle from the trees. To Doran, there was but the sound of his heart thundering in his ears and his laboured breath. It had been some time, years even, since he had killed anything that couldn't be found in Asher's bestiary. Monstrous as Viktor's men were, there was something different about killing people; an extra factor that increased his bloodlust and put him right back on the battlefields he had escaped.

So enraptured by the feeling, the dwarf missed the sound of the trap door opening and the Stormshields approaching from behind. When Danagarr put a hand on Doran's shoulder, he turned on the familiar dwarf and took him by the collar of his shirt, a feral growl building in his throat. Perhaps it was Kilda's yelp of surprise or Deadora's gasp, but Doran's fog of war dissipated enough for him to stay his raised fist. Another thunderous heartbeat and he managed to release his friend's shirt and even back away.

"Apologies," he mumbled, adjusting the hang of his cloak.

Kilda stepped forward and placed a mothering hand to his cheek. "For once, Heavybelly, yer timin' was perfect."

"Aye," Danagarr agreed, smoothing his shirt down. "We'd been down there all day. I wasn' sure how much longer we could hold out."

Deadora rushed between her parents and wrapped her small arms around his leg. "*You saved us!*" she exclaimed in their native tongue.

Doran was suddenly aware of the bodies scattered about the Stormshield homestead. It was no sight for a child. "It seems me timin' could o' been better," he opined, his voice gruff.

"They're dead an' we're not," Danagarr remarked as a matter of fact. "Yer arrival is nothin' short of a miracle, praise Grarfath."

"Still," Doran continued, nodding at Deadora, "we should see to buryin' 'em. Don' want to be givin' the folk in Darkwell a reason to hang us."

"We heard them talkin'," Danagarr said, his eyes finding Revus's body in the distance. "They were sent by that Viktor fella."

Doran's brow pinched at the name. "Aye," he confirmed. "This should never 'ave happened but..." The dwarf shrugged hopelessly. "Varga's too vindictive to honour his half o' the deal."

"Deal?" Danagarr echoed. "So ye made one with 'im?"

Conscious of the corpses he had made, Doran only replied, "Aye, we did. I'll tell ye all abou' it after we've dealt with this lot. Maybe Deadora can play inside for a while?" he suggested.

As the son of Dorain moved to begin piling the bodies, Kilda held him back with a light touch to his arm. "Asher has not returned with ye?"

Doran could see the ranger, wrists bound and surrounded by enemies, as The White Horse sailed away from Dragorn. "No," he answered grimly. "No, he hasn'."

CHAPTER 28
INTUITION

Fraedan - Perhaps it's my age, but I was raised to call them Imps or Sprites. Regardless of their name, the best word to describe these little creatures is mischievous. I've never seen one taller than my hand but it's their size that lends to their vexatious behaviour. They can get into everything and, thanks to their nimble fingers, I've even seen one reach into the keyhole of a door and undo the lock.

Who can say what drives these wicked beasts? I say it is no more than boredom, though I have heard others—of the religious sort—claim they are sent by the Goddess Atarae to keep our individual destinies on track. I'm sticking with my theory. You're free to make your own and add it to the next edition of this bestiary.

You will know a Fraedan when you see one. The homunculi look strikingly like us, with all the features you would expect to see in a human. There are some added features, such as their small horns and mouse-like tail. They're also a deep purple, though I have seen a few with red skin.

When they're not setting mills alight or leading several thousand rats from tavern to tavern, Fraedan sleep together in one big pile. This pile will be inside the largest bird nest you have ever seen and high up a tree.

*If you catch them sleeping, a flaming arrow should do the trick. If you tackle them while they're awake, they'll likely swarm you.
Just look for the nest.*

**A Chronicle of Monsters: A Ranger's Bestiary, 12th Edition,
Page 114.**

Osmand The Mute, Ranger.

He had been seen.

There was no going back. No convincing the witnesses they were mistaken. No hiding in the shadows. Spectators and gladiators alike had watched a blindfolded man kill four men with seemingly choreographed steps. The Arakesh had been made flesh.

In the days since, the training grounds had become unbearable. For years, Asher had moved through the world with insubstantial steps, a ghost who drifted from place to place. But now, within those high walls, the ranger's every step was like thunder in the ears of his fellow gladiators.

Wherever he was, eyes regarded him with curiosity and fear. Even inside the confines of his private cell he could feel eyes on his door. They would always be watching him now, like the fish that always keep the shark in sight lest it turn on them. It still didn't feel right, to be *seen*. It was like an itch inside his skull that he could never scratch.

Whether he liked it or not, he needed it now, the fear that kept those eyes on him. It was a tool he could use to stay alive, though to what end he still could not say.

Moving through the training grounds, through that haze of fear, Asher couldn't rightly say how many days had passed since his bloody display in the arena. The days and nights had blurred together. Under the summer sun, he honed his body through relentless exercise or watched those around him move through their routines—futile as they were. Within the gloom of his cell, when the day was finally behind him, he dreamt of real violence, always of memories past. Every morning he would awake in a sweat, sure that his hands would be coated in blood.

His fellow gladiators—prisoners by any other name—had witnessed Death incarnate, yet Baal and Grift still regarded him with palpable contempt. As did their small cabal of followers, though they remained cautiously behind their fearless leaders. Still, the pair hadn't provoked him. If they had planned to, his recent display in the arena would have likely given them something to think about. Asher could live with the looks and the sneers. They would only last until they met in the arena anyway.

That last thought plagued the ranger for most of the day. Every gladiator he looked upon would potentially die by his actions. They must have been thinking the same thing. And how many more were there yet to come, men who had wronged the system Dragorn called justice? How many more would enter this foul place and meet their end on his sword? It would be a cycle of never-ending death.

"Water?"

The question broke his spiralling thoughts, turning the ranger to Mouse and the proffered waterskin. As always, he accepted the water and sniffed the contents before swigging it back.

"I was thinking," Mouse began, "maybe you could show me one or two moves? I saw you..." The young man faltered and he licked his lips. "In the erm... In the arena. Maybe you could—"

"No," Asher told him bluntly, taken back to his days serving as a mentor for Nightfall's younger Arakesh. "I'm done teaching people how to kill people."

Mouse was already nodding along. "Of course," he said, pondering. "Maybe then, you know, if we're ever in the arena at the same time... Maybe we could work *together*."

Asher regarded the diminutive figure of a man. He would need all the help he could get on the sands. "Do yourself a favour, kid, and stay away from me. Nothing good ever came from being around me."

"Mouse!" the magistri barked. "Pick up a sword! You're rotating in!" Once he recovered from the surprise of hearing his own name, Mouse skittered off and did as he was told. Kad Gorson gave the ranger a pointed look as he approached. "I think it would be better," he suggested, "if you rested *inside* today."

"You mean you want me out of sight," Asher corrected.

Gorson took a breath. "Having you in here right now is like having one of those monsters around. The men see you and they see their death. It's off-putting and they need to focus. Five of them are heading into the arena tonight."

The ranger responded with a questioning look.

"Not you," Kad replied. "But you're up soon," he added. "Outside these walls, you're the talk of the city. I've even heard there's mainlanders due to arrive. When the frenzy is to Mr Varga's satisfaction, you can expect to hit the sand again. Until then..." The magistri nodded his chin at Asher's cell.

With nothing more to say, Asher turned away and crossed the training ground as if there weren't gladiators sparring on it. Those in his path were quick to pause and stand aside, two of whom averted their gaze, as if the assassin could kill them with his eyes alone.

As he reached the threshold of his cell, Asher noticed Salim at the other end of the corridor, beyond the eating area and the baths. There were a collection of odd rooms back there, including a place for the guards to rest in between patrols. There was nothing that held any meaning for a gladiator.

Asher was on the verge of ignoring the scene when something about the southerner screamed at the ranger's senses. He was unusually still, as if he had become stuck while contemplating. When he did finally move, it was with a stride of purpose that felt wrong to Asher.

His hand resting against the doorframe of his cell, the ranger's fingers tapped the wood repeatedly. His curiosity, a characteristic of his ranger-self, demanded investigation. As did his humanity that suspected something terrible was about to happen to Salim. But why should he care? They were all doomed to die on this island and he didn't even know if Salim's life was in danger. He should simply retire to his cell.

But he was walking down that same corridor, following in Salim's steps.

He passed a handful of gladiators who had been assigned to clear up after lunch and the single guard who observed them. None seemed to care where he was going or why, testament to the fact that there was no way out of the complex. Beyond the baths, the ranger turned a corner—it was a dead end with three doors either side. There was no sign of Salim.

After glancing back the way he had come, the ranger moved on, checking the first door he came to. Locked. As was the door opposite and the next two down. The final door on the left, however, opened without protest. It was gloomy therein, the only light provided by a slit set high into the wall that revealed a column of dust.

And Salim, hanging by his neck.

Asher darted forward, a slave to his instincts. He wrapped his arms around the southerner's waist and heaved him up, taking the pressure off his throat. Salim's thrashing stopped almost immediately and his hands—notably free of binding—slapped maniacally about the ranger's face and head. Under the oscillating movement, something gave way and the noose slipped through the loop that had secured it. Carrying Salim's weight, Asher went down with the southerner on top of him.

An awkward manoeuvre untangled them, allowing Salim to roll away, coughing and cursing the ranger as he did. Asher inspected the noose extending from around the southerner's neck —a handful of random pieces of clothing all knotted together.

"Why?" Salim rasped, the first coherent word Asher had ever heard the man utter.

"Why would you try to kill yourself?" the ranger countered. It was easier to ask the question than answer the one posed to him.

Sitting against the wall, the southerner removed the noose and rubbed his neck. "Hell will hold no surprises for me," he said, in his thick Karathan accent.

Asher rested his back against the adjacent wall. "There's always something worse," he muttered. "You couldn't wait until the arena?"

Salim didn't answer, his chest rising high with laboured breaths.

Questioning whether he had done the right thing or not, Asher gave a short nod and made to rise. "Alright then," he said gruffly.

"I cannot die in the arena," Salim stated, halting the ranger mid-stand. "By my honour, I will not die by the blade of a lesser man. And I have no desire to die to the cheer of a crowd."

Asher returned to the floor, beside one of the empty shelving racks that lined half the room. "Your honour?" he echoed incredulously, a characteristic he had never given much weight to. "Your honour doesn't mind if you die swinging from some pitiful noose though?"

"If I must die, then I will die on my terms and by my hands."

Asher gave a shrug. "Fair enough."

"I do not expect an assassin to understand," Salim said, with an edge to his damaged voice.

"And you'd be right not to," Asher agreed, deciding he couldn't be bothered with an argument about his title.

"Nor would I expect an assassin to save my life," the southerner added, again halting the ranger from making his leave.

Asher met his companion's gaze. "I suppose we'll just have to live with not understanding each other then."

"I saw you fight," Salim went on. "I have never seen a man fight like that without his sight."

"And I haven't seen you fight at all," Asher quipped.

Salim glanced at the wall between them and the corridor. "For all his sins, the magistri cannot break the foundations of his conditioning. I imagine you know something about that yourself."

Asher had no response to the latter; at least none he felt like voicing. "His conditioning? What's that got to do with you?"

"He is an old captain of Karath," Salim informed, his breathing under control now. "I believe the Serpent Legion were under his command. Good fighters all."

"You're army too if ever I saw it," Asher remarked, putting it together.

"For a time," Salim admitted. "But I was called to a higher path..." The southerner gave a soft laugh, robbing him of his own words. "I haven't heard the sound of my own voice in some time," he explained. "The irony that I would confide in one lacking such honour as you. Perhaps I truly am in Hell, and there is no need for this." He picked up the noose and tossed it away.

Having stomached all the insults he could from a man whose life he had just saved, Asher stood up to leave. "You only know what I was," he told the man. "You know *nothing* of who I am." Even as he said the words, the ranger could only hope there was still a distinction to be made.

"Wait," Salim beseeched, a hand held up towards the ranger. "I speak of honour and show none. You saved my life." He considered his own words. "Perhaps you have even saved something of my honour." Picking himself up, he offered Asher his hand. "I am Salim Al-Anan, former Honour Guard to Emperor Kolosi."

The ranger hesitated before clasping the man's forearm in greeting. "Honour Guard?" he repeated. Were there any better fighters in The Arid Lands than the emperor's personal guards? Asher had never fought one—there had never been a contract to kill the emperor—but he recalled Nasta Nal-Aket comparing them to the Graycoats. They were also revered by the general armies of the south, with only the best of the best being chosen to ascend to such a position. That certainly explained his special treatment from the magistri.

"I'm Asher," he managed, recovering from the revelation.

"I know—"

"Ranger," Asher interjected, before Salim could claim to know what he was.

"A *ranger*? I have not heard of this."

Asher took his hand back and stepped away. "We... *I* hunt monsters. For coin," he added, wishing to be honest.

Salim frowned. "You are Arakesh, no?"

"I was," he confessed. "Now I'm not," he said simply. "What I *was*, however, is of far more interest to Viktor Varga than what I *am*."

"He is a collector of dangerous things," Salim commented, crouching to roll up his makeshift noose. He considered it in his hands for a moment before placing it on one of the empty shelves, clearly abandoning it.

Approaching steps brought an end to their conversation. "One of the guards," Asher deduced by the sound of their boots.

"We should not be found here," Salim warned.

Asher agreed and opened the door enough to peer out and spy the guard. Handling a ring of keys, the ranger concluded that the guard was entering one of the locked doors. Salim stepped closer, curious perhaps, but the ranger held a hand up to impose patience.

"Now," he eventually whispered, after the guard had disappeared behind one of the other doors.

Upon reaching the training grounds, the pair went their separate ways and without another word.

It wasn't until the evening meal time that Asher caught up with Salim again. Deliberately steering away from Mouse and the others, he took the seat opposite the southerner, who always aimed to sit a few seats away from everyone else. The Honour Guard's stoicism was equal to the ranger's, a quality that endeared him.

They ate in silence for several minutes, their apparent alliance putting the others on edge. Asher enjoyed it.

"How did Viktor come to collect you?" the ranger asked, breaking their mute accord.

Salim finished his mouthful and glanced at the gladiators over Asher's shoulder. "There are only four laws on this island," he began. "The Trigorns, Fenrigs, Yarls, and the Danathors. If you threaten their standing or even question it, you end up belonging to Viktor Varga."

Asher was almost amused by the analogy. "And which *law* did you break?"

"The Yarls," he answered, with obvious derision. "I stopped two men from murdering a man who owed them... how do you say? *Protection money*."

"Protecting and threatening mean the same thing here," Asher said, continuing with his meal.

Salim nodded in agreement. "And how does so skilled an assassin end up in the clutches of Viktor Varga?"

"Poor choice in friends," Asher replied, before wondering if friends was to overstate the reality. He shrugged. "I tried to cut a deal on behalf of another hunter and his kin. They live, I fight."

Salim appeared to be watching him now, as if he could see through his skin and into his soul. "Perhaps I was mistaken about your honour. You are not the Arakesh I have heard stories of."

"I was *everything* you've heard," Asher admitted. "Maybe worse. I found a way out though. It didn't last long," he added, his demeanour deflating. "In here, I can feel it all coming back to me." The ranger stopped himself before his emotional state could translate into further words. "Viktor," he said instead, "has turned me into Dragorn's new executioner."

"Not today," Salim pointed out. "Today you saved a life," he said quietly, his fork twisting his food rather than gathering it.

Asher looked around, his gaze enough to redirect others, before turning his attention back to the Honour Guard. "*Will you try it again?*" he asked in perfect Karathan.

Salim looked up at him, a hint of surprise at hearing his native tongue from an outsider. Of course, he had no idea that Nightfall was located in The Arid Lands or that most training excursions were in Karath itself. Not that such a detail would have mattered, Asher thought. Had Nightfall been in the snows of the north every Arakesh would still be expected to know the various languages and dialects of the south.

"*I don't know,*" Salim answered honestly, returning the language of his ancestors.

Asher left it there for a minute, his thoughts cast back to his own attempt, four years prior. "*You went further than I did,*" he said, his voice still nuanced despite the foreign language he was conversing in. "*I tried. But I never went through with it.*"

Saying it out loud hadn't been nearly as painful or exposing as he had thought it would be. The memory of it was still so clear in his mind; on his knees, the blade to his chest. His courage had faltered. Or perhaps it was his cowardice that had faltered. The ranger always struggled to decide which it had been.

It then struck Asher as a bizarre thing to have told the man he had met only two hours earlier. Perhaps, he wondered with irritation, this was another effect of his maturing humanity. Intuition had always been a tool for profiling those around him, allowing him to reduce all to a walking list of attributes and little else. In Doran he had seen a kinship, a bond born of guilt from a life they would both rather forget. In Salim, he saw an honest man who did not belong among the worst of Dragorn—a warrior of discipline still.

That wasn't to say he could trust the man. Trust was hard earned, if such a thing was even possible. But what were a few truths between the damned? And it made a change from talking to Hector.

Salim let the words hang between them for a moment. "*Because you didn't go through with it, I am alive.*"

But how many more had died? Asher didn't voice that question, or the subsequent question of how many *more* would die?

"*I'm sorry,*" Asher eventually offered. "*You didn't ask me to stop you.*"

"*I haven't asked anyone for anything in a long time. It doesn't mean I shouldn't have.*" Salim sighed. "*I would have found no honour in that room, only a meaningless death.*"

Asher regarded the southerner for a moment, recalling all that he knew of the emperor's protectors. "*Honour Guards should die protecting their emperor,*" he stated from their ancient code.

"*Yes,*" Salim confirmed, and with a heavy heart by the tension in his jaw. "*Should we see our service through, we are expected to instruct future Honour Guards until our death.*" He let his hand fall to the table and his fork clatter against the plate. "*That is not to be my fate,*" he said, taking in their surroundings. "*I will not even have the honour of dying in true battle. In Viktor's world, it is all a performance.*"

Asher finished his cup of water and poured them both another from the jug they shared. "*How did you end up in Dragorn? You're a long way from your post.*"

An element of Salim's discipline and poise fractured, if only for a second. "*Your Karathan is exceptional,*" he complimented, evading the question.

"*It's been a long time since I have made use of it,*" Asher replied. "*I'd forgotten how much I enjoy the feel of the words.*"

Salim nodded along, happily agreeing, even if his mind was elsewhere. "*I was exiled,*" he said eventually.

Asher tried to keep the surprise out of his expression. "*From Karath?*"

Salim paused. "*From The Arid Lands,*" he replied, his voice almost breaking.

The ranger could think of only one thing that would lead to the exile of an Honour Guard. "*What happened?*" he asked, not wanting to make assumptions and risk insult.

"*Six months ago,*" Salim recounted, "*there was an assassination attempt on Emperor Kolosi and his wife. The first attempt in two generations,*" he added.

Asher suddenly felt foolish for not being aware of that fact, though he was hardly one for gossip or even talking to the people he encountered on his travels. "*I hadn't heard.*"

"*On that day, the attempt was seen through to its end,*" Salim continued. "*The emperor and his wife were both slain. Two of my fellow Honour Guards died trying to defend them. I alone survived the ordeal, and with naught but bruises to show for it.*" It was clear to see that the latter stung deeply, as if he should bear terrible scars in exchange for his survival.

Asher was about to enquire about the killer, sure that the

description would match the garb of an Arakesh, but Salim beat him to it. *"I have never seen anyone fight like that,"* he explained, his eyes seemingly cast into the recent past. *"Not even your display in the arena could be compared,"* he mused, bringing genuine surprise to the ranger's face.

"How so?" he asked, with hardly a breath.

"He was fast," Salim reported, eyes flashing with remembered awe. *"And strong. I saw him throw the emperor as if he were no more than a child."*

Asher sat back, the mystery already gnawing at his bones. *"They never caught him?"*

Salim shook his head. *"The blame was placed on a group of rebel slaves known as The House of Owls. But I know that not to be true. There are dark forces at work in the south. An evil stirs there. I fear my kinsmen are only aiding it."*

That all sounded rather theatrical to Asher, but he wasn't going to argue with the man about his homeland. *"And you were exiled,"* he concluded.

Salim raised his chin an inch. *"I was. And rightly so. I failed in my duties. Now the safety of The Arid Lands falls on the shoulders of an infant who cannot even crawl yet."*

"Why Dragorn?" Asher asked.

"I believed there were people after me," the southerner divulged. *"I can't be certain, of course. It was more of a sense. I asked the wrong people too many questions before my exile."*

Asher knew what it was like to be hunted, to always be looking over your shoulder. *"I think you chose poorly,"* he said with a hint of amusement.

Salim saw the humour in it. *"I think you are right. As did you,"* he commented.

Asher responded with something close to a shrug of agreement, though he knew he was where the Stormshields needed him to be.

"This friend," Salim pondered, his tone improving upon the pivot in conversation, *"the hunter. He is still on Dragorn?"*

Asher gave a short laugh. *"Doran? He's long gone. He'll have already seen the bottom of so many tankards he won't even remember me."*

Survive, the dwarf had said. What little hope Asher had glimpsed of his companion finding him a way out of this hell was gone now. He could rely only on himself. Such thoughts gave strength to the *Assassin*.

Three loud knocks tore through the room, silencing the hubbub, and turning every head to Kad Gorson and his baton. "Time's up, boys!" he yelled. "To your cells!"

Salim stood up before Asher. *"I thank you for today, for both deed and word. I hope not to meet you on the sand. Viktor would be most displeased if I was to kill his champion."*

Asher used his own rise from the chair to stifle his amusement. Meeting the Honour Guard eye to eye again, he simply nodded, agreeing with the sentiment.

He watched the man from The Arid Lands walk away as the *Assassin's* dark thoughts crept through the alleys of his mind. If and when the time came, Salim's blood would wash the sands red.

Saving one man's life would not be enough to defy the monster within anymore.

CHAPTER 29

ONE MORE WAR

Khalighast - *Easily identified by the three thick tendrils protruding from the back of their head and shoulders. Here's a monster that can take to the water as swiftly as it does the land. I've hunted these beasts in both and, honestly, they're fiends to kill in either. They're fast runners, fast swimmers, and damned fast killers. They move predominantly on four legs but they can stand on two if they wish—which puts them somewhere between six and seven feet tall.*

Their grey hide is that of a rough leather, not dissimilar to a Gobber's, if a little tougher. In fact, after you've brought the Khalighast down, I would recommend turning them into a good saddle.

When it comes to distinguishing between the sexes, you need to get a good look at those tendrils I mentioned. The female's are longer and darker than their male counterparts. You might be wondering why you need to know the difference—a monster is a monster. But, when it comes to Khalighasts, targeting the right one can make all the difference to your hunt. Due to the fact that they live in a female hierarchy, if you can identify and kill the matriarch first, the pack loses its cohesiveness. When these creatures aren't working together they're more mindless animal than dangerous predator. That's when you wade in with your sword, but I'm not going to teach you how to suck eggs.

Doran apologised by expression alone, his shoulders hunching up.

Danagarr flexed his fingers from the flat of the table, a gesture to cool Doran's temper. "*We're all a bit frayed after recent events.*" The smith took a breath. "*The way I see it,*" he said calmly, "*we need to get out from under the gaze of this Varga fella. If we're not in danger, he's no leverage to hold against Asher. Now, I know that doesn't equal his freedom for he can't exactly break himself out if he doesn't know we're safe. But, if we can evade Varga's men for a while, it will give us the time needed to free him ourselves.*"

That last word clogged up Doran's thoughts. "*Ourselves? What are you about?*"

"*Aye,*" Kilda echoed. "*What are you about?*"

Danagarr thumbed at the front door. "*I heard what you were saying today, about them fancy cells you were being kept in. There's only one at this table with the skills to open them.*"

"*You must be joking!*" Kilda replied.

"*They're Novian cells!*" Doran protested at the same time. "*With erm... Hyperia locks or some such. They just can't be opened!*"

Danagarr waved his words away. "*I don't care what fancy names they have. If they've been crafted by human minds and forged by human hands they might as well have been constructed by a child. I can open them,*" he added confidently.

"*You can't go to Dragorn!*" Kilda insisted, as if it was obvious.

"*Aye,*" Doran reinforced. "*It's going to be hard enough getting about on my own, never mind two of us! And don't forget, even if—by some miracle of Grarfath—we rescue Asher, we still need to get out of there and off that damned island.*"

The smith appeared unfazed by the allied reproach. "*I don't think you understand my intentions,*" he said slowly. "*There's more to this than freeing Asher, gods help him.*" The dwarf laid his hands flat on the table top. "*My family is in danger,*" he began again, his gaze burning with quiet rage. "*They will remain in danger for as long as this Viktor Varga holds power. I cannot, will not, let that be. I am a Stormshield, and if he knew what that really meant, he would never have threatened my kin.*"

The rousing, yet menacing, speech brought goosebumps to Doran's arms. "*What do you mean to do?*"

"*There's no meaning about it, lad. Not anymore. I'm going to that island, with or without you, and I'm going to undo this little man's kingdom with my bare hands.*"

Doran swallowed, wholly taken in by the crusade. He turned to Kilda, however, sure that the healer would bring a swift end to such tough talk. Her eyes were glassy orbs, a sight that lent her a softness Doran was unaccustomed to seeing in the Stormshield.

"*He's right,*" she said, if reluctantly. "*This won't end until Viktor has bigger problems than us. Destroy his world,*" she said, nodding along to her own words, "*before he destroys ours.*"

Doran didn't miss Kilda's gaze fall on her daughter's bedroom. "*I'd kill more than I can number to keep that girl safe—to keep all of you safe. But you don't know what you're talking about. You don't know Dragorn and you don't know Viktor. Two dwarves going to war against all that he can bring to bear? Even if we did bring him down, it might cost you your life. Both our lives.*"

"*Sounds like Heavybelly talk to me,*" Kilda stated.

Doran sighed, his fists clenching into knots. "*I'm getting mighty sick of that,*" he told her. "*Dhenaheim or Illian, being a Stormshield doesn't make you better than a Heavybelly. They're just the names of two long-dead dwarves whose deeds have been bloated beyond all truth.*" He stood up and pressed one finger into the table. "*But I am alive and I can tell you the truth...*"

The tirade building in the son of Dorain fled his lips at the sight of Deadora. Without a sound, the girl had come to stand in the doorway of her bedroom. She was staring at him with her innocent features and big doe eyes. How many times had he looked at her and wondered if the gods might have blessed him with a daughter one day, had he stayed the course his father intended? And were she to be like Deadora, what a blessed dwarf he would have been. But there were no children on the path he had chosen.

That couldn't be true, he then realised, frozen in that moment with her. How could it be, when a child was the very thing he was fighting for?

Deadora hurried to her father's side and complained of a nightmare in the comfort of his arms. *"Like I said,"* Danagarr reiterated, looking at Doran from across the table, *"I'm going with or without you, lad."*

"You're not going without me," Doran said quietly, humbled by his own love for the girl. He looked at Kilda and made peace with her by expression alone. *"I reckon I've one more war in me,"* he added.

A wicked grin spread Danagarr's beard. *"I'm glad you said that. I've something to show you."* The smith kissed his daughter on the head and ushered her to accompany Kilda back to bed. *"Follow me,"* he bade Doran.

Each carrying a blazing torch, the dwarves departed the house and crossed the yard to the workshop. For the first time that day, Doran noticed the smith's stride and was pleased to see he had overcome his previous injury fighting the Troll. Having a healer for a wife was never a bad thing, he reasoned.

Inside the workshop, Danagarr ignited the hearth and put his torch to a handful of others, illuminating the benches and tools.

The smith moved to the corner, where a dusty tarpaulin concealed something tall beneath. *"When you left, it was to make a deal that would keep me and mine safe. Grateful as I was, it left me feeling awfully idle. When my hands get that itch, I've got to put them to work. So,"* he drawled with a shrug. *"Expecting you back as I was, I made you something."*

Doran folded his thick arms across his chest. *"What've you been up to, Stormshield?"*

Rather than explain any further, Danagarr gripped the folds of the tarpaulin and dragged it. Revealed was a crude mannequin, the sort used by soldiers to improve their sword techniques. Of course, it was the armour fitted around the wooden structure that captivated the son of Dorain.

His mouth slightly ajar, the dwarf approached the cuirass and pauldrons with his torch held forward to better appreciate the details. Polished black and gold, it was a quality of armour he hadn't seen since his days as Grimwhal's War Mason. His rough fingers ran over the smooth surface of the chest plates and curved with the gold lines, taking his grip to the edge of the cuirass. It was damned strong, that much his dwarven intuition informed him.

He turned to Danagarr. *"It's not..."*

"No," the smith answered, *"it's not silvyr. I honestly didn't think you'd want it."*

"Aye," Doran replied softly, his eyes cast back to the exquisite armour. *"You'd be right."*

Coveted as the mineral might be, Doran had rid himself of the shackles that bound his kin to silvyr. Walking away from that life meant walking away from the trappings that appealed to so many others. In his opinion, silvyr should be reserved for the heroes among them, of which he knew there were none. That golden age had long passed.

He was happy with his steel.

And steel worked by hands so skilled as Danagarr's made it all the better. He rapped his knuckles against one of the pauldrons and gave a silent chuckle. It was perfect.

"And these," the smith said, presenting him with a pair of matching vambraces.

Doran beamed as he took them in hand. *"You honour me, Danagarr."*

The smith matched his smile before something occurred to him. *"Oh!"* he exclaimed, snapping his fingers. *"There's more!"*

"More?" Doran questioned in disbelief.

"Well," Danagarr replied, his tone coming down a notch, *"it's not to the standards of the armour but..."*

From one of the benches, the smith returned holding an axe in one hand and a sword in the other. Doran placed his vambraces down with care and gladly accepted the weapons. The warrior in him scrutinised every inch of them, his eyes running up and down the haft of the axe before flitting to the blade of the sword.

"I purchased them in Darkwell some time ago," Danagarr explained. *"Not sure what I was going to do with them,"* he muttered. *"Anyway, I've reforged them both to some degree; made them fit for dwarven hands."*

"*That you have,*" Doran agreed, hefting the weapons.

The sword was single-handed though it seemed Danagarr had thickened the hilt and, perhaps, even shortened it, as he had the length of the blade itself. It felt sturdy in Doran's grip as he rolled his wrist. The axe looked more a work of art than a piece of steel attached to some wood. Either side of the leather straps, the haft possessed carvings in the same intricate pattern as the armour, which then spread across the curving blade in a display of the smith's incredible talent.

Danagarr stepped closer to the armour and tapped it with the back of a finger. "*Try not to lose this lot like you did the last, eh?*"

The comment sent Doran right back to The Mer Seed and the tumultuous journey to Dragorn. There was no getting around the fact that they would have to do it again. Approaching steps cut through his thoughts and turned him back towards the house. Kilda walked into the torchlight with a shawl draped over her shoulders.

"*A fine suit of armour if ever there was one,*" she voiced with genuine praise. "*I would say there aren't many in the realm fit to wear my husband's work.*" The dwarven healer took a breath and eyed Doran. "*I think for the likes of a Heavybelly... it's just right.*"

Her smile was infectious and quickly spread to Doran's face. "*Thank you,*" he said quietly, appreciating what was a compliment and an apology all in one.

Kilda moved close enough to put a hand on one of his large shoulders. "*You are a good dwarf, Doran, son of Dorain. I have not met so many of those. You will be a friend to this family for the rest of your days.*"

"*Thank you,*" he replied, slightly flustered by the kindness.

Kilda squeezed his shoulder before stepping away. "*Right,*" she announced. "*I suggest we all get a good night's sleep. Tomorrow, I will take Deadora north, to Dunwich. It's a damned long walk for her little legs, but you're going to need the donkey if you're to reach Velia in good time.*"

"*You're sure?*" the smith checked.

Kilda waved away his concern. "*We'll be fine. We can purchase supplies in Dunwich and camp in The Black Wood. We won't be found."* She turned to Doran. *"I'm sure you know the fastest route back to Velia."*

"Aye," he confirmed.

"Very good," Kilda replied. *"Come along husband,"* she bade, making her way back to the house.

Doran grinned at Danagarr, who was only too happy to accompany his wife. He watched them disappear inside their home, another thing he would never have on his path. But, like Deadora, that didn't mean there wasn't a home to protect.

The dwarf looked down at the sword and axe in his hands. *"One more war,"* he whispered into the breeze.

CHAPTER 30

THE CHAMPION OF DRAGORN

Creeper - You'll never hear them coming. It doesn't matter the terrain, Creepers move like the silent hand of Death. I've seen the needle legs walk through snow, forests of fallen leaves, and caves awash with puddles. Despite being four feet tall, their arms and legs are such fine points of bone that there isn't that much to see of them. By the time you realise one has crept up on you, it will be too late.

Of course, you will know about it when they are upon you. If they don't impale you with their needle arms they will clamp their jaws around a limb and they will not let go. I saw a fellow ranger stab a Creeper in the back repeatedly and it never once relented its bite. It's a tactic of the males, used to slow you down until the females can attack. Nasty buggers.

If you do find yourself with a Creeper's jaws wrapped around your leg or arm, use fire to free yourself. It's the only thing that will make the creatures retreat.

A Chronicle of Monsters: A Ranger's Bestiary, 12th Edition, Page 331.

Trantor Vane, Ranger.

. . .

Returned to the weapons room, to the same spot in fact, Asher stood with his arms out while Fengil and Roin suited him in clean leathers and a red cloak. While the two wittered between themselves about fitting and shape, Asher listened to the drone of the announcer through the closed gate. The mage was in the process of working the crowd up, promising them more blood and more coin than they could ever imagine.

Asher could feel the *Assassin's* anticipation building inside him. It wanted out. Violence was its way and violence it would have. With slow and steady breaths, the *Ranger* retreated into the background.

Before he could complete the ritual, however, Viktor Varga and his usual entourage arrived. "Excellent!" the crime lord praised, his hands held out to encompass his champion. "How quickly you look the part," he remarked, walking right up to him. It was a display for all of them as much as Asher - a show of strength if not dominance. "Ah, the new armour looks just as I imagined," he continued, a single finger taking in the curve of a pauldron.

The comment tugged at Asher's attention, turning his eyes down to the leathers that had been fitted neatly around his muscle groups. The detail had escaped his previous notice—a fact he chalked up to his switching personalities. He could see now that Fengil and Roin had equipped him with brown leathers not unlike the ones he had worn as a ranger. Upon closer inspection, Asher decided the armour was an improvement on the dark leathers he had been stripped of after his first appearance in the arena.

"You like?" Viktor enquired, head tilted as he observed Asher. "The black armour will have its moments, of course, but I felt tonight called for the look of a *hero*."

Asher raised an eyebrow. "A hero? How twisted *is* this crowd?"

Viktor laughed the question off. "There will be time for the Arakesh in all its shadowed glory. Tonight, I wish for you to display the talents of an Arakesh while channelling the ranger in you."

Varga clapped a hand around each of Asher's arms. "Can you do this for me? Can you walk the line between the two? The crowd wants to see the supernatural abilities they've heard so much about. *But*," he emphasised, "Lady Trigorn prefers a more traditional story of good versus evil. So the winner *must* be the hero." Viktor beamed at him. "That's you!"

Something akin to a groan rumbled deep in Asher's throat—he didn't care who was watching him. "And how many evils will I be *vanquishing* tonight?"

"Just the one," Viktor replied casually, stepping away.

"One?" the ranger questioned.

"Just the one," Viktor confirmed with a knowing smile.

"It's to be a monster then," Asher concluded.

"Indeed! Though I shan't ruin the surprise." Viktor noticed something beyond Asher. "Speaking of surprises," he said, that knowing smile curling in a wicked way.

Asher paid no heed to Fengil and Roin's work as he pivoted on the spot. The ranger maintained his passive expression as Grift and Baal were being escorted into the chamber by Kad Gorson and a pair of guards. Neither gladiator offered their usual look of contempt but adopted a rather blank expression. Grift especially looked paler than normal, his features beginning to lend him an almost sheepish appearance. The magistri gave Viktor a bow of respect and Asher a curt nod before handing Baal and Grift various pieces of armour.

"Why are *they* here?" Asher demanded.

"They are to be the hero's companions!" Viktor answered dramatically.

Asher turned back to the gates. "Whatever the beast," he told Viktor, "I don't need *companions*."

"True enough," the crime lord agreed. "But it's a visual thing," he explained, his hands out before him as if he was seeing the arena from his viewing box. "The hero may rise victorious and evil may be defeated, but there have to be *casualties*. The crowd want their pound of flesh and I can't have that taken from you yet.

Besides, from the reports I've heard, these two fellows want you dead," he added, no care given as to whether Baal and Grift could hear him.

"So they're here to die," Asher surmised.

"That is up to them," Viktor said, and certainly loud enough to reach the gladiators. "But yes," he added with a shrug. "And should any more threaten my champion," he went on, his words now directed at Kad Gorson, "they too will find themselves in the arena."

The magistri responded with a short but slow bow of the head. He didn't need Asher's ears to hear the threat laced between Viktor's words, and it wasn't a stretch to imagine the crime lord throwing Kad in the arena for failing him.

Viktor placed himself directly in front of Asher and brushed the top of his pauldrons. "Don't kill the monster too quickly," he instructed. "'Tis a show after all, and there are those among the crowd who have travelled from the mainland to see the *Arakesh*. Perhaps it could eat them first," he suggested, patting the ranger on both arms. "But, most of all, just enjoy yourself, hmm? Do what you do best," he added with a wink.

Asher locked Viktor's gaze into his own. "You don't want me to do what I do best."

Varga's jaw shifted uncomfortably and he stepped back as drums began to blast from the arena. "Ah," he voiced. "Your moment is almost upon you. I shall retire and watch from on high. Happy hunting, *Ranger*."

Soon, there was naught but four guards to oversee Asher and the gladiators, as even the magistri had left them to the sound of the beating drums. Asher glanced over his shoulder at Baal and Grift, each wielding a spiked mace and a sword. Grift was staring at the gate, the whites of his eyes stark against his dark skin. Baal, already sweating in the heat, was staring hard at the ranger. Asher was beginning to wonder if it was the only expression his face was capable of.

"You think 'cause Viktor butters your arse you're a worthy

champion?" They were Baal's first words to him, his accent betraying his Ice Vales heritage—at least that explained his size, and that of his brother. "I've put assassins in the ground before," he continued, his breath hot on the back of Asher's neck. "I'll drop you like I did the rest."

The drum beat was increasing.

"Good luck with that," Asher uttered, confident he needed no more than muscle memory to deal with the fool. The monster they were about to fight, however, would require more of him. There wasn't a single creature in the bestiary that didn't come with a warning about planning ahead.

The gate began to rise, its chain links barely audible over the thunderous beat of the drums and the clamorous roaring of the crowd. The guards ushered them onto the sands, Grift a step behind Asher and Baal. They stopped just short of halfway and let the crowd get a good look at them. Baal knew his part and raised his weapons with a cry of his own. Grift didn't move a muscle.

"Whatever monster we're to face," Asher yelled, speaking to any who might listen to him, "just keep moving. If you stay still, you're dead."

"I don't need advice from a dead man," Baal shouted back.

"LADIES AND GENTLEMEN!" the announcer boomed. "YOUR HEROES! THEY HAVE TRAVERSED LAND AND SEA TO FACE THE NIGHTMARISH BEAST THAT PREYS ON THE INNOCENT! ONCE AN ARAKESH, A FIENDISH ASSASSIN OF THE FABLED NIGHT-FALL, ASHER HAS TURNED HIS SWORD TO THE EVILS OF THE REALM! ONLY BY SLAYING MONSTERS MIGHT HE REDEEM HIMSELF IN THE EYES OF THE GODS!"

The crowd lapped it up and cheered for Asher, unaware just how close the story was to the truth. He turned his eyes up to Viktor's viewing box and found his telltale outline. He wasn't alone. A slender woman cupping a glass of wine stood by his side —Lady Trigorn, he guessed. Beyond them were the usual leeches who never wandered too far from their masters.

Movement to his right guided the ranger's attention to Darya

Siad-Agnasi. The Shadow Witch was striding across the sands with his red blindfold in hand.

Baal and Grift retreated a step as she cut between them and came to stand behind Asher. The *Assassin* was clawing at his insides, desperate to feel the fabric against his eyes. When darkness at last fell over him like a curtain, the world was set alight with detail.

The *Assassin* floated in that soup of information, absorbing everything about the environment. Baal and Grift were close behind him, their very being thrumming like the drums. The stink of fear clung to Grift especially, his bladder on the verge of losing control. There was a note of fear to Baal also, but the big man was doing his best to convert it into fuel, his closed fist repeatedly hammering his chest.

Then there was the menagerie of monsters below, their roars, howls, and shrieks always crying out between raking claws and flicking tails. Asher ignored them and turned his attention to the monsters above, watching him from the viewing box. Viktor was the prominent figure, scented in his usual lilacs and honey. The woman beside him was younger by a decade perhaps, her skin tighter and more flexible. Her heart carried the sound of youth, suggesting she kept herself in good shape. Her dress was a fine silk with an intricate lattice that broadcast her wealth. Asher had no doubt now that it was the illustrious Lady Trigorn.

The side gate closed behind Darya, the lock snapping into place like a bolt of thunder in Asher's ears. Above her, behind the top of the wall, Malak raised his hand and with it the silvyr short-sword, its ring, as it sliced through the air, unique among all other weapons. The *Assassin* tilted his head, curious for a moment as to why the thug was holding the blade high. When Darya had thrown it before his first match, the blade had been tossed from low to high, so that he might catch it mid-fall.

Malak had no such intentions.

His arms tensed, the muscles coiling from shoulder to wrist, in preparation to launch the weapon. Asher's mind had already calculated the distance, speed, and trajectory Malak was capable of and remained perfectly still, as if he were no more than a blind man with no idea what was happening around him.

When the short-sword left Malak's grip it was in a fast spin, thrown aggressively from high to low. Had he aimed for Baal or Grift, the blade would have impaled them and brought their time in the arena to a swift end. Fortunately for them, its intended destination was Asher's chest. The *Assassin* relished the opportunity to use his reflexes like no other. Avoiding death was as simple as pivoting his shoulders, favouring his left side, so the silvyr blade flew naught but an inch from his leathers. At the same time, his left hand shot out and caught the hilt mid-spin.

The crowd gasped before erupting in cheers, their expectations met before the fighting had even begun. Asher tilted his head towards Malak again, showing the thug that he had the *Assassin's* attention. There was a notable increase in his heart rate and the glands beneath his skin produced more sweat. He soon retreated and joined the Shadow Witch in her climb to the viewing box.

In his wake, the gate on the far side of the arena began to open, drawing the crowd into a hush.

"LADIES AND GENTLEMEN," the mage continued in his enhanced voice, "WHAT YOU SEE NEXT IS NOT FOR THE FAINT OF HEART! THE FEARLESS VIKTOR VARGA HAS REACHED INTO THE DEPTHS OF HELL TO BRING YOU THE MOST TERRIBLE OF CREATURES! FOR YOUR SAFETY, DO NOT CROSS THE SPEARMEN!"

Asher's senses took in the oval ring of guards stationed at the top of the walls. They each hefted a considerable spear that clearly wasn't intended for the gladiators.

Before the gate could reach its apex, monstrous legs unfolded onto the arena's sand like a desert spider emerging from its burrow. Asher could feel its moist exterior, smoother than silk. Its sloped-back head pushed up against the bottom of the gate as it screeched something from the darkest reaches of man's primal fears. The general disquiet was kept in check by that terrible shriek. It was, however, the last straw for Grift's bladder.

Six horrifying feet brought the monster's advancing body into the torchlight. Asher's senses worked their way around those feet, determining their shape and size. They were almost exactly the same dimensions as a human's hands, each possessing the correct number of knuckles and articulating joints.

While the *Assassin* in him didn't much care for its features, the *Ranger* rose to the surface just long enough to remind Asher of the bestiary. He knew this creature. He had read about a monster with hands for feet.

"Naerwitch," he muttered under his breath.

Further matching the bestiary's description, the monster's beetle-like body was ridged. Its torso, however, rose up in a similar fashion to a Sandstalker's. Unlike a Sandstalker's slim and muscular build, the Naerwitch's torso was a protruding structure that suggested nature had stopped investing in its kind and left them to their ugliness. Its head, too, was an unfinished moulding, lacking any eyes or obvious nostrils. What it did not lack was fangs, translucent points that dripped with thick saliva.

It was a true monster.

Asher could hear the sand piling upon itself as Grift's feet shuffled backwards. Baal, on the other hand, was widening his stance and tightening his grip on his weapons.

The announcer stepped onto his dais again, wand tip to his lips. "IT SEEMS OUR MIGHTY HERO AND COMPANY HAVE COME ACROSS A FIEND OF THE UNDERWORLD, FOR WHAT YOU SEE BEFORE YOU, LADIES AND GENTLEMEN, IS NONE OTHER THAN A NAERWITCH! THESE CREATURES ARE HARD TO CAPTURE AND EVEN HARDER TO SLAY! THEY ARE DEATH INCARNATE, CAPABLE OF KILLING A MAN IN MERE SECONDS!"

Asher almost chuckled to himself—anyone could be killed in mere seconds, Naerwitch or not. Still, the mage wasn't wrong—everything about the monster spoke volumes of its capacity to reduce a man to bloody shreds.

The Naerwitch immediately explored the wall to its right, hand-like feet pressing flat to the sandy stone. The front half of its body reached over the lip of the wall, where three spears were waiting for it. The beast shrieked and thrashed before dropping back down into the arena, each limb creating a plume of sand. Only then did the audience in that part of the arena find their seats again. The exhilaration of it brought out an uncivilised cheer that spread like wildfire all around them.

By now, Grift had retreated so far he was against the wall, his mace and sword clattering against the stone. Baal had succeeded in holding his ground, though his breathing had become heavy and his skin slick with sweat.

Asher reduced everything about the men to background noise and focused on the Naerwitch. It had noticed them. Its sloping head of curves tilted one way then the next before its feet padded rapidly across the sand. It appeared the monster had just remembered how hungry it was.

Asher was able to hear, as well as feel, the strange clicking sound that tapped away beneath the Naerwitch's smooth hide, either side of its elongated head. He couldn't say what it was, though he guessed it to be some biological method of locating prey.

"WHO'S READY FOR THE BATTLE OF THE AGE?" the announcer queried, sending the crowd into a bloodthirsty frenzy.

Asher tilted his head up so that Viktor could see his face. *"Don't kill the monster too quickly,"* he had instructed.

The *Assassin* within was diminished by the righteous anger of Asher's true self. He raised his arm, twisting the hilt of the silvyr blade round and round as he did so. Then it flew from his grip, set to sail in the manner of a spear.

The dwarven weapon slammed into that misshapen chest, stopping only at the hilt. The Naerwitch moaned once, its monstrous throat reverberating, before it keeled over, its limbs heaped into a pile upon itself.

There wasn't so much as a whisper from the crowd.

Asher turned his head back up towards the viewing box, the hint of a smirk curling his lips. The distance between them did nothing to conceal Viktor's sigh from the ranger's ears.

The announcer held his wand in front of his mouth again, hesitating, before finally saying, "YOUR CHAMPION!"

Impressed or not, the crowd had little to say in response, with only a handful of cheers and hollers. The jeers soon mounted, much to Asher's amusement, until the entire arena was up in arms.

The violence, however, was yet to end.

From only a few feet away, Baal charged Asher, barrelling him with his shoulder and launching him across the sand. He was quick for his size—quicker than his brother had been. Still, Asher hit the ground knowing the fault lay with him, his attention too focused on Viktor's displeasure, and he chastised himself for not anticipating the assault.

"You want a champion?" Baal growled, his arms held out to the audience. "*I* will show you a champion!"

The crowd responded with glee, hoping they would yet witness the bloodshed they had been promised. It also invigorated Baal, who believed they were cheering for him rather than his inevitable death.

Asher knew Baal's mace was coming down on him long before it was a real threat. He rolled out of the way and let the spiked ball blast the sand where he had been lying.

"A BETRAYAL, LADIES AND GENTLEMEN!" the announcer was quick to declare. "CAN OUR HERO SURVIVE THIS TREACHERY?"

Feeling the muscles, tendons, and bones in his opponent's right side moving like falling dominoes, the ranger's senses informed him that another mace attack was coming his way; this time from low to high as he rose from the ground.

Turning his rise into a sideways spin, he was able to roll in time with the incoming mace and evade its spiked tips. Landing like a cat, Asher then sprang to his feet and weaved between Baal's successive attacks, his sword and mace taking turns. The gladiator's aggression escalated to a leap that saw him come down with a thrust of his sword. To Asher's senses, which picked up all the micro-movements that proceeded his foe's actions, Baal might as well have informed him verbally of his every intention.

The ranger side-stepped and pivoted as the gladiator touched down, avoiding the tip of the blade with ease. He then slapped the top of Baal's wrist, causing the big man to relinquish his hold on the sword. Before it hit the ground, Asher had already swung his arm around and caught his enemy across the jaw with the rigid edge of an open hand. Baal was stunned, unable to stop himself from staggering back. Using little effort, Asher jumped lightly into the air and thrust a boot into the gladiator's chest, sending him reeling across the sand.

The audience gave a resounding, if sharp, cheer of approval.

Turning his keen senses to Grift, he knew the man had stepped away from the wall since the Naerwitch's untimely death. His fear had abated somewhat but he was yet to find his way into this new fight that Baal had started.

Ignoring them both for the time being, the ranger made his way over to the Naerwitch, there to reclaim his weapon. With one boot pressed to its chest, its open mouth still twitching, he slid the blade free. He was still surprised by the lack of resistance, the monster's hide no match for the silvyr's edges.

He didn't need to turn around to know that Baal was on his feet again, and with a hair-line fracture to his jaw. The gladiator shouted something indecipherable at Grift and waved the man to join him. Grift took a breath and rolled his shoulders and neck; something of the fighter returning to him. He needed to do something to prove himself now, lest he suffer Viktor's whims and find himself being served up to the monsters below.

Of course, that meant surviving the monster in the blindfold first.

Together, Baal and Grift advanced, spurred on by the baying mob that watched from on high. They parted just enough to force an ordinary man to choose one direction or the other, relying as they would on their eyes. Asher remained exactly where he was, directly in front of the Naerwitch's open maw, with his silvyr blade held low.

"I promise to kill you quickly," he told them, straining his voice to be heard over the crowd.

Baal let loose a snarl that sent a jolt of pain through his jaw.

"I'm not dying today!" he managed, slapping the flat of his recovered sword against his chest. "My blood is that of a champion!"

"Take another step," Asher warned him, "and your blood's going to be everywhere."

His words fell on deaf ears where Baal was concerned. Grift, however, became a lot lighter, shifting his weight onto the balls of his feet.

Instead of moving as one—a pincer attack that would have increased their chances of victory—Baal alone advanced, his mace going up and wide. Asher casually stepped back and allowed his opponent to close the gap. Once Baal had replaced his position in front of the Naerwitch, the ranger lightly kicked the top of its curved head, exciting reflexes that worked long after death.

Those unforgiving jaws shot forwards and clamped shut. Everything between Baal's ankle and knee disappeared inside. The gladiator managed no more than a sharp intake of breath before collapsing under his own momentum and with no right leg to take his weight. The crowd roared at the blood splatter and demanded more.

The Assassin wanted to loom with superiority over Baal, who had finally given in to his dire situation and begun screaming. The smell and taste of blood would normally ignite the creature of shadows that dwelled in Asher, and the *Assassin* desperately wanted to loom with superiority over Baal. But, despite the conditions, the *Ranger* won out and took mercy on the big man. It was the same mercy he had once shown to Everic in those cold snows, four years previously.

By the time he retrieved the blade from Baal's chest, the gladiator was already dead, his heart stopped by cold silvyr. Lacking the dramatic fashion that gratified the crowd, they responded with little enthusiasm for the execution.

Quite panicked by the beast's animation, Grift's fear had returned in earnest and saw him fall back several steps. His gaze—terror-stricken—was fixed on Asher, his feet in full retreat. He dropped the mace on his way, the weapon no more than a heavy object now. Calls for his death soon followed and the ranger felt Viktor's eyes on him.

"I won't let one of those things eat me," he said, tears streaking his face. Gone was the brash gladiator who believed himself invincible. Now he was just a scared man who didn't want to die as Viktor had intended.

Asher walked towards him, prepared to share his mercy with the man—it would be better than facing the fangs and claws of some monster in the pits below. "It'll be quick," he promised, taking no pleasure in it.

Grift seemed to hear him, his features relaxing into realisation. He knew he was about to die; no easy thing for any man to comprehend. And now, at the end, his only comfort came from his killer and a handful of words.

With no choices left to him, Grift charged ahead, a defiant cry of rage on his lips. Asher ducked under the obvious swing and slashed his silvyr blade once across his opponent's midriff and a second down the length of his spine. Spine severed, Grift was dead before he hit the sand.

The crowd cheered, though not nearly as enthusiastically as they had on previous occasions. Asher didn't care. As far as he was concerned, his job was done. If anything, he was pleased to have taken no joy in it all, the *Assassin* muzzled. For now.

Giving in to his curiosity, he removed the blindfold so that he might behold the monster with his eyes. Being capable of perceiving colour again didn't add much to the Naerwitch's profile. Every inch of the beast was so black as to appear to be the absence of light altogether. Perfect for a creature that dwelled in the dark of the mountains.

Beside its corpse was an unmistakable red where Baal's blood pooled out and stained the sand. Asher felt nothing for the man, nor even Grift, who had shown a glimpse of a real person before the end. They were both fiends in the world of man and had both threatened him. Killing them before they killed him felt like one of the only fair things that actually existed in the world. What he loathed, however, was the way in which Viktor wielded him, a puppet of death and nothing more.

He looked up at the viewing box. Lady Trigorn's silhouette was no longer up there, but Viktor had remained. He stared down at Asher and, even in shadow, the ranger could feel the hard edge of that gaze. He had angered the crime lord.

Asher smiled inwardly. At least something good had come of this.

CHAPTER 31
LOOSE ENDS

Luxun - *I have been laughed at for this comparison, but the resemblance between a giant tortoise and a Luxun is most certainly there. Rather than being housed inside a hard shell, Luxun find safety inside their carapaces of jagged stone. In fact, when head and limbs are retracted, these creatures are often mistaken for boulders. I myself have walked right past a family of Luxun while on the hunt. I can tell you quite humbly, it is damned embarrassing to drive your spear into no more than a large rock, only to discover the real thing is slowly flanking you.*

Now, there are obvious differences between a tortoise and a Luxun— besides their shells. The head and neck of one of these beasts is closer to a snake. It will slither out of its stony shell and spit venom at its prey (their spit has been known to reach ten feet).

Thankfully, killing Luxun is as simple as cutting off their slimy head. You just need to lure them out of their shell first. Oh, and avoid the venom, of course.

A Chronicle of Monsters: A Ranger's Bestiary, 12th Edition, Page 68.

Renley Killinger, Ranger.

Near on three days since watching Kilda and Deadora head north for Dunwich and the safety of The Black Wood beyond, Doran and Danagarr finally arrived at the gates of Velia. Having discussed it many times on their journey south, the dwarves decided that trying to enter the city during the day would prove more fruitful than trying at night.

"It's the busiest city in the realm," Doran had argued. "We can pass right through with all the others."

Danagarr had looked at him with a frown pinching his bushy eyebrows. "All the other *what*? We're dwarves last I checked. We don' exactly blend in."

Doran had waved his concerns away. "Ye've never seen a city the size o' Velia: Darkwell don' compare. The main gates will be packed with people comin' an' goin'. Ye'll see."

"That's a lot o' eyes on us," the smith had rightly countered.

"A lot o' eyes is better than jus' a few *suspicious* ones," Doran had replied. "We jus' need to find a caravan o' sorts an' stick close to it."

Danagarr hadn't been convinced and, now, standing outside the high walls of Velia, the smith still didn't look convinced. "Reminds me o' home," he remarked, looking at the city overcritically. "Only, ye know, upside down."

Doran tore his eyes from the constant trail of visitors and merchants to take in the scale of Velia. He could see what Danagarr meant, though he had only visited Hyndaern once, and as a child at that, on some diplomatic trip. To his memory, Hyndaern was large enough to swallow Velia whole and have room to spare. Still, to any dwarf's eyes, all the kingdoms of man were upside down.

"Do ye 'ave the coin?" he asked the smith, changing the subject.

Danagarr adjusted his cloak to reveal the purse knotted to his belt. "If ye 'ave to ask me again, Heavybelly, I'm o' a mind to hit ye with it."

Doran nodded along apologetically. "A'right, a'right. I jus' think it best if they don' go any further," he said, gesturing to Pig and Danagarr's donkey. "There's a decent enough stable round the corner from 'ere."

"So ye've said," the smith replied dryly. "Let's be on with it then. The quicker we get this done the quicker I'm returned to me kin."

Doran considered the task that lay between now and then. If only it was so easy.

After paying a hefty price for several nights' lodging, the Warhog and donkey were left in the lower town with naught but an empty promise that their masters would return. Admittedly, Doran found it harder to part with the animal. How many years had they spent together, the other's only companion? They had seen it all together, battling wars and monsters alike.

"Get some rest, eh?" he had said upon leaving the Warhog. He had also advised the owner of the stable to keep Pig away from any and all alcohol, lest he become insufferable. The owner's expression suggested it was strange advice but he took it on all the same.

Returned to the main road that led right up to Velia's entrance, the dwarves leaned against an alley wall and continued to watch all those who travelled in and out of the city. They had to pick the right crowd to adopt.

"Is this really necessary?" Danagarr asked, frustration in his voice.

Doran would have rolled his eyes were he not so keenly watching the road. "I told ye o' the manner in which I departed this city. A dwarf on a Warhog ain' an easy thing to miss. If we jus' walk through those gates, bold as brass, we take the chance that I'll be arrested. Ye too probably, jus' for bein' with me. Then we'll never reach Dragorn."

The smith tutted. "Can' ye do anythin' without makin' a scene?"

Doran chose to ignore the jibe and doubled his efforts to find a way inside. "Wait, what's that?" he questioned, directing Danagarr's attention further up the road.

The smith narrowed his eyes. "A juggler," he concluded, seeing the man throwing balls into the air, much to the delight of several children who followed him through the lower town.

"Aye," Doran agreed enthusiastically. "An' look who he's with. It's a whole troupe o' entertainers!"

Beside the juggler, a caravan of costumed performers traversed the lower town with a number of wagons and carts. Some wore face paint while others even approached the city on tall stilts.

"What's all this abou'?" Danagarr asked.

Doran shrugged. "Humans do strange things when the sun's out. That's our way in," he declared.

The smith sighed and the son of Dorain shared his apprehension. Demeaning as it was, however, a way in was a way in and they couldn't afford to waste it. He instructed Danagarr to follow his lead and, when the group passed them by, he strode out of the alley and cut through the children until they were walking between two tall wagons at the back of the caravan. They each hefted their bags over their backs, their weapons and armour concealed therein, and made themselves out as no more than stagehands for the performers.

Following the procession, they were soon passing under the stone arch of Velia's entrance and beyond the sight of those towering kings. The dwarves hadn't even been seen by the guards, who had mostly been distracted by the man and woman on stilts. When the opportune moment arose, the two companions slipped away and disappeared down a quiet side street.

"I wish gettin' out o' Hyndaern had been that easy," Danagarr commented, adjusting his hood to keep his face in shadow.

Doran chuckled. "Humans have the attention span o' a fish. Come on," he bade, eyeing an alley that cut through to another part of the city.

Their journey through Velia's curving streets and back alleys was a slow one, the pair always having to take the city watch into account. Here and there people pointed or stared; the children always asked them questions. The dwarves were always careful to keep to themselves and use their large bags to conceal their general shape.

When the breeze brought The Adean's salty air, they knew their destination was close. Doran tried not to think about the sea that lay between him and Dragorn but, instead, put his mind to the task of how they might get there. Moving out onto the docks, a sprawl of jetties that came close to rivalling Dragorn's, the dwarves were quick to find an adequate space between stacks of crates awaiting transport into the city. From there, they were able to peruse the multitude of trading vessels and smaller boats that bobbed in the water.

Danagarr peered over a crate. "Ye weren' exactly clear about this part, Doran. How were ye imaginin' we'd get to Dragorn?"

The son of Dorain pointed a stubby finger at the docks in general. "We're goin' on one o' those obviously."

The smith planted two stern eyes on him. "I'd figured as much out meself, ye stupid sack o' hammers. I mean, *which* boat did ye think were goin' to take us."

Doran hardly noted the insult amidst Danagarr's response. "We need to find one o' Viktor's boats," he said plainly, eyes peeled for such a vessel.

The smith glanced at the docks before his scrupulous gaze returned to Doran. "One o' Viktor's? Are ye mad? How are we to sneak into Dragorn under his very nose?"

Danagarr had been particularly prickly since leaving Darkwell. Doran understood why given the upheaval and threat to his family, but it was still a growing irritation that was making the dwarven hunter equally prickly.

"Look at all 'em damned boats," he spat. "Who knows where they're all goin'. We need to be on one that is definitely goin' to Dragorn. Well, the only boats I know for sure are goin' to that blasted island are the ones ferryin' Viktor's sundries an' the like."

The smith groaned. "Well how are we to know it's one o' his boats when we see it?"

"We won'," Doran replied. "That's why we're not lookin' for

boats. We're lookin' for his *men*. Viktor hires a breed o' thug that's hard to miss."

Danagarr inspected the sun in the sky, now well past its apex. "How long's that goin' to take?"

Doran sighed, and would have sighed all the more had he known the answer to his question would come just over four hours later, when the sun was beginning to slip over the horizon, behind the city. Doran had seen them first, his sight better trained to spot the likes of Viktor's thugs. They had made their way across one of the jetties, escorting the transport of several barrels. From their vantage, the dwarves had been able to trail them by sight alone, all the way back to one of the warehouses in the south. The building bore no signs or markings to identify its owner; another indication that it belonged to Varga.

On the other side of the warehouse there rested a large vessel, moored to the jetty. One agonisingly slow hour later and the pair had successfully navigated the docks while remaining relatively unseen. Now, from the edge of the warehouse, they could see those working inside as well as the vessel. Doran narrowed his eyes to make out the name painted on the hull: The Duchess.

"Right," Doran began, his plan formulating in his mind. "Our best bet will be to sneak into the hold," he said, directing the smith's attention to the gangplanks that led up and into the bowels of The Duchess.

"Get down," Danagarr hissed, dragging the son of Dorain behind a partially broken wall.

Doran pulled his hood back a notch to see the men walking past. They left the warehouse via a side door and crossed the jetties to a smaller building that operated as an office of some kind.

"Undvig," he uttered, his fingers gripping the top of the broken brick.

"Undvig?" Danagarr questioned, peeping over the jagged edge. "He's the mage ye mentioned?"

"Aye, that's 'im," Doran confirmed. "Best avoid that lot."

"He's the one that sent 'em fellas after me family," Danagarr continued, steadily rising.

"He's also the one who blasted half the city tryin' to take me head off," Doran reminded, pulling his companion back behind cover. "Forget abou' 'em an' look to the ship," he insisted, turning back to spy The Duchess's hold through the window. "We need to time this jus' right, ye hear? If jus' *one* o' these laddies spots us it's goin' to be the end o'..." There was a notable absence in the dwarf's peripheral vision. "Danagarr?" he whispered frantically.

The smith had already left their hiding place and even his bag. The bag, of course, was missing one particular item that could now be seen resting over Danagarr's shoulder.

"What are ye doin' with that bloody hammer?" Doran demanded, though the smith had already crossed too much of the jetty to hear him. Retrieving his axe alone, the son of Dorain audibly huffed on his way to his feet, and gave quick pursuit.

"What in the hells are ye doin', ye old fool?"

Danagarr paused in front of the door to the smaller building. "This fella sent men to kill me wife an' daughter."

"I know," Doran agreed, his manner pleading. "But this ain' a fight to be 'avin' now. We *need* to be on that ship."

The smith looked him in the eyes as his sledgehammer knocked twice against the office door. "He sent for me daughter's head," he said ominously, drawing his hood back.

Doran's grip tightened around the haft of his axe. "That he did," the dwarf agreed, seeing no way around that fact. "Best he don' get another chance, eh?"

Danagarr responded with a wicked grin. "My thinkin' exactly."

The door was opened by one of the mage's halfwits. He looked out before looking down on the dwarves, his gormless expression an accurate representation of his mind's inner workings.

"Evenin'," the smith greeted pleasantly enough. Then his sledgehammer swung up to meet the thug's jaw. His teeth exploded from his mouth, which was undoubtedly shattered beyond recovery, and his eyes quickly rolled into the back of his head before he collapsed back like a plank of wood.

The pair stepped inside and closed the door behind them, there to stand before Undvig and five more of his underlings. Slack-jawed, the mage looked on from behind a desk, the only piece of furniture in the large room. Along with his men, he stared in disbelief at their comrade on the floor before his gaze fell on the defiant dwarves.

"The name's Stormshield," Danagarr announced, his hammer beating steadily into his palm. "It'll be the name ye take to whatever hell ye're bound for."

Doran couldn't help but look at his companion—this was not the same dwarf he had known all these years. Disturbing as that was, this was exactly the kind of dwarf he needed by his side right now. "Aye," the son of Dorain added, for naught else to say. "What he said."

Undvig's shock slipped from his face until only amusement was left in its place. He pointed from one to the other. "Stormshield. Heavybelly." The mage scoffed. "You're making my job a lot easier, boys."

"Say whatever ye will," Danagarr told him. "These are to be the last pointless words o' ye miserable life."

Undvig leaned over his desk and reached for the black wand that rested there. His hand hesitated, hovering over the length of wood. Instead of picking it up, he sat back in his chair and intertwined his fingers. It seemed he was in the mood for entertainment over direct violence.

"Gentlemen," he said, addressing his men. "Do me a favour and kill these little dwarves."

Doran deliberately avoided looking at their faces lest he commit more of the dead to his long memory. What he did note, however, were the weapons they brought to bear. Short-swords and studded clubs, all easily concealable but perfectly deadly.

"Come on, laddies," he goaded. "We 'aven' got all day."

The first to lunge attempted to drive his short-sword through Danagarr's face. The old smith made quick work of him, batting the blade aside before swinging back to catch the thug in the knee. The bone snapped and dropped the fool down upon it. His pain was momentary, ended by a third and swift arc of Danagarr's hammer, this time caving in his skull.

As the corpse hit the floor, a second was coming down on Doran with a studded club. The son of Dorain side-stepped and swiped his axe across his foe's wrist, a clean cut that parted limb from owner. Doran's follow up attack was not so merciful, the blade of his axe hacking through skull and brain alike.

That left three on their feet, and two of them moved on the smith. Danagarr deflected the club of one but suffered a gash across his arm from the other. The pain made him recoil and lower his guard just enough for the first to strike him across the shoulder with his club. No reprieve was given by the swordsman, who planted a boot in the smith's chest and sent him to the floor.

Doran growled as he moved to intercept the pair, but the third of their surviving gang lashed out with his short-sword and drew a red line down the back of the dwarf's shoulder, unprotected while his armour remained in the bag. The pain sent a bolt of rage through the son of Dorain. He pivoted on one foot and met the next attack with his axe and the ring of clashing steel.

A flicker of movement from the mage's desk drew the dwarf's attention. The wand was in Undvig's hand and, worse still, it was pointed directly at him. With no cover and no shield, the son of Dorain did the only thing he could, grabbing the swordsman roughly by the shirt and thrusting him into the path of the spell. Though quiet, like a sharp inhalation of air, the magic that burst forth from the mage's wand was blindingly blue. It struck the swordsman in the middle of his back and shoved him hard into Doran, knocking them both to the floor.

Dazed by both the light and the weight of the body on top of him, Doran blinked hard and looked into the face of the swordsman, who was not blinking at all. The dwarven hunter cursed magic and heaved the smoking corpse off him, and all in time to see Danagarr jump to his feet and charge one of his two attackers. He barrelled the man into a wall with such force that the thug dropped his club. One swing of that hammer knocked all sense from him. The second ensured he would never rise again.

"Behind ye!" Doran warned, the swordsman and last of Undvig's men flanking the smith.

It should have been the end of Danagarr Stormshield, but the son of Dorain would be damned if he didn't see the smith returned to his family. His axe flew like a whistling banshee and crossed the room in a heartbeat. The curved blade imbedded itself in the side of the thug's head and threw him into the adjacent wall.

That was not to be the end of Danagarr's peril. Undvig had rounded his desk now, his long coat fanned out in his wake. Magic was again brought to bear and upon the Stormshield at that. Doran cried out his friend's name but his voice was lost to the sound of the spell, louder than its predecessor. Blinding as the purple flash was, it didn't stop Doran from seeing Danagarr take the magic directly to his chest. It cast the smith back and off his feet until he slammed into the back wall and crumpled to the floor.

"NO!" Doran bellowed.

Undvig snorted and swivelled his wand on the son of Dorain. "You're next," he promised.

Doran slowly rose to his feet, eyes narrowed on the mage and full of murderous intent. "Ye best not be missin'," the dwarf told him, his voice threateningly low.

A toothy grin spread across Undvig's face. "It'd be hard to miss a squat thing like you."

Danagarr's sledgehammer came from nowhere and impacted the mage in the shoulder joint of his wand arm. There came an audible crack of bone before the hammer knocked against the floor and Undvig yelled in pain. Staggering back, he tripped over one of the bodies and was sent sprawling, his wand lost under the desk.

Doran turned to the back wall, where he should have seen a dead smith. Instead, he saw Danagarr sitting up with a smoking patch in the centre of his chest.

"Good throw," he complimented, for loss of all else to say.

The dwarf coughed once, blowing some of the rising smoke away. "Ye can' beat a flyin' hammer," he rasped, picking himself up. "Even better if they don' see it comin'," he added determinedly.

Unable to argue with the poignant fact, Doran watched in stunned amazement as the smith crossed the room in pursuit of Undvig, who was desperately trying to crawl back to his desk.

Along the way, Danagarr paused to retrieve his sledgehammer, showing no outward sign of discomfort from the dark bruise that stained his chest. Coming alongside the mage, he kicked the man over onto his back and dropped the hammerhead onto his broken shoulder. There was a look in the smith's eyes, a menace that was not to be trifled with, and so Doran kept his distance.

Undvig squirmed and groaned under the pressure of the hammer. "You should be dead," he spat through the pain.

Danagarr added more of his weight to the hammer and cut the mage off. "Ye've had yer last words, little man." The smith leaned down. "When ye get to wherever it is ye're goin' an' they ask ye what ye're doin' there, be sure to tell 'em abou' the little girl ye tried to 'ave murdered."

Undvig's eyes bulged as he watched the hammer swing up and round. When it came down, the steel head could be heard to impact the hard floor beneath the mage's head.

There was no denying the strength of a dwarven smith.

The blood-splattered room was quite the scene to behold, and even more so for Doran who beheld Danagarr in the middle of it, his face speckled red. This had not been the doing of a smith or even a dwarven soldier. This had been the unbridled wrath of a father.

Doran looked from what was left of the mage to his companion. "Shouldn' ye be dead?" he said, echoing Undvig's last words.

His chest heaving, Danagarr brushed some of the singed edges of his shirt away. "I told ye," he replied gruffly, "we dwarves 'ave a natural resilience to magic." With no further explanation, he hefted his hammer—dripping with blood—and made for the door.

Doran shrugged and stepped over the bodies to follow him. "Good to know."

CHAPTER 32
A MENAGERIE OF NIGHTMARES

Ydrit - *The White Bears our ancestors called them. If only they were as easy to kill as a bear. Ydrits are suited to cold environments, the harsher the better. Most are found north of Longdale and around The Shards. The myth is that they prefer the mountains, but they are more commonly located near to water—typically the sea.*

On two feet, Ydrits stand at nine foot and, let me tell you, they make for a tower of muscle and white fur the likes of which you've not seen. If you find yourself in the shadow of one of these beasts, you had better be at the top of your game. Their flat faces are partially hidden behind curtains of fur, but their large lower fangs can't help but stand out. And don't be looking into their black eyes for they'll be sure to rob you of your courage and leave you in a puddle of your own making.

Their two arms are comparable to logs, thick and strong, with five wicked claws. One swipe will send you to the next world so keep your distance.

Now, they usually hunt fish and the like with little interest in the taste of humans. That doesn't mean they can't be persuaded. In the winter, when the ice is thick and the fish harder to come by, they have been known to turn their sights on Longdale's outlying villages.

A Chronicle of Monsters: A Ranger's Bestiary, 12th Edition,
Page 285.

Isold The Hook Hand, Ranger.

"Four days," Salim commented, his tone conveying disbelief. "Those are four days you should not have had, my friend."

Asher was inclined to agree with him. "It would have been worth it," he opined, still savouring Viktor's displeasure with his performance in the arena.

Salim checked his four remaining Galant cards before choosing to put down the knight. "Were you any other, I fear Viktor would have fed you to his pets by now."

The ranger considered his own cards, worn and dog-eared as they were. "He still might," he pointed out, playing the dragon card. "Perhaps he can't decide which monster will devour me the slowest."

Salim chuckled. "True enough."

Asher took a moment to cast his eyes over the newcomers. Seven new prisoners had been added to the compound over the last four days. Mouse had spoken to all of them of course. Of the seven, the ranger had only identified one as a potential threat, but word of Grift and Baal's demise had already reached the man. Indeed, Viktor's solution to both men's threats had granted Asher an even wider berth than before. None dared challenge him now.

Returning his attention to Salim, he noticed a single spot of blood under the man's left earlobe. "You fought well last night," he told the southerner, his tone a matter of fact.

The old Honour Guard shifted in his seat. "Is there any other way to fight?" he posed, crafting his own path through the new conversation.

Asher recalled the image of Salim standing bloody and alone in the arena, his scimitar red with victory. "Not for survivors, I suppose."

"Is that what we are?" Salim questioned, putting down the plague card. "I thought we were the damned."

"In here," Asher replied, "that's the same thing." The ranger chose the castle from his four cards, confident that he was only one move away from winning the game.

"If you keep upsetting Viktor Varga," Salim noted quite succinctly, "you are going to discover you are more one than the other."

Asher nodded along. "You don't like to fight?" he asked casually enough, intoning no sense of judgement.

Salim's brow pinched in a flutter of tension that ran through his strong features. "I love to fight," he admitted. "I taught my sons how to fight," he continued, mentioning his children for the first time. "But, more importantly, I taught them *why* we must fight. The cause must be measured, it must be balanced against why *not* to fight." The southerner sighed and played his next card. "Alas, there's no end of causes to pick up one's sword for in The Arid Lands."

The ranger absorbed every word while assessing the river card with two faded skulls in the top right corner. It was a good card to play, but it couldn't beat his battalion on horseback. "You must loathe your time in the arena then," he concluded, placing his card atop Salim's. He sat back with the humility of a man who was accustomed to winning and had forgotten the sense of satisfaction that came with it.

"What I truly loathe is myself," Salim confessed, his response entwining them all the more, "for the fight is the only thing that makes me feel alive anymore. Well, that..." He played his last card, the gallant knight with sword and shield. "And beating you," he finally said.

Asher sat forward to better examine the old card. He was confounded and, for once, failed to hide it. "Well played," he grumbled.

"I have seen it in you," Salim stated, his dark eyes boring into the ranger. "You *hate* what you are. And you hate that you *enjoy* it."

Their conversation was taking a turn down a personal path, one that Asher did not wish to travel. He enjoyed the Honour Guard's company and saw something of himself in the man, even if it was just a shard, but he couldn't divulge much more than he already had—it just wasn't natural to him.

"I found an outlet," he said, instead of directly addressing Salim's comments.

"An outlet?"

"Men like us weren't built for life out there," Asher explained, thrusting his chin at the high walls. "It doesn't want us and we don't really want it. With a sword in my hand..." The ranger trailed off as memory brought with it the taste of freedom. "With a sword in my hand I know who I am. There's not much outside of soldiering that requires our skillset. Mercenary work was too close to... Too close to what I was."

Salim leaned forward. "You speak of this *ranger* business." The southerner gestured at one of the archers patrolling the wall. "I've heard the guards talking about you."

Asher nodded. "I didn't have the best introduction to that world but..." He flicked one of the cards back onto the table, his fingers having straightened its edges out a bit. "It's a life," he eventually said. "You move around and see the realm off the beaten track."

"And you get to use your sword," Salim put in.

"There's plenty of work out there for those willing to do it," Asher told him. "There's always someone willing to put coin in your pocket if you can put a monster in the ground." He tossed a casual gesture at the Honour Guard. "You'd be quite suited to it."

Salim laughed through his nose. "Are you pitching to me?"

Asher mimicked his laugh. "No. I wouldn't want the competition."

The loud, yet now familiar, crack of Kad Gorson's baton striking a wall drew the ranger's attention. "Assassin!" he snapped. "With me!"

Asher watched the magistri move to the gate that led out of the training ground and into the arena.

"It seems you have been summoned," Salim reasoned ominously.

The ranger stood up, his response more guttural than anything else. Before walking out of earshot, he turned back to the southerner. "Shuffle the cards. I'll be back to beat you soon enough."

The arena was eerily quiet during the day, something made all the more obvious by Kad Gorson's apparent vow of silence. They moved through the hallways with two guards at their backs, the sound of their heavy boots bouncing off the walls. Asher glanced down at the magistri, gleaning what he could from the man's demeanour.

Was he to be punished finally?

Kad was a figure of solitude, the mould of a soldier that could never be truly broken. Regardless of his own rigid training and confident strides, the magistri hesitated before they turned the final corner. Seeing the size of the gates that awaited them there, Asher understood that hesitancy. They had journeyed down, below the arena floor, where the corridors widened beyond reasonable need.

They had arrived at the monster pit.

"No guards?" Asher questioned, curious as to why the gate to some of Viktor's most valuable assets was left unattended.

Kad moved to open the normal sized door situated in the middle of the right-hand gate. "What madman would try and break in to a place like this?" he replied rhetorically, unlocking it with a key from his belt.

Asher paused before following the magistri through—his bound wrists cause for concern now. "I'm to be monster food then," he surmised aloud.

"Surely that is the fate of all rangers," Gorson concluded.

"We don't usually have our hands tied," Asher quipped, walking down the slope.

"You will choose to displease the master," Kad pointed out evenly.

Asher couldn't argue with that, and so he kept in step with the magistri as they descended ever lower into the arena's bowels. It was cooler, and pleasantly so. The only light came from torches on the walls, the flames setting the shadows to dance.

Then came the noise of monsters.

Their movement. Their breathing. Their very existence. It was a general hubbub, but every individual detail about the creatures cried out to the ranger's senses. They padded their cells and scraped claws down walls. Others licked their bars and hissed as the potential prey passed them by. Most were concealed by the natural darkness, or perhaps it was the nature of some to become the darkness.

"Stay in the middle," Kad advised.

Indeed, a tentacle snaked out between a set of bars and attempted to molest the ranger. There were some cells that lacked bars altogether; simply covered from wall to wall in thick sheets of iron. Some of those iron walls were notably scarred by large bulges. The sound of beating wings came from the adjacent cell and Asher turned to see a Grendel strike the top of its cage and squawk in defiance.

He had no love for the monster, nor any of them, but he knew this wasn't right. They had a right to live their lives. If they crossed the line and threatened the human populace, they were fair game as far as the ranger was concerned. But not this. They weren't meant to be caged and used for entertainment. Let them live or kill them. That's all there should be.

There was a dead end in sight, and far more illuminated than the path. The chamber rose up, like the bulbous tip of an infected finger, its walls lined with more torches. The first detail to catch his eyes were the three human bodies laid out in a row. Asher suspected they had been men, but there wasn't much left of them to confidently identify their sex. The only thing he could say for sure was that they hadn't died well.

Curiously—and the ranger was pleased to see that his curiosity could still be piqued—the curved ceiling of the natural chamber was interrupted by protruding bones.

Massive bones.

At a guess, Asher would have said the bones he could see were similar to the small ones that sat beneath the muscles and tendons in his feet, or hands perhaps. But if they once belonged in the hand or foot of a living creature it would be gargantuan in size, unfathomable even.

"Incredible isn't it?" Viktor's voice, quiet as it was, filled the tall space, though it possessed a humble note of awe rather than his usual excitement.

Asher tore his eyes from the fossils above and looked upon the man who would be his master. With his hands resting behind his back, the crime lord slowly walked towards him, his gaze drawn to the bones. Beyond him, lingering in the shadows was Darya Siad-Agnasi and the hooded mage known as Alissandra. The mage's presence informed Asher that Varga was likely cocooned inside her protective spell. He wondered if she had upgraded it since his little display in the weapons room.

"Nobody knows what it is," Viktor continued, his voice full of reverence. "Or how old it is." He considered for a moment before adding, "Well, there aren't many outside of this chamber who even know there is such a creature entombed within the island. I would love to see it in its entirety. Could you imagine?" he asked, his excitement inevitably returning. "I would need an arena the size of Dragorn!"

Of course Viktor assumed he would enslave the creature. His cruel characteristics were just as overt as the monsters he procured.

"Recognise any friends?" Varga asked, looking over Asher's shoulder.

The ranger half turned to regard the caged monsters, only to notice that Kad Gorson had slipped away. "I was in the middle of a game of Galant," he said, quite bored. "Is there a reason I'm down here?"

The smile that ruled Viktor's expression faltered subtly before increasing across his face. "You are refreshing, I'll give you that much. No one has spoken to me like you do since... well, since my father was alive. You wouldn't have got on with him like you do with me. My father was a severe man. He took everything very seriously. Especially the authority of the ruling houses," he added, intoning a joke. "Take your last fight for example. Had you ignored his instruction and killed the Naerwitch as quickly as you did—and all in view of Lady Trigorn..." Varga's smile was no longer reaching his eyes. "You would have already been digested by some beast."

Asher was perfectly comfortable in the tense atmosphere. "Then it's a good thing he's dead," the ranger remarked.

Viktor's mouth twisted in amusement. "I couldn't agree more. That's not to say *I* wasn't disappointed. Some might even have categorised my mood as *murderous*," he clarified. "Being aware of your potential, however, I decided to take a few days, get some space. A clear head is a profitable one, my father always said."

"You have a way of avoiding the point," Asher told him bluntly.

"And you have a death wish," Viktor replied. "That must be frustrating given your instincts to survive. Or perhaps it's this weakness you've developed for others." Adding action to words, he revealed Deadora's blue ribbon again, the fabric pinched between finger and thumb. "Leaving Nightfall hasn't done you any favours. Either way, I would remind you that there are many ways to inflict torment. Or, if I must, inflict torment on your behalf."

The binding around Asher's wrists began to creak. He put all of his focus into his feet and ensuring they remained rooted to the spot, lest he start forward and attack the man.

"Now that we've got that out of the way..." Viktor announced, excitable elasticity returning to his demeanour. "Passionless and uninspiring as your performance was, you still managed to capture the Lady Trigorn. Even your execution of the gladiators impressed her," he added with a shrug. "I thought it was... *unimaginative*. You must do better."

Asher accepted the knuckles that Viktor rapped against his chest. "I'm glad the Lady was pleased," he said dryly.

"Indeed," Viktor agreed, circling the ranger. "So much so, in fact, that she has requested a more *intimate* display of your abilities."

Asher located the crime lord, over his shoulder, and shot the man a questioning look.

"Nothing like *that*," Varga reassured. "Though such a special request is not unheard of. No, Lady Trigorn wishes to see you up close. To see an *Arakesh* up close! Most who have had the pleasure do not live long to tell of it."

"That we can agree on," Asher said, his ominous threat not lost on Viktor.

"The Lady's interest in you gave me an idea," the crime lord went on, ignoring the comment. "I'm putting on a smaller, more personal, show for the island's elite."

Asher didn't bother suppressing his sigh. "Just put me on the sand."

"Oh, this won't be in the arena," Viktor explained, clearly enjoying the power he held over so skilled a killer. "I will be hosting it myself, in my home. I have a little place just outside the city, on one of the islands."

Quite naturally, Asher was already thinking about escaping. His chances always increased when they moved him, even from one building to another. Moving him across the city and actually putting him on a boat was almost inviting him to try. He was already envisioning the death of a dozen faceless thugs before taking control of the boat and heading to the mainland.

The ranger looked down at the blue ribbon clutched in Viktor's hand and his fantasy faded like smoke.

"When do I leave?" he asked, his hope reduced to embers again.

"Tonight, of course!" Varga exclaimed, as if it was obvious. "And you will not be coming alone," he added with a sly smirk.

Asher raised an eyebrow.

"Come now," Viktor cajoled, "you didn't think attending my exclusive party would absolve you? Were you any other I would have fed you to my monsters by now—disobedience cannot go unchecked. Instead, you have the opportunity to make it up to me."

"And if I refuse?"

Viktor paused, to reorganise his approach. "Let me put it another way then: you're going to do exactly what I command you to do or the next time we meet, I will present you with one of little Deadora's fingers."

The urge to murder the crime lord was so overwhelming that Asher had no choice but to recall his training, specifically the time when he was beaten by his peers and forced to stand still. If he attempted to defend himself or attack one of the others, Nasta would punish him so severely that the beating would seem like a reward. It was, ultimately, a test of mental discipline, a part of his training that helped him to develop his fortitude and create that island inside his mind, where he might retreat from the pain.

Viktor's threat was akin to every one of those blows. But Asher remained where he was, hands clenched into knots.

"What do you want?"

Varga let out a breath of relief. "That's what I want to hear. Soon, that will be the only question you have when you see me." The crime lord clapped his hands together. "I have been reading your book," he stated eagerly, one hand held out to the shadows. Darya stepped into the light without a sound and gave her master a familiar book before retreating again. Viktor opened it. "A Chronicle of Monsters: A Ranger's Bestiary! It's quite the read. I have been meaning to put something like this together myself, but who has the time?" He flicked through a handful of pages before he made a sound of satisfaction and planted the book in the cradle of Asher's arms.

The ranger was drawn to the sketch before the title of the page, neither of which reassured him. "Mer-folk," he said gruffly.

"Yes," Viktor replied, beaming. "Have you ever encountered one before?"

"Can't say I have."

"Hmm. How long have you been in the business of monsters, might I ask?"

"Four years."

"Four years," Viktor echoed. "I have employed hunters with twice that on their record. Admittedly, they didn't have all their parts like you do," he said, waving a finger over Asher's limbs. "Nor did they have the skillset of an Arakesh to fall on. I suppose that's what makes you... *you.*"

Asher looked from the pages of the bestiary to the crime lord. "You want me to hunt down one of the Mer-folk?" He didn't mean there to be, but the note of disbelief in his voice was most audible.

"It's already been hunted down," Viktor informed. "I just need you to capture it."

"Just?" Asher repeated. "I'm a ranger—I *kill* monsters, I don't *capture* them."

"You captured the Rakenbak," Viktor was quick to point out.

Asher glanced at the sketch again. "This is *not* a Rakenbak," he stated, hoping his meaning was clear.

Varga held up a finger. "Regardless, you *were* a ranger," he corrected. "Now you are an extension of my will. Nothing more. And I *want* that creature. *Alive.* You are to bring it with you—the perfect addition to our little exhibition."

Asher required a moment to work the tension out of his jaw. "Where is it?" he managed.

Viktor appeared satisfied by the response. "South of the island, beyond the walls." The crime lord pivoted to gesture at the three corpses. "These gentlemen failed to capture the beast. Now they are bound for the gut of my Trakians—they do so love the dead meat." He let that gruesome scene sit between them for a moment. "They did, however, succeed in cornering the creature in a nearby cave. I have men guarding the entrance, though none have the courage to enter. I could encourage them, of course, but I fear they all lack the skills to get the job done."

The ranger looked down at the sketch, pulled in by the detail given to the creature's claws and teeth. "You're not afraid you'll lose your champion?"

Viktor pursed his lips. "Don't doubt yourself, Asher. You would have brought in that Rakenbak were it not for circumstances outside of your control. Then there's the Royal Gobber you slew in The Iron Valley—with your hands bound no less! I read Doran's missive more than once. No, I think you will be just fine. In fact, I am more concerned that you will kill the sea monster."

"It would be a mercy," Asher commented.

"Perhaps. But mercy is no longer yours to grant."

The ranger took a moment to consider it all. "Why would you want one of these? It's not a monster of our world." He threw his head towards the cages behind him. "Any Mer-folk you capture will surely die in here, and long before you can get them on the sands."

"I want it because I want it," Viktor said simply. Enjoying the sound of his voice, he continued, "Their existence is well documented and general knowledge, but they are rarely seen in the light. Much like your ilk in Nightfall," he added with a smirk. "And if I can procure an Arakesh, why not a Mer-man?"

"There is nothing about them that can be likened to a man," Asher protested.

"Most would say that about an Arakesh," Viktor pointed out. "Yet here you are; the myth made man. And better yet, you are such a man as to be a ranger. I don't see why I can't utilise all of your talents."

Asher found a crack in the floor to hold his gaze while his mind came to grips with the corner he was in. He had no choice, of course, but he had demands of his own. "I'm going to need some things," he insisted, tired of arguing with the man.

Viktor framed his hands in the air, his face a picture of happiness. "My resources are generous. You may have what you wish."

"We'll get to the weapons," Asher began. "I need Salim."

The crime lord glanced briefly at his allies in the shadows. "Salim?"

The ranger refrained from rolling his eyes. "Salim Al-Annan—one of your *prisoners*."

Viktor clicked his fingers. "The Honour Guard! Yes, he was quite the find. But no, you cannot have him join you."

Asher's brow twitched in surprise and disappointment. "Why not?"

Varga straightened his back a notch. "Is it not enough that I have said so?"

"No," Asher replied defiantly.

Viktor sighed. "Even my dogs weren't so hard to break in." He folded his arms. "You said it yourself, he is a prisoner. That is how the people of this city see the men who fight in my arena. The worst of the worst. They cannot be seen to be walking the streets."

"I need him," Asher insisted. He handed the book back and pressed one finger into the text. "Should a contract be posted concerning these monsters," he read aloud, "share the coin with your fellow rangers—your only hope is in numbers."

"As I said," Viktor countered, "there are men guarding the cave; you can command them as you see fit."

"None of them have the training of an Honour Guard," Asher argued. "He's a damned good fighter and I need someone by my side that I can rely on."

Viktor looked up at him, calculating. "I didn't take you for a man to rely on anyone."

"I can rely on him not to *run*. Can you say as much about the men you have on that beach?"

Varga turned away and let his hands fall by his side. The index finger on his left hand tapped his thigh repeatedly, a rhythm to accompany his thoughts.

Seeing the cracks appear, Asher doubled down on his argument. "Having him with me could be the difference between killing the creature and capturing it."

Viktor stopped pacing and swivelled towards the ranger. "Very well," he said crisply. "You both leave at sundown." Making his leave, Varga paused by Asher's side. "You know better than to attempt escape," he said, his voice lowered as he returned to his interest in Deadora's blue ribbon. "But Salim might not. He is your responsibility. Should he flee, I will have no choice but to take it out on—"

"I know," the ranger cut in, before he could hear another threat laid against the child.

Viktor nodded once. "You said something about weapons..."

CHAPTER 33
CROSSING PATHS

Nefaris - These pale walkers hail from the Shadow Realm, a dimension of fangs and claws that should remain behind lock and key. Sadly, the magic users of our fair realm have learnt of dark and twisted paths that lead to that hellish abyss.

One such creature that has been unleashed from that other place is known as a Nefaris. On two feet, they move like a man and even stand at our height, but they possess four arms, the upper pair of which are so long as to reach their knees. The arms protruding from their skeletal ribs are smaller, designed for shredding the flesh of any prey pulled in by those stronger, outer arms.

Their head is, in effect, a mouth, capable of opening from forehead to chin to reveal several rows of teeth.

Thankfully, there is nothing fanciful required when it comes to slaying the nightmarish beasts. A good length of steel or even a well-placed arrow will bring them down. If you ask me, it's the mages who should be hunted down and made to answer for the monsters they unleash on our world.

A Chronicle of Monsters: A Ranger's Bestiary, 12th Edition, Page 492.

Royce Wiggins, Ranger.

"Are ye quite done?" Danagarr pestered, taking cover behind a crate. "We need to be movin' on."

Doran spared a moment from suffocating the man beneath his knee to shoot the smith a hard look. "Do ye mind? I'm in the middle o' somethin' 'ere."

Danagarr sighed. "First ye take an age spillin' yer guts all over the deckin' an' now ye takin' yer sweet time with this fella."

The son of Dorain glanced at the horrendous pool of vomit he had thrown up minutes earlier. He had barely made it to their current hiding place before it burst from his lips and even his nose. Damned sea. Unfortunately for the crew of the ship, they would discover more of it inside the hold. Doran had decided early on in their secret voyage that being below deck was far worse than being above deck. Still, they had made it onto the ship unseen after dispatching Undvig and his thugs and, ultimately, survived the journey. It was certainly a better arrival than his last, though the man beneath his knee would disagree.

Having remained hidden in the hold, biding their time while the crew organised themselves, the dwarves had succeeded in departing The Duchess using the increasing stacks of cargo to move between. It had required good timing and patience. The latter was not one of Danagarr's strong suits.

Now, a little further away from The Duchess, hiding amidst empty cargo crates and broken fishing gear, Doran strangled the only man who had come across them. Whether he worked for Viktor Varga like the crew remained to be seen. After his eyes rolled into the back of his head, the dwarf removed some of the weight from his knee and waited to ensure the stranger was truly unconscious.

"Right," he announced quietly, rising to his feet while remaining in a crouch behind the wall of crates. "Are ye done witterin' on?"

"Are ye done muckin' around?" the smith countered. "An' why ain' he dead?"

The hard lines of Doran's face creased into the centre. "What is it with ye an' killin' everyone?"

"Me daughter's life is in the balance," Danagarr snapped, a feral look in his eyes. "As far as I'm concerned, everyone on this whole damned island can taste the steel o' me hammer."

Doran couldn't argue with the dwarf's motives. "For the love o' Grarfath, Danagarr, we can' jus' kill every person we come across. That lad might not even work for Varga."

The smith made a face. "Bah! Why else would he be round these parts after dark? This whole area probably belongs to that Viktor fella."

"I'm not..." Doran trailed off, his words replaced by an exhausted sigh. "We're not talkin' abou' this. *I'm* in charge an' I say who we kill an' who we don'. Got it?"

"I'm not to be takin' orders from a—"

"Don' say it," Doran interjected, his finger shooting up into Danagarr's face.

His family name died on the lips of the smith, who slid down the side of a crate and let his head rest back against the wood. "I'm sorry, Doran. I might 'ave been abou' to say it but it's not how I think. We're equal, ye an' I. I truly believe that."

The son of Dorain took a breath and let some of his frustration boil off. "Never has a Stormshield uttered those words before," he commented softly. "Nor a Heavybelly for that matter," he added. "But I agree," the dwarf finally declared.

"It seems I'm not copin' well bein' so far from me family," Danagarr admitted. "An' I hate to think o' em out there in the world without me."

Doran sympathised. "Kilda's damned tough," he pointed out. "An' her plan to hide in The Black Wood is nothin' short o' genius. Who's goin' to look for dwarves in the woods?" The pair shared a short chuckle at the ridiculous idea. "Listen," he began, "we're both 'ere for Kilda an' Deadora. I'm goin' to do everythin' I can to undo the mess I've made. But I've been 'ere before, so ye *need* to let me lead."

His jaw set behind his bushy beard, Danagarr nodded, accepting the terms of their partnership. "Where do we start?" he asked the son of Dorain.

Doran didn't need to consider his answer for long. "Ideally, we'd spring Asher first. Once we get a sword in his hands this'll all go a lot smoother."

"An' where are we to be findin' 'im?"

The grizzled hunter turned away from the smith and set his eyes over the high walls and inspiring towers of Dragorn. "In there," he answered reluctantly.

Asher looked up at the night sky where an incalculable number of stars looked back at him. Framed between them was the moon in all its glory, a glowing disc of light that brought some illumination in the sun's absence. The heavens were all the more beautiful to be observed outside the confines of Viktor's prison.

Admiring them at all was new to the ranger. Of course, it seemed a little late to begin appreciating the natural wonders of the world. Now there was only the stone of walls and the sand of the arena.

"A hunter's moon," Salim commented, coming up on his side, his own eyes captured by the majesty of it all. "If this is part of your pitch, I fear I will not survive long enough to give you an answer."

Asher regarded the man and felt the sting of guilt. "You don't have to do this," he told him, quietly enough so as not to be heard by Malak and the guards buzzing about them in preparation to move through the city.

Salim withdrew his gaze from the moon and stars. "That's not what he said," the southerner replied, nodding at Malak.

"*If I tell them to send you back they will,*" Asher assured, switching to Karathan.

"*Send me back?*" Salim appeared almost offended by the idea. "*I have not tasted freedom like this in months. And I cannot say this monster business does not intrigue me. At the very least, it will be practice for when I face one of Viktor's beasts in the arena."*

Asher wanted to apologise for putting the Honour Guard in this position, in danger, but the actual words remained behind an obstacle in his mind. *"If we work together we can bring the creature down,"* he said instead.

"Is it true what the brute said?" Salim enquired. *"We are to capture one of the Mer?"*

There was no trepidation in the Honour Guard's voice, though his doubt reached Asher's ears. *"It can be done,"* he stated evenly, tightening the straps of his left vambrace.

Salim observed one of the guards walk past them, a horse in tow. *"You have captured one before?"*

The ranger glanced at his companion before returning his attention to his armour. *"No,"* he admitted.

"But you are confident?" the southerner checked.

"I'm confident we'll try our best," Asher countered. *"But I'm equally confident that we'll slay the creature if it doesn't give us a choice."*

Salim folded his arms across the leather cuirass he had been given. *"Will killing the beast not incite Viktor's wrath?"*

"I can only hope so," the ranger replied without missing a beat.

"Oi!" Malak barked, knocking the back of his hand into Asher's chest. "You two don't get to talk until we're on the beach," he dictated. "And I'll have none of that southern talk either."

He would snap his wrist first, Asher decided. Perhaps even his elbow too before dislocating Malak's shoulder. All three assaults would require no more than a second to accomplish. Two more seconds and the brute's neck would be out of alignment with the rest of his spine.

"Where are the weapons we chose?" the ranger asked, in place of living out his violent fantasy.

Malak stepped away and accepted the reins of a horse from one of his men. "You'll get them when you have need of them," he beamed, enjoying the power he wielded.

It didn't take Asher long to locate the weapons, distributed amongst the various riders along with their own blades. At least their wrists weren't bound, though he suspected that was to prevent Salim and himself from looking like prisoners as they left the arena. Adding to that image, they were both presented with a horse each from the stables. Asher instinctively reached for the reins of the chestnut brown one.

"Hector," he greeted with a genuine smile, his hand running up and down the horse's forehead. "Have they been treating you well?" he uttered.

"Assassin," Malak called from atop his mount. "Mr Varga said you were to have this." The brute tossed a bundle of fabric down at him. "He said it was to inspire you."

Asher didn't much care what the crime lord had said, but he did unravel the fabric and hold it up for inspection. By touch alone, the ranger knew that it was his green cloak, taken from him after The Mer Seed had ploughed into the dock. Viktor, a man of detail and appearance, had even seen to it that the blood be washed off.

Asher's hands clenched the fabric, taking on more than the mere feel of it. Part of his identity could be found in that green cloak and, only now, did he truly realise how much of him that was. How much of him was the *Ranger*.

It made his incarceration all the more torturous.

Rather than dwell on his inevitable return to the training grounds, Asher cast the cloak over his shoulders and clipped it to his cuirass. Even the weight of it was a welcome familiarity. It made him look down at his right index finger, notably absent his ring. This wasn't the longest he had gone without the black gem, but it was definitely the longest he had gone without thinking about it. As refreshing as that was, he still missed it. The gem, for all its confounding mystery, was just as much a part of his identity as the cloak draped over his back.

"Let's go!" Malak ordered, directing his horse down the street.

Asher let go of his musings and mounted Hector, just as he had so many times before. It had been too long since he had felt like a ranger, with nothing but a monster in his future.

It felt good.

~

Doran couldn't believe his eyes. He blinked hard, his mouth ajar. Night it might be, with shadows abounding between the candle-lit gloom of the surrounding buildings, but the man riding away from the arena gates was most definitely Asher. The ranger was even wearing his green cloak.

"Are ye sure?" Danagarr asked, his own sight not up to the task.

"It were *'im*," Doran declared, moving to better see between the patrons that staggered between taverns. He had been unsure himself, at first, but once the ranger had taken to his mount and risen above the loud and jolly Dragornians, there was no doubt.

"Well, what's he doin' out 'ere?" Danagarr pressed. "I thought he were a prisoner?"

"He is," Doran replied confidently.

The smith made a face. "He didn' look like a prisoner to me."

"He didn' 'ave any weapons," the son of Dorain explained to him. "Can you imagine Asher goin' anywhere without a bloody big sword strapped to 'im?"

Danagarr shrugged. "So where's he goin' with that lot?"

"How am I to know?" Doran countered. "I jus' got 'ere, same as ye."

"Well, ye best get after 'im then," the smith suggested, picking up his bag and throwing it over one shoulder.

Doran looked him up and down. "What are *ye* abou'?"

Looking over the barrels that concealed them, Danagarr nodded at the arena. "I'm goin' in there before they get to closin' them gates."

Doran adjusted his hood to hide more of his face and stood up to look over the barrels as the smith did. "Ye're goin' in there alone?"

Danagarr opened his mouth to reply when a man, clearly inebriated, planted a hand on his shoulder and tried to turn the dwarf about. "You're a small fella ain't you!" the drunkard accosted.

The smith growled and shoved the man with a strong hand. "Push off!" he spat, sending the man on his way. Danagarr brushed the cloak on his shoulder and turned back to Doran. "Aye, I'm goin' in there. The quicker we get to it the quicker we can get off this wretched island."

The son of Dorain peered between the Dragornians to see Asher's company—they were almost out of sight. "What are *ye* goin' to do in *there*?"

Danagarr sniffed, pushing the bridge of his nose into his brow. "I'm goin' to upend Viktor Varga's little empire," he stated, his voice low, before patting his chest with one knotted fist. "Let 'im taste the wrath o' a Stormshield."

Doran was immediately torn. He knew the benefit of freeing Asher up to help them bring Viktor down and he also felt an overwhelming responsibility towards the ranger. But letting Danagarr go into the belly of the beast alone dramatically increased the chances that the smith would never see home again. How could he face Kilda and Deadora with that news?

"This ain' up for debate, Heavybelly," Danagarr interjected, cutting through his thoughts. "Go an' see to Asher. Then come back an' help me finish the place off."

The smith didn't wait for a response before walking round the barrels and making for the stable gates that led into the arena. Doran's eyes followed him for the moment, noting the lone man that had been left to close up the gates from the inside. Security around the arena didn't seem much of an issue when everyone knew what nightmares were kept inside.

With no preamble, Danagarr strode through the entrance as Viktor's employee was securing one of the gates. Doran watched him take issue with the smith's trespass and quickly follow after him, out of sight. The dwarven hunter could feel his heart racing already. Setting him at ease, Danagarr soon returned, absent his bag, to close the other gate behind him. Doran didn't need to investigate to know that Viktor's man was dead beyond the wall. It seemed every Stormshield had war in their blood.

With his armour and weapons slung over one shoulder, Doran kept his hood up and maintained a hunched appearance as he set off down the road. Harsh remarks and insults came at him from various patrons, their comments aimed at either his height or hurrying speed. The son of Dorain, however, was more insulted that he could ever be mistaken for a man, even a crippled one. Still, he bore it all to move through the streets unrecognised by Viktor's many eyes and ears.

He didn't catch up with Asher's company until they had exited the city through the much smaller southern gates. Once beyond the walls, Doran had to take even more care, for Viktor's men—Malak included—would not mistake him for anything but a dwarf. Adding to that dilemma, there were few places to hide, forcing the son of Dorain to hang back and watch the party ride up along the beach. He moved from patch to patch of long grass and crawled over some of the larger dunes in his pursuit. The light of the moon caught the gleaming steel of their weapons, but it was the numerous fires, further up the beach, that drew Doran's attention.

A small, but sheer, cliff rose up from the beach's end, a belt of rock that separated Dragorn's walls from the sand. At the base, forming a semicircle, a group of men stood with spears and bows between long torches embedded in the sand. They appeared to be guarding the cave entrance that sat inside the semi-circle, a pointed and jagged thing that reminded Doran of an arrowhead.

Hidden behind an outcropping of rock that extended from the cliff, the dwarf continued to watch as Asher and company finished their journey along the beach and dismounted to join those guarding the cave.

"What in the hells is goin' on?" he muttered, shaking his head.

To the sound of licking flames and the lapping sea, Asher's feet landed in the soft sand of Dragorn's southern beach. His eyes were naturally captured by the wave-worn cave cut into the side of the cliff. No such sense existed, yet he could *feel* the monster that dwelled in that chamber. He also knew it was looking at *him*.

Malak came into view, rounding his horse, with a two-handed longsword sheathed in its scabbard. He freed the blade in one clean motion and tossed it to the ranger, tip to the sky. Asher caught it easily enough and hefted it so the blade twisted one way then the next. It was unwieldy compared to his two-handed broadsword, but it would suffice, the steel meeting his lowest standards where its edge was concerned.

"And the rest?" he questioned.

Malak looked put out before nodding at one of his men. Asher accepted his short-sword—a weapon he was content to keep sheathed until they were beyond the touch of moonlight—and his folded bow with a full quiver to accompany it. After plunging the longsword into the sand, he strapped them all to his body, keeping the quiver, silvyr blade, and folded bow tight across his back.

"Remember," Malak began, his deep voice banishing the tranquil sounds of the night. "Mr Varga wants the creature *alive*. Do not disappoint him."

Asher ignored the brute and reclaimed the longsword. He rolled his wrist once, getting a feel for its weight—it would take longer to become accustomed to its length. Taking hold of a torch while it was still planted in the sand, he swiped the blade across the haft and cut it in half so that he might carry it better. Beside him, Salim was given the sabre he had chosen in the weapons room, the same blade he chose for every arena battle. There had been the option to take more, but the Honour Guard had refused, favouring only the curved sword.

With Salim at his side, the pair entered the semi-circle and stood sentinel at the entrance to the cave, each getting a feel for the environment they were about to enter. Inside, where the light of the moon could not touch, he would have mastery over his senses, an advantage in any fight. But the *Assassin* did not capture monsters—it didn't capture anything. Were he to soak up the dark, he would become a killing machine. Not tonight. Tonight he would remain the *Ranger*.

While he could.

"Do you have a plan?" the southerner asked, drawing him from his thoughts.

"Beyond not getting killed?" Asher responded. "No."

"What about that book you mentioned? The bestiary."

The ranger glanced back at Hector, where the book had once been tucked away inside the horse's saddlebags. According to Viktor, it was now in his possession.

"There's nothing in it that could help us," Asher insisted. "Very little is known about Mer-folk, especially their weaknesses."

"You don't have all night, boys!" Malak yelled from beyond the semi-circle.

A deep sigh rumbled from Asher's throat. "Ideally," he said so that only Salim could hear him, "we would use this lot as bait."

"And in the absence of bait?" Salim enquired.

"We put ourselves on the hook," Asher replied, striding into the cave.

Salim was close on his heel as he passed over the threshold, the light from his torch pushing back the shadows. The darkness moved around them like the mouth of some beast swallowing them whole. The sand continued until the path rose up and round, where uneven rock paved the way. Holding his torch out, Asher could see the puddles and small pools of sea water that dotted the interior chamber. It was a terrible environment to engage a monster.

With his own torch held up to his face, Salim used his hands to suggest that they split up and move around the cave's surrounding wall to check all the shadows. It was a good idea, since they didn't know if there were other chambers off this one, but Asher knew better than to separate when the bestiary's only advice had been to utilise numbers.

"You don't need to be quiet," he told the Honour Guard, his gruff voice awfully loud as it filled the cave. "It already knows we're here," he added ominously, his eyes roaming over the shadowy ceiling. The ranger nodded at what he estimated to be the centre of the chamber. "Back to back," he advised.

Together, they moved into the middle of the cave like the morning sun cutting through the dark of night. The shadows danced about them, revealing clumps of glittering rock and stalactites. Backs aligned together, the companions made a slow circle. When Salim stopped, so too did Asher. He glanced over one shoulder to see the Honour Guard staring up at the sloping curve of jagged wall. Following the man's gaze, the ranger scrutinised every shape defined by the torchlight.

The creature's tail stood out first, lining the curve in the wall. It was too smooth and too long to be mistaken for rock. The tail, however, took Asher's eyes to a hideous body, its back pressed to the ceiling and kept there by strength alone, a strength expected from a creature that navigated powerful ocean currents as easily as men walked the earth.

Hanging either side of its head were long curtains of what looked like seaweed, though any human would call it hair. Nestled between, he soon found its eyes. Two black orbs as big as a man's fist. It was impossible to discern what they were looking at, yet there was no doubt they were fixed squarely on the humans. Prey to the Mer-folk.

Most unnervingly, the creature didn't move.

Of all the monsters Asher had hunted down, he couldn't recall any that hadn't immediately attacked him on sight. And why wouldn't they? Though described as monsters, they were all mindless animals that lived by their instincts alone. But this monster, a creature of The Adean's black depths, didn't move an inch, content to observe them. The reason occurred to Asher and unnerved him all the more.

It was *thinking*.

They had been pitted against a monster that could think as they did, assess and plan as they did, and, right now, it was determining how best to kill them. It wasn't the first time on the cursed island that Asher realised he had made a grave mistake.

"Get out," he hissed at Salim.

But it was too late. The monster sprang from its high perch and came down on them like a spear. The ranger managed to shove Salim aside while diving in the opposite direction himself. The Mer-man met the cave floor and coiled about itself in a bid to correct its orientation. It did so with terrifying speed, towering over Asher before he had returned to his feet again.

Like a snake rearing to attack, the creature stood at least eight feet tall, its toned arms spread wide with black claws protruding from every digit. The webbing between its fingers was highlighted by Salim's torchlight behind it. When it opened its wide-set mouth, baring teeth akin to a shark's, it produced a series of clicking and hissing sounds. Asher gave very little thought to the noises monsters made, just as he gave little thought to the barks of a dog, but it was very possible the sounds he was hearing were words in a language he couldn't comprehend.

Behind the Mer-man, Salim let loose a cry of violent intent. Asher caught sight of his scimitar, flashing in the light of the torch at the Honour Guard's feet. The ranger tightened his grip around the hilt of his longsword, preparing to make his move as soon as the creature turned to deal with the rear attack. That crucial moment, however, never arrived. The monster flicked its powerful tail and launched Salim across the cave.

Still caught in its unwavering sight, Asher had no choice but to face the thing head on. He made the first move and lashed out with his torch, swiping it across the creature's face. He struck naught but air, the monster too fast for such an obvious attack, though he noted it recoil from the light and even raise a hand to block it out.

His second attack was more subtle thanks to the twist he employed, which saw his longsword roll around and up instead of swiping out wide as he had with the torch. It was unorthodox enough to catch the Mer-man off guard and so the tip of the sword drew a red line up its slimy flesh, marring its chest. The monster hissed and its tail coiled to bring its upper body into retreat.

Asher resisted the urge to advance. Instead, he observed the beast as it observed him.

Swaying as if it were a kite caught in a breeze, the Mer-man kept its shoulders hunched and its eyes within the shadows of its long and unusual hair. One clawed finger investigated the gash across its chest and brought the blood to its vision. Its head then jutted forward and unleashed a torrent of clicking and hissing again.

"Salim?" Asher called.

The Honour Guard made an indecipherable noise before discovering his words again. "*I live,*" he said in his native tongue.

"Get out," the ranger instructed him again, stepping through and over the small pools to put himself between the creature and Salim.

"I will not abandon you to this fiend," the southerner protested, his senses returned enough to use the common tongue of the northern kingdoms.

The Mer-man watched them both, its head cocked to one side. Was it listening to them? Did it understand them? Asher couldn't imagine it did, just as he couldn't understand it. But what did he or anyone truly know of these mysterious and deadly creatures?

"This monster is beyond you," the ranger warned him. "Get out while you can."

Asher heard the sound of Salim's scimitar scraping along the cave floor. "Tonight," he declared in his exotic accent, "I am *ranger.*"

Having given him all the chances he could, Asher decided to use the Honour Guard. "You go right," he instructed. "I'll go left." The ranger had no intention of following that plan; it was merely a test.

Before Salim took to his path, along the cave's righthand wall, the Mer-man swivelled its head in that direction before retreating a couple of feet. It could have been a coincidence, Asher decided.

"Salim," he called back, not daring to take his eyes off the creature. "When I tell you to, I want you to throw your sword at it."

"As you say," the Honour Guard replied, adjusting his grip on the scimitar.

The Mer-man's upper body flitted erratically left then right while its thick tail remained relatively still. Asher licked his lips, considering the revelation of his findings. Though he refused to face it, there was a degree of dread sitting like a stone in his gut.

"It understands us," he breathed, his lips barely moving. "*It understands us,*" he announced in the Karathan tongue, gambling that the monster's knowledge of man's languages was limited to the most common of them.

"*Truly?*" Salim questioned, apprehension in his response.

"*Come to me,*" Asher said, hoping the creature's snarl was a look of confusion in its kind.

Salim only made it half way before the Mer-man shot forwards, its claws raking high to come down on Asher. The ranger swung his sword, a deflection that would surely cut through the monster's arms, but the intelligent beast was swift and slithered past him at the last second. With no time to bring his sword back from the swing, he was struck by the tail that threw him down and across a series of small pools. The longsword clattered away, out of reach, while the torch was extinguished underwater, plunging half the cave back into darkness.

On the other side, illuminated by the only flames they had left, Salim was set upon by the Mer-man. Those terrible claws tore across his leathers until they pierced through and found the soft flesh under his ribs. The Honour Guard suppressed his pain to no more than a grunt and whipped his scimitar out with disciplined grace. The edge sliced the creature's arm, forcing it to retract the claws before simply backhanding him across the face, knocking him down again.

The surviving torch landed at an awkward angle, its flames kissing the surface of a shallow pool.

By now, Asher had not only got up but closed the gap between, his silvyr blade in hand. The Mer-man turned on him, its tail coiling beneath its humanoid upper body. The creature sprang, curling low before launching back up, there to grab the ranger by his leathers. Asher felt his quiver scrape across the curve of the cave wall, his legs kicking out against nothing. And up there, the Mer-man brought its nightmarish face within inches of his own.

He had the sense to swing his head back before the creature snapped at him with its razor-sharp teeth.

And then, with nowhere to go but down, the cave floor came rushing up to meet him. His feet, though, barely touched stone before the monster flung him sideways. For a brief, but painful, moment up became down and down became up as he bounced and skipped over the rock.

He was dead. There was no question in his mind. There would be no recovering before it was upon him again. Even now, his momentum having only just stopped, he could hear it slithering towards him at speed.

Your only hope is in numbers, Olav One-Eye had written so long ago.

It was in that moment that Salim Al-Anan proved the late ranger correct. The Honour Guard leapt from the shadows and scored two more blows, one of which chopped off two digits from the creature's right hand. He went on to evade the Mer-man's counterattack but his third strike was halted when it rushed forwards and slammed into him.

Asher gritted his teeth and jumped up to his knees, thrusting the silvyr blade as he did so. At least a quarter of the sword pierced the monster's tail, just below its humanoid waist. It wasn't a killing blow but it was enough to redirect the beast's ire from Salim to him.

Rounding on him with vengeance, the Mer-man hissed and shot one arm out to grab the ranger by the throat. He was soon lifted from the ground, his short-sword brought with him. Damn Viktor, he thought. This wasn't a monster to be captured alive. He raised the weapon, his arm bent and ready to spring, but the beast's larger hand wrapped around his own and held the silvyr at bay. He thought to release the blade and catch it with his free hand, but his own grip of the hilt was kept in place by the fiend.

"Salim!" he croaked, his voice quashed by fingers slick with blood. "*The fire!*" he rasped in Karathan. "*The fire!*" Asher reached out with his free hand, waiting.

The Honour Guard scrambled across the ground and grasped

desperately at the torch. Asher watched its brief flight before the wet haft met his hand. He didn't hesitate. He *never* hesitated.

The ranger drove the flames into the monster's eyes and it shrieked in instant agony, its large black eyes reduced to scorched pits. The Mer-man's reaction was sudden and violent. It knocked the torch away and hurtled through the cave in a blind rage, Asher still grasped in its hand. The creature collided with every surface, its muscular tail more than capable of launching it up to the ceiling. Asher too felt those rocks and did what he could to protect his head from serious injury. More than once he glimpsed Salim diving out of the way.

Inevitably, the monster threw itself into the curving tunnel that led to the beach. Yet the pain was driving it to madness. So much so, that even after discovering the sand and coming across the sound of the ocean, the creature's motion was still volatile, sending it into every jagged surface.

Dragged through it all, Asher was beginning to lose conscious-ness, the tight hold about his throat keeping the precious air from his lungs. He tried again and again to stab it with his silvyr blade but the Mer-man's uncertain and irregular movement kept his arm flailing ineffectually.

Over the sound of its constant shrieking, the ranger could just hear Malak and his men preparing to meet the beast. Whether it was injured or not, there was still every chance that they would flee at the mere sight of it.

Ultimately, the Mer-man's downfall was of its own making. As it approached the entrance to the cave, the creature misjudged its surroundings and propelled itself high, likely expecting to then hit the beach with enough momentum to aid its dash to the water. Instead, the monster's head slammed into the top ridge of the entrance, causing it to almost somersault backwards before crashing into the beach in the middle of the semi-circle.

It didn't move after that.

The same could not be said of Asher, who had been released from its grip and left to tumble across the sand. Everything hurt. Added to that, the stars above were doubling in number.

"Well I'll be damned," Malak said, walking into view above the ranger.

"Is it..." Asher coughed, interrupting himself. "Is it... alive?"

Malak ignored him and crouched down. When next he stood, he was holding the ranger's short-sword. Like any who looked upon silvyr in the moonlight, the thug marvelled at its glittering display.

That pit of dread returned to Asher's gut.

"You've been holding out on us, mate," Malak remarked, his gaze still enraptured by the blade. "Mr Varga's going to want to see this."

Asher could do nothing but lie back and give in to his coughing fit.

For the second time that night, Doran Heavybelly couldn't believe what he was seeing. His surprise, coupled with his continued struggles to don his new armour, caused the dwarf to fall backwards. The twisted cuirass dug into his side and made him wince and grunt.

While cursing the armour he also adored, the son of Dorain picked himself up and peered over the rocky outcropping.

He had no idea what manner of beast had burst from the cave but he was thankful it was down and still. He was also thankful to see Asher emerge with it, and alive by the look of him. After another man walked out of the cave, and was curiously disarmed by the others, the ranger was hauled to his feet and pushed towards the sea, where a number of small boats had recently arrived.

The strange monster was tended to by most of the others and bound tightly by several chains and ropes, before being heaved onto the largest of the boats. Asher was similarly bound, though only by the wrists, as he was forced into a different boat with the man who had been previously disarmed.

Pacing up and down the beach, Malak clapped his hands. "Come on! Let's go! Get a move on!"

Doran couldn't make head nor tail of any of it. "What in the hells..."

Once Malak climbed into one of the boats they were all pushed off from the beach and sent into the dark waters of The Adean. Doran looked ahead, further south of those black waters, and spotted torchlight in the distance. After guessing it to be one of the smaller islands that sprawled south of Dragorn, the dwarf began to wonder if they were all heading towards Viktor's private home. Then the dwarf feared such a thing. Why would Asher be sent there?

More talk from the beach returned Doran's attention to his surroundings. A few stragglers had been left to gather the horses and see them returned to the stables. There was one other, however, who was further down the slope from Doran. His tracks in the sand led back to a simple rowing boat that he had left unattended so that he might relieve himself.

"You best get on with it, Hadrik!" one of the riders yelled on their way back to the south gate. "Malak'll have your hide if you're not across the water soon!"

"Yeah, yeah," Hadrik replied wearily. "There's enough of them over there already to start a war!" he called back, but the riders had gone.

Doran quickly finished fitting his armour and leathers before strapping the axe to his back and sheathing the sword on his hip. Then he crept down the slope after Hadrik, who had begun to saunter back to his rowing boat, oblivious to the dwarf that stalked him.

"Excuse me," Doran said, politely enough. "Is there room for two in there?"

Hadrik jumped out of his skin, his feet almost leaving the beach as he turned to face the son of Dorain. He made to speak but Doran's sword was brought to bear and placed neatly under the man's jaw. The dwarf swiftly removed Hadrik's short-sword, a pitiful-looking weapon that he happily threw into the sea.

"I'll keep this simple for ye, laddy." He nodded at the boat. "Ye're goin' to take me wherever they've gone. If ye refuse, I'll take somethin' precious from ye. If ye try any funny business while we're at sea, I'll take somethin' precious from ye. If ye try an' warn yer pals, I'll take somethin' precious from ye. An' jus' to be clear, when I say somethin' precious, I mean yer—"

"I understand," Hadrik interjected hastily, his hands naturally moving to cover his crotch.

Doran grinned. "Very good, lad. Very good."

CHAPTER 34
NULL AND VOID

Grodel - I used to like birds. I thought they were exquisite animals and a reflection of the gods' beauty. I don't anymore. Not after meeting a Grodel.

How best to describe this monster of the sky? Even my worst nightmares could not conjure such a thing. Alas, I shall do my best to detail the creature.

On four scaly legs, a Grodel stands at around seven feet and can reach up to twelve feet in length when fully matured. Halfway up, black feathers conceal the rest of its hideous form and spread out across its impressive wingspan. Its head is that of an enlarged crow, though I have met rangers who state they encountered a Grodel with an eagle's head. I cannot vouch for that.

Just below their throat, you will find a pair of arms no longer than your own. Should you find yourself on your back, a Grodel looking down on you, they will use these arms to pin you and disembowel you with their beak.

Keep moving. Stay on your feet.

A Chronicle of Monsters: A Ranger's Bestiary, 12th Edition, Page 202.

Red Radigon, Ranger.

Hewn from the natural stone of the island, Viktor's fortress stood insurmountably above the dark seas of The Adean. It rose from the surface of the waves and continued on for six receding levels, all revealed where an outer wall had once been.

Asher beheld it from his place on the boat. He could tell it was old, the fortress comparable to the elven architecture that humanity had built upon and around while erecting their cities. The exterior, however, hadn't been maintained as well as such edifices were on the mainland, lending it a tired appearance that suggested it was older still.

The same could not be said of the interior, visible beyond the exposed edge. There he could see walls of modern construction, likely built to support the older framework or provide new and private quarters.

The ranger also spotted several guards, their patrols routinely blotting out the torches as they passed by. Given the guests Viktor was entertaining, the guards would no doubt be a mix of all the ruling houses. From an engagement standpoint, that fact made little difference to Asher, as they would all be relatively proficient fighters. The advantage would come in the form of miscommunication, as the factions were unaccustomed to working together.

Asher averted his gaze from the fortress and took a breath. What was he doing? Old habits, he presumed. His mind couldn't help but assess every new environment and deduce its strengths and weaknesses. There was no place for that now. He had no need of escape or infiltration. He was to do as commanded.

An echo of his former life washed over him like the waves that lapped against the ancient stone. Its sting was two-fold after having tasted the life of a ranger again.

Once the boats were moored, Asher watched the Mer-man be

received by one of Viktor's mages. Again, his tactical mind slipped between the cracks of his imprisonment and noted that there must be at least two mages present of the known four, as the other would be close to Viktor's side. He let it go and merely watched the mage levitate the creature and guide it towards the lowest entrance.

Having been stripped of his weapons, including the silvyr blade that now rested in the hand of Malak, Asher walked within the confines of his escort to the end of the jetty. He glanced over his shoulder to see that Salim was similarly surrounded, though the ranger was still curious as to why he had been brought along at all.

"You're later than expected," came the sharp voice of Darya Siad-Agnasi, her tone just as cutting as her words.

Malak could only shrug. "He's a better assassin than he is a ranger."

Asher eyed the brute, wishing he could prove the words true. "Maybe *you* should have captured the creature."

Malak clipped him round the back of the head. "I didn't say speak."

The ranger clenched his bound fists, fighting against the brief pain that urged him to kill the man. He instead locked his eyes on the Shadow Witch, who continued to passively watch the scene play out.

She looked over the ranger's shoulder, taking note of Salim, before saying, "Bring them." Like some spectre of the ethereal world, she turned around and led the way, her long coat trailing in her wake.

Inside the fortress, the aesthetics straddled the line between rustic and modern, with many of the walls left just as they were. The peering eyes of numerous portraits followed Asher down the halls, while painted landscapes of places he would never again see haunted his every step. Shelves and cabinets had been fitted throughout, there to display Viktor's endless collection of, apparently, everything.

Suits of armour that Asher couldn't place stood sentinel here and there. Weapons, both old and new, decorated the walls between the frames. Frayed maps and unusual trinkets were on display behind doors of glass. A good deal of it, though, was from The Arid Lands by the general look of it. Pieces of history from the desert's ancient past.

The deeper they penetrated the more Asher heard from various unseen chambers. It seemed Viktor's guests were partaking in a great many proclivities enjoyed by the rich and powerful. This was reinforced by the clusters of men and women, naked and sweating, seen moving between rooms. Such were the propensities of those who saw human life as no more than a product to be exchanged.

Before reaching the highest level inside the fortress, Salim and his escort peeled away. Asher turned to watch their diversion but was able to give the man no more than a curious look before stone separated them.

"Why has he been brought here?" he asked the Shadow Witch. This time, he bobbed his head to evade Malak's predictable response.

Darya stopped, her hand gripping the handle of the door that barred their way. "He is here because the master commanded it. Just like you."

Upon opening the door, the black of night and the stretching sea dominated the vista. The chamber was protected by a roof, but the adjacent wall—once the fortress's exterior wall—was entirely missing, leaving jagged edges above and below.

The ranger followed his dangerous escort inside, stepping on a large rug that overlapped several others. An ornate desk sat in the centre of the room, its top covered in carefully organised stacks of parchments, and all between exotic ornaments. The three walls were lined exclusively with bookshelves, leaving no space for paintings or decoration. It was in front of these shelves, to Asher's right, that he spotted Viktor Varga. He was holding a large leather-bound book, one finger delicately turning the page.

"Ah!" he exclaimed, shutting the book with all the dramatic flair Asher had come to expect from him. "The hunter returns!" Viktor shelved the book and performed a short dance of glee as he hummed his way across the room. "Do we have our prize?" he enquired, looking to Darya over Asher's shoulder.

"The creature is being prepared as we speak," she reported.

"Excellent!" Viktor declared, his hands clenching in the air. "I knew you could do it." He looked the ranger over. "And hardly a scratch too." He glanced at Darya and gestured to the ranger's binding. Once freed, Asher unconsciously rubbed his wrists, the restraints having been tied a notch too hard by Malak.

Movement from the corner of the room, where one of the bookshelves met the open wall, drew the ranger to the mage, Alissandra. As always, her large hood concealed her face, leading the ranger to wonder if she could see only her feet. Her presence in the corner also revealed a narrow door that granted access to an unseen room.

"I cannot wait to see it," Viktor continued, moving towards his desk. "And I am sure Lady Trigorn will love it," he added eagerly. "She has had a fascination with the Mer-folk since a young age. Combined with yourself, of course, this will prove to be the party of the age."

Testing the limits of his freedom, Asher slowly walked over to the open wall, where the sea breeze blew his hair out. From the edge, he could see the next two levels spread out beneath him. The immediate floor below was cause for concern.

"Is that an arena?" he questioned, observing the circle of sand, half of it surrounded by broken pillars.

"That it is," Viktor confirmed. "A more intimate space than the one you're accustomed to. Still, it will do nicely for tonight's entertainment."

Asher looked up from the small arena and paused. "I'm to fight then," he concluded, his thoughts racing to the Honour Guard. "Is that why Salim is here?"

Viktor wandered over, his fingers clasped at his waist. "And others," he remarked casually, taken in by the view of his own property. "Do you know what this place was?" he asked the ranger, not in the least concerned by the inevitable deaths.

Asher tried to look past his vision of the imminent and violent future. "It's elven," he finally answered.

"Indeed," Viktor agreed, folding his arms. "But not just any elf," he explained. "Structures like this one are dotted throughout The Lifeless Isles, though none so intact as what you see before you. There are also claw marks," he added provocatively. "Scars left on the cliffs eons past. Do you know what creatures made those marks?"

Asher didn't have to think for very long, given the history of the isles and the fact that very few creatures could make visible claw marks so high up. "Dragons," he uttered.

"Dragons!" Viktor repeated, and with great solemnity. "Who can speak of such a time, when dragon and elf lived together? It would certainly make for a great story," he considered. "Can you imagine it, Asher?" he went on, his voice full of wonder. "Elves stood in this very room and looked out on a world of dragons. We're in the midst of history itself."

Varga shrugged in an effort to dampen his excitement. "I suppose history isn't for everyone," he said, perhaps in light of Asher's disinterest. "And you're right to keep your focus," he continued, almost admiringly. "You will have quite the audience tonight." The crime lord walked Asher towards the door and regarded the Shadow Witch. "See him prepared."

"Mr Varga," Malak interjected, halting the ranger's departure.

Asher had been anticipating this moment. He had even hoped, if for only a second, that the brute would keep the silvyr for himself, thereby keeping the Stormshields' secret. But, like everything else that had happened to him since stepping foot on Dragorn, it was out of his control.

Malak stepped forward. "He dropped this on the beach," he said, presenting the short-sword to his master.

Viktor appeared non-plussed, irritated almost. "And?"

Malak maintained his confidence, sure of the value in what he held. "Take it to the edge," he urged, offering it again.

Somewhat bewildered, Varga accepted the weapon, glancing at Asher as he did so. His curiosity, as ever, was insatiable, and so he made his way across the room. The sword was held in both hands, his fingers deliberately running up the flat of the blade until they reached the point. Upon reaching the edge, where the moon shone unfettered by clouds, he stretched out his arms and bathed the rare mineral in that pale light.

The silvyr revealed its beauty to all.

Viktor was inspired, his cautious curiosity and annoyance hollowed out and refilled with unbridled wonderment. He turned it over to marvel at both sides. Experimenting, he withdrew the weapon beyond the touch of the moon's light and watched its glittering surface dull to the appearance of steel. Then he would extend his arm once more and observe the event anew.

"I do not believe it," he whispered in one of the Ameeraskan dialects, his pronunciation and accent second to none.

Asher was deathly still, his instincts on the verge of taking over. He could feel Darya and Malak watching him closely; the Shadow Witch even had one of her fine daggers halfway out of its sheath.

"This is..." Viktor trailed off in favour of a laugh, the sound full of disbelief. "This is silvyr!" he eventually exclaimed. "I have only ever heard of such a thing. Never did I think I would see it. Nor touch it," he added incredulously, letting the flat of the blade rest on his palm. "Exquisite."

The crime lord took another moment to swish the blade in and out of the moonlight, laughing as he did. It was clear to see that he was falling in love with the weapon, and clearer still that Asher would never wield it again.

"It is said that Lord Tyberius Gray possessed such a weapon," Viktor began, walking back into the room. "An entire sword of silvyr, gifted to him by *the* Gal Tion, the first king of Illian. It is also said that silvyr never dulls nor rusts, and that Tyberius's sword resides to this very day inside West Fellion, protected by the Graycoats. Were it only possible to claim such a prize from them," he said wistfully. "And now look what I hold!" he declared, his excitement mounting. "And brought to me by a lowly ranger no less..." Viktor's train of thought appeared to wander before sharpening.

"'Tis not the weapon of a ranger," he mused, his eyes captured by the blade. "But it is a weapon of the *dwarves*." Now he looked at Asher, his amazement replaced by cold calculation. "Tell me, how did you come by the silvyr?"

Lying was as easy as breathing to an Arakesh. "From Doran Heavybelly," he replied without hesitation. "He had brought it with him from Dhenaheim. It was my payment for aiding in the capture and delivery of the Rakenbak."

"Curious. I had occasion to meet Doran before you. I do not recall him possessing such a thing." Viktor looked to his Shadow Witch.

"He carried an axe and sword," Darya clarified, without a hint of doubt.

Viktor pointed a lazy finger at her, as if his suspicions had been proven right. "Yes, that sounds like the dwarf." Varga moved closer to Asher, his gaze penetrating. "I think you acquired the silvyr elsewhere, though I *do* believe the source was a dwarf." He reached into his pocket and retrieved Deadora's blue ribbon. "You wouldn't be lying to your master would you?" Viktor brought the ribbon to his nose as he asked the question, as if he could detect the girl's lingering scent.

"I got the sword from Doran," Asher repeated evenly.

"I don't believe you," Varga responded, an edge creeping into his voice. "Furthermore, I am greatly disappointed that you have kept such a secret from me. To think there has been a blade of pure silvyr simply lying about in the weapons room." The crime lord tutted at the thought. "I could purchase kingdoms with just a few pounds of this. What a joke it is that you've just been walking around stabbing monsters with it!" Viktor licked his lips, his gaze drawn back to the blade. "I think I will hold on to this from now on. And thank you, Malak, for bringing this to my attention," he added, eliciting a bow from the larger man.

A nod from her master, Darya gripped Asher by the arm and began to direct him towards the door. The ranger resisted and turned back to Viktor, his actions enough to lure one of the Shadow Witch's daggers to his throat.

"What will you do?" he demanded.

Varga's eyes narrowed on him, curiosity and revelation colliding behind his expression. "Is that fear I detect? Surely not, for what could grip the heart of an Arakesh so? Hmm." Viktor considered his own questions, his head tilted to one side. "Unless it is the ranger who is beset by fear. The man you have become betrays you, Asher. You acquired the silvyr from the Stormshields," he deduced.

"I told you—"

"You are only here because you *fear* for the dwarven family," Viktor cut in. "And so you should. Were you not here their heads would adorn the walls of my arena." The crime lord moved away, his attention continuously returned to the blade in his hand. "But this does change things," he stated. "Do they have more?"

Asher started forward and felt the bite of Darya's knife against his skin. "We had a deal," the ranger reminded.

Again, Viktor scrutinised everything about Asher. "I'd say that's a *yes*. How interesting."

Asher pushed through the pain of Darya's blade. "If you harm them I will—"

"Calm yourself," Varga bade the ranger, his hand gesturing for the Shadow Witch to stand down. "You think me only the butcher, but I am also a businessman. There is no reason why I cannot reach out to the Stormshields and offer some kind of exchange."

"We both know," Asher growled, "the only deal you'll offer is their life for the silvyr."

"You think you know me so well," Viktor said.

"Don't I?" Asher retorted, a single run of blood trickling down his throat. "Right now you're wondering how you can get both their silvyr and me. That leads you to the inevitable conclusion that you can't. Now you're trying decide what you want more: me or the silvyr."

Viktor didn't say anything—telling in itself. Instead, he beheld the ranger with an unimpassioned stare, as if he were a man merely examining an uninspiring painting. "Silvyr never dulls," he eventually uttered, repeating himself from earlier. "Can the same be said of you?"

Viktor might as well have said he was going to slaughter the Stormshields for their silvyr.

Such a declaration rendered their deal null and void which, in turn, gave Asher permission to decimate Varga's whole operation; starting with the man himself. He could feel the throes of the *Assassin* coming over him, like a curtain of death that was prepared to kill anything that threatened the dwarves. After all, the Arakesh within him had its uses.

Asher sprang into action, his target located no more than six feet away. The Shadow Witch, however, found him before *he* found Viktor. The two killers collided and slammed into the front of the desk before wrestling over the top of it. Parchments and ornaments were scattered as fists and elbows were exchanged with abandon. They hit the floor together, the torchlight bouncing off Darya's scalp so much so that it concealed the tattoos that lined her skin. She looked up on the ranger with measured wrath and hissed as if she were no more than one of her master's pet monsters.

Asher knew how to handle monsters. Before even fully rising from the floor, he backhanded her, his attack swift and powerful enough to lay the Shadow Witch out flat.

On his feet again, he was quickly faced by Malak, who leapt over the desk to challenge him and protect his employer. Unfortunately for the brute, Asher wasn't holding back anymore—he intended to kill them all and suffer whatever guilt he might.

The ranger's hand shot out like a cobra and caught Malak in the throat. It stopped the man in his tracks, leaving him vulnerable to the elbow Asher then hammered into the side of his head.

Without hesitating, he jumped over the desk and advanced on Viktor with murder in his eyes. Varga, however, stood perfectly still, his demeanour unreasonably calm, and with a slight smile of amusement.

Then there came a light, a blinding flash that erupted from the corner of the chamber. Asher had barely turned his head towards it before something far more substantial than light struck him.

By the touch of magic, the ranger was sent into blissful oblivion.

Doran looked upon the ancient stone of Viktor's home. He didn't think much of it. Typical elves, he thought. The immortals, ironically, couldn't make anything to last and humans were little better than children when it came to masonry. Still, it looked to be something of a maze, with multiple levels and untold depth.

He caught the man named Hadrik grinning like some fool, as if he was unaware of the fatigue pressed upon him by the constant rowing. "What's amusin' *ye* then?" he asked, dryly.

"You're dead as soon as we reach the dock," the young man informed him, his breath a touch laboured.

"Is that so?"

"Every lord and lady is at that party," Hadrik went on, flicking his head over his shoulder. "It's the most guarded place in the realm right now."

Doran scrutinised the approaching dock, though it wasn't easy to make out between all the luxury vessels that had brought the aforementioned lords and ladies. He made out one or two higher up, stationed on the makeshift walkways where the walls had once stood.

"Doesn't look that guarded to me," he commented.

"You'll see," Hadrik assured.

"Jus' shut yer gob an' row," Doran instructed, deliberately gesturing at the oars with his sword, "an' ye might survive the night."

His last few words robbed the young man of his sense of humour. They continued in silence for a handful of minutes, closing the gap and bringing those luxury vessels into towering view.

Something bumped the front of the rowing boat.

Doran looked at the young man, each sharing the same look of confusion. "What were that?" the son of Dorain demanded.

"How the hells do I know?" Hadrik spat.

Doran sighed and moved to look over the side. There was no hiding his surprise as he watched a dead body float past, face down.

Hadrik paused his rowing to observe the gruesome sight. "Is he dead?"

"No," Doran replied, his voice dripping with sarcasm. "He's probably jus' takin' a nap."

The young man looked to have a response of his own but something caught his attention, something further out than the dead man. Doran followed his eyes and quickly discovered half a dozen more bodies drifting in the waves.

"What in the hells?" he muttered.

They closed in on the jetty, keeping close to the starboard side of one of the larger vessels. Five more floating corpses passed them by before Hadrik tethered the rowing boat to an old iron ring that had been fixed into the stone.

"Ye 'ave me thanks, lad," Doran offered, his polite words preceding the pommel of his sword. He was already gripping the man's shirt when he struck the blow, allowing him to lower the witless thug without a sound. There was, however, a small splash when the dwarf climbed out of the boat and used the steps carved into the stone foundations.

Cautiously, he rose above the steps and onto the hard ground at the base of the fortress. An eerie atmosphere had beset the place. He could hear distant music playing and the hubbub of a party well underway.

He couldn't find a single guard.

No one was patrolling the dock. Even the figures he had seen higher up had disappeared. Regardless of his esteemed guests, surely Viktor's home would be better guarded than this.

He looked out to sea, where so many bodies now floated in the currents. He put the pieces together and still didn't understand the picture they made.

Who could have killed them all?

CHAPTER 35

WOLVES AMONG THE SHEEP

Draugur *- Monsters breed legends and legends breed monsters—this is the way of things. Draugur have a particular myth about them that has always stuck with me. It is said that they were made by the elves during the Second Age, though it could easily have been during the First Age, as we know the elves called Illian home in that time. I believe this myth is part of the reason Draugur are also referred to as Forest Witches, just as their creators are referred to by some as the Forest Folk.*

If this is true, I could not begin to guess at the reason for their creation. What I do know is that these creatures form considerable nests in the heart of forests, often manipulating the surrounding environment to blot out the sun. After that, everything begins to die. These monsters are the definition of blight and must be eradicated as soon as possible. The decay that spreads from them can have detrimental effects on nearby civilisation.

A Chronicle of Monsters: A Ranger's Bestiary, 12th Edition, Page 452.

Tarwen Evensin, Ranger.

. . .

A strong hand gripped Asher's jaw, the intensity enough to rouse him from his numbing slumber. "There you are," Viktor purred. "I was worried you would be out all night." The crime lord released him and stepped back with that all too familiar smile on his face.

The ranger blinked hard and absorbed as much information as he could, sure that his time would be short before execution followed. He wasn't in Varga's office anymore. This new room was considerably smaller and without windows. It was also barren, lacking the decoration the rest of the fortress boasted. That was not entirely true. The room did possess a set of chains and manacles fastened to the ceiling.

Hanging by his wrists, the tips of his boots scraping against the stone floor, Asher looked down and noted his bare torso before discovering his cuirass and gear piled up to one side. With nothing else to see, his gaze roamed over Darya and Malak, positioned behind Viktor. They both sported dark bruises where he had landed decisive blows. Were he not suspended from the ceiling he might have spared them some amusement.

Then there was the crime lord himself, and with the silvyr blade resting on his hip. He wore the composure of a humble victor, one accustomed to winning. "That was quite the display," he complimented. "Darya and Malak are among my best and you tore through them like they weren't even there." The two in question shifted on the spot, clearly seething. The Shadow Witch especially looked as if she could happily peel him clean of flesh.

"Alas," Varga continued with a sigh, "I believe you and I have gone as far as we can. Don't get me wrong, I would have loved to own both you *and* the silvyr in the Stormshields' possession, but, as you pointed out, they will likely die in the exchange. Without them I have no leverage, no *leash* that is. And every mad dog needs a leash. Otherwise," he explained with a shrug, "you have to put them down."

"So get on with it," Asher rasped. "I'm getting sick of hearing your voice."

Viktor stifled a laugh. "Come now, I thought you knew me so well. You might be a mad dog, but that doesn't mean you aren't a valuable one. I'm not going to put you down as it were. No, I'm going to sell you to someone who has the time to break you in." Varga looked over his shoulder. "Won't you show Lady Trigorn in," he prompted. "And where in the hells is Alissandra?" he demanded through clenched teeth. "I don't pay her to stand in the hall."

Malak opened the double doors and passed on a message to invite the lady in. Alissandra appeared first, though her arrival only preceded Lady Trigorn's by a second, saving her from Viktor's lambasting. The mage, instead, stood to one side as the lady and her entourage of servants filled the threshold.

Lady Trigorn was a vision of beauty. In her late thirties perhaps, she greeted Viktor as if he were no better than one of her maidens. She was far more interested, it seemed, in exploring every facet of the ranger's body.

The lady had a sheen about her, her silky skin coated in a fine sweat. Her heart-shaped face was framed by a mane of black hair, several strands of which were obviously out of place. She wore just enough clothes to protect her modesty, though Asher felt the lady lacked any concerns for such matters. When these details were combined with the heavy rise and fall of her chest, the ranger deduced that she had very recently been entertained by some of the men and women he had previously seen walking between rooms.

"He is a specimen, Viktor, I'll give you that," the lady declaimed on her approach.

Darya took the liberty to place the tip of a dagger between his ribs, just below the heart. Lady Trigorn hardly noticed, so accustomed was she to those around her always keeping her safe. With one hand, she ran her fingers down Asher's chest and over the muscles of his abdomen, stopping only when she reached the waistband of his trousers.

"You say you're selling him," the lady continued, referring to a conversation that Asher hadn't been privy to.

"I am, My Lady," Viktor confirmed.

Lady Trigorn looked Asher in the eyes and pursed her lips. "I find that suspicious given what he is," she said bluntly.

"I have certainly made good coin from what few fights he has performed," Viktor reassured. "And his procurement came at no cost, so it is all profit."

"Then why not keep him fighting?"

"I'm afraid Asher here is little better than the monsters in my pit," he began. "An Arakesh without a strong hand to guide them is a *wild* creature it seems. Though, as you saw in the arena, he retains his considerable skill. I merely lack the patience required to break him in, nor can I afford the gladiators he kills outside of the arena," he lied. "I fear as time goes on he will only cost me." Varga angled his head to see the lady's face, who stood a few inches taller than him. "Perhaps in your capable hands he can serve many a task..." He let his words and their implications hang there for the lady to fantasise about.

"I would see him fight up close," she commanded. "If he impresses as he did in the arena, I will pay your price."

Asher let his head hang. Lady Trigorn didn't need him for his fighting abilities. Owning him would be no more than a novelty. He would be added to her collection of expensive things and paraded for entertainment, for no more than boasting rights. Not that any of this really mattered. Asher didn't care who he was to belong to or what lies were used to sell him—he needed to protect the Stormshields.

That meant killing them all.

Viktor beamed. "Very good! Let us move on to the main event then."

After the people who were deemed important had been moved on, Asher was escorted to the small arena he had seen from Viktor's office. Malak led the way, dragging the ranger along by the chain that connected his manacles. To Asher's left and right were a handful of men, each maintaining a spear in his direction lest he try anything foolish. Darya, of course, followed from the rear, her eyes prickling the back of his neck.

The open area was filled with Dragorn's rich and powerful. Like Lady Trigorn, who had been seated close to the arena, the family heads and those of their inner circle were scantily dressed and surrounded by servants who presented them with food and wine. The general clamour came to a hush upon the ranger's arrival.

Asher cared nothing for them—his attention drawn to the sands of the small arena. There he saw Salim, two gladiators he recognised but could not name and, most curious of all, Mouse, who looked to be on the verge of crying. They were each chained by the wrists to one of the broken pillars that surrounded only the back half of the arena.

The ranger was secured to the last pillar on the left. "When Lady Trigorn gets bored of you," Malak whispered, close to his ear, "and she gets bored of *everything*, she'll probably have you tortured to death just for the fun of it. In the meantime," he added menacingly, "I suppose I'll be sent off to Darkwell. Find me some dwarves, hmm?"

The urge to kill the brute was overwhelming but, given his restraints, Asher settled with headbutting him. Malak cried out and staggered back, his nose bloody and broken. Pushed by the pain, he raised his hand to strike the ranger.

"Enough!" Viktor hissed, halting the reprisal, as he came up on Malak's side. "Let's not damage goods we intend to sell." A flick of the head dismissed the brute, who could only shoot the ranger a fierce look. "You should be happy," Varga had the audacity to say, now face to face with Asher. "After tonight you won't have to fight in the arena. And I'm certain Lady Trigorn will... *treat* you every now and then," he remarked, with a devilish smirk. "And, besides, won't it be so freeing to rid yourself of the burden placed on you by the Stormshields? They'll be dead," he stated casually. "You can just move on. The Trigorn compound is quite something you know. Luxury compared to the training grounds. Of course," he trumpeted, with a callous laugh, "I'll be richer than the gods and likely own the Trigorns within the month. Perhaps, upon consideration, your time there will prove no more than a light reprieve."

Asher started forward, his advance halted by the chains. "All the coin in the world isn't going to stop me from killing you," he promised.

With a pleasant smile, Viktor turned away from the ranger and crossed the sand to address his valued guests. "We've had the wine! We've had the food! We've had the flesh! Now who wants blood?" His every statement was met with cheers, but his question elicited something more primal in the audience. "As you can see, we have our Arakesh! And let's not forget the poor souls he will send into the next world!" Asher's introduction was accompanied by an excitable fuss, while the others received jeers and calls for their death.

The crime lord waved his hands to quieten them. "And that's not all!" he continued, drawing them in. "Could there ever be a Viktor Varga party without a monster?" Viktor looked around the semicircle of rich and powerful, enjoying the anticipation he had instilled in them. "For your entertainment, if not your nightmares, I present to you... A creature of The Adean!"

Double doors were thrown open with dramatic effect, turning the heads of every gathered man and woman. Asher looked over the heads of those who were seated and sighted the cage being wheeled into view, dragged by a team of men pulling on chains. The criss-crossing bars were strong enough to contain the Merman, though it was still able to fit a whole arm between them, long fingers grasping at would-be prey.

"When we've had our fill of blood," Viktor explained, one hand gesturing back at the gladiators, "we shall begin the auction! That's right! Tonight, one of you will be taking ownership of this fine and terrifying beast! I shall house it for you, of course, and for a minimal fee, but the coin it earns in my arena will be yours!" The audience lapped up the unique opportunity and applauded the crime lord.

There came no such applause from the arena. One pillar over,

Mouse began to frantically squirm against the stone. "No, no, no…" he muttered over and over again.

While the crowd swarmed around the Mer-man, Asher took his moment to speak with his fellow prisoners. "Calm yourself," he instructed Mouse gruffly, his mind racing to find a solution. "You heard him," the ranger reminded. "He's selling the beast. We're not fighting it."

"How can you be sure he won't do both?" Mouse asked.

"Because he's selling me to her," the ranger answered, thrusting his chin at Lady Trigorn. "He won't risk the loss of coin."

Mouse was shaking his head, sweat dripping down his temples. "*You* maybe. The rest of us might just be fed to it."

"No one is getting *eaten*," Asher firmly reassured. "Viktor wants a contest to drive my price up."

"We are to fight then," Salim clarified morosely.

Asher nodded. "It'll be last man standing. But we don't *need* to fight."

"That's not how this works," one of the nameless gladiators spoke up. "We don't get to choose."

"He's right," Salim concurred. "It's death to any who refuse."

"So we might as well fight," the other gladiator pointed out.

"I say we fight *them*," Asher suggested, his tone fierce. "If we work together—"

"You're mad!" one of the gladiators hissed. "If fighting back was an option someone would have done it by now."

Salim offered a shrug and an expression that spoke of his agreement. "We are just as outnumbered here as we were within the walls of the training ground."

It wasn't the numbers that weighed on Asher's mind, tilting his strategy, it was the mages. Alissandra was visible from the arena, not far from her master, and the second mage, who had levitated the Mer-man from the boat, was beside the cage, wand in hand. The ranger was confident he could kill any of the guards who confronted him, including Darya and Malak, but the magic users were an undeniable threat. Without the black gem in his possession, he was just as vulnerable to their spells as everyone else.

They must die first, the *Assassin* decreed in the shadows of his mind.

"*If I don't kill Viktor,*" Asher said in Karathan, laying out the truth of his situation for Salim alone, "*he will kill the Stormshields. They have something he wants.*"

"*Something he wants more than you?*" the Honour Guard asked incredulously.

"*A lot more.*"

Mouse had conquered enough of his fear to monitor their conversation. "What are you two talking about?"

Asher ignored the question and kept his attention on Salim, waiting for the southerner's answer—he really didn't want to have to face him in combat. Though he was sure he would win, the ranger was certain his victory would come at a great price, both physically and mentally.

"*Perhaps I will die with honour after all,*" Salim finally replied.

Asher nodded his appreciation before glancing at Mouse. "When the fighting starts, stay behind me."

After the blind Mer-man had been prodded with spears and even maimed by the mage who watched over it, the audience resumed their seats and prepared for the bloodshed they had been promised.

The Shadow Witch was the first to approach the arena and, as always, with Asher's blindfold in hand. Had this been another fight in the arena, he would have worn it reluctantly, hating the part of him that enjoyed what came next. Not tonight. Tonight, he welcomed the darkness.

Behind the blindfold, his senses were immediately struck by the monster and its stench, a tangible thing that took root in his nose and on his tongue, blinding him to most else. The sea clung to it, though not nearly enough to overwhelm its raw flesh and the rank oils it produced. Then there was the burnt flesh where its eyes had once been—now black craters of charred scales and flesh.

Married to it all were the unmissable odours of sex and spilled wine, and all between the scents of the most expensive of silks and fabrics that Asher could also feel between his fingers.

Malak's thunderous heart beat like a hammer on steel as he replaced Darya on the sand. Along with a handful of his men, they freed Asher and the others of their manacles and dropped several weapons onto the arena floor, slightly out of reach.

Viktor took centre stage, between the edge of the arena and the crowd desperate for violence. Asher could hear the man's lips move over his teeth as he displayed a broad smile. "'Tis simple!" he announced, speaking to the fighters. "The last man standing earns his freedom!"

There was a pregnant pause from the audience, like the beach drawing up the tide before pushing it back. Then they erupted in laughter at the absurd statement, believing as much as Asher did that any under Viktor's thumb could possibly earn their freedom.

The two nameless gladiators, however, took the man at his word, their hesitation turning to an eagerness that could be felt in their muscles. Mouse, on the other hand, was clearly convinced he was taking the last breaths of his life, his hands and back pressed to the pillar. Asher was pleased to note that Salim was looking beyond Viktor, taking stock of his real opponents.

Viktor held his hand out until a goblet of red wine was given to him by a servant. "Begin!" he exclaimed, his shoulders rising with giddiness.

The two nameless gladiators exploded forwards, partly diving to reach the swords left in the sand. "If we work together," one of them suggested, speaking to all but Asher, "we can take him! After that it's every man for—" His next word was a garbled mess, his life suddenly in Salim's hands.

The Honour Guard had quietly advanced towards the weapons, his demeanour more casual than predator. Once he was within reach of the closest man, his hands snapped out and took possession of the blade in his enemy's grip, twisting the steel round and up into the gladiator's jaw before pressing it on into his brain.

The gladiator was dead.

Asher was impressed.

As was the crowd, their roar far worse than anything the Merman behind them was capable of. Those on the very edge of the arena jumped to their feet in ecstasy, their bare flesh sprayed with blood.

The surviving gladiator was quick to respond, his blade lashing out to put Salim into retreat. No fool, he then turned to swipe at Asher, who he had expected to advance from the other side. The ranger was not there, however, his primary goal being the sword not far from his pillar. Using the tip of his boot, he flicked the weapon and a handful of sand into the air, where his hand eagerly awaited the flipping hilt. Weapon in hand, Mouse was reduced to no more than a figure on the ranger's periphery.

The gladiator beheld him, blade in hand, and his heart rate increased all the more. His sweat became a melting pot of fear and adrenaline, a concoction that excited the *Assassin*.

Embrace it, Asher told himself. *Kill them all.* The voice was like silk, alluring and provocative. The fact that he *could* kill them was intoxicating. And why shouldn't he? How many innocents would die because of these people?

Asher moved slowly across the sand, his mind in turmoil. He could feel the *Assassin* in him wielding the truth like a weapon. He was trying to give himself permission to unleash, to show these monsters what they had brought upon themselves. But the *Ranger* desperately held on to the reasons *why* he must fight. For *who* he must fight for. He was a protector. Not a killer.

Viktor's laugh cut through it all, focusing him. There was only *one* who needed to die, though more would die defending him. Asher could live with that.

The bones inside the gladiator's right shoulder scraped against each other, informing Asher that a heavy one-handed swing was about to come down on his head. Keeping his back to the man, Asher made a minor adjustment to his stance and evaded the edge of the blade by no more than an inch. It was child's play to an Arakesh, but the crowd still gasped and renewed their cheers.

The next attack was just as obvious to the man with Nightseye elixir flowing through his veins. He could feel the air pressure change as his opponent altered his stance. He could taste the steel of his blade as its direction was reversed from the recent swing. He could hear muscles and bones groaning to drive all his strength into the backhand.

Asher blocked the incoming sword and made a tactical side-step towards his real target, who was currently whispering in Lady Trigorn's ear. "He will make a fine plaything."

Varga's comment irritated Asher far more than his foe's attempts to kill him. And so he continued to allow the attacks, using the choreography of their fight to subtly close the gap between him and Viktor. He would lift a leg to avoid a low swipe, tilt a shoulder to evade a thrust, and deflect anything that came for his centre mass. Soon, Asher could feel the vibrations of Viktor's speech washing over his skin.

And that was not all. He detected the ribbon scrunched into the crime lord's robe. How many times had Viktor put it in his face and threatened Deadora by his mere possession of the blue silk? Yet, the ranger failed to detect anything of the dwarven girl. It lacked her scent and that of her home or the woods about where she lived. Instead, he found traces of a woman and cheap perfume. It was subtle, but he could taste spices and smoke, each stubbornly clinging to the fabric.

There was but one conclusion: the ribbon had never belonged to Deadora Stormshield. Judging by the various notes he could taste and smell, it had been purchased for Viktor from one of the market stalls in the city.

The lie of it set Asher's skin on fire, urging him on.

His plan was simple enough: launch the sword at Alissandra, who stood no more than ten feet away from Viktor. The mage would either die or be forced to use magic to prevent her death. Asher didn't care which option she chose as both would leave Varga vulnerable and he would be damned if he wasn't going to kill the man with his bare hands now.

Salim was moving in from the gladiator's blind side, his blade coming up aggressively. Asher adjusted his defence and put himself briefly between the two, giving him just enough time to raise a hand and push the southerner back a step, not wanting him to interfere with his plan.

Something akin to a dance was then required to manoeuvre his opponent back on track.

Their swords rang out again and again. The ranger resisted delivering the killing blow a dozen times over. Only when Viktor was close and his sword had a clear path to Alissandra did Asher finish it. He flourished the blade in one hand, bringing it dramatically over and around his head. The steel sliced through most of the gladiator's neck, though killing the man was only half of the reason for the ranger's method of execution.

He needed the momentum.

In the same instance he decorated Viktor's guests with more blood, Asher repeated the flourish, swinging the blade over and around his head, while pivoting to face the mage. The sword was about to leave his grip, and with undeniable accuracy. But it was then, in that inestimable moment, that his acute senses detected multiple things out of place.

Alissandra's hands were hidden inside the large folds of her sleeves, much like her face, but Asher could taste the blood on her fingers. He had never seen what lay beneath her voluminous robes, but he doubted it was hardened leather, the very thing he could hear creaking beneath the dark fabric. Her boots possessed a thick tread that smelt and tasted like the ocean, though she had undoubtedly stepped directly off a boat and onto the dock. Most telling of all, however, was her steady heartbeat, an anomaly compared to those around her.

Asher redirected his attention to what his senses were telling him about Viktor. Everything about the man was exactly as it always was with the exception of one thing: he lacked the tenuous vibrations that accompanied his personal shield.

The *Assassin* should have been screaming inside his head, urging him to cut down the vulnerable crime lord, but the Arakesh in him possessed a quiet voice now, like a whisper in his ear that could cut through the noise of the storm. Numerous thoughts bombarded him but they all boiled down to one word that the instincts of every animal knew all too well.

Danger.

The *Assassin* demanded he stop and assess his full environment, just as he was trained to do. The sword came down to his side and he even took a step back from Viktor. He could feel the crowd revelling in the death of the gladiator. Their anticipation for more was mounting, though he felt a few grow curious as to why the violence had suddenly slowed. It was all noise.

Putting them all aside, he let his mind swim in the ocean of information that his senses soaked up. He was searching for more anomalies like Alissandra. Some instinct that had been instilled in him told the ranger that there were more of them out there. He needed to find them, and, even though he couldn't define the reason why, he knew he needed to find them fast.

He sharpened his focus again and again, stripping back everything he considered inconsequential.

There. Two more of them.

Unlike Alissandra, they remained out of sight, extensions of the darkness beyond the touch of the scattered fires.

The most obvious one was up high, observing alone from the jagged edge of Viktor's office. His scent was carried away in the sea breeze, hiding his existence all the more. The second was harder to find, hidden in the shadows on the far side of the dilapidated level, behind the masking wall of the Mer-man's entire being. That particular anomaly was also positioned behind the mage that watched over the sea creature. It was a strategic placement—the same Asher would have chosen—that left no doubt as to who these uninvited guests were.

Nightfall had come to Dragorn.

As the revelation took shape in Asher's mind, so too did he feel the bite of cold steel pierce his back and slip under his ribs.

CHAPTER 36

UNINVITED GUESTS

Ghost - My fellow rangers and I feel it prudent to include mention of ghosts in this edition of our fine bestiary. Let me tell you why. Should you be hunting some monster out there and you decide you're chasing a ghost, you're going to turn to this book for advice. You would then discover that there is no advice concerning ghosts and would, perhaps, wonder if your predecessors had failed to collect an accurate library of the beasts that prey on our world.

Well here it is, the advice you are looking for.

There are no such things as ghosts.

Whatever it is you are hunting, it is not the spirit of the departed. It is something else inside this book. Try harder.

A Chronicle of Monsters: A Ranger's Bestiary, 12th Edition, Page 431.

Melisanda Shadow-Born, Ranger.

It was a mortal wound.

He knew that, just as he knew his life could now be calculated in minutes or hours.

At least one organ had been perforated, the damage irreparable.

Death had finally laid its cold hand on his shoulder, patient in the end, content to wait out whatever time the ranger had left after so many years of eluding the inevitable.

Asher had always wondered what he would feel when that final blow came for him. What would he think? How would he react? Nightfall didn't train its Arakesh to prepare for death. They were to *embody* Death and avoid it at all costs.

And now, in that fateful moment, when death was assured, he could only conjure a memory of Nasta Nal-Aket. The years between could not be counted accurately, but Asher had been young enough that only wisps of hair had taken root in his young face. And it had been hot, the sun of The Arid Lands unforgiving compared to that which hung over Dragorn, even at the height of its summer.

"Don't fight it," Nasta had said so long ago, his voice always close to the boy.

Or was it? Was his master on a different rooftop? The Nightseye elixir made everything feel like it was right next to him while other things felt as if they were reaching out and touching him. It was all so much.

"Don't fight it," Nasta repeated. "Your body is an instrument. Let it tune in to the very harmony of the world around you. Feel it on your skin. Taste the textures on your tongue. Take in the scent of so many secrets."

Standing on a rooftop in the centre of Karath, under a midday sun, Asher's young mind began to fracture. "There's... too much," he managed.

"The vastness of your mind supersedes that of the world," Nasta uttered. "Make it small. Conquer it. You *must* comprehend all that surrounds you. An Arakesh cannot be stabbed in the back. Focus, Asher."

There was a note of desperation in his master's voice. Asher had detected such a tone before, during their private lessons together. While the other masters of Nightfall treated him like any other, a child to be bent or broken, Nasta *wanted* him to survive, *needed* him to.

"Have you found him?" The question was added to the torrent of information flooding Asher's senses.

"No," the boy replied through gritted teeth, a slow trickle of blood worming out of one nostril.

"Find him," Nasta implored. "He wears a bracelet of silver beads."

The target's identity, beyond being *the target*, was inconsequential. Asher hadn't even questioned his master as to why this particular man had been chosen for the lesson. But finding a single person among thousands by no more than the bracelet he wore seemed an impossible task to the young boy.

He heard broken pieces of every conversation. He could smell and taste the sweat on the air, all bleeding together into one acrid musk. The sound of so many feet pounding the dusty streets was akin to a cacophony of out of beat drums. Vibrations ran up through the rooftop and into his feet, filling his mind with an accurate picture of the floors below and those who inhabited them.

Then there was Nasta, only feet away. He was blindfolded too, his dark curls spilling over the edges of the red fabric. In one hand he wielded a fine stick, though Asher was yet to glean the point of it.

The aroma of food struck him, reminding the boy that he hadn't eaten in some time. A legion of vendors were selling hot and cold meals, their constant hollering a deafening rabble. They most of all crowded Asher's mind, masking the passersby and, more importantly, the target.

"You're running out of time," Nasta warned, his words interrupting what precious little focus he had managed.

Asher stepped forwards, intending to perch on the lip of the roof.

"You do not need to move," his master instructed. "The sound of your own bones and muscles can be distracting. Be still, child. Focus."

Tap.

Asher tilted his head, willing his senses to home in on the metallic sound. He heard it again. Every time the target's arm swung from forward to back, the beads knocked together. To his ears, the colliding silver spheres was an unmissable noise, as if that silver bracelet was the only thing that existed in the whole world.

The boy raised an arm, his hand gesturing to the general direction of his target.

"Very good," Nasta praised. "Listen to your senses. Find the street. Feel his speed, the gate of his stride, the obstacles around him. With this, you will learn to interpret your target's intended direction and when they will arrive."

Through desperation and a swirling storm of emotions, Asher hard-pressed his focus, his teeth clamped shut against the jarring cacophony of city life. Now there existed naught but the target, a lone man walking through an ether of nothingness. He knew what the man had eaten and when, based on the sounds of his digestive tract. His beard had been trimmed that very morning, the ends sharp and even.

Asher felt like a god in that moment. He had achieved a level of omniscience that no mere man could dream of. If he wanted to, he could pick the target apart and strip him of every secret he owned and he could do it all unobserved from the rooftop.

Pain, however, had a way of cutting through everything, and his knuckles felt like they were on fire.

Asher retracted his outstretched hand and clutched it close to his chest. Gone was the target and all his secrets. The noise of the world came rushing back, bombarding the boy. Sound, taste, touch, smell, they all clawed at him until he tore the blindfold from his eyes.

The light brought with it more pain, though he certainly

welcomed the comparative quiet of the capital city. When, at last, his eyes adjusted, he discovered his master wiping blood from the end of his stick. Asher examined the back of his hand and found the source.

"Why?" he questioned, doing his utmost to conceal the level of pain he endured.

"Why not?" Nasta said with a shrug. "It was you who gave me the opportunity to strike." The wizened Arakesh gestured at the streets below. "If you sharpen a blade too much, you damage its edge. This will leave its wielder vulnerable. Do not make the same mistake with your focus, child. If you strip the world back to your target alone, you will be left vulnerable to those around you. An Arakesh cannot be stabbed in the back," he reiterated. "This is our way."

Asher had let his emotions guide his focus that day, a path that always narrowed his view, blinding him to all that surrounded him. And now, on the sands of that small arena, he had made the exact same mistake, only he hadn't been whipped with a stick.

The ranger pulled his blindfold down to his neck and blinked hard as his heightened senses transitioned to that of an ordinary man. He looked over his shoulder and discovered the eyes of a monster staring back at him.

Mouse.

No... Not Mouse. There was nothing remotely human about him, as if he had been wearing a mask all this time, concealing the ice behind his eyes and the manic glee that curled the edges of his thin lips into a cruel smile.

Caught in the well of those lifeless eyes, Asher recalled Viktor's description of his prisoners: "*...how wicked do you think your cell-mates are—those who have been so evil as to be imprisoned by criminals of the highest order?*"

How could he have been so naive? How could he have misjudged the man? Or any man for that matter? He was an expert profiler, a common trait among the Arakesh, and he was supposed to be among the best of them. The blade in his back said otherwise.

"Asher!" Salim hissed, his voice cutting through the silence that had captured the crowd.

Mouse withdrew his dagger with a quick pull and the ranger fell to one knee, a hand pressing against the wound. Mouse leapt back and fell upon all fours, as if he truly was one of the monsters from the ranger's bestiary. Even his laugh, which spilled out of him much like the blood did from Asher's wound, was distinctly inhuman. Without warning, he jumped to his feet again. It was impossible to discern his incessant mutterings, though they were certainly no more than the wild musings of a mad man.

Salim diverted his attention from Asher and put himself between them, a shield against the knife-wielding psychopath. He waved his sword and dashed left and right trying to match the killer's erratic movements.

"I'm just a little mouse," he squeaked. "Don't hurt me," he pleaded, before his face creased into rage and he lashed out at nothing at all. Then his laughter returned tenfold, until drool and spit escaped his mouth.

Asher pushed through the cold realisation that he would inevitably die from his wound and turned back to the audience, who watched in stunned amazement. Narrowing his vision on Viktor, he found the man's expression to be the very definition of disappointment, though there seemed a hint of embarrassment about him too.

He was not the only one. Lady Trigorn stood up from her seat and looked down on Varga. "How very regrettable, Viktor. I would have enjoyed him." No instructions were required to rouse her entourage, who followed her departure. "I did enjoy the beast though," she added as an afterthought.

In Lady Trigorn's wake, so many others lost interest in what had become an ordinary fight. It was the Arakesh they had come to see. Now he was just a man bleeding out, soon to meet his end.

Asher tightened his grip around the hilt of the sword and set his jaw as he looked past Viktor. The mage guarding the Mer-man was already gone, likely executed without a sound and his body disposed of without anyone noticing. It was an impressive feat few in the realm were capable of.

"For a monster hunter," Viktor remarked, "you're not very good at recognising one when you see it." His gaze flashed over Mouse, who had been sent into retreat by Salim's aggressive advance. "What a pitiful death yours is to be. Still," he added, managing a smile and patting the silvyr short-sword on his hip, "you have proved more profitable than my wildest dreams."

The ranger ignored his every word for it was naught but dead air from a dead man. He was more concerned with the mage's executioner, who now stood between the doors and the departing guests, twin short-swords drawn by his side.

"I think your party's over," Asher concluded.

Viktor frowned and turned to follow the ranger's gaze. He froze, gripped by real terror and only a fraction of a second before all of his guests exhibited the same reaction. Then, as expected, came the flash of steel and unbridled wrath, all to the sound of panicked screams. Darya and Malak were quick to respond, positioning themselves between the Arakesh and their master while barking orders at their subordinates. Their defence would matter little when the assassin came for them, but Asher didn't care; he was determined to be the one to finish it. Viktor Varga would be his last kill.

The ranger took his moment.

The pain from pushing himself up so fast forced a grunt from his lips and alerted Viktor to his sudden movement. Asher still made his move, a desperate lunge that saw him swing his sword up from the sand. Varga's very human instincts kicked in, sending him back a step. Since Asher was already falling back to his knees, the tip of the blade scored no more than a red line up Viktor's cheek, threatening his right eye. Amidst the dying screams, he gasped and pressed a hand to his cheek, surprised to discover blood on his palm.

Naturally, his rage mounting so very fast, he snapped his head around to admonish Alissandra, who should have shielded him from the attack, but the mage pulled back her hood to reveal that she was no such thing.

Viktor's burning ire was immediately tempered by a cold revelation that pitted his gut with dread, as he now faced a true Arakesh clad in dark leathers and blindfolded by red cloth. Varga staggered away, knocking aside chairs and spilling goblets of wine.

Only Asher's next words could tear his eyes from the assassin. "What was it you said?" the ranger began, looking up at the damned. "Word will spread and then the world will come." He was paraphrasing, but Viktor's intentions were undeniable. The crime lord had brought this down on himself. Asher spared the advancing Arakesh a brief glance. "I'd say the world has come," he added through the pain, and with a mean smile at that.

The next moment saw the chaos erupt to new heights.

The Shadow Witch had taken note of the Arakesh's deception —her guise as a mage abandoned—and deserted the defensive line to protect her master from the more imminent threat.

The Mer-man, roused by the spread of death, doubled its efforts to be free and hammered the end of its cage, damaging its integrity.

The Arakesh blocking the doors already had a dozen bodies at his feet and was now challenged by Malak and his men—all doomed to die.

Salim, dangerously close to the jagged edge on the other side of the arena, cried out in pain as the skittish Mouse scored a hit, his knife cutting across the Honour Guard's leg.

As Darya and the female Arakesh collided in a flurry of blades, the third Arakesh dropped down from his high vantage and rolled across the sand. When he rose from the manoeuvre his blades were already in his hands, the fine edges angled at Asher.

The ranger gritted his teeth. He wasn't dead yet, a fact that he used to bolster his resolve. Instead of fighting against the pain of his wound, he welcomed it. It pushed him on, urging him to rip through the Arakesh and finish the task he had assigned himself: killing Viktor Varga, the same man who now cowered behind strewn chairs while his guests were butchered for no more than being witnesses.

The Arakesh advanced with fury, eager to kill the exile. Whether he was too eager or had simply overestimated Asher's wound and fatigue remained to be seen, but his opening attack was all too obvious to the ranger, even without his blindfold on. With his gladiator's sword, he rose up and deflected the first swing before batting away the second, a defence that preceded the elbow he drove into the man's face.

The overextension intensified the pain in his back, however, threatening to damage his resolve. *"Never give them an inch,"* Nasta's old voice echoed in his mind, ever a close companion to pain.

Asher pressed his attack, pushing the assassin further into the arena. He brought his sword out before him, twisting it threateningly into various shapes and thrusts, each movement designed to put his opponent off balance while he sought out the weak spot. Of course, the Arakesh was blindfolded and so was able to interpret the ranger's eventual attack a moment before he struck.

Steel rang out across the whole level, and all between the screams and wails of the dying and the shrieks of the imprisoned Mer-man.

"Salim?" Asher called out, working hard to evade the incoming blades.

The Honour Guard sounded frustrated. "He won't stay still!"

"Just kill him!" Asher barked, weaving between a cluster of spinning steel.

Salim groaned and swung his sword one last time at Mouse, giving himself enough time to retreat and join the ranger. The Arakesh sensed the flanking attack and immediately adjusted his stance and fighting style. He simultaneously blocked both Asher's and Salim's incoming swipes, giving him space to lift a single boot and whip it from left to right, catching each across the jaw. While the southerner managed to stay on his feet, the ranger's wound got the better of him and he met the sand in a heap.

Get up, he told himself.

Beyond the edge of the arena, Darya was holding her own against the Arakesh, though she had been forced back again and again until their duel was only a few feet away from Viktor. The crime lord's death was inevitable, though it irked the ranger to think that final blow might come from someone else. He considered abandoning Salim to the fight and moving in for the kill while there were none to stop him.

Hearing Salim's blade clash with both of the assassin's, Asher knew where he was needed, and where else could he be if not where he was needed. Such were the constraints of a conscience.

He pushed up from the sand only to receive a swift kick to the wound on his back. He yelled in agony and gave in to the force of the blow that rolled him across the arena, his sword left behind.

Mouse's hysterical laughter drowned out the carnage as he pounced on top of the ranger. He looked down on Asher with those black eyes, perhaps the most unhinged person he had ever seen.

"What a lovely, lovely party!" he spat, the dagger dancing between his fingers.

Asher could feel warm blood between his back and the sand as he regarded the man who had killed him. A pitiful death indeed. And deserved given the error in judgement he had made. If only Nasta could see him now.

Mouse plunged his dagger, its point aimed at Asher's heart. The ranger's left hand shot up and intercepted the attack at the wrist, halting the blade half an inch from his bare chest. He had never attributed any degree of impressive strength to the man but, while Death smiled upon him, Mouse might as well have possessed the strength of Malak.

Tears welled in the eyes of the maniacal lunatic, a contradiction to the sharp grin that ruled half of his face. "I'm just a little mouse," he whispered. "Don't hurt *me*."

Had any healer the time they might have gleaned some great tragedy from Mouse's past that had driven him to madness, but Asher was no healer and nor did he have the time. The same could be said of Salim, who was disarmed and thrown to the ground by his skilled opponent, his death just as assured as the ranger's.

Asher's tactical mind required no thought to produce a solution.

His free hand snapped up and wrapped around the back of Mouse's head. Then, with all the strength he could muster, the ranger threw them both sideways, towards Salim and the Arakesh. Somewhere in the middle of their roll, he broke Mouse's wrist and took control of the dagger in one smooth motion. Once their positions were reversed, and Mouse found himself on his back, Asher continued his own momentum and rolled again.

"Salim!" he shouted, giving the man some warning.

The ranger's arm followed in the wake of his body's roll and brought Mouse's dagger with it. The blade was launched in a spinning arc that would take it directly into the Arakesh's temple. As predicted, the assassin raised one of his short-swords—his timing supernaturally perfect—and knocked the dagger from its path. It was then, of course, that Salim, having retrieved his fallen sword, thrust upwards, impaling the Arakesh.

Asher didn't wait to see if the assassin dropped to his death—he still had the crazed Mouse beside him. He swung his body back, reversing his roll, and dropped an elbow onto the man's throat, robbing him of the inexplicable laugh that accompanied the pain of his broken wrist.

It couldn't be compared to the pain that continued to spread throughout Asher's abdomen, draining his skin of colour. The ranger pushed through the wave of nausea and the temptation to pass out, opting, instead, to pick himself up and quite casually rest one knee over Mouse's swollen throat. While the madman choked and clawed at the leg blocking his airway, Asher took what precious time he had to assess the environment.

Violence and death ruled the night.

On the far side, the Arakesh was surrounded by bodies, the floor slick with the richest blood in all of Dragorn. Lady Trigorn and the other heads of the ruling houses lay among the dead, their corpses added to the tally of witnesses that could not be allowed to live. At some point, Malak had seen his impending death and left his men to it, choosing to rally by his master's side, who continued to survive thanks to the efforts of his Shadow Witch.

Then there was the Mer-man. The beast threw itself at every bar of its cage, determined to find its way back to the sea.

Looking over his shoulder, Salim was standing over the dead

Arakesh, his sword dripping with blood. The Honour Guard's glistening torso was marred by a patchwork of gashes and cuts, but he stood tall with an air of strength about him. He had survived an encounter with an Arakesh, an accolade few—if any but Asher—could boast.

The ranger couldn't say as much about his own survival. His left trouser leg was wet with blood and he couldn't shake the hollow feeling that was spreading to his fingertips. How long did he have left before he lost consciousness? Once his mind slipped from the world he knew there would be no returning to it.

The clawing at his leg had stopped.

Beneath his knee, the ranger beheld Mouse's final moment, his face livid with burst blood vessels. Asher felt nothing for him, his humanity stretched to its absolute limits.

He returned his focus to the action and scooped up the dagger deflected by the Arakesh, the weapon having landed in the sand beside him. With the blade in hand, he attempted to stand and implement his plan. He would flank the female Arakesh and kill her before moving on to the Shadow Witch. When they were both dead at his feet, he would snuff out Malak's pathetic existence. Then there would be nothing between him and Viktor. No bodyguards. No magic.

Perhaps the third Arakesh would be the end of him, beating his wound to it. Asher couldn't muster a care. Killing Viktor was all that mattered. His only hope was that Salim would use whatever distraction he could to escape and find a new life in Illian.

All of his intentions, however, hinged on his ability to fight, and he could hardly stand. His perceived orientation shifted, as if the entire floor had suddenly tilted under his feet. He staggered trying to correct himself and succeeded only in falling onto the stone edging the arena.

Turning his head, he watched Darya Siad-Agnasi receive three successive kicks to the torso and head, the third of which sent her from her feet. Malak hesitantly replaced her, his axe coming up. It did not deter the Arakesh from advancing, nor the second assassin who had finally finished murdering Viktor's guests, Malak's men, and even the poor band members.

Salim arrived at the ranger's side. "Come!" he hissed. "Their fate is sealed. It does not have to be ours."

Asher looked up at the Honour Guard. By his expression alone he conveyed the truth of his dire situation. Salim looked to argue the unspoken point but there was no opposing the severity of the wound.

Forlorn, Salim hefted his sword. "If you wish it, I will end your pain."

Asher groaned. "I'm not going before him," he stated, looking at Viktor. "Just help me up." As Salim hooked an arm under his own and pulled him up, the ranger had but one piece of advice for the Honour Guard. "When I tell you to, remain as still as possible." Salim responded with curiosity but their elevated stance had gained the attention of the female Arakesh.

She halted her attack on Malak, who was only too happy to have some reprieve, and turned her head over one shoulder. "Asher." Her tone was dripping with anticipation. "Still with us, I see."

The ranger grunted through the pain in his back and straightened up. The second Arakesh walked into view, joining his sister of Nightfall. His blades were so slick with blood that there remained no steel to be seen.

"He is weakened," the male Arakesh observed with audible disappointment.

"He is still of the Father's making," the woman remarked, identifying herself as the more intelligent of the two killers.

Behind the Arakesh, the Shadow Witch had recovered and found her feet again. Wise enough to watch events unfold, she stuck close to her master, daggers in hand. Through them all, Asher planted eyes on Viktor. Gone was his familiar smile, his easygoing demeanour having died with Alissandra. Now he had the look of a man who knew his death was no more than the toss of a coin.

"Stand aside," Asher commanded gruffly.

The female tilted her head, her expression somewhat bemused. "You mean to kill him yourself?"

"I *mean* to kill them all," Asher replied as a matter of fact. "After that, we can settle up."

"I thought you had left our ways behind," she said.

The ranger had no intention of getting into a conversation—he certainly didn't have time for it. "Stand aside," he repeated.

The male assassin stepped forwards. "You aren't nearly that intimidating."

Asher regarded him as he would any fool who confronted him. "If that was true," he goaded, "you would have made your move already."

The assassin's jaw stiffened, the bait taken.

"Don't move," Asher reiterated, his instruction to be understood by Salim alone.

The male assassin lunged at the ranger with bloody swords raised. Behind him, the woman fell into a crouching stance, prepared to fight whatever the outcome.

Asher knew there would be no beating the Arakesh in his current condition, let alone two of them. It was a miracle he had survived one of their ilk already. It was for that reason he had devised the only plan that would ensure they all died that night.

Before the Arakesh could strike at him, the ranger let fly the same dagger that had ensured his eventual death. The blade, however, went far wide of the assassin, its intended target on the far side of the chamber. When it drove home it did so to the sound of clashing metal, the tip embedded in the flat iron of the creature's bars.

The dagger had missed its target, the lock, by inches—Asher swore under his breath.

The profanity still hung on his lips when the Arakesh was upon him. The ranger twisted his body at the last second, avoiding the short-swords just enough to reach out and grasp the assassin's wrists. Their ultimate collision sent both men to the floor, the impact forcing one of the blades from the Arakesh's grip. Salim, a slave to his training, came to Asher's defence only to be intercepted by the female Arakesh.

Beyond the aid of the Honour Guard, Asher wrestled the man on top of him, acutely aware of the short-sword grazing his throat. Should his strength falter for even a moment, that blade would spill what precious blood he had left.

To the sound of a sweeping crash, the double doors opened on the far side of the floor. So surprising was the figure standing over the threshold that, for just a second, Asher reconsidered his lack of faith in the gods—if not humanity itself. Of course, it was no human who had burst through those doors but a dwarf.

Doran Heavybelly.

The son of Dorain, the last person the ranger had ever expected to see again, exploded into the chamber with axe and sword. His dramatic entrance stunned them all, offering Asher one last chance at executing his plan.

"The cage!" he bellowed. "Open the cage!"

The Arakesh on top of him renewed his efforts and pushed down until the edge of his blade was cutting into the ranger's neck, adding to the wound Darya had given him earlier. Asher paid it no heed, his head arched back to see an upside down Doran. It was impossible to see his expression from such an awkward position, but his hesitancy to unleash the sea creature was evident in his lack of action. The female Arakesh suffered from no such hesitancy. She broke the sword-play and delivered a swift roundhouse to Salim's face, knocking him to the floor. Without challenge, she broke into a sprint towards Doran.

"Do it!" Asher roared. "Do it, now!"

The dwarf was too far away from the cage to reach it before the assassin reached him. Unlike Asher, though, he wasn't suffering from blood loss or internal bleeding, and so his aim was far more accurate. When his axe had finished its short journey, the curved steel had cut through the cage's lock and jarred the door open an inch.

The Arakesh sprinting towards Doran tried to skid to a stop but the stone beneath her boots was slick with blood. She hadn't even come to a halt before the Mer-man shot out of its cage and slammed into her. They tumbled across the floor, amidst the mutilated corpses her companion had left behind. It was difficult to discern exactly what deadly methods the creature employed in their violent struggle, but its claws and fangs, and considerable weight, made short work of the assassin, splashing more blood up the wall.

Asher pressed himself as flat to the floor as he could, his strength reserved for keeping the Arakesh's blade out of his windpipe. Then he let loose a primal roar, a dinner bell to the blinded Mer-man. The assassin on top of him realised the truth of his situation all too late.

With terrifying speed, the creature from the sea slithered through the debris, over Asher, and collided with the Arakesh, taking man and beast onto the sands of the arena and away from the prone ranger. Only feet away, Salim had recovered from the assassin's kick and retained sense enough to follow Asher's previous instruction and remain as still as possible.

As his vision began to blur, the ranger pushed his head forwards and watched the Mer-man open up the Arakesh, turning him inside out in a matter of seconds.

Its work done, the monster slowly rose and turned its torso to face the rest of them. It swayed gently, listening. Salim's arm crept up, sword in hand.

Another wave of disorientation washed over the ranger and he lost control of his head. The resultant *thud* it made on the stone was all the creature needed. It bolted forwards, its humanoid torso wet with blood.

Salim swung his sword with both hands but even the Honour Guard's reflexes were too slow for the Mer-man; the tip of his blade scoring no more than a shallow cut across the monster's ribs. No reflexes were required, however, when the weapon itself was two-hundred and eighty pounds of armoured dwarf.

Doran leaped over the ranger and smashed into the oncoming Mer-man with abandon. The pair's trajectory saw them fly sideways, crashing down only a few feet from Asher. The monster snarled and clawed at the son of Dorain, its webbed hands a frenzied blur. All the while, Doran roared in its face and repeatedly stabbed the beast with his sword. One such blow struck harder and, perhaps, luckier than the rest and plunged straight through the creature's chest, piercing through to the other side. Its shriek increased to that of an impossible pitch and for all but a second before dying away with its last breath.

Unfortunately for the dwarf, it then died on top of him.

"Bah!" Doran cursed the monster. "Get off me, ye ugly swine!" With some effort, he managed to shove the beast aside and sit up in his scratched armour.

Asher was only partially aware of what was happening around him now. He wasn't entirely convinced that Doran was real and he entertained the possibility that he was either dead already or hallucinating on the verge of death. Darya Siad-Agnasi, however, appeared very real. The Shadow Witch was standing over him, her daggers catching in the torchlight. How and when she had reached him he could not say.

"You will both surrender," she ordered, her tone as sharp as her weapons.

"The hells I will," Doran grumbled, rising to his feet.

Darya dropped into a crouch and let one of her daggers hang over the ranger's heart. "You *will* surrender."

Asher heard Salim's sword clatter against the stone, though the ranger's eyes were fixed on Doran's grimace. From behind the dwarf, Viktor emerged, his steps slow and precise, so as to avoid the blood where possible. His gaze roamed over the slaughter and paused over each of the dead Arakesh. The ranger's mind might have been slipping away, but he could still identify that look in Varga's eyes. He was disturbed, afraid even. The bedrock of his world, a world in which he was untouchable, had been shattered.

The crime lord swallowed. "Have the bodies disposed of. *Discreetly*," he specified, his voice as shaken as he was himself. "Have every inch scrubbed clean. Then see to the cleaners yourself. Not a word of this can get out."

"And them?" Malak asked.

Viktor merely glanced at Doran and Salim, his attention soon secured on Asher.

The ranger called on every scrap of his reserves so that he might twist the knife while he still had breath in his body. "You thought... you could tell the world you had an Arakesh in your pocket... and there would be no consequences?"

Varga's expression cracked, his eyes glassy. "Kill them," he uttered, his voice yet to reach its usual pitch or cadence.

"You're a dead man," Asher pressed upon him, his vision doubling now. "They'll never stop... coming for you."

"He's right," Darya announced, sending a flicker of surprise across her master's face. "Nightfall will come again. They will not stop." The Shadow Witch regarded Asher beneath her blade. "There might, however, be a deal to be made."

"A deal?" Viktor enquired, clearly uncomfortable in his own skin—the same skin the Arakesh wished to strip him of.

"A bargain of sorts," Darya explained. "His life for ours."

A ripple of interest, if not hope, ran through Viktor. "You believe it that simple?"

"You saw how they reacted to him. How they loathe him. He is a great prize to them."

"You're banking he's a greater prize than any of us," Varga concluded.

If their conversation continued Asher could not say. He tried to hold on, but even Nasta's whispering voice had abandoned him at the end. He looked to Doran, if the dwarf was, indeed, standing there. The ranger wanted to thank him for returning, for proving him wrong, but there was nothing left to avail him, words beyond all grasp.

As if by some supernatural ability, Viktor Varga was now standing over him. His fear and rage had collided, making a ruin of his expression. Without warning, he raised one foot and stamped on Asher's head.

The pain would come when he awoke.

CHAPTER 37
HOPE IS FOR THE LIVING

Harpy - What beautiful critters these monsters are. At only a foot tall, bodies like the bark of trees, large doe eyes, and wings like lush summer leaves, they will lure you in with the innocence of a child—even their smile is a twisted mimicry of our own. Whether this appearance is by evil design or unfortunate coincidence is unknown.

Make no mistake, Harpies know exactly what they're doing when it comes to us humans. Woodland dwellers, one or two will make contact, appearing as playful things to lower defences. If you are foolish enough to follow them back to their forest nest, you will be set upon by thirty or more of the buggers. Then you'll see their teeth.

It's not typically our way, but I would advise donning a suit of armour before tracking them down. They'll bite through leather as easily as they do flesh, but iron will give them something to think about.

A Chronicle of Monsters: A Ranger's Bestiary, 12th Edition, Page 182.

Tobias Noon, Ranger.

The line between life and death was a tenuous thread not many could walk. For most, slipping into the dark, into those numbing depths, was inevitable and certainly hastened once consciousness was lost. Too few could sleep a deathly slumber and recover enough strength to open their eyes again.

But open they did, and Asher looked upon a world that refused to let him rest.

The first of his senses to return with any clarity was his hearing. Flames dancing on torch heads. The quiet rasp of his shallow breathing. Doran Heavybelly swearing profoundly.

"Ye're awake!" he gasped, hurrying to the ranger's side. "Ye're alive!"

Strong dwarven hands grasped Asher's arms. In his weakened state they felt like the hands of a Giant. There was more pain to follow, sprouting from a sharp pinch in his back to emanate in waves of hot fury. Adding to his discomfort, there was a throbbing pain in his head that he couldn't ignore. Experimenting with the muscles around his eyes, he quickly discovered the source of the pain was his right eyebrow.

Salim stepped into his vision, a tall block of toned muscle to tower over the son of Dorain. "Either the gods love you," he determined, "or they will not have you."

Asher couldn't imagine the former. "What happened?" he croaked, becoming aware that he was lying flat on a hard floor. He was also cold, colder than he could ever recall.

"Your friend here saved us all," Salim explained, planting a hand on Doran's right pauldron. "Had he not arrived when he did, we would have died on Arakesh steel."

The recounting jogged some of Asher's memories. So much of it was blurry and ill-defined in his mind. But he recalled Doran colliding with the Mer-man above him. He retained a fractured image of the monster lying dead, the dwarf's sword buried in its chest.

"You..." The next word failed to get any further than his tongue.

Licking his lips, he tried again. "You came back," he finally managed.

"Aye," Doran replied. "I told ye to survive didn' I?" The dwarf took in the ranger from head to toe. "Ye're doin' a piss poor job o' it by the way."

Despite the dire situation he found himself in, Asher was amused and exhaled a short sharp laugh through his nose. It still hurt.

"I'm still alive aren't I?" he managed, one hand moving to investigate the binding he could feel around his abdomen.

Doran glanced at Salim. "Aye, lad, that ye are." His lack of optimism was all too clear. "Ye owe me a cloak by the way," he added, gesturing to the material tied around the ranger.

Asher looked at Doran's cloak and noted the jagged edge where a strip had been torn free. He also noted that the dwarf remained entombed in his armour, new as it was. "I'll get right on that," he groaned, attempting to move.

"Easy, my friend." The Honour Guard crouched as Doran did and placed a hand on the ranger's chest. "You have lost a lot of blood."

Asher shook his head. "I need to sit up," he decided.

"Ye're goin' to upset that wound o' yers," Doran warned.

Asher sighed, chastising himself all over again. Of all the would-be killers on that island, three of whom had been fully-trained Arakesh, he could not believe that the one to put him in his grave was Mouse. What a fool he had been in the end.

"I'm not dying," he began, "lying on the floor of some dungeon."

Doran raised a bushy blond eyebrow. "But ye'd settle for dyin' while *sittin'* on the floor o' some dungeon?"

Asher shot him a pointed look. "Just help me up."

It took both Doran and Salim, but they succeeded in propping his back against the nearest wall without inducing too much pain. Nausea instantly assaulted the ranger and his perception swerved, threatening to drag him back down to the cold floor. The pain in his back and throughout his gut began to build, numbing the pain in his head. It was several minutes before he was able to look about and acquire his bearings.

They were in the arena dungeons, returned to the confines of those Novian cells.

"Back where we started," he commented, feeling the red cloth of his blindfold still tied around his neck.

Doran nodded. "The place is startin' to grow on me."

"How long?" Asher enquired.

"An hour maybe," the dwarf estimated.

The ranger's head rested back against the stone, his mind, as always, drawn to the art of survival. He had lost a precious hour, an hour in which he might have figured out a way to escape the quicksand his life had become. How futile it was, he mused. Even if they could break out of the Novian cells, what would he do? His death was inevitable and he had nothing to offer that would aid in ensuring his companions' freedom. There was naught left but death itself.

"Have you seen him?" Asher asked.

"Viktor?" Doran checked. "No. Not since we got back to the arena. For a man who enjoys the sound o' his voice, he was damned quiet on the journey. I didn' think anythin' could rattle that man."

Exhausted as he was, Asher still managed half a smile at the image conjured by the dwarf's description. Viktor would squirm before Nightfall came for him, and they *would* come. The crime lord had broken the strict rules put upon those who sought the services of an Arakesh. As long as he breathed, he would be viewed as any target was.

There remained very little of the *Assassin* in Asher, here at the end, but he couldn't deny the need he felt to be the one to silence Viktor forever. He had met few people in his life who he truly believed deserved the edge of his blade, but Varga had more than earned his place near the top of that list.

"I do not understand why *we* are still alive," Salim remarked, glancing at Doran as he wandered over to the bars, his long black hair hidden in the shadows.

Salim's musings brought back the last of Asher's memories. "He's going to make a deal with Nightfall," he said, too weak to intone his disbelief.

"He's goin' to *try*," Doran replied with half a laugh. "As for us, lad," he continued, looking to Salim, "he's likely goin' to devise a way to make some coin out o' the most gruesome execution he can imagine. Ye can bet it'll involve a monster or two."

Asher turned his head as much as he dared to look at the dwarf. "You should not have returned," he lamented. "You had your freedom."

Doran shifted where he sat, an uneasy, if fleeting, look given to the Honour Guard's back. "Ye thought I'd leave ye to rot?"

Asher gave a barely perceptible shrug. "You said it yourself..." Here the ranger paused to brace against a new wave of disorientation. "You owe me nothing," he finished.

The shadows danced across Doran's face, making it hard to say whether he winced or not. "In all this mess—*my* mess—ye've only ever tried to do the right thing. I'm not knowin' another man who lives by such a code. Stupid as it was," he went on, his usual gruff bravado returning to his voice, "maybe I thought ye were worth savin'. Now I'm not so sure," he added with wry grin. "Salim 'ere told me abou' the fella that stabbed ye. How could ye be so daft?"

Asher groaned in place of nodding his head. "It's a mistake I'm paying for," he assured needlessly. For a short while there was naught but the sound of the torches, their flames flickering between the ranks of cells. "For what it's worth," the ranger whispered, "thank you." As painful as the words felt to say, they felt *right*.

Doran chewed over his response. "Better to die amongst friends than enemies," he muttered. Then he gave a stifled laugh. "That might be the most *un-dwarven* thing I've ever said."

Friends... The word became stuck in his mind. To have friends implied a degree of trust. To Asher, *trust* meant *trap*. Or, perhaps, it didn't. At least it didn't have to. The *Assassin* within him could never trust another person, a belief that had been affirmed after his experience with Geron Thorbear and the other rangers. But, to the *Ranger,* it could be something new, something *real.* After all, how could he ever break away from his life as an Arakesh if he didn't embrace the qualities Nightfall abhorred?

The concept seemed a strange thing to consider while the life in question had somewhere between minutes and hours left to go. At the same time, Asher knew he wouldn't mind dying as the man he wanted to be rather than the monster he had been for so long. Too long. Rather than dwell on his regrets, however, he focused on the positive, if there could be such a thing in death, and that was those around him. There were only two, but neither wished him dead and both had tried to save his life. They were two statements he couldn't apply to anyone else in all the realm.

"So," Doran drawled, breaking the quiet atmosphere. "That were the Arakesh back there then... the real deal."

Asher was slow to respond, his mind growing sluggish. "*Three* of them," he said, voicing his own incredulity.

"They know ye don' go down easy, eh?"

The ranger disagreed but lacked the energy to shake his head. "I wasn't the target," he corrected. "Though they would gladly kill me given the chance."

The dwarf rocked his head back and eyed the ranger. "Ye weren' the target?"

"Viktor broke the rules," Asher explained. "He brought Night-fall into the light. He sealed his own fate the moment he invited the world to watch me kill for him."

"And everyone else?" Salim enquired.

"No witnesses," Asher replied bluntly. "They can't kill everyone from the arena, but what they saw could be argued the world round. Those at Viktor's party were too close to the truth. They had to die."

Doran's eyebrows reached for his hairline. "Scary buggers, eh?"

"They tend to have that effect," Asher acknowledged. "Though most don't live to dwell on it."

Doran held his hands up to the four walls that contained them. "If I'm supposed to consider us the lucky ones..."

"It was not luck but great cunning," Salim pointed out, eyeing the ranger. "The Arakesh would have butchered us all were it not for your quick thinking. Releasing the beast was quite the gamble given your condition."

Asher tucked up his bottom lip in thought. "I could have taken it," he stated, thankful he didn't need to prove such a thing.

The dwarf scowled at it all. "Oh, so *he* gets all the credit now does he? I thought I were the one who *saved us all*."

Had he the energy, Asher might have managed a laugh. "Your timing was good. It could have been *better*."

"Bah! That bloody place was all stairs!" The dwarf thumbed the black and gold armour across his chest. "This ain' exactly light ye know."

"I must say," Salim cut in, one hand cupping his goatee, "I was surprised the legendary Arakesh were defeated so quickly by the creature. You, however, seemed so confident."

The ranger flexed his eyebrows, the extent of his ability to make expressions. "They're not trained to kill monsters."

"And you are?" Salim asked with genuine curiosity.

"No," Asher confessed. "I'm just better," he quipped.

"Well I can tell ye, I wouldn't mind if I never saw one again."

The Honour Guard was still smiling from Asher's remark when he responded to the dwarf's statement. "The Mer-man or the Arakesh?"

Doran pinched his lips together in consideration. "Both."

Their good humour was scored through by the all too familiar sound of a monster's ear-splitting roar. Asher frowned, wondering if he alone was hearing the call of some hellish beast come to take him to the next world. Seeing the apprehension in Salim and Doran alike informed him otherwise.

"You heard that?" the ranger whispered.

"I'm wishin' I hadn'," Doran quipped, slowly rising to his feet.

"It was close," Salim observed, his voice brought down to a hush as he stepped back from the bars.

That single step saved the Honour Guard's life, for had he remained so close his torso would have been pierced by the monstrous claw that gripped between the bars. Man and dwarf jumped back, Doran deliberately placing himself between the creature and Asher. There was no concealing the beast, however, its other claw gripping the bars of the adjacent cell in its effort to move through the dungeon.

Asher scrutinised the monster from his place on the floor and realised they weren't claws at all, but the hook-like ends of thick black pincers. Upon noticing the prisoners, the creature desperately thrust those terrible pincers towards them. It succeeded only in bending a handful of the bars, but its attack was jarring enough to rain a fine debris down from the ceiling.

"What in the gods is this fiend?" Salim questioned.

Asher had the answer but he paused before giving it, taking a moment to admire the Honour Guard's calm composure in the face of a living horror. "It's a Kruid," he breathed.

Doran looked down at him. "A what?"

The ranger summoned a notch more energy. "A Kruid," he repeated. "And a young one at that."

It wasn't even a minute later before the monster thought better of penetrating the bars and moved on. Its black carapace and long tail were dragged down the corridor and out of sight. In its wake came the cry of monsters—lots of monsters—and all frighteningly close rather than far below.

"Our new jailer?" Salim queried.

"Not likely," Asher murmured, desiring to change his position. The ranger gave the son of Dorain a double take, noticing the dwarf's face so laden with uncertainty. "Doran?"

The stout warrior licked his lips but said nothing, the silence, instead, filled by the howls and moans of unseen creatures.

"Doran?" he repeated, his soft tone lacking the urgency he felt.

The dwarf grew serious as he met the ranger's gaze. "He sent his men, Asher," the son of Dorain began. "He sent killers to Darkwell. He wanted their heads. Mine too."

"We knew there was a chance he wouldn't honour the deal," Asher interjected. "That's why you *had* to go."

The heavy lines of Doran's face creased all the more into

shadow. "Aye, but the Stormshields would never be free so long as Viktor held a grudge, an' he's not a man to let his grudges jus' lie."

Asher tilted his head. "Why do I sense there's more?"

Doran scratched an eyebrow with his thumb and took a breath. "We decided the only way to be free o' Viktor's threats was to be done with the man 'imself. *Indefinitely.*"

"We?"

Doran made to speak before rethinking his answer. "Dwarves don' take well to threats. An' the higher up the hierarchy ye go the worse their response. Threatenin' Deadora was a declaration o' war."

The ranger didn't have the energy to display the alarm he felt, managing no more than a slow blink. "You didn't bring the Stormshields here," he stated, refusing to believe that the son of Dorain would be so foolish as to bring the family to the most lawless place in all of Verda.

"No," Doran protested. "Well," he added, countering himself, "not *all* o' 'em. Kilda an' Deadora are safe; they're hidin' out in The Black Wood. But erm... Well, if I'm honest, there was no stoppin' Danagarr."

"Danagarr's *here*?" Asher gasped.

"Oh aye," Doran confirmed. "An' I tell ye what, he's bloody dangerous with a hammer in his hand. I forgot he served in Hyndaern's army for near on a century before he turned to smith's work."

"Doran," Asher interjected, focusing the dwarf.

The son of Dorain held his hands up in brief apology. "If I were a bettin' dwarf," he continued, gesturing toward the departed Kruid, "I'd say this was Danagarr's handiwork."

Asher sighed. Since the question of how the smith had infiltrated the compound was a moot point, the ranger moved on to a question he didn't have an answer for. "This was your grand plan? Unleash *all* the monsters?"

"It wasn' me first plan." The response came from behind Doran and beyond the bars. "But when things started to get a little hairy," the old smith went on, "I had to... What's the word? *Improvise!*" he declared with a beaming grin.

Doran rushed to the bars. "Danagarr!"

"I see things went well on yer end," the smith commented dryly, taking in the confines of his fellow dwarf. He then noticed Salim, standing tall on the other side of the cell. "Well met, stranger. Be ye friend or foe?" he asked boldly.

Salim stood a little taller, if it was possible. "I am friend, good dwarf."

"Good to hear it," Danagarr replied. "'Cos gettin' out o' here is goin' to be damned hard." The smith moved so that he might better see Asher behind Doran. "Oh," he voiced, seeing the truth of Asher's situation.

The ranger didn't want to talk about it—there was no hope for him but, thanks to Danagarr's reckless actions, there was now a sliver of hope for his companions where only moments ago there had been none. "I'll be fine," he lied, moving things on. "What did you do?"

The smith's seasoned eyes roamed over Asher one more time before sharing a look with Doran, who confirmed the ranger's critical state by mere expression. "I was gettin' a lay o' the land," he finally told them. "Ye know, scoutin' the place out while I looked for Viktor. Then *ye* lot returned from wherever—with Viktor no less—an' the guard presence doubled. One o' 'em saw me. Or, at least, he thought he did. Anyway, in me bid to evade the fella, I ended up in a place where me nightmares would 'ave been more welcome."

Doran shrugged his heavy pauldrons. "That don' explain why all the monsters are on the loose."

The smith caught Doran in his gaze and held him steady with a look that could cut granite. "I told ye, boy, I came here to upend his world. Well, ye can bet it's bloody upended now, eh?" he posed, thumbing over his shoulder to the sound of monsters and men clashing in blood and steel.

The irrepressible chaos of it all brought a true smile to the ranger's ashen face. "Who are we," he croaked, "to argue with the battle plans of a Stormshield?"

Doran was shaking his head. "Ignore 'im," he insisted, "he's lost too much blood. Now," he said pointedly, his hard gaze returned to the smith, "how in the hells are we supposed to get out o' 'ere with monsters at every turn? Hmm? Did ye think abou' that when ye were springin' the lot o' 'em? I'll be damned, Danagarr Stormshield, if I don' see yer sorry self returned to the arms o' yer wife! Grarfath knows what Kilda'll do to me if I return without ye..."

The smith looked upon the dwarf mockingly. "I didn' know ye were one for frettin', Heavybelly."

"Danagarr," came the growling response.

"Easy, lad. It's the madness o' it all that'll ensure our escape. O' course, we jus' need to make sure Viktor Varga goes down with it all. I didn' jus' come 'ere to ruin his coin purse. I want his worthless *life*."

"Either way," Salim said, joining the conversation with steel in his voice, "we must reach the weapons room."

There was a brief discussion between the dwarves and the southerner, and all in agreement by their shared tone, but Asher heard not a word, his mind having wandered the moment he heard *weapons room*.

Empty seconds passed him by as he focused his thoughts, grasping hopelessly as to why the weapons room felt important to him. After all, what could be overly important to a dead man? The question opened a door in his memory and led him back to the last time he had been on the verge of death. He should have died four years ago with Basilisk venom in his blackened veins, yet he had survived.

In his crippled state, his mind lost the thread and returned to the memory of Doran signing the barbarian word for survive. It felt like a lifetime ago and only yesterday all at once.

Survive... He was good at surviving.

"It doesn' really matter," Doran grumbled, his hands coming up as he interrupted Asher's drifting thoughts. "These are Novian cells or some such. I don' know. They're *inescapable*. Ye're goin' to 'ave to check every corpse ye can find for the blasted keys."

Danagarr wrapped his knuckles against one of the bars. "Even the dungeons o' Silvyr Hall could never boast inescapable cells, lad. Take it from a smith o' the old ways, there's no such thing as *perfect* engineerin'." The dwarf scoffed. "Even more so when it comes to the clumsy hands an' muddled brains o' humans. No offence," he added immediately, looking to Salim.

"None taken," the Honour Guard assured.

"Give me a minute," the smith bade, retrieving a pouch of tools from his belt and crouching to inspect the lock.

Doran looked over his shoulder at Asher. "I'm not sure all o' us 'ave a minute," he muttered gravely to the others.

"I'm still here," the ranger informed them, though he could feel his life falling away like water through a sieve.

"Ye don' die easy, ranger man, I'll give ye that."

Danagarr chuckled on the other side of the bars. "Humans," he uttered with a tut. "Me grandfather used to give me puzzle boxes more complicated than this." The sound of his fine instruments, so intricately invading the lock, was momentarily drowned out by the low rumble of heavy limbs hammering the ground somewhere. An almighty roar spread throughout the arena and must have surely reached the residents beyond.

The smith paused in his work. "What were that?" he asked tentatively.

Doran turned to meet Asher's eyes, where the pair came to a silent agreement. "Lumber Dug," the dwarf answered reluctantly.

Danagarr returned to his task. "Should I be particularly worried about that?"

The son of Dorain craned his neck to scrutinise the space inside the dungeons. "No Lumber Dug's gettin' in 'ere."

"Oh. Big laddy then," the smith concluded.

A few minutes went by while Danagarr huffed and sighed, his implements twisting and jostling the lock pins.

Doran's eyes were boring into his kin. "What's takin' so long?"

The smith wiped the sweat from his brow across one sleeve.

"I'll admit, the human that devised these cells was havin' a good day. There's some real dwarven inspiration 'ere."

"Is that another way o' sayin' ye can' open it?"

"I can open anythin', laddy!" came the biting retort. "Ye're the dolt for gettin' yerself locked up in the first place. Ye only had one job!" Danagarr flicked his head towards Asher. "I'd say that went abou' as well as it usually does."

"One job?" Doran echoed in disbelief. "That *one job* was infil-tratin' the most secure compound in The Adean an'..." The dwarf stopped himself. "Ye don' know what ye're talkin' abou'. Jus' open the damned door."

"Oh, is that what I'm supposed to be doing?"

Salim stepped forward. "Peace, gentlemen," he said in his soothing voice. "Do you feel that?"

Asher couldn't be more still than he already was and his focus had grown slack. Yet he still felt the rhythmic vibrations through the floor. It was likely the heavy footfalls of the Lumber Dug, coupled with its unique ability to create vibrations in place of an audible roar.

It was getting closer.

A thunder-clap of ruin split the ceiling and walls, scrawling them with a cobweb of cracks. In its wake came the cries of men who ran with death on their heels. They were inside the passage that cut between the adjacent cells, sprinting towards Danagarr. The look on the smith's face said it all.

"The other cell," Asher rasped. "*Now,*" he urged.

"Go!" Doran snapped.

Danagarr needed no more encouragement, dropping his lock picks and dashing to the open cell opposite their own. He didn't even have time to close the gate before three of Viktor's men came rushing past, ignorant of all but the fiend that gave chase.

The Lumber Dug's arrival was apocalyptic.

Its ungainly advance and hulking proportions destroyed every-thing around it and extinguished most of the torches. The vibra-tions its rocky hide created cut through the sound of twisting iron and snapping bolts. Debris was launched in every direction and clouds of dust masked its passage. No better than a living battering ram, the Lumber Dug pushed its way through and out the other side. The entire event was over in a handful of chaotic seconds.

Doran managed to call out Danagarr's name between coughing fits. Salim's dark shadow staggered from wall to wall before he inevitably tripped over a chunk of loose stone. Asher remained seated on the floor, his back resting against the wall. His lower position appeared to have spared him, though he struggled more than the others with the dust thickening his air.

"I'm a'right!" the smith called back.

"Praise the Father," Doran uttered, wafting the dust in front of his face. "Are ye hurt?"

Of the few torches that had survived the catastrophe, the one nearest to their cell cast Danagarr in a gloom as he navigated the debris and returned to the passage. "I'll live," he reported.

"Asher?" Doran then checked, turning back to the ranger.

He could but cough in response, though it informed the dwarf that he yet drew breath. For how much longer he could not say.

"Look," Salim said, directing them to the warped bars and framework of their cell.

Asher blinked the water from his eyes and observed the wrought iron. The top of the framework had been knocked loose from the stone above and bent inwards.

"With me," the Honour Guard instructed.

Following his lead, Doran jumped up and grasped the top of the frame. With Danagarr adding his weight to the other side, the three were able to rend the damaged bolts keeping it pinned to the walls and bring it further into the cell.

"We can climb over it," Salim instructed.

"Ye go first," Doran told him. "I'll get Asher."

In the near dark, Asher groaned through the pain of being manhandled up and over the bent frame. He was pushed, pulled, and dragged over the debris until all four of them were in what remained of the shattered passage.

"Stay with me now," Doran chanted close to his ear.

Asher was too busy trying not to pass out to offer any kind of response. He was only partially aware that Salim had taken over his care and hooked one of the ranger's arms over his shoulders. A firm hand wrapped around his waist, dangerously close to his wound, and he was soon being aided out of the dungeons.

"Which way to the weapons room?" Danagarr asked, careful to step over one of the bodies of the men flattened by the Lumber Dug.

Again, while the three fell into discussion, Asher's mind collapsed in on itself, falling down a rabbit hole created by the words *weapons room*. It was important. So much so that he was convinced his life was tied to that room.

The gem...

The answer finally came to him and with it he glimpsed a future he might yet live to see. "Weapons... room." The words left his lips like a light breeze through a crack in the door.

"Weapons room?" Salim repeated. "Yes, my friend. That's where we're going."

"Ring," he wheezed. "Need... ring."

The ranger struggled to follow all that happened next. There were times when it felt like Salim's breathing was extremely laboured, suggesting there were periods where he lost consciousness and the Honour Guard was forced to take all of his weight. Asher had a brief memory of being on the floor at one point on their journey and surrounded by the clatter of fighting. Then there were times where he would open his eyes to discover he was being furiously dragged down one corridor after another, and all to the background noise of stalking monsters and men dying.

"Here!" Salim's voice snapped, rousing Asher from his latest bout of unconsciousness.

The ranger looked hazily to his left, where Doran crouched close by with one hand out to keep Asher sat upright. "Stay with me, laddy," he ordered.

The Honour Guard shoved his body into the locked door before stepping back to kick it in. "Go," he commanded of the smith.

Asher was unceremoniously dragged inside the weapons room by Doran. Salim moved from torch to torch, igniting each with the one he had brought in with him, though the ranger could not recall him ever acquiring it in the first place.

Armour, plated and leather, weapons, old and new, were all revealed in the light. The ranger's eyes fluttered to take in the large gate on the far side—the entrance to the arena itself. To his left was the tall locker stacked high and haphazardly with a multitude of belongings confiscated under Viktor's rule.

"They were right behind us," Salim began, his gaze drawn to the door he had broken.

"Let 'em come," Doran replied eagerly, reclaiming the same axe and sword he had possessed in Viktor's fortress home. He examined the steel of both. "At least the scrupulous bastards brought everything back, eh?" he commented, nodding at Asher's gear and green cloak, all left in a pile by the wall.

The ranger recognised his folded bow among the brown leathers and recalled something Viktor had said about cleaning the massacre up. No one could know, he had said. It would have been more fortuitous if he still had the strength to draw the bowstring or even don his leathers and cloak.

"I've got all I need," Danagarr stated, his sledgehammer hefted in both hands.

Salim's focus passed along the wall of weapons and armour, a single hand outstretched as if he could feel them all as an Arakesh might. He stopped in front of a single-handed scimitar and claimed it as his own.

The steel flashed as the Honour Guard twisted his wrist to get a feel for its weight and balance. "This will do."

"Throw this on, laddy, an' be quick abou' it." Doran tossed a leather cuirass at the southerner, its high sleeves and chest plates laced with chainmail. "Keep an eye on the door," he commanded of the smith.

Asher's world was suddenly dominated by the son of Dorain, who came to crouch over him. "We'll do our best to keep these beasties away from ye, but beyond 'ere..." The dwarf trailed off, unable to voice the burden that Asher had become. "I'm so sorry," he whispered. "It weren' meant to go like this. I was to free ye..."

Doran's mouth continued to move but he was lost for words. "Ye gave yer life... ye gave yer life for me an' me kin. Ye deserve more than a knife in the back."

Asher turned to see the door of the grated locker. "Ring," he breathed.

Some inhuman noise came from the broken doorway, diverting the dwarf's attention over his shoulder. "Salim?"

The Honour Guard, secured within his cuirass now, advanced to put himself between them and the door. Shadows given life lurked over the threshold, pierced only by the reflective eyes that peered in at the companions.

"Ring," Asher repeated, squeezing Doran's arm. "I need... the ring."

"What's that?" Doran questioned, but there was no time to hear the ranger's response.

Monsters were upon them.

CHAPTER 38
HERE AT THE END

Ghoulist - I have transcribed the passage from the eleventh edition of A Chronicle of Monsters: A Ranger's Bestiary, despite the fact that no ranger has identified a Ghoulist in over a hundred years. I know from experience that just because a thing hasn't been seen for a long time doesn't mean it can never be seen again. So I warn you not to skim over the details but commit them to memory, as you might be the first to cross a Ghoulist and, as you have probably learnt by now, facing any monster unprepared is a good way to lose your life.

If you are reading this, my fellow ranger, then I say well done to you. It would take even the most learned of men some time to reach this page, which means you must have many a monster under your belt.

If you must add another, pray to the gods it is not a Ghoulist. With six legs and the musculature of a horse, you can bet they are bigger, stronger, and faster than yourself. Should you manage to stay on your feet long enough to actually fight it, beware its twin-tails, each ending in razored bone. Then there's its head, a hideous thing. If you have ever come across a Scudder, that's exactly what their head and neck look like. Wicked beasts.

I only survived because the damned thing was more interested in devouring my horse.

A Chronicle of Monsters: A Ranger's Bestiary, 12th Edition, Page 488.

Harndel Goft, Ranger (transcribed by Barnwen, son of Farngorn).

There wasn't much of Asher's mind left, but what did remain identified the monsters as Nefaris, creatures of the Shadow Realm likely brought forth by one of Viktor's mages.

They burst into the room on seemingly four legs, though their front two were, in fact, extended arms that could reach the floor when they stood on their back two. A pair of smaller, clawed, hands protruded from their ribcage, each digit fluttering rapidly in anticipation.

They attacked Doran and the others with open jaws, a terrifying sight given that their mouths stretched from brow to chin.

The three companions met them with grit and cold steel, their frantic battle chaotic to Asher's failing mind. The ranger struggled to follow any of it and so his head eventually fell back so that he was flat to the floor.

A new figure stepped into view, towering over Asher's frail body. He had come from nowhere but, then again, it always felt as if he came from nowhere.

"Nasta..." Asher wasn't sure if he truly said his old master's name or whether it had simply echoed from somewhere deep in his mind.

Nasta Nal-Aket crouched beside him, his movement so effortless he could have glided down. His hair sat upon his head like a helmet of dark ringlets, a contrast to his immaculately trimmed beard. He looked down at Asher with eyes so brown as to be pure wells of colour that drew him in and held him firm. They were wells of experience and knowledge and cunning. The things he had seen, the places he had visited, the people he had met: Nasta's life was a rich tapestry and it was all right there in his eyes.

It had been a long time since Asher had seen his master's eyes. He could still conjure the memory of his ascension ceremony, the day Nasta had allowed his fellow Arakesh to remove those dark orbs that spoke of so much life.

"You're not real," Asher whispered. Or, perhaps, he didn't.

Nasta gave no reaction to the statement, but continued to look over the ranger. There was something about the way his eyes roamed over him that tugged at Asher's memory. He looked up at his master and knew he had seen this before. Exactly as it was happening now.

"It is only by falling that we learn to rise," he said, his calming voice and accent not dissimilar to Salim's. "It is in my heart to help you, child, but we all rise alone... or not at all."

It made sense to the ranger then, hearing those words from his past. It was from a time so early on in his life that all else had faded. But never that moment. Never those words. He had been but a boy, absent even a single hair on his now stubbled jaw. He remembered it, of course, because of the sentiment, a sentiment Nasta never shared with him again. But, for just a moment, he had felt loved. Twisted as it was.

"The ring," he reiterated, head turning towards the locker. "I need... the ring."

Nasta's mirage followed his gaze and looked upon the small sack, just beyond the barred door. "Then take it," he simply instructed. "I did not train you to die."

Asher knew those words were similarly from some distant memory and did not directly apply to the gem in question, yet his mind had conjured just what he needed to hear from the one person who had always pushed him beyond his limits.

While Doran, Salim, and Danagarr fought for their lives and his own, the ranger rolled onto his front and began the arduous crawl towards the locker door. He heard steel sink into pale flesh and claws rake along iron plates. The monsters shrieked and the companions raged against the beasts that would feed upon them. Still Asher crawled.

Every inch of ground he gained saw another inch of his life ebb away. His fingers, crusted with his own blood, reached out for the edges of the door. Had it been fully closed, his journey would have ended right there and then and his life with it. Taking what luck he could get, the ranger curled his fingers around the frame and pulled to open it. The door groaned in protest and he nearly lost his grip.

Finally, the task complete, his palm slapped back down on the stone, where his body seemed determined to die. Through strands of hair he could see the small sack sitting upon a short stool in the corner. The black gem and its promise of life was so close now.

One of the Nefaris hurtled into the side of the grated locker, the impact enough to knock almost a whole wall of items to the floor. The creature stamped its long arms and shrieked in defiance at Doran's charge, his axe and sword slick with the obsidian blood of the monster's kin.

Asher paid their fight no more attention than that. He urged his knees to find purchase and aid his flat crawl across the remaining feet. Short though the stool was, the sack might as well have been on top of the locker's flat roof. With Nasta leaning against the doorframe behind him, watching intently, the ranger reached out, determined to live. He toppled the stool and the small sack with it.

The stool made a clatter beside him but the sack was sent back the way he had come, beyond the locker door. Worse still, the contents had spilled across the stone, spreading Doran's jewellery and the ranger's ring into the midst of the heated battle.

"Where is it, boy?" Nasta questioned, crouching to meet him as he awkwardly turned to crawl out. "Where is the fire I saw behind your eyes that day?"

The question gave Asher pause and he looked up at his old mentor. He had been referring to the day they had met. The ranger couldn't picture it clearly in his mind, the edges of the memory frayed after decades of brutal training and hard living. He had been threatened. That much he remembered. By whom or what eluded him, though he vividly recalled a blindfolded Nasta Nal-Aket leaping over his small body to protect him.

"I saw so much in that young face," Nasta purred. "Your drive. Your tenacity. Your recklessness. All bound to that feral animal that lacked purpose. *I* gave you purpose. But you were a survivor *before* Nightfall, child." Nasta stood up and regarded the scattered jewellery. "So survive," he commanded.

Asher dragged himself onwards, over the locker's threshold and back into the weapons room proper. Figures danced about him, blood splattered the stone, and ghastly noises broke the air, but forwards he crawled, oblivious to the details. He scraped Doran's bracelets aside and swiped at the dwarf's necklace, his blue eyes searching desperately for the gem.

There it was.

The black crystal absorbed the torchlight, making its rough edges hard to see. The iron band, to which the gem had been fixed by his own amateurish hands many years ago, shone in the gaze of the surrounding flames, drawing him in. Seeing it now, so close, he felt so much of himself yearn to be reunited with it.

A pale fist of three bony fingers and three curling claws touched down between the ranger and his salvation. Looking up, through his matted and dust-coated hair, he laid eyes on the opening mouth-head of a Nefaris. The vertical jaw continued to extend, each side connected by strands of thick saliva.

A sledgehammer caught the monster in the ribs, jarring the fiend into the sweeping arc of a scimitar before a dwarven axe split its head truly in half. The Nefaris staggered a step and dropped dead, its hideous corpse added to the rest.

The ring came back into Asher's view. His hand moved instinctively, fingers flexing, yet the gem remained inches from reach. The urge to give up and fall asleep was becoming overwhelming. The ranger knew if he blinked for just a moment too long he would never open his eyes again. But in sleep there was the promise of rest, at last. The pain would be gone. The shame and the guilt of his past deeds would finally fall away.

His life upon a precipice, the end was most alluring.

The thick and stubby fingers of a dwarf dropped into his fading vision, ignorant of the one last spark of life within him. Dread welled up in the ranger, for he knew it to be Doran's hand and so too did he know the dwarf's fate should he touch the hostile gem. He tried to voice a warning but his breath was too shallow to form any words.

As he intended to, Doran Heavybelly took the ring in hand.

Asher, helpless to prevent the inevitable, watched frozen at the dwarf's feet. Be it pain or simply the mysterious power of the gem, his meaty hand was immediately drawn into a clenched fist. The knotted hand was mimicked by his expression, his features pulled into silent agony. Danagarr and Salim rushed to his aid though neither could fathom the cause of his distress.

Only seconds after picking up the gem, the son of Dorain was brought to his knees before Asher. The ranger clawed at his companion but he hadn't the strength to bring him down to the floor, where he might prise open those strong dwarven fingers. Danagarr and Salim called out his name and pawed at his clothes and armour, but Doran remained fixed in his silent cage of pain.

How long did he have? Seconds? Asher had seen this twice before and knew that death or severe disability was all that awaited Doran now. Surely his would be another death added to the ranger's conscience, a death he could have prevented if he had but found the damned strength.

The dwarf opened his eyes and they beheld naught but Asher.

Taken aback by the raw defiance he saw in those eyes, the ranger could only watch the son of Dorain perform the impossible. His tight fist extended towards Asher, every muscle in his arm shaking from the strain, as if he was lifting an anvil. Dark veins bulged across the surface of that hand, worming under his vambraces in search of his heart.

Teeth clenched and glassy eyed, the dwarf fought his own end and slowly but surely opened his hand like the petals of a flower come the dawn. Stunned by disbelief, Asher glimpsed the black gem between Doran's fingers.

A growl worthy of rolling thunder rumbled forth from the dwarf's throat. He tilted his jerking hand. Bit by bit, the ring slipped across his palm until it sat on the very edge, beneath his little finger. With the last vestiges of his strength, Asher sluggishly reached out one hand, his fingers sliding over the cold stone until they were under Doran's.

The ring fell from one hand to the next.

The ranger enveloped the ring so that his fingers made contact with the black gem. He could feel its power resting in his palm, ready and waiting to be called upon. Closing his eyes, Asher imagined himself healing, his blood replenishing, and his pain evaporating. The curious gem did not disappoint.

Death's cold hand fell from his shoulder and its black shadow retreated. Warmth. He had almost forgotten the feel of it. Life-giving, the warmth coursed through his limbs and into his frigid fingers. Instances of pain flashed across his body and he writhed as numerous injuries were miraculously healed. Worst of them all, the stab wound in his back took longer to recover. It pinched and burned and his organs ached under the thrall of the magic.

Rising from the very edge of death, Asher's mind sharpened. He gained control of his arms and legs and managed to push up to his hands and knees. Doran was beside him, still on his knees with shoulders hunched. Like the ranger, the dwarf's chest was laboured in its recovery breaths. Unlike the ranger, he did not have magic to return him so quickly to his feet.

Three startled faces watched him rise to his full height and remove the cloth from around his waist.

"What," Doran began, face drenched with sweat, "in all the hells... is that?"

Asher followed the dwarf's gaze down to the ring in his hand. "I don't know," he answered honestly, slipping it over his right index finger.

Doran swallowed. "Ye don' know?" He glanced at Danagarr and Salim for support. "But ye knew it would save ye?"

Asher delayed his response, waiting for the son of Dorain to find his feet with an extra hand from the smith. "I've had it for as long as I can remember," he said, continuing his streak of honesty. "I don't know how I came to possess it or why, just as I don't know how or why it can heal only me." The ranger observed Doran for a moment, a sentinel of strength where there should have been a dead dwarf. "You are not the first to feel its biting touch. But you are the first to *survive* it." He looked to the spot where Doran should have taken his last breath. "You should be dead."

The dwarf nodded at him. "The same could be said o' ye, lad."

Danagarr held a tentative hand towards the ring on Asher's finger. Only when the ranger offered the hand did the smith take it in his own and examine the black gem. He was careful not to touch it, not even the band.

"I'd say there's magic abound," he uttered. "An' heaps o' it too. There ain' much known abou' healin' magic, especially among dwarves. Our oldest stories talk o' elves usin' magic in such a way." The smith looked over his shoulder at Doran and chortled. "I told ye, Heavybelly: natural resistance!"

"Aye," the son of Dorain remarked dryly. "Lucky me." He was still massaging the hand that had held the ring.

Danagarr turned back to the ranger. "Ye say ye don' know how ye came by it?"

Asher shook his head. "I have kept it secret all my life. Even from the Arakesh."

Even from Nasta Nal-Aket, he wanted to say. A subtle glance at their surroundings revealed his old master's absence. Focused once more, the ranger wondered if he had truly hallucinated the Father of Nightfall. The last few minutes felt more a dream than reality.

Doran had the look of revelation about him. "That's how ye did it!" he exclaimed, pointing an accusing finger up at him. "On the cliff top. With the Trolls. I did see ye bloody an' broken!"

Asher confirmed the truth with a nod of the head. "You saw

what you saw. I am not nearly as good a monster hunter as my reputation would have you believe. This," he said, turning his hand to see the gem, "has saved me from death many times. Just as it has today."

Doran's eyes shifted one way then the next, as if such movement stirred his thoughts. "An' the fire? Ye started that fire like a mage I'm tellin' ye."

Again, if reluctantly, Asher nodded in the affirmative. "I learned the word for fire from a mage... some years ago," he settled on, deciding now wasn't the time for a story. "The ancient word," he clarified. "I can't shape it like a mage, but I can start a fire now and then."

"Without a wand?" Danagarr asked. "No Demetrium?"

Asher nodded but said nothing in the hope the discussion would die away.

Managing to find something of a smile, Doran wagged a finger at him. "Ye're wily, ranger man, very wily."

"It serves only you," Salim stated, though his tone suggested there might have been a question in there.

"I have no idea why," Asher confessed, keeping his answer clipped.

Danagarr's head tilted to take in the ring from a different angle. "Fascinatin'," he drawled.

"I would appreciate it if this remained a secret," Asher voiced. "I fear in the wrong hands it could be made to *do* wrong."

"Aye," Doran agreed. "Better it be wasted on *yer* finger, eh? I won' speak o' it, ye 'ave me word."

"And mine," Salim added with a short bow of the head.

Danagarr held his hands up. "I will take the truth o' it to me grave."

"Thank you," the ranger replied, feeling the quiet but powerful touch of friendship. Nevertheless, he was uncomfortable with the attention he was receiving and so thrust his chin at the monsters lying dead behind the trio. "You made short work of them," he complimented.

Doran thumbed at the door they entered through, where the

sound of distant beasts and wretched creatures filled the halls. "There's plenty more where they came from."

Asher moved to retrieve his gear and folded cloak. "They'll have to wait," he said, thumbing the small lever on his bow and snapping the limbs to life. "I'm hunting a different monster."

CHAPTER 39

AN ARMY OF FOUR

__Vogan__ - Now here's an interesting creature for you, dear learner. Though these little beasts do not directly hunt humans, they are undoubtedly a threat should the two ever meet. Vogan can be typically found in the wake of Giants. Not always, I should say, but their presence is not uncommon.

These beasts come in at no taller than the average man's waist with a naturally hunched back and long arms that aid in their movement. On their own, any Vogan is easily killed by even an amateur swordsman but, due to the numbers they travel in, they can overwhelm a person or potentially a group if motivated enough.

As I said, however, they trail Giants, preferring to pick clean whatever they leave behind. There's nothing fancy to be done here—there's no bait or poison to employ. If you take on a contract regarding a Giant, it's always good to be aware of these creatures lest they surprise you. It's rare to see a contract come up specifically for the Vogan but should one arise, be mindful that the Giant they're following is likely dead, leading to the Vogan creating trouble for humans directly. If the Giant is dead, you have to wonder what could kill it. There's always something worse out there.

*A Chronicle of Monsters: A Ranger's Bestiary, 12th Edition,
Page 361.*

Rogan Vane, Ranger.

Doran could hardly believe his eyes. Standing before him, Asher was attired in his weathered brown leathers, draped in his rough green cloak, and equipped with a multitude of small blades and throwing knives, most of which he managed to conceal from sight. On his hip rested a two-handed longsword, taken from the wall of weapons. In his grasp, and strong it was now, he effortlessly wielded his bow with an arrow nocked neatly onto the taut string, ready to launch.

The sight of him made no sense, not when the dwarf held such a fresh memory of the ranger bleeding out and being so close to dying.

The red blindfold caught Doran's eye, knotted around the ranger's belt now. Had he ever met such an extraordinary human? Or dwarf for that matter? Every layer that was peeled back from the man only revealed more mystery and intrigue. Questions aside, he enjoyed more and more the person that existed beneath all that stoicism.

Dare he call him a friend?

A human friend sounded preposterous to the son of Dorain. After all, their kind were only one up from an elf... not that he had ever met one of the undying. Yet here he was, standing side by side with a man, ready to die fighting as something more than a mere ally.

"Do we have a plan?" Salim asked, his voice strained as he pushed a heavy cabinet across the doorway.

"Viktor's the target," Asher said, a curtain of assertiveness drawing over him. "He'll likely be hiding in his office. If I leave via the arena I can ascend the steps and breach the higher levels from his viewing box. That should help to avoid some of the monsters."

Doran's sense of hearing felt jarred by the distinction Asher had made. "What's this *I* business? Are we not in this together?"

"I will move quicker on my own," the ranger told him. "Trust me, I've done this before."

"Aye, ye 'ave," the dwarf agreed, and darkly so. "But I thought ye didn' want to be that man anymore. The *assassin* an' all that."

"Those skills have their uses," Asher replied gruffly.

"Not today, laddy," Doran said. "*Today* ye fight with us."

The ranger's jaw tensed and his eyes found not a one of them, trapped as he was inside his own contemplation. It was clear to see that the man was fighting demons, the darker parts of his soul where Nightfall had left its mark on him.

At last, Asher looked down at the son of Dorain. "Together," he said.

Doran nodded. "Together," he echoed. "Now, do ye know where Viktor's office is?" he questioned, not wishing to wander the halls.

Asher shook his head. "No. But he does most of his work from here, so it's a safe assumption there is one. In all likelihood, it will be located close to his private viewing box."

Danagarr moved to the turning wheel beside the arena's gate. "Well what are we waitin' for?"

Doran held out a hand. "Wait," he commanded. "Maybe it's best if ye stay behind. Ye can shut the gate behind us an' lock yerself in there," he suggested, thumbing over his shoulder at the tall locker.

"Why would I do that?" the smith argued. "I've come this far, 'aven' I? Ye thinkin' I can' hack it, Heavybelly?"

"I'm thinkin' ye've already done enough," Doran countered. "One way or another, ye freed us all. But let *us* see to Viktor. He's not goin' to be unguarded. We three can see to his end. We'll make yer family safe again."

"Bah!" Danagarr spat, waving the caution away. "Ye're jus' afraid o' Kilda."

"O' course I am," Doran agreed.

The smith began to turn the iron wheel, his corded arms

bulging with effort. "I can'—I *won'*—return to me kin until I've seen 'im dead. Be it by my hand or any o' yers—I don' care. I jus' need to know it's done."

With his every word, the gate rose higher and higher, bringing into view the field of sand and surrounding arena. Doran wanted to double down on his argument and see the dwarf made safe, but the Stormshield was just as stubborn as he was, and Doran knew he wouldn't have hidden himself away. He knew, however, that Danagarr's part in the fight to come would prove to be a complication, for the son of Dorain always preferred to fight with nothing but his opponent to think about.

His fears for such a complication came all too soon.

Upon rising five feet, the gate's ascension came to a sudden halt when a scarlet red tentacle snaked around the wall and wrapped around Danagarr's leg. The dwarf was swept from his feet and dragged from the weapons room and into the arena. His hands clawed at the stone floor before he reached the sand and was lifted from sight.

"Danagarr!" Doran bellowed, scooping up the smith's hammer with his free hand.

While the men ducked under the gate, Doran ran straight into the arena without obstacle, his gaze going high to find his kin. What a monstrosity he found, there upon the stone-cut benches of the arena. As garishly red as its tentacle, the beast was an eyesore against its sandy surroundings. Eight, or possibly ten, tentacles whipped about in the air, one of which dangled poor Danagarr by his ankle. From that mass of rubbery limbs and jagged suckers emerged the bulk of its main body.

"What in the hells is that?" the son of Dorain yelled, taking in the humanoid monster that rose up to meet the smith.

"Praitora!" Asher growled, his bow coming up.

"How do we kill it?" Salim asked.

"An' fast!" Doran added, hefting his axe to throw.

"You don't," Asher stated calmly, his gaze narrowed down the shaft of his arrow. "Get ready to grab him and run," he instructed tersely.

The ranger's arrow took to the air and closed the gap in less than a second. It plunged into the creature's side, where a human would expect to find ribs. A wet shriek burst from its circular mouth, rising up to the pale sky of dawn. The tentacle holding Danagarr prisoner unfurled and the smith was unceremoniously dropped, leaving him to tumble over the benches until he slammed into the top of the arena wall.

"Jump!" Doran barked at him.

Asher had already nocked another arrow and taken aim before the dwarven smith had come to his senses. The arrow sailed, closing the gap, and impacted the Praitora on the underside of one of its tentacles. The monster recoiled, giving Danagarr more time to climb over the lip of the wall and drop down onto the sand.

"Run!" Asher cried, turning to the steps that cut halfway along the arena.

The Praitora was not to be deterred by a couple of arrows. The creature's body writhed, moving it down the sloping arena and onto the sand, its tentacles reaching out like grasping hands. More than once, Doran had to heave Danagarr up from where he fell and partly drag him onwards.

"Up here!" Asher yelled, darting up the steps that led to the base of Viktor's viewing box.

Doran had only to glimpse those steps to know that neither he nor Danagarr stood any chance of outpacing the Praitora. Even if they reached the top without falling prey to it, there was another climb awaiting them to ascend to the viewing box. With a silent prayer to Grarfath on his lips, he handed the smith his hammer back and urged him on behind Salim. After taking five steps himself, the son of Dorain turned around and drew his sword so that he might delay the monster with both blade and axe.

"Doran!" Danagarr's voice, bristling with alarm, rang out across the arena.

"Go!" the dwarf snapped over his shoulder, his eyes fixed on the Praitora squeezing its body through the gap in the arena wall. "Come on then, ye ugly son of a—"

A dark mass blurred across the sands, unseen behind the wall, and collided with the Praitora with such force that both were taken far from the steps. Doran felt the rush of air pass over him and leave him standing, a stunned dwarf. For just a moment, he wondered if Grarfath Himself had pummelled the creature and saved his life.

It was no god, however, that had saved the son of Dorain but another monster. The flap of its wings drowned out the reverberating shrieks of the Praitora and the new beast soon rose into view, topping the arena wall and with the Praitora clenched in its talons no less.

"Is that a Dathrak?" Doran muttered. He hadn't seen one in nearly two decades and had nearly died fighting the dragon-like creature.

Squirming in the grip of a greater predator, the Praitora reached up with its tentacles and began to ensnare whatever it could of the Dathrak. Soon, both were eclipsing the open top of the arena and ascending into the dawn. Doran's mouth fell open when the Praitora coiled a pair of tentacles around the Dathrak's throat, robbing it of breath. Try as it might, the beast could not maintain its place in the sky and the pair fell upon the sloped roof of the arena and dropped from sight, into the streets of Dragorn.

"Doran!" The call came from Asher, who had already climbed into the viewing box with Salim. The two men were in the process of pulling the smith up and over by his wrists.

Surprised to still be alive, the son of Dorain dashed up the steps and jumped as high as he could, into the waiting hands. His armour scraped against the wall but he was promptly heaved into the viewing box. After rising to his feet, he looked back and observed two more monsters scaling the arena to find freedom beyond its open roof. Dragorn would soon come to despise the name Viktor Varga.

Doran wiped the sweat from his brow. "So much for avoidin' the monsters, eh?"

Asher flashed him a glance before returning to monitor the corridor through no more than a hairsbreadth opening in the doorway. "It's clear," he whispered.

Doran was sure to take up the rear, keeping Danagarr in the middle of the group. Ahead of the smith, Salim moved with all the grace of a cat, creating even less noise than Asher who carried significantly more gear than the Honour Guard. Either way, both men moved with hardly a presence at all when compared to the dwarves. No matter how hard he tried, Doran couldn't seem to land a single step without it adding to the cacophony of his armour. The company's movement, however, was mostly drowned out by the sound of monsters echoing through the halls. Now and then they heard one of Viktor's men scream in terror before they met their end. Those particular sounds only tightened Doran's grip around his weapons.

Following Asher's lead, the four pressed themselves flat to the nearest wall, and only a second before three of Viktor's thugs ran past them. When the companions made to move on, a fourth appeared from the same corridor and nearly collided with Asher. The ranger was quick to react and pushed the man back so that he could level his sword. The thug, round of face and slightly larger than his friends who had long fled, raised his hands immediately.

"No quarrel," he managed between his panting breaths. "We don't get paid enough for this," he added, slinking away.

Asher maintained a level blade and kept the tip pointed at the man as he jogged to catch up with the others. He only made it as far as the next corner. To the eyes of any man it was a white spider that emerged, its body glistening like diamonds, but, to the dwarves of Dhenaheim, who dwelled deep in the mountain roots, it was an Ice Spider, a *Skitter*. The creature dared enter the gloomy light of the torchlit corridor to ensnare its prey, its eight legs scuttling out of the darkened corridor for naught but a heartbeat. A brief yelp was all that escaped the thug before a more terrible and gruesome sound echoed from that shadowy place.

"Let's not go that way," Salim suggested.

"Agreed," Asher said, leading them in the opposite direction.

Doran continued to follow from the back, though he did so with his head permanently turned over his shoulder, lest the Skitter grow bold and brave more of the light.

A short hiss drew his attention, leading him to Danagarr who was again pressed against the wall behind Salim and Asher. The ranger flicked his head, indicating that Doran was to copy them and quickly.

Shoulder to shoulder with the smith, the son of Dorain leaned out. "What is it?" he asked, his voice as hushed as a dwarf's could be.

"We found his office," Asher replied quietly, displaying an inconceivably low volume to Doran.

"An'?" he continued with a shrug.

Asher blinked slowly. "There's one guard."

Doran frowned. "One?" He licked his lips and felt the hairs of his moustache. "So, what are we waitin' for, lad?" The dwarf hefted his axe to speak for him.

Again, Asher's exasperation came in the form of a slow blink. "It's a mage."

It was Danagarr who sighed. "Ye're sure?" he asked, rubbing his chest where Undvig had struck him with a spell.

Asher didn't bother answering the question. "Stay here. I'll deal with this."

"Best we go," Doran advised. "It'll take 'im longer to put *us* down."

The ranger responded with a devilish grin that Doran had never seen on his face before. "Stay here," he repeated.

Bold as brass, Asher stepped out from cover and revealed himself to the mage. Doran moved with the others so that he might peer around the corner and watch the madman.

"Viktor!" Asher yelled, his voice a growl.

The mage remained calm and collected despite the ranger's sudden and loud appearance, a testament to his confidence. Of course, that confidence came from the wand he was raising. Doran was already narrowing his eyes, bracing against the explosion of light to come. The mage didn't disappoint. Magic ignited the air and an unbelievable flash of blue outshone the mounted torches. Whatever spell tore free from the mage's wand ripped through the air and hammered the ranger square in the chest.

The son of Dorain blinked hard, and not because of the blinding light.

Asher's cloak had blown out behind him and nothing more. Equally baffled was the mage, who stared, slack jawed, at the ranger. He glanced at his wand and licked his lips, perhaps formulating new spells in his mind. It did him no good. Asher advanced down the corridor at a slow pace, letting the mage unleash his magic with spell after spell. Fire, ice, lightning, and all manner of unexplainable flashes poured out of that wand, exhausting the mage's knowledge.

Asher remained untouched by it all. "Viktor!" he called out at the top of his lungs.

Dumbstruck, Doran could only chalk it up to the strange gem worn on the ranger's finger. Just the thought of such mysterious magic sent a shiver up the dwarf's spine. Though the son of Dorain held none in contempt for their use of magic, he was still the *son* of Dorain, an old dwarf from an even older time and, as king, it was also his father's place to maintain a good level of distrust for magic —an example to his people.

It was still a sight to behold. The ranger walked as a god might. Invincible. Untouchable. Beyond the understanding of those around him.

"Viktor!" Asher bellowed again.

Almost backed up to the door now, the mage appeared desperate. He looked at the floor either side of him, seeing something Doran could not. Amidst his unintelligible chanting, he lashed out at the floor with his wand, striking to left and right with unknown spells. A ring of previously unseen runes came to life in a glowing violet.

"Now what's he doin'?" Doran demanded.

The answer came from the rings themselves as the stone inside the runes turned to quicksand before darkening to a pitch black. From both portals, grotesque and dreadful limbs of claws and talons reached out from the Shadow Realm.

Doran cursed under his breath and rushed into the hallway. "I'm comin'!" he cried.

Asher required no such assistance, bringing the dwarf to a skidding stop. One swipe of his longsword all but decapitated the mage. With his death, the magic he commanded fell silent and the portals to the Shadow Realm collapsed on themselves, severing fearsome limbs before the bodies could follow.

The hallway was saturated with the acrid stink of magical discharge and the foul stench of unnatural monsters. Wisps of smoke rose from the patches of stone where the mage's spells had rebounded off Asher and struck his surroundings. The ranger himself was entirely unharmed, without so much as a loose thread on his cloak.

Doran thrust his chin at the ring on Asher's finger. "Ye got any more o' those?"

The ranger gave a dry smile and turned to kick Viktor's door in.

Salim and Danagarr soon joined them as they strode into the office, an army of four. Doran already had the exact insult he intended to throw Viktor's way, though he was yet to decide whether he would kill the man with sword or axe.

The room that awaited them was awash in the glow of the rising sun, the light breaching the room through the open window that stretched from one wall to the other. The ceiling was unusually low for one who enjoyed the grander things in life, though it suited Doran's dwarven sensibilities.

It was immediately obvious that there was no desk but, instead, a number of plush sofas and armchairs in the centre of the room, forming a rough circle. The furniture could only command the dwarf's attention for so long, as he was drawn to both left and right of the wide chamber. To his left, a thick iron door stood ajar, revealing a walk-in alcove of bare shelves, strewn sacks, and small chests left fallen on their sides, bereft of their contents. A vault, Doran mused.

An *empty* vault.

Turning to his right, he was somewhat disturbed by the stone carvings that protruded the entire length of the wall. Painted black to match the rest of the room, every carving was the top half of a man, woman or child, all reaching out towards the centre-most carving with desperate expressions. The figure they reached for with such anguished verve was carved in the likeness of a man, his expression the only one among them that knew peace. The figure held out a single arm, its hand the source that drew the reach of those across the wall.

Doran narrowed his eyes but there was no mistaking the very real coin pinched between those stone fingers. The dwarf had no idea what ugly piece of art he was looking at, but everything about it screamed Viktor Varga.

"The first coin," came a silky voice from nowhere.

Doran pivoted on his heel and raised his sword. Likewise, Asher, Salim, and Danagarr assumed some form of fighting stance, weapons held at the ready. The son of Dorain laid eyes on Darya Siad-Agnasi, though where the Shadow Witch had emerged from was a mystery to him. Her title, he decided, was well earned.

"It was his first coin," she went on, glancing at the coin held on display. "The first he earned, at least."

"Where is he?" Asher demanded, his voice evenly cool yet menacing.

"Gone," the Shadow Witch answered simply.

Danagarr hammered the floor with his hammer. "She's lyin'!"

The ranger eyed the assassin from the south. "No she isn't," he deciphered.

Something about the smith's expression cracked. "No!" he fumed. "He can' be gone!"

"I assure you, master dwarf, he is," the Shadow Witch stated again, moving across the length of the open window like a Wraith, her ornate daggers bathed in the light. They hadn't been in her hands a moment ago, baffling Doran as to when she had retrieved them.

"He fled," Asher concluded, his tone dripping with judgement.

"He has *retreated*," Darya corrected. "He wasn't given much of a choice," she added after the distant roar of some monster. The Shadow Witch came to a sudden stop, her bald head perfectly outlined against the golden sky. "How is it you are still alive?" she asked bluntly.

Asher ignored the question and regarded the plundered vault. "He couldn't have made it out of the city yet. What ship is he taking?"

Doran looked up at the ranger. "What makes ye think he'll leave the city?"

"Because right now," Asher theorised, "the most powerful families on the island will be waking up and wondering why their heads of house have yet to return from Viktor's party. When the truth comes to light—that they were all *butchered*—there will be *chaos*. In-fighting will break out on every corner. *But,*" he emphasised, "all four families will suspect Viktor's hand in it. Then they will come for his head." Asher gestured at the empty vault. "He was going to flee whether his monsters got free or not, wasn't he?"

As the ranger had ignored her question, Darya ignored his. Instead, she tilted her head and scrutinised him all the more. "You should be dead," she told him. "I suppose that can be corrected," she added, looking past the mystery of his healthy appearance with all the practicality of a stone-cold killer.

"Tell me the name of his ship," Asher dictated, "and you can walk away."

"The hells she can!" Danagarr snarled. "She knows abou' me kin! Where we live. She can' be allowed to live!"

The Shadow Witch stepped forward, the light defining the features of her face. "The Stormshield," she purred. "My master would like to make a deal with you, for your silvyr that is."

The smith was rocked back, his face suffused with rage. He looked Asher up and down as if suddenly realising some terrible truth. "Ye don' 'ave it," he muttered. "Ye don' 'ave it!" he repeated, louder this time, eyes shifting left and right. "Varga's got the blade," he reasoned, and ominously so. "Ye dolt!" the dwarf barked at the ranger. "Ye were to keep it safe! Ye were to keep it secret!"

"I didn't exactly hand it over," Asher replied through a clenched jaw.

"Your family's safety will be assured upon the delivery of the silvyr," the Shadow Witch articulated in her southern accent.

Danagarr pointed his hammer at her. "Ye can shut yer mouth

an' all! I've seen the worth o' his word, an' unlike these idiots I'm not so daft as to get into bed with yer so-called *master*! I'm not to be satisfied until he's dead!"

"Then you are not to be satisfied," Darya stated coldly.

Doran could see the smith's aggression rising to foolish heights, but all his years and experience wielding that hammer would be for naught when pitted against the lithe assassin. "What exactly are *ye* doin' here?" he questioned, cutting through the heated exchange. "If yer master's buggerin' off, why aren' ye by his side, eh? I thought he was afraid to go anywhere without ye."

"I am to act as his liaison during the..." Here, Darya trailed off and looked to Asher. "*Chaos*," she intoned, using the ranger's word.

"The League of Silk and Ink," Asher drawled mockingly. "*Liaisons* to the rich and the wretched."

The muscles beneath Darya's expression flickered, ruining her facade of stone. "We act as our clients instruct," she replied, her words clipped.

The ranger smirked. "He's got you on a retainer? That's not an assassin. That's a *bodyguard*. Is The League running out of coin?"

"Bah!" Danagarr spat, his hammer swinging round to shatter an ornamental vase. "I'm done with all yer talk! Ye're to die!" he threatened, directing the head of his weapon at Darya. "An' yer master will follow!" he promised.

"Danagarr, no!" It was all the warning Doran managed before the smith burst into action and charged the Shadow Witch.

Darya struck first, her movements as precise as an attacking snake. Danagarr took her boot to his face and was damn near flipped round onto his front. Before his back had even flattened to the floor, the Shadow Witch was leaping over him, her leg whipping out to catch Salim across the jaw. The Honour Guard, however, was swifter still and bobbed his head to evade the incoming kick. His counterattack would have been savage, the curve of his scimitar splitting the assassin up the torso, but she too was equally swift. Her daggers blocked the edge of his blade before her head snapped across the gap and slammed into the southerner's nose, splattering his blood across the glyphs that adorned her scalp.

Instantly stunned by the blow, Salim was vulnerable to the dagger now being levelled at his face and would have succumbed to its biting tip had Asher not intervened. The ranger flicked his longsword up, forcing the Shadow Witch to abandon her kill and dive away.

While Asher advanced from one side, Doran pressed from the other, rushing to the spot where her dive and roll would come to an end. Axe raised, he had but to drop it and end the witch's life, but somewhere in the middle of her manoeuvre she had seen the dwarf coming and, at the last moment, turned her roll into a sweeping kick that claimed his footing. From his back, he had the good sense to immediately roll to one side and, in doing so, avoid the dagger plunged into the floor where he had landed.

A second and fatal attack was coming for him but it was not to strike true, the blow deflected by his sword. The tip of the dagger came to a stop a mere inch from his throat. With a growl of defiance, Doran swung his axe from his prone position, but the Shadow Witch was too close and he struck with fist alone. Still, a dwarven fist to the ribs was enough to displace even the strongest of foes and Darya was shoved aside.

In a feat of acrobatics, she was quickly returned to her feet and just in time to meet Asher's blade. The ranger had ascended one of the armchairs and pushed his weight forward to knock the chair back, his longsword coming down from on high. It was a heavy attack, forcing Darya to retreat post deflection.

Doran pushed himself up, determined to aid his friend, and saw that Salim and Danagarr were similarly recovering and moving to back up the ranger. It soon became apparent, however, that Asher required no such support from any of them. Both he and Darya had entered into a dance of sorts, their weapons flashing in the light and often moving faster than the eye could reasonably follow. They pivoted around each other, ducked, jumped, and twisted their bodies into unorthodox positions. Theirs was a fury that held the others back, each unsure where they could contribute to the fight.

To the sound of ringing steel they moved across the open window, a pair of silhouettes existing in their own private world, each vying for dominance. There was something about Asher, a reservation, that Doran could see in his attacks. Having witnessed his savagery in the arena, when that demon Doran knew himself all too well had been very much in control, the style he now employed against Darya seemed almost tame, if surgically proficient.

Perhaps, against the odds, the ranger had beaten the demon within.

Perhaps...

For all her skill and prowess, the Shadow Witch was clearly working harder than the trained Arakesh. Doran could see it. She appeared to be working twice as hard and was almost entirely on the defensive, always on the back step. Asher hadn't been trained to give an inch and he certainly wasn't now. This wasn't to be like their first meeting on the deck of The Mer Seed—a surprise attack. No. The ranger saw her coming.

Darya's end seemed all the more assured when one of her fine daggers was knocked from her grasp. She now faced Asher's longsword with a single knife, reducing her options.

So taken by the fight was he, Doran missed Danagarr's aggravated sigh. Nor did he notice the smith raise his hammer until it was already held aloft in both hands. There was no warning the smith this time. The sledgehammer was given short flight and a sudden stop, the head buried deep in the Shadow Witch's skull.

She dropped dead as if her body were made of the very iron that had killed her.

Doran looked from the dead assassin to his fellow dwarf, recalling his words from Velia's docks. The son of Dorain didn't feel like complimenting the smith's throw this time—the desperate fool had dashed their chances.

Asher slowly emerged from the attack he was in the middle of, his shoulders rounding into a defeated hunch and head bowed.

With laboured breath and chest heaving, he stared down at the corpse and said, "I wasn't going to kill her." He turned his head to spy the smith. "She was the only one who knew where to find Viktor."

Danagarr stormed across the room and yanked his sledge-hammer out of the assassin's skull. "He's gone," the dwarf growled, visibly pained by the resignation of it all. "Now me family will never be safe. We'll be livin' in those damned woods for years waitin' for that fiend to die! Ye were supposed to make things right!" he yelled at Doran. "An' *ye*," he fumed, turning on Asher. "I gifted ye the most precious thing a dwarf can give, an' not only did ye lose it, but the man ye lost it to will kill me kin for more o' it!"

"Danagarr," Doran beseeched, but the smith was having none of it.

He waved away the son of Dorain and crouched beside Darya's body. The smith quickly found the Shadow Witch's coin purse and took it for himself. "This should see me off this wretched island," he calculated. "The rest o' ye can rot for all I care!"

"Danagarr," Doran tried again.

"I will make this right," Asher promised, crouching to retrieve one of Darya's blades, though Doran couldn't guess for what purpose.

Danagarr paused as he reached the threshold. "The hells ye will," he retorted. "It's *over*. Viktor gets to live an' me an' mine get to look over our shoulder for the next few decades. Ye failed." The smith sighed. "We all failed."

Doran's heart sank as he watched his old friend walk away. This wasn't how it was supposed to end. And, of course, this had all started because he had got into bed with Viktor Varga in the first place.

"We best go after 'im," the dwarf croaked. "He'll be lucky if he makes out o' here, never mind off the bloody island."

"Agreed," Asher said, though the ranger hesitated to follow as he passed one of the sofas, his attention captured by a pile of books stacked on top of each other. When next he caught up with them, A Chronicle of Monsters was tucked under one arm.

The smith offered no protest when the companions joined him again, and nor did he seem to mind following their direction to find the way out of the arena. There hadn't been many monsters left inside the arena walls, a fact that was already causing great alarm in the streets. All manner of beastly noises rang out across the city and even a growing fire could be seen down the road.

The stoical smith ignored it all and continued his march towards the port, shoving any aside who staggered into him.

"You will return with him to The Black Wood?" Asher enquired of Doran, his tone laden with expectation.

"Aye," Doran replied, keeping an eye on the departing Stormshield. "I'll see them settled as best I can."

"*Can* you get off the island?" Salim posed.

"We'll make the coin stretch," Doran reassured. "What will ye two do?"

"I have no coin to my name," Salim pointed out.

"Nor do they," Asher said, gesturing to the lone side door of the adjacent building, where a one-eyed man, was ushering gladiator after gladiator into the street. He was urging them all to run as fast and far as they could. He caught sight of the three companions after the last of Viktor's prisoners had fled and offered them a simple nod before disappearing down an alley.

Doran raised an eyebrow. "Who were that?"

"Captain Kad Gorson," Salim answered, as if that was an answer.

"The magistri," Asher specified. "I'd say he's earned a second chance, just like the rest of them."

Doran frowned. "Weren' they the worst o' the worst?"

Asher looked up, to where some monster scuttled over the rooftops. "Not anymore." The ranger nodded at Danagarr. "You should go. Make sure he returns safely to his family. *We*," he emphasised, turning to Salim, "will earn the coin we need to put Dragorn behind us."

"We will?" the Honour Guard asked incredulously.

"Ye're stayin'?" Doran checked with the same tone of disbelief.

"There's plenty o' boats that would make use o' two such as yerselves."

"There are monsters to be hunted," Asher began, "and an island full of people who will pay good coin to be rid of them. By the time we're finished, we can buy our *own* boat."

Doran assessed the ranger for an extra second, searching for any sign of the truth lurking beneath his words. The dwarf had a feeling the monster Asher intended to hunt was of a different breed to those who had escaped the arena's dungeons.

Salim was nodding along, a tight smile bringing his lips together. "A ranger," he mused. "At least I will have a good teacher."

Doran let his musings go and gave a short laugh. "Good huntin', lads," he offered, envious even, for his path led to the waves of the ocean and an extremely angry dwarf. "I err... I hope to see ye both again some day. I really do."

Asher planted a hand on the dwarf's pauldron. "I have a feeling I will never escape you, son of Dorain."

The dwarf chortled. "Too bloody right," he uttered.

The three broke apart, Asher and Salim making for the stables while Doran navigated the panicked streets to catch up with Danagarr.

The dwarf paused, turning back to spy the men. They were all departing into uncertain futures, some bleaker than others, but he dared to hope that Asher had finally put the Arakesh in him behind, that the *Assassin* would never leave the wretched island.

He dared to hope.

CHAPTER 40

ONE MORE DEATH

Mergossa *- The trees that eat, my mother called them. There are many myths surrounding the Mergossa, and from many cultures and times, but they all agree that these beasts have a taste for human flesh. Personally, having observed them in the wild, I have seen no such propensity. I have witnessed the devouring of everything from baby rabbits to bears, depending on the size of the Mergossa. I cannot say what power put them on our fair world or how it came to be that they are able to so closely mimic the trees around them, though I would wager there is evil at work within them.*

I also cannot say where the myth came from that Mergossa are static creatures. Perhaps it is because of their likeness to the trees they live between. I can tell you for a fact, my fellow ranger, that Mergossa can move as they like, and swiftly too. I believe, however, that they choose not to move so often because of the great noise they make, their heavy legs thundering into the ground.

A Chronicle of Monsters: A Ranger's Bestiary, 12th Edition, Page 138.

Nathaniel Crawly, Ranger.

. . .

Viktor Varga sat at the head of his dining table as a king might. The open balcony beside him granted the man one of the most spectacular views in all of Tregaran, The Arid Land's most northern territory. A sea of stars hung over the city, a canvas of silent watchers to his lonely meal.

Months had gone by since the collapse of his empire on Dragorn, yet here he sat, popping one baby tomato after another into his mouth. He wiped the juices from his chin and let his hands dance across the buffet laid out before him. He enjoyed a handful of grapes and sampled two different kinds of hummus, each with a piece of flat bread.

The world he had built was in ruins behind him but, by the easy smile he wore, it was most definitely *behind him*. How easy it had been to relocate to the south and start again. The wealth he had amassed bought him security and his earlier years in the desert lands afforded him a network of waiting allies and business opportunities.

And now, after changing his name and rewriting his history, even the enemies he had left on Dragorn could not find him. The Arakesh, of course, would come for him eventually, forcing him to call upon more than a degree of cunning to stay a step ahead. Still, he had survived longer than most who found themselves a target of Nightfall.

Viktor tapped his cup twice against the table, indicating his need of more wine. "And I'll take the chicken now," he called over his shoulder, one finger tracing the fine scar that ran up his right cheek.

An oval dish, covered by a rounded lid, was placed in front of the crime lord and he rubbed his hands together. "And the wine," he reminded irritably.

The servant said not a word but removed the lid and stepped back. Viktor looked down expectantly, his mouth naturally curling into his telltale smile of anticipation. It never quite formed, however, but slipped from his face, dragging his expression down into wild shock.

Much like the final expression on Malak's severed head.

His heart racing and sweat soaked with fear, Varga slowly turned his head and looked up at his servant, only it wasn't his servant who looked back.

The *Assassin* plunged Darya Siad-Agnasi's blade down through the back of the man's hand and into the table, pinning the limb in place.

Viktor wailed and rocked back in his high chair, his blood spilling across the table. A spasm of pain wracked his features and flushed his face an angry pink.

Asher couldn't have asked for a more satisfying feeling.

Moving round to perch against the head of the table, beside Viktor, the *Assassin* removed his blindfold so that he might take in the view with his eyes. There he looked upon the man who had named himself master, the man who had caged him and used him. The man who had threatened the life of a child and her family. Asher seethed at the thought of it all.

For any other in his position, they would have been described as seeing red, their vision obscured by a haze of vengeance and wrath. This is not so for an Arakesh. That kind of primal rage has no place. Rather, they see black, a shapeless void of untold depths. It robs them of feeling, morality, and, of course, their humanity. Only the predator remains. Always hunting. Always hungry.

"You left this," he said gruffly, tossing the crime lord's first-earned coin into the pool of blood before him. He then tossed a wand onto the table. "And there will be no mage coming to your aid this evening," he added ominously. Reaching over the table, he picked up his silvyr short-sword, the blade concealed within its scabbard. "This is mine."

Teeth clenched and eyes watering with agony, Viktor looked from the coin to the Shadow Witch's dagger and finally back to his henchman's decapitated head.

"He didn't die well," Asher informed him, putting the silvyr blade to one side.

He relished in the memory of the kill. He had approached Malak from behind and purposefully on the man's left, where his hip bone had been damaged years earlier. The *Assassin* could have murdered the fool before he even knew what was happening, but he had wanted Malak to know his end was upon him and who it was that delivered the final blow. So when Viktor's chief thug turned to confront the predator creeping up on him, his old injury slowed his movement and gave Asher all the time he needed to dominate his foe.

"Neither did the other fourteen men you hired to guard you here," he added, noting only then that his black leathers and even his face were splattered with so much blood. Picking off the guards one by one had been exhilarating, a feast for the *Assassin*.

"You left quite the mess in Dragorn," Asher went on, enjoying the moment he had been working towards for the better part of ten months.

Just the thought of so much time led his memories to the dozens he had threatened, maimed, and killed to find the crime lord. How many times had he left Salim asleep to take to the night and hunt down any and all who whispered of Viktor Varga's whereabouts? How much blood had he spilled even before reaching Tregaran?

"The ruling families are still in open war," he explained. "The only thing they all have in common now is their desire to hold you in their grasp. To trap you like that Radonian Red-back," he described, recalling the spider Viktor had caged beneath his glass. "The things they would do to you," he mused, watching the man squirm. "They believe you responsible for the deaths of their family members. I suppose, in a way, you are." Asher let his hand fall on the pommel of Darya's dagger, sending a new ripple of pain through the crime lord.

When his scream died away, the *Assassin* narrowed his eyes on the man. "No target has taken me so long to hunt down before. I applaud your efforts. But it gave me time to think about this moment. For a long time I considered dragging you back to Dragorn and handing you over to the Trigorns. Let their hound,

Lucas Farney, carve you up before the end." Asher took a breath. "One less death on my hands, I thought." He gave a silent laugh. "As if such a thing would ease my conscience. As if one less death even matters anymore."

The *Assassin* beheld his prey and fell deeper into that shapeless void. It swallowed him whole and drove him to action. His name managed to escape Viktor's lips before Asher closed his hand around the man's throat and forced him backwards.

"You've already said your last words," he seethed.

The chair toppled over with its occupant and the crime lord's hand was sliced open when Darya's blade refused to budge. He tried to scream again but the impact, combined with Asher's vice-like grip, robbed him of speech.

Crouched by his victim's side, the *Assassin* kneeled over one arm, pinning it down, and took whatever punishment Viktor could dole out with his other. His clumsy attacks only got worse as his air supply dwindled. His legs thrashed and kicked out against the underside of the table, but it was all for naught.

Giving in to that abyss that had opened up within him, Asher relaxed his grip just enough to allow Viktor a lung full of air, prolonging the kill. Then he squeezed again. Tighter and tighter. Varga's eyes bulged and the small vessels burst, staining them red.

"You should have taken the deal," he told him, thinking back to the original terms he and Doran had brought to the crime lord. But greed had corrupted Viktor Varga as entirely as the *Assassin* now corrupted Asher. Slaves to their conditioning, they were both no better than animals that lived by instinct alone.

Asher was fine with that.

He maintained eye-contact, watching for that final moment. And, inevitably, the moment did arrive. Viktor's thrashing and protests came to a dying stop. His eyes remained open, lifeless. He belonged to Death now.

Asher took the breath that Viktor could not and stood up, bringing the chair and the body with him. Still seated, Varga's corpse flopped over the table, knocking Malak's head aside.

He looked down at his victim, his face lying in the blood, eyes forever fixed on that single coin that sat as an island in a sea of red. There might have been some poetry in that, but the *Assassin* never mused over such things. The deed was done.

Time to move on.

CHAPTER 41
A PROMISE KEPT

Triffid - A four-winged bat would be a better name for these creatures, but I suppose it doesn't roll off the tongue quite so well. Still, there is no better description for these flying monsters. Worse still, they are equal in size to a fully-grown hound and perfectly capable of lifting a man from the ground. What happens to the man thereafter I leave to your imagination, dear ranger, but rest assured, it does not end well. These nocturnal hunters can be found in deep caves (see A Charter of Monsters, Page 110, for known locations), though be warned, their colonies number in the hundreds. I say this so you do not take the contract lightly. A monster hunter you may be, but some jobs are simply beyond the skills of an individual or even a group. Should a colony of Triffids pose a real threat, escalate the job to whomever rules over the threatened. You're going to need an army.

A Chronicle of Monsters: A Ranger's Bestiary, 12th Edition,
Page 439.

Hadrian Bossem, Ranger.

Asher's boots crunched through the snows of the north. How he had welcomed the cold air when first it had washed over him. Dragorn's summer had been a relentless heat and moving on to The Arid Lands, where winter hardly touched, had offered no reprieve. But north of The Vrost Mountains there was naught but snow and ice.

For near on a week he had traversed beyond the city of Darkwell and adopted the frigid air as an old friend. Now, having skirted around the town of Dunwich and put its great lake, The Old Well, behind him, the ranger looked upon The Black Wood.

He gave the trees very little of his attention, for it was the ground that demanded he crouch to better examine it. With one hand still gripped to Hector's reins, he ran his other hand over the deep impression left in the snow. There were more, all leading away from the town and into the forest.

The footprints were short and wide, but just as deep as any grown man's. A dwarf then, he reasoned. "Come on, Hector," he bade, pulling the horse along.

Together, they pressed on, pushing through the trees and into the thick of the forest. The tracks disappeared here and there, where the owner of the prints had deliberately climbed over a series of rocks. It didn't take much work, however, to find them again and continue the hunt. In one patch, where the tracks had disappeared, Asher discovered a fine branch hanging by a single strand where someone had clearly snapped it on their way past. Then there was the black thread blowing in the breeze from where it had snagged a bush.

Asher soon came to conclude that he wasn't following in the wake of just any dwarf, but, in fact, a Heavybelly dwarf. He was surprised to find a smile flash across his features.

"We're getting close," he told the horse, detecting the scent of dwarven cooking on the air.

Proving himself correct, he caught sight of smoke between the trees, rising high into the pale sky. He soon laid eyes on a camp of sorts, with great canvases stretching from trunk to trunk and different stations beneath that clearly functioned as various living areas. In the centre of it all was a fire and a spit-roast slowly cooking above the flames. As quaint as it was, the camp was no replacement for a real home.

Snuffling through the snow, Pig walked into view and boisterously shoved the family's donkey aside so it might scour more ground. How suited to its owner the animal was.

"Asher!" His name had come from a young voice, turning the ranger to one Deadora Stormshield. His smile returned.

The girl bounded over and crashed into his legs. He possessed no natural instincts for the situation and so he ruffled her hair affectionately. "It's good to see you," he said, the girl having no idea how true that was.

"Dee!" her father growled, before emerging from the main tent, hammer in hand. Asher couldn't help but notice the iron head had been cleaned of Darya's blood.

Moving past the image, the ranger greeted the smith. "Well met."

Danagarr slowly lowered his weapon and took a breath. "Well met," he echoed, his expression and tone full of regret. "I didn' think we'd be seein' *ye* again."

Before Asher could respond, Kilda and Doran appeared from the other side of the clearing. "What are *ye* doin' here?" the son of Dorain yelled cheerily.

Kilda whipped out a hand and struck the dwarf across the chest. "That's not how ye greet me guests," she chastised.

"Guests?" Doran repeated, rubbing his chest. "We're in the woods!"

Kilda just shook her head and met Asher with a tight embrace. "Ye are a welcome sight," she told him.

"Aye," Danagarr agreed, leaning his hammer against a post. "Though, if I could ask, how *did* ye come to find us?"

"Even the blind could track Doran Heavybelly," Asher quipped.

The smith scowled at the son of Dorain and immediately threw a wet cloth at him. "Ye dolt! Ye weren' to leave any tracks!"

Doran caught the cloth as it struck his shoulder, soaking his shirt. He rolled his eyes and sighed before finally settling on the ranger again. "Please tell me ye've come because ye need me help killin' somethin'."

Asher stifled his amusement and stepped towards Danagarr, leaving Hector where he stood. "I've come because I've already killed something," he replied cryptically. In his hands he presented the smith with a bundle of navy cloth.

"What's this?" he asked, accepting it from the ranger.

Without a word from Asher, Danagarr unravelled the cloth to find an ornate dagger bejewelled with rubies. It was not the red of those precious stones, however, that captivated the dwarf, but the red of the blade.

Danagarr looked up at the ranger. "Is this what I think it is?"

"I don' understand," Kilda confessed, joining her husband's side.

"Tell me it's true," Danagarr implored.

"Viktor Varga is dead," Asher confirmed, living through another moment he had long envisioned. "So too are those closest to him who knew of you and the silvyr. There remain none to threaten you."

The smith's eyes glistened. "Truly?"

"You're safe now," the ranger reassured. "You can go home."

Again, Kilda wrapped her arms around Asher and squeezed hard. Danagarr quickly added his considerable strength to the embrace, a signal to Deadora that she should join them. Soon, the ranger was engulfed by the Stormshield family.

When, at last, he was freed from their affection and gratitude, Asher had one more thing to present to the smith. Danagarr looked from the ranger's blue eyes to the silvyr short-sword resting in his hands.

"Ye got it back," he declared proudly. "What're ye givin' it to me for?"

"I am returning it," Asher said simply. "I do not deserve so fine a weapon. It belongs with its people."

The smith pushed the edge of the scabbard back, not accepting it. "I made it for *ye*, laddy. I presented it to *ye*. I have no claim to it now an' nor do I wish to make one. It's yers."

Asher hadn't expected that, not after the smith's outburst in Viktor's office. He stood a little straighter and looked down at the blade, unsure how to proceed.

"I'm sorry abou' what I said," Danagarr began. "I was... well, frightened for me family. I should never have taken it out on ye. Ye've done nothin' but help me an' mine since we met. An' now ye've come to me with this," he added, lifting up Darya's bloodied knife. "I don' know what ye had to do to see this done, or what sacrifices ye might 'ave made to keep yer promise, but ye've saved us again. I will call ye friend to the end o' me days."

Asher was honoured in a way he could never have imagined. He held the silvyr blade by his side and offered a short bow of the head. "I would like that," he admitted, if quietly.

"Ha!" Danagarr cheered, landing a heavy pat against the ranger's arm. "It's damned good to be seein' ye again!"

Asher responded with a tight smile. "And all of you." He took a steadying breath. "Until the next time," he added, turning to leave.

"Where do ye think ye're goin'?" Kilda shot, halting the ranger in his tracks.

"I would take my leave," he replied.

"Nonsense!" she cried. "Ye'll camp with us for the night ye will. I'll rustle us up somethin' hot. We can *all* think abou' leavin' tomorrow."

Asher was torn by the invitation. He could still feel the *Assassin* residing beneath the surface, reminding him of the trail of blood he had created from Dragorn to Tregaran. It felt wrong to be around so loving a family, he who held a monster within. But the Stormshields were like a warmth he could not deny, a fire that pulled him in from the cold.

"Thank you," he managed, turning back to the camp.

The family blurred into motion, making preparations as they would. Off to the side, where Doran had remained, the dwarf chuckled to himself. "It's not that easy to escape is it?" he muttered, walking away from the camp and with Asher in tow.

When they were a little way from the others, Doran turned to him. "I'm damned happy to see ye, lad. One more week here an' I would have lost me mind." He bobbed his head to make certain he wasn't being overheard. "I love 'em like family but they drive me nuts."

Now it was Asher's turn to chuckle, and with it he felt more the man he desired to be. Perhaps, he considered for the first time, the company he kept was the sustenance the *Ranger* required. It seemed outlandish to one who had operated his entire life in the manner of a lone wolf, but he couldn't deny the feelings that stirred in him.

"So ye did it then," Doran continued, his eyes finding the red blindfold on Asher's belt. "Ye actually killed the bugger."

"It took longer than I had hoped," Asher said. "He was better at covering his tracks than *you*."

Doran looked away and resisted the obvious urge to roll his eyes again. "What of Salim?" he asked.

"We parted ways in Velia. He was to make his way to Vangarth, where he had heard rumour of unnatural deaths. From the description I would guess it to be a Jaxyl. Nothing Salim couldn't handle."

Doran was nodding along, his thoughts clearly one step ahead of their conversation. "Maybe we could journey back to Darkwell with this lot," he suggested. "See if there's any beasties that might require say... a *couple* o' rangers."

Asher folded his arms and looked upon the dwarf with a smug grin. "A couple of rangers? Such as me and..."

Doran shrugged. "Ye an' me," he said innocently enough.

"I thought you were a *monster hunter*."

"Aye, well, *ranger's* got a nice ring to it. So, what do ye think?"

Asher thought of the *Assassin* and its recent victory in Tregaran. It felt now like he had taken two steps forward and one step back, giving Nasta Nal-Aket's monster precious ground in the silent war that raged in his soul. It was just so easy to be the predator, a killer of men. If the *Ranger* was to win out he needed to continue moulding that aspect of his life. It seemed clear now that he could not do such a thing on his own, painful as that thought was.

"I think we could make some good coin," he finally answered, his throat catching.

Doran didn't make a big deal of his response but he appeared somewhat elated. "Good," he said. "The bigger the better, eh? I could do with choppin' down some fiend o' a monster. Anythin' but more blasted fire wood."

Asher was happy to be led towards the fire, where he took a small log for a seat and accepted the drink Deadora brought to him. Before long, all four dwarves were positioned around the fire with the ranger, drinking and laughing. Stubborn as he was, Asher couldn't help but be swept up in their ways. It was like coming up for air.

Absorbing it all, his very soul soaking up the atmosphere of family and companionship, the ranger looked into the flames before him. If only he could toss the monster inside of him into those flames and be done with it. Perhaps then he wouldn't feel the fraud among those who were the salt of the earth.

As it was, the *Assassin* still held a claim on him. Worse still, he wasn't sure he was ready to give it up either.

For now, though, he would take what he could from such good company. And so he enjoyed the drink and the food that followed. After all, there would always be tomorrow to renew the battle.

Always tomorrow...

The morrow would have to wait, the ranger awoken in the dead of night by the tormenting sounds and images of his deeds. Sitting up, his face dripping with sweat, Asher's blankets and cloak fell away and he turned to regard Doran. The dwarf was snoring only a few feet away beneath the same stretch of canvas.

Asher released a long breath, filling the air with hot vapour.

How could sleep feel like fighting? His heart thundered within his chest. All of his instincts were on edge. Without conscious thought, his hand had reached out and grasped the hilt of his silvyr blade. His rational mind knew there was no threat, yet his fingers refused to part with the weapon.

Closing his eyes, it all came back to him as it had in his dreams. He was moving through Viktor's Tregaran compound again, slipping from shadow to shadow, opening arteries as he went. He could see them all, every face expressing its last emotion before he opened them up. Their gasps of shock and pain rang in his ears.

They were wicked men all, rotten to their cores. Asher felt nothing for the lives he had extinguished that night, least of all Viktor Varga's. The true weight that pressed upon him was something else, something deeper that came from the root of him.

He had loved every second of it.

The very feel of taking a life was intoxicating. It made him feel superior, invincible even. There was nothing comparable to being an apex predator. Even so far removed from the event itself he could still smell the blood, taste it. Worse, he craved it still.

Ahead of the ranger, the Stormshields' tent flapped in the wind, taking his mind to the family of three. This wasn't where he belonged. That thought was as pure as the light snow that sprinkled down across the clearing. They were good people. They should not have his ilk casting a shadow over them. No one should.

Before he knew it, Asher was on his feet, cloak draped over his leather pauldrons, and gear strapped to Hector's saddle again. The horse had roused with relatively little noise, though the sound of its hooves cut sharply through the night.

He regarded the longsword nestled between the saddle and a rolled-up blanket. It was too long, he decided, having held on to it since Dragorn. It would have to be replaced and sooner rather than later. Had he not the urge to depart, the ranger would have likely engaged Danagarr to forge him a new two-handed broadsword, for he knew of no better smith. But he would do without, just as he would do his best to steer clear of their lives. They didn't need a killer hanging around.

His hands braced on the mount, Asher prepared to climb up and take his leave. It was the movement in the corner of his eye that stopped him, turning him back to where he had been sleeping. Doran walked out from under the canvas, his blond beard quickly brimming with snowflakes.

"Ye're off then," he assumed, and quietly so. "I had a feelin' ye might."

Asher stepped away from his horse and faced the son of Dorain. "They are good people," he began, gesturing to the tent. "They deserve better company."

Doran shrugged. "What are ye abou'? They're good people, aye, but so are ye, laddy."

"I am not their people," Asher told him.

"O' course ye're their people," he declared boldly. "We've all walked away from them that made us what we are. Us exiles 'ave got to stick together, eh?"

Asher was shaking his head. "I can't... I just can't, Doran. I'm not... *whole*. I'm not *good*. I'm not good for *them*."

The dwarf sighed and looked pointedly at the strip of red cloth hanging from the ranger's belt. "We've all got our demons, Asher."

"Mine aren't always on the inside," he replied, almost exhausted by the truth of it. "Better if I keep moving."

Doran nodded in the absence of a reply. "I'm not to change yer mind?" he posed, hopefully.

Asher answered by mounting his horse. "See them home," he said, looking down at the dwarf.

"An' what are ye to do then?"

The ranger considered the question, his gaze roaming the trees ahead. "Find monster. Kill monster. Move on."

Doran's bushy eyebrows rocked up as he absorbed the simple answer. "Take me word for it, Asher," he replied, his tone grave, "that won't banish yer demons; it jus' keeps 'em a step behind ye."

"It's the only path I have," Asher responded, and honestly so. With that he spurred Hector towards the break in the trees and the world beyond.

"Oh, I'll be seein' ye on that path," Doran called lightly after him. "Don' ye worry, ranger man. I'll be seein' ye again..."

PHILIP C. QUAINTRELL

Hear more from Philip C. Quaintrell including
book releases and exclusive content:

PHILIPCQUAINTRELL.COM

FACEBOOK.COM/PHILIPCQUAINTRELL

@PHILIPCQUAINTRELL.AUTHOR

@PCQUAINTRELL

ABOUT THE AUTHOR

Philip C. Quaintrell is the author of the epic fantasy series, The Echoes Saga, as well as the Terran Cycle sci-fi series. He was born in Cheshire in 1989 and started his career as an emergency nurse.

Having always been a fan of fantasy and sci-fi fiction, Philip started to find himself feeling frustrated as he read books, wanting to delve into the writing himself to tweak characters and story-lines. He decided to write his first novel as a hobby to escape from nursing and found himself swept away into the world he'd created. Even now, he talks about how the characters tell him what they're going to do next, rather than the other way around.

With his first book written, and a good few rejected agency submissions under his belt, he decided to throw himself in at the deep end and self-publish. 2 months and £60 worth of sales in, he took his wife out to dinner to celebrate an achievement ticked off his bucket list - blissfully unaware this was just the beginning.

Fast forward 12 months and he was self-publishing book 1 of his fantasy series (The Echoes Saga; written purely as a means to combat his sci-fi writers' block). With no discernible marketing except the 'Amazon algorithm', the book was in the amazon bestsellers list in at least 4 countries within a month. The Echoes Saga has now surpassed 700k copies sold worldwide, has an option agreement for a potential TV-series in the pipeline and Amazon now puts Philip's sales figures in the top 1.8% of self-published authors worldwide.

Philip lives in Cheshire, England with his wife and two children. He still finds time between naps and wiping snot off his clothes to remain a movie aficionado and comic book connoisseur, and is hoping this is still just the beginning.

AUTHOR NOTES

Welcome to the waffling stage of the book! If you've made it this far I hope you enjoyed the second book in Asher's trilogy.

For me, it has been something of an emotional ride as Asher takes his next step on a journey that is, ultimately, preparing him for an epic destiny.

But here we find him, before The Echoes Saga, and he's a man who doesn't know who he is. Or what he is. I knew I wanted to continue exploring the idea of trust, otherwise he would never be the man we meet in Rise of the Ranger, but out of that came a whole new side of him that needed dealing with.

The *Assassin*.

This trilogy takes place only a few years after his last mission as an Arakesh, a time in his life where he could easily be identified as a stone-cold killer. It felt important to me that we explore that side of him as it would be very hard to simply drop that aspect of his life.

So, for me, Blood and Coin was more about taking Asher through a time in his life where he was not only forced to face his demons, but also embrace them to survive. This internal war between *Assassin* and *Ranger* is the main story of the entire trilogy

—how could it not be? The thought that Asher could just stop being an Arakesh overnight is absurd.

With both aspects of his personality in mind, I had to consider the needs of both. What fuelled them? What did they each desire? What triggers opened the door for them to assume control over Asher's way of thinking?

These questions were easily answered when surrounded by characters like Doran, Salim, and the Stormshields. They feed the *Ranger*, informing Asher that he needs good people to mirror, to remind him the world and its inhabitants are worth something. In this vein, his humanity is allowed to grow and explore avenues that were shunned by Nightfall.

Perhaps the greatest of all things then is *trust*. Without trust he would remain forever a pillar of solitude, growing no further than a man with a guilty conscience. But how does an Arakesh come to trust anyone?

Enter the dwarf...

Like Asher, Doran is someone who defines himself through action over words. It seemed natural then that Asher would respect this response more than anything else. Doran's return to save him, therefore, was the greatest example of trust to Asher. The same could also be said of Doran, who had come to expect nothing but disdain from humans. In this, they are kindred, a bond neither could ignore.

On the other side of Doran—a dwarf of action—was Salim, a man of words and emotions. I never planned on bringing Salim into the trilogy, but my writing is organic and, well, he just kind of appeared, so I went with it.

His presence, however, proved fruitful for Asher, who had yet to meet anyone else who had attempted suicide. As a nurse, I have looked after people who have attempted and, unfortunately, succeeded in suicide. It's something I take seriously and write delicately. With that on my mind, I wanted to revisit it with Asher, as his suicide attempt would have been a monumental moment in his life and he hasn't had the opportunity to talk about it.

Salim's own attempts at suicide felt natural given his situation

—a situation further explored in The Echoes Saga. I know from experience that talking to someone about something changes the way your brain interprets that thing, rather than always internalising it. So bringing these two men together over their shared experience was an opportunity I couldn't miss.

My hope is that you can see the growth in Asher, if not both men, from the book itself.

The Stormshields provided the perfect example of family, the one thing Asher knows he will never have. As an Arakesh, it was something he knew he was never permitted to have. And so, meeting this wholesome family, and in need of him no less, left a strong impression on the *Ranger*. They are the perfect example of why he does what he does.

They also provide a tether to something he can't have. I like to think of them as his first experience of family, setting him up for meeting the likes of Faylen, Nathaniel and Reyna in The Echoes Saga.

On the other side of this war, the *Assassin* was also being fuelled by characters surrounding Asher. I very much enjoyed writing Viktor Varga. I had wanted to delve into the crime guilds more, but Viktor was an opportunity all of his own, having direct ties not only to Nightfall but Asher himself.

Ultimately, his part in the story itself is inconsequential. It's the lasting effect he has on Asher that truly means something. After four years, the *Ranger* was winning and, there was even a chance Asher would have emerged a free man from Viktor's clutches with that virtuous part of his life intact. But his determination to track the crime lord down and assassinate him was two steps back for Asher. Because of Viktor, Asher finishes the book in turmoil, with the *Assassin* closer to the surface than ever before. This will be a thread that continues into A Dance of Fang and Claw...

Speaking of which, I have already made a start on book 3 and I'm loving it! It's less grounded, geographically speaking, taking Asher back to his adventurous roots. And he's not alone. For those who have read The Echoes Saga, you might recall a certain pick-axe wielding character.

As always, I like to be relatively transparent with you all. After this trilogy is completed later this year, I will begin writing the next EPIC saga and, yes, it is set in Verda! I've been planning the next saga since before I finished writing A Clash of Fates, so it's been in the works for a while and I'm very excited to begin a new sweeping story, and in Verda's most ancient past too! I will reveal the new saga title soon enough.

So, I hope you've enjoyed your time in Verda again, and your spiralling trip down the rabbit hole of Asher's fractured mind. If you could spare the time, I would always appreciate any review you might leave on Amazon etc. As a self-publisher, it's your love of these books and this world that helps spread the word.

You can also reach out to me via my website or social media pages. I try my best to respond to everyone.

Until the next time...

APPENDICES

<u>Kingdoms of Illian:</u>

1. ***Alborn*** (eastern region) - Ruled by King Rengar of house Marek. Capital city: *Velia*. Other Towns and Cities: Palios, Galosha, and Barossh.

2. ***The Arid Lands*** (southern region) - Ruled by Emperor Faros. Capital city: *Karath*. Other Towns and Cities: Ameeraska, Calmardra and Tregaran.

3. ***The Ice Vales*** (western region) - Ruled by King Gregorn of house Orvish. Capital city: *Grey Stone*. Other Towns and Cities: Bleak, Kelp Town and Snowfell.

4. ***Orith*** (northern region) - Ruled by King Merkaris of house Tion. Capital city: *Namdhor*. Other Towns and Cities: Skystead, Dunwich, Darkwell and Longdale.

5. *Felgarn* (central region) - Ruled by King Uthain of house Harg. Capital city: *Lirian*. Other Towns and Cities: Vangarth, Wood Vale and Whistle Town.

6. *Dragorn* (island nation off The Shining Coast to the east) - Ruled by the four crime families; the Trigorns, Fenrigs, Yarls, and the Danathors.

~

<u>Dwarven Hierarchy:</u>

1. *Battleborns* - Ruled by King Uthrad, son of Koddun. Domain: *Silvyr Hall*.

2. *Stormshields* - Ruled by King Gandalir, son of Bairn. Domain: *Hyndaern*.

3. *Heavybellys* - Ruled by King Dorain, son of Dorryn. Domain: *Grimwhal*.

4. *Hammerkegs* - Ruled by King Torgan, son of Dorald. Domain: *Nimduhn*.

5. *Goldhorns* - Ruled by King Thedomir, son of Thaldurum. Domain: *Khaldarim*.

6. *Brightbeards* - Ruled by King Gaerhard, son of Hermon. Domain: *Bhan Doral*.

~

<u>Significant Wars: Chronologically:</u>

The Great War - Fought during the First Age, around 5,000 years ago. The only recorded time in history that elves and dwarves have united. They fought against the orcs with the help of the Dragorn, the first elvish dragon riders. This war ended the First age.

The Dark War - Fought during the Second Age, around 1,000 years ago. Considered the elvish civil war. Valanis, the dark elf, tried to take over Illian in the name of the gods. This war ended the Second Age.

The Dragon War - Fought in the beginning of the Third Age, only a few years after The Dark War. The surviving elves left Illian for Ayda's shores, fleeing any more violence. Having emerged from The Wild Moores, the humans, under King Gal Tion's rule, went to war with the dragons over their treasure. This saw the exile of the surviving dragons and the beginning of human dominance over Illian.

~

<u>The Gods:</u>
    Atilan - King of the Gods
    Paldora - Goddess of the Stars
    Krayt - God of War
    Naius - God of Magic
    Ymir - God of the Harvest
    Zephia - Goddess of Music
    Sebela - Goddess of Marriage
    Ibilis - God of Shadows
    Athar - God of Agriculture
    Mydowna - Goddess of Night and Day
    Farg - God of Blacksmiths
    Balgora - Goddess of the Afterlife
    Atarae - Goddess of Destiny
    Oemis - God of the Sea
    Fimira - Goddess of Wisdom
    Ikaldir - God of the Hunt
    Nyx - Goddess of Life and Death

Nalmiron - God of Thunder
Lethia - Goddess of fortune
Vidilis - God of Dreams

A Chronicle of Monsters: A Ranger's Bestiary 12th Edition:

Skalagat - A mistake of nature to be sure. These monsters are often referred to as forest knights or knights of the wood. They are not so noble as knights, however.

Their black hides produce a sticky substance that binds whatever they can find to their bodies. Most commonly, they are found to be using bark from the trees, lending their exterior a look something akin to a suit of armour - hence the reference to knights.

It should be noted that Skalagats will use anything they can find, not just parts of the forest. They have been seen to wear the skulls of their victims like masks or even utilise the claws of other animals.

If you can get close enough to bring your sword to bear, they are vulnerable between these makeshift plates of armour. Getting close can be difficult though. Fully grown Skalagats can reach twenty feet in height, a fact that allows them to blend in with the trees.

Margotta Elysabef, Ranger.

Spider - If you can squash it with your boot, it's not the breed of Spider I'm writing about.

There are parts of the world where Spiders grow and grow until they could stand side by side with a horse (see A Charter of Monsters, Page 22, for known locations).

If possible, bring a mage into the contract; they're worth their weight in coins when it comes to Spiders. You see, Spiders hate the light, despise it. Now don't be thinking you can just take a torch into a nest - you're going to need a weapon in both hands. A mage can bring light to the hunt and it could mean the difference between life and death.

Your next advantage will be to keep moving. If you remain in one spot, which will be tempting when faced by waves of the fiends, you will be overwhelmed. See below for extensive list of strengths and weaknesses.

The knight with no name, Ranger.

Lech _- To the common folk, these monsters are known as Mudslugs. It's an apt description, though Lech are closer in size to a large dog. Typically found in bogs and marshes due to their preference for wet environments. If you can't see through the water and it's past your knees, take a care. The bite on these beasts is almost as painful as it is strong. Once they've got you in their maw, you're going to need fire to make their fangs retract._
Thankfully, they're easy to kill. They have no outer shell or any natural protection beside their ability to blend in with their surroundings. They don't taste too bad either.

Dane, son of Heslin, Ranger.

Stravakin _- So wicked and foul a creature could only have been born of nightmares I tell you. Bone eaters our ancestors called them and rightly so. The first one I came across had left a bear carcass in its wake. Can you imagine finding a dead bear with all but its bones? A more unnatural thing I never saw._
The bite on these beasts is next to none, their jaws capable of reducing bones to splinters. And, as large as their pointed maw might be, don't bother attacking it - those jaws will blunt your blade. Fire is your best bet. Set your trap and make certain you've plenty of oil about it. Don't hang about to watch it burn, mind you. Something in its gut gives off poisonous fumes when put to fire. Those fumes, however, are the perfect lure for the mate, and Stravakin always have a mate they're paired with until death.

Welek Tysarion, Ranger.

Basilisk _- These are likely to be among my last words, certainly my last written words. I have recently returned to Lirian after taking a contract in Longdale._
It's a miracle of the gods that I made it back. I slew the Basilisk plaguing the outer villages, but not before it sank its fangs into my arm. There is

no cure for their venom save for a touch of magic perhaps. A simple ranger, I possess no such talents.

I was able to make a small amount of Selvin paste (see Nature's Secrets, A Ranger's Companion, Page 88) with local resources. This helped with the pain and slowed down the deadly venom.

Now for what might help you. I found that luring the Basilisk was made all the easier using a blend of Gorsk oil and sheep fat. If you can also get your hands on a vial of Weet Green, add this to the bait. It will make the monster gag until it spills the contents of its stomach. This will be your moment to—

Amaya Hawkyns, Ranger.

Scudder - *Just because you've killed yourself a Lech or two, don't be thinking you can tackle a Scudder. These beasts are faster and far more aggressive than Mudslugs.*

And when I say fast, I don't just mean in the water - they're equally fast out of it. And when I say they, I do mean they. *These buggers do naught but eat and breed, increasing the size of their nest as they go.*

Thankfully, they're prey to a number of other monsters who help to keep their numbers down, but should they encroach on civilisation, they need rooting out as soon as possible.

There's always a female at the heart of the nest and she's the one you want if you're to put a stop to the nightmare. She's no fiercer than the males, though she is somewhat larger.

Now, there's nothing special required to kill the wretches. You just need something sharp and a strong swing behind it. (Read on for known sources of natural bait).

Handor Grain, Ranger.

Werewolf - *'Tis a curse, simply put. How this began is up for much debate, though talking about it makes little difference. Werewolves are real and they are among us.*

Contracts concerning these beasts should be left to the most experienced of our kind. I don't just say that because these beasts are seven feet tall with claws as long as your fingers. I urge the young among our ranks to leave these contracts because a wise ranger knows you don't hunt the wolf. You hunt the poor soul who received the cursed bite. They're stronger than the average person but they're weaker in their human form. Still, it's going to feel like killing a person. A deed like that will weigh on a good man.

Oh, and don't stock up on silver, it's a myth most likely started by a werewolf. You can kill it the same way you kill anything - with a good swing of steel.

Arnathor (the old hunter), Ranger.

Dragons *- The addition of this creature is a point of contention among my fellow rangers and for more than one reason at that.*

Firstly, no one has seen a dragon since the time of the elves, a thousand years ago. Some say they're extinct, others say they migrated to lands unknown. The truth is beyond this humble ranger.

Secondly, what legends there are speak of intelligent creatures of innate wisdom. Of course, we're still talking about an animal that has the power to level cities and torch entire forests.

Should you meet one, as unlikely as that is, pray to the gods that your death is swift and worthy of history's note.

** I would also add that more than one report has come from The Shining Coast in years of late. Rumour has it the mages of Korkanath have one under their spell, a pet of some sort perhaps.*

Fenrid Arlvark, Ranger.

Golem *- The first thing to know about these brutes is that they aren't natural. Golem aren't born, they're made out of pieces of the dead. Make no mistake, this is dark magic, necromancy work, crude as it may be.*

The most important thing to keep in mind is that they cannot be killed. Burn them, break them, cut them into bits - nothing stops them except a command from their maker.

That leads me to my next point, so be sure to read it twice. You're looking for people, not the Golem itself. Be it a mage, wizard, witch - whatever you want to call them. They're the key. You either trap the monster in something it can never get out of (good luck with that) or you convince the wretch who brought it into the world to stop it.

But be warned; a Golem will protect its master, and most Golems can rip a man in half with their bare hands. Trust me, I've seen it.

Hamish Lancet, Ranger.

Troll - *There exist variants of this creature, both big and enormous (read on for the breakdown of all types). They are brutes all and of limited intellect at that.*

Solitary beasts, they are rarely found in any numbers, though, be aware, their breeding season runs through winter. These areas can be found by following the sounds of recurring landslides.

Weak spots for most variants include the face, in particular their large eyes, and their softer midriff. I would advise using a surprise attack and with a spear, utilising the distance of such a weapon. If possible, coat the tip in Oylish poison (see A Ranger's Guide to Alchemy, Page 97) so that you might slow the Troll down first.

Gallad Corsair, Ranger.

Mer-folk - *The darkest depths of The Adean are said to be home to numerous creatures of intelligence, some even equal to our own (though that's entirely debatable), but it is those who dwell closer to our shores that move my quill this day. They be real monsters.*

Depending on when you are reading this, you may or may not know of Haven Run, a fishing village on The Shining Coast, just north of Velia. The creatures of the sea came in the night, slithering across the beach like snakes. All but myself were dragged from their homes into those murky waters, reducing the village itself to a lifeless husk.

I found no weakness in them other than with the swing of my sword, a skill the fishermen did not possess. Should a contract be posted concerning these monsters, share the coin with your fellow rangers - your only hope is in numbers.

Olav One-Eye, Ranger.

Vorska - *These monsters have gone by many names over the centuries. Your great grandparents likely called them Vampeer or Vampire. Before that, they were Gorgers and Blood Fiends. Whatever you wish to call them, know this: they are the real hunters. They have been preying on humanity since the dawn of time.*
Should you cross them in the light of day, you will see their true appearance and what a monstrosity they are, their nightmarish features forged in the pits of the lowest hell. But, by night, they will appear as the most beautiful person you could imagine. They will charm their victims into seclusion before their beastly tongue drains them of blood.
Silver, my friends. They abhor its touch. Use this to reveal them, then take their head with a good piece of steel.

Dobrin Vansorg, Ranger.

Sandstalkers - *Don't run. Never Run. Sandstalkers are among the most confident predators the world of monsters has to offer. Standing your ground will put them off balance and lend you an edge in the fight. If faced by one on its own - and this is unlikely - seek out the monster's weak spots, the softer flesh between the joints; their chitinous exterior can blunt the best of steel. That said, it is more likely you will encounter a nest. In this instance, run. Run until the heat of The Arid Lands beats you into the sand. A nest of Sandstalkers is not to be taken lightly, nor ever alone.*

Jorven Dorn, Ranger.

Gobbers - *Gangly creatures of muscle and claw. What they lack in intelligence I have found they make up for in ferocity, a feature that is amplified all the more by their pack-like behaviour.*
They have speed on their side and you won't see them coming until they have you ambushed. Their scales are tough but not impenetrable - nothing a good axe can't deal with.

Kel Kregor, Ranger.

Wraith - *This foul creature is not of this world, but that of the Shadow Realm, a nightmarish place that only the most experienced mages can access (see Monsters of the Deep World).*
Half in this world, half in another, most folk call them ghosts but, as we all know, there's no such thing. Though, fighting these beasts can sometimes feel like fighting smoke.
Killing the mage who conjured the Wraith won't change a thing; once it's here it's here to stay. Studying Wraiths is near impossible due to their hyper-violent nature, so we have no idea what they crave. We only know that their victims are drained of vitality and life: a painful process from all reports.
While magic is the best weapon against a Wraith, they can be killed with traditional means, including an unusual weakness to salt. For reasons unknown, salt disrupts their ethereal nature and reveals more flesh and blood. Good hunting.

Gudvig, son of Gendervig, Ranger.

Giant - *Not to be confused with Trolls. Their heights might cross over, especially where the Mawclaw Giant and Mountain Troll are concerned, but the Giants are, as their name suggests, the largest of Illian's monsters.*
Their level of intelligence varies across the subspecies. Through all my travels and all the contracts I've taken, it is my strong belief that the Ice Giants of West Vengora are the smartest and, therefore, the deadliest. Regardless of the subspecies, however, all Giants appear to suffer from bad hearing. Either that or they can't hear us tiny folk. Keep this in mind when springing your trap or ambush.

Bragen Durth, Ranger.

Rakenbak - *If you haven't come across one of these beasts there's no mistaking them when you do. Imagine, if you can, a hedgehog and a* *bear brought together by monstrous forces and you have an idea what a Rakenbak looks like.*

They're fiercely territorial and their boundary grows as they do. This becomes a problem when the mother drops a litter close to a town or city, though you'll mostly find them in a woodland environment.

Now, once you've engaged a Rakenbak there's no walking away - or running away for that matter. At a flat-out run, they're faster than any man and they can climb anything you can. So don't attack the fiend until you know exactly how you're going to kill it. Read on for a list of suitable poisons and baits.

Weylan Ganes, Ranger.

Yarxal *- So fair a voice has never been heard, for it is like honey to the ears. How many travellers have fallen prey to this lure I cannot say, but I have discovered Yarxal nests decorated with more human bones than I could count.*

They are proficient predators that kill with admirable swiftness. This is a blessing in disguise I feel, as the beasts don't waste any part of their prey, whether it be devouring the flesh they strip from bone or using those same bones to secure their nests. These monsters prefer to hunt alone, only gathering in significant numbers for breeding purposes (don't even try hunting a Yarxal during this time).

Upright on three legs, they also possess three slender arms, their third limb protruding from their chest. Their grotesque heads will spread like the petals of flower, revealing a combination of suckers and fangs. It is also from where their unusually hypnotic voice comes from. The survivors I have encountered described the voice they heard as a lullaby, though they were all convinced it belonged to a beautiful woman.

Now, their skin breaks as easily as ours do, but I have found they suffer greatly when exposed to a particularly high pitch. I would recommend capturing a Banshee first (see page 400) and transporting it to the Yarxal nest. It's a lot of work, but a disorientated Yarxal is an easy kill.

Gelethaine the Grey Knight, Ranger.

Banshee *- Keep your head on a swivel with these noisy buggers. They've well-earned their name and they'll use their wretched screech to disorientate you - make you look one way while they attack from the other, and always from above.*

They live in swarms of up to twenty and prefer high vantages (see A Charter of Monsters, Page 107, for known locations). If you ever come across these pale predators, you'll understand why they're so well-suited to high vantages. You see, they possess a thin membrane that connects their limbs and hooked claws to the main body. Once they leap from their perch, their limbs spread out and this membrane allows them to glide without a sound.

Once they've got their hooks in your back their razored beaks will take chunks out of your head, so don't go blundering into a swarm. Locate them, then smoke them out (add Harlergrayde to the smoke and they'll get drowsy - see A Ranger's Guide to Alchemy, Page 214). Once they start dropping, get to work.

Yurik (The Beast of Bleak), Ranger.

Arkilisk *- A distant cousin of the Basilisk, though, thankfully, much smaller and easier to trap. Having said that, the bite of an Arkilisk has a much faster acting venom and is capable of killing a man in mere minutes rather than the hours Basilisk venom requires.*

You will find these most deadly of creatures in forests, their preferred habitat due to their bark-like hide that allows them to blend in with the trees.

Now, in all honesty, it is going to be rare that a contract comes up to hunt an Arkilisk down. They don't actively hunt humans and they never stray from their woodland domain. As a ranger, however, it is likely that you will share that same domain at some point or another and it's best to know your neighbours when they could kill you with a single bite. Speaking of their bite, don't even think about an antidote. Even if one existed, you couldn't ingest it before their venom paralysed you, a symptom that begins in the hands of all places. Your only hope is to kill it fast or, better yet, from a distance. Just bear in mind that Arkilisks have six legs and move with significant speed.

The best advice I have for you is this: leave them well alone. If you don't pose a threat to either the Arkilisk or its prey, then it will leave you alone.

Korkali of the Oseki Tribe, Ranger.

Darkling - *The addition of this monster is something of a special case, but the rangers' council has agreed it warrants inclusion. The first thing you need to know when dealing with Darklings is this: they're already dead.*

These abominations are the creations of dark mages and the foulest of magic. From our archives, it appears I am the only ranger to have ever encountered Darklings and I pray to the gods that this will forever remain the truth.

I came across these dark mages in Snowfell. Their insidious cult, whose name I was never able to learn, was in the process of digging up the dead from their graves and breathing new life into them. Only, it was not the life they had known. No, these people were brought back as monsters, fiends who know only their master's command.

They're fast, ferociously violent, and they feel no pain, no fear, and they never tire. Under their master's spell, they hunt in packs and consume the flesh of any poor soul they come across.

Darklings do not return to death idly, and they killed my ward in the time it took us to discover a viable method of destruction. You must take their head or set them alight with fire. Nothing else works. They can lose limbs and take enough damage to drop a Rakenbak, but they will never stop coming for you. So I will say it again. Take the head or set them alight. Better yet, use both methods.

As I said though, these are not naturally occurring monsters. They are products of magic, the machinations of mad men. Though I never got the opportunity to kill one of these dark mages, there is a possibility that their death would end the spell and the Darklings with it.

Omas Ban-Harqen, Ranger.

Praitora - *Also known as the Fisherman's Bane. Praitora are most defi-nitely the creatures that slithered out of the ocean's nightmares. If you've* *ever spent any time by the sea you probably have an idea about what an octopus is. For the sake of this passage I will assume you have. They are similar in appearance to the more harmless octopus, but they are considerably larger and have no qualms about encroaching on the shore. They hunt in the shallows and often claim nearby caves - the damper the better - as temporary dens while hunting on land.*

Some of the larger ones have even been known to capsize small fishing boats. Now don't even bother hunting these or even the smaller ones if they remain in the water; that's their territory. If one has come ashore, hunt it down or use bait to lure it from the sea if you must (see below for list of appropriate baits).

Logan Hackett, Ranger.

Drayga - *If Scudders and Mud Worms weren't enough to steer you clear of swamps, let the Drayga be the warning you need. These pale beasts move on two legs as we do and even stand with the height of an average man, but they are feral to the bone.*

Their sloped heads are more fangs than anything else but if you look into their black eyes you will see the sickness that lives there. Drayga are one of few monsters who hunt prey for no more than sport. Hungry or not, these creatures will rise from the swamps of Illian and tear you to shreds. They do not, however, cope well out of water. Their ghostly pale hides dry up fast, a fact that causes them pain by all reports. If you can lure them onto dry land, away from their precious swamps, you will stand a better chance of whittling their numbers down. And they will have the numbers. Drayga move in family pods and always attack with every member, no matter how old or young they are.

Not to fear. If you are a competent swordsman these monsters will fall to your blade as easily as any man.

Arthur Penvin, The Dancing Sword, Ranger.

Trakian - *There's nothing in this world more appetising to a Trakian than a dead body, and a human one at that. These fiends haunt graveyards up and down the six realms, disturbing the departed and leaving a* *ghastly mess in their stead. They might have no interest in the living, but that won't stop them from defending their feeding ground. Best to hunt them by day since they're nocturnal by nature. You can find their warren around the graveyard in question; they won't stray far from it, not even to sleep. Smoke them out and chop down anything that emerges from the den.*

Varlan Bard, Ranger.

Lumber Dug - *I don't know who named these monsters but lumbering will come to mind if you ever cross one. Hulking beasts of stone they are! At least most of their body is. If you dare face one from the front, and contend with the enormous horn protruding from its face, you could take a swipe at their soft underbelly. I wouldn't advise it though. What they lack in speed they more than make up for by being able to crush every bone in your body with one meaty fist.*
You are better off poisoning their food (a dead deer will do nicely) or using fire depending on the environment.

Sedwig The Trapper, Ranger.

Lewsha - *Of all the monsters you might face during your career, I guarantee you will never come across one so beautiful as a Lewsha. Beware these creatures, for they will appear to you as one thing when, in fact, they are something else entirely.*
The glands in their neck produce a toxin of some kind. It disturbs the air around them like the heat of The Arid Lands. Once you have inhaled this poisonous air, you will see only what you want to see: a beautiful maiden, a lover, even an old relative. With this they will lure you in, revealing their true and hideous nature when it's too late.
If Lewsha are your prey, you must ingest a potion of Hackweed and Lindis Grass. It will rob you of taste and smell but once it is in your gut it will counteract the Lewshas' toxins. Just try not to lose your nerve when you see their true form.

Arnor Grimbold, Ranger.

Howling Matron - *What devil gave birth to such a creature I could not guess nor would I care to meet it, for this offspring of evil is wretch enough. It boasts a dozen pincer legs, giving this beast its scurrying speed. Its carapace, sizeably comparable to a horse, is plated like armour and capable of chipping our blades and keeping back our arrows.*

And what hellish sight its monstrous jaws are. Upon attack, the largest of the Matron's armoured plates retreats just enough to reveal the six blood-red tentacles that surround a razored beak. It will howl almost continuously, altering its pitch until it finds one that disorientates its prey. Once thoroughly dazed, those tentacles will have you; then there's no getting away from that beak.

All that in mind, you'll be wanting to tackle this monster with a spear— to give those tentacles something to do. Then push the beast back and lever it up to expose its soft underbelly. That said, I would advise bringing another ranger into the contract. If that's not possible, you're going to need more preparation time. First, hunt down a Narkul - you're going to need the natural acid their mushrooms produce as it's one of the few things capable of burning through the Matron's carapace.

Just try not to die extracting the acid from the Narkul first.

Keldrik The Grey, Ranger.

Centaur - *The scourge of The Moonlit Plains, to be sure. Most would describe these creatures as part man, part horse. They'd be wrong. There's no shred of man to be found in these beasts. Now, I know the legends as well as anyone—ancient friends of the even more ancient elves. But whether they were once friends to the elves or not, one thing that isn't a legend is their brutality towards humans. Stray too far from The Selk Road while traversing The Moonlit Plains and it's said you'll meet your end by way of a Centaur. And they would be right. Why the beasts hate us so much has been debated by scholars of The All-Tower for centuries but we rangers know the truth, don't we? Centaurs are like any animal we hunt—they're territorial. The Plains are theirs, it's that simple. But, sometimes, it's they who stray from their territory. In these cases, most contracts for a Centaur will come out of Vangarth or*

Tregaran. But be warned, they hunt and live in teams of forty or more. They are not likely to be brought down.

Hadrik Delaney, Ranger.

Humming Swarm - *Twenty-six years. That's how long I've been in this business. That's a long time for a ranger. I tell you this because in all my years on the job, only once have I come across a contract for a Humming Swarm.*
The swarm I was contracted to destroy was on the west coast, not far from Ameeraska. The little buggers prefer a hot and dry climate. They also devour their prey within three to five seconds and they leave naught but nibbled bones in their wake. The closest creature I could compare them to is a piranha fish—if it had wings.
Most mistake them for leaves, and a whole swarm will fill the branches of a fully-grown tree. Unfortunately, each individual Hummer (my preferred name for them) is no bigger than the end of your finger, so your sword, axe, bow— whatever your preference—is of no use with these monsters. You could swing at them for hours and hit naught but air. Not that they'd give you the chance.
The only way to kill the critters is with smoke. Since they sleep at night, I would suggest creeping under the canopy and starting a few fires. Either that or don't take the contract. The latter is probably more sensible.

Arslef, Ranger.

Dopplegorger - *Once you've learnt of these demons you'll have enjoyed your last night in a tavern or upon the cosy bed of some sleepy inn. I thank the gods Dopplegorgers are rare (almost wiped out in the fourth century of the Third Age).*
These monsters will infiltrate villages or towns, lurking on the outskirts until they find a suitable candidate (often a loner with little to no family). Once they do, they not only kill their victim but assume their identity. I am yet to understand how they accomplish their devilry, but it seems they skin the victim and then proceed to wear it. Beyond this, the

fiends are able to transform their bodies until their resemblance is flawless.

It is then that the fox is able to walk among the chickens. Should you find yourself hunting one of these monsters, be sure to thoroughly question everyone—leave no stone unturned. Their level of intelligence is only passable in brief encounters; extensive questioning will reveal them. Just make sure your sword is in hand when you do.

Borvun the butcher, Ranger.

Naerwitch *- These be demons of the dark I say. The pitch-black is their home and they know it well. How these cave-dwellers are able to detect their prey remains a mystery but, make no mistake, they will find you. And while you will need fire to hunt them down, the light will not deter them. It's for this reason we believe Naerwitches lack eyes altogether. These creatures move on six legs, though it should be noted that some have been discovered to possess eight or even ten. I hesitate to describe their feet but it is a feature that remains unique to these monsters. It doesn't matter how many legs they have, they all walk on feet that look exactly like human hands.*

Why this is the case remains as much a mystery as their perception. As for killing a Naerwitch, aim for their protruding torso and swing hard—you don't want to get into a prolonged fight while your fire is dying. Once you lose the light, you lose your life.

Anther Grane, Ranger.

Greyking *- Like the Arkilisk, the Greyking is another sub-species of the Basilisk, which is itself a sub-species of the incredibly rare King Basilisk. Firstly, I would like to talk about their size as I'm sure that would be on any ranger's mind when something as big as a Basilisk is mentioned. The Greyking sub-species fits nicely between the dog-sized Arkilisk and the Basilisk which, of course, is comparable to a horse. I believe the largest Greyking on record was just shy of seven-feet in length, so no easy beast to bring down.*

Unlike those of the broader species, the Greyking does not possess a venomous bite. That's not to say its bite can't kill you—it most certainly can. However, depending on the season, the Greyking will either remove your limb with a single bite or implant a number of eggs into your body. I, personally, have come across two victims who believed they had survived their encounter with a Greyking by some miracle. Of course, once those eggs mature they poison the blood, resulting in a deadly fever. Once the victim has died, the newly-hatched Greykings begin to eat their way out.

It is not a sight for the faint-hearted.

Eletta Gelding, Ranger.

Banefisher - *Devils of sea and land I say. They plague the coasts from north to south paying the weather no heed, for neither heat nor blistering cold can bother them. Their outer layer is that of a crab, a natural armour that can also lend them the appearance of a rock should they curl up on the beach. Upon their two feet—webbed claws—they stand at six-feet tall. Now these beasts are fast on land and even faster in the water, so mind your surroundings.*

I've seen the buggers eat, or consume I should say. They have four rows of translucent fangs and an extendable jaw that can fit a man's face neatly inside. Don't let them get that close. You're going to need something with a bit of weight behind it if you're to crack their shell exterior. I would recommend a war-hammer or spiked mace even.

Hamish Harclaw, Ranger.

Red Daliad - *At two-feet tall, these monsters might not appear all that threatening, especially since they seem all legs with an almost indiscernible body. But hunt these beasts with caution in your step. Should you wander into their nest (see A Charter of Monsters, Page 212, for known locations) they will quietly, almost innocently, approach you with feigned curiosity. Do not be fooled. They regard you as naught but prey.*

When close enough, the Daliads will leap for you, their hooked legs fanned out. It is then that you will see their mouths, located on the underside of their small body. They'll take chunks out of you while their hooks barb your skin to keep them anchored.

One of my earliest contracts was to exterminate a nest, just west of Vangarth. There were two of us, in fact, and I was the novice. I watched my mentor disappear, his body overtaken by these red monsters.

Now, depending on the size of the nest, you can either take your sword to the task or - as I did - use a portion of the contract money to hire a mage. If you take the latter route, for the larger nests, insist that the mage uses a freezing spell. The Daliads have a curious resistance to fire. I will continue to research the reason for this.

Rogaer the Blueblood, Ranger.

Ghola - *If I'm being honest—and I know I've been discouraged by my peers to voice as much—it would be easier to relocate the village or town plagued by a Ghola than to kill the monster.*

I have checked the records and found only one instance of a ranger killing a Ghola. The records are limited, however, as that same ranger died from injuries only moments after defeating the beast.

Luckily for all of us, Ghola dwell solely in the mountains. They rarely venture beyond them, only doing so if they feel their territory is threatened. Such was the case of Harvest Snows, a small village outside of Longdale. As you know, this area of the world is nestled well within the stony walls of The Vengoran Mountains (known colloquially as Vengora).

As you might not know, Harvest Snows no longer exists. Or, rather, it is no longer inhabited. Should you happen across the village site you will find naught but the shell of a village. From what I can tell of the records from the time, the village was in the process of expanding, soon to become a town in fact. That must have been when the Ghola felt threatened.

Now, the reason I suggest relocation over tackling the monster is their speed. Ghola can only be described as supernaturally fast, despite appearances being likened to a human. Before dying, the ranger who fought the beast described it as no more than a blur with claws.

Folaf Ingerson, Ranger.

Dathrak - _In the cities, I have oft heard the pigeons be referred to as 'rats with wings'. If such a phrase was to be coined for Dathraks, it would be something akin to 'a Basilisk with wings'. In truth, one of the strongest theories I've come across actually suggests the Dathraks are distant cousins of dragons._
If the true size of dragons is to be believed, then Dathraks are considerably smaller. That's not to say they aren't large monsters in their own right. The largest recorded possessed a body close in size to a shire horse. Believe me when I tell you, a Dathrak will have no trouble snatching you in its claws and returning you to its high nest (see A Charter of Monsters, Page 112, for known locations).
On two legs, their stance is not dissimilar to that of a vulture's. Their snout is even beak-like, with a razored hook on the end. 'Tis their hide that sparks the debates regarding their relation to dragons. Dathraks are scaled from head to tail and hard it is too, harder than any scales a Basilisk might boast. See below for list of viable poisons and proven traps.

Arn Grawly, Ranger.

Urgal - _It is highly unlikely you will ever encounter this creature, but there are two accounts in our oldest archives that detail Urgals, and so I have chosen to make an addition to our growing bestiary._
Having thoroughly read the reports from our long dead colleagues (it should be stated that neither man ever met, with forty years between the death of one and the birth of the other) I can see that their descriptions of an Urgal are identical. And disturbing.
The Urgals were seen north of Snowfell, at the base of The Vengoran Mountains. This alone would suggest that their species inhabits the area. There are local myths and legends about Urgals, though most in The Ice Vales refer to them as Goblins.
At a reported three-feet tall, they are green of colour with large pointed ears. They've sharp teeth and lethal nails on their six-fingered hands. Now for the disturbing part.

According to both late rangers, the Urgals they encountered could speak and even wore clothes, if a little shabby in their appearance. Furthermore, it was reported by both that the creatures possessed a level of intelligence on a par with a human. It was the creatures who named themselves as Urgals, in fact.

The second ranger to meet an Urgal made note of tools hanging from several belts around its waist, though their purpose was never recorded. Nor was their reason for being around Snowfell.

With that, they remain a mystery.

Elswyn Palona, Ranger.

Harkon - *Vicious aquatic hunters, the Harkons could best be described as eel dogs. They hunt in fresh water such as lakes and rivers (see A Charter of Monsters, Page 203, for known locations). They can reach up to twenty feet and weigh up to four hundred pounds.*

It's a myth that these creatures possess a venomous bite—as far as humans are concerned that is. To the fish it shares a habitat with, the bite of a Harkon means death within seconds. That's not to say their bite doesn't mean death for a human, for their jaws are extendable and capable of taking a limb, given the opportunity. A fully grown female could snap a man in half.

As with any monster who calls the water their home, Harkons can be difficult to hunt (see below for suitable list of bait).

When it comes to killing them, I would recommend using poisoned bait. Failing that, you're going to need a spear and a lot of patience.

Good hunting.

Cal Phesto, Ranger.

Fade - *A nightmare of the Shadow Realm, of that there is no doubt (see Monsters of the Deep World). 'Tis a plane of existence that should never have been tampered with, but I could write a book on the arrogance of mages.*

The Fades are either brought through from their world and let loose or they find a way through to our world due to a mistake on the mage's part. Either way, they will seek to create chaos in our world. Fortunately, in most cases, these creatures of the abyss are taken care of by the mages of Korkanath (they don't want magic's reputation to be tarnished after all).

Rangers are called upon when these monsters find people—and they will find people. They seem to be drawn to civilisation, as if we are no more than play things for their entertainment.

Fades are categorised by their appearance: unnaturally tall and thin, cloaked in black, they attack with claws the size of your hand. Unlike Wraiths, kin from the Shadow Realm, salt will not aid you in your fight. It is known, however, that Fades cannot cross iron. Even a fallen sword is as impassable as a stone wall. This makes for subtle traps—use them well.

Kasira Cornwell, Ranger.

Kruid - *A good old-fashioned monster if ever there was one. If you're yet to accept a contract on one of these beasties, perhaps you haven't spent enough time in The Arid Lands, typically Karath. Kruids hail from The Undying Mountains, a place no man can say much about. Adding to the mystery of the mountains is, in fact, the Kruids themselves. It is unknown why they only appear during the summer months, though I would guess it has something to do with their food supply.*

When it comes to slaying these monsters, you would be better off sharing the contract with another ranger, maybe even two. They're easy enough to kill, but they're big. The best description I can give would be to compare a Kruid to a scorpion, except they can reach twenty feet in length.

Now, as long as you have a sharp enough sword, you'll do just fine. I would suggest assaulting as a team so you can distract the beast, specifically its pincers. Keep them busy, and you can attack from the sides.

Robyn Kobb, Ranger.

Skitter - *Sometimes referred to as Ice Spider. These buggers start out life no bigger than your hand and can grow to the size of a small house. If* *you come across the latter, leave well alone. No contract reward is worth the risk.*

I should also say, if you come across the smaller ones, there will be hundreds of them and their mother, one of the big ones, won't be far away. Leave them all alone too.

Anything in-between is manageable. They appear to go through a phase in their adolescence that sees them isolate themselves, especially the males. When taking them on, use fire. Their icy hides are so sensitive to heat that even light has been known to burn them.

Elgor Thrice-Bitten, Ranger.

Cruul - *A Cruul, pronounced 'Cruel', is well suited to its name. These monsters—a distant cousin of the Hell Hag—dwell in deep lakes, the darkest depths their home.*

The majority of their bodies are made up of tentacles, and long ones at that. They reach up, towards the surface, and wrap a single tentacle around their victim's leg. Once their human prey is ensnared, they will drag them down and then let go, allowing the person to swim back to the surface. This is by design. The Cruul wants its victim to shout for help, thereby bringing more into the water.

With up to a dozen tentacles, the beast can easily drag down numerous people. There is no escaping it then. There are no records in the older archives that detail any ranger ever killing a Cruul. Most are slain when the problem is escalated to the local lords or even kings and queens, who have access to court mages.

Suesh Nas-Arteese, Ranger.

Narkul - *Known as the Mushroom Folk to some, these monsters do not actively hunt out human prey, though they are more than capable of killing humans.*

When left to themselves, Narkuls will simply get on with their lives but, should their territory be disturbed, they will not only protect it but consume those who have wandered into their path.

Their true form is unknown due to the sheer number of mushrooms that protrude from every inch of their bodies. We do know they are capable of standing on two feet and possess two stubby arms.

Their main form of attack is to rear up and burst a number of mushrooms on their chest. The spores and flesh that explode from these mushrooms will melt you to the bone. (If harvested correctly, this substance can be used as a weapon against other monsters).

Killing Narkuls is relatively easy, though it does feel cruel to kill an animal for no more than defending its territory. Still, a contract's a contract.

Wovun Bhear, Ranger.

Wither - *Forest dwellers—the darker the better. In fact, a prevailing myth surrounding these creatures suggests they possess some ability to darken the areas they inhabit.*

At six feet tall, they are entirely covered in coarse black hair. Beneath all this hair stands a beast not unlike a wolf. This likeness ends, however, when taking into account the ram-like horns on their heads.

Exclusively meat eaters, these monsters have no problem eating humans should they cross paths. Of course, it is not very often the two encounter each other, as most people avoid these strangely dark areas of the forest. When a contract arises though, and they do from time to time, you need to know how to tackle the creatures.

Firstly, they live in groups of male or female. The two only mix when it comes to mating season during the autumn. From studies, there seems no difference between the male and females when it comes to facing them, but it should be noted that the females are more territorial.

Galus Kroma, Ranger.

Husk - *These skeletal monstrosities haven't been seen for some time, though they are worthy of note in our fine bestiary. Their origins is unknown to our order of hunters and, perhaps, even the mages of Korkanath. What we can all agree on, however, is that magic had its part to play.*

The beasts do not have brains or working minds as we do—they do not

even possess organs. Their bodies are capable of reshaping its form to match whatever prey has endured the misfortune of crossing it. They simply engulf their victim from head-to-toe, wrapping around them like strips of filthy cloth, and leech every ounce of energy. You see, these creatures are not named for their appearance, but for the manner in which they discard their prey.
Steel, neither sharp nor blunt, will aid you here. Fire is key when it comes to destroying Husks. Until fire and flame are required, prey to the gods that the monsters stay in seclusion.

Beregor Nine-Fingers, Ranger.

Scelda *- Known as Gremlins to those who call The Shining Coast their home. Scelda burrow in and out of the white cliffs in the east - excellent climbers. The people of Velia and Barossh, in particular, have started many a legend about these small creatures. Most of them are absolute twaddle, the spindled tales of storytellers with nothing better to do. Ask any along the coast and they will warn you of Scelda, the baby-snatchers! 'Tis ludicrous, of course, since these sO-called Gremlins prefer to eat stone over meat. The only real threat these monsters have ever had was nigh on three centuries ago, when they displayed a liking towards the hewn stone of Velia's walls. Small as they are, however - and none have ever been recorded as being taller than one's knee - it would take hundreds, if not thousands, to weaken Velia's walls.*
Still, if you piss the little bastards off you can imagine the bite these stone-eaters are capable of. Best kill them quick, eh.

Old Bill, Ranger.

Hell Hags *- You best be having some years behind you before taking on a contract for a Hell Hag. One wrong move—or if you're too stupid to plan ahead—and you're Hag food. These wicked specimens of life call swamps their home, and the worse the better. If you can't see through the water or you feel the trees around you have gathered to defy the light, you're probably right in the middle of their lair.*
Now, I've heard some talk of this evolution rubbish, as if monsters can

change according to their environment, but no one can argue that Hell Hags were designed by the very scaled hands of demons themselves. Atilan protect us.

To see a Hag from the shore, you would think you were watching some poor girl drowning in the swamp, even crying out for help, arms flailing. You'd be wrong. And if you dived into the water to save that girl, you'd be dead too. That girl—at least what you can see of her—is the humanoid bait that protrudes from the top of a Hag's back. The spider-like creature that dwells below the surface is a monster you wouldn't soon forget. They vary in size, but I've never seen one dredged out of the water that was smaller than my horse.

You can see below the numerous methods used against Hell Hags over the years but, more than anything, you're going to need a big set of lungs.

Veador Hemsmith, Ranger.

Royal Gobber - *I'm sure you will agree that slaying Gobbers is nothing short of fun for the experienced and exhilarating for the recruits, but— and there is a but my fellow rangers—a Royal Gobber is a completely different beast.*

Coming in at somewhere between seven and eight feet, these behemoths are sheer walls of muscle, rage, and speed.

Not much is known about them, though we believe they are asexual creatures and responsible for hatching the lesser Gobbers that trail them. Like I say, we believe. This is only a theory and there are there credible theories where these beasts are concerned. I've heard it said that the Royal Gobbers serve to impregnate some kind of Queen Gobber, though there has never been any proof that such a monster exists.

When it comes to killing these things, well, you just need to know your way through the beats of a good fight. They don't go down easily, known for taking a damn good beating before giving it up. Personally, I found a nice heavy axe to the skull did the trick. On the third swing.

Mosef Gibbs, Ranger.

Cruxta - Wherever the dead have fallen, these monsters will be sure to follow. They move in small packs of three or four, all with a nose for the stench of rotting flesh. Make no mistake, though Cruxta prefer the taste of the dead, they will settle for the living and they have the claws to see it so. If there is a big enough battlefield, where chaos reigns, they have even been so bold as to begin feasting amidst the fighting. It should also be known, if the battle goes on and on it is likely more packs will arrive. This can be advantageous as the packs will consider each other rivals and fight amongst themselves.

I have to say, in most cases, we rangers are not called upon in these circumstances. The last contract I accepted for a pack of Cruxta was in an old crypt just outside of Kelp Town. This is more typical for our line of work.

If it's possible, I would recommend hunting them during the day, while they sleep in their nest (see A Charter of Monsters, Page 301, for typical locations).

Don't however, think that light and dark will have a part to play beyond their natural sleep periods. Cruxta have no eyes but rather a whole face of nostrils. And a mouth. A very big mouth in fact. I should probably have mentioned the mouth earlier. Anyway, back to the nostrils. Always approach from up wind.

Kalem Bifson (oldest ranger on record).

Dhisha - I have no intention of dying by the fang or claw of any monster but, if I had to choose one of their foul kind to end my days, it would be a Dhisha.

I am fairly confident in stating that there is no other creature in the realm that kills its prey quite like one of these beasts. You can see from the crude drawing below what they look like, but it does nothing to explain how their unique venom works.

Dhisha will always attack their prey while they sleep (they have not mastered lock and key but they have no trouble opening doors). When they do attack, a pair of retractable fangs, so fine as to be mistaken for strands of hair, will sink into the victim's skin and do a number of interesting things.

As the venom is not powerful enough to paralyse a person, it instead seeks out the mind, working its way into their very thoughts. Those who have survived these attacks state that same thing. They are all-consumed by their dream-like condition to a point that the mind chooses not to wake up. The victims also stated that this was accomplished through some shadowed figure in their mind, a figure who grants them three wishes. They are then able to play out their greatest fantasies while the Dhisha drains them of life.
I don't know about you, but I know what my three wishes would be.

Ryfe Fenlock, Ranger.

Broxon - *A bullish monster that enjoys the taste of cattle over a human. That said, the loss of cattle is often the catalyst for a contract to be drawn up. Thus enters the ranger.*
My first description was, perhaps, deliberate as Broxon resemble bulls. That is in shape and by the horns on their head. All else is quite different. For starters, they are twice the size of any bull. Their hide is difficult to look at, well, at least it is for those unaccustomed to the musculature of any animal. You see, Broxon hide is the deep red of muscle, as if the beasts have been stripped of their skin. That would certainly explain their bad temperament.
There are a number of ways to slay a Broxon, some easier than others. By far the easiest way is to poison the beast with suitable bait, but I would advise killing the monster the old-fashioned way. Granted this comes with greater risk, but doesn't such a thing always come with greater reward?
A fully-grown Broxon can feed a village for a week. They taste like pork of all things. Now, if you can put the beast down with steel instead of poison, you can then sell the carcass and add the coin to your reward.

Fenley Klum, Ranger.

Dredling - *A parasite to be sure. These squid-like creatures will secure themselves to travellers who wander through bogs and the like, finding purchase under the concealment of clothing. Most prefer a nice juicy* *calf. Once they are attached, they will immediately begin to poison the mind of the host, turning them violent and mad. This usually results in several deaths before the Dredling is discovered.*

There have been numerous cases of Dredlings injecting their eggs into their host and forcing the victim to seek out civilisation before the offsprings slither out of their mouth to find hosts of their own.

There are signs to look out for, of course, before the violence begins. The eyes of the host are always extremely bloodshot for the thirst few days. Then they begin to turn black. By this stage, madness will have its firm hold. Other signs include a slight tremor in the hands, loss of appetite, paling skin, and muttering to oneself.

If you can identify a Dredling host before their eyes turn black, there is a chance you can save their life, though you must sever the limb. This, however, might result in their death anyway.

Selene (the maiden of Snowfell), Ranger.

Jaxyl - A monster of cruel design and, in my opinion, further proof that some thing truly wicked has put monsters on our fair Verda. You will know a Jaxyl when you come across one or hear of their description. In fact, I have never met a witness who didn't tell me they had seen a creature of wolf and ram. 'Tis an apt description. To put it simple, they possess the head of a very angry ram (with four eyes mind you) and the body and claws of a wolf.

Something drives these beasts to rage and I have seen as much on my hunts. They roam the wilds with a very particular look on their four golden eyes. Yo've probably seen that look, in a tavern or pub, before a fight breaks out. It's as if the Jaxyls go looking for trouble, and not always fr sustenance. They just like to kill, as if they've something in them that must be unleashed.

Killing them is just as easy as swinging your sword into the right body part, just be sure to avoid those horns though—even at a short charge a Jaxyl will break your legs.

Sabine The Red, Ranger.

Fraedan - *Perhaps it's my age, but I was raised to call them Imps or Sprites. Regardless of their name, the best word to describe these little creatures is mischievous. I've never seen one taller than my hand but it's their size that lends to their vexatious behaviour. They can get into everything and, thanks to their nimble fingers, I've even seen one reach into the keyhole of a door and undo the lock.*

Who can say what drives these wicked beasts? I say it is no more than boredom, though I have heard others—of the religious sort—claim they are sent by the Goddess Atarae to keep our individual destinies on track. I'm sticking with my theory. You're free to make your own and add it to the next edition of this bestiary.

You will know a Fraedan when you see one. The homunculi look strikingly like us, with all the features you would expect to see in a human. There are some added features, such as their small horns and mouse-like tail. They're also a deep purple, though I have seen a few with red skin. When they're not setting mills alight or leading several thousand rats from tavern to tavern, Fraedan sleep together in one big pile. This pile will be inside the largest bird nest you have ever seen and high up a tree. If you catch them sleeping, a flaming arrow should do the trick. If you tackle them while they're awake, they'll likely swarm you.

Just look for the nest.

Osmand The Mute, Ranger.

Khalighast - *Easily identified by the three thick tendrils protruding from the back of their head and shoulders. Here's a monster that can take to the water as swiftly as it does the land. I've hunted these beasts in both and, honestly, they're a bugger to kill in both. They're fast runners, fast swimmers, and damned fast killers. They move prominently on four legs but they can stand on two if they wish - this puts them somewhere between six and seven feet.*

Their grey hide is that of a rough leather, not dissimilar to a Gobbers, if a little tougher. In fact, after you've brought the Khalighast down, I would recommend turning them into a good saddle.

When it comes to distinguishing between the sexes, you need to get a good look at those tendrils I mentioned. The females' are longer and darker than their male counterparts. You might be wondering why you need to know the difference—a monster is a monster. But, when it comes to Khalighasts, targeting the right one can make all the difference to your hunt. Due to the fact that they live in a female hierarchy, if you can identify and kill the matriarch first, the pack loses its cohesiveness. When these creatures aren't working together they're more mindless animal than dangerous predator. That's when you wade in with your sword, but I'm not going to teach you to suck eggs.

Agnes Stone, Ranger.

Creeper *- You'll never hear them coming. It doesn't matter the terrain, Creepers move like the silent hand of Death. I've seen the needle legs walk through snow, forests of fallen leaves, and caves littered with puddles. By the time you realise one has crept up on you, it will be too late.*
At four feet tall, they can also be something of a pain to see. Adding to that, their arms and legs are such fine points of bone that there isn't that much to see of them.
Of course, you will know about it when they are upon you. If they don't impale you with their needle arms they will clamp their jaws around a limb and they will not let go. I saw a fellow ranger stab a Creeper in the back repeatedly and it never once relented its bite. It a tactic of the males, used to slow you down until the females can attack. Nasty buggers.
If you do find yourself with a Creeper's jaw wrapped around your leg or arm, use fire to free yourself. It's the only thing that will make the creatures retreat.

Trantor Vane, Ranger

Luxun *- I have been laughed at for this comparison, but the resemblance between a giant tortoise and a Luxun is most certainly there. Rather than being housed inside a hard shell, Luxun find safety inside their shells of jagged stone. In fact, when head and limbs are retracted, these creatures are often mistaken for boulders. I myself have walked* *right past a family pf Luxun while on the hunt. I can tell you quite humbly, it is damned embarrassing to drive your spear into no more than a large rock, only to discover the real thing is slowly flanking you. Now, there are obvious differences between a tortoise and a Luxun— besides their shells. The head and neck of one of these beasts is closer to a snake. It will slither out of its stony shell and spit venom at its prey (their spit has been known to reach ten feet).*

Thankfully, killing Luxun is as simple as cutting off their slimy head. You just need to lure them out of their shell first. Oh, and avoid the venom, of course.

Renley Killenger, Ranger

Ydrit - *The White Bears our ancestors called them. If only they were as easy to kill as a bear. Ydrits are suited to cold environments, the harsher the better. Most are found north of Longdale and around The Shards. The common myth is that they prefer the mountains, but they are more commonly located near to water—typically the sea.*

On two feet, Ydrits stand at nine foot and, let me tell you, they make for a tower of muscle and white fur you've not seen. If you find yourself in the shadow of one of these beasts, you had better be at the top of your game. Their flat faces are partially hidden behind curtains of fur, but their large lower fangs can't help but stand out. And don't be looking in their black eyes for they'll be sure to rob you of your courage and leave you in a puddle of your own making.

Their two arms are comparable to logs, thick and strong, with five wicked claws. One swipe will send you to the next world so keep your distance.

Now, they usually hunt fish and the like with little interest in the taste of humans. That doesn't mean they can't be persuaded. In the winter, when the ice is thick and the fish harder to come by, they have been known to turn their sights on Longdale's outlying villages.

Isold The Hook Hand, Ranger

Nefaris - *These pale walkers hail from the Shadow Realm, a dimension* *of fangs and claws that should remain behind lock and key. Sadly, the magic users of our fair realm have learnt of dark and twisted paths that lead to that hellish abyss.*

One such creature that has been unleashed from that other place is known as a Nefaris. On two feet, they move like a man and even stand at our height, but they possess four arms, the upper pair of which are so long as to reach their knees. The arms protruding from their skeletal ribs are smaller, designed for shredding the flesh of any prey pulled in by those stronger, outer arms.

Their head is, in effect, a mouth, capable of opening from forehead to chin to reveal several rows of teeth.

Thankfully, there is nothing fanciful required when it comes to slaying the nightmarish beasts. A good length of steel or even a well-placed arrow will bring them down. If you ask me, it's the mages who should be hunted down and made to answer for the monsters they unleash on our world.

Royce Wiggins, Ranger

Grodel *- I used to like birds. I thought they were exquisite animals and a reflection of the gods' beauty. I don't anymore. Not after meeting a Grodel.*

How best to describe this monster of the sky? Even my worst nightmares could not conjure such a thing. Alas, I shall do my best to detail the creature.

On four scaly legs, a Grodel stands at around seven feet and can reach up to twelve feet in length when fully matured. Halfway up, black feathers conceal the rest of its hideous form and spread out across its impressive wingspan. Its head is that of an enlarged crow, though I have met rangers who state they encountered a Grodel with an eagle's head. I cannot vouch for that.

Just below their throat, you will find a pair of arms no longer than your own. Should you find yourself on your back, a Grodel looking down on you, they will use these arms to pin you and disembowel you with their beak.

Keep moving. Stay on your feet.

Red Radigan, Ranger

Draugur - *Monsters breed legends and legends breed monsters—this is the way of things. Draugur have a particular myth about them that has always stuck with me. It is said that Draugur were made by the elves during the Second Age, though it could easily have been during the First Age, as we know the elves called Illian home in that time. I believe this myth is part of the reason Draugur are also referred to as Forest Witches, just as their creators are referred to by some as the Forest Folk.*
If this is true, I could not begin to guess at the reason for their creation. What I do know is that these creatures form considerable nests in the heart of forests, often manipulating the surrounding environment to blot out the sun. After that, everything begins to die. These monsters are the definition of blight and must be eradicated as soon as possible. The decay that spreads from them can have detrimental effects on nearby civilisation.

Tarwen Evensin, Ranger

Ghost - *My fellow rangers and I feel it prudent to include mention of ghosts in this edition of our fine bestiary. Let me tell you why. Should you be hunting some monster out there and you decide you're chasing a ghost, you're going to turn to this book for advice. You would then discover that there is no advice concerning ghosts and would, perhaps, wonder if your predecessors had failed to collect an accurate library of the beasts that prey on our world.*
Well here it is, the advice you are looking for.
There are no such things as ghosts.
Whatever it is you are hunting, it is not the spirit of the departed. It is something else inside this book. Try harder.

Melinda Shadow-Born, Ranger

Harpy - *What beautiful critters these monsters are. At only a foot tall, bodies like the bark of trees, large doe eyes, and wings like lush summer leaves, they will lure you in with the innocence of a child—even their* *smile is a twisted mimicry of our own. Whether this appearance is by evil design or unfortunate coincidence is unknown.*

Make no mistake, Harpies know exactly what they're doing when it comes to us humans. Woodland dwellers, one or two will make contact, appearing as playful things to lower defences. If you are foolish enough to follow them back to their forest nest, you will be set upon by thirty or more of the buggers. Then you'll see their teeth.

It's not typically our way, but I would advise donning a suit of armour before tracking them down. They'll bite through leather as easily as they do flesh, but iron will give them something to think about.

Tobias Noon, Ranger

Ghoulist - *I have transcribed the passage from the eleventh edition of A Chronicle of Monsters: A Ranger's Bestiary, despite the fact that no ranger has identified a Ghoulist in over a hundred years. I know from experience that just because a thing hasn't been seen for a long time doesn't mean it can never be seen again. So I warn you not to skim over the details but commit them to memory, as you might be the first to cross a Ghoulist and, as you have probably learnt by now, facing any monster unprepared is a good way to lose your life.*

If you are reading this, my fellow ranger, then I say well done to you. It would take even the most learned of men some time to reach this page, which means you must have many a monster under your belt. If you must add another, pray to the gods it is not a Ghoulist. With six legs and the musculature of a horse, you can bet they are bigger, stronger, and faster than yourself. Should you manage to stay on your feet long enough to actually fight it, beware its twin-tails, each ending in razored bone. Then there's its head, a hideous thing. If you have ever come across a Scudder, that's exactly what their head and neck look like. Wicked beasts.

I only survived because the damned thing was more interested in devouring my horse.

Harndel Goft, Ranger (transcribed by Barnwen, son of Farngorn)

Vogan *- Now here's an interesting creature for you, dear learner. Though these little beasts do not directly hunt humans, they are undoubtedly a threat should the two ever meet. Vogan can be typically found in the wake of Giants. Not always, I should say, but their presence is not uncommon.*

These beasts come in at no taller than the average man's waist with a naturally hunched back and long arms that aid in their movement. On their own, any Vogan is easily killed by even an amateur swordsman but, due to the numbers they travel in, they can overwhelm a person or potentially a group if motivated enough.

As I said, however, they trail Giants, preferring to pick clean whatever they leave behind. There's nothing fancy to be done here—there's no bait or poison to employ. If you take on a contract regarding a Giant, it's always good to be aware of these creatures lest they surprise you. It's rare to see a contract come up specifically for the Vogan but should one arise, be mindful that the Giant they're following is likely dead, leading to the Vogan creating trouble for humans directly. If the Giant is dead, you have to wonder what could kill it. There's always something worse out there.

Rogan Vane, Ranger

Mergossa *- The trees that eat, my mother called them. There are many myths surrounding the Mergossa, and from many cultures and times, but they all agree that these beasts have a taste for human flesh. Personally, having observed them in the wild, I have seen no such propensity. I have witnessed the devouring of everything from baby rabbits to bears, depending on the size of the Mergossa. I cannot say what power put them on our fair world or how it came to be that they are able to so closely mimic the trees around them, though I would wager there is evil at work within them.*

I also cannot say where the myth came from that Mergossa are static creatures. Perhaps it is because of their likeness to the trees they live between. I can tell you for a fact, my fellow ranger, that Mergossa can move as they like, and swiftly too. I believe, however, that they choose not to move so often because of the great noise they make, their heavy legs thundering into the ground.

Nathaniel Crawly, Ranger

Triffid - *A four-winged bat would be a better name for these creatures, but I suppose it doesn't roll off the tongue quite so well. Still, there is not better description for these flying monsters. Worse still, they are equal in size to a fully-grown hound and perfectly capable of lifting a man from the ground. What happens to the man thereafter I leave to your imagination, dear ranger, but rest assured, it does not end well.*
These nocturnal hunters can be found in deep caves (see A Charter of Monsters, Page 110, for known locations), though be warned, their colonies number in the hundreds. I say this so you do not take the contract likely. A monster hunter you may be, but some jobs are simply beyond the skills of an individual or even a group. Should a colony of Triffids pose a real threat, escalate the job to whomever rules over the threatened. You're going to need an army.

Hadrian Bossem, Ranger